White Buffalo (New Beginnings) Series

RAVEN AND THE GOLDEN EAGLE

Lauretta Beaver

PublishAmerica
Baltimore

Second printing

All characters in this book are fictitious, and any resemblance to real persons,
living or dead, is coincidental.

PublishAmerica has allowed this work to remain exactly as the author intended,
verbatim, without editorial input.

Hardcover 9781451241747
Softcover 9781448941612
PUBLISHED BY PUBLISHAMERICA, LLLP
www.publishamerica.com
Baltimore

Printed in the United States of America

To: Hedger

THE RISE OF THE SHAMAN

The Prophecy

One arises more powerful then any shaman in a hundred years!
Able to walk in others dreams, his powers will exceed all before him!
What he becomes in the future hangs in the balance as the choice between his powers
and life looms ever closer!

Laurel Weaver
Dec 16/15

This book is dedicated to my late husband, **Edward Milton Beaver**
Born April 21, 1958 died May 20, 2008.
It was a tragic tale that someday I might be able to tell.
Also to my two beautiful daughters, **Pamela Lynn Ryman** and
Jessica Alexandria Oper, who stole my heart the day they were
born. I loved you than, and I will love you two forever. I thank you
both from the bottom of my heart, for the love you two have shown
me over the years. As well as your patience, while putting up with my
constant writing.

I would like to thank my hairdresser at **Za.hair.a** for the beautiful hairstyle for my back cover. Also to Tracy Gagne for the gorgeous pictures especially on such short notice

Thank you, ladies.

A special thank you goes to my mother, **Irene Chaisson**, for her help with some of the editing on both of my books.

Extreme gratitude and love goes to my new partner, **Michel Pelletier**, for all his help getting both my books redone. Thank you!

I would also like to thank **God** for his enduring Love, even though at times it does not seem as if he cares. I would like to share a short story with my readers of my grief if I may. Edward had died a month before we were to be remarried. I lost my job a year later than to make things worse I hit a deer and almost totalled the front of my car. This all happened in less than two years, I was depressed it seemed **God** hated me at the time. I put on a DVD that Edward had bought before he had died, called the Isaac's. A song they sing called '**Stand Still And Let God Move' sent shivers down my spine.** I looked up imploringly. "Okay, God, obviously you are trying to tell me something! If that is what you want I will stand still but please tell me, what do you want from me?"

While I waited for **God** to tell me what he wanted me to do next, I picked up my pen and finished two books that I had started when I was twenty-four. Passionate Alliance and the second book to the series Raven and the Golden Eagle. Wouldn't you know it, I sent the first one in, and it was published! Just because, the Lord gives you hard times, does not mean he hates you even though it seems that way at times. Remember that if you stand still and let **God** move in your life after such tragedies something good usually follows. Not when we want it to but when the Lord says it is time! I pray that your dreams come true as mine have.

PROLOGUE

NORTH DAKOTA

Mell leaned back with a sigh of contentment as she sipped her tea. She eyed her daughter-in-law sitting across from her pensively as she thought back over the years. Pamela or Pam as she liked to be called married her oldest son, Daniel. They had named Daniel after Jed's first dead son. It had shocked all of them, especially her when Daniel had hung up his guns to become a Baptist Pastor. However, Mell was extremely proud of him anyway after the initial shock had worn off, of course.

Pamela was Giant Bear and Mary's only daughter. She had moved here to live with Mell so that she could go to a white school. Pam had her mothers light blonde hair with her father's deep black eyes. A slight dusky look to her skin plus the high cheekbones clearly pointed to her Indian heritage. She was willowy slim so had no need to wear a corset to get a perfect hourglass figure, she already had one.

Mell, as well as Mary, had both been ecstatic when Pam had fallen in love with Daniel then gotten married. The two newlyweds moved over to Mary's old ranch house, and Pam made it liveable once again. The two mothers-in-law, as well as best friends, were thrilled to have their families entwined by marriage at last. Now finally the shadow of Brian, who had plagued their lives even though they were unaware of it, was laid to rest as the kids brought love into Mary's old ranch.

Daniel's twin sister was named Patricia or Pat for short, named after Mell's mother. Pat was following in her mother's footsteps, as she became the second woman sheriff in their hometown.

Mell's third child another boy that they named John, after Mayor Elton who had died last year as well as Jed's father who also happened to have the name John, was becoming a rancher like his grandfather Alec. Much to Jed's fathers disappointment, but Alec's satisfaction.

The thought of Jed's father made Mell grin in amusement, Jed had been right about his father's reaction to Mell. After the initial shock of her being a sheriff as well as a soon to be marshal had worn off, of course...

John looked her over carefully in pleasure then he had smirked in satisfaction. "Well at least you picked someone as strong as you are this time. I expect to have strapping grandsons and tall ones too from such a good looking woman!"

Mell had laughed with Jed over that for many years.

Mell's father, Alec, after being married to Jessica for two years made Mell's dream come true then gave her a sister. Unfortunately, for the grief stricken Alec, Jessica had died in childbirth. Mell had to raise her sister as her own, so she had always felt that little Jessica was more like her daughter because of that.

Alec had given them all a scare after Jessica died and almost died himself. But little Jessica pulled him out of his grief with her large green blue eyes, fiery red hair that came with her fierce temper. He was starting to show his age now though at seventy-eight years old.

Right now, Alec, Jed, as well as their youngest son John was out checking on the new cattle that John had purchased a month ago. Now they had an even five hundred head, which had always been Jed's dream.

Mell's horse Lightning had died two years ago much to Mell's sorrow, but not before producing a few dozen healthy offspring.

Mayor Elton's prediction proved true; although he was a few years too early, as the railroad went through their town five years after Mell became the new marshal. The towns population doubled within a year then new towns sprung up everywhere across North Dakota. It had kept them extremely busy. They got so busy that Mell had to hire two more deputy marshals, just so that they could keep up.

Alec's gold mine had finally dried up, but he had found another one in town when he had invested in Chelsie's Goldsmith Shop. Alec along with Jed had tripled their investment since they had built the store for

Chelsie. She had sold the saloon shortly after the store opened since she was just to busy with her new shop to keep both.

Mell shook off her reflective mood then turned her attention back to Pam. "Well you look very grim today. What seems to be the problem?"

Pam shrugged dismissively, but the worry was evident in her voice. "I don't know! I have been having these dreams lately, and I am not sure what they mean."

Mell sat forward quickly in surprise as well as shock. She had been having strange dreams herself for about a week now. She motioned ominously describing her nightmares distressfully. "Dreams of your father calling for help then death and blood all around him?"

Pam shivered in fear as she waved incredulously in distress. "You have been having them too?"

Mell inclined her head that she was then her gaze became distant as she remembered the last dream two days ago. "Mine always starts out with a white female buffalo running towards your father. Sometimes she goes to him and tells him something then everything is fine. Other times she does not as the white buffalo leaves blood and death appear all around him!"

Mell touched her white buffalo medicine bag that she was never without. She now knew instinctively that she was the white buffalo in the dream. Somehow, she must go help Giant Bear immediately.

Pam shuddered in panic then dread as she thought of the last dream that she had two days ago before gesturing apprehensively. "All I see is blood and death with a feeling of urgency to go to my father! Do you hear what the white buffalo is saying in your dreams?"

Mell scowled in confusion as she shrugged pensively. "Yes, but I do not understand it. She just keeps repeating that they must not be forced to marry. An older white man pops into the picture a few minutes later than the white buffalo tells him something important, but I cannot hear what she says to him. It is all so very confusing."

Pam looked puzzled as she waved urgently. "But who must not be forced to marry?"

Mell shook her head in frustration totally baffled by it all. "I don't know that is all she says to your father."

Pam sighed uneasily as she opened both her hands in supplication to Mell as if she had the answers. "It does not make any sense, how can two people being forced to marry cause so much death. My father would have contacted us by now if he were in danger, right?"

Mell shrugged thoughtfully as she mussed reflectively. "Maybe he doesn't even know that he is in danger yet."

Pam frowned grimly. She looked at Mell knowingly already aware of the answer, but asked anyway. "You could be right! Are you going and when?"

Mell nodded emphatically as she waved towards town in explanation. "I will be leaving right away, but I have to go telegraph the governor first to let him know I have a family emergency. I also need to tell him that I am not sure how long I will be away. I will let my deputies know at the same time that they are going to have to look after things here for me."

Pam scowled grimly then got up as she motioned towards her ranch. "I will run home and pack. I am not sure if Daniel will come with us or not. Do you think Jed will come?"

Mell inclined her head decisively, as she got up to. She waved shrewdly having no doubts at all. "Of course, Giant Bear is his blood brother as well as his friend. I know he will do everything he can in order to help us save Giant Bear.

Pam nodded relieved. "Okay! I will be back here in a few hours or sooner if I can help it."

Pam turned skirts flying as she raced from the room without waiting for Mell to agree or disagree with her. More scared now than she had been earlier.

Mell sighed dejectedly. Well, so much for her well-deserved vacation. She turned and headed to the kitchen to ask Jane to pack provisions for their trip. Gloria had died the year before Mayor Elton had passed on, so Jane had taken over. She headed upstairs to her room after leaving the kitchen.

At fifty-seven years of age, Mell was still an imposing figure of a woman. Most people were shocked when they learned her age. The only difference now from thirty years ago was that her hair had turned almost entirely white. Her face had a few more wrinkles, but her body was still girlishly thin even after giving birth to twins than to one more boy afterwards.

Mell and Jed had talked seriously about retiring as marshals this year, but they had decided to wait three more years. Jed would be sixty-five by then, and she would be sixty, time enough to retire then spend the rest of their lives together in peaceful contentment.

Mell grabbed clothes from the closet before throwing them on the bed. She frowned thoughtfully as she stared in surprise at a pouch hanging in her closet. She had forgotten all about it again. Inside was her wedding certificate as well as one for Mary and Giant Bear, which they had added two months later. She had also added a deputy's certificate made out to Jed than one for Giant Bear. Getting a document was a new thing that had only started a few years ago. Mayor Elton had printed one out for their anniversary gift.

Mell had asked him to get one made for Mary and Giant Bear so that next time she saw her friends she could give it to them as a gift. There had never seemed to be an opportunity to give it to them though, until now. So she nodded to herself then grabbed the pouch and threw it on the bed to be packed with their things. It would be a perfect gift to bring them, they could laugh about the days when...

Jessica came bounding into the room unexpectedly, interrupting Mell's reflection. She waved imploringly in anticipation. "I heard you are going on a trip would you mind if I came along this time?"

Mell smiled indulgently at her sister, but shook her head in denial. "No! I am going to Giant Bear's village in Montana. It will be too dangerous for you!"

Jessica grinned knowingly then put her two hands together as if in prayer as she tilted her head beseechingly. "I know that I heard you tell Jane, but I would still like to come. Please! You have taught me how to protect myself so I will not be a hindrance. Who knows I might even be able to help out."

Mell harrumphed in disbelief at the idea of the rambunctious Jessica helping them. It was more likely that her sister would bring them more problems, as beautiful as she was. She finally gave in though with a smile of resignation at the replica of her mother, Jessica. Not once, in all these years had she been able to say no to her sister when she truly wanted something and this time was no different. She nodded reluctantly then pointed a finger at her and shook it in warning. "Okay! You can come to, but we are leaving in a few hours if you are not ready we will leave without you. It is going to be a hard ride as well, so you better wear pants."

Jessica squealed in delight as she grabbed Mell giving her a fierce hug in thanks. She picked up her long skirts so that she could run as she raced out of the room in a rush before her sister could change her mind.

Mell shook her head already regretting her decision then wondered if she had made a mistake. She forgot about Jessica a moment later as she cocked her head curiously at the sound of a door slamming and hurried footsteps racing up the stairs. She turned expectantly then waited in anticipation as Jed burst into their bedroom all out of breath. Her gasp of pleasure caught in her throat as she eyed her husband in appreciation. Even after all these years, he still made her heart race in need just by looking at him. His hair was now grey instead of black with a slight hint of baldness on top, but he still kept it long. Jed's face had gotten craggier over the years from spending so much time outdoors. None the less, it was still a handsome face, only older. He had not lost any of his muscles, if anything he had gained more. He still stood at six foot six, with no hint of slouching. Most men Jed's age tended to lose height as they got older, not Jed though. He did have a bit of a potbelly now though, but hardly noticeable unless you had known him all these years.

Jed inhaled in relief at the sight of his wife standing in front of him unhurt. "What is going on? Pam raced past us as if her skirt were on fire. So I came to see what the problem was then seen two packhorses outside being readied for a long trip by the looks of it."

Mell grinned relieved to see him here. At least now, she would not have to go running around looking for him. She told him everything about hers as well as Pam's dreams lately.

When Mell finished, Jed nodded not even surprised a little bit, as he motioned knowingly. "I have been waiting for this to happen; I just did not think it would be this late in the future."

Mell looked at Jed in shocked amazement as she waved angrily in demand. "You were expecting this to happen! Why ever for?"

Jed smiled reassuringly at her tone of disbelief and explained. "Do you remember when Giant Bear named you White Buffalo?"

Mell nodded mutely that she did, but did not say anything.

Jed frowned pensively as he thought back to that time. "When you were teaching Tommy knife tricks we were watching you. Giant Bear told me then that the Great Spirit had informed him that you would come to him when his people were in desperate need. He did not know at that time when or why he would need you, so I knew this moment would be coming for a long time now."

Mell sighed in confused understanding, not sure, if she liked this one little bit. Having her future controlled by higher powers would never have been something she would have thought possible or even about. She shook of her disgruntlement. Nothing she could do about it now, she could not help thinking. She waved at all the clothes laid out on the bed. "Well help me finish packing we are leaving in a few hours."

Jed nodded without argument then got to work helping her.

A few hours later they were all gathered together in the yard as Mell had predicted. Mell, Jed, Jessica, Pam, and an emphatic Daniel who refused to be left behind all mounted.

They waved goodbye to the people they were leaving behind before racing away to save their friend. Not one of them even looked back!

CHAPTER ONE

MONTANA

The sun was just topping the mountains when the rider on a roan mare stopped to admire the view. It was breathtaking to watch them turn spectacular colours as the sun slowly emerged above them. The rider stiffened in alarm then looked further left immediately at the sound of horse's hooves coming from the cliffs above as a ringing challenge pierced the air. Before finally relaxing, knowing the sound of that defiant squeal as the eyes of the human and horse collided.

The rider held perfectly still as the large black stallion snorted testing the air for a scent. When the sun materialized totally over the mountains, it shone directly on the brawny stud making his coat seem almost as red as the mare. At other times, his coat appeared blue.

The mare neighed in response to the stallions challenge then started shifting sideways in eager anticipation.

The rider stroked the mare to quiet her watching the stocky black paw the air as he reared. The stud turned before disappearing heading back into the canyon where he had come from.

Nudging the mare forward, they rode toward the same location that the stallion headed for. If one did not know about the crevice hidden behind the rocks ahead, you would ride right passed it. This would be a shame, since they would miss the most beautiful valley. They had stumbled on it about four and a half years ago when the idea of catching the black stud first occurred. It took a whole year to catch him, but after six months of trying to break the stallion, they had given up when he got sick. Knowing he would die if kept in captivity, they brought him back then set him free. Some horses were not meant to be tamed!

The rider desperately needed another stallion for the big herd of mares at the ranch. So they decided that if you could not bring the stud to the mares, the idea of bringing the mares to him was tried. Every spring they would bring the same mare here for breeding before they got too busy with the cattle drive. There were two reasons for this. One was because she was the herd leader. The second reason was that the rider knew this particular horse would stay close even when her life was threatened. One whistle is all it would take. Nothing would stop this mare from getting to her rider she was that reliable.

The mare with her rider would spend two or three days with the stallion. One-week later they would bring twenty-five mares into the valley and leave them with the stud for one month. Afterwards, these mares were herded back to the ranch then another twenty-five were brought in until all seventy-six mares were bred. It had been a challenge two years ago when they first tried it because the stallion kept trying to steal the mares, only about half of them ended up pregnant. But with the roan mare on guard, plus the two herd dogs working together, last year everything went off without a hitch. Luckily, all seventy-six mares conceived without a single loss. Most of the foals promised to have their sires height as well as muscular build.

The rider had come to an understanding with the stud as long as they did not try to catch him again, and he did not try to steal the mares everything worked according to plan. Somehow, the black always seemed to know when the rider was coming because he was always waiting on that particular ledge.

As the mare entered the valley, she stopped obediently when her rider pulled her to a halt so that they could admire the view. All that could be heard from the pair was a deep intake of breath then the release of air in a huge sigh of relief. This was the only time of relaxation permissible from the everyday stress of running the largest ranch in the territory.

The rider smiled in satisfaction before looking around, it was incredibly beautiful here with lots of trees and vegetation. A small pool fed by an underground spring was on the right hand side against the cliffs, they circled all the way around to the left hand side. These cliffs were the reason people did not know about the valley. The rider nudged the mare forward into a gallop without a trace of fear, knowing that the stud would not be here if there were any possibilities of danger within miles.

The mare stopped at the edge of the trees where she knew her rider would set her free. After dismounting then unsaddling the mare, they stood for a few moments listening to the sound of the stallion's hooves as he galloped towards the pond in excitement. The mares ears perked forward listening keenly, but she did not move as she waited for permission to go. Stepping back with a quiet murmur of approval the rider gave a low chuckle as the mare eagerly spun on her hind legs galloping towards the black.

The rider watched them run around the valley for a few minutes in pleasure, before turning to ready the camp that was used only for this occasion. Going to a cairn of rocks and digging up the supplies hidden underground to protect them from scavengers, the rider took them to the fire pit then prepared the camp. Once finished decided to take a swim so walked over to the edge of the small lake.

The transformation that took place at the lagoon would leave a stranger stunned in open mouth shock as the rider shook waist length raven black hair out from under her tanned hat. Only after her clothes were removed did one see her lush body. She was stunning! She stood five feet five inches tall with a muscled body that was every man's fantasy, with large firm breasts. She had slightly slanted light green eyes with long black luscious eyelashes. High cheekbones with a dusky complexion gave away her Indian heritage. She stood bold and proud against the shadows of the cliffs then dived gracefully into the water. Swimming until her body felt refreshed as well as relaxed, she finally got out. Raven sat in the warmth of the sun, to dry her golden bronze body. She shook out her long straight hair so that it could also dry faster.

Raven lay back thinking about her parents, which she had not done for quite a long time. Her mother had been a full-blooded Cheyenne. If you were to put mother and daughter together, you would swear that they were twins, except for Ravens green eyes as well as her slightly lighter skin. Her grandfather on her mother's side was Giant Bear a Cheyenne Chief of the Wolf tribe. Her father had been half-Cheyenne as well as half-British. Her grandfather on her father's side had been full British, surprisingly an Earl of the realm in Britain. He had been a general in the army stationed at the fort, which is how he met his Cheyenne wife. They were married by the Cheyenne first then later he had taken her to the fort where he had married her again in the white mans way. It had caused a scandal here and in England, she was told. They had one child Everett to the whites or Red Fox to the Cheyenne.

Ravens grandmother died giving birth to Everett, so Ravens grandfather quit the army then bought a thousand acres of good fertile land. He started what was to become one of the largest wealthiest ranches in the area. It was not until the Earl died that his son Everett decided to go find the Cheyenne and meet the rest of his family. There, he met Ravens mother Morning Dove. They fell instantly in love then married six months later. They returned to Everett's ranch where they got married again by a white preacher. They had two children, Raven who was twenty-three, as well as a boy Edward named after his British grandfather. Edward just turned sixteen years old; he was known to the Cheyenne as Dream Dancer.

Five years ago, Ravens parents both died in a stagecoach hold up on their way to Boston. Raven eighteen at the time had to take full responsibility of a grief stricken eleven-year-old boy, plus a thriving ranch that she had to learn to manage by herself.

One thing that Raven would like to thank their parents for was keeping their Indian culture alive. Since she was three, she had spent six months out of every year with her Cheyenne grandfather. It was the first time she had been away from her parents for any length of time, so it was quite frightening to a three-year-old child, but it did not take her long to adjust.

The first three years with the Cheyenne were spent playing with the other children then learning all their customs, as well as their language. When Raven was six the women took the rambunctious six year old in hand and taught her how to cook, tan hides, as well as make buckskins. This went on for two years. At the age of eight, Raven was banished from the women's presence unexpectedly, before being taken in hand by her grandfather as well as the other warriors. From that day forward, she learned everything a warrior did. She learned to hunt with a bow, as well as a rifle, then how to track game, and humans. She learned the art of using a tomahawk, the proper use of a bow, knife fighting, as well as how to use a coup stick, plus everything else a warrior learned.

This part she did not understand because in the Cheyenne society women were not even permitted to touch a warrior's weapon. She was the only woman to learn both that she was aware of anyway. So just after her parents died, she had approached the shaman curiously then asked him why she was allowed to be a warrior when she was a woman. What the shaman told Raven had flabbergasted her at first, but after it sank in it made her proud...

The shaman eyed Raven for a moment speculatively before nodding as if just deciding she was ready for the truth. "At your naming ceremony I had a vision of you as well as a boy, your brother of course, who would not be born for another seven years. It is highly unusual to have a dream of a brother and sister together, especially when the brother is not even born yet. Both of you were standing protectively over not only your ranch but also over the Cheyenne village, then the vision changed. You stood all alone like a warrior with Indian buckskins, war paint, and a gun with a raven in the background protectively keeping evil spirits away from both the ranch as well as the village. So you were trained as a warrior. It was quite a surprise when the raven claimed you since your mother had already named you Raven. Most warriors have a child's name at first until they become warriors then are renamed. Since you are white as well, you should have two names, but your mother named you true. A different vision was shown to me a few minutes later about your brother. He would also stand protectively over both the ranch as well as the village, but he had on the white man's clothes with a book that had white eyes scratch on it. I also saw him standing on one of the white man's giant canoes. Your brother was destined to have two names one white, as well as one Indian, but again he is unusual he will keep his childhood name and not receive another."

So far Raven mused the visions had proven true. The Cheyenne wintered every year in a canyon that was part of Ravens property so that no white man dared bother them. She always had men patrolling that sector of the ranch to make sure her people were safe.

There was one Cheyenne brave from each band that kept the younger braves in control at all times because one of the rules was that as long as the Cheyenne stayed on Ravens land no war, killing, or horse stealing from the town was allowed. There was one exception made though. Once a year the young braves who were close to becoming warriors were given a description of a horse that was hidden somewhere on her land. They were then told that if they could find that horse without being discovered they were allowed to keep it. This was their final test before they could become warriors, and Raven never made it easy for them.

Before Ravens father had died, they had gone to a town meeting to let the townspeople know that they planned to have the Cheyenne winter on their land. There was outrage as well as apprehension at first, but after six years of peace between them, the town accepted then even began trading with the Indians on occasions.

As word got around to other bands of Cheyenne that Ravens family was living in peace so close to a white town, more bands asked to join the winter procession onto Ravens ranch. Where once there were fifty tepees, now there were two hundred and fifty tepees. Every year they seemed to have more tribes asking to join. This concerned Raven at first, because not all Cheyenne were peaceful. However, every new band that joined not only had to talk to Raven, but also had to swear to keep the peace. They also had to be approved by all the Cheyenne bands that were already there. All white captives brought onto these lands were questioned first before being released if they wished, or they could stay with the Cheyenne then be adopted. There had only been one problem with a band that refused to give up a prisoner when she wanted to return to her own people, they would not release her. She happened to be owned by a war chief who refused to give her up. There was much arguing at first, but the band was finally asked to leave, which Raven was grateful for since she knew that they would have eventually caused problems.

The only other issue that Raven had when other bands started joining them was food. How were they to feed so many Cheyenne in the winter? Raven, her grandfather, and all the other chiefs that had joined the band deliberated for three days. It was eventually agreed that two months before winter all the bands would show up then every available hunter would hunt until snow started falling. It was also decided that two warriors from each band would work on the ranch as wranglers for one year to earn the right to fresh beef and other supplies needed during the winter. Every warrior had to take their turn so that all could learn how to deal with the cattle. This way if Raven ever had an emergency all the warriors knew how to help, so that they could be called on at any time.

Several old Indian women plus a few men that could not keep up when the bands were on the move, since they had no family to help them, stayed at the ranch year round. This way they could still contribute to their tribe's well being; it also helped them to feel useful. So far, ten Indian women took care of fifteen acres of gardens that grew every kind of vegetable, herb, as well as fruit that the land could produce. They harvested bottled then dried everything they could find. They even went further to collect wild vegetables, fruits, nuts, and anything else that was edible.

There were only six old warriors since most did not survive to old age. Two took care of about five hundred laying hens. Two looked after ten milking cows. Two more braves looked after about three hundred pigs.

So the town would not feel slighted there were fifty year round cowboys then at round up and cattle drives fifty more were employed. There were two ranch cooks, one for the house as well as one for the bunkhouses. Two camp cooks stayed with the cowboys at all times they were also from town. There were three maids, one for the two bachelor bunkhouses, one for the single women bunkhouse, as well as one for the main house. Three women plus two men from town was hired to assist in the gardens. Two men kept the barns, storage sheds, as well as the forge cleaned. Nobody was allowed to remain idle if your own chores were done then you helped someone else. Even the children were given light chores to do.

All Indians or cowboys who worked on the ranch were given their own gelding to ride and keep. No mares were used as they were only for breeding or on the rare occasion women mount. It was also decided that all the trade goods of the Cheyenne were sold for cash only then this money was given to Raven for the use of the land. It was quickly becoming apparent that another thousand acres of land would be needed soon if anymore bands were going to join them. She kept this money in a separate account, and she added a quarter of all money from the sale of her cattle as well as the horses. Next year she would be able to pay cash for the neighbouring thousand acres that was adjoining her property.

Raven let it be known that if her people needed anything during the winter; it would be taken from that particular account as long as everyone agreed it was necessary. That also included horses. If a warrior or maiden who was not working on the ranch needed a horse, it would also be taken out of this account. That is why it had taken so long to save for this other piece of land someone always seemed to need something. The same privileges were given to the people on the ranch. So far, this system had worked remarkably well for Raven. Everybody at the ranch plus the Cheyenne were more than happy with it so far. The townspeople were also happy because they could buy genuine Indian articles for a fair price, but they did not actually have to deal with the Indians personally. Raven handled all transactions, so that nobody felt cheated.

Raven thought about the other part of the dream it was also coming true as she sighed dejectedly. Her brother was leaving for university this fall. She would miss him terribly, but her brother wanted to be a lawyer. He always said that it is unjust how the white man takes advantage of the Indians, so he decided to become a lawyer to fight for Indian rights. Edward decided to go to school in England so that he could also take over the title and lands that belonged to him through their English grandfather. She knew the task her brother had chosen would not be an easy one, being three quarters Cheyenne in a white community would be extremely difficult to overcome. She knew though that Edward would make out all right since he was just as determined as she was. The fact that he did not look native would be to his advantage also.

Raven sighed forlornly as she got up to get dressed, before going then setting some snares for fresh meat. She decided to walk around before the sun went totally down. As she walked towards the little lake, she spotted her mare with the stallion. She watched in fascination as the studs long penis came out and he mounted her mare. The mare squealed in pleasure as the stallion entered her.

Since Raven took over the ranch, she had watched horses, cattle, dogs, as well as pigs breed. She had not thought much about it in all these years. After all, it was only to increase her herds. But two years ago when she first brought this mare here to be bred, something inside her changed. She started to feel shivery sensations whenever she watched the stud cover her mares. It was not too long after her first stirrings that she started having dreams about a man, but she could never seem to see him fully. The first time it happened Raven had awoken feeling hot, flushed, as well as scared. She also felt frustrated because she could not remember her dream fully all that she could recall when awake is a shadow of a man. Worried at first thinking that something was terribly wrong with her, she had gone to the shaman to ask him about it...

The shaman smiled in satisfaction as he chuckled knowingly. "Ah my daughter at last you are becoming a woman, not just a warrior!"

The shaman would say no more after that, so Raven had left his tepee with his cryptic words still ringing in her ears. The dream had returned often after that, but Raven tried to ignore them without much success.

Raven finished her walk then turned back to her camp to check her snares. She was in luck as she found two rabbits inside. While the rabbits cooked on the spit, she scrapped the hides automatically, without thought. She tried to ignore the shivery feelings she was still experiencing from watching the horses mate. She ate before curling up in her bedroll and went to sleep.

As Raven slept her dream lover came to her again, but this time it was different. The dream was so strong that it seemed as if she were there physically as she saw him clearly for the first time. He was riding a white horse straight towards her at a full gallop. Just as he came abreast of her, the man leaned down then swept Raven into his arms. She turned and looked fully into his face for the first time. She caught her breath in wonder he was gorgeous! He had eyes that would rival the storm clouds that swept in from time to time. He had unusual light blonde hair, almost white. The man's head started to drop for a kiss.

Raven was forced awake by a ringing challenge from the stallion as well as the sound of her mare's hooves galloping into her camp in excitement. She jerked into a sitting position then grabbed her revolver, which was never far from her side. She jumped to her feet instantly awake before grabbing her mare's mane as she vaulted onto her horses bareback in one swift motion. She turned her mare as she galloped towards the opening of the valley, to see what was upsetting the stud.

The mare stopped beside the black and they all waited tensely in silence for whatever was coming.

The only sound that could be heard at that moment was the faint sound of another horse as well as the cocking of Ravens revolver. She had to strain hard to hear the soft tread of the other horse, so she knew it could not be a white man's because the horse was not wearing shoes. Therefore, it was either another wild horse or an Indian. Just as the other horse came into view, a ravens call floated through the stillness as a large bay gelding slipped through the opening.

Raven sighed in relief then put her gun away when she recognized the signal of one of her family members. When she recognized her cousin Running Wolf, a shiver of apprehension shook her. She knew that Running Wolf would not come here unless there was an emergency. He would think it beneath him as the next chief of her grandfather's band to be a messenger.

Raven and Running Wolf clasped arms in the traditional warriors greeting then Raven turned her horse to take Running Wolf to her camp. She eyed Running Wolf speculatively out of the corner of her eye thinking how much he looked like his father Black Hawk, or Tommy as his mother sometimes called him. Running Wolf had his fathers blue eyes plus his build, but he had the darker skin with long black hair of the Cheyenne, his father had light brown hair. Running Wolf like Raven was three quarters Cheyenne as well as a quarter white. Black Hawk was Ravens uncle he had lived with Melissa Ray for most of his young life before Giant Bear had even known that he had a son.

Giant Bear's second wife, Mary, had found out that she was pregnant after Giant Bear had left to pursue the killers of his first wife. Being white and not growing up in the Indian ways, she had gotten scared so ran off to her brother's home to have her baby. She quickly learned that she had made a mistake in running to him because he hated Indians then tried to kill his nephew when he was born. Later he had tried to kill Giant Bear when the lovers were reunited after nine years of separation.

Raven and Running Wolf dismounted, which cut her contemplation short. She slapped her mares rump to send her back out to the stallion. She put more fuel on the fire to heat up coffee as well as the rabbit she had cooked earlier, but had not finished. They sat across the fire from each other as Raven served Running Wolf the remainder of her rabbit, like any Indian maiden would do for a man.

While he ate that, she took out her peace pipe, as tradition dictated must be smoked before anything serious could be discussed between two warriors. Running Wolf belched in appreciation than Raven lit the peace pipe. She took two deep puffs and blew smoke into the air then more smoke at the ground before blowing the rest of the smoke to the right and left. She handed the pipe to Running Wolf. He repeated the ceremony then they sat back to enjoy the peace pipe in silence.

After the pipe was smoked, Running Wolf sat forward intently. "I bring greetings to the Raven, 'Protector' of our tribe, and a message of urgency to come to the winter camp as soon as possible!"

Raven was speechless for a bit stunned then she motioned in apprehension. "But the winter camp has been empty for two weeks now. Why would our grandfather bring the tribes back there?"

Running Wolf exhaled noisily in irritation before shrugging perplexed. "I cannot say why our grandfather chose to go back to the winter camp, luckily it was only the Wolf tribe that needed to go back not any of the others. All I can give you is our grandfather's full message. He said to tell the Raven she must hurry to the winter camp or many deaths would occur and only she can stop it. He also said that you must come as an Indian with no white mans trappings. Grandfather said to tell you that he would explain everything when you get there."

Raven mussed over the cryptic message for a moment then frowned baffled. She gestured curiously at her cousin. "Running Wolf, do you have any clue as to what is going on?"

Running Wolf scowled in annoyance before shaking his head negatively. "No, I do not! All I can tell you is that seven days away from our winter camp right on the traditional route to our summer camp we came across a wagon that had been wiped out. Only two white survivors were left. One was a woman the other one was a man. The woman died despite all the medicine man's attempts to save her. The man was unconscious when we found them he was still unconscious when I left. The medicine man did not think he would live at first either. The shaman and our grandfather argued for a long time. Then the shaman went into seclusion to meditate and ask the Great Spirit what to do. He came out then called our grandfather to him, and they argued for a while again. When our grandfather finished talking to the shaman, he advised everyone that we would be returning to the winter camp. Our grandfather approached me then asked me to come here to give you his message of great importance. The only other thing I can tell you is that it was a Cheyenne war party who massacred those people."

Raven grimaced in anger. She already knew who was responsible, but asked anyway just to make sure. "Running Wolf, do you know which Cheyenne band?"

Running Wolf nodded decisively. "Yes! I recognized Slippery As An Eel among the dead. He is from the tribe that you turned away and shamed."

Raven inclined her head grimly her suspicions confirmed then waved anxiously. "Go tell our grandfather that I will be there as soon as possible, but I must go home first to get my Indian pony and gear. I will meet you there as soon as I can."

Running Wolf got up then jumped on his gelding without another word his mission accomplished.

Raven stood there in contemplation as she watched him leave, before giving a shrill whistle for her mare as she hastily broke camp.

The mare came galloping into camp at full speed when she heard the desperate whistle from her mistress and stood quietly as Raven saddled her for the trip back to the ranch.

Raven patted her horse in sympathy. "Sorry, old girl, it looks as if your love life is going to have to be put on hold for now."

The mare nickered as if she understood then waited patiently for her rider.

Raven mounted and bent down close to her horse's neck. "Come on girl get me home as quick as possible!"

As if the mare understood the urgency, she pinned back her ears then spun on her hind legs towards the cliffs and the short cut home.

As Ravens horse flew across gullies then through streams at a full gallop, her thoughts were flying just about as fast. It was obvious to her that the other group of Cheyenne was setting up her family, but until Raven learned all the facts it was hard to figure out exactly what they were up to. She was mystified by her grandfather's insistence that she was to come as an Indian, instead of as she was; it made no sense to her. She knew though that her grandfather would not tell her to do it if it were not necessary for some reason.

Raven shook off thoughts of her grandfather for now and tried to remember her dream from earlier. She remembered seeing her dream lover's face for the first time, but now she could not remember what he looked like. Darn! If she could have slept just a little longer maybe she would have remembered, but it was gone again. Someday she was sure they would meet until then she must put him out of her mind. Raven sighed in aggravation as she shook off all thoughts. She needed to pay more attention to where they were going, so she did not accidentally killed them both. She leaned closer to her mares neck for more speed urging her along as the feeling of forewarning increased.

CHAPTER TWO

Raven and her mare crested a hill, which gave a clear view of the large sprawling ranch. She slowed as she looked down in satisfaction then kept them at a walk for the last quarter mile to cool the mare down. She thought of her father and mother again, she knew her parents would be extremely proud of her if they could see how much the ranch had grown since she had taken it over. Not only was she going to expand to two thousand acres next year, which her father had talked about before he died. But in the last five years she had built a second bunkhouse for the single men as well as one for the single women. Three more cottages were built because three of her people living on the ranch got married. A second barn had been built as well as a forge with additional stalls for sick or quarantined animals. The blacksmith from town came out once a month for any major work, but a young fellow looked after any minor tasks that needed to be done on a daily basis.

The cattle herd had also increased from one thousand head to around two thousand head. So three more bulls had to be bought to increase the conception rate as well as to increase the quality of beef she was selling. Now there were twenty bulls instead of seventeen, which was another reason more land was needed. The horse herd also doubled now there was four pastures instead of two. There was the old stallion with his fifty head of mares, but he was getting too old for more than that. The next pasture consisted of geldings only, where once there was two hundred now four hundred head was used for ranch work as well as for sale. The third one held all the female offspring's from the first pasture.

About three years ago, a new stud was found for this group of mares. There was now seventy-five head of mares in that pasture. The fourth one held all the female offspring's of the second stallion plus the excess from the first stud.

Raven did not like it when the second stallion over exert himself because he was her main Indian pony, so she needed a third stud. There were now seventy-six mares in the fourth pasture, and it was growing every year. They were driven into the valley twenty-five head at a time. She knew a fifth stallion would have to be found soon because it was just too hard on the black stud. They had been lucky last year that all the mares had conceived. She had finally found a new stallion several months ago that was coming next year. He was a stunning silver white thoroughbred stud colt from Melissa Brown's ranch.

Melissa at one time was the sheriff in a town called Smyth's Crossing, but now she is the marshal of North Dakota. Raven had met Melissa as well as her husband Jed through her grandfather Giant Bear. She had grown up on stories of how her Cheyenne grandfather, Jed Brown as well as Melissa Ray had met then defeated a group of cold-blooded murderers. It was not until earlier last year that Raven actually met Melissa and Jed Brown though. That was when she first caught sight of the colt Melissa was selling, he was the last son to Melissa's stallion Lightning he would make a good addition to Ravens herd. Melissa had promised to keep him until next year for her.

Raven shook off her thoughts, it was almost suppertime of the next day, and they had galloped all the way home. Both were exhausted they had only stopped a couple of times to eat as well as to give her horse a needed rest. She reached down then patted her mares sweat encrusted neck in apology. "Sorry about that, girl!"

Raven guided her mare over to the lower pasture were Ravens Indian pony Brave Heart was kept. She gave a sharp shrill whistle as she called him to her. She jumped of her mare and loosened the saddle slightly on her horse before tying the reins around her neck so she would not trip on them. She slapped her on the rump to send her on her way. "Okay, girl, go to the barn. Steve will look after you."

Ravens mare nickered then turned to the stables where she knew oats would be waiting for her, before trotting off obediently, familiar with this routine.

Brave Heart came galloping to the fence in response to his mistress's call and waited.

Raven open the gate wide then let Brave Heart out, not one bit worried he would take off. While she was closing the gate, he turned to face his mistress without budging from that spot waiting patiently. She turned to him and walked around checking his feet then his legs to make sure he was ready for a long hard journey.

He was a beautiful stallion he stood sixteen hands high with perfect markings. He was a black and white pinto highly prized by the Cheyenne. He was wild when she first found him staggering around with a bullet crease in his neck. Even being creased he had managed to evade capture. It took a long time to get him to trust Raven enough to treat the wound, but eventually she managed to help him. They have been inseparable ever since.

Raven grabbed Brave Heart's mane then hoisted herself up bareback. She walked him over to the barn for her Indian tack, before jumping down. She turned to him in command. "Stand, Brave Heart!"

Raven went into the barn with no worries knowing that her horse would not budge from that spot, and that nobody would go near him. Everybody on the ranch knew that he would kill anyone who went to close so avoided him at all costs. She entered then looked around expectantly but did not see anyone. "Steve, where are you?"

"Over here, Raven!"

Raven saw Steve's head pop up from behind her roan mare, so she walked over to the stall. She leaned against it as she studied him carefully. He had golden blonde curly locks and was shorter than she was with brown eyes that were so light in coloration they appeared golden. He was a little over weight, but not fat. He was the best horse wrangler Raven had ever met, except for the Cheyenne of course. She paid good money to keep him around here.

Steve was bent over putting a wrap on the back leg of her mare.

Raven sighed in regret as she eyed her mare in concern. "Is her leg sore Steve?"

Steve inclined his head distractedly as he continued to work on Ravens mare, but did not look up. "Just the one, it looks a little strained, so I just want to wrap it for the night just in case. You sure rode her hard I have never seen a horse you were riding this bad before, what's up?"

Raven frowned thoughtfully in anxiety. "There is trouble at the winter camp! I am not sure exactly what the problem is, but it does not sound good."

Steve looked up at Raven perplexed for a moment before looking back down at what he was doing. "I thought they were gone. Shouldn't they have left two weeks ago?"

Raven sighed anxiously. "Yes, but they had to come back for some reason. I had to come here for Brave Heart before I could go find out what is going on up there. You might want to watch my mare closely for awhile, the black did manage to cover her a couple of times before we left so she might be pregnant."

Steve nodded as he got up. "Okay, I will keep a close eye on her."

Raven smiled in thanks before pointing behind her at the barn doors in warning. "I am leaving Brave Heart just outside for a few minutes while I go get ready, so be careful when you go out. Can you please take out a small bucket of oats to him?"

Steve inclined his head in agreement and went to get the oats.

Raven unhooked her Indian rifle holder from her usual saddle then grabbed the rest of her Indian tack. All three she had made herself, the bridal had no bit, and the saddle blanket had a few modifications. It had a girth strap, plus a small saddle horn woven in for mounting on the run.

Raven walked out of the barn so she could saddle Brave Heart. He was still standing exactly where she had left him. She walked up slowly as she praised him in Cheyenne for standing so patiently.

Steve nearing the barn doors started whistling a tune loudly to let both Raven, as well as Brave Heart, know that he was coming out. Only once had he made the mistake of walking outside without letting the stud know first. He would carry the scar on his hip for the rest of his life.

Brave Heart's ears went back in anger then he started to back away from the barn. A sharp command from his mistress was the only thing keeping him from bolting. It took him a few minutes to smell the oats, when he did instantly he calmed down.

Raven smiled when Brave Heart nickered, and she chuckled in amusement then called out in reassurance. "It's okay Steve, he knows that you are coming."

Steve stuck his head out the door cautiously, but when he saw the stallion standing with his ears perked up he slowly walked out the door. He set the bucket down close to Raven but stayed away from the horse.

Raven finished putting her Indian tack on Brave Heart and grabbed the bucket then let her horse eat. She turned to Steve inquiringly as she motioned hopefully. "I have to go up to the house, can you just stand here for a few minutes?"

Steve smiled calmly not worried now. "Sure you can go, I will make sure nobody comes and spooks him."

Raven inclined her head in thanks then turned and sprinted to the ranch house. She vaulted up the three steps then rushed through the door. She paused as she looked around, on the left side of the house was a large dinning room and kitchen with the maids room past that. On the right was a sitting room then a small hallway that brought you to stairs leading up. If you walked past the little hallway with the stairs, you would reach the den and just beyond that was the cook's room. There was a door at the end of the hallway; it led into a storage area then down to the root cellar. The root cellar ran the entire length of the house.

Raven went past the sitting room and turned right; she did not even stop to take off her outer footwear. She hurried to the end of the short hallway then turned left before taking the stairs two at a time. Once upstairs you were facing a blank wall, which was Edward's rooms, behind her was the library. But to get into either room you had to turn left and go down this short hallway to the very end. Which would lead you to a T then you could only turn left or right into a bigger hallway. Once you turned left down the bigger hallway there was two guest rooms on the right. They would be over the top of the dinning room as well as part of the kitchen; on the left was access to the library. If you turned right down the bigger hallway instead, and go down that hallway, it would take you to her rooms on the left. That would make her room right over the top of the maid's room, plus part of the kitchen. It was right across from Edward's rooms that would make his room over the top of the cook's room as well as the den. Once at the T she turned left, went about ten steps then turned left again to enter the library, which was directly across from the two guest rooms.

Raven rushed through the door slightly out of breath from the steep stairs. She scared her brother so badly that he jumped from his seat in fear as his book went tumbling to the floor in panic.

Edward stood with his mouth hanging open in shocked surprise for a moment before managing to get words past the tightness in his throat. "Raven! What on earth are you doing home, and why did you just try to give me a heart attack?"

Raven laughed at the astonished look on her brother's face, not in the least worried by his admonishment. She sat down in a chair as she studied him silently in affection. Edward at the age of sixteen was a half an inch away from reaching six feet already. He was powerfully built for his age thanks to his training with the Cheyenne. As well as the hard work that he had to do around the ranch in order to help, Raven out. His hair was shoulder length a light brown with auburn streaks throughout. In the summer, his hair turned lighter almost a strawberry blonde.

Their father always said that Edward looked so much like his father, the late Earl, that it was eerie. He had the same aristocratic nose as well as the strong stubborn chin. Edward's eyes were a deep green so dark in fact, that sometimes they appeared black especially when he was upset or angry. He had the high cheekbones of the Cheyenne with a slight dusky look to his skin, but it was a lot lighter than Ravens except in the summer when he got a tan.

Raven sighed as she shook off her reflection, before getting up and pointed down the hallway. "Come on, Ed. I will explain everything while I pack."

Edward nodded perplexed as he followed Raven obediently. He watched her grab an Indian dress that she rarely wore then moccasins, buckskin pants, and a matching shirt were thrown on the bed. He frowned in puzzlement then showed his youth in his impatience. "What is going on Raven? Grandfather and all our people are gone for the summer so what do you need your Indian clothes for?"

Raven jumped slightly in surprise. She had been so busy trying to find everything as she mumbled under her breath that she had totally forgotten her brother standing there impatiently waiting. She grimaced in exasperation at herself then sat down on her bed before looking up at Edward in apology. "I am sorry, I forgot you were there."

Edward inclined his head, pacified by the apology. "It's okay; now please explain to me what is going on!"

Raven told him everything that had happened since she had left.

Edward was frowning in concern by the time she finished. He motioned in apprehension. "Should I go with you in case I am needed?"

Raven shook her head negatively as she gestured calmly. "No, I need you here! You will have to take my mare, and a few hands then drive those horses into the valley for me. Do not forget to take Lady and King; they will keep the stallion from running the mares off."

Edward scowled in forewarning then leaned forward intently. "Okay, but I have to warn you that there is a late winter storm coming and it is going to be a bad one. I was going to send Josh later to warn you, it should be here…"

Edward stopped for a moment then looked off into the distance before turned back to Raven troubled. "In three or four days at the very most I would say!"

Raven nodded thoughtfully. She did not even ask him how he knew this, for as long as she could remember her brother had been able to predict storms. He even knew that there was something wrong with their parents before anyone else. She had questioned the shaman about her brother, he had told her that Edward could have been a powerful shaman or medicine man if he had decided to stay. However, he refused to teach him since he was leaving them to go to England.

Raven sighed in aggravation as she waved decisively. "I will take my wolf fur with me, but I still have to go storm or no storm!"

Edward grimaced knowingly as he waved grimly in caution. "I know you do just be careful, okay!"

Raven grinned reassuringly and hugged her brother before pushing him to the door.

Edward left the room so Raven could get dressed.

Raven took her hat off releasing her hair before dropping the hat on the bed. She plaited her hair into two long Indian braids then grabbed her wolf pelt out of the closet and put it on the bed so she would not forget it. She turned back to the bed to change into her buckskin pants then her shirt. Once done, she turned back to her closet as she took out an intricately designed carrier that she had made herself. She checked all twelve of her arrows, which she had also made herself, for breaks or missing raven feathers. Satisfied she put them back into her carrier and strapped it to her back. She turned to her bed once more then picked up her fur and put it over her shoulders. She turned back to the closet one last time then grabbed three hunting knives, all intricately made by her that were in a chest. She stuck one in each moccasin before strapping on her belt sheath with a knife already inside around her waist. When she was done, she grabbed her bow that was propped against her closet wall and turned to leave.

This transformation was even more dramatic than the one at the lake. Instead of looking like a man, she now looked full Indian, except for the eyes. Even her expressions and mannerisms from this point on would be mostly Indian, until she changed herself back. She rushed out the door then down the stairs.

Edward was waiting at the door with a saddlebag, mittens, as well as a beaver hat. On one side of the saddlebag, he had put in matches, jerky, a little chopping axe, as well as hardtack just in case she needed it. On the other side was the gift she was making for their grandfather. He looked deeply into Ravens eyes, guessing she had already changed he switched to Cheyenne. "May your journey be swift and without hardships!"

Raven locked arms with her brother in farewell then grabbed him and gave him a warm hug. She turned to leave, but not before she tucked the mittens with the beaver hat inside the saddlebag then she was out the door as she whistled for her stallion.

*****

Steve heard the whistle so backed away from the stud knowingly.

The stallion reared before spinning around as he galloped full speed to his mistress.

Raven just stood there waiting for him calmly. As her horse came towards her, she put the bow over her shoulder then slung the saddlebag around her chest by a rope that was made for this purpose. It not only freed up her hands but it also kept her wolf fur, bow, as well as her arrows in place. She waited expectantly. When it looked as if her horse would gallop right past her, she took two running strides and reached up then grabbed his mane and the saddle horn before vaulting onto his back.

At a full gallop, Raven pulled her saddlebag over her head then turned and put it behind her saddle tying it tight so it would not come off. She turned back around as she lifted her bow of her back then attached it to the strap made to hold it tight, so it did not bounce too much against her horse's side.

The two men watching went to stand by each other so that they could talk.

Steve shook his head in awe as he turned to Edward. "Every time I see her do that I wonder if one of these days she will miss and fall flat on her face."

Edward laughed in delight as he slapped Steve on the back in reassurance. "No, my friend, I do not think she will ever miss. As for me, I have tried to learn that, I am so inept though that I get dragged for a couple of feet before I can manage to get on my horse."

They both laughed at the mental image of Edward being dragged along the ground.

Edward sighed as his face sobered in question before motioning inquisitively. "Steve when will Ravens mare be ready to ride again?"

Steve shrugged in concern as he pictured the mare. "Not for two or three days at least, Raven rode her pretty hard."

Edward nodded thoughtfully as he waved in caution to the north. "Well there is a big storm coming in three or four days, so I guess we will just have to wait to go to the valley until afterwards."

Steve inclined his head without questions, familiar with Edward's predictions. He turned away to go back to the barn so he could check on the mare.

Edward stared after his sister a little longer still extremely concerned, before turning back to the ranch house with a worried frown. Something was just not right as he felt a shiver of foreboding. He had a strange feeling that he should have gone as well.

*****

Raven rode hard for the rest of the night. The direction she was taking would require at least three or four days of hard riding to reach the village. Two extra days than the direct route, but she needed to tell her men to drive the cattle closer to the ranch just in case. Her brother was never wrong, and she did not want to take any chances. She reached one of her herds of cattle around nine o'clock that night. She had only stopped once to water her horse then grabbed a quick bit. She saw three of her men turn their horses to meet her, so she gave her ravens call to let them know it was her.

Two men stopped and waited for her while one turned then rode to camp to tell everyone else that she was coming. She stopped as she inclined her head in greeting at the two men. Both were brothers and almost identical, except one had blue eyes the other one had light grey eyes. They were the same height at five foot nine, with light brown hair. Paul was skinnier than Jake was but Jake was more muscular.

Raven turned to Paul first, before motioning anxiously. "Paul, call in the rest of the boys and meet us back at camp."

Paul nodded without questioning why then rode off.

Jake eyed Raven in question, before beckoning ahead. "Follow me."

Raven rode beside her foreman and warily dismounted before turning her horse loose to graze. She walked over to the fire then hunkered down as she patiently waited for the camp cook to dish her up beans with pork and biscuits. He handed the plate to her then poured her a strong cup of coffee. She smiled in thanks at the chunky black haired typical camp cook and ate hungrily as the boys started coming in. She waited until they were all in then gestured at Jake in warning, but included all the men in her discussion. "Jake there is a storm coming in three or four days, so I want you to drive the cattle closer to the hay sheds. You will have to let Shorty know for me as well so he can get his cattle closer to."

Jake nodded before waving inquisitively at her clothes in surprise. "What's up Raven you are dressed to go see your grandfather, but I know that he left already?"

Raven retold the story to the men.

Jake frowned grimly when Raven finished as he motioned anxiously. "This could cause you lots of problems with the townspeople if they find out. You know that they only tolerate your people and even you because they have benefited too. We both know that there are still some, especially your neighbour, who keeps trying to get the townspeople to drive you out or call in the army. The only reason they have not done it yet is that they do not know how many Cheyenne are actually out here. If they find out, they will bring in the army for sure!"

Raven scowled knowingly then waved in aggravation. "I know! That is why I am going out there now and why I need you to make sure all hands stay on the ranch until I get back. I would not want anyone to say anything by accident. Running Wolf said that they found Slippery As An Eel, so we know who did it. Unfortunately, the white man was unconscious when my family rescued him so he will not be able to help clear my family of any wrongdoing. First, I will have to prove it was not them then track the real killers and bring them to town to hang. Or the townspeople might still try to blame my people just because they are Indians!"

Jake nodded decisively as he leaned forward earnestly then pointed at her to make his point. "If you need me to help track down the killers send for me! I will be watching for your signal."

There was a murmur from the men as they each vowed to help Raven and her family if she needed them. She thanked each one for their support then got up and turned away. She walked towards her horse before any of them could see the tears in her eyes. She knew that every one of her hands would die to protect her as well as the ranch if need be.

Raven walked around Brave Heart making sure that the hard journey was not affecting him. It gave her the time she needed to get her emotions back under control. Once she was satisfied that he was doing okay, she mounted. She turned back to Jake then gestured curiously. "Have you seen Bruno recently?"

Jake looked at the men, and they all shook their heads no. He turned back to Raven then waved towards the north. "I saw him once about a week ago with a female wolf."

Raven nodded in disappointment as she shrugged dismissively. "If he is around he will find me."

Jake inclined his head in farewell before turning to his men grimly. "Mount up boys it's going to be a long night. Paul you can go let Shorty know about the storm."

Jake turned back to Raven with a concerned expression. "You be very careful, and I will watch for your smoke signal. Do not be stubborn about it either!"

Raven reached down then took his hand in gratitude. "Thanks Jake and good luck to all of you".

Raven turned Brave Heart before galloping away without another word. They maintained that pace for the rest of the night. At dawn, she slowed down to a trot then to a walk to allow the stud cool down so they could stop for a needed rest. She wanted to stay at one of the established campsites that were hidden from strangers. There were four of them in total; they had passed one at dusk. At each one, there was a cairn of rocks with blankets, food, flint, water, and oats for the horses. All were buried in waterproof containers so nothing spoilt.

Twice a year one of her men took a wagon then replenished all the sites. That is why Raven had not bothered with a packhorse. She unpacked the cairn and gave Brave Heart some oats then a little water, before grabbing a sack with dried jerky and cakes for herself. The cakes were made with flour or cornmeal. Groundnuts were added as well as a variety of fresh berries that were mixed with animal fat then baked until firm and brown. You could live on the cakes they kept for a long time, which made them excellent travelling food.

Raven finished eating, before grabbing her blankets then rolled into them. She was just dozing off when Brave Heart gave a loud snort and pawed the ground in warning. She turned over then stared up into a pair of yellow eyes. Unexpectedly she felt a rough wet tongue lick her face. She smiled in pleasure as she reached up and patted the soft fur in welcome. "Hello, Bruno. I knew you would come if you were around, where is your girlfriend?"

Bruno looked behind him.

It was not until then that Raven saw the second pair of yellow eyes.

The female turned and disappeared.

Raven gave Bruno a final pat then waved her hand at him in dismissal. "Its okay boy, you do not have to go this time."

Bruno turned back and gave Raven another sloppy kiss in goodbye, before turning then disappeared after the she wolf.

Raven sighed dejectedly as she turned to go back to sleep wondering if she would ever see him again. She had raised him from a pup he was half wolf and half dog, the only one that had survived out of the litter. They were inseparable for a long time until recently that is, when he started wondering looking for a mate. She was glad he had found one.

Raven yawned then fell asleep, she slept for about two hours before jerking herself awake and broke camp quickly. She saddled Brave Heart then turned back once more to make sure everything was back the way she had found it, satisfied she mounted and galloped away. She did not go far when Bruno caught up then loped along beside her. She looked behind them and saw the female following at a distance. She looked back down at Bruno then smiled in delight. "Okay, Bruno, you can come along too."

Raven only stopped twice to feed and water the animals then she was back in the saddle again. Around evening, they passed the third campsite, but she kept going hoping to make it to the fourth one by dawn. She was getting worried now she could smell the snow coming, but they were so exhausted that they had to stop for a rest. It would still be another day at least until she reached her grandfathers if she could keep up this pace. On the other hand maybe two, if the snow slowed them but it would not help if she killed her horse or herself before they could get there. So she stopped at the fourth camp and fed the animals. She curled up beside Bruno then fell into a deep sleep.

Raven did not awaken again until the first few snowflakes fell on her face. Instantly she sat up in anxiety and knew that she had slept longer than she should have. She hurriedly got up and broke camp as fast as she could not even bothering with eating as she mounted. They were now in a race for their lives, the animals sensing the urgency broke out into a full gallop. They maintained that speed until Raven felt it prudent to slow down or possibly kill them. It was now a full out blizzard impossible to see two feet in front of them. She bent over to Bruno in urgency. "Find Grandfather, Bruno!"

Bruno trotted ahead as Raven tied herself to the saddle so exhausted now she could barely keep her eyes open. The animals knew the way they would take them safely to the canyon without any help from her. They were still a day away at this speed, but Raven was already partially frozen as the temperature dropped dramatically. She knew that if she did not tie herself on she could fall off then maybe freeze to death. She hunched under her wolf fur before dozing in the saddle off and on for the rest of the day. Twice she almost fell off her horse, but her bound hands saved her.

Raven did not awaken fully again, until Brave Heart stopped then Bruno started barking insistently at something. She tried to release herself, but the bonds shrunk and would not budge. They were cutting painfully into her wrists.

Giant Bear ran out of the tepee then hurried over to help his granddaughter. He was wary of the stud but too worried about Raven to let that stop him.

Brave Heart shifted uneasily, but he was too exhausted to put up a real fuss.

Raven barely able to speak managed to get a few words past her chattered teeth. "Bruno, go find Spotted Owl and bring him."

Bruno loped off with a little yelp.

Giant Bear got her bonds severed then caught her as she fell from her horse too exhausted and frozen to walk by herself. The chief was just lifting his granddaughter to bring her inside when Spotted Owl arrived with Bruno leading him. Giant Bear turned to him in concern. "Take Brave Heart to the pasture, you are the only one who can touch him besides Raven then get the shaman here as quickly as you can!"

Spotted Owl nodded in confusion wondering why the chief did not need the medicine man instead. He shrugged and picked up Brave Heart's reins then talking to him soothingly so he would not spook, he turned and trotted off. He stopped short in surprise when he saw the shaman already coming towards him.

The shaman stopped then motioned inquisitively. "How is she?"

Spotted Owl shook his head unknowingly. "It does not look good the chief had to carry her in!"

The shaman inclined his head in thanks before hurrying to the chief's tepee in concern. He rushed in and went straight over to Giant Bear without even looking at the white man huddled in the corner. All his attention was on Giant Bear as he lovingly, unwrapped his granddaughter. The shaman bent down to help his chief, totally cutting off the white man's curious gaze.

*****

The white man sitting in the corner sat huddled in silence fearfully. He had finally woken up today with his arm bound as well as tied to his chest. The pain was excruciating he knew by the feeling that it was broken in more than one place. When the medicine man probed at his ribs, he thought that at least one of them was broken. His face was in horrible shape also since his nose was broken with both his lips swollen. The white man could feel some cuts in his mouth they stung something fierce, and there was a distinct metallic taste of blood when licking his lips. Both his eyes must be swollen as well because he needed to squint to see, they hurt like the dickens also.

The medicine man had tried to straighten his nose, but he was not sure if he had been successful or not. All he knew was it had hurt like hell. He had been given food, water, as well as medication then told to stay. Why he was still alive, he did not know. He had asked about his sisters insistently, but the medicine man did not seem to understand English. He must have guessed at the question though because he had given a sad shake of his head, so the Englishman figured both were probably killed. He had sat in this very place all day afraid to move or speak, remembering all the horror stories he had heard about Indian torture and wondered when they would kill him.

The white man had been sitting here quietly watching the chief secretively when a dog started barking, he had stared in disbelief when the chief jumped up then rushed outside. The white man heard someone speak, but it was too low to understand or to make out whether it was female or male. He was even more astonished when the chief came back into the tepee carrying what looked like a wolf, until he noticed the long legs dangling. A few moments later, a wolf did walk in the white man jerked reflexively and groaned in pain as his ribs throbbed.

The wolf looked over at him curiously then came over to investigate. As the wolf sniffed him, the white man sat terrified holding his breath in fear. When the wolf was satisfied he licked the man's hand before lying down beside him.

The white man released the breath he had been holding as he tentatively reached out to pet the wolf with his good hand in wonder.

The wolf let the man touch him for a few minutes before getting up and then went over to the chief to watch him. The chief looked up in exasperation then spoke harshly in rebuke. The wolf whined plaintively and went back to the white man then laid down in a sulk watching the chief closely.

Giant Bear watched Bruno slink over to the white man and trustingly laid down beside him. He watched the man tentatively reach out to stroke the wolf's soft fur in awe. He nodded in satisfaction as he watched the terrified white man overcome his fear to pet the wolf. The man had courage maybe this crazy plan would work out after all.

Giant Bear turned to the shaman as he motioned in question. "Are you sure that your vision was correct? We do not even know who this man is, are you sure he is the same one we sent for, it might be just a coincidence?"

The shaman sighed in exasperation as he gestured in reassurance. "Yes, I am sure. In the first vision, I had I was told to find the owner of the neighbouring thousand acres then bring him here to meet Raven so that they could marry. The Great Spirit did not warn me that his sister and the two guides would be killed! If I had known, I would not have told you to ask Jed to find him then get him to come here. When we stumbled on the massacre, and I meditated on the matter again the vision changed if Raven does not marry him now all of us will die including Raven. The vision also told me that the man must stay here with Raven to become a white Indian without knowledge of Ravens ranch. He must accept us as we are; Raven as well fully before he can leave here! Remember also that at Ravens naming ceremony, the golden Eagle had also been present, but so distant I had a hard time distinguishing what it was. At that time, I did not understand why he was there. Now I know that those two were destined, right from birth, to marry."

Giant Bear mused over the shaman's words while he lifted the wolf hide off his granddaughter. They still must have done something wrong, but he could not figure out what it was. Even if, it was true that the two were fated right from birth for each other, something was still terribly wrong. The Great Spirit would not tell them to do this then change the outcome.

The shaman checked her over carefully and sighed in relief as he looked over at his chief. "She is not hurt physically, so you do not need the medicine man just exhausted from her ordeal. She looks half frozen also, to have gotten here so quickly she must have flown like the wind."

Giant Bear nodded in relief that his granddaughter was okay then turned to the shaman. He waved irritably still concerned that they had done something to cause all this. "How are we expected to make the two marry, you know Raven and the white man will fight this to the bitter end! Not only that, but how am I to explain this to my people! I have forbidden my warriors to make war on the whites or take captives for the last twenty-seven years. We have changed completely, now over half of my people are part bloods or whites, what am I to tell them?"

The shaman shrugged thoughtfully Raven had always been difficult as for the others well secrecy was the key. "I know they will fight this! Just tell the white man his life will only be spared if he marries your granddaughter. Tell Raven that she has to marry him to save us or he will go to the army. But do not tell her that we arranged for this man to come here, she would be very angry. As for the others, do not tell them anything we must keep it a secret!"

Giant Bear sighed in irritation; he was not sure if he liked this situation at all or even if it would work. He turned beckoning the white man to come forward impatiently, wanting to get this over with now. Before the white man got to them, the shaman covered Raven up again so he would not be able to see her.

The white man got painfully to his feet then limped over to the chief and shaman. Curious he wondered what they would want from him. He carefully sat down Indian style as he faced them. He looked down at the bundle of fur between them wondering if the person was dead and that is why they had covered up the body.

The chief cleared his throat noisily in annoyance.

The white man jerked his head up, hoping he had not offended the chief in some way. He stared in shocked surprise when the chief started talking to him in perfect English, until now he had thought nobody here knew his language.

Giant Bear scowled angrily at the stunned look in the white man's eyes. He pointed towards himself than the shaman as he talked in English before translating the conversation into Cheyenne for the shaman's sake. "I am Chief Giant Bear, and this is our shaman. What is your name? Why were you travelling on my land?"

The white man frowned surprised. He had been told he was on the late Earl's property, which now belonged to his grandson Edward. He scowled in puzzlement then pointed to himself. "My name is Devon Rochester, and I am from England. I have some property I come here to sell. I did not know I was on your land, I was lead to believe I was on Earl Summerset's property."

The conspirators looked at each other then Giant Bear nodded in apology at the satisfied, I told you so look on the shamans face. Giant Bear turned back to Devon curiously. "Why would you come here just to sell something?"

Devon shrugged bewildered by the questions the chief was asking, but answered truthfully anyway. "The property was bought on speculation a long time ago. The late Earl talked my grandfather into buying it. My father inherited it, but there were stipulations attached. One was that my father could not sell it, only give it to his second son, which happens to be me. I could sell it if I wished, but I had to come here first then live for one year on the property. Only after a year is up could I sell it. A man named Jed Brown got in touch with me a year ago wanting to buy my land. When I told him about having to live here for a year, he said that he could wait if he had to. When my year is up he will come to discuss the sale."

Giant Bear nodded musingly pretending he did not know any of that. He motioned calmly towards Devon. "We now know you had no bad intentions when you came to this land. Even though it was not our band that killed your people they were still Cheyenne, so we will give you a life for a life."

Devon scowled in disbelief then anger at the chief as he waved incredulously. "What do you mean not your band? You are the only Indians I have seen since I came to this godforsaken land. It was you who massacred my family, and it is you who will be punished when I leave here!"

Giant Bear sighed in disagreement then shook his head sadly, as he pointed decisively at the white man. "No, it is you who do not understand! I did not say you would be permitted to leave. I said you would get a life for a life. You will stay here and marry my granddaughter."

Devon jerked back as if slapped then thundered in amazement without even thinking of the consequences. "Marry a dirty murdering Indian squaw, I would rather die!"

Giant Bear jumped up with a roar of rage as he reached across the bundle for Devon's throat.

The wolf sensing the anger in the air jumped in between the two men unexpectedly, protectively covering the bundle of fur in warning as he growled menacingly.

Devon fell back in stunned surprise as the massive wolf jumped between him and the chief. He lay on the ground groaning in pain holding his side as his tortured ribs throbbed in angry protest at the sudden movement.

The bundle of fur whimpered plaintively then thrashed about for a moment, but did not wake up still to weak from her ordeal.

Giant Bear dropped back down beside the wolf fur before lifting it slightly. He bent over as he softly spoke in a soothing whisper until his granddaughter stopped thrashing and lay quietly once more. He put the fur back down calm once again then turned to the shaman grimly. "I do not think this is going to work, did you see the look of disgust on his face at the idea of marrying an Indian."

The shaman patted the chief's hand in reassurance that was still resting on the wolf fur. "We both knew it was not going to be easy, and we knew he would be as prejudiced as any other vi'hoI. That is why he is to become a white Indian before he can leave here. The vision stressed that he must marry your granddaughter to save us!"

Giant Bear nodded in resignation as he turned towards Bruno. He spoke reassuringly to the wolf. "Bruno it's all right now, go lay down!"

Bruno looked at both men intently, wanting to protect his mistress. Sensing the danger past though, he went then settled back down. He did not go far though still cautious as he watched them closely.

As the wolf left, Devon slowly sat back up painfully and watched the chief warily. Not sure what would happen now, he wondered if his careless words had just signed his death warrant.

Giant Bear faced Devon once more, but this time he left a hint of menace in his voice as he motioned decisively with determination. "Listen very closely Devon, you have two choices! You can either be handed over to the dirty squaws as you put it to be tortured to death or you will be adapted by the shaman so you can marry my granddaughter, but either way you will never leave here!"

Devon opened his mouth to speak angrily, but snapped it shut again when the chief lifted his hand for silence.

Giant Bear continued as if there had been no attempt at interrupting him. "Do not get me wrong, marrying my granddaughter will not be an easy task for you. She will fight this all the way, even though normally in our culture women do what they are told, she is different! There has been the rare occasion's throughout our history when a woman becomes a medicine woman or even a shaman. My granddaughter though is unique because she is a warrior, our first one ever in history. You will have to prove yourself worthy of her not only to my other warriors, who will be watching you closely, but also to her. My granddaughter will fight tooth and nail to avoid this marriage, but here my word is the law so she will marry you when I insist."

Devon stared hard at the chief in stunned disbelief. He saw anger as well as a steely resolve painted on the old man's face. He sighed dejectedly in frustration as he looked down at the bundle thinking fast not wanting to blurt out the wrong thing this time because he was sure the chief would kill him next time. Why would the old man be trying to get rid of his granddaughter, was she that offensive or scarred in some way? On the other hand, maybe it was because of the fact that she was a warrior. Or maybe she was grotesquely muscled, there had to be something not right with her! Devon grimaced in resignation then looked at the chief hopefully. "You do not leave me much choice, but I would like this night to think about it."

Giant Bear looked at the shaman inquisitively as he translated and saw him nod slightly in agreement. He turned back to Devon then inclined his head in consent, as he got up. "You have this night to resign yourself to marrying my granddaughter. We will leave you now to think. My granddaughter is sleeping, but she should wake up soon. I will be back in a few minutes with some stew for both of you."

Devon watched in amazement as the two men left without another word or backwards glance. He looked down wondering why the chief would trust him enough not to hurt his granddaughter while he was gone. He looked fugitively to the side at the dozing wolf, remembering how fast he had jumped between them. He knew that the wolf would kill him if he even tried something like that.

Devon tentatively lifted his hand to move the wolf skin aside so that he could see the woman he might have to marry to save himself. When the wolf skin fell away from her face, he sucked in his breath in shocked surprise. She was beautiful! Pitch black braided hair framed an oval face that was perfect not a blemish or a spot marked her skin. Her cheekbones were high with a complexion that was a light dusky brown, but not as dark as her grandfathers. His hand reached out to remove the rest of the fur curiously, but stopped suddenly. The woman's eyes sprang opened in bewilderment, and Devon was staring down at the lightest green eyes he had ever seen. She was clearly not a full-blooded Indian.

*****

Raven woke slowly to the feel of someone watching her intently. When she managed to open her eyes fully, it took her a moment to focus on the strange vi'hol sitting in front of her. She gasped in stunned surprise then panic before rolling away out of reaching distance quickly. She pulled her knife out of her moccasin instinctively, without thought, before squatting there with her knife held out threateningly. She was ready to defend herself as she waited for the white man to make the first move.

Bruno sensing his mistress's alarm woke quickly. Instantly he crouched as the wolf readied himself to jump at the horrified confused white man, before growling menacingly at him in warning.

Devon fell to the ground again for the second time in alarm, but this time he lost consciousness from the excruciating pain.

CHAPTER THREE

Raven hunkered down in bewilderment, ready to defend herself should the white man attack her, watched in stunned disbelief as the stranger fell over and passed out. She then looked around at the familiar tepee and wondered how she had gotten there. Then it all came back to her, the visit from her cousin telling her to hurry as well as her wild ride through a blizzard.

Bruno quieted when he realized Raven was no longer in danger. He walked over and whined at his mistress before going over to sniff curiously at the white man.

Giant Bear walked in with two bowls of stew then stopped short at the scene inside. Raven squatting there with a knife drawn and the vi'hol lying on the ground as if dead. He put the bowls down rapidly then rushed over to Devon in concern. He looked at his granddaughter in reproach as he past her before bending down to check on the Englishman. "What have you done to him Raven? I swear if you have killed him after it took us so long to heal him, I will kill you myself!"

Raven scowled disconcerted and quickly sheathed her knife as she stood up then grabbed her fur off the ground before draping it over the white man to keep him warm. She sat down across from her grandfather with the vi'hol in between them. She looked down studying the white man curiously, as she told her grandfather what happened to make the Englishman pass out. She spoke in English automatically, since her grandfather liked to practice with her from time to time. When she finished her explanation, Raven looked up and opened her mouth to ask her grandfather about the white man.

Giant Bear quickly raised his hand for silence when she looked up at him. "Raven, I do not want you to speak in English for now. I do not want the vi'hoI to know yet that you can."

Raven quickly switched to Cheyenne in confusion. "Okay, namshimi', but I would like to know why? I would also like to know what is going on around here! Who is this man?"

Giant Bear sighed then motioned in dread not looking forward to this discussion. "I will speak to you privately about what happened later. As for the name of this man, it is Devon Rochester."

Raven frowned in surprise, stunned she broke in incredulously. "Lord Devon Rochester who owns the neighbouring thousand acres that I want to buy, do you know why he's here?"

Giant Bear grimaced in annoyance. He had not realized that Raven knew the white man's name. He just hoped she did not know about the conditions of the will that Devon's grandfather had left. Or found out that it was because of him that Devon was here in the first place. Everett had gotten a hold of Devon's father before he died because he wanted to buy his land, so that is how Giant Bear had found out about it. But at that time, Devon was too young to come here. When the shaman told his chief about a vision that he had of Raven and the neighbour getting married Giant Bear had suggested getting in touch with his friend Jed then he could arrange it so that Devon would come out here right away.

Giant Bear stared through his granddaughter distantly thinking quickly. He finally noticed that she was scowling in annoyance at him, wondering why it was taking him so long to respond. He quickly cleared his throat then shrugged dismissively as he avoided Ravens glance by looking down at Devon. "No, I do not know why he came here! I have not asked him yet since he only just woke up today and found out that his sister is dead. So I left him alone to grieve."

Raven nodded in approval then frowned at her grandfather in confusion when he continued insistently.

Giant Bear looked up at his granddaughter for a quick second in dire warning before looking down again, hiding his guiltily look. "I also do not want you to asking him either, not for awhile anyway. He needs time to heal and get over his sisters death."

Raven thought it over for a moment wondering what her grandfather was up too. It was not like him to avoid her glance. She sighed thoughtfully then inclined her head in agreement. She was sure he would tell her eventually they were too close to keep secrets for long.

Giant Bear reached over and grabbed one of the bowls of stew before handing it to Raven. "Here eat this; it will warm up your insides. You gave us quite a scare."

Raven took the bowl as she smiled in thanks half starved. "I am sorry I scared you, Grandfather, I was more exhausted than hurt. I had to go all the way home first since I was with the black stud and had my mare. Than I had to go the long way to get here so that I could warn the men of the coming storm, I wanted the cattle moved closer to the hay sheds just in case. My brother warned me about the storm, of course. That is why I was so well prepared in the first place."

Giant Bear motioned inquisitively. "How is Dream Dancer doing?"

Raven looked down at the white man with a pensive frown studying him curiously, as she slowly ate her stew. She did not even hear her grandfather's question as she stared down at Devon wondering what he would look like once his face healed. His face was rugged it looked as if he had some laugh lines around his eyes, but it was hard to tell with both of them so swollen and black. He had a hawkish nose that had been broken. It was almost but not quit straight again with a slight lump in the middle that probably would never go away. His lips looked full, but again it was hard to tell because they were so swollen as well as cracked badly.

Raven reached out then touched his hair inquisitively, but it was greasy and it looked like he had a lot of dirt or soot mixed in. If she had to guess, she would say it was probably a light brown or possibly blonde. He looked vaguely familiar, so she wondered if maybe she had seen his grandfather's portrait somewhere at the ranch since he had been a friend of her English grandfather's. She nodded to herself as she remembered one in the library with both Earl's together. That would make this man an Earl, or the next Earl if his father were not dead yet. That thought disturbed Raven deeply, because he could go to the army and insist that her family had done the killing. She would not be able to do anything about it; they would take his word over hers, even though she was an Earl's daughter because in their eyes, she was still an Indian. Three quarters only, but that would not matter to them. So how would she stop this man from going to the army and demanding justice? The only way she could think of was to keep him here, but to keep him captive was not the answer either. Eventually, she would have to let him go or he would try to escape. If he succeeded, it would only make things worse.

If Giant Bear could have heard his granddaughter's thoughts at that moment, he would be jumping for joy because he had the perfect solution all planned.

Raven scooped up the last of the stew still contemplating the vi'hoI. She looked up at her grandfather inquisitively as he cleared his throat to get her attention.

Giant Bear gestured to the north side of the village. "Raven you go to your tepee and sleep for awhile. I will come tomorrow to discuss what happened when we found the white man."

Raven nodded then got up. She looked down wondering if she should take her fur.

Giant Bear grinned up at her and waved in permission, guessing at her thoughts. "Take it, Raven. I have lots here to cover Devon up with."

Raven inclined her head wearily then took the fur, before whistling to Bruno. "Come on boy, let's go to bed."

Devon woke to see Giant Bear putting extra furs on his bed for him. The whistle had disturbed him. He looked around wondering where that she-devil had gone, but was relieved when he could not find her or the wolf.

Giant Bear walked over and sat across from Devon.

Devon painfully sat up, still looking around suspiciously waiting for her to jump out at him again.

Giant Bear smiled in reassurance then waved towards the entrance. "She is gone if you are looking for my granddaughter. She went to her own tepee to get some much-needed sleep. I am sorry she scared you so badly, but you scared her just as bad. You should not have lifted the wolf fur to peek."

Devon shook his head in horror as he gestured angrily. "That is the woman you want to marry me to! She just tried to kill me, no wonder you want to get rid of her! It is also clear to me why you have to give her away nobody would want such a she-devil for a wife!"

Devon paused for breath ready to continue berating the chief, but stopped in astonishment and stared incredulously at Giant Bear as he roared with laughter. Devon watched in puzzlement as the chief tried to stop laughing, but he was having a hard time of it.

Giant Bear got himself under control then wiped tears away. When he looked into Devon's disbelieving eyes, Giant Bear sighed, before motioning in explanation. "Devon, try to think of it this way; my granddaughter arrives at my tepee half dead from the cold and unconscious. As she is waking up, she expects to see me or another Indian; instead, she wakes then sees a vi'hoI, a white man. Who looks like death since your eyes are black, your nose is still crooked, your lips are badly swollen, and you are as white as a ghost from fear as well as pain. If you are honest, you will realize that her reaction is no different from what yours would have been under the same circumstances. If I remember correctly, when you first woke and saw us if you would have had a knife you would have done the same thing. Just because she is a woman, does not mean that she has no right to protect herself when she feels threatened."

Giant Bear watched the amazement leave Devon's eyes to be replaced by a pensive look as he mulled over what the chief had said. He smiled pleased then nodded in satisfaction as he realized that Devon was not adverse to new ways of looking at things. He let Devon think about it for a few minutes before handing him the still warm stew.

Devon looked at it suspiciously. He sniffed it cautiously before tentatively taking a small amount of meat and tasting it. Surprise showed on Devon's face at the tangy rich taste of the beef stew. He wondered where the beef came from. It did not actually matter where, he was so hungry that he shrugged off his suspicions then hastily ate every bit of the stew.

Giant Bear grinned in approval as he watched Devon devour every morsel. He chuckled again as he remembered Devon's account of his first real experience with Raven. He wondered whether he should tell Devon that half the men here, at the ranch, as well as in town were in love with Raven. No, even better, he would just keep quiet and let Devon find that out for himself. He waited until Devon finished off the stew then cleared his throat and pointed behind Devon. "I put some extra furs on your bed; because of the storm it is going to be cold tonight."

Devon nodded his thanks then put the bowl down and stared intently at the chief. He wondered if he dared to ask the chief questions, or if that would just get him into trouble.

Giant Bear watched the uncertainty on Devon's face waiting patiently for him to overcome his fear enough to ask the questions that he new Devon needed, as well as wanted to know. However, the first question he asked surprised Giant Bear significantly.

The startled look on the chief's face almost caused Devon to change his mind, but he pushed his fear away then asked curiously again, when Giant Bear did not answer right away. The perfect English, as well as the laughter earlier, had him immensely curious. From all he had heard about Indians since he got here, the chief was certainly not how he had pictured them being. "How did you learn to speak such good English?"

Giant Bear grinned in delight at the question and decided to answer honestly except for names of course. His face sobered sadly, as he remembered the death of his first wife. "A white man taught me it was a very long time ago; I will not bore you with all the details. I will tell you though that three white men killed my first wife. They were going around raping as well as killing any woman or child in their path. No matter what colour of skin they had. They were known as the Shadow Killers of Montana. I had taken my family away from our tribe to go on a special hunt. When I got back to our temporary camp that we had set up, my wife had already been raped then they killed her. My sister had also been raped, but was not dead. Fortunately, for me, my wife had hid my daughter before the killers got to them. After telling me everything that happened my sister took her own life before I could stop her since she could not stand the shame. I took my daughter back to my tribe and took ten braves with me to hunt down the killers."

Giant Bear paused for a moment trying to decide whether he should go on. Devon had listened the whole time; the expressions on his face went from outrage at the killings to shame at what the white men were capable of doing. He frowned thoughtfully, wondering if he should tell him about Mary or if he should leave that out. He decided to take a chance that Devon would understand then forgive him for his mistakes. Besides, if Giant Bear wanted Devon as his grandson by marriage to accept him, he had better be as honest as he possibly could. Even when it showed him in a bad light, so he took a resigned breath and his face became expressionless suddenly. "Two weeks later we came across three white men camped with a white woman. She was separated from the men crying very upset. We did not even ask questions we just went in then killed all three men. The white woman screamed hysterically and ran into the trees, so I went after her in concern. I did not know very many English words at that time, but I did understand some. After I had calmed her down, I was able to convince her that I was not going to hurt her. It was then that I found out we had made a mistake. The white woman had not been crying because those men had hurt her or were even going too. She was crying because her brother had forced her to marry someone she did not know. Her new husband made her leave everything and everyone behind without even being able to say goodbye."

Giant Bear sighed in sorrow for killing innocent men, even if they were white. He watched Devon closely for his reaction. His face was extremely expressive. At first, there was outrage than revulsion for what Giant Bear had done. However, much to the chief's surprise Devon's expression turned to sorrow and finally acceptance that although Giant Bear was a chief of his people, he was not infallible to mistakes.

Devon looked at the chief in understanding as he waved consolingly. "I can't really condemn you for what happened. At first I was going to, but then after I thought about it for a moment I realized that if it had been me, I would probably have made the same mistake. I would like to know what happened to the woman, and I still do not understand where this man who taught you such good English comes in?"

Giant Bear got over his astonishment quickly. He was pleased that Devon was sensitive enough as well as intelligent enough to see both sides of an issue. He also realized that although Devon had blown up at the idea of marrying an Indian, the Englishman was not as intolerant as he first thought. If he were prejudiced beyond redemption, Devon would not have understood he would have just condemned the chief for killing white people regardless of the reason.

Giant Bear smiled in delight as he thought of his second wife then his expression sobered as he neared the end of his story. "Well I could not just leave the woman wandering around by herself with nowhere to go, so I brought her to my tribe. I was going to find a way to send her back to her brother, but even though we could not communicate all that well, we did manage and fell in love in the process. We were married a month later, in that time I learned to speak English better, but not by much. We spent a month together after the wedding, but I knew I would have to leave again. I had to avenge my first wife as well as my sister before I could have a good marriage with my second wife. I did not want to make the same mistake that I had made when I took my warriors with me last time, so I decided to go alone. Besides, the men that I was chasing had a full two months to get to wherever they were going, which probably included a few towns. I certainly could not take my Dog Soldier's there or the army would come looking for us without asking any questions. So, I gave my daughter to my second wife to look after then left the shaman in charge until I returned. Before I left, I had a vision that I was to look for a specific cabin and there I would find a man that would help me, without his help I would never reach the killers. Without him, I was also shown that I would die within a year. As the killers travelled across country, they hit every cabin or small community that they could find. They were killing every woman or child that they found alone, plus some that were not. Of course, that was not too many since Montana at that time was only thinly populated with not many women around. But, it was still enough to make you sick. For three-months, I followed those men trying to catch them or find the cabin in my vision. I had almost caught them when I found the cabin I was looking for. It looked deserted, so I waited, watching hoping to use it myself. The weather had turned ugly just before I got there. We were in for quit a severe lightning storm. I was just about to go to the cabin when a man on a horse leading a string of mules behind him showed up then disappeared inside. I waited for a bit and finally decided that I should introduce myself as the storm worsened, but then the door flew open. He came out and marched over to a huge tree with a shovel, obviously he was upset about something as he started digging a hole. The man went back in then came out with two pieces of wood; he sat on the ground carving something into one before going back in. A few minutes later, he came out with a white bundle. He carried it over to the freshly dug grave. I hid back in the trees and patiently waited, I did not want to intrude on his grief. I know who this man was. Not personally, you understand, but I had heard of him. He was the white man that the Indians called Grey Wolf, but I still was not quite sure, so I hung back waiting. I had the feeling that the bundle he was carrying over to the grave was a woman, a child or maybe both. When the man finished he bellowed out some words in rage, I did not understand them all, I realize then that the three men I was chasing had found this cabin too. I waited until his words were finished before showing myself. The Cheyenne had named him after the immense grey timber wolves because he was just as silent and deadly as the wolves when he was hunting. It did not matter either if you meant an animal or a human. Grey Wolf teamed up with me to pursue the killers after I told him about my sorrow. On our journey, he taught me your tongue as well as customs. I am not going to tell you the whole story because it is an extremely long one. I will finish it by telling you that it took us nine long years to track down those men. We finally did catch them though then they paid for their crimes with their lives."

Devon shook his head in disbelief as he gestured curiously. "How come it took you so long to find them? You had said that when you met up with this Grey Wolf that you were catching up to them. What happened?"

Giant Bear was extremely pleased that Devon was so interested in his story that he wanted to know more. He sighed irritably and looked sad for a moment trying to explain further without getting into the whole story. "We do not know why it was taking so long after we left the cabin the men just disappeared suddenly without a trace. We searched for a long time, but we could not find them anywhere. Once they started killing again, we continued the pursuit. They did this more times than I want to remember. Sometimes they would be behind us when they surfaced, at other times they were ahead of us. When that happened we would lose them altogether for a short time, usually a week or two, but sometimes they would disappear for a month or more. Twice for over a year, there did not seem to be any pattern or reason to what they were doing. We knew that in the end, they were going to Dakota. But, we did not know whether it was South or North Dakota. All we knew was that they were looking for some woman who had killed two of their brothers. We had no idea who this woman was or where she lived. All we could do was keep trying to track them hoping they messed up somehow, so that we could get them or that the law would catch them and do the job for us. But, unfortunately it, took us nine years before we could put an end to all the killings."

Devon shook his head disbelievingly in amazement as he waved inquisitively. "Didn't you or Grey Wolf ever think about quitting?"

Giant Bear looked at Devon solemnly then pointed at him intrigued, wondering if he were wrong about this Englishman. No he was sure he was not wrong about this mans character, but he had to ask anyway to be sure. "Would you have quit if it had been your wife and sister?"

Devon opened his mouth to say yes then snapped it shut again quickly. He looked the chief in the eye deadly serious. "No, I guess I would have done the same thing as you."

Giant Bear hid a smirk of satisfaction. He had known he was right about the Englishman. The Great Spirit would not match Raven up with a weak minded, snivelling, coward. The chief was absolutely sure of that.

Devon took a deep breath and hardened his courage to ask his next question, wondering if the chief would be just as open for this one. "I want to know why you attacked us then killed everyone, but left me alive!"

Giant Bear shook his head quickly in denial as he sat forward intently, motioning seriously as he tried to convey his heartfelt sincerity to his future grandson. Anyone else he would not have cared whether they believed him or not, but this man one day soon would be Ravens husband. "We did not kill your people I assure you, but it was another Cheyenne tribe who did. I know who they are. I just need to prove it."

Devon shook his head angrily in disbelief as he gestured decisively. "I do not believe you, why would they do such a thing? No! I know it was your tribe and sooner or later I will get away then you will regret it!"

Giant Bear shook his head sadly at the furious Englishman as he sat back, in a way he did feel responsible since he had sent for him. "I am sorry, but you will never be allowed to leave, and you will marry my granddaughter."

Devon got up ominously holding his ribs in obvious pain. "I promise that you will all pay for what you have done! I have a lot of influence in England. I will make sure that the army hunts you down! As for that story about those white men, I think you just made it up so that I would feel sorry for you. It would make it easier to convince me that you did not kill my people, but you have not fooled me. I have also decided that you are bluffing about marrying your granddaughter, so I am going to decline your offer of marriage to her!"

Giant Bear stood up instantly in rage then took a menacing step forward as he jabbed a finger irritably towards Devon to get his point across. "You have not been listening to me! When I said you had no choice in marrying my granddaughter, I meant every word! YOU WILL MARRY HER! Or you will die! As for not believing me about how I learned to speak English, I do not care whether you believe me or not. Now though, since you choose to be so obstinate, you will be confined to this tepee unless one of us is with you. You had better hope that I can find a way to prove that we did not do it! Or you will 'NEVER EVER' leave here, do I make myself clear!"

When Giant Bear had taken that menacing step toward him, Devon stepped back hastily in anxiety. This was the first time since he woke up that the Englishman felt real fear. Even after Devon had insulted the chief's granddaughter, he had not felt any actual threat to his life. He had no illusions that the chief meant every word that he said.

Devon knew that eventually he would give in because he did not want to die. He wanted revenge! Suddenly an idea came to him, and he frowned thoughtfully. "Giant Bear earlier you said that I was to marry your granddaughter as payment for a life. Does that mean, that if, after we are married I decide I want my revenge by taking her life? Is it my, right? Or will I have the whole village in arms against me?"

Giant Bear was flabbergasted for a bit surprised by that question. He was even more amazed that Devon was smart enough to figure out that a life for a life meant just that. Once the two were married, he could kill Raven if he wished. Or even tell her in front of a crowed that she had to kill herself, honour would require that she do so. The chief was sure the Englishman did not know about the last part though. He definitely was not going to tell him, this was certainly not what they had in mind. The shaman had waved away his chief's concern when he had mentioned it, figuring Devon would not find out about that custom until after he fell in love with Raven.

Giant Bear eyed Devon searchingly; trying to decide if he should lie or if he should take a chance that the Englishman was too soft hearted to kill a woman. Then he thought of Raven, his beautiful but headstrong granddaughter. He was so proud of her managing such a large ranch all by herself plus still finding the time to come spend part of each year with them. Every year she won every archery test, knife throwing, and horseback riding contests. The only ones she actually had any problems with were wrestling, tomahawk throwing, as well as the long distance running. His grandson, Running Wolf, always won them. The chief smirked in smug gratification for a moment then stared at Devon calmly.

Devon saw the smug look cross Giant Bear's face for a fleeting moment before it was gone. The wily old chief regarded him gravely, and the Englishman knew he was up to something, but had no idea what it was.

Giant Bear stared at Devon silently for another couple of minutes, watching the Englishman's eyes narrow in suspicion, in amusement. He finally cleared his throat so he would not laugh aloud then motioned calmly. "Well Devon I must say you catch on quick, I would never have thought that you were ruthless enough to kill a woman though. But, you are correct in our culture a life exchanged for a life means that you can kill for revenge and not pay for it. But you cannot kill my granddaughter until after you are wed then you must convince her that you are allowed to kill her. I think you might have a little problem with that!"

Devon grimaced in annoyance as he realized the chief was right. He distinctly remembered Giant Bear's granddaughter jumping out of that fur with a knife in her hand ready to kill him if he threatened her in any way. He had full confidence in himself though, he was no weakling; he had boxed as well as fenced most of his life. However, there was the other problem. Sure, he had shot a couple of men before in fair duels, but he had never shot a woman. He could also remember distinctly how beautiful that woman looked before she woke up and was annoyed when his mental picture of her caused a surge of unwanted desire. He hardened his heart to the image then banished it from his sight. He sighed in relief as he also realized that although he had to marry the woman here, in his culture the union would not be valid. So when he escaped from this place, he would still be available to marry someone of his own culture. This means that he would not have to kill her after all!

Giant Bear smiled as he watched the conflicting emotions flirt across Devon's face. He could see that the Englishman was trying to figure out how to get out of this wedding without actually killing Raven. The chief also knew by Devon's expression that he thought he would not have to honour the marriage, but the chief had a surprise for the Englishman even his granddaughter would be shocked when she found out.

Devon turned to the chief his mind made up as he nodded decisively, before waving irritably. "I will marry your granddaughter, but of course you knew that I would give in if I wanted to live. I still have not decided whether I will kill her after the marriage or if I will just make her life a living hell. So, when do you want us to get married?"

Giant Bear turned aside quickly so that Devon could not see the smug look of satisfaction on his face as the Englishman gave himself an out for not killing her. He managed an expressionless face as he turned back to Devon. "You will be married a month after your ribs and arm heals. The medicine man says your ribs should be healed completely in a couple of weeks. In that time, you will learn our language as well as our customs. After your arm heals, which should be about three to four weeks after your ribs are healed, you will be trained as a warrior."

Devon's dumbfounded stare was genuine as he gestured incredulously. "You want to train me as a warrior, even though I might kill your granddaughter! Why?"

Giant Bear eyed Devon pensively for a moment wondering how much he should tell him at this time. He shrugged deciding it would not hurt to tell him some of it. "Well there are several reasons; I will tell you a couple of them. First, as I told you earlier my granddaughter is a warrior. So for you to be happy with her you must match or at least come close to her skills, or you will never come to terms with your new life. The second reason, which is the most important to you even though you do not believe me, is that we will be going after the tribe that killed your people. I know you will want to be there for that!"

Devon tried to interrupt the chief angrily.

Giant Bear held up his hand for silence knowing he was going to argue that point.

Devon shut his mouth fuming in silence.

Giant Bear grinned at Devon's sulk then motioned knowingly. "I know you do not believe me right now and it really does not matter if you do or not. But this is how it is going to be, my wife will be here in the morning to start your lessons. Then my grandson, Running Wolf, will take over your training once you are healed enough. Oh, one other thing, you will have dealings with my granddaughter. She was not here when we found you, so she does not know anything about it. Until I give you permission to speak of it, I do not want you to tell her anything. Except about the actual attack, not why you came here to begin with or about our talks. If I find out you told her anything, 'I WILL' slice out your tongue! If she asks for more details use your grieving as an excuse for not talking about it, am I understood?"

Devon nodded puzzled. He shrugged off his confusion at the chief's insistence it really did not matter to him anyway, before waving curiously. "I take it your wife and granddaughter speak English?"

Giant Bear inclined his head in agreement. His first plan had been to lie then say Raven could not so the Englishman would have to teach her to draw them closer. But he knew that Raven would not go for that at all. It was better that they talked as long as Devon remembered to keep his mouth shut. Of course, the chief would never cut out his tongue. As long as Devon believed that he was that ruthless though, it served its purpose. "Yes, my wife is white as I told you earlier so speaks English. She is another one I do not want you to talk to about why you came here or about our conversations. My granddaughter speaks your language as well as you do. Running Wolf can also speak when he wishes, but he refuses to lower himself by talking in your language. He will not even teach you until you learn our language, that is why you need training in ours first."

Devon scowled confused by it all, but he did not actually care one way or the other he just wanted to get out of here. He nodded, before clearing his throat inquisitively. "Giant Bear would it be too much to ask what your granddaughter's name is. In all our conversations about her, you have never once told me."

Giant Bear frowned thoughtfully for a moment thinking back, he finally gestured in apology as he grinned sheepishly. "You are right, I am sorry, my granddaughter's name is Raven. I might as well tell you my wife's name as well her English name is Mary, and her Cheyenne name is Golden Dove."

Devon was silent for a time trying out Ravens name with his first mental image of her jumping out of that fur with knife drawn; it definitely suited her.

Giant Bear pointed to Devon's bed. "You will sleep there until you are married. I arranged for my wife to stay with Raven tonight. Go to bed now, you have enough to think about, we will talk more tomorrow."

Devon turned then went to his pallet before lying down obediently. As he was drifting off to sleep, unwillingly, an image of Raven was his last thought.

*****

Raven left her grandfather's tepee, and the first thing she did was walk to the corral to check on Brave Heart. He nickered when he saw his mistress then walked over for a scratch.

Spotted Owl materialized beside Raven quietly as he pointed at the stallion. "I wiped him down before checking his legs and hooves. He is fine no real damage from the hard ride."

Raven inclined her head in thanks as she turned to Spotted Owl curiously. "Have you met the vi'hoI yet?"

Spotted Owl shook his head negatively. "No, I only saw him from a distance. He was beaten up pretty bad the chief was not sure he would make it at first."

Raven nodded then turned to leave.

Spotted Owl touched her arm to get her attention, he continued when she turned back to him inquisitively. "Your grandmother is in your tepee waiting for you. She asked me to come and find you then tell you that after you are finish checking on your horse, she would have hot stew waiting for you."

Raven smiled, before chuckling at the image of her formidable grandmother that popped into her head. "Thanks, Spotted Owl. Please give Brave Heart some extra oats and put a warm fur on him for me."

Spotted Owl inclined his head in agreement, as he released her arm.

Raven turned then walked towards her tepee. Just before she entered, Bruno gave a little bark to say goodbye to his mistress. Now that she was safe, he could go. She squatted to pat the wolf in farewell. "Okay Bruno you can go find your girlfriend now, and thanks for leaving her to help me out."

Bruno licked her face then turned; he trotted away without looking back.

Raven sighed sadly at losing her friend as she watched him go. She turned and entered her tepee. She was immediately enveloped in a huge hug of welcome, laughing Raven hugged her grandmother back. Mary or Golden Dove as she was known here, held her granddaughter out at arms length. She looked her up then down assessingly to make sure Raven had suffered no real damage. She beckoned Raven over to sit and eat a bowl of stew.

Raven sat before accepting the bowl gratefully, she did not dare refuse even though she had already eaten. She watched as her grandmother moved about cleaning up the tepee. She knew better than to say anything until after she finished all the stew because Golden Dove would not respond until she was done every bite. Her grandmother had not changed much since Giant Bear had brought her home twenty-seven years ago. Her hair was still a golden blonde without even a hint of grey hair anywhere. Of course, she was not actually Ravens grandmother. Her real grandmother had been Giant Bear's first wife, but three white men had murdered her. However, Golden Dove was the only grandmother Raven knew, and she did not love her any less than she would have her real grandmother. She finished her stew as she sighed thankfully in pleasure, the warmth from the fire and stew slowly warmed up her insides.

Raven watched her grandmother for a few more minutes than could not help commenting. "Nisgii, you still look absolutely beautiful. Actually, every time I see you I think you get more beautiful."

Golden Dove turned to Raven in amazement as she blushed in pleasure. "Well thank you Raven that is such a lovely compliment from you."

Raven nodded, she sighed sadly before motioning in apology. "After almost freezing to death today, I realized that I had never told you how much I love and admire you."

Golden Dove sat down beside Raven then took her hand into hers in concern. "We were all really worried about you. The storm hit so suddenly that we thought you would be caught off guard and maybe lost to us, but you are here now that is all that counts. How is your brother, by the way? He has not been out to see us this year, we miss him a lot?"

Raven smiled at her grandmother's abrupt change of topics as she impulsively hugged Golden Dove again then sat back to regard her lovingly. "Dream Dancer is fine, he is just so busy getting ready to leave for England that he has not had time to visit. I will make sure he comes to see you before he leaves though, I promise."

Golden Dove grinned in delight at the thought of her grandson and changed the subject. "I fixed your bed up then put extra furs on it. I hope you do not mind if I stay here tonight with you. I have been banished from my own tepee until tomorrow."

Raven was extremely surprised by this, ever since Giant Bear had brought Golden Dove as well as their son home that long ago day. He had not let his wife out of his sight for more than a couple hours. Even after all these years, he still took her everywhere with him.

Golden Dove shrugged her shoulders just as perplexed as her granddaughter was at the shocked look on Ravens face. "I was just as amazed as you are; he is definitely up to something. The shaman and your grandfather have had their heads together ever since we found the white man. Actually, that is not totally true; the two of them have been scheming something for the last two years. But every time I try to find out what they are up to, they say it's nothing to worry about then refuse to say anything else."

Raven pondered her grandmother's words for a moment before waving incredulously. "You don't think that whatever they are up to has anything to do with that man, do you?"

Golden Dove thought about it for a moment; finally, she shook her head negatively. "No, it couldn't be we have never seen that white man before we stumbled across the massacre. Giant Bear and the shaman were just as shocked as we were. Although, they did seem a little more upset about it than anybody else was and there was definitely relief on their faces when we found the Englishman alive. They argued for a few minutes out of hearing of course then they decided to come back here after the shaman had his vision. I don't know, maybe it just made whatever they were up to impossible now and that is why they were so upset."

Raven frowned grimly then sighed in relief as she motioned reassuringly. "Yeah, you are probably right. What did they do with all the bodies?"

Golden Dove was not so sure that was all there was to it, but let the matter drop. "We brought the bodies with us for a decent burial. Giant Bear figured the white man would want it that way. We also cleaned up everything so that nobody would suspect anything. We brought all the evidence with us so you could look at it, before deciding what to do. Slippery As An Eel was among the dead, so was Squatting Dog. We brought them both here as well as their arrows and anything else we thought you might want to see."

Raven inclined her head in approval. "That's good I will look at everything tomorrow. Slippery As An Eel is with the Eagles tribe. Squatting Dog is with the Badger tribe. I wonder if they have banded together or if it is just a coincidence. Squatting Dog might have left his own band to join the Eagles. I will have to find out for sure one way or the other."

Ravens grandmother nodded then shook a finger at her in warning. "But not tonight, it is time for you to go to bed and recover from your ordeal."

Raven grumbled good-naturedly under her breath then went towards her bed obediently. She stopped suddenly then turned back as she asked her grandmother inquisitively. "Is my saddlebag here, nisgii?"

Golden Dove inclined her head as she pointed in a corner. "Yes dear it's over there."

Raven grinned in relief. She did not want to lose that gift, and climbed into her furs. Her last thought as she fell asleep was of the white man.

CHAPTER FOUR

At first light, Giant Bear left Devon sleeping as he slipped out to go see Black Hawk. He stopped in front of his son's tepee then scratched on the door and waited for permission to enter. The chief was just about to leave when the flap was pushed aside for Giant Bear to enter.

Black Hawk's wife Gentle Doe was just putting coffee on, so Giant Bear sat down across the fire from her then waited for Black Hawk to sit down beside his wife.

Giant Bear spoke to Gentle Doe in Cheyenne first. "Good morning, Gentle Doe. How are you this fine day?"

Gentle Doe shyly looked over at the chief. "I am fine I'ho, how is your morning?"

Giant Bear smiled tenderly, even after all these years Gentle Doe was still shy when he came around. He motioned inquisitively. "It is going very well. My son is treating you well I hope. Not asking too much of you?"

Gentle Doe turned to Black Hawk questioningly for approval before she said anything.

Black Hawk nodded solemnly in permission for her to tell his father their news.

Giant Bear looked from one to the other curiously, wondering what was going on.

Gentle Doe turned back to Giant Bear with a smile of pride. "No, he is not asking too much of me, I will be glad to give him another son."

Giant Bear's mouth fell open in disbelief for a moment. He grinned as he shook off his amazement and gestured in pleasure. "You are pregnant again? Well congratulations, I know you have been very disappointed about not having another baby since Running Wolf was born."

Gentle Doe beamed shyly at Giant Bear. She waved confidently. "I will get breakfast you will stay of course, will you not?"

Giant Bear inclined his head in agreement; as he watched Gentle Doe get up then go outside. He turned to Black Hawk and saw the sad look on his son's face. He switched to English so that Gentle Doe would not understand if she came back in. "You do not think she will survive this time, do you?"

Black Hawk shook his head anxiously at his father before sighing dejectedly. "I do not know I'ho. She has had so many miscarriages since Running Wolf, but this is the longest she has gone without losing it. I am afraid for her! She is so tiny as well as very frail plus she is twenty years older. I would rather lose the baby than lose my wife!"

Giant Bear frowned in understanding as he motioned consolingly. "I know you do not want to hear this right now, but the Great Spirit has plans for all of us. If your wife is fated to die giving you a baby, do not throw the sacrifice away. Go talk to the shaman; see if there is anything he can do to help your wife. How far along is she?"

Black Hawk grimaced dispiritedly. He knew his father was right, but he was still afraid. "Two weeks into her seventh month. She did not want to tell mom until she was sure she was not going to lose it this time. Nissgo gets so upset when Gentle Doe loses a baby. Especially since mom could not have any more after Morning Star was born."

Giant Bear scowled remembering some of his fights with his daughter, in the end she still got her way. She had wanted to go to a white school. He wanted her to stay here then marry one of his braves. It was not until Golden Dove interfered on her daughter's behalf that the chief gave in before getting in touch with Melissa and Jed Brown. He arranged for Morning Star to stay with them so that she could go to school. She went by the white name of Pamela there. After she had finished school, she married Jed's oldest son who then went on to become a Baptist Pastor. The two of them had taken over Golden Dove's old ranch in

North Dakota. He smiled in joy that was the only good thing to come of Morning Star's desire to go to school. Now he was related to Melissa and Jed, not just through blood bonds, but also by marriage.

Giant Bear shook his memories away then looked closely at Black Hawk in speculation. "I was going to ask you a favour, but with this news of a baby I do not think I should ask you. Maybe I will ask Running Wolf instead."

Gentle Doe came in, so the two men quieted. She handed each of them a bowl of porridge proudly. Golden Dove had taught Gentle Doe how to make it. She also told her to try putting nuts or fruit that was preserved by Ravens ranch in it.

Giant Bear and Black Hawk smiled their thanks, before digging in as Gentle Doe poured coffee then handed one to each of them. She turned to the door leaving quietly to do her chores for the day.

The two men finished eating as they sat there both immersed in their own thoughts, drinking their coffee in companionable silence.

Black Hawk took out his peace pipe and lit it then handed it to his father to begin the ritual. After the pipe was done, Giant Bear sighed in contentment. He patted his ample belly in appreciation. "You know before we came here and started living on Ravens ranch we never ate so well. I remember many days when we would be half starved before winter finished. Living here has brought many changes to this tribe we owe her so much. I never thought when we first started coming here that this would work out. We only started coming here because of Everett, after he found his family he suggested having our rituals or celebrations here where no one would bother us or interfere. So Everett's grandfather sent runners to all the tribes with directions on how to get here. We all came of course then Everett met my first daughter Morning Dove. You know the rest of course since you were here for that celebration."

Black Hawk nodded thoughtfully remembering when he had first come here. He had been scared to death to meet so many Indians, but thrilled at the same time that he had a father after not knowing who he was for so long. His mother had never told him, always terrified that her brother would find out he had not actually killed her Cheyenne husband as he thought. For most of those years, he had lived with his aunt Melissa. She was not actually his nhai, but he always thought of her that way since she had looked after him for most of his younger years.

It had not taken him long to learn the customs as well as the language of his new family after he got here. For the first time in his young life, he found complete acceptance for who he was. The colour of his skin or the shade of his hair or eyes did not matter here. All that mattered was what he made of himself, it did not take Tommy long to become Black Hawk. Especially with the training Mell had given him in the art of knife fighting. He had won every knife contest after that until he taught Raven that is.

Giant Bear was also still thinking about that time. His people were known as the Bear tribe. Everett's grandfathers band was the Wolf tribe. They had both stayed after the celebration so that they could marry Everett to Morning Dove. Afterwards, both chiefs promised to come again on their first anniversary to celebrate. So, both chiefs showed up as promised the next year. Not only did they celebrate the anniversary, but the birth of their first granddaughter and great granddaughter, as well.

Just before they left, Everett's grandfather died unexpectedly. There was considerable confusion at first because Everett's grandfather had left nobody to replace him. After Giant Bear had everyone calmed down, he suggested that they join his band. The oldest among the tribe deliberated for a whole day, but finally agreed on the condition that Giant Bear would adopt the name of their tribe. So instead of being the Bear tribe, they were now known as the Wolf tribe. The other condition was that they kept their medicine man for healing, so Giant Bear's medicine man became the shaman dealing with the spirit world only. Everyone was happy with the new arrangement.

Giant Bear made arrangements with Everett to meet in this valley every summer so that Raven, when she was three, could discover the other side of her heritage. This went on for seven years, in all that time Ravens mother had not conceived again. In the seventh year, Giant Bear arrived right on schedule. An ecstatic Everett and Morning Dove met him with a squirming bundle. A boy they named Edward William Charles Summerset after his white grandfather, Earl Summerset, or Dream Dancer as he was to become known to the Cheyenne.

Giant Bear remembered as well how angry the town was, even terrified, to have so many Indians that close to town. But Everett, having his fathers charm, managed to talk the town into accepting the Indians so close. He promised the townspeople that there would be no horse stealing, murders, kidnapping women, or children. So it was agreed, and everything had been peaceful until now. The massacre of the white mans guides who had unfortunately, been from town. As well as the white woman, would create a full-scale panic. It would not be long before the army showed up; he was quite convinced about that.

Black Hawk watched his father for a moment in speculation wondering what he was up too. The scheming had started about two years ago at a powwow on the border of North Dakota. Melissa accompanied by her husband, Jed Brown, had shown up to celebrate with them. It was not unusual for Melissa or Jed to come to their celebrations when held so close to their home. However, it was unusual for them to go into hiding with Giant Bear then leave two days later before the powwow was even over.

Black Hawk had not paid too much attention at that time. But just after they got to the winter camp that year a rider from Dakota showed up, sent by Jed no doubt. The messenger talked to Giant Bear, and the shaman for about an hour then left. For about a week after that, his father and the shaman huddled together scheming. Black Hawk enquired curiously, but he was told to mind his own business. He was crushed by the rejection at first until he saw his mother starring at him. Then Black Hawk had realized that he was not the only one being shut out, his mother had also been told it was nothing. He had talked to her about it several times, but she would just shrug and tell him that when his father was ready to confide in them, he would. Until then, they could spend a little more time together.

It was not until they came across the massacre a few days ago that Giant Bear had started acting weird again, first by arguing with the shaman not once but twice. Afterwards, he brings everyone back here with the white man and all the dead bodies. Then he sends for Raven who has a ranch to run to fix things, how she was supposed to do this nobody knew. The final act to all this madness is that his father sends his wife away so that he could stay with the white man alone. He had never once since he had been reunited with Golden Dove slept alone or left her behind when travelling. Now all of a sudden, he sends her away because of a vi'hoI. This whole thing was odd, and it was clearly time to find out what was going on.

Black Hawk watched a guilty look cross his fathers face then cleared his throat loudly to get Giant Bear's attention. "I'ho you know I love you and would do anything to help, but if you do not tell me what the problem is I cannot help you. I also know that you have been up to something for the last two years. Does it have something to do with the white man we found?"

Giant Bear looked at his son in surprise, he had not thought he was that transparent, but he clearly needed another ally to pull this off. He just hoped Black Hawk did not get too mad at him for trying to arrange this marriage. He took a steadying breath then shrugged in apology for his thoughtlessness. "I guess I have been a little obvious. I was not going to get you involved after hearing about the baby, but I need your help. I will start at the beginning; you already know why Raven was trained to be a warrior since it is no secret. In a dream the shaman had when she was three, Raven was to be the 'Protector' of this tribe, and it has all come true of course. She keeps us fed as well as protected all through the winter months, not once has she ever asked for anything in return. Two years ago, just before we left for the powwow, Raven came to the shaman worried about a dream that she had about a man that she could never see. Well the shaman sent her off with reassuring words, but he wanted to help her since she has done so much for us. So he spent the last two days of our stay here meditating on Ravens problem, asking the Great Spirit to help her. On the last day, the shaman got his vision. In it, Raven as well as a white man was standing close together holding hands as they surveyed their land. They were standing on a cliff wall looking towards Ravens ranch; behind them was the valley she always uses to breed her mares to the black stallion in. Of course, that land Raven wants to buy since she does not own it. Raven as well as the man she was with turned towards the valley still contemplating all the property that they owned. Then right behind them two images appeared, behind Raven was a black raven of course, and right behind the white man was a golden eagle. That is where the vision ended! The shaman had to interpret the dream, so he came to me asking my opinion since he did not understand the vision. We figured out right away that Raven was supposed to marry this man. But, who was the man? The shaman asked me since both of them were surveying her land than the thousand acres that she wants to buy together if it might be significant. At first, I could not see it, but suddenly I remembered a conversation that I had with Everett before he died about trying to buy the neighbouring thousand acres. Everett had thought it strange that his father would convince his friend in England to buy that land. It was even stranger that he got him to make a will that stated his first-born son would inherit it, but with stipulations that he could never sell it. He could only give it to his son, but it had to be given to his second grandson only. Now his grandson could sell it if he wished, but he had to live here for a whole year before he was allowed to sell. Well when I remembered that conversation, it did not take us long to figure out that the man in the dream was the owner of the thousand acres. All we had to do was get him down here from England so that the two of them could meet and fall in love. But how were we to get the man here; Jed of course was the first one I thought of to help us. He could contact the Englishman then pretend to want to buy his land, which would mean that the white man had to spend a whole year here. Since there was no house at the Englishman's place, he obviously would have to stay at Ravens as the Earl's granddaughter she would have to let him stay for the whole year. We were sure that by the end of the year, they would be madly in love. Last winter just after we got here Jed sent me a message; the white man would be coming this spring. His name was Devon Rochester, and he is the second son of Earl Rochester in England. Well we were thrilled of course that everything was going according to our plans."

Giant Bear stopped talking as he paused to put tobacco in his pipe. He got a refill on his coffee as well before gathering his thoughts together unhappily.

Black Hawk waited patiently knowing his father was not done yet. He was not quite sure how he felt about what his I'ho was telling him. He figured he would allow him to finish before deciding how he felt.

Giant Bear took a fortifying sip of coffee as he continued talking sorrowfully. "Well when we left here two weeks ago for our summer camp, I was still extremely happy about how events had turned out. Then we came upon the massacre, and I figured everyone was dead. I knew this group was the one with Devon in it. I was heartsick every time I turned over a body. It was my fault the Englishman was here! How could the Great Spirit steer us so wrong, why did the Great Spirit want us to bring this fellow here if all he was going to do was let him die? The shaman was the one who found Devon, as well as his sister. She was not dead yet, but unfortunately within an hour she died. As for Devon, he was pretty beaten up, but we were confident he would live. I argued with the shaman thinking that maybe we had been wrong about the vision. The shaman was adamant saying we were right, but something had obviously gone wrong. So we set up the shamans tepee so that he could try to find the answers. An hour later the shaman called me to him; he had been shown two visions. The first one was the same one as before with the two happily surveying everything they owned, with both birds over their heads. The following vision scared the shaman badly. He saw Raven, as well as Devon standing apart glaring with hatred at each other. In between them were dead white men as well as Indians lying everywhere. The shaman interpreted the dream as this, either the two would get married then live happily ever after or we are all dead. Including Raven and Devon since she had a dead black raven hovering over her head, he had a dead golden eagle over his head. So I sent Running Wolf to get Raven then I brought everybody back here, including the dead. As well as all the proof that I could find to convince the white man that we did not do it. When we got back here, the shaman and I came up with a plan. We would tell the white man that he would have to marry my granddaughter in payment for a life. Plus he would never be allowed to leave here. We would tell Raven that she had to marry the white man in order to save us so he would not go to the army. I already told Devon last night he agreed to marry Raven to save his own life. I will tell Raven later. What I want you to do is to stay with the white man while your mother is teaching him our customs. You will be guarding him plus protecting her!"

Black Hawk stared in disbelief at his father, speechless for a moment. If he had not been present at the discovery of the massacre then been a witness to some of Giant Bear's descriptions, he would think the chief was trying to pull his leg. He knew his father was deadly serious though. Black Hawk shook his head in bewilderment, not sure what to say at first. "I am not sure how to take this story; I will think about it and let you know later. While I am thinking about it, I will go stand guard in order to protect my mother. As for making Raven marry this man, I think you might be making a big mistake. Instead of pulling them closer it might backfire then pull them farther apart."

Black Hawk got up slowly and pointed towards the entrance. "I will go check on Devon. If he is still asleep, I will go get mother. If he is awake I will take him with me, a little exercise would be good for him."

Giant Bear nodded then watched Black Hawk disappear out of the tepee. He sighed in frustration. Black Hawk might be right when he said forcing Devon and Raven to marry could backfire on them. He was already committed though, so it was too late to turn back now. The chief got up reluctantly to go tell Raven she had to marry the vi'hoI.

*****

Devon woke up about a half hour after Giant Bear left. He did not bother getting up it was still dark in the tepee, so he did not even realize that the chief was gone. He had slept surprisingly well considering everything that had happened to him lately. He thought of his home so far away in England where his ancestral castle was. It was not far from London; actually, they were not his they were his brother's now that their father had died two years ago. Then again, it had never actually felt like home just a place he had to go to occasionally as a duty.

After Devon had grown to manhood, was when the feelings had first started. He had watched his father as well as his older brother treating the servants like dogs, but it was the serfs they actually treated the worst. All of his life he had watched them shame as well as beat the serfs, for what purpose he could never figure out. It was not until he grew older that Devon started questioning the conduct of his father and older brother. One day when he was about sixteen Devon had caught his father trying to rape a female serf; he had received a severe beating for trying to stop him. Since then Devon had stayed away from his home as much as possible.

When Devon's father had died, he tried to get his older brother to lighten up on them. All his older brother did was laugh at him before tell him that he should consider a female serf. It might change his tune then make him a man. Devon had left in a rage and had not set foot in his home since. Luckily, his father had willed him a small estate in Sussex where he now lived. Of course, he owned a thousand acres here in Montana too. He also had a trust fund that his grandfather had willed to him.

Devon had been smart he knew that eventually he would cut all contact with the new Earl, his brother, so he took his trust fund then invested it. His father had given Devon a living allowance while he was alive, so he had lived on that while continuing to invest his inheritance. Now he was prosperous in his own right, but he still was not happy something always seemed to be missing. The older he got the more disillusioned he became, especially, about the way the Royalty treated the poor. It bothered him more and more each year. He had always figured that there must be more to life somewhere, but it just never got any better.

After his father died, Devon began thinking of the land he now owned in Montana. Should he sell it or should he just go start a new life for himself. He had enough money to do anything he wanted, but he had heard so many stories of people disappearing. He had also heard all the stories about the fierce Indians torturing as well as murdering white people, now he knew it was all true. There always seemed to be a little doubt about it all in England though, because some of the people he talked to said the Indians kept breaking their treaties. Then you talk to a different group of people, and they tell you it's the whites that keep breaking the treaties so that the army can go out then chase them down to take their land. It was hard to determine who was right.

Two weeks after his father died a letter from a man in North Dakota changed everything. A man by the name of Jed Brown wanted to buy his property in Montana. Devon had written him back and advised him that because of the conditions of the will he could not sell until he had lived there for one year. Jed Brown had written him back then said he could wait a year, so Devon had started preparing to go to Montana eagerly willing to try something new.

Devon's two sisters found out where he was going and begged to go, as well. He had said no at first, but changed his mind later after he thought about it. His older sister was widowed, with nothing left since their father managed to steal it all from her. So she also wanted to start a new life somewhere else. His second sister was a year younger than he was and had always been sick. The doctor said my sister had a weak heart, so she would never be able to get married because she could not have any children or it would kill her. She had begged, when that did not work she pleaded, but what had actually convinced him to take her was her belief that she would die in the next two years anyway. She wanted to go so that she could see something new before she died, even if it killed her to come. His older sister stated that she too would rather die anywhere but England. So he had taken them both with him, now they both were gone, their desire to die somewhere other than England was granted.

It still hurts unbearably even though Devon knew it was what they both wanted. He would never be sorry though as he remembered his younger sisters pleasure at every new experience. Like the day that the dolphins followed them, her tinkling laughter as she watched them dance and frolic in front of the ship would always be etched in his memory. As well as the sheer joy she had experienced in Boston when he took her all over the city to see the sights. Then her blissful appearance as they travelled through Montana. He would never forget that he had given her so much joy before she died. One thing he did wish for though was that he could see them once more and give them both a proper burial. Devon curled up then mourned for his sisters.

*****

Black Hawk opened the flap on Giant Bears tepee before closing it immediately when he heard the white man grieving for his sister. He did not want to intrude, so he turned heading to Ravens to get his mother. He met his father in front of the tepee then they scratched at the door to be let in.

Raven opened the flap for them.

Golden Dove turned with an ecstatic smile of welcome before rushing over to give her husband a passionate kiss.

Black Hawk and Raven moved off respectfully, politely turning their backs to give the lovers a moment to themselves. Raven grinned at Black Hawk as she motioned curiously. "How are you, I have not seen much of you lately."

Black Hawk embraced Raven warmly then stepped back. "I am fine. I just came to get mom, I am suppose to protect her while she is with the white man. I also have some good news, but I will tell you at the same time as nissgo so I will wait till the love birds are done."

"What good news?" Golden Dove walked over and asked as she gave her son a loving embrace of welcome.

Black Hawk returned his mothers hug enthusiastically. "Well it looks as if you are going to be a nisgii again."

Golden Dove stepped back in distressed surprise. "Gentle Doe is pregnant again? How far along is she?"

Black Hawk winced at his mother's worried voice, remembering all the frustrated miscarriages. "It's all right mom she is two weeks into her seventh month. So she should carry it full term this time."

Golden Dove sighed in relief as she waved in reproach. "Why didn't you tell me sooner? I could have been helping her with the chores so she would not have to do so much."

Black Hawk shook his head sadly. "No mom, Gentle Doe did not want you to know because you get too upset when she loses the baby, so she did not want to tell you until she was at least past her seventh month to make sure she would carry it full term."

Golden Dove eyed Black Hawk shrewdly in suspicion. "You are worried that she has carried the baby this long, aren't you?"

Black Hawk frowned sorrowfully. "Yes I am, I do not think she will survive this time. If she does not, I do not know what I will do!"

Golden Dove hugged her son again in reassurance. "It will be all right. I will help her as much as I can."

Black Hawk hugged his mother before looking at Raven miserably over Golden Dove's shoulder. "I know it will mom, I am sure Gentle Doe will be glad to have your help."

Golden Dove stepped back then gave her son a reassuring look before pointing towards the fire. "Come everybody and have some coffee. Did you both eat yet?"

Black Hawk walked over then sat beside his mother as she sat down. He waved away the offered food. "Yes mom we both ate. Gentle Doe fed us that excellent tasting porridge you taught her to make."

Golden Dove grinned pleased that Gentle Doe liked porridge. "Good, I suppose we had better bring some to the white man. Do you know whether he is awake yet?"

Black Hawk grimaced with a frown of concern. "Yes he is awake, but he was occupied, so I decided to come and get you first. I am sure father has lots to talk to Raven about, so they should not miss us too much."

Golden Dove got up to get a bowl ready to go.

Black Hawk turned to Giant Bear then motioned curiously. "Do you want me to tell the white man that his sister is here, he might want to see her before we have a ceremony to help her on the way to the Great Spirit?"

Giant Bear inclined his head in permission. "Yes you can tell him, but wait until the sun reaches its highest point. I need to talk to Raven first, we also need to go over all the evidence we collected before deciding what we are going to do first."

Black Hawk nodded as he got up quickly to help his mother. "Here nissgo, let me take that porridge and coffee pot."

Golden Dove smiled gratefully then gave them to her son as they were leaving. On the way to her tepee, Golden Dove looked at her son curiously. She waved sharply in demand wanting answers now. "Tommy did your father tell you what is going on?"

Black Hawk grinned knowingly, the only time his mother called him Tommy now was when she was mad at him or wanted to know something that instant. Whether you wanted to give an answer or not of course, it always worked except for this time. She would have to wait until father told her. "Yes mom, I now know. But I cannot tell you, you will just have to wait until dad decides to tell you!"

Golden Dove opened her mouth to demand he tell her, but snapped it shut angrily when Black Hawk held up his hand pleadingly. He frowned unhappily, as he scowled grimly. "I am sorry nissgo I have never kept anything from you before so this is hard on me, but I will make you a promise. If father does not tell you by the time the new moon is full, I will tell you myself. That is the best I can do for now!"

Golden Dove thought about it for a moment before nodding her assent. She motioned angrily in annoyance. "Okay Black Hawk I will wait for now, but you better tell your father to confess to me himself, and very soon! I would also like to know what the white man's name is, no one has told me yet?"

Black Hawk nodded that he would give father her ultimatum. He sighed relieved as his mother called him by his Indian name once again. "I will tell I'ho what you said, I promise. The vi'hoI is called Devon Rochester; he is the second son of an Earl in England."

Golden Dove inclined her head pacified by her sons promise. They reached her tepee, so she scratched at the flap to let the white man know they were coming in. They looked at each other in dismay at the subdued response from inside. "Come in."

Black Hawk went in first then held open the flap for his mother to enter. When they were both in, they turned and looked for the white man. The first thing they noticed was that it was cold, as well as pitch black inside the tepee since no one had built a fire.

Golden Dove shook her head in angry disapproval. "Tommy make a fire while I open this tepee up."

Black Hawk winced at his mother's use of his white name then hurried over to do as he was told. You never argued with Golden Dove when she was in this mood, no matter how old you were. Even his father stepped lively when she used that tone. He got a good fire going before putting the coffee pot there, and setting the bowl of porridge beside it to heat them up again. He also pushed open the smoke hole so that the sun would shine in.

Golden Dove tied up the door flap then went to the flap on the windows. When she had first come here to live she had made Giant Bear cut out two windows, so it was not so dark inside. She turned once done to inspect the white man curiously.

Devon was still sitting on his bed, he wondered if he should get up to greet the white woman or not. However, his good manners got the better of him as he stood up then gave a deep bow of greeting. He smiled devilishly at Giant Bear's wife. "To see any woman as beautiful as you are when a man wakes up, even when he is a prisoner, is all a man could ask for."

Golden Dove blushed in pleasure before grinning shyly at the white man. It had been a long time since anyone had flirted with her. At first, she felt flustered wondering if she still knew how, but it did not take her long to remember. She lowered her eyes in modesty and held out her hand so that Devon was able to, very gently; touch his lips against the back of her hand.

Black Hawk chuckled in delight at his mothers blush then walked over to the white man as he held out his hand in greeting. "My white name is Tommy, and my Indian name is Black Hawk. My mothers name is Mary her Indian name is Golden Dove. You may use our English names for now until you become familiar with our language if you prefer."

Devon inclined his head in greeting then grasped Tommy's hand firmly with his good one as he joked. "My white name is Devon Rochester, and I do not have an Indian name yet."

Tommy smirked teasingly at Devon. "I would not be too sure of that if I were you!"

Devon let Tommy's hand go then looked at him in surprise.

Tommy just grinned before waving at Devon to sit by the fire without further comment.

Golden Dove checked the porridge to make sure it was hot and handed it to Devon. She poured coffee for the three of them then sat back to watch the Englishman eat.

Devon hesitantly took a small bite of the porridge before looking up in stunned appreciation. "Porridge with nuts and raisins, this is great! But where did you get them at this time of year?"

Golden Dove smiled at Devon mysteriously. She was not allowed to disclose to this man anything about Ravens ranch. Her husband had been extremely clear about that last night, so she shrugged then fibbed a little. "We collect the nuts at our summer camp, sometimes if it is a good year we still have some left over in the spring. As for the raisins, we trade for them. When I first came here, I insisted on having porridge with raisins, so my husband always manages to find me some."

Devon nodded at this simple explanation as he finished the porridge. He picked up his coffee cup and sighed relieved he had been starving. He sipped his hot coffee then grimaced at the strong bitter taste he was use to tea. He looked over at Mary pleadingly. "Your husband would not happen to get you sugar as well?"

Golden Dove shook her head negatively as she motioned in apology. "No, sugar is very hard to get. We do harvest our own honey though, would you like some? I forgot that you are English, so prefer tea. I do have several different kinds. I make my own so I will get you some later."

Devon grinned in delight as Mary promised him tea later.

Mary got up and went over to the area where her three trunks were stored.

Devon was surprised to see the trunks at first, he had not noticed them last night then remembered that Mary was not a prisoner she was here of her own free will.

Golden Dove came over with a jar and opened it then took a small spoon before dipping out some honey to put in his coffee.

Devon raised his eyebrows in surprise.

Mary just shrugged as she put the spoon back in the jar. "I did bring a few things with me from my old life. Actually, when you get to know us better you will find that we are a little more inclined to accept some of the useful white inventions. You will also find that this group of Indians is not as adverse to change as most of the other Indian tribes. Most of our people here are mixed bloods with a few white people also. We keep to ourselves most times trying to get along with both whites and the Indian tribes that surround us. The next chief after my husband is three quarters Cheyenne, as well as a quarter white, so there is even a few white customs we follow now."

Devon was extremely surprised by this conversation as Mary settled across the fire from him. He had heard that Indians hated the whites so wanted nothing to do with them. He had also heard that the Indians tortured then killed any white person they found. Except on some rare occasions when a child is stolen and kept. A few women had also been adopted Devon had heard then willingly married an Indian like Mary.

Black Hawk saw the surprise on Devon's face, and he shook his head in annoyance. He had not thought by looking at Devon that the white man would allow gossip or other people's prejudices rub off on him.

Devon saw the disappointed look that Tommy flashed his way then remembered how the Royalty in England always degraded the serfs and servants. Why he had never quite figured out, as well as how frustrated it had made him feel when trying to stand up for them. Maybe he was wrong in his thinking, could it be possible that he was doing the same thing now that he had stood against back home. Just because, someone was different did not mean that they were wrong. It only meant that they had unconventional ways of looking at things or other customs to observe. He had come to this country to get away from prejudice, and here he was doing the same thing. Well this was his chance to learn the other side of life in this country. Maybe it was time to be quiet then listen instead of thinking only of himself and his losses. Both his sisters had died the way they wanted it was time to put them away in his heart then go on living.

Black Hawk could see the conflict plain on the vi'hoI expressive face. As he debated with himself on whether he should open his mind to new ideas, or whether he should shut himself off completely. He was surprised and then relieved as Devon's face became more open.

Devon inclined his head now ready for Mary to continue.

CHAPTER FIVE

Raven and Giant Bear sat across from each other staring soundlessly. The only thing that could be heard in the tepee was the crackling of the fire, as well as an occasional voice from outside.

Giant Bear was the first to turn away with a guilty look on his face.

Raven frowned in surprise usually her grandfather could out stare anybody. She remembered one time when Giant Bear had a staring contest with a chief from another band. It went on for two days until finally the other chief looked away.

Raven took a sip of her coffee reflectively then grabbed her pipe and tobacco pouch. As she was filling the pipe she peeked at her grandfather again, but he was staring into the fire intently, he did not seem to notice what she was doing. She was not fooled though she knew that her grandfather was aware of every move she made. He used this tactic to confuse his opponent that he was using it on her did not bode well for her peace of mind she was sure. She passed the pipe to her grandfather first.

Giant Bear looked up as he took the pipe from her before taking two puffs and blew the smoke into the air, towards the ground, right then left and passed it back to Raven. She put the pipe down after she was finished then looked at her Grandfather intently as she motioned sharply in demand. "Well namshimi' are you ready to tell me what is going on now?"

Giant Bear winced at Ravens angry tone and sighed resignedly as he told his story, with a few missing facts of course. Once finished telling her about finding the Englishman, he continued grimly."We did not understand at first what was going on it was not until we found Slippery As An Eel than Squatting Dog that we figured it out. When we followed their tracks we realized that they had followed the wagon for quit a long time, it was not until they were on your property that they struck. They did not seem to want any of the other tribes that stay here with us involved though because they waited until we got past the spot White Antelope's tribe usually leaves us. They stay with us almost to the end of your land, about six miles from your border. I also think they left the two dead braves there to let us know who did it, taunting us. I am not even sure that Squatting Dog was involved. He could have been put there to make us go down the wrong trail."

Raven inclined her head having already thought of that earlier. Squatting Dog was from a different band altogether. She waited anxiously for her grandfather to go on, not saying a word, knowing he was not done.

Giant Bear cleared his throat then waved beseechingly. "Well we still did not realize the full danger to ourselves. Not until, the shaman went into seclusion in order to get a vision from the Great Spirit did we get scared. I decided to send Running Wolf to get you after the shaman said we had to return to the winter camp. I told him to get you and meet us back here."

Raven mulled over everything her grandfather told her suspiciously. It was exactly what Running Wolf had told her almost as if it were rehearsed. She shrugged off her qualms as her mind whirled with plans. Well the first thing she needed to do was to find out if Squatting Dog was involved intentionally or involuntarily. Suddenly she looked over at her grandfather sharply in reproach as she realized that he had not said anything about the shaman's vision at all. She knew he had one it was written all over her grandfather's face.

Giant Bear looked down in guilt as Raven stared at him in wariness. Raven pointed at him in ultimatum as he looked back at her. "Namshimi', what did the shaman say about his vision?"

Giant Bear cleared his throat uneasily, now not so sure that this was such a good idea. He opened his hand in apprehension almost pleadingly trying to stall. "You are not going to like it!"

Raven frowned in exasperation as her grandfather tried avoiding the issue than she nodded wearily she was sure she would not, but she needed to know. "I figured that out already, but tell me anyway!"

Reluctantly Giant Bear told her about the vision. The only thing he left out was the golden eagle and that it had been present at her naming ceremony when she was a child as well as in this one. He also left out the fact that the shaman had seen the first vision before, which is why the white man was here to begin with. The chief watched his granddaughter's face go from disbelief to outright refusal then to resignation at the trap she found herself in.

Raven could not believe it! Why? She had sacrificed her whole life to look after her Cheyenne people, and she had never asked for anything in return. Now she was being asked to give up the only thing she had left. Her freedom! It just was not fair, how could the Great Spirit ask her to give up more!

Raven remembered Giant Bear's description of the carnage that would occur if she did not marry this white man. She knew that she would do it to save her family, no matter the cost. "Grandfather you do realize that this white man will not actually recognize our marriage?"

Giant Bear smiled in relief at Ravens calm voice. He had expected hysterics this was going better than he had thought it would. He shrugged dismissively as he waved that problem away, not bothered by that at all. "Do not worry about that right now, he has agreed to marry you. We will just have to trust in the Great Spirit for the rest."

Raven frowned dejectedly. "Namshimi', you also realize that if he does decide to stay with this marriage that I will have to move away. I can't see an Earl wanting to stay here; he has other responsibilities in England."

Giant Bear shook his head in reassurance. "No, Raven, I forgot to tell you that when Devon woke up he told me that he was the second son so has nothing holding him in England."

Raven sighed in relief before gesturing curiously. "Good, but why did you not want me to talk in English around him?"

Giant Bear grimaced uneasily he had hoped she had forgotten about that. "Well at first I thought that you could pretend not to know English, so he had to teach you in the hope it might draw him to you."

Raven tried to interrupt angrily, but stopped when her grandfather held up his hand.

Giant Bear shook his head knowingly as he dropped it. "No, do not say it; I had already decided it would not work. In the first place, your grandmother is white so speaks perfect English. He would never believe that you would not have been taught also. The second reason is that you will need to talk to him about what happened at the massacre. The final reason and the most important one is that you are just too honest. Sooner or later you would say something; I think this Devon fellow prizes honesty before anything else."

Raven inclined her head grimly. "You are right I would not have even gone along with it. Did you happen to ask this Devon; didn't you say his name was why he came here in the first place?"

Giant Bear quickly nodded his head. He hated to lie to her, wanting to get it over with he answered in a rush. "Yes, his name is Devon. I did ask, but he would not tell me. I think it had something to do with his sister because every time I questioned him about it he would get very upset. I do not want you to be asking him right now either it just upset him. There will be lots of time later for questions."

Raven frowned in agreement, she would wait for now.

Giant Bear sighed in relief then looked sheepishly at Raven as he fidgeted in dread not actually wanting to tell her this, but she needed to be prepared just in case he was wrong about the Englishman. "There is one other thing I have to warn you about. You have to realize that just as you are being forced to marry this white man, so is he being forced to marry you. I got his agreement in two ways. First, by telling him that he had to marry you or he would die. The second is by telling him I was giving him a life for a life. I did not realize he would know what I meant!"

Ravens mouth fell open in stunned indignation as she leaned forward in ominous foreboding. "You actually told him that you were giving me to him as payment for the death of his sister? Namshimi' how could you, now if he demands my death I would have to kill myself!"

Raven jumped up in a rage as she stormed around the tepee furiously. "Grandfather, how could you do this to me?"

Giant Bear got up as well and grabbed Raven by the shoulders. "I am sorry Raven if I had known that he would guess correctly at what that meant I would never have told him. He only figured out part of it though he thinks that he has to kill you himself. He does not know that all he has to do is tell you to do it. If I thought for one moment that he would actually demand your death, I would never make you marry him. I would rather die first!"

Raven stared at her grandfather earnestly looking for reassurance. "Are you sure he will not demand my death?"

Giant Bear let go of Raven then sighed dispiritedly as he shrugged. "No I am not totally sure that is why I had to warn you, but I did tell him that he would have to convince you first. He did not seem to be very anxious to try it though after he remembered you jumping out of that fur."

Raven stared off into space for a few moments desperately trying to think of a way out of this. "Grandpa, do I have to marry him now or can I have some time to think about it first?"

Giant Bear shook his head negatively. "No, you do not have to marry him today. Actually, he has to become a white Indian before you marry him. So you have about a month or so to find out who killed his sister and to resign yourself to your marriage."

Raven nodded in relief; maybe she could get out of this yet with a little patience as well as a lot of work. If she could find the killers before the month was up maybe she would not have to sacrifice her freedom. She frowned grimly then looked at her grandfather in question. "Grandma told me that you brought all the evidence and all the bodies back with you. I would like to see them now before I decide what I am going to do next."

Giant Bear turned then beckoned her to follow him outside; he led her to the south side of the village.

As they walked Ravens mind was turning over possible courses of action that might work for proving her family's innocence, she had not come to any conclusions by the time they arrived at the spot. She walked over to Squatting Dog and Slippery As An Eel first both had been shot by a rifle, but she could not tell whether it was from the same gun or not. She turned to her grandfather hopefully. "Did the white man say anything about the massacre that might help me?"

Giant Bear shook his head negatively. "No, I have not really asked him too many questions yet. I figured you would want to ask him yourself before you go anywhere."

Raven inclined her head in approval as she walked over to the two guides then groaned in dismay. She knew both of them, brothers Patrick and Scott they were from town. They both had wives as well as several children plus both had been strong supporters on her behalf. She stroked Scott's hair tenderly for a moment then whispered softly. "I am so sorry, I promise to look after your families they will never want for anything this I swear!"

Raven turned to her grandfather angrily as she motioned in demand. "I want two coffins made for their bodies. If you cannot do it contact Dream Dancer he can bring out two, no make that three coffins. The white woman should also have one."

Giant Bear frowned thoughtfully it would take to long to make them. "I will send Spotted Owl to the ranch with your message."

Giant Bear turned before trotting away.

Raven walked to the white woman next; she was exceptionally beautiful and not that old. The Englishwoman had no visible wounds that she could see. Raven turned her over to check her back, nothing there either. She was just easing her back down when a harsh voice made her spin around.

"DO NOT TOUCH HER! You filthy squaw!"

Raven drew herself up angrily then watched the white man storm towards her with a look of hatred and rage plain on his face.

Black Hawk walking beside Devon suddenly reached over then grabbed the vi'hoI. He spun the unfortunate Englishman around furiously before he could reach Raven. The half Cheyenne warrior hissed warningly, infuriated. "You will be careful how you talk to my niece, or you might find yourself lying on the ground with another broken arm."

Devon stepped back in shocked surprise. This was a different side to Tommy that he had not seen yet. It was easy to forget that the mild tempered Tommy was a Cheyenne warrior.

Raven pushed between the two men quickly. She turned to Black Hawk in reassurance as she spoke in Cheyenne. "It's okay uncle he is just upset, I need to question him so you can come back here in an hour to take him back to grandfather's."

Black Hawk scowled a warning at Devon before turning as he walked away.

Raven spun around and glared at Devon angrily as soon as her uncle was out of sight. She jabbed a finger hard into his chest menacingly. "I will ignore your insult this time because I know how upset you must be, but if you ever call me a filthy squaw again, you will regret it! Do you understand me?"

Devon frowning just as furious, but he nodded slightly ashamed of himself, although he hid it well. He motioned anxiously towards the bodies. "What were you doing to my sisters, haven't you people done enough to them already?"

Devon stopped in confusion at the stunned look on her face. "Why are you looking at me that way?"

Raven scowled in uncertainty. "Did you say sisters as in more than one?"

Devon frowned and motioned grimly. "Yes, I brought two sisters with me why?"

Raven moved aside so he could see all the bodies. "There was only one at the massacre."

Devon walked over to his youngest sister before looking around, but did not see his older sister anywhere. He spun around anxiously as he waved in wild demand. "Where is she? My older sister Janet is not here!"

Giant Bear came back just then. He looked from one to the other in apprehension. "What seems to be the problem here, the whole village can hear you two shouting?"

Raven turned to her grandfather thoughtfully. "It seems that there should have been one more sister. Are you sure you got all the bodies?"

Giant Bear looked at Devon in surprise and nodded decisively before turned back to Raven. "Yes we searched the whole area there was no other woman, could the killers have taken her as a captive?"

Raven shrugged unknowingly. "They must have there is no other explanation."

Devon looked from one to the other suspiciously. He waved furiously in demand. "You must have her here somewhere, what have you done with my other sister?"

Raven shook her head sadly in sorrow. "My people have not done anything to them; didn't my grandfather explain to you that it was not our tribe of Cheyenne who did this?"

Devon snorted in contempt then motioned angrily. "Do you really expect me to fall for that nonsense? I do not believe anything your grandfather told me. Indians attacked us, and the same Indians hold me prisoner! I do not see any differences in looks or clothes."

Raven grabbed Devon's good arm before hauling him towards the bodies of the warriors furiously.

Devon tried to pull away, but was in for a shock when he could not get away from her. She was certainly stronger than she looked not too many people could hold him.

Raven held on to him until they reached the two dead Indians before letting go as if burned. It had taken almost all her strength to pull him; he was clearly no weak white man. She had a feeling that the only reason she had been able to manhandle him was that he did not have his full strength back yet. She pointed at the dead warriors legs ignoring the strange feeling in her hand. "Look at the moccasins of both these men and tell me what you see?"

Devon scowled at Raven suspiciously then did as he was told. At first, he could see no difference between the two, so he bent closer. The pattern on both moccasins was slightly different, but not by much. He looked at Raven as he shrugged dismissively.

Raven frowned at the shrug and waved impatiently, even a fool could see the difference. "Now look at their knife sheaths as well as the arrows."

Devon looked at them closely then spotted the differences this time on the design and colours of the knife sheaths. The arrows were even more complex, he looked at Raven inquisitively.

Raven nodded at the questioning look. "They are from two different Cheyenne tribes."

Raven beckoned to her grandfather then spoke in Cheyenne to him. Giant Bear nodded and left again.

Devon had not even realized that the old chief was right behind him; he scowled in annoyance at being surprised.

Raven bent over then took off one of her moccasins and handed it to him. "Now look at my moccasin, do you see the differences now?"

Devon saw the variation right away now that he knew what he was looking for. He reached out then touched her knife sheath as he handed her moccasin back. While she was putting it back on, he turned and watched curiously, as the old chief came towards him with a quiver full of arrows as well as something on his face.

Raven stood up then pointed at the dead warriors again. "Now look at the war paint on both of these men and look at the war paint on my grandfather's face."

Devon looked at all three faces. He took the arrow that Giant Bear handed him then studied it. He handed it back before the chief turned and left again without saying a word. The Englishman looked back at Raven then shrugged in exasperation. "So all you have proven to me was that there were three Cheyenne tribes instead of two!"

Raven folded her arms under her breasts in anger and tried to explain again as she shook her head in exasperation. "No, we know there was one tribe for sure, but we are not certain Squatting Dog's tribe was involved yet. He could have broken off from his tribe to join the others or he could have been captured then killed before being left to try and throw us off the trail."

Devon shook his head in puzzlement. "How do you know this? Couldn't it have been the other way around? Maybe it was Squatting Dogs tribe then the other Indian was left."

Raven sighed sadly in disagreement. "No, Squatting Dogs tribe would have no reason to do this, but Slippery As An Eels tribe hate me and my grandfather for shaming them."

Devon scowled in frustration as he motioned in anger. "Are you telling me all this was done to get back at you? It just happened to be our misfortune to get caught in the middle!"

Raven nodded unhappily then waved in apology. "Yes, it looks that way. I am still not sure though. I need to question you first before I ride to Squatting Dogs camp and make sure they were not involved to. Afterwards, I have to track down Slippery As An Eels tribe, when I have done this I will be back to gather a war party to go after them. Grandfather says you will be ready to come along by then. I will also try to find your other sister. If I can safely get her out without help I will, if not we will go get her when I get back."

Devon turned to look at his youngest sister sadly. He reached out and tenderly stroked her hair then he sighed in resignation. "I do not have much choice but to trust you and your grandfather."

Devon turned back to Raven before clenching his good fist in rage as he shook it threateningly. "I do promise you this though! If you do not return in a month with either my sister or the whereabouts of my sister, I will find a way to escape. When I do, I will make sure that the army wipes every one of you out. You have my promise for now that I will not try to run."

Raven clenched both her fists in impotent rage. Who did he think he was anyway threatening her? Who was the prisoner here, her or him?

Devon watched the conflicting emotions on Ravens face in interest than could not help the surge of desire that shot through him. She was certainly one of the most beautiful women he had ever seen. He quickly squashed that emotion, before turning away towards his sister to hide the evidence of his desire.

Raven got her emotions under control and moved closer to Devon as she gazed down at the beautiful blonde. "I was not trying to hurt your sister earlier I was only trying to find a wound to see how she died. But I could not find anything; do you happen to remember how she died?"

Devon shook his head sadly, as he stared down at his younger sister reflectively. "No I did not see what happened, but I would guess her heart finally gave out. She had a bad heart, she was born with it. The doctor did not even think she would make it to her first birthday, but she fooled him as well as everyone else."

Devon looked behind him then saw that Giant Bear had returned and was watching him expressionlessly. He turned back to Raven at the chief's warning scowl. "All I can remember is riding along talking to my older sister when the guide in front of us dropped from his saddle as a dozen or more riders shooting arrows came out of nowhere. My older sister fell out of her saddle that is the last I saw of her. My younger sister, as well as a guide, was behind us in a wagon. I heard her scream hysterically then two Indians pulled me out of my saddle and started beating me. I did manage to shoot the one you call Slippery As An Eel, but there was too many of them. I passed out from the pain, when I woke up I was in your grandfather's tepee."

Raven nodded in sympathy. "Would you be able to recognize any of them?"

Devon shrugged grimly. "I do not know for sure, maybe the ones who beat me so bad, but I will not know until I see them again."

Raven frowned seriously, as she waved in promise. "I will find them, I promise! If I can, I will bring your sister back with me alive. You must not get your hopes up too high though, she could still be dead. Or be a totally different person when we find her."

Raven waited for Devon's nod of understanding then turned before walking off toward her tepee. She passed Black Hawk on the way and nodded, but did not stop. She entered her tepee in a rage then started throwing extra clothes and things together for the trail. All the while she mumbled under her breath about stubborn men who could not see the proof right in front of them, even if they were bashed in the head with it.

Raven stopped short as she stood there staring off into space with a pensive look on her face. Remembering how she had grabbed Devon's arm then nearly dropped it at a tingling sensation from the contact. However, she had stubbornly held on, the feel of the hard muscles under his shirt had felt good. She shook herself in impatience for what she was thinking, she did not even know the man, and she certainly did not like him. It had just been a surprise to realize that he was not a weak vi'hoI.

Raven finished packing her saddlebags then put them in the corner for tomorrow. At least the storm had broke and by tomorrow afternoon, there should not be any snow left.

Giant Bear walked in then saw the saddlebags in the corner. He turned to Raven and motioned calmly. "I see you are already packed to go. I will have a packhorse readied for you with enough provisions to last you a month. I would like you to stay for a couple more days though."

Raven frowned in frustration at her grandfather. "I want to get started right away, the sooner I find the killers as well as the white woman the sooner I can get rid of the white man."

Giant Bear scowled in annoyance. "Look a few more days will not hurt anything. You know where both tribes are camped; it is not as if you have to follow a trail. Besides you are the best at breaking horses, I want Devon to learn from the best. He needs a horse to go with you later, so I want you to teach him."

Raven grimaced in aggravation at her grandfather. "It will take more than two days to teach him. I would need at least two to three weeks, and I do not have that much time to waste."

Giant Bear shrugged placatingly. "Take a week show him everything you can. Whatever you cannot teach him in that time; Black Hawk will show him while you are gone. Besides, you two need to get to know each other better. We will also have Devon's adoption ceremony before you go."

Raven waved sharply in anger at her grandfather. "I do not want to marry him! That is why I want to go find the real killers now then I do not have to!"

Giant Bear grabbed his granddaughter by the arms and shook her angrily. "The Great Spirit said you must marry him, or we will all die! The vision did not say if you find the killers, we would live. Only through your marriage will we survive."

Raven pulled away furiously then stood with tears streaming down her face. She hastily wiped them away, livid that she had let her emotions take control of her. "I do not want to marry him, namshimi'! The Great Spirit cannot ask me to do this, it is not fair! I want to marry for love like my parents did, as you did. Why should I have to sacrifice my life to a loveless marriage? Has Heammawihio, our Great Spirit turned away from me? What did I do to deserve this?"

Giant Bear turned away so that Raven could not see the guilt on his face. "I am sorry Raven; we all must make sacrifices that we do not like sometimes."

Giant Bear turned back once he got his face under control before opening both hands in supplication as he pleaded. "Please do not close yourself off, give Devon and yourself a chance to get to know each other. Maybe you will come to love him in time. The Great Spirit always does things for reasons we do not understand until later. All I ask is that you will give this a chance to work."

Raven inclined her head sadly in resignation. "I will try grandfather, but I can't promise I will love this man. It is just too much to ask of me! I think we will both end up hating each other in time."

Giant Bear sighed miserably as he motioned helplessly. "For all our sakes I hope you are wrong. All I can ask is for you to try."

Raven hugged her grandfather in reluctant agreement then moved back so he could see her nod before changing the subject. "Which horse are you letting Devon have?"

Giant Bear grinned mischievously. "I am giving him Devil."

Raven stood there with her mouth open in stunned surprise for a moment then she snapped it shut incredulously as she gestured angrily. "Why ever would you give that mean brute to Devon?"

Giant Bear smiled smugly at her shocked reaction. "Devil is not beyond hope; he has just never been tamed. I have been observing Devon for the last few days, I think Devil will suit him very well."

Raven grimaced in distaste as she thought of the stud. She had been the one to give him the name Devil. The grey stallion stood sixteen hands plus a little, with a muscled body that was perfect. He was certainly made for speed; he was so powerful that none of the other horses that were kept with him could outrun him. But he also had a nasty temperament to go with it, he hated people. So far, only Spotted Owl could get near enough to handle him.

Giant Bear smiled knowingly at Ravens scowl. "I figured Devon could give it a try at least. If I am wrong and he has not made any headway with the stallion in a week, I will give him a different horse. I had Spotted Owl bring him in from the pasture before he left to see Dream Dancer."

Raven inclined her head reluctantly as she walked over to the corner then grabbed her training whip as well as a rope that she used as a halter. "I will meet you and Devon at the corral. Oh, can you ask Black Hawk to bring that mare I gave him last year. Tell him to put her in the corral beside the stud, but not together. I do not need him trying to mount her while I am working with her."

Giant Bear left.

Raven grabbed her lariat as well as a bridle, even though she did not think she would need them today. She walked out of her tepee then over to the large pasture and whistled for Brave Heart. She unlatched the gate then waited for her stud to come, before letting him out. She turned to lead him towards the breaking pens with a soft whisper. "Come, Brave Heart."

Brave Heart nickered obediently as he followed his mistress. He made sure not to crowd her keeping his nose close to her left shoulder, but not too close.

Giant Bear and Devon were already standing by the corrals watching Devil frisk then paw the air angrily.

Devon turned and stared in amazement as he watched Raven leading another stud without any ropes or restraints that he could see. He took a step towards her to help with some of the things that she was carrying, but stopped short when Giant Bear grabbed his good arm to stop him not wanting him to get hurt.

Raven took Brave Heart to the opposite side of the corral where nobody would get to close then softly commanded. "Stand, Brave Heart!"

Raven turned away and went to the gate.

Giant Bear moved to open it for her, now that the stallion was not with her.

Raven smiled in thanks then walked to the center, she put everything down except the whip. Devon walked in as well, but stood with his back to Raven staring in awe at the stallion standing there looking at them. The horse had not moving an inch from where he was told to stand. She walked over then stood beside Devon as she motioned towards her pinto. "Magnificent isn't he?"

Devon grinned in admiration. "How do you get him to follow you like that and stay when you tell him to?"

Raven shrugged dismissively. "It takes a lot of patience, as well as many days working with a horse to teach them that. The Indians believe though that for every warrior, there is one horse that will suit his or her personality. My grandfather thinks that grey stud over there will be your perfect match."

Devil picked that moment to rear then paw the air in challenge at Brave Heart, but Ravens stud ignored him.

Devon grimaced as he looked over at the grey in disagreement. He turned back to Raven shaking his head grimly. "I do not think that stallion will let anyone near him!"

Both studs interrupted Devon as they loudly neighed enticingly. Devil raced to the end of the corral with his neck arched. Brave Heart also arched his neck and pranced in anticipation, but he did not budge.

Devon looked at where both stallions were staring then smiled at the dainty palomino mare that was being led towards the pen.

Raven touched Devon's arm to get his attention. "I am going to teach you how to break your stud, but I will do it with the mare. I brought along my stallion to show you what can be accomplished with patience and training. I need to explain a few things about him first though. I was out hunting a few years ago in the foothills when I heard a horse neighing in painful frustration. I followed the sound then came to a gully where that stud was trapped. There was blood on his neck, and he was staggering around badly. There was no food or water down there, so I hobbled my mare before gathering as much grass as I could then threw it down. I took my two water bags and slid down to the canyon bottom then made a camp on the opposite side so that the stallion would not get to upset. I put the grass and a large bowl of water in the middle of the canyon. This went on for a week, the stud on his side and me on the other. I finally decided that the stallion was strong enough to get out by himself, so I broke camp. I was not entirely sure, but figured that a bullet had creased the stud. I scrambled up the bank then saddled my mare. When I was up on her back, I looked behind me, and there was the stallion watching me. I had talked to him quite a lot while he was getting his strength back. I was always calling him my Brave Heart so continued doing so. He followed me all day, but stayed at a distance. I decided to make an early camp to see if he would stay. He did, but well back watching me. I took the bowl that I had used for watering him as well as some oats that I had stashed away in my saddlebag then went to the edge of my camp. I sat down with the bowl in front of me singing softly. We did this for two days; on the third day, he came over to me and ate the oats. The next day when I brought the dish I did not even have to sit down, he came right up to me. I finally got to touch him then was able to treat the crease in his neck. He has been with me ever since, but he still will not let anyone else near him. There is one exception though; Spotted Owl who brought your horse here can also handle Brave Heart. Spotted Owl seems to have a way with horses, so remember that if you need help with Devil in the future. So, while I do this demonstration you will have to stand outside the corral."

Devon nodded and left with Giant Bear following. The two men took positions away from the gate. The Englishman watched silently as Black Hawk brought the mare in then handed Raven the rope. When Black Hawk was clear, she gave one high shrill whistle.

Brave Heart galloped into the pen obediently.

Black Hawk shut the gate, before walking over to Devon so he could watch with him.

Raven released the mare and watched her sidle up to Brave Heart.

The only response Devon could see the stud make was the ears twitching as well as his nostrils flaring. Other than that, Brave Heart never moved from in front of Raven.

Brave Heart lowered his head hoping for a scratch. Raven obliged him as she smiled in delight at her horse. She stepped back and shook the whip out. She then lifted it up to him so he could smell it. She walked around him and moved the whip along his sides touching him everywhere with it. Brave Heart did not even twitch, familiar with this routine. Satisfied Raven stood in front of him again. She pointed the whip to the right then murmured. "Walk, Brave Heart."

Brave Heart turned right and walked around the corral. Raven turned with him as he walked around keeping the whip pointed in the direction she wanted him to go. She gave two distinct whistles so that her horse would pick up more speed. He trotted two full circles around the corral then Raven gave a long low whistle. Brave Heart broke into a canter immediately. She gave one strong whistle, and he went back to a walk. She lowered the whip then took a step in front of him. The stallion stopped and turned towards her instantly waiting patiently. Raven pointed to her left with the whip then gave a long low sharp whistle.

Brave Heart spun to the left and went directly into a gallop. He maintained this pace for two full circles of the pen. Raven dropped the whip on the ground then gave a strong sharp intense whistle. The stud spun on his hind legs and in a full gallop bore down on his mistress.

Raven waited patiently then reached up at the last minute and grabbed his mane, before vaulting onto his back in one running step. She directed Brave Heart to gallop down the middle of the pen then jumped down and grabbed the whip off the ground then was back up on Brave Heart within two strides. She slowed Brave Heart and stopped him in front of Devon then gave another command. The stallion rose up on his hind legs to paw the air squealing as he did so. Feeling another nudge from his mistress, he dropped onto all fours again before bowing deeply to the Englishman. Devon was impressed he had never seen a horse so well trained or so eager to please.

Black Hawk smiled proudly at Devon as he waved towards his niece. "Raven is our best horse trainer. Of course, we all know how to train our own horses. If we can convince Raven to do it though, the value on our horses goes up double. She is known all over Montana as the best, even by the whites."

Raven led Brave Heart out of the corral and took him back over to the spot he was in before. She beckoned Devon to enter the corral as she walked back inside alone.

Devon went in, he stood beside Raven as they watched the mare.

The mare totally ignored the two people as she pranced around the corral, first facing the grey stud then going over to the pinto.

Raven scooped the whip up in preparation before turning to Devon. "See how the mare totally ignores us. The first thing we want her to learn is that when she is in this pen or around people, she is to pay attention. So I will take this whip and run her until she will stand facing me no matter the distractions. Every trainer is different some use whistles, some use words, some use body language with no words or whistles. Black Hawk does not use whistles or words so because this is his horse I will not use any either, unless I have to. Try to stay close to me so I can explain as I go along, but I will be moving really fast so try not to get in the way."

Devon nodded then followed close behind.

Raven walked towards the mare and clucked, but was ignored. When nothing happened, she cracked the whip loudly to get the mares attention. The mare jumped then spun away from the loud noise at a full gallop. She let the mare run without giving her any direction at first, but every time the mare would try to stop in front of one of the studs, Raven would crack the whip again to keep her running. She called back over her shoulder to Devon as she explained. "Now I want her to go the other way, so I will step in her path and point the whip the way I want her to go. If she does not turn, I will crack the whip until she does."

Raven stepped in front of the mare then pointed the whip in demand before clucking at her in urging. When she did not turn, Raven cracked the whip and the mare spun away. She tried twice to turn wanting to go the other way, but each time Raven was there to stop her. She turned the mare twice more then dropped her arm and stepped in front of the mare. "Whoa girl!"

The mare stopped then turned to the stallion. As soon as she did, the whip cracked loudly, and she was running again.

Raven called back over her shoulder explaining what she was doing to Devon as she stopped the mare again. "What I am doing now is letting the mare stop, but even while she is stopped I want her attention on me. Every time she turns away or neighs at one of the studs, I will force her to run again. Some learn fast others take two or three days to learn this. When she decides she has had enough, she will stop then turn to face me. When she does I will praise her and let her rest for a few minutes."

The mare turned to the woman totally ignored the stallions this time as she stood there quivering in exhaustion watching Raven.

Raven squatted patiently waiting, letting the mare rest. One of the studs neighed loudly, so the mare turned away. Instantly Raven jumped up then started running the mare again.

Devon stayed where he was holding onto his side and just watched, in too much pain to keep up. When the mare stopped again then turned to Raven, the Englishman went over and squatted beside her. It took Raven three more tries before the mare would stand still, entirely ignored both the stallions. Even when one called out she did not move a muscle.

Raven smiled in approval at the mare as she turned towards Devon. "Now I will get up then walk towards her talking quietly if she backs up or turns away I will run her again until she lets me pat her."

Devon stayed where he was and watched Raven walk towards the mare talking soothingly to her in Cheyenne. It took Raven another half hour before the mare would stand then let Raven come to her. She touched the horse all over and handled her feet the mare did not even twitch.

Raven smiled at Devon then beckoned him to come closer. He got up and walked toward her slowly. He was just about there when the mare turned away. So Raven spent another half hour running the mare until she let him touch her.

Raven then beckoned to Black Hawk to come in. Black Hawk climbed over the fence railing and walked over to them. The mare did not even twitch this time. She smiled at her uncle. "What did you name this fine lady?"

Black Hawk grinned mischievously at her. "I named her after all the ladies in my life. Her name is Stubborn Lady."

Raven laughed in delight. "Well she certainly lived up to her name today; I think she has had enough. We will work on her tomorrow afternoon around the same time."

Black Hawk nodded then went to get the rope to take the mare back to her pasture.

Raven turned to Devon. "I am going to take Brave Heart back to his pasture as well, when I will get back we will talk about your horse."

Devon watched her walk away without comment.

Giant Bear came over and looked at Devon proudly as he motioned inquisitively. "Well what do you think about your first lesson on breaking horses Ravens way?"

Devon shrugged then walked out of the corral towards Devil's pen. "I am not sure yet I have never seen anyone break horses this way, not in England anyway. I will have to let you know after the mare is broke."

Giant Bear nodded as they silently watching the grey stallion pace angrily.

Raven trotted up to the men. She watched the stud in interest for a moment then turned to Devon as she waved towards the stallion. "I named him Devil, but now that he is yours, you can call him anything you want. He will remain in this pen until you have trained him. I want you to come every morning before you start your lessons and talk to him. Always stand by the fence so that you can watch him, make sure that he can see you too. After lunch, we will meet here so that you can continue to help me break the mare. Every night before you go to bed I want you to come out here again then do the same thing. We want the stallion to get to know you as well as rely on you. You need to realize that out here trust is the most crucial component in a human and horse relationship. If you do not have confidence in your horse, you can never be sure of him when your life is threatened. I have been fortunate that way I have two horses I can depend on with my life. You have met one today, but the other one is away. If you can break that stud, he will be your friend as well as companion until he dies. He is also like Brave Heart he will never let anyone else on him. He is a one person horse, whoever has the courage to try winning him over will have one hell of a horse."

Raven waited, for Devon to nod his head in understanding. She then turned to her grandfather as she gestured decisively. "You do not need to keep a watch on Devon, he promised not to run until I come back with the whereabouts of the murderers and his sister. So show him where everything is as well as where his boundaries are."

The old chief nodded without argument then beckoned Devon to follow him.

Devon looked at Raven in amazement at the faith she was showing in him, before following Giant Bear quietly without comment.

After the men left, Raven turned to Devil. "Well you handsome devil you, I hope you can keep Devon so busy breaking you, he will not even think of running."

Raven returned to the other pen and grabbed her stuff then went for dinner.

CHAPTER SIX

Devon woke the next morning and stretched experimentally making sure to keep his broken arm still, but his ribs only hurt when he overstretched. He lifted his good hand then touched his face curiously. Some of the swelling had gone down, but not much, it was still extremely sore. He rolled out of his blankets slowly and quietly got dressed so that he would not wake the chief or his wife. He picked up the bag by the door on his way out then headed to the corrals to visit his new horse. In the sack were some oats as well as a handful of crab apples that Mary had given him. She had told him that they were left over from winter storage. He approached the corral slowly and watched the stallion run around in admiration.

Devil saw the strange man so stopped abruptly as he tested the air cautiously. He could detect no fear, but he gave a loud squeal of challenge anyway as he pawed the ground in warning.

Devon smiled at the horse calmly unafraid. He was in total awe at owning such a beautiful animal. He had always loved horses never having been afraid of one in his life he decided to sit up on the top rail to see what the stallion would do. Mindful of his arm he carefully made his way up before carefully sitting.

The stud pawed the ground again as he snorted irritably then pinned his ears back as he tested the air once more. There was a strange smell, but it was not unpleasant so he did not charge.

Devon gave a loud whistle of command and tried to call him over.

The stallion's ears went up, but other than that he ignored the whistle.

Devon smiled in delight. "Well you are a handsome devil, aren't you? I think your name suits you just fine, so I will not change it."

The stud snorted and bobbed his head up then down as if in agreement.

Devon laughed softly in pleasure before trying to talk to the horse instead of whistling. "Come Devil, come on boy."

Devil blew softly through his nostrils testily and shook his head ignoring him.

Devon chuckled not discouraged then lifted the sack he still held and started taking out apples. "Well I brought you some treats; I will leave them here for you anyway."

Devon took out three apples then rolled them around in his hands. He did this so that the stud would get his scent off the apples. He put them on the fence and watched the stud hopefully.

The stallion tested the air again then took a hesitant step forward at the enticing scent of the apples. Suddenly he stopped short and spun away as he ran to the other end of the corral.

Devon grinned encouraged by that small step then got down off the fence. He dug in his bag and pulled out a handful of oats then put some in between the apples before turning and walking away. When he was far enough, the Englishman looked over his shoulder then saw his horse eating the apples. He smiled, but did not go back as he headed towards the chief's tepee.

Devon took a deep breath of the mouth-watering smells that were coming through the tepee and realized he was starving. He ducked inside once permission was given before putting his sack by the door. He walked over to the fire before sitting down.

Mary turned with a smile and handed him a plate of pancakes. She poured him a tea that she had made special for him then put some honey in it before handing him the cup and honey to put some on his pancakes.

Devon grinned gratefully between mouthfuls. "Thank you Golden Dove. Where is Giant Bear?"

Golden Dove beamed in delight at Devon's first use of her Indian name then sat down across the fire from him. "Giant Bear is already closeted with the shaman, but he did ask me to tell you about what to expect at the burial of your sister and the guides."

Devon frowned perplexed. "I did not know Indians buried their dead. I heard they put them up on a platform then burn them."

Golden Dove inclined her head in admiration at his knowledge. "Most Indian tribes burn their dead but not all of them do, we will discuss that later though. Eat your breakfast first; afterwards we will talk about who the Cheyenne are."

Devon nodded and dug into his breakfast. He was about half done when a scratching sound was heard at the door.

Golden Dove got up then went over to open the flap; she warmly hugged her son Black Hawk in welcome.

Black Hawk returned the hug before walking over to the fire he sat down beside Devon. "How are your ribs and arm today, Devon?"

Black Hawk smiled gratefully at his mother as he accepted a plate as well as a cup of coffee then turned his attention back to Devon inquisitively.

Devon grinned before shrugging casually. "My ribs are better only a slight twinge if I move too fast or overstretch. I do not think they are broken just bruised or maybe cracked a little. My arm still hurts a lot, but hopefully not too much longer."

Black Hawk sighed relieved that Devon was feeling better as he motioned curiously. "Did you go visit your new horse this morning?"

Devon inclined his head eagerly. "I did, but he would not have anything to do with me. I did leave three small apples that your mother gave me, as well as a handful of oats, on the top railing of the fence. As I was walking away, I peeked over my shoulder. Devil was eating the apples."

Black Hawk laughed in humour. "Well nobody said Devil was stupid only stubborn. I put some hay in his corral a few minutes ago there was no apples or oats anywhere."

Devon chuckled knowingly. "You will have to show me where you keep the hay so I can feed Devil myself."

Black Hawk nodded before finishing his breakfast in companionable silence.

After they ate, Golden Dove sat across the fire from the Englishman and began his lessons while she worked on a pair of moccasins for him. "Devon yesterday you learned a few words in Cheyenne, but I think today I will tell you about the Cheyenne as a whole. I will also tell you how this tribe came to stay here. I have to go back in history so please bear with me."

Golden Dove waited until Devon inclined his head that he understood then continued. "The Cheyenne were originally farmers they planted corn, squash, beans, as well as other vegetables. They migrated to the Sheyenne River in eastern North Dakota around the seventeen hundreds; they lived there for about a half a century. There the Sioux as well as the Assiniboin Indians surrounded them. They lived in an earth lodge most of the year, which was situated further up towards the northern region. Once they acquired the horse, around seventeen-sixty they ranged further out. They had their own political system as well as their own religion. It was believed that they are the direct descendants of their creator, which they call Heammawihio, the Great Spirit. They have different societies some of them included the dog, wolf, fox, and bull societies or soldiers as the whites come to call them later. They also have the red shield as well as many others. Rivalries developed between the societies, which caused some of the tribes to break off then head into Montana. The constant fighting with the Sioux also contributed a great deal to the move. They crossed the Yellowstone River before slipping around the Blackfoot people. As they travelled, groups continued to break off and they branched out more. All Cheyenne tribes have their own Sun Dance at the beginning of the summer. Every five years though, they have a powwow where all the Cheyenne come together as an entire nation once again. The Cheyenne refers to themselves as Tsis-tsis-tas. It was not until the white people started settling in Montana that the Cheyenne started going on the warpath again, except for a few tribes that kept to themselves refusing to go to war again. Giant Bear was one who kept his tribe friendly, but then three white men killed his wife so Giant Bear put on war paint once more. You already heard this story from my husband I have been told, so I am not going to go into details. I will say that because of the white man Giant Bear was travelling with he learned to trust the white people again. When Giant Bear brought Black Hawk and me home, we started looking for a place where we could live in peace. I cannot tell you how we came to settle in the Bear Paw Mountains because it is not my story to tell. But I am sure Giant Bear will tell you either before you marry Raven or after. Anyway, we winter here than every spring we go to the Bitterroot Mountains where we stay until fall. Normally we would be gone before now, but finding you changed that. Now Giant Bear has decided to stay here instead of going to our summer camp. When we first came here to stay for the winters, we had fifty tepees in total. As word spread to other Cheyenne that we lived here in peace, more tribes came to join us and ask permission to winter here with us. Giant Bear agreed on the condition that all white captives were to be questioned then either released back to their people or if they wanted to stay they would be adopted into a family and treated like a Cheyenne. This of course was Ravens doing even though she hides it she cannot stand to see anyone suffer, so now we have four tribes of Cheyenne who live here. In total, we now have two-hundred-fifty tepees' that remain throughout the winter months. You will find that we have adopted many of the white man's ways, but do not be fooled all Indians are dangerous even peaceful ones. This is all for now. It should be time for you to join Raven at the corrals. After you finish with her we will talk about your sister's funeral as well as your adoption than I will try to include some of our other customs."

Devon nodded and left the tepee, he had not even realized what time it was. He had been so engrossed in the story Golden Dove was telling.

Black Hawk caught up to him then touched his good arm to get his attention. "Well, what do you think about us so far?"

Devon shook his head perplexed. "I do not know what to think, I have always heard so many horror stories of Indians that I am finding it hard to believe."

Black Hawk shrugged dismissively. "Some of the stories you hear are true, and some are not. All the Indians really want is to live in peace, except for a few that have always been on the warpath like the Sioux. But the whites keep stealing our land then break their promises. Take scalping for instance it was the white man who started that!"

Devon shuddered at the mental image of someone being scalped. "I did not know that, I had heard it was the Indians way of proving their courage in battle."

Black Hawk shook his head with a snort of distaste. "No, I think it was the French who first started it. They paid the Indians a bounty on any scalp they brought in of their enemies, which were the British I believe. After it was started, the Indians quickly took up the practice. They figured it was the whites way of keeping their enemy's out of heaven as you whites call it. Actually, the Indians always used counting coup as a means of showing bravery. Counting coup means that, in a battle you ride up to an enemy and touch him. If you use your hand only it is considered the ultimate bravery test, or you can use a spear. We also have a special staff made up especially for this purpose; a brave will put a notch on it every time he is successful. After counting coup you ride away without killing anyone this is how we show our courage, not by killing. We only take scalps now to stop our enemy from reaching the happy hunting grounds."

They arrived at the corrals a half hour late.

Raven was standing near Devil's pen waiting impatiently.

Black Hawk went over then hugged Raven. "I am sorry we are late, but you know mother when she starts talking you better not budge until she is finished."

Raven laughed in agreement and squeezed her uncle back before turning to Devon. "How are you feeling today? I see some of the swelling has gone down in your face, but it is turning some interesting colours?"

Devon touched his face experimentally. "It feels a little better my ribs too only a slight twinge, but my arm is the worst off."

Raven nodded in sympathy than turned to indicate Devon's stallion. "You spent time with him this morning, how did it go?"

Devon shrugged regretfully. "Not great! I sat on the top railing for a bit, but he would not come anywhere near me."

Raven looked at Devon in disbelief for a moment. "He did not charge?"

Devon shook his head negatively. "No, but I did not go into the corral with him. I just sat on the top railing and talked to him."

Raven frowned still surprised then turned to Black Hawk before pointing at the corral. "Uncle go over and sit on the top railing for me."

Black Hawk scowled irritably at Raven. "Do I have to?"

Raven raised an eyebrow at Black Hawk chidingly then folded her arms across her chest impatiently.

Black Hawk held up his hands in defeat as he chuckled. "Okay, I'm going!"

Devon watched in puzzlement as Black Hawk walked over reluctantly and carefully climbed the fence. He straddled the top railing half in, half out of the pen ready to make a quick getaway.

Devil stood watching Black Hawk with his nostrils flaring to catch a scent as he had done with Devon. Suddenly he reared then screaming a challenge he charged the fence where Black Hawk sat.

Black Hawk quickly jumped off and almost ran over to them.

Raven chuckled in amusement then turned to Devon. "Now you see why I was surprised that Devil let you sit on the fence. If I would try sitting there he would come after me as well, only Spotted Owl can handle him."

Devon watched the stallion race back to the middle of the pen and stop.

Devil stared in their direction irritably as he pawed the ground in warning.

Devon slowly walked over to the fence.

Devil watched him then tested the air for a scent. Again, he could smell something different about this man; it wasn't unpleasant. He pawed the ground before bobbing his head.

Devon climbed up onto the top railing mindful of his injured arm. He had no fear or hesitation at all, since he was a child he had an affinity with horses it had even amazed his parents at times. He had not even realized that it was anything unusual until now because he had never been around wild horses before.

The stallion just watched him and did not charge.

Devon gave a sharp whistle.

The stud's ears perked up but still he did not move.

Devon climbed down then walked back to Raven awed by it all. He shook his head in disbelief. "Does that mean Devil will let me train him?"

Raven shrugged unknowingly. "It is too soon to tell the stallion lets Spotted Owl handle him, but will not let him ride or train him. Just keep coming here and talking to him for now. Later we can see if he will let you actually go in the pen with him."

Devon inclined his head in agreement then turned. They walked over to the pen with the mare in it.

Lady was standing at the opposite end of the corral staring at the grey stud ignoring the humans.

Raven handed her whip over to Black Hawk. She had noticed the problems Devon had yesterday with keeping up so had decided it was too much for him. "We will stay here and watch you. I want you to get that mare to pay attention to you then I want her to follow you. I will explain everything to Devon as you go along."

Black Hawk took the whip and climbed over the fence before walking towards the mare, she totally ignored him until he cracked the whip.

Raven chuckled as the mare stubbornly spun away from Black Hawk refusing to face him. She turned to Devon then waved at the mare. "She is definitely living up to her name, but she should not take as much time as she did yesterday. If she is a quick learner, she should only take half the time. Tomorrow she should pay attention as soon as we walk into the corral. After my uncle gets her attention, we will go in and make as much noise as possible until she does not flinch from any noise. I brought my rifle because we want her to stand still, even when somebody is shooting at or around her."

Devon looked surprised as he motioned incredulously. "You are going to shoot at her?"

Raven grinned before shaking her head negatively. "No, but I will shoot in the air. We will not shoot at her until she is almost fully trained."

They stood together quietly watching Black Hawk work the mare. It took two hours for the mare to stand then face Black Hawk and another half an hour for him to walk up to the mare without her turning away.

Raven grinned in satisfaction. It had taken almost half the time. She stood up on the corral fence then hollered at Black Hawk. "Uncle cluck to her and walk away if she does not follow you run her again."

Black Hawk nodded then turned away clucking at the mare, but it was not until the third time she had to run around the corral that she followed him obediently.

Devon smiled at Raven in excitement. "So that is how you train a horse to follow you without a rope."

Raven smirked before chuckling at Devon's enthusiasm. "Yes! Now let's go in and walk up to the mare."

They opened the gate then walked slowly towards the mare and Black Hawk. The mare took off running again, so the two stopped then waited until Black Hawk quit running her. Finally, the mare let them come to her.

Raven smiled at Black Hawk. "She is a quick learner she will make a good horse for Gentle Doe."

Black Hawk nodded in satisfaction, but did not comment.

Raven turned to Devon. "Okay let's go get our noise makers to see what she does."

They spent the next hour working with the mare until Raven was satisfied then she called a halt until tomorrow.

Black Hawk took the mare back to her corral after he wiped her down.

Raven and Devon gathered all her stuff together to take back to her tepee.

Devon looked at Raven curiously. "Where is your wolf? I have not seen him around lately."

Raven pointed to the west. "He went to be with his girlfriend I imagine, he is only part wolf. I will probably never see him again now."

Devon walked ahead to push the flap open for Raven then followed her inside. He looked around curiously after handing Raven her things. The tepee was almost empty except a sleeping pallet and some cooking items. He looked at Raven suspiciously. "You do not live here all the time?"

Raven looked at Devon then away again guiltily. "No, I only live here part of the year."

Devon scowled in puzzlement before gesturing in demand. "Where do you live most of the time?"

Raven turned her back to Devon ignoring his question. "I have something for you."

Raven took a step towards the far corner, but halted suddenly when Devon grabbed her by the arm; he spun her around angrily. Devon growled in frustration. "Answer me damn it! Where do you really live?"

Raven pulled her arm away then glared at Devon furiously. "It is none of your business where I live. Now get out of my tepee!"

Devon met Ravens angry glare with one of his own and stormed out in a rage.

Raven sat down on the ground in a huff as she glared at the tepee opening, wishing that he would come back so that she could punch him in the nose. Who did he think he was anyway demanding answers? She got up then walked over to the package that was lying against the back of the tepee before opening it. She had made them for her grandfather, but had decided to give them to Devon instead. Inside the bundle were a shirt, pants, moccasins, as well as a sheath with a knife in it.

Raven had spent nearly a year making them, she had only finished the moccasins last night; everything had been made out of a white elk hide. About a year and a half ago, while in the valley that she used to breed her mares, an unusual large albino buck had wondered into the valley. She had killed him for the meat as well as his hide. The leather was soft, very supple the interior had a light fluffy feel to it. The shirt was beaded, but the pants were painted because beads did not stay on pants that long. The designs on them were spectacular. The knife sheath, as well as the moccasins, was intricately designed. The knife blade she had bought in town, but Raven had made the handle; it was made out of the antlers of the elk. She had spent two weeks scraping then filing it until it was smooth. Once done she had carved a design on it, which gave it a distinctive appearance as well as a good grip. When she had first started making this outfit she was only going to put a horse and cow on it. However, once she had begun a vision of a golden eagle as well as a wolf in the background had come to her. Putting the raven on the knife, sheath plus the moccasins was only natural since it was her personal symbol.

Raven had gotten the idea yesterday of giving them to Devon instead of her grandfather. Since according to her grandfather, she had to marry the man whether she liked him or not. At least he would have some decent clothes for their wedding, that way he would not embarrass her by wearing rags. Her mind made up she bundled everything back up then left the tepee with the bundle under her arm.

Raven marched into her grandfather's tepee angrily. She spoke to her grandmother in Cheyenne so that Devon would not understand. "I am sorry nisgii; I just need to give this vi'hoI something. I have to go meet Dream Dancer and bring up the caskets for the burial. I do not want the Englishman to meet my brother yet."

Golden Dove frowned troubled at the furious look on her granddaughter's face, guessing it had something to do with the matching scowl on Devon's face. She got up then brought a bowl of stew with her to Raven. "Okay, but you must eat first."

Raven nodded to upset to argue. She ate quickly and quietly not looking at Devon.

Devon looked from one woman to the other. He frowned even more infuriated now when neither would talk to him.

Raven handed the bowl back then gave her grandmother a hug. She turned to Devon irritably. "I will be away for a couple of days so you and Black Hawk can work on the mare. I brought the gift that I was going to give you before you so rudely stormed away."

Raven threw the parcel at him then stormed out of the tepee. She ran to the pasture and whistled shrilly for Brave Heart. She let him out then they immediately went to her tepee for his tack as well as her gear. She was just galloping out of camp when she heard her name called, but she did not stop or slow down.

Raven rode hard for the next hour in frustration; finally, she pulled up a little and slowed her horse to a trot calm once more. She was not in any real hurry, so she slowed to a walk. It was a beautiful evening twilight was just starting, so there was still some sunlight to see by. The ground was almost entirely dry now with no snow was evident at all. It was as if the snowstorm had never happened.

Raven had decided to ride out to meet her brother. It was a spur of the moment decision, done more out of anger. As she took a deep breath of the mountain air then slowly relaxed for the first time since she left the valley, she figured it was a good idea. She needed some time alone right now to think. She would camp at the first campsite and wait until her brother came. It would be at least another day or two before he arrived so it would give her an opportunity to hunt. It should not be her brother coming anyway. He should have driven the mares into the valley by now. She had just used that as an excuse to get away. It did not matter anyway if it were not him then it would be one of her ranch hands. She certainly did not want Devon to see one of them yet. She had no worries about missing whoever came because a wagon could only get through this way. The way that she had arrived after leaving her men, the night of the storm was only passable by a horse; it was generally a five-day trip. Coming this way though was only a day and a half by horse, two days by wagon, so it was much shorter.

Raven undid the strips of rawhide that held her hair in two braids then reached behind her and unravelled one braid than the other. She reached up to dig her fingers into her scalp messaging deeply in pleasure before running her fingers through her hair spreading it out, so it surrounded her in a cloud of raven black. When she was at the ranch, she always wore it coiled up and tucked under her hat so that it would not get in the way. When she was in the Indian village, she always wore it in two braids as tradition dictated an unmarried maiden wear her hair. Only when she was alone could she let her hair down. Her hair was so long that it covered Brave Heart's hindquarters then fell on each side of him a little way down his sides.

Brave Heart was so used to this ritual of his mistress's that he did not even flinch at the feel of her hair tickling him.

Raven unhooked her bow and reached behind her then took out two arrows. One she put in her mouth. The other one she notched on her bowstring so that it would be ready to fire at a moments notice. Dusk was falling rapidly, but she hoped to flush something before full dark. She rode along leisurely and kept a little pressure on her bow, using her knees to guide her horse. She halted her horse unexpectedly in anticipation then turned to her right at the sound of a sharp bark. She automatically drew her bow and waited to see what was being flushed out for her. A young buck charged out in front of Brave Heart wildly trying to get away from the wolves.

Raven did not even hesitate as she aimed then shot. Her second arrow was notched in preparation before the buck took an extra step. Instead, she released the tension as the buck dropped dead almost immediately. She hastily gathered her hair over her left shoulder as she jumped off her horse. She unsheathed her hunting knife as she walked over to cut the buck's throat. As she let the buck bleed, she looked around expectantly in anticipation. She smiled as Bruno came loping over to her and gave her a wet sloppy kiss of greeting. She ruffled his fur in affection as well as appreciation. "Good boy, but where is your girlfriend?"

Raven looked at the edge of the woods then saw the female pacing back and forth impatiently, hungry but too scared of the woman to come any closer. She smiled then turned aside quickly before she pulled her hair into a hasty ponytail. She cut the buck's stomach and pulled out intestines then the guts. Normally she would keep most of it for use later, but she figured Bruno and his she wolf deserved a reward for helping flush out the deer. The only thing she kept was the liver as well as the heart. The rest she took to the edge of the trees then threw it as far as she could manage. The female grabbed an intestine and dragged it away to eat in privacy.

Bruno stayed with the buck than watched his mistress clean out the buck's cavity waiting patiently.

Raven took the liver and cut it into four. She quickly dug a hole then chanting her thanks to the buck as well as to the Great Spirit. She buried two pieces in the ground. Normally she ate the other two pieces, but since Bruno had shared in the hunt, she gave him one piece while she ate the other one. The eating of a raw piece of the liver was a tradition to acquire the animal's strength and spirit. She groaned in pleasure as the still warm liver slithered down her throat. The warm blood dribbled down her chin, but she ignored it.

Once done Raven went to her saddlebag then pulled out a waterproof container that was designed to keep the heart or any other parts that you wanted to take with you. This way it would not make a mess in her saddlebag. She dropped the heart inside before sealing it tightly and put it back in her saddlebag. She took her little chopping axe out of her holder then walked around until she spied two saplings that would be strong enough to keep the buck off the ground and chopped them down. When she came back to her horse, she reached into her saddlebag once more then pulled out a bunch of rawhide ropes that were kept for this purpose. She tied a rawhide rope around each pole and tied one on each side of Brave Heart's saddle. Then she took a third rawhide rope before bringing the two ends of the poles closer together, she tied them so that they would not catch on anything.

Raven clucked to Brave Heart in command so he dutifully walked up beside the deer. She heaved the deer carcass onto the travois before taking the rest of her rawhide and tied the deer onto the poles securely than to Brave Heart's tail so that the carcass would not slip off. Brave Heart bore this treatment with a slight snort of indignation.

Raven laughed in delight. "It's not far Brave Heart, I promise."

Raven still chuckled gave him a consoling pat before hoisting herself up into the saddle. She smiled down at Bruno and saluted him in farewell. "Goodbye Bruno, until next time we meet."

Bruno barked in farewell then left his mistress to go eat what his mate had left him.

Raven urged Brave Heart on down the trail and tied her bow back where it belonged. She took out her rifle then laid it across the saddle, so it was convenient. The scent of fresh blood would attract predators and the rifle would be used to scare them off. It took her another two hours to reach the camp. By that time, it was full dark.

Raven jumped off her horse quickly. She untied the buck from her horses tail then unhitched the travois and dropped the poles on the ground. She took out two rawhide ropes to hang the deer up into a tree so that scavengers could not get to it. She looked up wishfully at the platform above her, way up in top branches of the tree; even flies would not go up that far. If she had help she would have used that, but it was too high. There was no way that she could get him up there by herself, even with her horses help.

Raven tied one rawhide rope to each leg before throwing the loose ends over the highest thickest tree branch she could reach. She went then gathered the two loose ends and wrapped the rawhide around her horse's chest so he could help her pull. Slowly she encouraged Brave Heart forward, inching the deer up gradually. The heavy buck finally reached a good height, now completely off the ground. Satisfied she went then grabbed the dangling rawhide that she had used to attach the deer to Brave Heart's tail and tied him securely in place. Going over she untied the rawhide that was secured to her horse then tied them to a lower limb just to make sure it stayed up there.

Raven unsaddled Brave Heart next and wiped him down before making camp. She got the fire going then went over to unpack the cairn of food and blankets that was always there. She got three sticks to use as a spit then took out the deer's heart and skewered it before putting it over the fire to cook. While it was cooking, Raven made herself a bed then made coffee waiting impatiently. When the stick holding the heart was lifted off the fire, she held it out in front of her and just ate it like that without removing it. When she had eaten her fill, she put the rest on a rock beside the fire for breakfast then sat back to enjoy her coffee and gazed up at the stars reflectively.

*****

When Raven had thrown the bundle at him, Devon had automatically reached up to catch it, not thinking. Then he doubled up in pain as his severely cracked ribs protested at his quick reflexes.

Golden Dove rushed over to him to make sure he was not hurt before eyeing the package Raven had thrown in surprise. She knew what was in it and was shocked that Raven would give it to the white man. She had not seen the finished garments of course, but had watched Raven work on it several times.

Devon sat up straight then slowly untied the rawhide string one handed. He watched the package spring open with a shirt on top. His mouth dropped open in admiration as he reached out in awe and felt the velvety texture of the white elk hide. He looked up at Golden Dove pleadingly. "Can you hold it up for me so I can look at it properly?"

Golden Dove nodded speechless then reached down to pick up the shirt first.

Devon gasped as the shirt fell open to reveal a golden eagle. Its wings were outstretched with the Eagle facing forward as if it were just about ready to take flight. He noticed a raven under the left wing of the eagle. Its wings were outstretched with the tip of one wing just touching the golden eagle. The raven was staring at you intently with its beak part way open ready to scold. Under the right wing was the head of a wolf and it looked as if it were staring straight at you! The beadwork was extraordinary, how she had managed to find so many different colours way out here was fantastic.

Golden Dove turned it around then watched Devon's expression of incredulity in satisfaction as he looked at the rearing black stallion; under the stallion's front hooves was a black and white cow. Both were done as a side view. She folded the shirt then handed it to him before picking up the pants and let the legs drop so he could see.

Devon gazed at the pinto foal in admiration then looked at the black and white calf, this time they were painted instead of beaded. On the other pant leg was a wolf cub, a raven, as well as a golden eagle chick. The raven was first with both wings outstretched so that the wings would go part way around your thigh. The wolf cub with the eagle chick was both below the raven. They were staring up intently at the raven mouths slightly open. Devon frown thoughtfully, it almost looked as if they were waiting to be fed by the raven. He shook his head at his foolishness it could not be that.

Golden Dove folded the pants then handed it to Devon. She reached down and picked up the moccasins then displayed them to him. She reached down again and brought out the knife sheath with a knife inside. The moccasins as well as the knife sheath were beaded, they both had raven designed on them.

Devon put down the clothes then reached out and tentatively pulled out the knife so that he could examine it. The blade was long obviously bought or traded for. The handle was certainly unique, made out of an antler by the looks of it. It had a little carving of a raven on one side as well as an eagle on the other. He gripped the knife in his hand experimentally. He was surprised that the knife did not slide right out of his hand since she had worked the antler until it was so smooth it shone. However, with the carvings on either side of the handle it made for a sturdy secure grip. If she had left the carvings off the handle, it would have been too slippery to hold. He returned the knife to its sheath then put them with the clothes before looking up at Golden Dove in speculation. "Did she make all this herself?"

Golden Dove smiled in pride. "Yes, she has been working on it for a year now. She must have just finished them recently because they were not done two months ago when I saw them last."

Devon nodded thoughtfully wondering why she would give them to him. "They are very beautiful. I understand why she would put the ravens, the eagles, the wolves, and the horse. But why would she put a cow, what significance do they have to an Indian?"

Golden Dove thought quickly she could not tell him the truth of course then an idea came to her, and she grinned in relief. She hated lying. "Well all animals are sacred to the Indians, even domesticated animals."

Devon nodded in understanding at this simple explanation.

Golden Dove sat back down then waved enticingly. "I will take you to the lake after our lesson so that you can bathe and you can try on your new clothes."

Devon inclined his head in thanks then listened attentively while Golden Dove continued his lessons.

*****

Giant Bear called out to Raven in demand as she galloped away, but she did not even look back or stop. He turned to Black Hawk angrily as he pointed in disapproval at his retreating granddaughter. "Now where is Raven going in such a hurry? She is supposed to be teaching Devon how to break his horse!"

Black Hawk shrugged in confusion. "I left them alone while I was putting the mare away. Maybe he said something to set her off."

Giant Bear sighed in irritation. "Let's go find out!"

Giant Bear stormed into his tepee furiously and growled at Devon without even looking at his wife, interrupting her in mid-sentence. "What did you say to Raven to make her mad enough to leave?"

Golden Dove got up quickly then frowned at her husband in disapproval at his offensive behaviour before switching to Cheyenne. "She went to meet her brother. She said she did not want Devon to meet him yet."

Giant Bear nodded only slightly pacified, but continued speaking in English wanting the Englishman to understand him. He motioned down at Devon suspiciously. "Maybe, but he still must have said something to upset her. She galloped out of the village like a mad woman!"

Devon stood up as he faced Giant Bear defiantly. "I helped her bring her stuff to her tepee. When I looked around, I could tell that she did not live there permanently. So I asked her where she lived, and she would not tell me, so we argued."

Giant Bear looked at Devon imperiously then gestured decisively. "Well first off, it is none of your business where she lives. Raven is a warrior she can live anywhere she chooses!"

Devon harrumphed angrily and waved at the chief sarcastically. "That might be true now, but she is going to be my wife. Or so you say, so I do have a right to know!"

Giant Bear shook his head negatively then pointed at Devon threateningly. "No! Until you are married you will not ask any more questions regarding my granddaughter, is that understood?"

Devon nodded irritably as he balled up his good hand in an impotent fist. "Loud and clear!"

Devon turned then stormed out.

Golden Dove eyed her husband furiously in disapproval before turning to Black Hawk and motioned sharply in demand after the retreating Englishman. "Tommy, go find Devon then shows him where he can bathe!"

Black Hawk sighed plaintively as his mother used his English name and gave his father a sympathetic look before leaving in a hurry. He definitely did not want to be around for that conversation.

Golden Dove turned to her husband once they were alone. She pointed in command at Giant Bear. "I think it is time you told me what is going on. NOW!"

Giant Bear grimaced resignedly. He knew that there was no getting around telling her this time; if he ever wanted to sleep in his own tepee again, that is. Only once before had she used that tone with him. It was when their daughter wanted to go live with the whites so that she could go to school. He had given in than, and he knew he would give in now. He sighed in resignation then sat down. His hand brushed the package Devon had left behind. Curiously, he opened it and examined the contents. He looked at his wife in stunned admiration. "Where did these come from? Who are they for?"

Golden Dove watched his reaction closely, curious to see what he would think of Ravens gift to her future husband. "Raven made them then gave them to Devon as a wedding gift."

Giant Bear looked up at his wife in amazement and picked up the shirt to examine it more closely. When he saw the prominent golden eagle on the front, he smiled widely in pleased satisfaction.

Golden Dove watched grimly as a look of glee come over her husbands face. She cleared her throat noisily to get his attention as she sat down. She stared intently at him in demand. "Okay, what is going on? You had better not leave anything out either. I want to know all of it this instant!"

Giant Bear folded the shirt then put it back. He took a deep breath to gain some courage as he faced his angry demanding wife. He told her the truth, the whole truth, leaving nothing out as he had with Black Hawk and Raven.

CHAPTER SEVEN

Black Hawk went out searching for Devon, he found him at Devil's paddock. He was sitting on the top rail talking to the stallion. The stud was in the middle of the pen watching the Englishman with his ears cocked forward listening curiously.

Black Hawk chuckled then cleared his throat noisily to get Devon's attention.

Devon turned in surprise at the noise and carefully climbed down off the fence.

Black Hawk smiled in approval then waved towards the stallion. "I think he likes you. He sure pays attention when you talk to him."

Devon shrugged as he turned and looked at the stud. "I am not too sure of that yet, but I definitely like him."

Black Hawk nodded knowingly then turned to Devon before beckoning him to come with him. "I am supposed to take you to where we bathe so follow me."

Devon smiled in anticipation and fell into step beside Black Hawk. He motioned towards the east end of the village curiously. "Why haven't they buried my sister or the guides yet?"

Black Hawk sighed sadly at not being able to be honest with Devon; it went against all the training his aunt Mell had given him when he was younger. "We are waiting for something that is all I can say. You will see in a day or so we will be lighting the piers for the dead braves tonight though."

Devon inclined his head irritably then lapsed into silence sullenly.

Black Hawk took Devon to the north side of the village and followed a path until he reached a small lake at the bottom of a steep hill. He searched along the side until he found a particular weed then waved Devon over and showed him what to look for. "This is where you will find a soap root."

Black Hawk pulled it out then let Devon inspect the plant as well as the root. He broke off the bottom before passing it to Devon. "When you are in the water and totally wet take this root then crush it in your hand. It will foam as you rub the fluid into your skin and hair. It cleans even better than the soap you whites use."

Devon pointed down at his bound arm eagerly. "Can you help me with these bandages and with my clothes please?"

Black Hawk nodded then helped Devon unwrap his arm from his chest. He took off the Englishman's shirt so that he could unwrap the binding from around his ribs. He took the bandage off Devon's arm next; it was still grotesquely swollen. He stepped back before pointing behind his shoulder towards the tepees. "I will bring you some of my clothes, they should fit you."

Devon inclined his head in thanks and finished undressing himself. He picked up his root then walked into the cold lake carefully, mindful of his injured arm. He shivered as the icy water hit his warm skin, but still he sighed in ecstatic pleasure as he laid full length in the water tired of being filthy. It did not take his body long to adjust to the cold water thankfully.

*****

Raven finished her coffee as she stretched sleepily. She banked the fire for the night before curling up in her blankets. She was just too tired mentally and physically to bother with the deer tonight. Slowly she dozed off, enjoying the delightful sounds of the gentle warm breeze rustling the leaves as well as the crickets chirping. Just as Raven was falling into peaceful dreams, the frogs joined in as they also started croaking their nightly song.

Ravens eyes popped open immediately in deep concern. Instantly she was wide-awake as the crickets then the frogs stopped their songs unexpectedly. Deadly silence fell as she listened intently in dread! Straining, she finally heard a faint distinctive grunt of an animal that she had hoped never to hear.

Raven reached over quickly and grasped her rifle that thankfully she had kept close, just as a massive grizzly bear rushed into her camp then went after her horse. She rolled out of her blankets as fast as she possibly could as her stallion screamed a challenge at the grizzly.

Brave Heart reared up on his hind legs before desperately striking out at the huge bear. All that Raven could hear was a powerful thwack, as her horses front hooves connected with the bear's thick skull. She quickly lifted her rifle and sighted on the grizzly, but could not get a clear shot as Brave Heart got in the way.

Brave Heart spun around in a frenzy to hit the giant bear with his more powerful back legs. Raven saw the grizzly stagger back at the impact as both her stallions' hooves connected solidly. The grizzly raging now rose to his full height; with a savage growl, he took a swipe at the stallion. Brave Heart squealed in pain as the bear's claws raked his hindquarters.

Raven screamed at the black monster in desperation trying to divert it as she ran forward. The grizzly turned to face the woman suddenly in fury, before dropping down on all fours as he charged the smaller easier prey.

Raven raised the rifle then shot the beast in the head twice in quick succession, but he was too close by that time. The gigantic black grizzly leaped just as the second bullet ripped through its skull killing him instantly, but the momentum carried it straight into Raven. She screamed in painful shock as she fell backwards as blackness overtook her.

*****

The five people riding hard for the North Dakota border were only two days away from their ranch. The man leading was a tall broad shouldered white man with long black hair although the grey throughout was fast taking over the colouring. He had craggy features that had not shown his age until recently. On his chest pinned to his vest was a deputy marshal's badge. He was just slightly ahead of the two riding on either side of him.

The person riding just behind his left shoulder, on his horses left flank, was not as tall with narrow shoulders that tapered down to a slim waist. With distinct feminine features, older also, a white buffalo hide was draped around her with a black hat that effectively concealed hair that was almost as white as the hide. She was all woman white as well, but on her vest hidden by the robe was a marshal's badge.

On the other side of the deputy marshal just passed his right shoulder, on his horse's right flank, was another woman. She had a dark complexion, long blonde hair done in two Indian braids, with dark brown almost black eyes. She was obviously a half-breed Indian.

Directly behind the deputy marshal, in-between the marshal and the half-Indian maiden were two others. One was another white male leading a packhorse. He was riding on the left side of the Indian maiden just past her left shoulder on her horses left flank. He was tall as well as lean. He looked a lot like the man leading, but younger with blonde hair. Around his neck he wore a necklace with a large cross that proclaimed to everyone his profession as a Baptist Pastor. Right beside him was another white woman, younger then all of them. She had her fiery red hair done in one braid down her back. She was leading a silvery white two-year-old stallion with a light load on his back. She was riding on the right hand side of the marshal just past her left shoulder on her horse's right flank.

The man in front slowed his horse to give them a rest. The woman on the left nudged her horse forward a little then looked at the leader curiously, as she motioned in question. "Jed how many days will it take?"

Jed shrugged, unsure. "It should take about twenty days if we push our horses hard, twenty-four days if we take it a little easy on them. That is with no problems arising at all it could take more if we have any major difficulty."

The woman scowled anxiously. Jed reached over and took her hand consolingly; he gave it a reassuring squeeze before letting go. "We will make it in time Mell, I promise!"

Mell gave her husband a slight smile of relief, but still sighed dispiritedly as she dropped back slightly. She looked on the other side of Jed's horse at the Indian maid then frowned distraughtly. Mell's daughter-in-law smiled over in confidence and turned away not wanting Mell to see the fear in her face.

*****

Raven came to half an hour later with the massive grizzly lying on her legs. She groaned in pain, its claws had raked her thigh. Already she could feel her leg throbbing with infection. Luckily, her buckskin pants had provided some protection, but not enough. As she tried to move, she winced at the sharp stinging sensation in her leg.

Raven lifted her head when she heard her horse limp over to her. She managed to get up on her elbows then tried to push the black monster off her. She fell back in frustration she could not budge the animal. At least she had managed to hold onto her rifle, it still had four bullets in it, so she was not entirely helpless.

Raven looked up at her horse in concern. He was standing not too far from her with his head hanging down in exhaustion, and he had his left leg slightly lifted in obvious pain. Suddenly she heard another menacing growl of an animal. She swore in frustration as she cocked her rifle in fear then looked around wildly. She could not see anything at first, but suddenly she heard a familiar low whine and sighed in relief as she eased her grip on the rifle. "Bruno, come boy!"

Bruno slunk slowly towards her with his hair all bristled, growling fearfully at the grizzly laying on top of his mistress.

Raven called out in encouragement as she snapped her fingers impatiently. She could not help the sound of desperation in her voice. "Bruno, please come here boy!"

Bruno finally ignored the bear at the urgent plea of his mistress then rushed to her.

Raven sighed thankfully. She reached up and grabbed his thick fur then pulled his head down close to hers as she gasped out in beseeching demand. She could feel the blackness of unconsciousness coming once again and desperately she tried to keep it at bay. "Go find Black Hawk, Bruno! Go get Black Hawk for me than bring him here!"

Bruno barked sharply in understanding. He turned away and raced towards the Indian village as soon as his mistress let him go. He ran past his mate, but paid her no attention fully focused on finding Black Hawk. Very rarely did his mistress ever use that intense desperate voice with him, when she did he knew something was terribly wrong. His strides lengthened as he ran flat out nothing would stop him now, except death!

Raven thanked the Great Spirit that she had the foresight to teach him to get certain people when she asked. As a pup, they had made a game of him finding her grandfather, Black Hawk, the medicine man, or Spotted Owl. By the time he was a year old he could find any of the four anywhere then bring them to Raven, no matter where she was. It would be quite a few hours before Bruno would return. She pulled the rifle in closer to her for reassurance and knew no more as she let the blackness claim her once again.

*****

Black Hawk brought Devon some clothes then walked down the trail carefully. It was full dark with only a half moon to see by. He reached the lake without incident. He called out knowing the white man was still in the water. "Devon I brought you some clothes, come here I will re-wrap your arm and ribs."

Devon got out reluctantly, even though it was getting too cold anyway then walked over to him.

Black Hawk smiled and teased him playfully. "If you stayed in there any longer you would have turned into a fish or an ice burg."

Devon chuckled in agreement. "It felt so good to stay in the shallows soaking. I did not really want to get out yet even though I was starting to freeze."

Black Hawk nodded, but made no comment then put his bundle down within easy reach. He took a fresh bandage from the pile and wrapped Devon's ribs. Then took the other bandage and wrapped the Englishman's arm, before helping him put a clean shirt on. He picked up the last cloth then wrapped Devon's arm tight against his side so that he would not bump or use it. He helped the Englishman put on his pants and handed him a loincloth before stepping back then looked Devon up and down in approval. "Well my clothes fit you pretty good. You can keep them if you like, I have a lot more. The loincloth you can put on later, we usually sleep in them. Some of the other Indians will only wear a loincloth in the summer no pants."

Devon grinned in pleasure as he stroked the soft buckskins appreciatively. "Thank you; I like the feel of buckskins better than itchy wool."

Black Hawk inclined his head knowingly with a chuckle. "I felt the same way the first time I wore them."

Black Hawk turned to lead the way back to the village. They were almost there when he stopped suddenly and turned to his left listening intently.

Devon cocked his head curiously, but he could not hear anything. Just as he was opening his mouth to ask Black Hawk what the problem was, he finally heard a bark.

Black Hawk whistled in response then waited. Bruno came running towards them and jumped up on Black Hawk in demand then licked his face with a pleading whine. The wolf dog jumped down, and trotted a few steps away before coming back then jumped up on him again with another woeful desperate whine.

Black Hawk turned to Devon anxiously as he pushed the wolf away. "Sorry, you are going to have to find the way on your own. There is something not right with Raven, and I have to go!"

Before Devon could answer, Black Hawk was sprinting towards his tepee. He shrugged at Black Hawk's strange behaviour then went to Giant Bear's to sleep.

*****

Black Hawk quickly grabbed his tack out of his tepee before sprinting to the big corral to saddle his gelding. He raced out of the village with the wolf leading. He pushed his horse as fast as he dared in the dark. He prayed to the Great Spirit as he rode that they would not be too late or that his horse would not step in a hole and kill them both.

It was close to three in the morning when Black Hawk heard a horse whinny painfully in challenge. He slowed his horse then took out his rifle cautiously. His horse snorted at the scent he caught and sidled sideways refusing to go any further as he backed up snorting in fear.

The wolf growled uneasily as his fur bristled, but he slunk ahead anyway.

Black Hawk jumped off his horse then tied him securely to a tree and advanced cautiously on foot. He could smell the grizzly before he saw the ugly behemoth lying on top of Raven dead. He rushed forward apprehensively; as he went by, he glanced briefly at Brave Heart. He saw the claw marks, but did not stop. He quickly bent then heaved the grizzly over and out of his way. He knelt down then ripped open the tear in Ravens buckskin pants so that he could examine the claw marks closely. They were festering already and burning to the touch.

Black Hawk jumped up then built up the fire quickly before running to where he had left his horse. He untied him and lead him into camp. His horse tried to balk once, but Black Hawk spoke harshly to him in Cheyenne, so he settled down following obediently.

Black Hawk tied him near Ravens stallion and took out bandages as well as a medicine bag he always carried with him. He took the pouch over to the fire then went and pulled Ravens blankets closer to the firelight. Now he would be able to see better before going back to pick his niece up, he then carried her over to the blankets. He put her down and touched her forehead. She was burning up; if he did not get that poison out of her immediately, she would probably die.

Black Hawk hastily poured out the coffee then filled it with fresh water from Ravens canteen sitting beside the fire pit. He dug in his pouch once more and pulled out two different types of leaves, he crushed them into the pot to steep. He took out one of his knives next then laid it in the fire to sterilize it. While he waited, he bent over so he could remove his niece's buckskin pants before examining her wounds critically. It needed stitching, so he took out a little awl as well as a piece of thin sinew that he would use to sew up the gaping wounds. He had learned this technique from his aunt's maid in North Dakota.

While Black Hawk waited for the tea as well as his knife to heat up enough, he ran his hands over both Ravens legs to make sure that they were not broken. He sat back with a sigh of relief at finding no breaks. Next, he ran his hand through his niece's hair checking her scalp for any lumps or cuts. He found one lump, but not too large. When he pulled his hands away he examined it critically, but there was no fresh or dried blood. That was good, so he did not worry about it after that. He lifted each eyelid to check her reaction, but she did not even move and it was still too dark out for him to see anything.

Black Hawk added more wood to the fire then checked his knife as well as the tea water. Neither was ready yet, so he got up and walked over to the grizzly then slit its throat with his other knife to let it bleed. He dragged it over to the edge of the camp, but not out of the light. Raven would want the skin and maybe even the meat. He walked over to Brave Heart next chanting soothingly to him in Cheyenne, he cautiously advanced wanting to see how severe the stallion was hurt.

Brave Heart snorted in warning, but let the man check the wound in too much pain to put up a fuss.

Black Hawk sighed in relief. It was not as serious as it looked there was only a small amount of festering. He decided it could wait a little while for treatment. He backed away from the horse then went over to Raven. He would need a poultice for the stallion, but until the sun came up enough for him to identify the right plants it would have to wait.

The tea was ready, so he poured some in a cup and blew on it steadily until it was cool enough not to burn his patient. He lifted Raven a little then forced some down her throat. She choked a little, so he put the cup down quickly to free up his hand as he tenderly stroked her throat to get her to swallow. He did this several times until finally he got enough in her to satisfy him before laying her back down.

Black Hawk took the awl and sinew he had waiting then put it into the rest of the tea. He took his knife out of the fire and satisfied at the red-hot glow he poured a little tea over the blade. He nodded in approval as the blade hissed before letting off a little bit of smoke. He straddled Raven backwards to hold her down as he gently inserted the knife tip into her festering wound then quickly withdrew it to treat the other four gashes in a similar manner.

Raven sat up in response for a moment as she screamed in agony, before mercifully passing out once more.

Black Hawk held her down not relenting until he had drained all the putrid wounds of pus. When he was satisfied that he had gotten all the poisoned fluid out and only fresh blood was flowing, he poured some tea in the open wounds. He took the awl with the sinew attached from the bottom of the cup so that he could sew her wounds up. She would have five nasty scars later to tell the tale, but he was sure now that she would survive. He turned back when finished than made her swallow some tea.

Black Hawk looked up at the sky in satisfaction it was almost dawn. He would have to leave the wound open for now until he could find what he needed for a poultice. He got off Raven as he looked down at Bruno, who had not moved a muscle since they had gotten there as he sighed warily. "Well I have done everything I can; it is now up to her."

Bruno whined in anxiety and thumped his tail in agreement before laying his head back down on his paws watching Raven intently.

Black Hawk went over to his horse then stripped him of his saddle blanket and saddlebags. He took his bedroll over to the fire then made a bed beside Raven before putting his hand on her forehead. She still had a terrible fever. He moved his hands further down and laid one on each side of her gashes then sighed in relief when there was no heat.

Black Hawk turned away from Raven to pour the last of the tea into the cup before filling the pot with fresh water for coffee. He noticed a heart lying on the rocks; he had been too busy earlier saving his nieces life to see it. He looked around expectantly until he found the buck hanging in a tree. So that is what the grizzly was after, they did not usually eat meat unless it was easily gotten or they were hungry enough. However, sometimes you would get a bear that preferred meat to their regular diet of fish, berries, ground squirrels, fruit, grain, grass, birds, and bugs.

It was now light enough out to see better so Black Hawk walked over to the grizzly first. He checked its mouth to make sure it was not rabid; if the bear was they were in big trouble, but thankfully, he found no foam around its muzzle. He pushed him onto its back then noticed that it was not a he at all, but a she and nursing a cub by the look of it. He walked over then looked down at the massive bear tracks; he slowly followed them into the trees. If she had a cub, it would not be too far away, probably up in a tree waiting for its mother. He looked down every once in a while as he tracked to make sure he was still going in the right direction, but most of his attention was up in the trees. He stopped suddenly as he saw a black bundle clinging to a tree bawling for its mother.

Well Black Hawk had two choices he could either shoot it since it would not survive without its mother anyway, that would be the humane thing to do. On the other hand, he could cajole it down and take it home to raise it. It would not be the first time he had raised a bear cub, but it would be the first time he tried raising a grizzly cub. They were more brutal than a regular bear, so it would be difficult to say the least. He stopped at that thought and chuckled at himself. He had already made up his mind without even realizing it. The easiest way to get the cub out of the tree would be to go back to camp then skin the mother and bring the hide here. He could wrap the skin around himself afterwards, so that the cub would smell its mother. Hopefully, it would come down then Black Hawk could take the cub back to camp. His mind made up he turned and headed back. As he walked along, he looked for the plants he wanted; he was just about back at camp when he spotted what he needed. He took enough for a two-day treatment for Raven as well as Brave Heart.

When Black Hawk got back, Raven was thrashing around moaning pitifully. He rushed over then held her down as he picked up the cup of tea and made her drink the rest. The tea did the trick as she settled back into a deep sleep.

Black Hawk fixed the paste then put some on his niece's wounds before wrapping her thigh. He picked up the rest of it and the awl then walked towards Brave Heart talking soothingly, hoping the stud would allow him to treat his wound. The stallion surprisingly stood still and let him drain the infected wounds. Before Black Hawk put the paste on, he touched the wound to make sure it was not hot; satisfied he smeared it on then backed away slowly.

The stud snorted at him and bobbed his head as if saying thank you.

Black Hawk laughed in disbelief. "Sometimes I think you understand us humans."

Brave Heart just stared at him.

Black Hawk shook his head at his own foolishness then took out a knife from his moccasin and started skinning the enormous black grizzly.

Bruno trotted over then whined pleadingly.

Black Hawk nodded guessing what the wolf dog wanted and slit the belly of the bear then pulled out all the insides. He smiled at Bruno in permission. "Go ahead boy you can have it all, you deserve it."

Bruno yipped in thanks and grabbed an intestine then dragged it into the trees. A few minutes later, he came back and got some more before dragging it off too.

Black Hawk watched Bruno in puzzlement then caught a flash of silver fur and grinned in understanding. Bruno's girlfriend must have been just out of sight all night watching, but she had not once showed herself.

Black Hawk turned back to the grizzly then carefully skinned it. Raven would have his head if he wrecked the hide. It took him two hours since she was monstrous, when standing at her full height, she would be around eight feet or so. She probably weighed well over a thousand pounds. It was small compared to a male grizzly. He would stand about ten feet and weigh between fifteen hundred to two thousand pounds easily.

When Black Hawk was finished, he walked over to his pack then pulled out some rawhide ropes and hoisted the bear up into a tree. Without its hide, she was easier to hang. He left the hide where it was for the moment then walked over to the cairn of rocks where the supplies were kept. He grabbed a small bucket that was kept there for water and walked into the trees. He went a little way until he came to a small creek. He washed himself off first then filled the bucket with water, before looking along the bank until he spotted a good place. He layed on his stomach before putting a hand in the water and waited patiently. All of a sudden, his arm shot out as a big plump trout flew through the air then lay thrashed about on the grass trying to get back into the creek. He did this twice more before getting up; he carried the fish and the bucket of water back to camp with him.

Black Hawk looked down at his clothes then over at the grizzly hide and grimaced. He would have to go naked, except for his loincloth;

he had not thought to take any extra clothing with him. He shrugged dismissively naked would do. He put all but one fish by the fire then turned looked for Ravens wolf; he had seen him a minute ago. Spotting him lying beside his niece once again, he shook a warning finger at him. "Stay here with Raven and do not touch the fish."

Bruno looked up and whined then put his head back on his paws obediently.

Black Hawk stripped and went over then picked up the skin before putting it around himself with a grimaced of distaste at the wet slimy feel, but left with it on. With a trout in his hand, he trotted quickly to the place where he had found the cub. He looked up and sighed relieved to see it still there, he squatted then grunted a few times and put the fish in front of him enticingly.

The little cub stopped crying immediately then slipped down the tree a little way before stopping undecided. He was very confused by the scent he was getting. He could smell his mother and the fish, but he could smell an unfamiliar scent also. Finally, his hunger drove him the rest of the way to the ground.

Black Hawk picked up the fish then made some more grunting sounds in encouragement as the cub came towards him. Once the cub was close enough, he brought the fish closer and held out his hand for the cub to smell him.

The cub hesitantly smelt the hand held out to him then walked closer. He squatted and ate the fish to hungry to care.

Black Hawk let him eat, but made sure to run his hands all over the cub at the same time so that he would get use to being touched.

When the cub finished eating, he snuggled up to his strange smelling mother.

Black Hawk picked him up then carried him back to camp.

Bruno jumped up in warning as he growled at another bear coming into camp, protecting his mistress. He immediately laid down again at the familiar voice coming from the black grizzly.

Black Hawk heard a chuckle and turned quickly in relief to face Raven.

Raven was propped up on an elbow watching him. "I knew she had attacked for a reason, but trust you to figure it out then go save the cub."

Black Hawk grinned as he brought the cub over to her before laying the sleeping baby in her arms. "Well if he were a little older I would have left him there, but he is only about three weeks old and was up in a tree all night. So it did not take much convincing to get him to come down."

Raven grimaced as the wind shifted causing her to get a good whiff of Black Hawk then looked him up and down teasingly. "I think you better go wash, do not forget to put some clothes on too, you are a mess!"

Black Hawk scowled down at himself then his nose wrinkled in disgust as he caught the scent. "Don't I know it, and I stink something awful!"

Black Hawk took the hide then threw it over a low hanging branch; he would work on it later. He grabbed his clothes and trotted to the creek for a much-needed wash.

Raven watched him disappear than layed back down with the cub curled up against her. She turned her head and saw Bruno staring at the cub curiously, so snapped her fingers in command. "Bruno, come here!"

Bruno crawled over to his mistress then licked her face in greeting.

Raven brought up her hand with the scent of the cub on it so that he could smell it, and pointed at the cub when he licked her hand. "Smell Bruno!"

Bruno leaned over then smelt the cub and wagged his tail. Raven nodded at him in agreement as his tail wagged. "Friend Bruno!"

Bruno smelt the cub again then laid down on her other side contentedly.

Raven grinned teasingly as Black Hawk trotted back into camp. "Well you definitely look better with your clothes on."

Black Hawk laughed in delight. "Well I do not think my wife would agree with you. Stay still while I check your wound. How do you feel by the way?"

Raven chuckled softly as she waved in jesting. "Like I was run over by a grizzly! Actually, not really that bad, a slight headache and my leg is throbbing. But mostly I feel thirsty, really hungry as well."

Black Hawk checked the wound then inclined his head thankfully; hunger was good. He looked critically at the elegant stitch work as he talked distractedly. "Well I have coffee on, so I can help you with the thirsty problem right now. I will use the rest of your deer heart and make you some soup too. That will take care of your hunger then just before you go back to sleep I will brew up some more tea for your headache and for the pain in your leg. Can you wiggle your toes then move your feet and legs for me?"

Raven did as he asked than watched him nod in satisfaction.

Black Hawk glanced up at Raven for a moment chidingly before looking back down at what he was doing. He decided to leave the wound open for a moment to give it some air. "You are very fortunate you did not end up with two broken legs. You are also extremely lucky that I got here when I did or you might have lost your leg to poison or gangrene."

Raven nodded with a grimace of agreement. "I know, but I could not get the grizzly off of me to clean it properly. I am just glad I trained Bruno to get someone when I am in trouble. How is Brave Heart doing did he let you treat him?"

Black Hawk smiled in reassurance as he walked around the fire to sit across from her. "Yes he let me treat him, and yes he is fine. His scratches were only superficial, so they were not as festered as yours were. He will still have a scar, but not as bad as the one that you will have. I had to reopen your wounds then drain the poison and pus before I could sew them closed properly."

As Black Hawk talked, he cooked their dinner then poured Raven a coffee.

Raven propped herself up on her elbow trying not to disturb the cub and sipped it gratefully. She looked down at the cub then chuckled at the little ball of fur. "Well he sure must have been exhausted he has not moved once. What are you going to call him?"

Black Hawk shrugged undecided as he looked over at Raven. "I am not sure yet. Oh, by the way I hung up your grizzly. I was not sure if you would want anything besides the hide."

Raven frowned thoughtfully before waving irritably at herself. "You can cut off the head, and the claws then throw the rest in the trees. I never even thought of reaching out to cut its throat. The meat is probably no good now, but it will not go to waste with Bruno and his mate around. This is the second time he has come out of nowhere then saved my life."

Black Hawk looked over at the wolf gratefully and handed Raven a fish as the little cub came awake. She held the trout to his nose then let him smell her hand before he dug into the fish.

Bruno stood up and reached around Raven so he could smell the cub again, but was growled at. He lifted his head away then cocked his head inquisitively and eyed the cub curiously for a few moments before trying to sniff him again.

When the cub looked up to see what was sniffing at him their noses touched. The black ball of fur pushed back against Raven with a frightened cry. The wolf jerked back at the cry then bent again to sniff, this time he gently nudged the cub.

Raven laughed in delight as she looked over at her uncle. "I think he remembers the last bear cub you used to have and want's to play with him."

Raven turned then swatted at Bruno reproachfully. "Okay, he does not want to play right now, lie down and let him eat."

Raven let the cub settle back down a little then pushed the rest of the fish towards him and watched him finish eating. She looked over at Black Hawk. "Can you pass me some water uncle the little fellow is probably thirsty."

Black Hawk found a bowl in his saddlebags then put some water in it before bringing it over and setting it down in front of the cub.

The cub drank it thirstily then curled up to Raven contentedly and went back to sleep.

Black Hawk went over then rummaged inside Ravens saddlebag for another bowl and filled it with soup then gave it to her. He washed out his own bowl and put the rest of the soup in it before rinsing out the pan that he cooked the soup in then put some fresh water in to boil. He took out some leaves from his medicine bag and crushed them into the water to steep. He sat down to eat hungrily; it had been a long day for him already. When the tea was ready, he poured some in a cup for Raven to drink. Afterwards, he dipped a soft buckskin cloth that he used to disinfect wounds with into the rest of the tea.

Black Hawk picked up the paste before going towards Brave Heart. He talked soothingly to the stud in reassurance then gently cleaned the dry stuff off and checked the wound. Nodding in satisfaction he put more paste on then backed off.

Black Hawk turned and walked back to the fire before squatting then washed the cloth out good with water. He dropped it into the tea to purify it. When it was done, he took the pan off the fire and let it subside before taking the cloth out of the tea. He walked over to Raven then removed the blanket and cleaned her wounds with the cloth. He put more paste as well as leaves over the wound then smiled at her before looking down as he bandaged it. "It looks good; all the infection seems to be gone so far. I made a paste for the stud because I knew there was no way he was going to let me put a bandage around him."

Raven laughed at the mental image of her uncle trying to get a bandage around her stallion and sipped her tea; she grimaced in distaste. "This is awful tasting stuff!"

Black Hawk smirked with a grin of agreement. "I know, but I want you to drink every drop. It will help your headache as well as the pain in your leg. It will also make you sleepy, which is the best medicine for you right now."

Black Hawk reached over then touched her brow in concern. "You still have a slight fever and until it is gone you will stay right where you are. Now before you fall asleep on me do you want me to skin then dress your deer?"

Raven nodded sleepily the tea was already working. "Yes, please. I already gutted it, so you do not need to do that."

Black Hawk smiled knowingly, but made no comment already aware of that.

Raven finished her tea and curled up around the cub to sleep. With the wolf sleeping against her back she was almost too hot, but it was not long before she drifted off.

Black Hawk smiled at the picture of the three of them sleeping contentedly. He picked up her cup then put it beside the fire before going over to start the butchering.

CHAPTER EIGHT

Devon left quietly so he would not wake Giant Bear and his wife. He made sure to grab the bag of goodies for his horse on the way out of the tepee. He walked over to the shed that had hay inside. After putting the sack down, he grabbed an armload then took it over to the corral before pushing it under the fence. Trying to do this one handed was extremely difficult, but Black Hawk was probably still absent or sleeping, so he had to do it himself. He had not mentioned Black Hawk's leaving to Giant Bear last night, maybe he should have. He shrugged dismissively if it were that serious Black Hawk would have told him to tell someone.

Devon went back to the shed and grabbed another armload then pushed it under. He went back for the third time and closed the door before grabbing his bag off the ground then went back to the corral. He climbed the fence this time and sat watching the stud.

The stallion snorted at him then walked over to eat seemingly ignoring the human.

Devon was pleasantly surprised this was the first time Devil had come this close to him. He was not close enough to touch of course, but he was only a few feet away. He smiled in delight and sat quietly not wanting to scare him off.

A few moments later the mood was shattered as Giant Bear came around a corner with a young boy who had a bucket of water.

Devil squealed angrily then raced to the other end of the corral and stood there watching them.

Devon sighed in disappointment as he carefully climbed down. He pulled out a couple of apples as well as some grain then put it on the fence.

The boy brought the water over and set it in the corral before trotting away.

Giant Bear beckoned Devon to follow him. "The medicine man wants to check your ribs and arm."

Devon nodded agreeably then walked beside the chief quietly.

Giant Bear looked at Devon sideways in speculation. "You sure look different after a bath and different clothing. Your hair is very light even more golden than my wife's."

Devon grinned as he touched his hair. "You should see it in the summer it turns lighter and in the winter it is different again, darker. It all depends on how much time I spend in the sun."

Giant Bear smiled then changed the subject as he motioned curiously. "Did you see Black Hawk today; his wife said he never came home last night?"

Devon shook his head negatively. "No, he was walking back with me last night when Ravens wolf came out of nowhere. Black Hawk took off running; all I heard was something about Raven needing him."

Giant Bear swung around with a look of anger and reproach. "Why did you not tell me this last night?"

Devon shrugged as he frowned troubled at the chief's distressed look. "Well you were already in bed; Black Hawk never said anything about telling anybody. So I did not think it was that important."

Giant Bear glared at Devon for a moment before sighing in annoyance, it was not Devon's fault. He did not know the meaning of the wolf coming here for help. He turned away grimly, more irritated at himself than at the white man now though.

Devon sighed in relief as Giant Bear turned his angry stare elsewhere. He scowled in anxiety and gestured inquisitively. "Why did the wolf come here to get Black Hawk, if you do not mind me asking?"

Giant Bear grimaced bleakly worried now, but continued leading Devon over to the medicine man's tepee. "If the wolf came here looking for help, it could mean Raven is in danger or hurt somewhere."

Devon winced he did not want to marry the woman, but that did not mean he wanted to see her hurt either. Not right now anyway, he needed her to find his sister for him. After that, he did not care what happened to her or so he kept insisting to himself. He waved in demand apprehensive now. "Well aren't you going to go find them to save your granddaughter than?"

Giant Bear shook his head negatively. "No, they could be anywhere. Black Hawk will find and help her."

Giant Bear stopped in front of the medicine man's tepee then scratched on the door.

The medicine man opened the flap and beckoned them to come inside with him.

Devon followed then copied Giant Bear as he sat cross-legged in front of the fire.

The medicine man undid the binding that held his arm to his side before helping him remove his shirt. He unwound the bandage from around Devon's chest and probed at his ribs. They were turning some fascinating colours, but were not broken.

Devon winced at a few sensitive areas, but drew in a deep breath then let it out without any major pain.

The medicine man nodded in satisfaction and threw the binding into a corner. The old crusty looking Indian appeared at least a hundred years old, with a face that was so full of deep wrinkles you could not tell if he were frowning or smiling. His hair was snow white it was so thin that Devon could see most of his pink scalp. The old man unwrapped Devon's arm then said something in Cheyenne and Giant Bear translated for him. "Wiggle your fingers please."

Devon frowned in concentration as he tried to wiggle them. He got a couple to move slightly, but then groaned as searing pain shot up his arm unexpectedly.

The medicine man probed at his arm a little more and satisfied he re-wrapped it. The old man cackled then spoke in Cheyenne to his chief as he poked his finger into Devon's chest and bicep for emphasis.

Giant Bear chuckled as he dutifully translated. "He said your ribs are not broken, only cracked, so you do not need to bind them anymore.

Your arm is healing well, so you do not need to keep it fasten to your side any longer. Keep it in a sling for another two weeks, but try not to use it yet. You should wiggle your fingers every morning for a few minutes if you can though. He also said you have nice muscles for a vi'hoI, a white man. Raven will be pleased."

Devon scowled in annoyance, but did not say anything as the medicine man helped him on with his shirt.

Giant Bear turned to Devon then waved vaguely towards his tepee after the old man made him a sling. "Golden Dove is waiting for you."

Devon nodded sullenly and got up then left.

*****

Black Hawk sighed in exhaustion as he sat back and rested for a moment. He could hear Bruno as well as the female feeding in the distance in satisfaction. The Great Spirit can be extremely angry when you killed his animals then left them to rot.

The grizzly's head was hanging from a tree and the claws were all collected. He had put them by the fire to dry. The hide was stretched out now that it was scrapped clean of fat, with no membranes evident that he could see. The three-year old buck was done, as well. They would need to be cured properly once back at the village, but this would do until then.

Black Hawk looked down at himself in disgruntlement, naked again. He grimaced distastefully it was time to go for a bath before Raven woke up.

Black Hawk got up and put fresh coffee over the fire then looked down and smiled at the picture of Raven sound asleep with the grizzly cub curled up against her belly. He grabbed his rifle then turned to leave, but stopped short when he heard the rumble of wheels.

The stud looked off in the same direction and called out a challenge.

Raven woke instantly. She looked up at Black Hawk in reassurance. "That will be Dream Dancer or one of my men."

Black Hawk inclined his head then handed her his rifle. "Here I need to go bathe."

Raven took the rifle then crinkled her nose in disgust. "I would say so, you stink!"

Black Hawk laughed in delight at her face before gesturing towards the hides teasingly. "Well if I were not reduced to doing women's work I would not need a bath. I suppose I had better go fishing also. The little fellow will be hungry again."

Raven waved her hand towards the creek in encouragement. "Go I feel better, even my fever is gone!"

Black Hawk grinned thankfully and grabbed his clothes then trotted off towards the creek without anymore urging.

Raven ran her hands down her legs and feeling no other injury's she lifted her dressing then looked at her wounds. She nodded in satisfaction at the neat stitches and healthy skin. She moved her legs experimentally, but she only felt a slight twinge when her stitches pulled a little. She slowly stood up then put some pressure on her injured leg. It held her up with only a little pain.

Raven could hear the wagon getting closer it was travelling fast. She limped over and slipped into her torn buckskin pants, even though like the men she wore a loincloth. She found it more comfortable than the cotton bloomers the white women wore.

Raven went over to the underground cairn and took out some cakes before going over to the buck to cut off a chunk of meat. She limped back to the fire then cut up the meat and cakes, she threw them in the skillet then started cooking it. She stood up and turned expectantly as the wagon came into view.

Black Hawk trotted back into camp with four fish then dropped them beside the bucket by the fire. He walked over to Raven and watched the wagon coming. "How is the leg feeling?"

Raven smiled gratefully at her uncle. "A little sore, but not bad thanks to you."

Dream Dancer jumped down in a panic then rushed over to Raven for a hug of reassurance. "Are you hurt? I felt your need for me, but could not get here any faster?"

Raven laughed in delight and patted his cheek tenderly. "I am fine love. I had a run in with a she grizzly, but Black Hawk came then patched me up. I thought you were taking the mares to the valley for me?"

Dream Dancer shrugged guiltily as they walked over to the fire. He stopped short and eyed the black bundle that was still sleeping on top of Ravens blankets. He turned to his sister with a knowing look as he motioned incredulously in warning. "Trust you two to kill the mother then look for the baby. This is not just any bear cub though, it is a grizzly cub, are you sure it is wise to try raising it? They can be so unpredictable at times."

Black Hawk smirked as he pointed at the cute black bundle of fur. "Well I am not sure it is wise, but I could not leave the adorable little fellow to die now could I?"

Dream Dancer chuckled then shook his head in exasperation. "No, I suppose you could not."

They sat around the fire eating Ravens hastily made meal.

Dream Dancer filled them in as they ate. "I sent Steve with the mares because the sheriff showed up at the ranch. Did you know Scott and Patrick disappeared with no trace?"

Raven sighed sadly then nodded grimly. "I know they were the guides that were travelling with the white man."

Dream Dancer frowned in concern. "I was afraid of that! The sheriff put a posse together so now they are out looking for them. The town is supposed to have a big meeting in a week. If the men are not found by then they are going to vote on sending the army to grandfather's village and drive them out. They figure that if they are all dead that the Indians did it. There are a few people demanding action now, but the sheriff said he talked them out of doing anything hasty. He will try stalling them at the meeting to give you an extra week to get our people out of here, but he is not going to be able to stop them for long."

"Damn!" Raven swore grimly. "I knew I should have left immediately. Now I have even less time than I first thought."

Dream Dancer scowled suspiciously and waved in demand. "So tell me what is going on at the village?"

Raven sighed dispiritedly then sat back and told him everything that she knew.

*****

Jed kept them at a walk for half an hour then judging the horses rested enough, he picked up the pace again. He slowed them to a walk again an hour later and looked back. "There is a good site up ahead for a camp. We will stay there for an hour for lunch. We all need a brief rest, especially the horses. There is a creek just behind it for fresh water as well so we can refill canteens."

Mell nodded without arguing they had been riding hard since sunrise the rest would be appreciated.

Jed found the place he was looking for, so they set up a quick temporary camp. Mell, Jed, as well as their son looked after the horses while the others cooked a light meal.

Everyone settled around the fire then ate quietly. Once everyone finished, Jed looked around and smiled in encouragement. "So far we are making good time. If we keep this up we could be there before the twenty days are up, but do not count on it, we still have a very long way to go! We will be travelling through Indian Territory after we pass this next town, so I would like to stay there for the night. It will mean stopping an hour early, but the horses need a rest. We all could use a bed for at least one night, as well. Once we leave this town, we will not see another one for three or four days until we reach the Montana border. I want Jessica as well as Pamela to hide their hair as Mell does, so we will grab hats at the store. The Indians will be less likely to attack five men than two men and three women."

Everyone agreed. All of them were looking forward to a bed as camp was dismantled quickly. They rode on once Jed was satisfied that there was no trace left of them ever being there.

*****

When Raven finished explaining everything to her brother there was a complete stunned silence for a long moment. Dream Dancer leaned forward intently as he shattered the silence by growling furiously in denial. He gestured sharply in finality. "They can't make you marry this man, it's just not right!"

Raven shrugged dejectedly then lifted her hands imploringly. "Well unfortunately, it looks like I do not have a choice."

Dream Dancer frowned shrewdly, knowing his sister the way he did, he knew there would be consequences. He motioned uneasily afraid to ask, but did so anyway. "If you have to do this what will happen later?"

Raven shook her head sadly in sorrow. "I do not know for sure! If the Great Spirit forces me to marry this man, it might be the last time I ever go back to the Indian village or follow my Indian heritage. My people will always be allowed to remain on this land, but I will not protect them anymore!"

Black Hawk shared a concerned look with Dream Dancer. Raven had never talked like this before, and it scared both men.

Raven got up painfully then waved towards the ranch. "Well I must hurry back! I have to find the killers, as well as Devon's sister as soon as possible. I need to prove to everyone that my people did not do it. Dream Dancer you go back to the ranch and look after things for me."

Dream Dancer shook his head no emphatically. "I can't I did not bring an extra horse with me, plus if you must marry this man I want to meet him anyway. Besides, maybe the Great Spirit will give me a vision to help you."

Raven looked at her brother solemnly then nodded in acquiescence as she gestured in warning. "Okay, but only on the condition that you leave for the ranch as soon as I leave to find the killers."

Dream Dancer grinned in agreement and helped clean up the camp. They loaded the wagon with the hides as well as the deer meat then headed out.

*****

Devon sighed in relief as he slipped away from Giant Bear's and walked to the shed to feed his horse. His head was spinning Golden Dove had drilled him hard today. His adoption ceremony would be held tomorrow night, so he had learned what to expect for that. Then she had quizzed him on the Cheyenne words he had already learned plus added quite a few more. She was angry with her husband for some reason and taking it out on everyone. He chuckled in pleasure to himself, but not as hard as she was taking it out on her husband. Giant Bear had slept by himself in a corner last night.

Devon took three armloads over to his horse then put them in the corral before climbing up on the fence. He sat quietly hoping the stud would come over and eat with him sitting here again.

The stud frisked a little before cautiously walking over to eat.

Devon smiled in satisfaction then sat as still as he possible could, not wanting to spook him.

All of a sudden, the stallion lifted his head before calling out a challenge as he rushed to the other side of the pen. He stared towards the west keenly waiting.

Devon saw two riders coming followed by a wagon. He climbed down then squinted in the fading light. He recognized Black Hawk and Raven then looked behind them anxiously watching the wagon. As the wagon got closer, he noticed three coffins in the back. He looked at the driver and sighed in disappointment, it was only a kid sixteen or seventeen maybe not old enough to help him.

Raven rode past him without even look down to acknowledge him.

Devon stared after her miffed then followed curious to see what was going on.

The strange procession went to Ravens tepee and stopped.

Black Hawk jumped down off his horse immediately, before rushing over to Raven. He lifted his hands to help her down. Raven looked down at him as if to bat the offered help away.

Devon watched Black Hawk gesture angrily then say something harshly in Cheyenne that he did not understand. She finally nodded reluctantly before slipping off her horse into his arms. The Englishman was puzzled by this exchange for a moment until Raven tried to stand and her leg buckled under her. She would have fallen if Black Hawk had not been holding her up.

*****

Black Hawk scowled up at Raven irritably. "Do not be a fool you have been in the saddle for hours, your leg will not hold you if you try to get down by yourself. I can also see by looking at you that your fever has returned. Let me help you into the tepee then I will go get the medicine man!"

Raven nodded in exhaustion and grimaced in pain as she lifted her injured leg over her horse. She sat sideways for a moment before slipping into Black Hawk's arms. He held her steadily as she tentatively put pressure on her injured leg then she gasped in pain as it buckled beneath her.

Black Hawk swept her into his arms and turned to his nephew. "Go get the medicine man as well as your nisgii than bring them here please?"

Dream Dancer nodded grimly and jumped out of the wagon immediately then hurried past the white man before disappearing around the corner.

Devon watched Black Hawk carry Raven into her tepee. He turned away and left for the chief's tepee. The medicine man, as well as the shaman, rushed past him. A moment later Giant Bear, Golden Dove then the youth all rushed by him. He continued on to the tepee where he stopped short, remembering the bag lying by the corral. He shrugged irritably he would get it tomorrow. He went inside to bed still wondering what was going on.

*****

The marshal's party slowed their horses for the last half hour of their ride. It was dusk and would not be full night for another two hours.

Mell rode up beside Jed. "We have not been in this town for awhile; I hope it is quieter than the last time we were here!"

Jed grimaced in agreement. "I am hoping it is too, we will go to the sheriff's office first to get a run down on what is happening in town."

Mell nodded thoughtfully. "Good idea I need to get his reports anyway, he has not sent us one in a long time. I also need to tell him that he will have to call on the other deputy marshal's if he has any trouble while we are away."

Jed smiled teasingly. "I know."

In the last twenty-seven years as marshal and deputy marshal, they had worked well together. The first year had been a little rough though. They had argued quit a bit, but they had come to an understanding finally after that things had gone smoothly. Now they hardly ever fought plus they knew each other so well by this time that they did not need to ask the others opinion. They just automatically knew what the other was thinking.

Mell sighed in disgruntlement as they came into sight of the town. It was aptly named Wild Rose they called it. Every time they came to the town they were pricked by a thorn, it just never failed! It was very wild too, most of the time they had to fight their way in. Being only four days to the Montana border it was a haven for outlaws as well as gunfighters. They had gone into town several times over the years then cleaned out the vermin, but somebody always gave away the fact that they were coming. Which is why they always had to fight their way in, but this time no one knew that they were here. So hopefully, they would not have any problems getting in or away in the morning.

They rode into town looking around uneasily. It was quiet, way to quiet!

Mell took off her white buffalo robe before putting it behind her saddle with her bedroll. She unfastened the strap holding her gun in its holster when she was riding. She took out her repeater rifle next and laid it in front of her across the saddle.

Jed, as well as all the women in his party were also taking out their rifles. The only one who did not was her son; he did have one although he would not use it. Mell shook her head then sighed in annoyance. Maybe she should have left Daniel behind; it worried her that he would not protect himself. Even though he had the same training as the rest of her children, and was even faster with a six-shooter than she was. He just refused to lift a gun anymore.

They got to the sheriff's office and dismounted then loosely tied the reins, just in case they had to make a fast retreat. Mell took the lead at this point. Jed and Jessica stayed close protecting her back. Pamela was beside her husband so she could protect him as they brought up the rear.

Mell entered then hastily looked around. Within seconds, she had the whole room mapped out plus knew that there was someone in the cell and only an unfamiliar deputy was at a desk.

He jumped to his feet in fear as he eyed the group coming towards him suspiciously.

Mell pushed open her vest so that he could see her marshal's badge.

The deputy sat down heavily with a sigh of relief. "Am I ever glad to see you, marshal! I was just writing out a telegram of urgency to you!"

Mell nodded having spotted the paper in front of him then motioned curiously. "What is going on here? I do not know you! Where is the sheriff or the original deputy?"

The deputy ran his hands through his hair in agitation. "Both are dead earlier today! We had a band of desperadoes ride in several days ago. The deputy caught the sheriff taking a bribe so he shot him and the man who was giving the bribe. The desperadoes shot the deputy later when they robbed the bank. We tried to stop them, but they got away except for the one that killed the deputy. I shot him out of his saddle; luckily, he had all the money so the towns people elected me as the next deputy. The leader came here about an hour ago, said if I did not release his man by sunrise he would be back. Oh, before I forget to tell you the deputy left you a message. He said to tell you that he had suspected the sheriff of tipping off all the outlaws as to when you were coming. He did not want to say anything until he had proof though."

Mell sat down grimly then sighed thoughtfully. "Well I was getting suspicious, but I was not sure which one was doing it. It looks like we got here just in time. Continue that telegram, but send out two one to Deputy Marshal Dusty and one to Deputy Marshal Tyler. They should be in Smyth's Crossing by now."

She turned to Pamela then motioned towards the hotel across the street. "Pam, you and Daniel can take the horses to the hotel, book three rooms. Then stable all the horses, except mine and Jed's leave them tied to the hitching post in front of the hotel."

Pam with Daniel following got up then left immediately.

Mell turned to Jessica next. "Jess you can also go to the hotel, bring us something to eat, please. It is going to be a long night!"

Jess inclined her head and left.

Mell turned to the deputy next then pointed down at the paper. "You can finish the telegrams and send them out right away. Then go get a couple of hours of sleep, but be back here before midnight. I doubt very much that the outlaws will wait until dawn, they will probably hit right at midnight."

The deputy frowned anxiously he had not thought of that. Hastily he finished writing, before leaving.

Mell turned to Jed and sighed dejectedly. "No rest for us tonight!"

Jed nodded not surprised then got up to make fresh coffee.

*****

Golden Dove, Giant Bear, and Dream Dancer all rushed into Ravens tepee.

The medicine man, as well as the shaman were already checking Ravens wound.

Golden Dove rushed over to help them.

Giant Bear with Dream Dancer following went over to Black Hawk. The chief grabbed Black Hawk's arm in demand. "What happened?"

Black Hawk sighed at his father's scowl then waved to his nephew.

Dream Dancer turned and trotted out of the tepee knowingly.

Black Hawk turned to his father then told him everything except Ravens forewarning. He was not quite finished when his nephew returned with the grizzly cub. Black Hawk pointed to Raven without stopping his explanation to his father.

Dream Dancer took the cub over to Raven and laid him beside her. The cub had been crying when he went out to get him, but he quieted as soon as he was put beside Raven. He snuggled against her contentedly before going to sleep.

Golden Dove raised her eyebrows at this, but did not say anything.

The medicine man smiled in relief then turned to Golden Dove. "The wound is okay, but she has a slight fever. I will give you some medicine and it should be gone by tomorrow. She is more exhausted than anything else, a couple days of rest, and she will be good as new."

Golden Dove accepted the herbs then nodded her thanks as he left the tepee.

The shaman relieved also got up then went over to the men.

Golden Dove turned to her grandson in delight. "Well it is nice to see you, but I thought Raven was not going to let you come here right now?"

Dream Dancer moved over to his grandmother and hugged her in greeting. "I did not bring an extra horse, so Raven had no choice but to let me come. Besides, I insisted after I found out that she had to marry a vi'hoI. I want to meet him!"

Golden Dove beamed; pleased he would be staying then stroked his cheek tenderly. "Well I am glad you are here, I have missed you. You have stayed away too long and soon you will be leaving for England then I will not see you again for a very long time, if ever."

Dream Dancer smiled reassuringly as he motioned in certainty. "I would never leave before coming to see you to say goodbye, I promise. I am going to help the men unload after we can visit."

Golden Dove nodded as Dream Dancer got up and left.

Black Hawk gestured towards his nephew curiously, as they walked out of the tepee. "I forgot to ask you where Spotted Owl is hiding."

Dream Dancer grinned as he waved to the northeast. "I asked him to help Steve with the mares since he is so good with horses."

Black Hawk pointed towards the paddocks. "Can you take Brave Heart then, and put him in the empty paddock for me? His wound is healing nicely, but we need to keep a close eye on him just in case."

Dream Dancer frowned he did not like handling Ravens stallion at all. "I will try, but he has only let me come near him once or twice."

Dream Dancer left reluctantly.

Giant Bear pulled out the grizzly head; he eyed it in disapproval before shaking his head in amazement. "Fool woman could have gotten herself killed."

Black Hawk sighed, he could not disagree with that statement it was all too true. He unhitched the horses then took them over to the large pasture. He returned and helped Giant Bear as well as the shaman unload the deer than the bear head. The head went into Ravens tepee. The buck was taken over to a permanent structure that Raven had built for them that held all the meat in storage before being butchered. There was also a trap door on the ground by the back wall. When opened, there were stairs that went down deep underground it ran the whole length of the building. Once the meat was sliced, it would be taken underground to keep it cool as well as away from disease infested flies. Once everything was put away, they all gathered in Ravens tepee.

Raven was still awake obediently sipping the tea her grandmother made of the herbs the medicine man had given her. She sighed as everyone gathered around her. "I am too tired to explain now, but I will be leaving tomorrow to look for the killers."

The chief and the shaman both shook their heads negatively. However, the shaman spoke first. "No! The medicine man said at least two days rest. You must stay off that leg for at least one day if the fever is to go away, the wound will not heal properly otherwise."

Giant Bear waited until the shaman was done then gestured in decisiveness at his granddaughter. "Besides, tomorrow we will bury the dead in the white man's tradition. We will also be having Devon's adoption ceremony tomorrow night and you need be here for that as well."

Raven grimaced resignedly then looked at both men in warning. "Fine I will stay tomorrow, but I am leaving the next day first thing in the morning. Black Hawk can finish teaching the white man."

The shaman and Giant Bear looked at each other in consternation both knew that they could not hold Raven here any longer, so they nodded grudgingly.

Raven smiled at her brother in invitation as he came back in then waved towards the corner. "You can sleep here with me."

Dream Dancer inclined his head in agreement before going out to gather his pack and bedroll. Then came back in and made his bed not far from Raven.

Good nights were said then everyone left for some much needed sleep.

*****

Mell sighed as she pushed her plate away; she was just finishing her meal when the deputy walked in.

Michal sat down with a sigh of irritation. "I could not sleep anymore; every little noise would make me jump."

Jed frowned then pulled out his pocket watch that Mell had given him before they were married; he looked at it speculatively. "It is almost midnight anyway we should take our positions now."

Mell and Jed picked up their rifles then went out to sit on the porch in clear view.

Jessica crooked her finger at the deputy, and he followed her outside.

Michal turned away obediently to take his position when the marshal pointed him towards the opposite end of the building.

Pam sat at the only window then broke open a pane of glass so that her rifle could be fired from there.

Daniel went into the prisoner's cell. He had a rifle as well, but it was only for show. He brought a chair with him as he sat tensely watching the prisoner before looking at his wife in concern. She had promised not to use her rifle unless given no choice.

Mell frowned then called to the deputy curiously. "How many are there in total?"

Michal peeked around the corner of the building at Mell. "Well there were only six when they came to town, but I am not sure if that was all of them."

Mell grimaced knowingly, of course there would be more, it would be just their luck. She sat back in the chair and lounged back as if she did not have a care in the world.

Jed was not fooled he knew that she was wound tighter than a spring. He sat in a chair not far from Mell and propped his rifle across his knee to wait. He took out his watch again to look at the time as they heard the faint sounds of horses coming. It was two minutes to twelve just as Mell figured. The outlaws had planned to spring their comrade all along.

The outlaws came into sight, but they did not see Mell or Jed until they were at the hitching rail.

Mell then Jed stood up and walked over to the edge of the porch cradling their rifles in their arms.

Mell had been right there were now ten of them. She nodded cordially at the group. "What can I do for you gentleman?"

The men looked at each other in confusion. They had heard that there was a woman marshal in North Dakota, but had not believed it until now. The leader looked at her badge in contempt then spat on the porch just ahead of her. "You have my friend locked up and I want him released. NOW!"

Mell looked back at him in anger, but did not flinch. "Sorry to disappoint you gentleman, but your friend robbed the bank. He also killed a deputy so he will be hung for his crimes. If you are smart, you will turn around then ride away, since we have recovered the money you are free to go. If you do not ride out of town you will be arrested as well."

Mell and Jed had decided to encourage these men to leave instead of trying to capture them. Her deputy marshal's could chase them later, right now they did not have time to waste on them. Their crimes were not severe enough yet to warrant killing them outright, unless they gave them no choice.

Jed let the safety off on his rifle, as the tension in the air grew heavier.

Finally, one of the outlaws made a fatal mistake as he pulled his gun; the rest followed his example. Within moments all the outlaws lay dead or dying in the street.

Mell walked off the porch then sighed dejectedly. "Well, I did try to give them a reason to leave."

Jed reached over as he squeezed his wife's hand quickly in sympathy knowing how she hated to kill before turning to the deputy. "Call the undertaker and have these bodies removed. We are going to the hotel for some much-needed rest. When the other deputy marshal's arrive, have them take any outlaw still alive to the capital for trial than have the town select another sheriff. Make sure you run as well, you did a good job tonight and we will give you a recommendation if you want the job."

The deputy held up his two hands grimly as he shook his head negatively. "No, thank you! The judge already offered it to me, but being a deputy is bad enough in this town. Thank you for your help though; they would have killed me if it were not for you folks."

Jed nodded in farewell as the others joined them. They crossed the street before entering the hotel.

CHAPTER NINE

Devon got up in the morning then went to grab his bag, but remembered that he had left it by the hay shed. He walked quietly out of the tepee and hurried over towards the paddocks, wondering where the boy had slept last night. He walked around the corner then stopped short when he saw the object of his speculation walking towards the second paddock with some hay and threw it into the pen for Ravens stallion. He watched in fascination as the boy croon something in Cheyenne to the big stud before climbing the fence then jumped in with the horse.

Devon watched intrigued as the stallion snorted and pawed the ground in warning. The boy continued crooning softly almost as if hypnotizing him. The stud stood still then let the youth walk up to his hindquarters. The boy took a cloth and wiped the horse down before smearing something on the stallion. He backed away carefully then went to the fence, climbed it and sat on the top rail.

Devon continued on his way. He went to the shed first then grabbed some hay for his own horse. He started whistling a loud tune to let the boy know that he was there, so he would not scare him. He turned still whistling as he walked towards Devil's pen. He looked at the boy out of the corner of his eye as he walked past, but did not stop. He awkwardly put the hay under the fence and turned to go back. The boy was gone when Devon turned, so he quit whistling then went for more hay. As he got there, the boy came out with an armload and smiled at him then took his load over to Devil's pen without saying a word.

Devon grabbed one more load as well as his forgotten sack and went over to the paddock. The boy helped him dump the rest of the hay over the fence then he turned and trotted off, still without saying anything.

Devon watched him disappear then sighed in disappointment and climbed up on the top railing. He had hoped to talk to the boy he shrugged, oh well. He turned to Devil then whistled.

The stud took a couple steps, but stopped and snorted in warning instead.

Devon turned towards Brave Heart's corral at a noise then saw the boy coming back with two buckets of water. He stopped at Ravens horse first and put one in there then grabbed the other one and came over to Devil's pen. He put the bucket beside the hay.

Dream Dancer walked over then leaned against the fence not far from Devon. He smiled in admiration at the beautiful stallion and started crooning softly in Cheyenne.

The stud perked up his ears then took a hesitant step forward before rearing in anger and running to the opposite end of the paddock.

The boy chuckled at the horse then looked up and stuck out his hand to Devon. "Names, Dream Dancer."

Devon took the hand then squeezed it gently in introduction. "My name is Devon. How did you get the stallion to react like that to you?"

Dream Dancer grinned cheekily as Devon let go of his hand. He waved toward the stud in explanation. "It is not really a secret you just need to remember that the horse you are talking to has been here all his life. So the only language he knows is Cheyenne if you want before I leave here to go home I can teach you the words to that song."

Devon eyed the boy speculatively as he cocked his head curiously. "And where is your home?"

Dream Dancer shrugged then motioned vaguely towards the west. "That way one and a half to two days ride by horse. Three by wagon unless you are in a hurry, you can make it in less than two if you push the horses hard."

Devon eyed the boy inquisitively, hoping that he could get more information from him. "And who are you?"

Dream Dancer chuckled in amusement. "I am Ravens brother, of course! Who are you?"

Devon looked at the boy more closely as he nodded. Yes, he could see the resemblance now although Dream Dancer was fairer in colouring than Raven. They both had the same high cheekbones of the Indians, the same nose, and face structure with an arrogant chin. They both had green eyes as well, but Raven's were much lighter in colouring. Her brothers were a dark green, very unusual, almost black looking. Where did he see eyes like that before? The boy was close to six feet now; by the time he reached full growth Devon was sure, he would be six foot one to six foot three.

Dream Dancer was studying Devon just as closely then smiled thoughtfully, yes, not a meek man by any means. The Englishman was powerfully built, but would he be able to handle his sister, Raven. He was not to tall about six feet. It was hard to say what his face and eyes looked like though because it was still pretty swollen in some places with bruises covered the rest. His handshake had been firm, but not overpowering.

Devon finally answered his question. "I am Devon Rochester from England."

Dream Dancer cocked his head intrigued then motioned inquisitively. "Well why are you here in Montana if your home is in England?"

Devon sighed in aggravation. "I have some property next to Earl Summerset's somewhere out here in this Godforsaken land. That is all I am allowed to say right now if I want to keep my tongue that is!"

Dream Dancer frowned puzzled by that statement, but did not push the matter. He felt guilty enough at not being able to tell him that he was Earl Summerset, but Raven had forbidden him to mention it.

Devon smiled enticingly down at the boy hoping to get a few more questions that he had resolved. Although, he did feel slightly ashamed using Dream Dancer's open honesty to get answers nobody else wanted to give him. He pushed his guilt away and continued optimistically. "Does your sister live with you? Where are your parents?"

Dream Dancer grinned knowingly, aware that Devon was using him then he shrugged not seeing any harm in telling him the truth. "My parents are both dead, they were killed in a stagecoach hold up. My sister lives with me sometimes at other times she lives here."

Devon nodded in disappointment. He had hoped for more information, but with none forthcoming, the Englishman changed the subject thoughtfully. "Why do they call you, Dream Dancer?"

Raven's brother smirked gravely. "The shaman says it is because when he had his vision of me, I was holding a dream catcher and dancing by the fire chanting. The moon was full, but as I chanted black clouds with a touch of mauve interwoven throughout covered the moon, when I was finished the misty clouds dissipated almost instantly."

Devon looked confused. "What is a dream catcher?"

Dream Dancer chuckled at Devon's curiosity then tried to explain. "A dream catcher is exactly what its name implies. We weave into a pattern symbols using thin strips of rawhide. Usually the patterns are circular, but not always. A shaman or a dreamer weaves an enchantment into the dream catcher as he is making it. You put this dream catcher over your sleeping pallet and it is suppose to keep away evil dreams or nightmares. It is also supposed to help us to remember any dreams that we have. Indians place great significance in their dreams so we always want to remember them, that way they can be interpreted properly by a shaman. Since I am a dream dancer my dream catchers hold greater power, according to the shaman anyway."

Devon grimaced not truly believing in that nonsense, but did not want to hurt the boy's feelings. He motioned teasingly. "Maybe you can make me one after I marry your sister?"

Dream Dancer sobered inquisitively as he pointed at Devon curiously. "Are you going to marry my sister?"

Devon's smile slipped away then he scowled furiously. He waved angrily as he looked away irritably. "I do not have much of a choice do I! I either marry her or die I am told!"

Dream Dancer sighed loudly in apprehension at the livid defiance in Devon's voice.

Devon heard the anxious sigh and looked down at the boy once more. Ravens brother was staring at the stud with a troubled distressed look. He cleared his throat to get the boy's attention then changed the sensitive subject when he looked up. "What happened to Raven while she was gone?"

Dream Dancer gestured calmly in explanation. "Well she came to meet me..."

Raven's brother told Devon the whole story before grinning in humour. "She is fine now though, but she will have another scare to add to her many others."

Dream Dancer grinned at the Englishman mischievously; he had forgotten to mention the cub. He beckoned Devon to follow him enticingly. "Why don't you come with me, I need to check on her anyway? I can also show you what we brought back with us."

Devon climbed down off the fence immediately, not suspecting a thing as he followed Ravens brother curiously.

Dream Dancer stuck his head in the tepee to make sure Raven was decent. He smiled pleadingly at his sister, who was sitting up sipping her coffee. "I brought Devon with me to see the grizzly head, is it all right if I bring him in?"

Raven set her cup down and eyed the wicked gleam in her brother's eyes suspiciously, wondering what he was up to then nodded her consent.

Dream Dancer ducked back out, and they both entered. He pointed to the corner where the grizzly head was displayed.

Devon examined the head then shivered in revulsion. "Good Lord, that animal must have been huge!"

Dream Dancer nodded in agreement before waving at the other end of the village. "It was, and after we are done here I will take you over to where the women are working on the hide."

Dream Dancer than grabbed Devon's good arm gleefully and pulled him over to Raven. "Can you show Devon your wound Raven? Please!"

Raven frowned at her brother distrustfully, she knew that he was up to no good, but she nodded curiously wanting to see where this was leading. She pulled the blanket away from her thigh so that they could see. Both of them squatted down for a closer look. When Devon leaned forward, Dream Dancer grinning at Raven innocently as he poked the grizzly cub hard.

The black ball of fur jumped up with an indignant wail at being so rudely, awakened.

The unsuspecting Devon gave a cry of panic before falling backwards then landed hard on his rump. He had such an expression of shocked amazement on his face that Dream Dancer and Raven both doubled up in hysterical laughter.

Devon watched the two having hysterics at his expense than could not help but grin at the trick Ravens brother had pulled on him. The offended cub settled down once more and curled back up against Raven then went back to sleep.

Devon eyed the cub distrustfully as he got up and sat down beside Dream Dancer. He watched Raven intrigued, this was the first time he had heard her laugh. It was deep as well as robust lighting up her whole face. It took his breath away just watching her.

Dream Dancer chuckled once more as he wiped tears away before poking his gullible victim in apology to get his attention. "I am sorry; I just could not help myself."

Devon grinned in delight at the shamefaced Dream Dancer. "Well I suppose I looked pretty funny. I am sure that if I could have seen my face I would have laughed to."

Devon pointed to the cub in demand. "Now tell me what that is?"

Raven answered him instead of her brother. "He is the reason that the she grizzly attacked my horse. She could smell the blood from the buck that I had killed, so figured to get an easy meal for her cub. Usually bears will not attack humans unless they have a very good reason or are starving. She had left her cub up in a tree to keep it safe, not far from my camp. Black Hawk went looking for it as soon as he realized she had a cub then coaxed it down, but he seems to have adopted me. If the cub had been a little older, Black Hawk would have left him in the tree or shot him depending on his age."

Devon frowned fascinated. "Why, what is the difference?"

Raven beamed at the inquisitive Devon, pleased that he wanted to know more. "Well, at this age they are easier to fool into adopting you. If they are young enough, they can be trained easier. An older cub would fight you all the way they would be impossible to manage. At five or six months old he would have had to be shot, it would be the humane thing to do since he would be too young to survive and too old for training."

Devon nodded then shrugged in apology. "I will take your word for it, I do not know much about animals out here."

Raven changed the subject as she pointed towards the paddocks. "How is it going with your stallion, any progress yet?"

Devon sighed forlornly not being a horse trainer he had no idea. "I am not sure; yesterday when I fed him I went and sat a little distance away from the hay on the top railing. He came over then stood not far from me and ate while I watched him. Then this morning when I whistled he took two hesitant steps towards me, but stopped and backed away."

Raven smiled satisfied that he was getting better results than anyone else ever had with that stallion. "Good you are making progress, later today after your lessons I want you to go into the pen. If he does not chase you out, take about three steps and sit down on the ground. If you have some apples left put them with some grain in front of you then stay there for fifteen minutes. Afterwards come back here and let me know what happens. If the stud does chase you out, do not get discouraged. He might not be ready yet, so you can try again in a few days."

Devon nodded then got up and turned to Dream Dancer. "We will have to go see that hide later. I am already late for my lessons your grandmother will be angry."

Dream Dancer inclined his head in agreement then watched him leave. He finally got up and made Raven some more coffee before settling down across from her as he asked inquisitively. "Devon seems like a very nice man. He did not get mad or anything at being tricked by an Indian, most white men would. Don't you like him?"

Raven shrugged dismissively irritated. "I do not know him so I can't say whether he is nice or not."

Dream Dancer frowned then looked at his sister shrewdly. "Are you fighting this marriage because you dislike Devon, or find him repulsive? Or is it the fact that you are being forced that is making you fight it so much?"

Raven eyed her brother in surprise before waving angrily. "Why would you even ask such a question, of course I hate being told that I have to marry someone I do not even know! How dare the Great Spirit or my grandfather demand this of me after all I have done for my people! I want to marry for love not to save myself or others!"

Dream Dancer leaned forward intently as he took her hand pleadingly. "I know Raven; I would hate it too, but try to think of it this way. If we had been born in England, as we should have been, it would be even worse. Not only do your parents pick out who you marry, but also you usually never even meet the man until your wedding day. At least you have a chance to see Devon as well as get to know him before you have to marry him. It is also good that he is not old or ugly."

Raven grimaced reflectively knowing that her brother was right, but did not want to talk about it anymore so changed the subject. "Go find me a walking stick; it should be almost time to go out for the funeral."

Dream Dancer nodded not wanting to push her too hard, she would just fight it more if he did. He squeezed her hand in reassurance before getting up to leave.

Raven sat there stroking the cub absently thinking about Dream Dancer's question.

*****

Jed and Mell met the rest of their party in the dining room for breakfast.

Jed critically inspected Pam then Jess as they sat down. He grinned in approval at their clothes both were wearing buckskin pants. They had also bound their chests tightly to hide the fact that they were women. They had changed into fringed buckskin shirts with their hair tucked away under their hats. The two now had revolvers on their hips as well as moccasins on their feet.

Pam must have loaned Jess a set of buckskins because she did not have any of her own. From a distance they would pass as men, but up close nobody would be fooled.

Jed smiled up in thanks as the waitress brought them breakfast, as well as coffee, but he did not say anything just sat eating quietly as did everyone else. Once they finished Jed sighed contemplatively. "Okay it is a hard four day ride to the border between Dakota and Montana. There are no more towns until then, so we will be sleeping on the ground again. We must keep a close watch for Indians and any more outlaws like last night. We have one fast flowing river to cross, two days after the border town that is dangerous. If we are vigilant as well as careful, we should make it with no problems. Let's get the horses ready then we will stop at the store for more provisions, any questions?"

They all shook their heads no.

Jed nodded decisively as he pushed his chair back. "Good let's go!"

They got up to collect their belongings, made a quick stop at the store before heading out of town.

*****

Dream Dancer was just helping his sister up when their grandfather stuck his head in. "It is time you two, come on let's go!"

Raven grimaced at the rush. "Be out in a moment grandfather!"

Giant Bear ducked back out without another word.

Dream Dancer helped Raven into her pants and held out the walking stick.

Raven smiled in thanks as they left the tepee together. They reached the spot for the funeral then walked to the front of the crowd.

Giant Bear, Devon, Golden Dove, and the shaman were all together waiting for her.

Raven went then stood by her grandmother and smiled at her.

Giant Bear stepped forward then raised his hands for quiet. He spoke in Cheyenne before repeating it in English so that everyone could understand. "Since this is a vi'hoI funeral, Devon will speak. I know some of you understand English, but for those of you who do not I will translate. We need complete silence so that everyone can hear."

Giant Bear nodded to Devon to go ahead as he stepped back. Devon stepped forward to start the service. The shaman chanting, blessed the dead as well with Giant Bear translating. Two warriors lifted each coffin into the ground with more coming over to help fill in the graves. Devon said a final prayer to finish it off as he said goodbye to his youngest sister. It was a beautiful service and for the first time in history, the dead were blessed not only by the white man's God, but by the Cheyenne Indians Heammawihio also.

Raven hobbled over to Devon then touched his arm, but snatched her hand back at the weird tingling sensation she felt. "I just wanted to say that was a beautiful service and I am very sorry about your sister."

Devon nodded in thanks at the words of sympathy, but turned away without saying anything. He walked towards the creek without looking back.

Raven sighed in distress at the rejection then turned to her grandmother. "I better go back and feed my cub before he wakes up, he is liable to rip apart my tepee looking for food."

Golden Dove smiled before kissing her cheek in farewell. "Okay, I will be there shortly with some lunch. We will not be having supper until the adoption ceremony so I will make sure it is enough to hold the two of you until than."

Raven inclined her head in agreement and turned away then walked towards Black Hawk. She motioned hopefully. "Did you go fishing this morning? My cub should be hungry by now."

Black Hawk chuckled in delight. "Oh, now it is your cub is it well it's good that you feel that way because my wife refuses to have anything to do with it. She will not let me bring him into our tepee either. So he will have to stay with you and yes I went fishing I will bring some fish over to you in a few minutes."

Raven grinned gratefully then left. Her leg was actually feeling much better and she was only limping slightly by the time she got back to her tepee as she ducked inside.

The cub was awake walking around sniffing at everything curiously.

Raven beamed in pleasure at the cute ball of fur then walked over to the fire before putting coffee on. She sat on her blankets as she regarded the cub thoughtfully.

The cub came trotting over to her and sniffed at her then cuddled up as he went back to sleep. Raven reached down and stroked the cub tenderly as a name popped into her head, which made her chuckle in delight. "I think I will call you Cuddles because all you want to do is cuddle."

Golden Dove ducked into the tent, followed by Black Hawk then Dream Dancer. Black Hawk carried a half dozen fish and her brother carried a pot of stew. A few minutes later Giant Bear with Devon arrived then they all sat around the fire eating lunch together.

Giant Bear turned to his grandson inquisitively. "When are you leaving?"

Dream Dancer shrugged dejectedly. "Tomorrow at the same time Raven does, I have some work I have to do."

Devon looked at Raven in surprise. "You are leaving tomorrow, but what about your bear cub and helping me to break Devil?"

Raven sighed plaintively as she looked down at the cub wondering what condition her tepee would be in when she returned. She looked over at Devon then pointed to her uncle. "Black Hawk will finish teaching you. As for the cub he will have to stay here alone, Black Hawk's wife will not let him take the cub to their tepee."

Devon sat up straight and put a hand on his chest pleadingly. "I can stay here with him while you are gone, that will give Giant Bear some privacy with his wife."

Raven looked at her grandfather then saw him nod in agreement. She turned back to Devon as she inclined her head in thanks. "Okay, that would be a great help. You must take him out during the day. There are trees behind my tepee that the cub likes to use as a scratching post, as well as a place to go to the bathroom. You will find that bears very seldom go to the bathroom in their own caves. They are clean animals so you can take him down to the creek once a day as well for a bath. The reason a bear stink so much is because they do eat carrion, but if there is water around they prefer swimming and playing in the water as well as fishing. You can feed the cub, fresh fish, nuts, fruit, berries, eggs, birds, snakes they also like ground squirrels. Grizzlies like carrion more than regular bears, but we do not want to feed this cub any since he will be living inside, and will start to stink after awhile."

Devon grinned eagerly before sighing in pleasure, anticipating a little time to himself. He sat back to enjoy the rest of the visit.

*****

Devon sighed in pleasure as he looked down at himself. The buckskins that Raven had given to him fit perfectly, but he could not see what he looked like. Golden Dove said he looked good in his new finery, but he was not too sure. He sat down on his blankets so that he would not get his new clothes dirty then ran through what he had to say at the ceremony. He was getting better at the Cheyenne language and understood more as long as they did not speak to fast.

Devon smiled in delight as he thought of the afternoon he had spent with Dream Dancer. They went then looked at the she grizzly's hide first. He found it hard to believe that Raven and Brave Heart had survived being attacked by that enormous black monster. Afterwards, Ravens brother took him to the creek where he taught him the crooning song for his stallion.

Dream Dancer had then proceeded to teach Devon how to catch fish for the cub using his hands only. This totally amazed him, never having seen it done before now. Ravens brother explained that they tickled a fish's belly until they were docile and quickly grasped it by the gills, once caught you had to throw them on land. It even worked he would never have thought of trying such a thing. They had laughed uproariously together as Devon tried to learn. Twice he ended up in the water, instead of the fish winding up on dry land.

After they had gone to Devil's pen. Devon had gone in then sat down crooning softly. The stallion had let him come in and sit, much to everyone's surprise. After a hesitant step towards him at the start of the song, the stud refused to come any closer. He grinned ecstatically in anticipation he was clearly getting results. Even that one-step towards him was progress at least he was not charging him.

Devon sighed in trepidation. He would meet all the Cheyenne tonight. After the ceremony was finished, they would all come over to introduce themselves as well as their families. He would not meet the other bands until fall if he remained here that is, of course, he did not plan to be here than. He was hoping to be on his way back to England before fall. He felt a little disappointed for a moment, but shook it off and berated himself angrily.

*****

Raven smiled in approval at her brother. "You look absolutely gorgeous tonight!"

Dream Dancer blushed slightly in pleasure. "Well I brought an assortment of clothes with me because I was not sure what was going on here or how long I would be staying. I am glad now that I did."

Raven hugged her brother affectionately. "I am definitely glad you are here. Devon seems to like you; he has been much more relaxed. Calmer to since you came."

Dream Dancer grinned in delight as he thought about their fishing expedition. "I like him too. It is just too bad he was caught in the middle of this. I think if he had made it to the ranch, you would have liked him too."

Raven scowled warningly at her brother, but did not say anything. She walked over then put a fish beside the sleeping cub for when he awoke.

Dream Dancer smiled innocently when his sister glared at him. He did not tell his sister about his dream last night since he was not sure what it meant yet. All he could see was a white buffalo leading some people and the buffalo kept repeating in a feminine voice. 'I'm coming'. Other than that, the Great Spirit was surprisingly quiet on the subject of Ravens marriage to Devon.

There was only one female named White Buffalo that Dream Dancer knew of and that was his grandfather's friend Mell. Did the dream mean that she was coming here to help them? If so, was he supposed to delay the wedding until she arrived? On the other hand, there could be another meaning to the vision! Most of the time, his dreams meant two or three different things. It was trying to figure out which meaning he was supposed to use that always had him confused.

Dream Dancer had talked to the shaman several times, but he could not actually help him. All the shaman would say is that the meaning had to come from within himself. As he grew older, interpreting the dreams would come easier. The shaman refused to teach him since he was leaving for England soon. That worried Dream Dancer, what if he did something wrong accidentally. He could hurt someone or even kill them unintentionally.

Raven watched her brother's expression go from a teasing smile to a fierce frown of apprehension at his thoughts. She cleared her throat to get his attention wondering if he had a dream. "Has the Great Spirit given you any hint about what I am supposed to do about Devon yet?"

Dream Dancer shook off his anxiety then shook his head negatively at his sister. "No, I am sorry nothing yet."

Raven sighed dejectedly as she went over to refill her coffee cup.

*****

Black Hawk sighed in apprehension as he watched his wife move around the tepee. She had been in her seventh month of pregnancy for two weeks now and she was not looking good. But no matter how he tried, he could not convince her to stay off her feet. Maybe he should talk to the medicine man again, see if he would mind coming over then ordered her to take it easy, she might take his advice. He would also talk to his mother about keeping Gentle Doe with her so that she could keep an eye on her.

Gentle Doe walked over to pick up a pail of water.

Black hawk jumped up and rushed over before she could pick it up. "Do not lift anything, I will do it!"

Gentle Doe nodded patiently at her worried husband, but did not say anything.

Black Hawk picked up the pail then put it beside the fire. He turned and looked at Gentle Doe in concern as he motioned in demand. "I want you to go see the medicine man tomorrow."

Gentle Doe looked at her husband sorrowfully then shrugged dismissively. "I will go if you insist, but I will die having this child and there is nothing anyone can do. I do want you to promise me something though."

Black Hawk looked at his wife in shocked surprise then shook his head vehemently. "You will not die, I will not let you!"

Gentle Doe sighed knowing he would be difficult, but she had already resigned herself to her death willing to sacrifice herself for her unborn child. She sat down before telling him what she wanted. She reached up and took his hand imploringly. "I have seen my future; I will die giving birth to a healthy boy child this I have accepted. But someone comes who will love you as I do, so all I ask is that you do not turn away from our son or from a new love. It will ease my mind if you will give me your promise!"

Black Hawk stared at his wife incredulously, but the look on his wife's face permitted no refusal. He finally nodded reluctantly. "I promise!"

Choking back tears Black Hawk rushed out to go see his mother once his wife let him go, satisfied at his answer. He rushed into her tepee without knocking.

Golden Dove looked up then started to smile in welcome, but quickly sobered at his grief stricken face. She turned to Devon quickly and waved towards her granddaughters. "Why don't you go to Ravens to show her how good your new clothes look?"

Devon looked from Golden Dove to Black Hawk in concern then nodded uneasily as he saw the stricken look on Black Hawk's face. He left immediately without argument or questions.

Golden Dove waited until he left and patted the spot beside her so her son would sit.

Black Hawk sat down heavily in distress then grimaced fretfully as he looked at his mother imploringly. "Gentle Doe said she is going to die in childbirth."

Golden Dove sighed sadly not surprised by that disclosure. "It looks that way! The medicine man and I discussed her the other day. We also feel that she will not survive the birthing. The medicine man figures the baby is way too big for her. The shaman had a vision, but we were going to wait until after the adoption ceremony to tell you. We know it will come down to a choice on either saving the baby or saving your wife. You will have to make that decision yourself I am afraid."

Black Hawk jumped up in agitation as he raged all the while shaking his head in denial. "I cannot let her die, I love her?"

Golden Dove nodded regrettably. "I know you do, but what does she want?"

Black Hawk stopped his frantic pacing then turned to his mother distressfully. "She wants the baby to live and she made me promise not to turn away from him. She also said something about some woman coming who will love me as much as she does. I do not want another woman or another child. I want my wife alive as well as healthy!"

Golden Dove frowned in disapproval. She wished Gentle Doe had not told him that. She got up then took Black Hawk's hands she squeezed them compassionately. "I am not sure if she is right about another woman, but you must realize that even if we let the baby die Gentle Doe will probably still die. If it's her time to go to the great hunting grounds there is nothing you can do to stop it. If you let the baby die and your wife survives, she will hate you. I know her well enough to know that she will take her own life later if she thinks it is her time to die. If the baby dies too than all that you will have accomplished is losing both of them."

Black Hawk scowled dejectedly as he waved grimly. "I know, but I cannot just sit back and watch her die. It will tear me up inside I will probably hate the child for killing her."

Golden Dove shook her head negatively. She knew her son better than that it was the grief talking now. "No, you could never hate a child especially your own! You have time yet to spend with your wife. Do not throw away her sacrifice or the time you have remaining with her by letting your feelings of anger and resentment get in the way. We all must go when our time is up; there is no way to stop it. At least you are prepared for what is to come so can tell her every day how much you love her. Most people do not have any warnings."

Black Hawk grimaced in thought then smiled appreciatively at his mother for her good advice. "You are right of course; I must spend as much time with her as I can. Thank you and I love you!"

Golden Dove grinned in relief as the despair eased on her sons face. It was not gone entirely, but more manageable now. She hugged her son in encouragement. "I love you too; now go hug that pretty wife of yours."

Black Hawk sighed in relief then nodded at peace now and turned before sprinting to his tepee, not wanting to waste another minute with his wife.

*****

Devon walked slowly towards Ravens tepee wondering what had upset Black Hawk so much. He still had not figured it out by the time he got to Ravens. He scratched on the door flap then waited.

Dream Dancer popped his head out and smiled in greeting at Devon. "Well hello there, come on in."

Devon walked in then saw Raven sitting on her bed patting the cub. He turned to see Dream Dancer staring at him with his mouth hanging open in disbelief.

Ravens brother turned his shocked look to his sister. "You gave Devon the buckskins you have been working on for a year! I thought they were for grandfather?"

Raven shrugged dismissively ignoring her brothers knowing gaze. "Well I was not exactly sure who they were for. I was thinking of giving them to you as a going away present, but they ended up being too big for you."

Raven stopped talking and bit her lip in annoyance at giving away this information to Devon. The Englishman leaped on her mistake immediately as he looked at Ravens brother speculatively in surprise. "Oh, where are you going?"

Dream Dancer smiled at Devon eagerly. "I am going away to school this fall; I am going to be a lawyer so that I can try to help my people."

Devon grinned in delight at the exited Dream Dancer. "Well congratulations, I hope you make all your dreams come true. Where are you going to take the law? I am not very familiar with schools out here."

Dream Dancer looked at his sister in rebellion then answered truthfully, as he turned back to Devon. "I am going to school in England; I am already enrolled for next fall."

Raven's mouth tightened in disapproval, but she did not say anything. He would not listen to her anyway.

Devon stared at Dream Dancer in shock, impervious to the dispute between brother and sister. "Well England has some of the best schools, but it is very expensive. How are you planning on paying for tuition?"

Ravens brother bit his lower lip not sure what to say for a moment. He looked at his sister again as he got an idea then grinned devilishly as he waved towards her. "My sister is paying for some of it. She has been saving money for my schooling since our parents died. My father left me an inheritance as well."

Raven scowled in anger at her brother for involving her so that he could get himself out of the tight situation that he had gotten himself into.

Devon looked at Raven in question, but when she refused to answer, he shrugged dismissively. Remembering Black Hawk saying she trained other peoples horses, even the whites considered her the best. He turned back to Dream Dancer in enthusiasm. "Well, when I get back to England I hope you do not mind if I come visit you. If you ever need help or a friend while you are there, just let me know."

Dream Dancer frowned intently at Devon, hoping to convey how serious this was to him. "Whatever happens between you and my sister has nothing to do with me. I like you so you will always be welcome to visit. I hope you feel the same way about me. No matter what happens or what you discover, I hope you will stay my friend."

Devon motioned reassuringly at Dream Dancer's pleading expression. "Well I have the same hope, I like you too. No matter what happens here, you remember that you will always be welcome in my home."

Raven cleared her throat in aggravation then gestured irritably. "Now that you two are done proclaiming your undying friendship, can you turn around Devon and let me see the whole outfit."

Devon scowled at her sarcastic remark, but did what she asked.

Raven nodded thoughtfully satisfied that it looked good on him, it was also a perfect fit. That worried her a little since he was taller than her grandfather was and broader in the shoulders. She frowned perplexed at how good a fit it was. She eyed Devon broodingly in suspicion. "Why are you here anyway, I thought you were not suppose to leave my grandfather's until the ceremony?"

Devon shrugged in bewilderment. "I thought so too, but Black Hawk came storming into your grandmother's tepee. He looked upset about something. She told me to come here to show you how well the buckskins fit so they could be alone."

Raven shared a sad look with her brother as Dream Dancer handed Devon a cup of coffee.

Devon looked from one to the other in confusion. "Well are you going to tell me or must I guess."

Raven sighed sorrowfully. "I suppose you will find out sooner or later, Black Hawk's wife is pregnant again. She is now two weeks into her seventh month."

Devon frowned perplexed at the sad looks. "Well what is so upsetting about that? It should be a happy time."

Raven inclined her head forlornly then explained to the baffled Devon. "Well, Black Hawk and Gentle Doe have been married for twenty-three years. The first three years of their marriage, she had one miscarriage after another. Finally, in the third year she managed to get pregnant again. This time she went the whole term, both were thrilled when she delivered a healthy boy child with no problems. After he was born, the miscarriages started again. Until seven months ago, she could not hold a child past her sixth month. Now she is going to give birth again, but she is thirty-eight years old very tiny as well as fragile. We all know that this baby will kill her, she must know it too. She must have told Black Hawk tonight that she would not survive."

Devon sighed dejectedly. "You are right it is not good news, poor Black Hawk I know what it is like growing up without a mother."

Devon was interrupted when Giant Bear popped his head into the tepee. "Oh there you are Devon; it is time to start come on."

Dream Dancer helped his sister up then followed Devon out.

CHAPTER TEN

Mell nudged her horse forward as she rode up beside Jed. "I think we better stop soon. The horses are in need of a rest and I think that somebody is following us."

Jed slowed his horse as he looked over at his wife in surprise. He had not noticed anything then motioned curiously. "Someone's following us, when did you first notice?"

Mell grinned at her irate husband." A couple of hours after we left town, they are still a little way back, but riding hard trying to catch up."

Jed shook his head in exasperation as he gestured in anger. "Why didn't you tell me before?"

Mell shrugged dismissively. "Well I was not sure that they were following us at first and I am still not absolutely sure. It could be someone on their way to Montana like we are."

Jed sighed in irritation at his wife's logic as he started looking for a camp that was in a good defensible position. He found what he was looking for a few minutes later. It was defensible on three sides with a small creek running through it for water if they had to whole up for more than a day.

They quickly made camp and Jessica started dinner as they waited tensely for whoever was coming. When they could clearly hear a horse, Mell grabbed her rifle then walked over to Jed at the edge of the camp.

Two horses could be seen, but only one rider. The rider approached slowly before taking off her hat when she judged that they could see her clearly and let her long coal black hair fall loose.

Mell looked at Jed then grinned in relief as they turned back to watch their daughter in disgruntled disapproval.

Patricia squealed in pleasure as she jumped off her horse and ran over to envelope first her mother then her father in a big hug. "Shame on you guys for running off on an adventure without me. I was only about a day behind you to start with, but I just could not seem to catch up much at first. It was not until you stopped in town that I almost caught you. I was only about two hours away by that time."

Mell grinned unperturbed by her daughters chiding voice. "Well if you had not been out of town at the time, we would have told you. Speaking of town, who did you leave in charge?"

Pat smirked at her mother in delight. "John is looking after things for me."

Mell groaned in horror as she waved dramatically in incredibility. "The town will be in shambles when we get back!"

Pat laughed in hilarity at her mother's theatrics. Suddenly she was enveloped in a gigantic bear hug without any warning.

Daniel lifted her off her feet and chortled in glee. "I knew that you were coming sis, I could feel you getting close."

Mell sighed loudly in irritation as she threw her hands up in defeat. "That is why you stalled us this morning in the store then again when we stopped for lunch."

Daniel grinned devilishly, not in the least concerned that his mother disapproved. "Well I could not very well ruin the surprise or make it too easy for her to catch up, now could I?"

Daniel chuckled at his mother's put upon expression and turned back to his sister with a wink of devilment before motioned inquisitively. "Where is your dog?"

Pat smiled then whistled.

A massive black monster of a dog came running at the whistle and stopped beside Pat then sat down quickly, waiting patiently as she looked up at her mistress adoringly. She was one of the biggest dogs they had ever seen, her shoulders when on all fours where past her owner's waist and Patricia was as tall as her mother was. She was pure black with silver on the tips of her hair. Her fur was long like a sheep dogs as well as slightly curly. She only had a stub for a tail it had not been cut off either that is the way she was born. They had no idea what kind of a dog she was. She looked exactly like a miniature black bear except for the silver tips on the ends of her fur. When the dog stood up on her hind legs, she was taller than Jed was. She stood a good seven feet, and her head was enormous. She could put a ten year olds head in her mouth without leaving a mark. However, she was one of the gentlest dogs they had ever owned. Unless you threatened Patricia that is then you had better run for the hills.

Pat had found her as a pup wandering the back alleys of town, so had brought her home. She now used the dog as a deputy and they worked well together.

Pat smiled down in approval at her dog then nodded in assent. "Okay, Silver Tip, you can greet everyone now."

The dog went to Daniel first, her second favourite person and stood up on her hind legs then put her front paws on his shoulders for a wet kiss.

Daniel laughed in delight and grabbed her around the neck for a hug.

Silver Tip jumped down then went to Jed next. She greeted him ecstatically her whole back-end wiggled back and forth as her stub of a tail wagged furiously. She butted against him insistently almost knocking him off his feet until he bent over with a chuckle for a hug.

The dog went to the two women sitting next. Silver Tip sat down before whining eagerly as she lifted her giant right paw for a shake first. Once they finished shaking her paw both bent down to give her a hug of welcome.

Only Mell got different treatment.

Mell squatted down as the dog crept towards her on her belly whining plaintively. Silver Tip sat up when she got close to Mell before carefully enclosing Mell's chin in her mighty jaws, but did not bite down. When the dog released Mell, she rolled onto her back then waited for Mell's approving rub on her belly. The dog had done this since she was a pup. The only explanation anyone could come up with is that the dog figured Mell was the female leader of their pack. So always treated her as such afraid she would be driven from the pack. If it had been a male dog, it would have probably treated Jed that way, instead of Mell. This treatment suggested to them a wolf breed, but they had never heard of a wolf that looked like a bear before.

Jess called them for supper, so everyone sat around talking as they laughed together enjoying Pat's company. After dinner was eaten, Pat turned to her mother inquisitively. "Well where are we going in such a hurry and how long till we get there?"

Mell smiled fondly at her daughter then frowned in concern as she explained her vital need to get to Giant Bear before it was too late. When she was done Pat scowled decisively then motioned imploringly. "Okay I see your urgency now. I want to come too and help Uncle Bear."

Mell smiled in humour at her daughter. Pat had called Giant Bear, 'Uncle Bear' since she was five years old.

Jed laughed in delight at his daughter then reached over and ruffled her hair affectionately. "Well squirt, I do not think we will be sending you back now that you have come this far to find us."

Jed looked up at the three quarter moon then nodded in relief as he looked back at the others. "We have plenty of light from the moon, so I want to keep going for another couple of hours. There is a sight I stayed at years ago with Giant Bear it is just down a little way so we will camp there for the night."

There were nods of agreement, with a lot of laughter as everyone saddled back up.

Jed rearranged their order slightly so that they were now riding in a triangle formation. He was still out in front by three quarters of a horse length. On his right riding on his flank was Pam she was leading a packhorse. On his left flank was Pat she had taken over her mother's place with her dog loping along beside her. Directly behind Pat on her horses right flank was Jessica, she was leading the white colt. Beside Jessica, riding on Pam's horses left side, was Daniel who also lead a packhorse. In-between Jessica and Daniel, but slightly behind them half a horse length back was Mell. She would protect their back trail.

*****

Raven was sitting beside Devon with her brother on her right as they ate the feast the women had made. There was a hug pot of rich beef stew plus they had roasted a hindquarter of the buck Raven had killed over an open fire. There were potatoes with corn from Ravens ranch as well as a dessert made out of last years bottled fruit.

Raven sighed in satisfaction as she sat back. The ceremony had gone well. Devon had done everything right even remembered everything he was supposed to say in Cheyenne. She frowned disgruntled suddenly as she looked at him out of the corner of her eye. It had been a complete surprise to everyone, especially her, when the shaman had named him Golden Eagle. The fact that the golden eagle was prominent on the buckskins that she had made then given to him caused goose bumps to appear all over her body in reaction. She grimaced, thinking back to the time she started making the buckskins; she had put the rearing horse and the cow on the back first to represent her ranch. Then she was going to put a bear standing on its hind legs, as well as a wolf because it was supposed to represent Giant Bear's Cheyenne tribe on the front. They were called the Wolf tribe now, but they had been the Bear tribe before that, so she wanted to show the difference between now and then. She just about finished the back design when an inspirational dream came to her of a golden eagle with its wings outstretched. A wolf head staring intently at you was under the right wing of the eagle. A raven, wings outstretched, with one wing just touching the eagle was facing forward. Its beak was opened slightly in warning as it stared at you relentlessly. It was under the left wing of the golden eagle. The golden eagle was shielding both animals as if protecting them. Its stare was piercing, almost compellingly so. So, Raven had been inspired to put the design on the front of the buckskin shirt instead.

Raven shuddered at being manipulated by the Great Spirit. She grabbed her glass of corn whisky that had been made by the Cheyenne before downing it. It burned all the way down causing her to almost, choke.

A young girl came around refilling everyones cup.

After Ravens cup was refilled, she took a more cautious sip of the strong alcohol. She turned to Devon sarcastically. "Well Golden Eagle how do you feel now as an adopted Cheyenne and named as well."

Golden Eagle looked at Raven in concern she seemed upset about something, but he could not figure out what it was. He smiled in contentment as he gestured in amazement. "Actually I am quite surprised at the feelings of being whole. Like a part of me was missing all this time that I had not realized until now was not there. As for being named Golden Eagle I like it, it even fits with my new clothes."

Golden Eagle laughed in delighted satisfaction as he stroked the soft buckskin shirt in pleasure.

Raven just scowled fiercely back then took another hefty swallow of the alcohol, not in the least amused. Golden Eagle stopped chuckling immediately and frowned in confusion as he eyed her sour expression apprehensively. He watched her take a large gulp of the fiery liquid then motioned cautiously. "You are drinking a lot of that stuff don't you think you should ease off a little?"

Raven waved decisively at him in anger. "It is none of your business how much I choose to drink!"

With that furious statement, she turned her back and started to talk to Dream Dancer ignoring Devon completely.

Golden Eagle sighed in uncertainty then shook his head at her foolishness as he went back to eating.

The food was finally cleared away.

The shaman added more wood to the fire until the flames were so high that it looked as if they were part of the night sky. Dressed in his best and most impressive outfit the shaman danced around the fire as the drums beat a rhythmic cadence, keeping pace with his spectacular awe-inspiring dance. He finished then sat as the braves began chanting steadily.

All the braves got up, except for the ones beating on the drums. A few minutes later, the women joined in. They all danced together around the vast crackling fire. Occasionally sparks popped loudly, sending shooting flames everywhere, it just added suspense with a touch of magic to the spectacular scenes happening around the fire. Suddenly all the braves sat, but the women remained. A few minutes later the women sat as one brave got up to dance alone. Now the braves told of their skills as well as their bravery, one by one. They tried to outdo each other as they showed off their story telling abilities to the newest member of the Cheyenne.

Golden Eagle watched spellbound until the last brave sat down.

Instead of the chanting stopping though, it got louder and louder then changed in tempo as if in demand. When that did not produce the desired results, the chanting was accompanied by sticks and rocks being pounded together until the noise was deafening, even the women joined in this time.

Raven sighed in defeat beside him then got up unexpectedly. The braves all cheered as Raven walked up to the fire a little unsteadily having drank way too much.

Dream Dancer scooted over closer to Golden Eagle. He smiled enticingly as he pointed towards the retreating Raven. "I will interpret the dance for you if you like?"

Golden Eagle nodded eagerly, but did not look away from Raven.

Dream Dancer smiled thoughtfully at Golden Eagles rapt attention fixed on his sister. He began as he waved around at all the braves hunkered down around the circle surrounding the firelight as they beat on drums continuously. "Well every brave that you have seen so far has told his story of the last heroic deed they had done, so Raven will do the same. She will dance of her courage in facing the grizzly to save her horse, which was her last act…"

Golden Eagle listened to Dream Dancer distractedly as he told the story, but continued to watch Raven closely throughout the dance and could not help but feel a surge of intense passion as he watched how gracefully she moved. He had never seen anything like it before it was so incredibly beautiful.

When she was finished, a thundering cheer arose from the braves then three braves surrounded Raven talking earnestly, but she was shaking her head insistently.

Golden Eagle frowned uneasily and turned to Dream Dancer. "What are the braves discussing with Raven?"

Dream Dancer smiled mischievously. "They are asking her to come to their tepee, if she agrees then goes that means she has chosen him as her possible husband."

Dream Dancer stopped what he was going to say with a knowing chuckle as Golden Eagle jumped up and stormed towards Raven furiously.

Golden Eagle was surprised to find himself on his feet almost running over to Raven. The surge of jealousy he felt was shocking to him. As he got closer, a bunch of Indian maidens converged on him then would not let him pass. One woman who spoke broken English but not particularly well gestured around at the five other women surrounding him trying to explain. "We all think you are um... hand...some."

She stammered the word unsure if she had gotten it right. She tried again not deterred by his frown of confusion. "We would like the Golden Eagle to share blankets with one of us."

Before she could finish, Raven stormed into their midst and said something harshly in Cheyenne that Golden Eagle did not understand. The woman shrugged unrepentant then smiled at the Englishman invitingly one more time before reluctantly leaving.

Raven was fuming and she rounded on Golden Eagle in a furious temper. "How dare you flirt with those women when you are supposed to marry me! If you had gone with one of them, you would have had to marry her if her father insisted."

Golden Eagle was taken aback by her angry ravings then smirked in disbelief. "I was not flirting with them they were flirting with me! Are you jealous?"

Raven stopped surprised by his question and snorted in angry denial. "Absolutely not!"

Raven turned then stormed off without another word.

Golden Eagle watched her leave in bewilderment before turning to go back to Dream Dancer.

*****

Dream Dancer had watched Golden Eagle go storming off towards Raven in a fit of jealousy and chuckled in glee as a bunch of women waylaid him then would not let him go. He laughed uproariously suddenly as he watched Raven storm into the group in a rage and not only admonish the women, but then she turned on the Englishman as if it were his fault. Dream Dancer watched Raven storm away even more infuriated now at whatever Golden Eagle had said to her. By the time his friend reached him, he had himself under control once again. He did not want the Englishman to know he was laughing at him. Golden Eagle might take it the wrong way.

Golden Eagle sat down again dejectedly and looked at Dream Dancer beseechingly. "Can you explain the Cheyenne customs on marriage to me?"

Dream Dancer had to clear his throat a couple of times before he could answer, still trying not to laugh. "Well it is a little complicated, but I will try. A brave who is not wed can ask a maiden who is untouched to go to his tepee. If she agrees, the brave goes to her family the next day then offers whatever he feels that she is worth, since it is now assumed that they will marry. If the father does not agree to the bride price, the brave must come up with a better offer if he wants the maiden that is. Now a brave who is married already can decide he wants another woman. If he is rich enough to afford a second wife, he does not have to ask his first wife for permission. He can just go ahead and get one, although not many braves will do this without asking their wife's permission first if he wants peace in his tepee that is. Sometimes a brave takes a maiden to his tepee then decide they do not want to be married afterwards. This happens infrequently as it is frowned on of course, but it does happen occasionally. If it does happen, the brave must make up for taking the girls maidenhood. Sometimes a maiden's family wants their daughter to marry a certain brave. If she does not want to the parents can pressure her into accepting, but the maiden cannot be forced into marriage. Now a maiden can refuse a brave if she wants and he cannot take her against her will. If he does, he is banished from the tribe then marked so that all who see him will know of his shame. A brave who wants to share a blanket for one night with another man's wife can do so, only if her husband agrees. This is rarely done as well since most men do not want to share their wives. But if a brave has three or four wives, he might encourage them to find other braves when he wants to be alone with a certain wife. Take the woman who was talking for the others. They are all married to one man, he must have given them permission to ask you to share their blankets. So that is what they were doing, you could have picked one of them or all of them if you can handle that many."

Golden Eagle shook his head in bemusement. "I could not take another man's wife or share my own wife and I definitely cannot handle more than one wife at a time."

Dream Dancer chuckled and held up his hand to quiet his friend. "I am not quite finished yet so let me tell you one more thing. Now, in our culture women are not normally allowed to do anything the men do, or visa versa. But there are women who do go to war with their husband. They stay on the edge of the battle though watching; some even participate if the war is going badly. The Cheyenne call these women brave hearted women. In our culture, there is only one woman who became a shaman, two who became medicine women. We also had a chief named Godasijo. She was the first chief in our recollection. She was the only woman ever named as a chief that I am aware of anyway. Now Raven is the only woman in our history to become a full-fledged brave. So there is some confusion by the braves on how to approach her for marriage. She is highly sought out because not only is Raven the chief's granddaughter, but she has her own wealth plus she has proven her bravery repeatedly. She is also known as the 'Protector' of her people, which is a first also. I guess you could call her a war chief, but than that would not be the right term either. She does not usually take them to war, but she prevents wars. She is the buffer between the whites and the Indians. At one time, we had dog soldiers as well as other societies that protected our people or went to war for us, but they were disbanded when we moved here. Now they are called the Raven Society, protectors only. So Giant Bear has had to fend off more offers than he knows what to do with for her to marry a brave in almost every tribe of Cheyenne there is. Raven has refused them all though and Giant Bear cannot make her marry anyone she does not want to."

Golden Eagle scowled in puzzlement then motioned in bewilderment. "Well if her grandfather cannot force her to marry why is she allowing him to force her now?"

Dream Dancer shrugged in confusion. "I do not know why she agreed, she does not have to marry you if she absolutely refuses. He is our chief though, so he does have the right to make anyone do what he wants if he feels the tribe is endangered for some reason, when this occurs his word is law."

Golden Eagle sighed in aggravation as he watched the chief and Raven standing together arguing. Raven finally threw her hands up then stormed away furiously.

*****

Raven marched towards her grandfather in a ferocious rage, the nerve of the man implying she was jealous.

Giant Bear saw her coming; he frowned anxiously at his infuriated granddaughter, wondering what Golden Eagle had said this time to set her off. Raven halted in front of the chief. She did not even looking at her grandmother she was that angry. She waved in finality. "I absolutely refuse to marry that man now or ever!"

Giant Bear grimaced enraged as he motioned in exasperation. "Oh yes you will and that is final! As your chief, I am ordering you to do so!"

Raven scowled in promise as she pointed a finger at her grandfather deadly serious. "If you make me marry that vi'hoI, you will regret it!"

Giant Bear growled then sputtered incensed as she stomped off without another word. Golden Dove stepped in front of her husband with her hands on her hips in warning. She glared at him for a moment and shook her head in bewilderment. "You will stop this madness now before it is too late! Or so help me you will sleep on the other side of the tepee by yourself for the rest of your days!"

Golden Dove whirled away not letting her stunned husband say a word as she also marched off towards Ravens tepee to try calming her down.

Giant Bear threw up his hands in dismay as the two most important women in his life left him fuming by himself. He sighed in regret. He could not stop this now even if he wanted to, all he could do was pray to the Great Spirit for help to get him out of this mess. He left for his tepee dejectedly not feeling like celebrating anymore. With shoulders slumped in hopeless despair, he shuffled grimly back to his tepee looking very old at that moment.

*****

Golden Eagle mumbled some excuse to Dream Dancer then followed Raven to her tepee and stood outside for a bit, chewing his lip in indecision. He was not sure why he had followed her in the first place, except that she had lied to him about having to marry one of those women since they were already married. He entered then feigned surprise that she was there. "Oh! I am sorry I thought you were still at the party, I just came by to check on your cub."

Raven scowled at him angrily as she swiped at her face trying to hide her tears. "What do you care? Go away and leave me alone!"

Golden Eagle stepped forward in concern at the tears running down her face. He reached out then gently touched a teardrop as it rolled down her cheek and put it in his mouth thoughtfully.

Raven stared in confused surprise at his actions.

Golden Eagle's brow wrinkled apprehensively at her pain then he gestured curiously. "Why are you crying? You are not hurt are you or is it your leg? Is it bothering you that much, maybe the dance strained it some?"

Raven grimaced distraughtly before motioning sharply in anger. "I am crying because I hate you and I do not want to marry you!"

Raven was taken totally by shocked surprise when he grabbed her around the waist with his good arm then ground his lips onto hers unceremoniously without warning.

*****

Golden Dove slowed as she saw movement in front of Ravens door and stopped in surprise then stared at Golden Eagle standing there undecided. He went inside, so Ravens grandmother smiled hopefully before turning away to go to her own tepee. She looked up towards the heavens with a pleading look as she lifted both her hands in supplication praying desperately. "Heammawihio, God! Please make it right between them; they desperately need each other even though they do not realize it yet. However, as long as my husband keeps interfering they will never come to grips with their love. There has to be a way to stop my husband, but so far, I am unable to figure out how. I implore you to help me to help them!"

Golden Dove sighed grimly as she dropped her hands. She grimaced dejectedly and ducked inside her tepee for another sleepless night, not use to sleeping alone.

*****

Raven struggled slightly for a moment then unwillingly at first she started to respond before finally melting against him in surrender. Her traitorous body quivered ecstatically as he pressed her so intimately into his hard muscular body. Her arms crept up slowly and went around his neck then she was kissing him back suddenly, just as passionately.

Golden Eagle groaned deep in his throat in pleasure when Raven responded by kissing him back. He brought his hand up under her shirt and stroked her bare back then he brought his hand around and caressed her breast for the first time.

Raven moaned in desire then pushed against him insistently wanting more.

Golden Eagle pulled back a little and tried to remove Ravens dress one handed, but she batted his hand away then did it herself. He gently lowered her to the furs that were spread out against the wall before straddling her and awkwardly tried to remove his sling that kept his arm at his side.

Raven sat up impatiently to help him then stripped him of his shirt, as well.

Golden Eagle pushed her down gently and laid full length on Raven, making sure to keep his broken arm above her head out of the way as well as his weight off her injured leg. He ran his lips down her neck then continued down her upper chest until he reached her engorged nipple. He gently suckled and licked her nipple before biting it gently.

Raven gasped in pleasure then held his head against her breast in demand.

Golden Eagle lifted his head away from Ravens insistent hands with a chuckle and started kissing his way down her stomach before running his hand up the inside of her thigh. He was extremely careful not to touch her wound. He reached her inner heat then brought his mouth back up to her nipple. He tilted his head wanting to watch her expression as he touched her intimately for the first time.

Raven groaned before raising her hips up encouragingly as he stroked her inner heat. She pulled his head back for another deep kiss. She whimpered against his lips in surprise and pushed against his hand harder as she started erupting deep inside.

Golden Eagle smiled in satisfaction knowingly as he broke the kiss feeling Raven climax hard. While she was recovering, he rolled off her to remove his own pants then loincloth before lying fully on top of her once more.

Raven automatically opened her legs to accommodate him.

Golden Eagle propped himself up on his good arm and looked down at her earnestly. "I want you desperately, but if you say no I will leave."

Raven looked up at his keen expression before ignoring it as she pulled his head down for a demanding kiss. She locked her legs around his without answering him, not wanting any talking at this moment or even time to think. This position pulled at her wound, but not enough for her to release him.

Golden Eagle moaned knowingly in understanding against her mouth then probed with his manhood until he found her opening. He lifted up so he could see her expression as he gave one hard thrust. He stopped in surprise as he broke the barrier telling him that she was still a maiden. The way she had responded to him, he had figured she was not a virgin and his shock was genuine.

Raven cried out in surprise at the slight pain then watched Golden Eagle's expression turn to disbelief. She tightened her legs around him and pulled his mouth down to hers, not wanting any questions.

Without saying a word Golden Eagle obliged her, he sighed regretfully, too late now anyway. The Englishman brought his mouth down to hers for a tender kiss before he pushed his hips against hers.

Raven groaned then lifted up to meet him.

Golden Eagle lost control suddenly as he surged up then ground his hips against hers again and again frantically. He could hold back no longer as the Englishman let go of his control then his seed fill her.

Raven pushed up against him eagerly wanting to feel that rush of intense pleasure once more, as she released her own control too. She would have screamed if he had not fused their mouths together smothering her cries of ecstasy.

Golden Eagle lay gasping for breath on top of Raven. He lifted himself up slightly then looked down at her in apology. "I am sorry if I had known I would have gone slower."

Golden Eagle's words stopped dumbfound when she put her finger over his lips for silence. Raven hushed him still not wanting to think or speak as she whispered wistfully. "Shush, do not say anything right now."

Golden Eagle nodded agreeing fully and lightly bit her finger. Raven jerked her hand back in surprise.

Golden Eagle chuckled at her stunned look then bent over as he kissed her again tenderly. He gently stroked her nipple before bringing his mouth down again. He was quite taken by surprise when he felt his manhood harden inside her as it rose to the occasion so soon. He laughed in delight at Ravens expression when he lifted up to watch her reaction. As his manhood slowly filled her, he proceeded to make love to her once more, but more slowly this time. Finally, both were replete and exhausted they slept curled up together.

*****

Dream Dancer slipped away quietly then went to his grandfathers to sleep in Golden Eagle's bed. He smiled in satisfaction as well as relief at witnessing Golden Eagle and Raven coming together as they let their emotions lead them. He reached his grandfathers tepee then ducked inside to sleep.

*****

Jed and his family wearily dismounted when they arrived at the camp he had wanted to use tonight. He smiled in pleasure as he looked around remembered Giant Bear sitting here with him talking about the white mans customs. It seemed so long ago, almost a lifetime away. He sighed forlornly praying that they would make it in time.

Mell sensing her husband's anxiety came over then put a reassuring hand on his shoulder. "Come to bed now dear, Pat will take the first watch. We have a long day ahead of us tomorrow."

Jed nodded, and a quick camp was made as they all fell into their bedrolls in exhaustion. There was no laughter or joking now they were all too fatigued even to smile at one another.

CHAPTER ELEVEN

Raven woke before the sun was up then slipped out of her blankets. They had ended up in her brother's blankets, which is why the cub had not bothered them. She quickly got dressed, fed the cub a fish and gathered her things. She stood over Golden Eagle watching him sleep for a few minutes before she quietly slipped out of the tepee. She went to the paddock where her stud was then whistled for him. She let him out and saddled him.

Brave Heart snorted then pawed the ground in warning.

Raven turned and saw Dream Dancer bringing the promised packhorse piled with supplies. She turned away then finished saddling her horse. She turned around and took the lead for the packhorse from her brother, before tying it to a loop on her saddle blanket designed for this purpose. When she was done, she turned back to Dream Dancer then gave him a farewell hug before mounting Brave Heart. She frowned curiously, as she looked down at her brother. "Where did you sleep last night?"

Dream Dancer smiled up hesitantly not sure of her mood yet. "I slept in nam'shimi', tepee. I quickly left this morning before they realized it was me, not Golden Eagle."

Raven nodded her thanks and motioned calmly. "You can stay for a few days if you like, but go back no later than a week to check up on the ranch. Make sure you go see how things are progressing with the horses. Get a list from grandfather on what he will need to stay here for the rest of the year. Tell Jake to let you have two or three two-year-old steers, two pigs, half a dozen chickens, eggs, and whatever else nam'shimi' needs. There is a lot left over from last years harvest, so go into the cellar than get whatever is needed. Try not to go to town if you can help it right now. If the sheriff comes back to the ranch, tell him that I am looking into the disappearance of the men from town and I will let him know what I find out when I get back. Tell him to try to stall the townspeople for as long as possible."

Dream Dancer inclined his head without comment then waved goodbye as she galloped away. He never said a word about what he saw last night and she never volunteered any information on the subject either. He turned then headed to his grandmother's and entered when permission was given.

Golden Dove turned to her grandson then smiled knowingly in satisfaction. "Golden Eagle stayed with Raven all night?"

Dream Dancer sighed fretfully; you could not hide anything from his grandmother. "Yes! She just left and was not looking too happy about it. I hope he did not do anything foolish."

Golden Dove beamed reassuringly, glad to hear that. "She is probably just confused; she will need time to think."

Dream Dancer frowned in bewilderment. "Nisgii, I think I will not ever get married or fall in love. It is way too difficult."

Golden Dove chuckled knowingly, not believing that for a moment. "Yes it can be very complicated sometimes, but if you can sort it all out it is worth it in the end."

Dream Dancer shrugged, unconvinced. "Maybe!"

Golden Dove handed him two bowls of porridge, tea, as well as a small jar of honey. "You can take this to Golden Eagle tell him that he can have the honey for his tea."

Dream Dancer nodded then got up to go. He stopped and turned back around to his grandmother. "Oh, I almost forgot can you tell grandfather to give me a list of everything he needs to stay here for the rest of the year. Raven already told me what she wants me to bring. She said to bring you whatever you need since we still have lots left from last years harvest."

Golden Dove smiled gratefully. "I will tell him then we will start a list for you immediately."

Dream Dancer left his grandmother's reluctantly. He was not sure if he wanted to be there when Golden Eagle woke up and discovered Raven already gone. He shouldered his way inside then put the porridge beside the fire pit before adding some kindling to the hot coals. He got the fire going and grabbed the pot then filled it with water. He put it back on a rock in the fire pit to heat and grabbed some coffee grounds then put it in the pot to steep. He put another coffee pot on, but it just had water so he threw in some tea leaves for his friend. When he judged the fire was hot enough, he grabbed the porridge and put it on a rock beside the fire to keep it warm. He got up then grabbed one of the fish to feed the cub.

The cub was eating noisily when Golden Eagle woke up. He sniffed loudly and turned around. He smiled at Dream Dancer sleepily before looking around expectantly. Not seeing Raven, he frowned perplexed as he looked at her brother suspiciously. "Where is Raven, Dream Dancer?"

Dream Dancer sighed unhappily. "She already left to track the kidnappers of your sister."

Golden Eagle scowled angrily. "She did not even say goodbye!"

Dream Dancer shrugged in reassurance. "I would not take it personally, she does not say goodbye very often. The only reason I know is that I had to bring the packhorse to her. Grandma said she is probably just confused, so will need time to think."

Dream Dancer's expression brightened suddenly. "But she did give me permission to stay for another week."

Golden Eagle's frown of disappointment disappeared then he nodded thankfully. "Well that is good news anyway. Do I smell the porridge burning?"

Dream Dancer yelped then grabbed the porridge away from the fire.

Golden Eagle grinned and sat up before tucking the blanket around him.

Dream Dancer handed him the bowl of porridge then poured him a tea. He scowled disgruntled that he had let the porridge burn. "Oh, I almost forgot, grandma sent over a small jar of honey and some tea."

Golden Eagle smiled his thanks and dribbled a little honey in his tea then a little on his porridge. He ate it all, scorched taste or no scorched taste he was too hungry to care.

Dream Dancer sighed in relief at Golden Eagle's calm reaction to Ravens leaving as he grinned enticingly. "If you hurry up and put on your clothes, I will show you something. It should be about the right time, but you have to be really quiet."

Golden Eagle eyed Dream Dancer distrustfully, remembering his passion for playing jokes then nodded as he quickly finished eating. He hurriedly put on his clothes from last night, at Ravens brother's insistence that he hurry up. He would have to make a stop at Giant Bear's and grab his other two changes of clothes. He looked down at the bear cub still eating his breakfast then figured the cub would be awhile yet so they should have time before he needed to be taken out. He followed Dream Dancer out and into the woods.

They walked on a pathway for ten minutes then Dream Dancer put a finger to his lips to indicate that he should keep quiet before leading him into the trees away from the path. They came to a clearing and squatted down waiting, for what Golden Eagle had no clue. A few minutes later Black Hawk came striding into view only wearing a loincloth as well as his moccasins. He walked to the middle of the opening then put down the two things he was caring. He stood still for a few minutes and closed his eyes.

Golden Eagle watched in amazement what could only be called a dance, but one he had never seen before. Black Hawk flowed from one move to the next gracefully without missing a step. He did high kicks, low kicks then a roundhouse kick. He did forward rolls, backward rolls, his hands, and arms were constantly moving at the same time. Every move he made flowed into the next move in a dance like pattern.

Black Hawk took out his hunting knife from the top of his moccasin then redid the dance again. He finished with the knife and took a large stick, almost a pole, from the ground where he had put it. It had intricate designs painted on it then he danced with it, as well. His last dance was done with a tomahawk. When he was finished, he stood in exactly the same position he had started in and facing the same direction.

Dream Dancer touched Golden Eagle's arm to leave, but they both stopped short when Black Hawk spun around then pointed directly at them.

Black Hawk crooked his finger demandingly. "Come out here you two!"

Dream Dancer and Golden Eagle shared a surprised look then left their hiding place and showed themselves.

Black Hawk scowled as he put his hands on his hips impatiently. "Well I am sure I do not have to ask which one of you had the bright idea of spying on me."

Black Hawk stared at Dream Dancer accusingly. Dream Dancer flushed guiltily then looked away first. Golden Eagle stepped forward quickly trying to take some of the blame away from his young friend. "It is partly my fault for encouraging him and it will not happen again, I promise. I am very sorry!"

Black Hawk eyed the two of them then sighed appreciating the confession and let them of the hook. "Your apology is accepted, as for you Dream Dancer I have felt you watching me before. I waited patiently for you to come to me if you wanted to learn, but you never did."

Dream Dancer shrugged slightly embarrassed. "I am sorry uncle I did want to ask, but I was afraid that you would be mad at me for watching you."

Black Hawk smiled then pointed at both of them. "Well since the two of you are together, I will teach you together."

Dream Dancer and Golden Eagle looked at each other ecstatically then grinned and turned back to Black Hawk nodding gleefully. Black Hawk smirked at their identical looks then waved at the ground. "Okay both of you sit facing me, while I explain a few things."

Both walked over eagerly and sat. Black Hawk turned to Golden Eagle. "Dream Dancer already knows some of this, but I will start from the beginning for your benefit."

Golden Eagle inclined his head as Black Hawk waited for his nod of acknowledgement. Black Hawk sighed wishfully as he thought back; missing his aunt so darned much at that moment. "Well believe this or not I learned this dance from a woman sheriff named Mell. She looked after me for most of my young life. Until I was almost ten then my father found my mother and me. You already heard that story from my father so I will not get into it again. But before I left to come to the Indian village, she gave me two gifts. One was the new repeater rifle the other was her knowledge of the art of knife fighting."

Both leaned forward then listened eagerly to everything Black Hawk told them.

*****

Raven rode hard for the next few hours her plan was simple so far. She would ride to the edge of the Bitterroot Mountains and visit the Badger tribe then find out whether Squatting Dog had left on his own, or if Chief Spitting Badger had sent him. After that, she would go into the mountains and look for the Eagle tribe then make sure that they were still at their summer camp. She also had to find out if the whole tribe was involved or if it was just the War Chief Howling Coyote. Hopefully, she would find Golden Eagle's sister there as well, alive.

Normally the trip to the Badger tribe would take a week, but she was hoping to make it in three days. Once there she had to get the chief alone to find out if he had any knowledge of Squatting Dogs activities, without accusing him directly and possibly causing her tribe more problems by starting a war. Afterwards, Raven would ride hard for the Eagle tribe's summer camp, which would take four days of hard riding to reach. Then she needed to get Chief Red Eagle alone to see if he were involved, as well.

Hopefully, with Golden Eagle's sister Janet in tow Raven would cut across the country and get back to her tribe within five days; if Janet was able to ride that is. Therefore, if everything went well, she needed a total of fourteen days with no troubles before she could get back to her grandfathers.

Ravens thoughts turned to Golden Eagle suddenly, but she quickly banished that thought she was not ready to think of that yet. She heard a bark so turned to her right; Bruno was loping along beside her. She smiled down at him then looked behind her shoulder and saw the she-wolf keeping pace, but not getting to close. She grinned down in delight.

"Well I did not think I would see you again, but you are both welcome to come if you want."

Raven bent slightly urging her horse for more speed.

*****

Mell's group broke camp at first light then galloped off.

Pat rode up beside her father inquisitively. "How far is it to the Montana border?"

Jed grinned over at her and sighed thoughtfully. "Three days at the most, two days if we are lucky!"

Pat nodded then fell back slightly. They were still riding in a triangle formation, but after they left the next town and got into the Montana wilds, the pattern would change. They would be in a diamond formation than, with Daniel and Pam in the middle leading the packhorses as well as the white colt. Jed would be further out in front then Pat as well as Jess would take up side positions to protect the packhorses as well as Daniel and Pam. Mell would still be riding behind to protect the rear.

Pam had not liked the idea of riding in the center, but since she had two small children who needed her safe she agreed reluctantly.

Pat's dog Silver Tip was keeping pace with Jed's horse; he would still be there even after the formation changed.

Jed slowed the horses for a while then picked up the pace again once he was sure the horses were rested enough. They rode all day with no problems arising.

*****

Black Hawk finished talking before getting up. He looked around in the bush until he found two sticks the approximate length and weight of a good hunting knife. He went back then sat facing Dream Dancer and Golden Eagle again. "Now take these sticks, I want you to use them for your wrist exercises."

Black Hawk turned to Golden Eagle in caution. "You will have to do the exercises with only your good hand for now, but try exercising your bad one as soon as you can."

Golden Eagle inclined his head in agreement.

Black Hawk passed them each a stick. "Now take the stick in your hand then hold it at the top with your thumb on the end of the stick the rest should be against your arm. Now twist your wrist to the right and left, but keep the stick tightly pressed against your arm. Now twist your wrist in a circle to the right then turn it to the left. Make sure you go both ways completely around in a circle. I want you to twist your wrist around now and bring the stick up horizontally. Now tuck the stick back against your arm. There is another exercise that I want you to do, but you will need to find a longer stick for this one. When you find one, I want you to grasp the stick in the center then twirl the stick on the left and right of your arm. I also want you to twirl the stick between your fingers. You can actually rest the stick on the back of your hand after twirling it through your fingers then flip your hand and catch it with that hand or even the other to continue doing the exercises with your other hand."

Black Hawk watched for a moment then nodded in satisfaction. "Good now watch me closely as I show you what it should look like when you get good enough to use a knife."

Golden Eagle watched avidly as Black Hawk passed the knife from hand to hand. His wrist was constantly in motion, but he never once moved his shoulders or any other part of his body.

Black Hawk put his knife away. "Now put the sticks down and I will give you some more exercises to do with your hands, as well as your wrists. Make a fist then bring it down as far as you can and up as far as you can it should look as if you are nodding. Now open your fist then do the same with your hand open. Always go as far back as you can even if you have to push your fist or open hand back further and hold it there for a count of ten. Make circles with a closed fist as well as an open hand. You want to supple up your wrists so that your knife will go in any direction you want it to. So do these exercises with an empty hand then with your sticks. Now remember most people when they knife fight hold their knife straight out and use their whole body to lunge forward to stab someone. That means their wrist, as well as their arm is locked, so all they can do is stab straight ahead then hope their opponent does not have a longer reach. If you learn my technique, you will find that you have way better control on how deep and at what angle you want the knife to enter your opponent."

Black Hawk paused for a moment remembering the first time he had seen this unique way of training. He grinned as he remembered the awe he felt watching his aunt perform her dance like exercises. He shook of his thoughts than he turned to his students and continued. "Now every person who learns the dance has a different way of doing things, no two dances are the same. For instance, Mell can kick straight up then touch her knee to her nose for a split second. I cannot do that, but I can stand sideways and balance on one foot then control my kick. I start at waist height and bring my foot up higher than go over your head and balance there without touching the ground to do it. So what you two need to do is discover your weaknesses as well as your strengths. You learn this by pushing your body beyond its limits. You have to train your body to go further than it ever has before. Only with practice can you do this. It can take over a year to perfect your dance and at first, all you will be doing is exercises. When you find your limits with all your exercises being done fluidly with no pain or effort than you know it is time to put your own dance together. It took me six months before I began putting my dance together and a year to perfect it, but Raven took less time. I think Raven learned faster because she learned younger. Right from a toddler she would come here then watch me, afterwards we would play at it. Raven can do things with her body that I did not think were possible, when she gets back you will have to watch her dance. For now, I will give you some exercises to do."

Black Hawk turned to Devon sympathetically. "Golden Eagle because of your arm and ribs you will not be able to do all of the exercises at first, but do what you can. Later you can add to the ones you can do now. So, up both of you let's get started."

Dream Dancer as well as Golden Eagle got up then eagerly watched and learned.

*****

Raven slowed her horse then looked around for a likely camp; they had ridden hard most of the day, so both her and her horses needed a break. She reached down then touched her injured leg it hurt like hell, but it was not hot to the touch. Her fever had not returned thankfully, but she needed to stop and change the dressing then take some medicine or her fever could return. She found a good defensible place and made a quick camp.

Raven fed Brave Heart, as well as the packhorse then threw some raw meat to the wolf and to Bruno. She built a fire after her animals were seen to than cooked herself some lunch. While she was waiting for her food, she changed the bandage on her leg and boiled up some medicine for herself. Once done she broke camp then remounted before galloping away.

*****

Dream Dancer and Golden Eagle limped painfully back to Ravens tepee. They went inside then stopped short, they had both forgot about the cub and the tepee was in shambles. The cub had gotten into everything. The furs were scattered from one end of the tepee to the other. Cooking utensils, as well as pots had been dumped then scattered around; the water bucket had also been dumped. Dream Dancer's clothes as well as his packs were all over the place. The cub was sitting in the middle of the tepee bawling loudly.

Golden Eagle heaved a sigh of regret. "Well, I guess this will teach us not to forget about him again. This place is a mess I think we should leave it and take the cub outside now. We can clean it up later."

Dream Dancer nodded with a chuckle then walked over to the cub and picked him up. The cub stopped crying immediately then snuggled up against him.

Golden Eagle laughed in humour. "I think he was just lonesome. Come on and we will take him behind Ravens then you can take him to the creek for a swim while I go for my lessons with your grandmother. We will meet at the corrals later and I will try to get Devil to come to me again, afterwards we can clean the tepee."

Dream Dancer nodded forlornly then walked towards the door. "Okay, I will look after the baby while you are gone."

Golden Eagle grinned at Dream Dancer's put upon expression, but did not feel one bit sorry for him as he followed him outside.

*****

Jed slowed down and looked for a good camp; he spotted one then rode towards it.

Groaning in pain everyone dismounted and a quick camp was made before all of them gathered around the fire to eat some lunch. Once everyone finished eating, they sat around talking quietly as they sipped their coffees.

Jed cleared his throat for quiet as he waved in praise. "Well we are making very good time. We should make it to town almost a day earlier than I had first thought. I think we will be in the border town sometime late tonight if everything goes well and we continue pushing hard. It will still mean riding all night, but since the moon will be almost full, it should be bright enough to see. If we can reach it tonight we will have at least one night in a bed, but I do not want to get there tomorrow then waste a whole day just for a little comfort."

Jed turned to Mell inquisitively. "What do you think?"

Mell nodded thoughtfully unwilling to lose a whole day, as well. "I agree we should try to reach it tonight or we will have to bypass the town."

Jed smiled sympathetically at the groans of distress at the idea of having to avoid the town and their last chance to sleep in a bed for a while. He grinned in encouragement. "Okay let's get mounted everyone then get going."

They hastily broke camp and were galloping away within twenty minutes.

*****

Golden Eagle left Giant Bear's with a sigh of relief. Golden Dove had growled at him for being late then grilled him hard again today; she was still very upset at her husband. He did not know what Giant Bear had done, but he wished the chief would make up with his wife soon.

Golden Eagle carried his extra clothing to Ravens. He had not seen Dream Dancer at the corrals so decided to bring his clothes here first.

He ducked inside then laughed at Dream Dancer who was comfortably sprawled on his blankets patting the sleeping bear cub. He looked around and grinned in appreciation over at Dream Dancer. "Well thank you for cleaning up the mess, your grandmother would not let me leave, sorry I am late."

Dream Dancer smiled not in the least put out by his friends tardiness then got up. "Well I did not have much else to do, so I figured I would clean up the mess while I waited. Black Hawk was here a few minutes ago and said we are to come to the paddocks when you got back."

Golden Eagle inclined his head in agreement then put his clothes in a corner.

Dream Dancer put a fish, a bowl of berries, and a cooked squirrel beside the cub. Golden Eagle eyed the dead squirrel in disapproval. "I thought Raven did not want the cub to eat meat?"

Dream Dancer shrugged nonchalantly. "Well he can't eat just fish; these berries are the last of our winter storage. So he needs something else to eat until the berries are ready again. I cooked the squirrel, so I do not know if he will even eat it. As long as it is cooked he should be all right."

Golden Eagle nodded in agreement, as they left.

Black Hawk was standing beside the paddock watching his mare running around the pen. Dream Dancer then Golden Eagle walked up to him. They stood quietly watched the mare, as well.

Black Hawk turned to Golden Eagle inquisitively as he motioned curiously. "Well how are the lessons going?"

Golden Eagle grimaced unenthusiastically as he gestured in annoyance. "Tough, your mother is mad at your father for something, but she is taking it out on me!"

Black Hawk smirked knowingly as he waved grimly. "I know I can always tell when she is mad or upset because she starts calling me Tommy, she has been calling me by my white name continuously for the last couple of days. That is why I have been staying away!"

Golden Eagle motioned in aggravation. "Don't I know it; she has been calling me Devon too. I wish your father would do something to make up with her before she drives us all crazy."

Black Hawk sighed forlornly. "Well until he tells you and Raven that you do not have to marry I think we will just have to live with her bad mood. I am pretty sure he is not going to do that!"

Golden Eagle looked at Black Hawk in surprise. "Is that what she is upset about? Well I will talk to her later about it."

Black Hawk raised his eyebrows in inquiry. "Oh, are you going to marry Raven now without a fight?"

Golden Eagle shrugged dismissively. "I do not know yet."

Black Hawk frowned at the Englishman then changed the sensitive subject. "Okay today I am going to go in with the mare and see what she has learned. If she is a quick study, she should turn to face me as soon as I walk in. If she is stubborn I might have to run her again, but it should not take as long only once or twice then she should stand. I want you two to come into the pen and bring the noisemakers in, make as much noise as you can. She should stand still faster today. If she does, I am going to put a saddle blanket on her than a bridle also. If she does not take long getting used to something on her and we have time, I will put those two big sacks on her for weight. The sacks are tied together to give her the weight of a person on her back. Plus the rope tied between the sacks is long enough so that the sacks are against her sides. That way if she runs they will bounce against her so that she can get the feel of someone's legs against her sides."

Golden Eagle nodded then watched Black Hawk grab all his things before going into the pen, he watched avidly.

*****

Black Hawk finally finished his training session and beckoned to the two watching. He stood away from the mare as he turned to face them as they walked up to him. "She has had enough for today I am going to walk her around a little before I put her away. Can you take my things to my tepee for me? I will meet you at my mother's for supper after I pick up Gentle Doe."

Golden Eagle inclined his head in agreement. "Sure, I have to check on the cub anyway so we will meet you there."

Golden Eagle with Dream Dancer's help grabbed everything then walked away. They stopped at Ravens tepee first, but the cub was sleeping, so they went over to Black Hawk's.

Dream Dancer scratched on the flap; he waited patiently for Gentle Doe to open it for him. When the flap was lifted, he smiled at Black Hawk's lovely wife as he switched to Cheyenne. "Good evening Gentle Doe, Black Hawk asked us to come and put these things in your tepee."

Gentle Doe nodded then backed away as she held open the flap for them. They ducked inside and put their things in the corner where Gentle Doe indicated that they should go.

Dream Dancer turned to face her then smiled gently. He indicated Golden Eagle making introductions. "This vi'hoI is now called Golden Eagle; he will be your nephew by marriage soon."

Gentle Doe looked at Golden Eagle and smiled shyly. "I hope you will like it here. Raven has been lonely for a long time, so I hope you will make her happy."

Golden Eagle had understood some of what she said, but not all so he turned to Dream Dancer to translate. Dream Dancer obliged his friend as he told him everything she had said.

Golden Eagle turned to Gentle Doe then hesitantly answered her in Cheyenne. "I will try."

Golden Eagle turned back to Dream Dancer. "Please tell her congratulations on having another child and I hope she has a healthy baby."

Dream Dancer translated for Golden Eagle then watched Gentle Doe smile her thanks sadly. He also added his own wishes of good will before they left.

Dream Dancer turned to Golden Eagle and sighed then waved miserably as they walked towards his grandfather's. "Black Hawk and all of us are very worried about Gentle Doe."

Golden Eagle frowned pensively. "She is so tiny no wonder everyone thinks she will not survive."

Dream Dancer nodded sadly then motioned grimly. "The Great Spirit has given the shaman a vision, Gentle Doe will die! The baby will survive it will be a boy."

Golden Eagle shook his head in confusion. "I do not understand what you mean by visions; you will have to explain it to me later."

Dream Dancer smiled enticingly. "If you want I can help you have a vision of your future, although I cannot guarantee that you will have one or even like it. The Great Spirit only comes to us when he so chooses. Except the shaman who can usually get visions when he wants them and will dream as he is sleeping about the future or the past. The shaman says if I want to stay, I could become the most powerful shaman the Cheyenne have seen in many generations. I have seen my future though I am destined to go to England, there is something important that I must do there that will protect my people. When I try for a vision after I go to England I see a future where I will return, I think. Why I think that is because I have seen two women in my future one white than one Indian. I do not know whether I will love them both or only one, but I will meet them. In some way they will affect my life."

Dream Dancer stopped talking for a moment as he shuddered in fear remembering some of his more disturbing dreams lately. Suddenly he waved grimly as he continued fretfully. "When I try to see a vision of my future if I stay here, I see and feel nothing! All I get is a grey wall as if I am no more. No, that is not the right description; it is more like nothing is out 'THERE' at all! So no future is possible, not just for me either, it is as if the whole world is empty. I feel no life anywhere! It has scared me so bad that I must go because I feel that I am the only one who can stop that future of nothingness! You were also in my visions, but I do not know what significance you will have other than marrying my sister."

Golden Eagle frowned in disbelief still not believing in all that hocus pocus nonsense. Suddenly he stopped as he turned to look at Dream Dancer incredulously in shock. "You saw me in your dreams before I came here? That is hard to believe, how long ago did you have this dream?"

Dream Dancer smiled at Golden Eagles stunned expression. "Well my visions still comes in bits and pieces; I do not always know what they mean yet. I had also dreamt about you two weeks before I came here. I saw great turmoil surrounding you as well as Raven. She was holding your hand one minute then turning away from you a moment later. I saw the death of many Indians and white people if Raven turns away from you. Then I saw her death or that is what I thought I saw at the time. A conversation I had with her the other day before I met you made me rethink that scene. She will not actually die physically, but her Indian self will die and she will turn away from her people. I do not know if you will cause this reaction in Raven or if her being forced to marry you will cause it."

Golden Eagle stood there thinking about Dream Dancer's vision then looked at him in surprise at a disturbing thought. "Do you think the shaman had the same dream and that is why I am being forced to marry Raven? If he had the same dream, but interpreted it like you first did about Raven dying could that be why your grandfather is forcing me to marry your sister."

Dream Dancer frowned thoughtful for a moment then nodded hesitantly as he gestured uneasily. "Yes, that is a good possibility. Maybe after they found you he had the same one I did."

Golden Eagle stared at Dream Dancer hard. "So if we go by your dream it could be that since in one part she is holding my hand willingly that we could assume she falls in love with me. In the second part where she turns away from me we can assume that she does not fall in love with me, but is still forced to marry me. So she comes to hate me instead then turns away from her heritage. If we put the two visions together, it would be worded like this. I have to make your sister fall in love with me in order to save her and your people. Is that right?"

Dream Dancer looked at Golden Eagle in disbelief at his uncanny reasoning then waved inquisitively in consideration. "Well yes, I think you could be right. I never even thought of it that way, but are you willing to try?"

Golden Eagle gazed at Dream Dancer pensively. "I do not know! I think your idea of helping me with a vision is a good one. Afterwards, I will let you know."

Dream Dancer nodded decisively. "Okay, but do not say anything to anybody. I am not sure if they will let me if they find out."

Golden Eagle inclined his head in agreement, as they started walking again. They ducked inside both wondering and worrying about what they would find out tonight.

CHAPTER TWELVE

Raven frowned not wanting to stop yet, but it was getting too dark to see. The moon was full, but with so many trees around it did not help her much, so she started looking for a camp. It did not take her long to find what she was looking for; it was surrounded on three sides with only the one side being accessible. She unsaddled Brave Heart then checked his feet and legs before checking his wound. Everything looked good, so she rubbed him down then gave him some oats before turning to the packhorse. She took his packs off and checked him over before wiping him down then gave him some oats.

Not until Raven finished with her horses did she attend to her own needs as she gathered wood and rocks for a fire pit then lit the fire. While it was getting a good start, she went over and grabbed her snares then walked into the bush and set them before heading back to camp to made coffee. She dug around in her pack then brought out the last piece of meat from the buck she had killed the other night. She sliced some up for her dinner and cut the rest in half. She threw some to the wolf than some to Bruno.

While Ravens supper was cooking, she went to check her snares and nodded in satisfaction at the rabbit caught in one. She took the rabbit out of the trap then reset it before going back to camp and skinned it. Raven cut it in half then threw part of it to the wolf and gave the other half to Bruno.

Raven scrapped the hide then rolled it up to be tanned later. She ate her dinner and had a cup of coffee before she got up then saddled the packhorse again just in case she had to leave in a hurry. The only thing she kept out was her coffee pot and the pan with the rest of her supper.

Raven grabbed her bedroll from beside Brave Heart's saddle blanket then made up her bed. After banking the fire, she curled up in her blanket as she went to sleep.

*****

Golden Eagle and Dream Dancer left Giant Bear's together then walked slowly towards Ravens.

Golden Eagle turned towards Dream Dancer hopefully. "Can you take the cub out again? I need to spend some time with Devil tonight before we talk to your Great Spirit."

Dream Dancer inclined his head in agreement. "Sure I need to be alone for awhile anyway to get ready for the ceremony. After you are done with your horse, you need to go to the creek and bathe. Afterwards, put the buckskins that Raven gave you back on make sure that your medicine bag is on as well."

Golden Eagle nodded then turned away and went towards Devil's pen. He went over to the shed that held the feed for the horses then gathered a large armload before carrying it over to Devil's pen. He did this twice more and checked Devil's water to make sure he had enough for the night before climbing up on the fence. He talked quietly to the stud musingly. "Sorry for ignoring you boy, but a lot of things have happened today."

The stallion bobbed his head before walking over then started eating while his master rambled.

Golden Eagle sighed in frustration as he watched the horse eat for a minute. "I hope you do not mind if I talk to you a bit while you are eating. I have a problem you see, I have come to know a few people in this village and I like them. They have accepted me completely, but now I find out that if I do not get Raven to fall in love with me most of them will die. I am not sure if I want Raven to fall in love with me though. I am not sure how I feel about her right now. If I do get her to fall in love with me that will mean I would have to stay here, I do not know if I want to do that."

The stud finished eating then regarded Golden Eagle intently. He did not go any closer though.

Golden Eagle smiled at the stallion and called softly in Cheyenne. "Come here Devil, come boy."

The stud turned away then walked back into the middle of the pen.

Golden Eagle grinned not discouraged as he got down. He went back to the shed to get some oats and the last three apples then went back to the fence and climbed over it. He took three steps then stopped and sat down on the ground. He put the oats as well as the apples in front of him before crooning the Cheyenne song Dream Dancer had taught him.

The stallion slowly walked towards him then stopped just out of reach. He craned his neck and ate one of the apples.

Golden Eagle kept singing as he reached down then picked up an apple and held it out to the stud enticingly.

Devil reached out then sniffed the offered fruit in Golden Eagles hand; he took the apple and ate it.

Golden Eagle kept his hand held out so that Devil could sniff at it.

Devil nuzzled his hand for another apple but then snorted in rebuke when none was offered.

Golden Eagle chuckled as he reached down and picked up the last apple then held it out to Devil.

The stallion ate it and let Golden Eagle feel his nose for a moment before he turned away.

Golden Eagle stopped singing then got up and grinned in satisfaction after the stallion as Devil went back to eating hay. He left the oats on the ground then turned and left the pen elated at having touched his horse.

Golden Eagle walked over to the creek then stripped out of his clothing. The Englishman found a soap root, a clean bandage for his arm, the buckskins Raven had given to him, and a clean loincloth to wear under his buckskins already waiting for him. He unwrapped his arm then looked at it closely. The swelling had gone down some and when he wiggled his fingers slightly it hurt a lot, but not as severe as it did yesterday. In another few days, the swelling should be down a little more than his arm would look almost normal again.

Golden Eagle picked up the soap root and walked into the water then laid back to enjoy his bath. He thought about Raven and about making love to her last night. Just the thought of her made his manhood rise in desire. Was it enough for a marriage though? He sighed unknowingly then started washing himself. Hopefully, he would find out more tonight. He was not sure if he believed a vision would come to him, but it was worth a try. He lay back after he finished washing and looked up at the stars. He still had another hour before they could start the ceremony, so he sighed in pleasure then relaxed.

*****

Jed slowed his horse and turned to beckon everyone forward. When they all got within hearing distance, he sighed in relief. "Okay the town is just ahead over that next rise it should be about midnight when we get there. Everyone stay together then follow my lead. I have not been in this town since the time Giant Bear and I passed this way. The town was only half finished then and pretty wild so be careful."

Mell nudged her horse closer in concern. "I think we should go to the sheriff's office first again even though it is out of our jurisdiction, just to make sure there is no real danger that we need to look for when we leave town."

Jed grinned already aware of her desire to go there first. "I know I had the same thought. Okay let's go, but stay close everyone."

They took their positions, but crowded closer together.

Pat called out in command. "Silver Tip come over here girl, I want you beside me."

The dog waited for his mistress obediently.

Jed nudged his horse into a slow trot to cool them down. As they got closer, he slowed to a walk looking around cautiously. The town was much bigger than the last time he had been here. He noted the hotel on the right hand side and saw three saloons before he found the sheriff's office on the left hand side. There was loud music coming from the saloons, but nothing seemed to be out of the ordinary. They stopped at the hitching rail in front of the sheriff's office then dismounted.

Pat looked down at Silver Tip. "Stay girl and guard the horses."

Silver Tip wagged her stub of a tail then layed down close to the horses keeping a close watch.

Everyone else gathered on the wooden sidewalk. Mell took the lead and the others followed her into the building. She stepped inside then quickly looked around. She had brought her whip with her just in case; she relaxed slightly though as she saw the sheriff asleep behind his desk. In the cell's, there were two men one sitting on the cot holding his head and one was apparently asleep.

Mell walked up to the desk then gently tapped her whip against it.

The sheriff jerked awake and reached for his gun lying on top, but stopped short as Mell laid the whip across the gun before he could get it.

Mell smiled at him calmly. "Sorry to startle you sheriff."

The sheriff looked from her to the rest of her party then glanced back at her and saw the marshal's badge. He lifted his eyes up to hers then raised his eyebrows in sarcastic surprise. "Well a woman marshal, I never thought I would see the day!"

Mell stiffened at his offensive voice as she straightened to her full height. "Well I am sure you will see more of us in the future. I am Marshal Brown and this is my husband Deputy Marshal Brown."

Mell introduced the rest of her family; they nodded stiffly none of them liked the looks of the dirty fat man then waited patiently.

The sheriff smiled nastily at Jed. "How does it feel to be out ranked by your wife?"

Jed's eyes turned hard as he observed the large sheriff; he did not like him one little bit. "Actually it feels pretty damn good. You should give it a try someday."

The sheriff smiled insolently at Mell. "Well I suppose she must be pretty good in bed to convince you to let her be the marshal."

Jed took a menacing step forward, but halted as Mell lifted her hand to stop him. She leaned forward and grabbed the sheriff by the front of his dirty shirt then lifted him bodily out of his chair. "We did not come here to trade insults with you so you will keep a civil tongue in your mouth! Now all I want to know is how things stand in this town and outside of it."

Mell let him fall back into his seat then straightened while she waited for his answer.

The sheriff shrank back in his chair in fear, being a coward at heart he did not like being confronted directly. The fact that the woman as old as she was could physically lift his two hundred plus weight shocked him. "I have no idea what is happening outside of town. I do not go out of the town very often, only when I have to. The town itself is quiet."

The sheriff looked towards the cells and snapped in anger. "Get away from there they are none of your business!"

Mell looked in that direction then saw her son talking to the man sitting on his cot. She turned to the sheriff and motioned warningly. "He is a Pastor so if the man wants to talk to him, it is his right to do so."

The sheriff shrank back again not say anything more.

When Daniel walked back to them, Mell waved to Jed then everyone except Mell turned and left. She smiled at the sheriff stiffly. "We will only be here for one night; we will be staying at the hotel if you remember anything."

The sheriff nodded with a scowl but did not comment.

Mell turned her back on him, but loosened the coils of her whip a little just in case he tried anything stupid then walked out of the sheriff's office uneasily.

Jed was waiting by the door and they quickly mounted then rode over to the hotel. Once the horses were looked after, they all went inside the hotel.

Jed walked up to the counter. "We need three rooms, a meal, and a bath all in that order."

The clerk looked at his badge then nodded nervously. "Sure deputy marshal glad to oblige you. I will have a lady show you to a private dining room while the boys get your things from your horses and fill tubs for you."

Jed inclined his head in thanks then signed the register and flipped him a silver dollar.

The clerk's smile of appreciation was a little friendlier now as he handed Jed three keys then rang a little bell.

A tiny skinny black haired girl with dark brown eyes came trotting around the corner. Her cheeks were sunk in which gave her a rather homely appearance, she halted in disbelief at the sight of them before she turned to the desk clerk. "Yes sir."

The desk clerk waved at them imperiously. "Take them to the private dining room and have tubs put in their rooms then filled. Rouse the boys to help you and to bring in their packs."

The girl nodded assent then beckoned them to follow her.

Silver Tip was hidden behind her mistress; they did not want her to be seen, Daniel, and Pam crowded Pat to keep her dog hidden while Jed kept the clerk busy.

When the girl saw the dog she opened her mouth, but closed it again as Pat held up her finger to her lips for silence. The girl nodded then motioned again and they followed her down the hallway. She stopped beside a door then opened it and waited until they were all in. She closed the door behind her.

Everyone seated themselves quickly. The girl waited until they were all seated then smiled shyly at them inquisitively. "What can I get you to eat?"

Mell beamed back at her encouragingly. "What was your special today?"

The girl sighed wishfully. "Beef stew it smells very good too."

Mell grinned in anticipation as she rubbed her hands together eagerly. "Bring eight bowls of stew, coffee, as well as eight pieces of pie for dessert."

The girl raised her eyebrows in surprise there was only six of them. "Eight bowls and eight pieces of pie are you sure?"

Mell smirked teasingly then waved down at the dog before pointing at her next. "Yes, one for the dog and one for you of course!"

The girl frowned hesitantly unsure then motioned uneasily in fear. "You want me to eat with you?"

Mell nodded decisively trying to put the girl at ease. "Yes, we are on a long trip and we need some information. I thought you might be able to help us, since we will be eating it would be disrespectful of us not to share. Just put it on our room, we will pay for everything before we go.

If the clerk asks just tell him the men want two helpings, also tell him that I asked you to stay here so you can wait on us for the rest of the night. But please do not tell anyone about the dog."

The girl inclined her head in anticipation not wanting to argue, too hungry to care. "Okay, I will be back in a few minutes."

The girl left then Mell turned to her son inquisitively. "Well what did you find out?"

Daniel sighed in disgust. "It looks as if we have another crooked sheriff. The two men in the jail would not give him money for a bribe, so the sheriff locked them up. Both men are brothers and they run the store in town, but that is not the worst of it! Do you remember that gang of bank robbers you took to the capital last year?"

Daniel waited for her nod then continued. "Well it looks like they broke out of jail and are holding up here, plus the sheriff is in with them."

Mell frowned in annoyance then waved in aggravation. "Well just great! Are we going to have to fight crooked sheriff's all the way to Giant Bear's village, if we have to fight all the way there and all the way back we just might not make it home again!"

Jed shrugged then gestured apologetically. They did not have any authority here. "Well what do you want to do? We have no legal right to interfere in Montana. I think we should keep going and at the next stop we can wire the Montana marshal to let him know what is going on here."

Mell scowled dejectedly. "I suppose you are right, but I hate to leave a town in the hands of a crook."

Mell was interrupted by a growl as Silver Tip let them know someone was coming. Pat shushed her as Mell got up then walked to the door. There was a soft knock, so Mell opened it and peered out. She saw the same girl holding a tray full of food. Mell opened the door wider before beckoning to the waitress to come inside; she closed it quickly as she took her seat.

The girl handed everyone a bowl of stew.

Pat took the extra bowl from the girl then put it on the floor for the dog. Silver Tip sniffed it cautiously before eating it. Everyone else dug in as soon as the dog let them know the food was okay.

The girl sat and wolfed down her food hardly even pausing for a breath between bites. She was finished before everyone else, so Mell handed her a piece of pie. The others were just finishing their stew when the girl put her empty plate down.

Mell nodded her suspicions confirmed, just as she thought the girl was half starved. She handed her another piece of pie than smiled encouragement. "The dog does not eat pie so you might as well have this one as well."

The girl beamed in gratitude and the rest of the meal was finished in silence.

Mell waited until everyone was done then having coffee before she turned to the girl enquiringly. "What is your name and how old are you?"

The girl frowned hesitantly unsure why the marshal wanted to know about her. "My full name is Black Rose, but around here they know me only by the name Rose. I will be seventeen in two days."

Mell smiled gently then pointed at her curiously. "And you are Cheyenne as well, are you not?"

Black Rose looked at Mell in stunned surprise. "Well yes, how did you know?"

Everyone perked up at that especially Pam; she was slipping she could not even recognize one of her own people anymore.

Mell frowned thoughtfully then motioned perplexed. "Well it was only a guess at the nation, but I figured you were Indian right from the start. Where are your parents and how did you come to be in this town?"

The girl sighed sadly then shrugged grimly. "I do not know who my parents are! The couple who raised me said they found me beside a dying Indian woman; she told the couple my name was Black Rose and that I was from a Cheyenne tribe in the Bitterroot Mountains called the Eagle tribe. She died shortly afterwards, so the couple took me in then raised me. Last year my adopted parents died so the hotel clerk gave me a job here because he felt sorry for me."

Mell looked at Pam inquisitively. Pam smiled in agreement aware of her mother-in-laws unspoken question. Mell looked at Jed next; he also nodded at the enquiry in Mell's eyes.

Mell turned back to Black Rose as she gestured curiously. "Do you like it here and wish to stay?"

Black Rose shook her head negatively then waved in denial. "No, I hate it here and now a man leading a group of outlaws keeps coming here then tries to talk me into going with him. I keep saying no, but I think one of these days he isn't going to accept that for an answer and will force me to go with him regardless of my wishes."

Mell reached over before taking Rose's hand in encouragement. "Well if you would like to come with us, we are going to the Bear Paw Mountains. I am sure we can find a way to get you to your tribe from there."

Black Rose looked at Mell then at the others in surprise. She turned back to Mell incredulously and shook her head bleakly. "I would like to go, but I have no horse, money, or clothes."

Mell let go of her hand then pointed towards her daughter, Pam, and Jess as she explained. "You do not need money where we are going. As for a horse, we will take care of that. Now for clothes I am sure the four of us women can come up with something to fit you."

Black Rose looked at Mell in disbelief then motioned sceptically. "You would really take me with you! But why?"

Mell shrugged dismissively. "Well we just happen to be going that way. I also hate to see anybody stranded in a town with a crooked sheriff in it and I like you."

Black Rose broke into a giant smile that lit up her face. It hid the obvious gaunt malnutrition look; she was cute when she smiled. She reached out then hugged Mell ecstatically. "Yes I would love to go with you. Thank you with all my heart."

Mell hugged her back and looked at Jed over Rose's shoulder then winked at him. Jed smiled back in delight at being able to help someone in need. Finally, they were in their room and able to relax for the first time since they arrived in town.

Mell climbed into her bathtub after Black Rose finished washing her long hair then left. She lay back with a contented sigh of relief, within moments she was fast asleep.

*****

Jed finished his bath quickly and got out of the tub to dry off. He looked towards Mell then chuckled knowingly as he remembered the first time he had found her fast asleep in the tub. He lifted her out of the tub and put her in bed then climbed in. He cuddled close to her and fell asleep with a loving smile on his face.

*****

Golden Eagle ducked into the tepee then stopped in surprise at the scene in front of him. Dream Dancer was sitting in front of the fire; he seemed to be in a trance, all he had on was a loincloth. His face was painted in different colours and patterns as well as his chest. He sat there rocking chanting in Cheyenne.

The bear cub was cuddled up beside him asleep.

Golden Eagle walked over to the fire then sat down Indian style on a fur that was waiting for him and sat facing Dream Dancer. Ravens brother reached down then picked up his peace pipe. He inhaled deeply on the pipe and blew the smoke into the air then down at the ground before turning his head first to the right and then to the left without hardly slowing his chanting. Without opening his eyes, he handed the pipe to Golden Eagle.

Golden Eagle copied Dream Dancer's actions and tried to give the pipe back. He stopped when his friend motioned insistently for him to draw on the pipe again. Obediently he did so.

Still chanting Dream Dancer got up with a hollowed out portion of antler then knelt down in front of his friend. He proceeded to paint designs on Golden Eagle's face. When finished he picked up another antler and painted a symbol of an eagle on his cheek.

Dream Dancer grabbed a bowl that had intricate symbols painted on it then held it out for Golden Eagle to drink. His friend drank the dark liquid and shuddered at the foul taste before handing the bowl back.

Dream Dancer put it down then picked up the peace pipe once again, he held it out for Golden Eagle to inhale one more time. He took the pipe back satisfied and sat back down in his place then made gestures for his friend to rock back and forth, as he was doing. He closed his eyes then reached out to Golden Eagle's mind to bring him on the vision quest for the answers he was seeking.

Golden Eagle eyes were becoming blurry, so he closed them as he started rocking back and forth slightly. Suddenly the room started spinning faster than faster totally out of control; he could not seem to stop it! He groaned in fear and acceptance at the knowledge that he was dying.

Dream Dancer grasped him abruptly then unexpectedly he was lifted away from himself. He gasped in shock as he felt himself flying away, but not actually moving. He saw himself arguing with his brother and storming out of his ancestral home vowing never to return. Instantly everything changed then he saw himself through a funnel as he became more and more cynical, dissatisfied with his life. Suddenly he saw himself packing to come here; it felt wrong as if he should not have come here yet. However, he was being pulled by another force to go now instead of when it was time. He saw his younger sister packing next, he knew instinctively that she should not have come with him it had altered things.

The scene changed again then he saw his older sister falling out of her saddle and watched his younger sister go into a coma from the shock than die. He moaned in denial, as he was being beat almost to death; he saw the Indians turn and leave. Next, he saw Giant Bear as well as his tribe looking for him as if they knew he was there.

Golden Eagle was lifted again then they were moving through time, suddenly they stopped. He saw a large ranch with lots of cattle and horses than he saw some old Indian women and men working around the ranch. The scene changed again, now he was inside the house. He felt welcomed immediately as if he belonged there. He looked around then saw Raven holding a child to her breast and a little boy looking at the new baby. He saw himself watching pleased with himself then all of a sudden the image was gazed directly at him and smiling in pure joy as if he knew he was there.

With a sickening lurch, Golden Eagle was back struggling for breath in amazement. He opened his blurry eyes then looked at Dream Dancer staring fixedly at him. His eyes were enormous and black instead of dark green. Suddenly they turned dark green again for a bit then black once more as if unsure which colour they should be.

Golden Eagle shook himself irritably, wondering if he was imagining things, but again they changed colour. He frowned puzzled waiting for Dream Dancer to come out of it, but he was still staring at him with a fixed expression unmoving.

The cub sat up unexpectedly and started bawling loudly as he pushed up against Dream Dancer insistently.

Golden Eagle got unsteadily to his feet in fear then dropped to his knees in front of his young friend and shook him anxiously. When he got no response, he slapped Ravens brother in the face then shook him again persistently. A hint of desperation entered his voice as he pleaded with his friend in anguish. "Dream Dancer wake up what is happening?"

Dream Dancer jerked in his arms without warning and went limp against him. Golden Eagle was frantic now as he held him close still calling his friends name urgently.

The cub stopped crying all of a sudden then stared at Dream Dancer intently for a moment before curling back up against him and went back to sleep in unconcern.

Dream Dancer opened his eyes a few minutes later then looked up into Golden Eagle's anxious face. "I am all right now, but that was definitely a close call. If you had not kept calling me, I think I would have been lost and died eventually."

Golden Eagle nodded shakily as he gazed down in relief at his friend's eyes that were once again a brilliant dark green. "I know I had felt the same sensation earlier before you took me with you."

Dream Dancer sighed thankfully then pushed himself up into a sitting position. "I know I felt you slipping away on me. So in desperation I lunged at you and then thankfully was able to catch you before you died."

Dream Dancer reached over and grabbed a pan of warm water as well as a soap root he had waiting. He took the cloth out of the water then put liquid on the cloth from the root before washing his face and chest. He rinsed the cloth then handed it to Golden Eagle to wash his face, as well. He put his head in his hands grimly and shuddered in apprehension. "Did you feel another presence with us?"

Golden Eagle stared at him in surprise having no clue as to what his friend was talking about. "No, I did not! Why?"

Dream Dancer looked up at him in apology. "I think that was why I had such a problem reaching you at first. I am not sure, but I think Raven was with us."

Golden Eagle gazed at him in shock then waved incredulously. "But she must be close to a hundred miles away from here by now! How could you find her and pull her in at that distance?"

Dream Dancer shrugged unknowingly. "Like I said, I am not absolutely sure that she was there. If she was, the only reason I can think of for being able to find her at such a great distance is that I used her when I first started learning how to do this. Since I knew her intimately, it would be easier for me that way, which means if I am right that I will be able to find you now as well no matter where you are."

Golden Eagle shook his head perplexed. "I am still not sure about all of this. How could you take my mind with you as you did?"

Dream Dancer frowned thoughtfully trying to explain. "It is not actually taking you with me that you felt. All I did while you were out seeing to your horse then bathing was to meditate before asking the Great Spirit to help me show you your future. I cannot always control what is shown yet. All I can do is go along and watch that is why we saw past as well as future because I could not control it. Now when you drank the liquid then smoked the distinctive tobacco harvested for these purposes it put you in the same trance that I was in. If you had been an Indian, the Great Spirit would have shown you the vision directly. But since you are not the Great Spirit used me as a guide so to speak, all I did was touch a part of your mind that is responsive to dreams and visions. When our minds touched you were shown everything that I was shown. Over a hundred years ago, shamans were able to read minds as well as walk in others dreams all the time, but slowly we lost the ability. Only a rare few since that time can do what I do; there has not been a shaman able to touch minds in fifty years. When our shaman found out that I could do so, he did not want me to leave. It was not until I reminded him that I was destined to go to England that he relented. Even though he already knew that since he had a dream before I was born that I would be going to England. Now since it has been fifty years since the last shaman could do this we have no idea what to expect or how powerful it will become. Take Raven for example, since I touched her mind five years ago, I have felt her need for me every time she is in trouble or needs me. I am sure that I felt her with us as well as we travelled to your past then your future. Now, since I cannot control my powers yet, it makes it difficult for me sometimes to let go again. I am hoping to find a way to control what I do, but so far, I have not been able to. But for some time now, I have had the feeling that on my journey to England, I will find someone who will help me. I have no idea who this someone is or even whether they are male or female."

Golden Eagle frowned in confusion as he nodded. "Well I understand better now, but I think we should go to sleep and tomorrow we will talk about the vision we had. Right now my mind is spinning; I can't make heads or tail out of anything we saw."

Dream Dancer sighed in agreement then let Golden Eagle help him to his bed, he was still extremely weak. He dropped down onto his blankets and went directly into a dreamless asleep.

Golden Eagle covered him up then went to Ravens blankets; he slept curled up beside the cub.

*****

Raven bolted straight up out of her blankets with a cry of despair. Her heart was racing so fast it felt like it wanted to explode in her chest and she was perspiring heavily. Her breathing was extremely ragged as she gasped desperately for a breath. She grabbed her chest trying to get her heart to slow down it hurt something awful. Finally, the pain eased as her heart slowed to its normal rhythm, so she dropped her hand thankfully.

Dream Dancer had reached out then touched her mind again, but this time it was different. It was so powerfully strong that she had not been able to fight it off even being a hundred miles away from him. She felt another strange presence as well and knew instinctively that it was Golden Eagle. She had sensed her brother's panic when he touched her mind instead of Golden Eagle's then felt his desperate lunge to reach Golden Eagle before he died. She felt relief from Dream Dancer suddenly when she sensed Golden Eagle brought in.

They travelled to England and she watched Golden Eagle's life as an English Lord unfold before her. She also felt the two forces pulling at him then sensed that he had chosen the wrong one to follow. She felt the same as Golden Eagle as she watched his younger sister getting ready to leave, it was wrong she should not have come here.

Next Raven remembered being in front of her house and going inside. She shivered as she recalled seeing herself sitting in a chair suckling a baby then looked over to see Golden Eagle watching her with loving pride. Suddenly she was outside the house and Golden Eagle's presence was gone then just her and Dream Dancer was left.

Raven still connected to her brother flew across the land to a field where she saw herself standing waiting for something. She watched in puzzlement as a rider came towards her then understanding as her dream lover again rode towards her. He swept her up in front of him and she looked fully at him in stunned disbelief, it was Golden Eagle. His hair was lighter than it was when she left almost a silver blonde. His eyes were a stormy grey; she had not been able to see the colour at the village because they were so black and swollen.

Raven felt her brother slipping away but not naturally, as if he were dying then nothing, she sat up in horrified shock. She screamed his name in horror as she tried to find her brother, but not being a shaman she could not of course. Suddenly she got a sense of well being and knew instinctively that he was all right. She lay back down to exhausted to think about what happened or what she had seen that night. Raven went back to sleep, this time with no dreams to wake her.

CHAPTER THIRTEEN

Golden Eagle woke to the smell of bacon frying as well as the aroma of coffee brewing. He sniffed the air appreciatively then turned over and looked at Dream Dancer sitting across the fire cooking breakfast. He sat up then lifted his eyebrows in surprise. "I did not know Indians ate bacon and eggs, I always thought that was a white man's trait."

Dream Dancer smirked in humour. "Well of course we do, if we can get it that is, besides I am part white too."

Golden Eagle chuckled not having thought of that then sobered as he thought of last nights near disaster. He motioned in concern. "How are you feeling this morning? No after effects from last night I hope?"

Dream Dancer shrugged dismissively. "A slight headache, but I took some medicine and it helped some."

Dream Dancer dished out the eggs then some bacon and handed it to Golden Eagle before making some more for himself. While his eggs were cooking, he sat back then eyed Golden Eagle. He pointed over his shoulder in the direction of the small clearing were they had spied on his uncle. "You will have to get dressed as soon as you are finished. We have to take the cub out and meet Black Hawk in the same place we met him yesterday for some more lessons."

Golden Eagle stopped eating then looked at his young friend in surprise. He frowned puzzled as he waved in apprehension. "You are not going to tell your grandfather about the vision and that he must not force us to marry?"

Dream Dancer shook his head negatively. "No, for one thing the shaman will say I am wrong, he will not listen. For another if I tell them what I did last night I will be in very big trouble then probably sent home."

Dream Dancer paused as he smiled reassuringly at the angry Englishman. He waved towards the west in explanation. "But do not worry someone is already coming who will stop the wedding, so just be patient."

Golden Eagle eyed his young friend suspiciously. "Who is coming that can sway your grandfather or the shaman? Why would they believe this person and not you?"

Dream Dancer rolled his eyes playfully as he leaned forward dramatically. He dropped his voice into a whisper mysteriously. "White Buffalo comes!"

Dream Dancer sat back up then laughed at Golden Eagle's dubious gaze and held up his hand to stop his questions. "Not now we will talk about it later, hurry up now finish eating. We will discuss the vision as well as who is coming later tonight."

Golden Eagle frowned pensively at his young friend's melodramatic light-heartedness; he seemed to be taking this too casually. He finally shrugged; Ravens brother was only sixteen after all even though he did seem older at times. They finished eating in silence before getting dressed then headed out of the tepee.

*****

Raven woke early and stretched, she got up then put some kindling in the fire. She blew on the few embers that were still alive until a small flame appeared. Once the fire caught, she made coffee and heated up the rest of her food from last night. While it was heating, she went to get her two snares then smiled in satisfaction at finding two rabbits in them. She took everything back to camp; she threw one rabbit into the trees for the wolf and gave one to Bruno. She did not bother skinning them this time because she just did not have time to waste on scrapping the hides.

Raven went over then fed and watered both her horses before sitting down to eat herself. While she was eating she thought back to the dream she had last night then sighed disgruntled. She should have known not to let her brother stay with Golden Eagle without her there. She was shocked at finding out Golden Eagle was her dream man and angry that the Great Spirit would try manipulating her.

Raven finished then started breaking camp, but her mind kept going over and over the vision. She was confused, who was the second group that had pulled Golden Eagle here at this time. It just did not make any sense. She mounted her horse then banished thoughts of last night and galloped away.

*****

Jed woke to the feel of someone feathering light kisses on his chest. He suddenly felt a wet tongue lap at his nipple and gently bite it. He groaned then lifted his wife up for a passionate kiss. He fondled her breasts before lifting her up until she was lying on top of him. He pulled her up further so that he could reach her nipples and suckled one gently.

Mell chuckled in delight then straddled her husband as she pushed up on her knees and lifted herself up to sheath him inside her.

Jed gasped in pleasure as she sat down on him taking his full length inside her.

Mell leaned back as far as she could to push him even deeper into her depths.

Jed moaned in anticipation then brought his hands up and teased her nipples for a moment before bringing one hand down between their bodies than stroking her bud of pleasure.

Mell panted in excitement as she lifted herself up until she only had the tip of his manhood inside her before sitting down hard. At the same time, Jed pushed up. They both gasped savouring the deep penetration.

Jed stroked Mell's bud harder and faster as she ground her hips against him. He could not take it another minute, so he grasped her hips then pushed her down hard against him repeatedly.

Mell dropped down onto her hands kissing him fervently.

Jed lifted his hips pushing himself inside her desperately.

Mell peaked unexpectedly long and powerfully, which triggered Jed's release as her muscles contracted around his engorged manhood intensely.

Jed pushed into her one last time then they climaxed together.

Mell fell on top of him unable to support herself another minute and laid there breathing heavily trying to catch her breath. She rolled off him finally then lay on her back with a smirk of satisfaction.

Jed rolled over and propped himself up on his arm so he could see her face then laughed deep in delight. "Don't you look pleased with yourself?"

Mell's smile widened mischievously. "Well we have been riding hard the last few days, and we have not once made love since the day we left home. So, I figured since we will probably not see another town for awhile we had better sneak a quick one before we leave."

Jed grinned down at her shamelessly. "I must say you can sneak a quick one anytime you have a mind to, I definitely would not object. But we better get up now before one of the kids comes to go for breakfast."

Jed combed the knots out of Mell's tangled long hair lovingly, savouring every moment. The two of them laughed then giggled as if still newlyweds as each tried to help the other get dressed. They just finished when a knock sounded at the door.

Jed raised his eyebrows comically and wiggled them mischievously with a smug look on his face. "See, I told you someone would be coming, a few minutes ago we would have been both caught with our pants down."

Mell blushed just as Jed opened the door. Pat walked in then saw the blush on her mother's face she rolled her eyes knowingly. "Don't you two ever quit, I could hear you next door giggling like children."

Mell's blush deepened. Pat laughed in delight and hugged her mother. "It's okay mom; I know you two are still children deep in your hearts."

Mell pushed away from her daughter then slapped her playfully.

Pat chuckled cheerfully. "Okay I will not tease you anymore, I promise. Are you two ready for breakfast?"

Jed inclined his head at his daughter, ignoring her banter. "Yes, we are just grabbing saddlebags and heading down to the dining room. Is Black Rose ready to go as well?"

Pat smirked smugly then could not help the humour from entering her voice. "Yes, she is! I already got her a horse, tack, as well as a rifle while you two were busy playing. My clothes fit her as well so she will meet us downstairs."

Mell and Jed looked at each other then grinned at their daughters teasing before grabbing their saddlebags, paying no attention to her mischievousness as they left the room to go have breakfast.

They were close to the dining room when they heard a commotion inside.

Mell hurriedly passed her bag to Jed and rushed directly inside when she heard Rose's frightened cry. She uncoiled her whip in preparation as she rushed in. Rose was trying to get away from a man that Mell knew all too well. "Jimmy, let go of her!"

Jimmy dropped Rose's arm immediately; he gave her a slight push to get her out of his way. Cringing in alarm at that familiar voice, he went for his gun as he spun around. However, he was not fast enough as he felt Mell's whip curl around him for the third time in his life as he groaned in disgust.

Mell held the whip tight as Rose rushed over to them. She walked up to Jimmy then smiled nastily as she shook her head and clucked her tongue in disbelief. "Well we meet again, still terrorizing the women I see!"

Jimmy stopped fighting the whip knowing it was useless then relaxed as he inclined his head in sarcasm. "Well hello there Marshal Brown!"

The outlaw looked behind her and saw Jed then frowned in annoyance. "Deputy Marshal Brown as well, really what a pleasant surprise it is to see you both here!"

Mell grimaced angrily then waved distastefully. "Well I am not sure it is enjoyable, but it is definitely a shock to see you here. How did you manage to escape from jail this time?"

Jimmy shrugged dismissively. "Bah, that was easy!"

Mell scowled in loathing as she uncoiled the whip from around her helpless victim. She had put him in jail three times now and he always manages to escape somehow. She knew there was no point locking him up here since he was in with the sheriff. "Lucky for you, we are not here to look for law breakers, but I will tell you this only once. Leave Rose alone! Now get out of here before I change my mind!"

Jimmy looked at Rose in regret cowering behind Jed. He nodded then left immediately in relief. Mell turned to Rose as she came out from behind Jed and put her arm around her in reassurance. "It is okay now he will not bother you again."

Rose sighed thankfully then squeezed Mell in gratitude before moving away.

Mell gazed at the people staring with one eyebrow cocked inquisitively. The townspeople quickly turned back to their food.

Mell looked around and saw a table back against the wall, so walked towards it as she coiled her whip back up. They sat down then Mell ordered coffee while they waited for the other three. Ten minutes later the others arrived and sat down. They ordered breakfast then sat sipping their coffees as they waited.

Mell smiled curiously at her daughter. "What did you do with Silver Tip this morning?"

Pat waved towards the back of the hotel as she explained. "I took her out the back way our horses are all ready and saddled, so I left her guarding them."

Mell inclined her head in approval. "Good."

Breakfast was served then everyone ate quickly and quietly. When finished eating, Jed went to pay the bill. The rest of them trooped outside then checked over their horses carefully. Jed came out a few minutes later and checked his horse over, as well. After they were all satisfied with the attention the horses had received, they mounted then rode out of town without looking back once.

*****

Golden Eagle and Dream Dancer limped to Ravens painfully. They entered then dropped down onto their blankets in exhaustion.

Golden Eagle sighed dejectedly as he lay back for a moment. "I think your uncle is trying to kill us!"

Dream Dancer chuckled in agreement, but did not say anything. There was a scratching on the tepee flap, so Ravens brother called out plaintively. "Come in."

Giant Bear entered and looked at the two of them lying in their blankets in surprise. He turned to Golden Eagle then pointed at the other end of the village. "The medicine man wants to look at your arm."

Golden Eagle nodded unenthusiastically groaning as he got up.

Giant Bear raised his eyebrows inquisitively. "What is the problem you two? You both sound like a herd of horses ran over you?"

Dream Dancer chuckled uncomfortably as he moaned painfully. "Not horses grandfather, but Black Hawk. He is teaching us how to fight with a knife."

Giant Bear smirked in satisfaction. "Good."

Golden Eagle turned to his young friend hopefully. "Can you take the cub out this afternoon I have to go for my lessons after I see the medicine man?"

Dream Dancer inclined his head resignedly, now the official grizzly sitter. "Okay, I will look after him for you."

Giant Bear and Golden Eagle left then turned towards the medicine man's. The chief looked at Golden Eagle out of the corner of his eye while they walked. "I think you should start talking in Cheyenne whenever possible now."

Golden Eagle shrugged dismissively. "I will try, but I am still not very good at it."

Giant Bear waved encouragement. "We will help you when you have a hard time."

Golden Eagle inclined his head agreeably, but did not say anything more as they stopped in front of the medicine man's tepee.

Giant Bear scratched on the flap and they waited to be let in.

The old man opened the flap then stepped aside for them to enter.

Giant Bear and Golden Eagle went in then sat around the fire.

The medicine man came over and helped Golden Eagle out of his shirt then he unwrapped his arm. He gently probed at the arm before smiling in approval. "The swelling is down and the colour looks better."

Golden Eagle looked towards Giant Bear so that he would translate. He had understood most of it, but not all. Giant Bear told him what the old man had said.

Golden Eagle frowned in concentration then spoke hesitantly in Cheyenne. "Yes it feels um, good."

The medicine man grinned in appreciation at the white man's use of the Cheyenne language and picked up an ointment than started messaging it into Golden Eagle's arm. The Englishman looked at the old man in awe at the tingling sensation of the ointment. "What is this?"

The medicine man smirked in humour at the white man's amazement. "It will help your arm to heal faster. It will also relax muscles so that you can exercise your arm for an hour. Plus, it will absorb through the skin right to the bone and it will help your arm become much stronger."

Golden Eagle turned to Giant Bear to translate. He turned back to the old man when the chief finished then smiled in delight. "It feels good!"

The Englishman wiggled his fingers slightly and sighed thankfully at least he could move them a little more now. The medicine man grinned then re-wrapped it before speaking to Giant Bear. The chief nodded and translated for Golden Eagle. "He said to take the ointment with you then put it on before exercising your arm and hand. Do finger exercises then stretch your arm muscles, but only twice a day and do not over do it yet."

Golden Eagle took the bowl with the cream in it. "Thank you."

The old man inclined his head appreciating his gratitude.

Giant Bear waved him towards the door. "Golden Dove is waiting for you."

Golden Eagle left obediently then went back to Ravens to drop off the ointment. He would feed Devil first before going for his lessons. Dream Dancer and the cub were gone, so he hurried over to the corrals after putting the cream beside his bed. When he came around the corner, he saw his young friend already watering as well as feeding Devil. So he turned away then went for his lessons instead.

*****

Raven looked around and smiled. She was making much better time than she had first thought. The mountains were just ahead; she might actually get to the Badger's summer camp tomorrow afternoon a day early. She decided to stop just ahead for lunch and a short rest.

*****

Jed slowed then looked behind him with a scowl of anger. He might regret taking Rose with them yet. They had placed her in the center with Daniel and Pam because she did not know how to shoot a rifle or how to ride particularly well, so they needed to keep an eye on her. Pat was riding close to her trying to give her lessons on how to handle a horse. Instead of riding in her designated spot to watch for dangers on her side as she was supposed to be doing. He slowed to a walk in disgust then started looking for a camp for lunch. He found a good one a few minutes later and pulled up.

Everyone helped make camp except for Rose; she was sitting on the ground crying.

Jed walked over to Pam then motioned in furious demand. "You will have to ride beside Rose from now on; I want you to help her. Pat is supposed to be watching out for you guys and the packhorses, not babysitting!"

Pam inclined her head in agreement immediately then sighed disgruntled as her father-In-law stalked off angrily. She walked over to Mell and pointed over her shoulder at Jed. "Your husband is very angry about Rose. Can you possible take her aside then talk to her? I have to give her horseback lessons on our way so Pat can ride where she is supposed to."

Mell frowned in annoyance and got up. "I will see what I can do."

Mell walked over to Rose then sat down beside her. She motioned in compassion and asked curiously. "Why are you crying? You can't be in that much pain already?"

Rose sighed dispiritedly then wiped the tears away before shaking her head in apprehension. "No I am not in pain, but your husband has been glaring at me since we started this morning. He is so disgusted that I can't ride or look after myself. So I could not help feeling sorry for myself."

Mell scowled knowingly now furious with her husband. She put her arm around Rose comfortingly. "I am sorry my husband has made you feel bad. Just ignore him, I promise he will not do it again. Now the only way for you to learn is for you to do it. Come with me, we will get your new rifle so I can show you how to shoot it. Afterwards, I will teach you a little about protecting yourself. Pam will teach you about what to look for in edible plants, when we stop for the night. She will also teach you the different medicinal properties of those plants. While you ride Pam will give you lessons on how to handle your horse, Pat can teach you how to identify the different tracks of an animal as well as men then how to draw a gun if you like. We will be teaching you every day while we are stopped, so no more feeling sorry for yourself. Come on let's get started."

Rose hugged Mell gratefully before getting up to get her rifle.

*****

Jed shook his head irritably and sighed, that girl was slowing them down. He could not do much about it though as he watched his wife take Rose into the trees for some target practice.

Jessica brought him over some lunch then sat down beside him to talk. She waved towards the retreating Rose curiously. "You know I have never seen you act this way about someone's inability to do the things you do before. You agreed to bring the girl with us and now you seem to be resenting the fact that you did?"

Jed sighed in exasperation. "I know I agreed, but I did not think she was totally useless either. She is slowing us down way too much!"

Jessica nodded she could see his point, but! She frowned cautiously not wanting him to get angry with her too. "Do you realize that your scowling at her is making it much worse?"

Jed grimaced then shrugged doubtfully. "No, I did not realize that I was making it worse."

Jessica smiled at him consolingly. "Well you are, so try to control yourself. I know we are in a hurry, but if we push the horses too hard or ourselves too much we might end up taking longer to get there because of exhaustion. One day taking it easy will not hurt anything it might even help. Especially when we get to that river you were talking about, we do not want to be too tired for that!"

Jed nudged her playfully calm once more. "And how did you get to be so smart, Jess?"

Jessica grinned in delight as she teased. "I think your wisdom has finally rubbed off on me."

Jessica looked up then saw Mell coming out of the trees. She saw her motion to Pam and they talked for a moment. Pam nodded then turned towards the trees.

Mell turned and stalked furiously towards them.

Jessica grinned devilishly at Jed as she quickly got up not wanting to get in the middle of this conversation. "I think I had better go now your wife is headed this way. She does not look too pleased with you at the moment!"

Jed nodded forlornly then watched Jessica's hasty retreat. He sighed knowingly and turned to his angry wife.

Mell stopped in front of him then put her hands on her hips in demand as she snapped in annoyance. "Well what do you have to say for yourself?"

Jed put his plate down before getting on his knees and put his two hands together as if praying for mercy as he looked up at his wife imploringly. "I am sorry! I promise I will not do it again."

Mell's lip twitched, but other than that her expression did not change. "Do you even know what you are sorry for?"

Jed tried to look utterly chastened. "Yes, I am a bad boy. I promise not to scowl at Rose anymore and I will try to find some patience."

Mell turned to look at Jessica then grinned at her in thanks so that Jed could not see. She turned back with a straight face not wanting to let him off the hook yet. "Well what kind of penance are you going to do to make up for being a bad boy?"

Jed smiled up at Mell innocently. "Well, I guess I could apologize to her and I could teach her how to use the rifle since I am a better shot."

Mell looked down at Jed in outrage then shook her finger at him threateningly. "That sounds a lot like insolence to me!"

Jed bowed down to Mell solemnly. "Sorry mistress it will not happen again. Please do not hurt me!"

Mell could not help laughing this time as she reached out and slapped him for his impertinence. "Oh get up, quit acting like an idiot. Yes, you can teach Rose about her rifle plus you will apologize to her!"

Jed nodded glumly as he got up pretending that the apology would hurt. He finished his lunch in two mouthfuls then brightened as he handed the bowl back. "Okay, but let's get going we can teach her tonight when we stop for the night."

Camp was quickly cleaned up and they were on their way once again. A little slower now as well as a lot calmer than the morning had been.

*****

Golden Eagle walked out of Giant Bear's tepee and headed for Ravens. He went inside then smiled at Dream Dancer and Black Hawk. He spoke in Cheyenne awkwardly. "How are you today, Black Hawk?"

Black Hawk smiled in approval at his nervous use of Cheyenne. He made sure to respond slowly in the same language. "I am doing very well today. How are you? Are you making any progress with your stallion?"

Golden Eagle sighed in disgust then switched to English. "I am just not good enough to converse in Cheyenne yet. I only got part of what you said."

Black Hawk grinned consolingly and repeated each phrase in English then in Cheyenne. Golden Eagle beamed in delight, but kept speaking in English. "I am fine thank you. I am making good progress with my stud. He came up to me while I was sitting in his pen this time. Devil ate two apples out of my hand and even allowed me to touch his nose before he walked away."

Black Hawk chuckled impressed. "Good, today you should try walking up to him. If he stands for you try touching him all over. If he does not let you walk up to him, do not get discouraged just sit down again then let him come to you."

Golden Eagle nodded enthusiastically in agreement. He motioned curiously, as he changed the subject. "Okay, are you working with your mare tonight?"

Black Hawk inclined his head in agreement. "Yes, we were just waiting for you. The mare is already in the corral waiting for us."

They left the tepee and walked over to the fence.

Black Hawk stopped then turned to them in explanation. "I am just going to repeat everything we did yesterday. If she stands fast today, I am not going to introduce anything new to her today. She needs a break for one day, but when you work with a horse you can't give them a whole day off you have to keep at them because they forget easily. Once they are fully trained though you do not have to worry about them forgetting anything."

Black Hawk went inside the pen.

Dream Dancer and Golden Eagle shared a satisfied look as the mare turned to face Black Hawk. Not once did she budge even when the stallion called to her. They picked up the noisemakers then went in the corral.

*****

Raven sighed tiredly as she shifted uncomfortably and slowed her horse; it was time to stop for the night. She started looking for a good camp, but it was another half hour before she found one. It was a little more open than she liked, but it had a creek running through it and it looked deep enough for a bath.

Raven dismounted then unsaddled her horses; she curried them both and fed them. She decided to go fishing first then take a bath before cooking herself something to eat. She rummaged in her saddlebags and pulled out clean buckskins.

Raven walked to the edge of the creek then stripped before looking for a good fishing spot. When she found one, she layed on the ground and put her hand in the water. She pulled out six good-sized fish. She threw one to the wolf as well as one to Bruno. Finding a soap root, she finally immersed herself in the creek with a moan of delight as she washed herself vigorously then got out and redressed.

Raven took her fish back to camp before gathering wood to start a fire. She cleaned then cooked two fish for herself and threw another one to her companions. She set her snares then made up a bed for herself. For the first time in a long while her sleep was undisturbed by dreams.

*****

Jed sighed in frustration Rose was riding better, but she was still slowing them down too much. At least she was not crying and Pam was staying close to her now instead of Pat. His daughter was riding in formation now with her attention focused where it should be. Rose was too inexperienced to ride in the dark, so Jed figured they would stop for the night early. It would give everyone a break, especially the horses.

Jed found a good place to camp with a good-sized creek running through it so everyone could bathe if they wanted. Camp was hastily set up before Jed took Rose into the trees for target practice.

Mell with Pam following went for a bath since they had to wait for their turn with Rose anyway.

Jessica, as well as Daniel was cooking supper tonight since it was their turn.

Pat left to do a little hunting with her dog; she walked away from camp then looked down at her dog. "Track, Silver Tip."

Silver Tip wagged her stub of a tail and put her nose to the ground. She walked ahead cautiously with Pat following slowly. Silver Tip barked suddenly in anticipation; she looked to their right steadily.

Pat spotted the two-year-old buck as he jumped out of the trees startled by the bark. It only took her a second to line up the buck than she pulled the trigger. The buck jumped once before falling dead. Pat smiled in approval at Silver Tip and reached down to touch her dog in praise. "Good girl."

Silver Tip wagged her stub of a tail furiously.

Pat went over then cut the deer's throat to let it bleed, she hoisted the deer up onto Silver Tips back before they turned heading back to camp.

Mell and Pam were just getting back from their bath when Pat with her dog following came into camp with the buck.

Mell chuckled at the pair in humour. Pat always used her dog to carry her kills around for her it looked funny. She grinned at her daughter in delight. "I heard the shot I figured you would be bringing something back with you."

Pat smirked saucily then waved dramatically. "Of course, I never miss!"

Mell hooted in amusement and shook a chiding finger at her in warning. "You are just as conceited as your father is!"

Pat grabbed her chest as if pained then shook her head in denial gleefully. "No way! Nobody could top dad for conceit."

"I heard that comment squirt!" Pat and Mell turned to see Jed walking towards them with Rose. Pat put on an innocent look then motioned decisively. "Only stating fact dad you would not want me to lie now would you, especially with a pastor around."

Daniel broke in indignantly with a laugh as he put up both hands in surrender. "Do not get me involved in this Pat this time you are on your own."

Pat stuck her tongue out at her twin. "Spoil sport."

Pam grinned at Pat and took pity on her as her twin refused to back her up. She winked at her then changed the subject to help her out of a tight spot. "Well if you do not have any objections I would like to confiscate your buck to show Rose how to skin and dress a deer. If you do not have any use for the hide, I will use it to make Rose a pair of her own buckskins."

Pat inclined her head agreeably then pointed at her father and volunteered him. "Okay, I am sure dad would be nice enough to carry the deer over to the trees out of the way for you. But you will have to give the intestines to Silver Tip here since she shared in the kill."

Pam nodded pleased. "Okay I have no objections to that."

Jed gave his daughter a dirty look for suggesting him then grinned good-naturedly and hefted the young buck onto his shoulders. He turned to Pam then swept his hand in front of him dramatically. "Lead on Ma'am."

Pam smiled at his teasing and led the way with Jed then Rose following her.

Mell beamed at her daughter enticingly. "You should go have a bath it is very refreshing."

Pat rubbed her hands together gleefully. "Sounds like a good idea to me."

Jessica broke in hopefully. "I will go with you too, I am sure Daniel can watch supper on his own."

Daniel sighed dejectedly with a long-suffering face. "Go you two; I can handle things if I have to."

Pat and Jess grinned at each other then turned sprinting for the creek with Silver Tip running beside them barking ecstatically.

Mell and Daniel grinned at each other as they heard the girls whooping in delight than a giant splash as they jumped in, clothes and all.

Mell sat down to help Daniel watch supper. She poured herself a coffee then smiled up at Jed as he walked over and sat down beside her. She poured him a coffee, as well. Jed nodded his thanks. Mell looked at him intently as she picked up her own coffee. "How long will it be until we reach the river that you were talking about earlier today?"

Jed frowned grimly then shrugged thoughtfully. "I was hoping to reach it tomorrow early. So we could cross in the daylight and camp on the other side tomorrow night. But since we had to slow down, we will not reach it until sometime after dusk. I definitely do not want to cross it then, so we will have to camp on this side and cross in the morning."

Mell nodded thankfully. "That means we will be stopping early again. Good, we need one more easy day before we get into Blackfoot country."

Jed scowled warningly in caution. "Fording that river is not going to be easy especially with an unbroken stallion as well as a novice rider."

Mell reached over then took his hand reassuringly. "We will make it okay do not worry so much."

Mell turned as she watched her daughter and Jessica sneaking up behind Daniel suspiciously. They smiled mischievously at Mell then Pat called out hastily. "Silver Tip, shake!"

With that command, the massive longhaired black dog, that had also been swimming shook her whole body vigorously. Water went flying everywhere. Not only did Daniel get soaked, but Mell and Jed got wet also. Daniel then Jed jumped up in outrage as they charged after the laughing girls.

Mell stayed where she was as she shook her head in exasperation after the four of them; they were always playing tricks on each other.

Rose walked over and handed Mell a large roast. Mell nodded her thanks then grabbed a spit before skewering the meat as she put it over the fire to cook. Afterwards, she handed Rose a coffee when she sat beside her. "How are you doing so far?"

Rose grinned in pleasure as she motioned in excitement. "I am doing well; I hit the target once already. I helped Pam skin and dress the deer, but I already knew how before. She described what parts the Cheyenne used though as well as what they were for it amazes me that they can find so many uses for everything; they do not throw anything away."

Mell chuckled at Rose's bemused look as she reached over then turned the spit before grabbing the coffee pot and refilled their coffee cups. She turned back to Rose then nodded in agreement. "Yes, they use almost every part plus most of their food as well as their medicines are harvested as they move from one camp to the next. It is amazing to watch them. Where you and I would starve or die of thirst, they can find enough food or water to feed several families. Until the white man came; now their lives are changing, I am afraid it is not for the better either."

Rose gestured gratefully. "I am so glad that I came with you, I have learned a lot already. But your husband is still a little upset because I am slowing you down a lot, I can see it in his face."

Mell smiled consolingly then waved in warning. "We will make up the time after we get across the river, once you have a couple more days of riding. Do not worry too much about it; we all needed a couple days of rest, so you actually helped us."

Mell sat up and stirred the stew then turned the spit. She called out loudly. "The stew is ready, come and eat everyone."

They all gathered around to eat then afterwards they all fell into their blankets in exhaustion. They were all in better spirits to finish the rest of the gruelling journey ahead.

*****

Golden Eagle followed by Dream Dancer left Giant Bear's tepee and headed for Ravens. He looked sideways at his young friend. "How is your headache?"

Dream Dancer shrugged irritably. "It is still there, but not as bad as this morning. I will take some medicine then take the cub out while you go see your stallion."

Golden Eagle frowned in worry concerned that the headache was lasting so long. "Okay, but afterwards I think we should talk about what happened last night."

Dream Dancer sighed unhappily, as he nodded before fidgeting uneasily. "Yes I know, I have thought of nothing else all day. I am looking forward to it one moment and dreading it the next. There is going to be a lot of truths come out that I have been forbidden to talk about, but now I think I must."

Golden Eagle looked closely at Dream Dancer as he frowned knowingly. He had already guessed at some of the truths that had to be told, but he did not tell his young friend that. He figured he would allow him to tell them in his own time. Just before reaching Ravens they split up. Dream Dancer went in as Golden Eagle continued on to feed his horse.

*****

Golden Eagle walked back to Ravens an hour later with a smile of satisfaction on his face. He went inside then grinned at Dream Dancer sitting on his blankets patting the cub. He sat down across the fire from his young friend and sighed in contentment. "Devil would not let me walk up to him or touch him, but after I sat down he came over then ate the oats out of my hand again."

Dream Dancer nodded satisfied and grinned encouragement. "Good you are still making progress; maybe tomorrow he will let you touch him."

Golden Eagle beamed eagerly. "I hope so."

Golden Eagle reached out then accepted the tea with a smile of thanks.

Dream Dancer pointed at the bowl on the ground enticingly. "Do you want me to put some ointment on your arm so that you can do exercises while we talk?"

Golden Eagle inclined his head in thanks. "Please it sure feels good when it tingles."

Dream Dancer smirked knowingly, but he did not tell his friend what it was made of or he would never let him put it on him. He got up and helped Golden Eagle with his shirt then took off the bandage and examined his arm critically. He nodded pleased with how fast the Englishman healed as he looked at him in praise. "Most of the swelling should be gone in three or four days, but it still will not be fully healed. So you will have to be careful you do not over do it too soon, after the swelling goes down it is very susceptible to breaking again. It will take another two weeks before you can use it fully. After the swelling goes down, I will get some flat sticks to brace it for you. That way you can use your hand, but will not overdo or strain the arm. It will also pad it just in case you hit it or something falls on it."

Golden Eagle nodded as he watched his young friend gently apply the ointment. Dream Dancer carefully massaged the ointment in as Golden Eagle watched him concentrate deeply on what he was doing. He was such an earnest young man, but he still had a mischievous nature at times, which was good.

Golden Eagle felt the tingling start then looked down at his arm in astonishment at the warm feeling spreading through it. He looked at Dream Dancer in awe as he saw him chanting something under his breath as he continued massaging the arm. The warmth travelled from the tips of his fingers all the way up his arm past his elbow and up into his shoulder.

Dream Dancer sat back feeling slightly light headed then stared at Golden Eagle's arm in shock, what had he done!

Golden Eagle eyed him pensively in amazement. "What did you do?"

Dream Dancer looked at his friend and shook his head flabbergasted. "I am not sure; I was massaging your arm when I felt this need to chant. I felt heat enter my hands suddenly as I chanted then slowly seep from them into your arm."

Golden Eagle wiggled his fingers and slowly moved his wrist around. The swelling was totally gone there was still some pain, but nothing compared to earlier. "It feels better not completely healed though, but like I have had the break for five weeks instead of three."

Dream Dancer stared off into space thinking aloud as he mused reflectively. "They say that over a hundred years ago a medicine man could heal by touch alone. I never believed that of course there is too much white blood in me for full belief of all Indian legends. Now I am not so sure, when I first learned that I had powers greater than any other shaman alive did right now, I was scared out of my mind. I hated it that the Great Spirit would choose me for this terrible burden. It would be so easy to misuse my gifts if you want to call it that. As each gift gets stronger or new powers reveal themselves, I get more and more frightened. I can touch minds now even at immense distances. I can predict storms before they happen now I can heal, as well. What will happen next? I do not think I want to know! What will I do if someone finds out, especially white people? They will try to use me!"

Golden Eagle gently turned Dream Dancer's chin towards him, so he was looking at him. "Nobody can use you unless you want them to. The things you can do are a gift; do not ever think they are not. It will be a tremendous responsibility to use your gifts for good, but the Great Spirit would not have given them to you if he thought you were not strong enough to handle them. Fear is a natural emotion, always remember that if you are frightened of something you will use it more cautiously, which is a good thing. The only time you want to be truly scared of your gift is if you actually lose your fear of using it. When that happens, you could use your gift without thinking then maybe hurt yourself or others. That is when you had better start being terrified because you will be dangerous to yourself and to others. Try to remember to think of every outcome that could happen if you do use your gift for something. Take healing me for instance. Think of what the consequences could be the medicine man or shaman could find out about it so make you stay here. Or, since my arm is now better, I could try to escape. I will not of course, but what I am trying to do is to get you to start thinking about all possible consequences. If you did this to a stranger when there are others around the story will spread then you would have a line up of people wanting to be healed. So I want you to think of what will happen before you do it, always remember that God makes things happen for a specific reason. So, for you to interfere would be terribly wrong. Listen to your inner voice or your Great Spirit, they will guide you so that you will know when to use your power, as well as when not to. I think you should rethink what you are taking in school as well if you become a doctor instead you can get away with healing a little as long as you are extremely careful."

Golden Eagle was surprised and pleased when his young friend hugged him fiercely.

Dream Dancer smiled gravely as he pushed himself away. He looked intently at Golden Eagle his face earnest. "Thank you! Now I know why you would be important to me, as well. I will never forget your words of wisdom."

Golden Eagle frowned solemnly. "Remember no matter where I am if you need me, I will come to you."

Dream Dancer nodded ecstatically as he took out Golden Eagles knife then cut his palm. He took Golden Eagle's good hand and cut his palm also. They clasped hands to blend their blood than Dream Dancer vowed indisputably. "We are now blood brothers if you ever have need of me, I will come to you!"

Golden Eagle repeated the words and they embraced once more.

Dream Dancer got up then found two soft hide cloths. He wrapped his hand and walked over to wrap Golden Eagle's before cleaning off the blade then gave it back. He sat back down across the fire and took out his peace pipe as well as his tobacco then filled the bowl. He took a stick from the fire and lit the pipe. He inhaled deeply then blew the smoke into the air and at the ground before turning to blow smoke to the right then left before passing the pipe to Golden Eagle.

Golden Eagle copied his young friend and they sat back to enjoy the rest of the pipe in silence. When the pipe was smoked, Dream Dancer sat forward then looked at Golden Eagle intently. "Everything I say must stay between us, I'm not supposed to tell you any of this and if grandfather finds out I will be in big trouble. After the vision that we had last night though, I concluded that the Great Spirit wants you to know. You are going to be angry with me after I tell you this, but I want you to remember that I never actually lied to you. I just did not tell you everything! My full English name is Edward William Charles Summerset the third; I am the person you came to see. Raven is Lady Raven Paulina Summerset. We are Earl Summerset's grandchildren."

Dream Dancer had watched Golden Eagle's expression closely. He was surprised to see no change.

Golden Eagle smiled knowingly. "I figured that out the second day we met; we have three different portraits of your grandfather at home. You are the spitting image of him, especially with those unmistakable Summerset eyes."

Dream Dancer relaxed with a sigh of relief. "I am sorry I did not tell you right away. I wanted to, but my sister would not allow it!"

Golden Eagle frowned thoughtfully then waved in bewilderment. "I understand completely, your grandfather threatened to cut my tongue out if I talked about the reason I came here. Although I am not sure why anyone but me, would care."

Dream Dancer motioned curiously. "Why did you come here?"

Golden Eagle shrugged dismissively. "I came to sell my land, but because of the conditions of my grandfather's will I have to live on the property for one year before I can sell it. A man named Jed Brown from Dakota wants to buy it."

Golden Eagle stopped short at the stunned look on his young friends face. "What is the matter? What did I say?"

Dream Dancer sighed in disgust. "Now, I know what the vision meant by two forces pulling you here. One was the Great Spirit, but he was not ready for you yet. My guess would be since your younger sister was supposed to die that you were not to come here until after she passed on. Your second sister is still a mystery she might have been fated to come, but we will not know until later. My grandfather must have asked the Great Spirit to help him find someone for Raven, for whatever reason. Once the shaman found you, my grandfather would have asked his blood brother to contact you and bring you here. That is the second force pulling you here before your time."

Golden Eagle shook his head in confusion. "I do not understand if the Great Spirit showed me to him why would it be too soon for me to come? Why would the Great Spirit show him the vision if he did not want him to contact me yet?"

Dream Dancer frowned anxiously. "It is hard to explain, but I will try. The Great Spirit does not always give us visions that are supposed to be acted on. Sometimes he just gives visions for reassurance that a way has or will be found, so let us use you as an example. My grandfather wants to help Raven find a husband, so he asks the Great Spirit if someone is out there who will love her. The Great Spirit gives him reassurances by showing the shaman you, this is not to be acted on, but grandfather had heard about you before somehow probably from my father. So instead of letting things progress naturally he decides to interfere by getting Jed to write to you to get you here now. If things had progressed naturally it might have gone something like this. In the vision, we saw you argue with your brother then you vow never to return. Next, we saw you becoming more and more dissatisfied with your life. I bet that you were already thinking about the property that you owned down here as an escape from your life in England?"

Dream Dancer saw Golden Eagle nod in agreement then continued in satisfaction, he was on the right track. "The only thing probably holding you in England was your sisters. So the Great Spirit is already finding ways to bring you and Raven together. If you would not have gotten that letter your sister would have probably died at home, that would have been the last straw for you. You would have come here on your own. Now do you see what I mean by two forces? Both were well intended, but ended up contradicting each other. So if what I think is true the Great Spirit had to find a way to fix things. Since your sister was fated to die on that day, he had to find a way to make it so. Although we do not think about it much, when it is our time to pass on, we have no choice. So the Great Spirit uses the War Chief Howling Coyote to complete his plan. Now though other deaths will happen if things are not set right. The only way to put things right is for you to fall in love of your own free will with Raven, not by force!"

Golden Eagle shook his head sadly. "I do not think our falling in love will fix everything now. I think it has gone too far for such a simple solution."

Dream Dancer smirked then motioned in reassurance. "I know, but remember when I said White Buffalo comes."

Golden Eagle inclined his head thoughtfully. "Yes, you said you would explain it to me later."

Dream Dancer grinned in delight. "Well do you remember Black Hawk talking about that woman sheriff who taught him how to fight with a knife?"

Golden Eagle shrugged in confusion. "Yes why?"

Dream Dancer chuckled at his obtuse friend. "That is White Buffalo, she also happens to be married to Jed Brown. The good part to all this is that White Buffalo is no longer a sheriff, but is now thankfully a marshal."

Golden Eagle sighed in relief now understanding where this was going. "Oh I see, so she is going to come here and help fix this mess we find ourselves in?"

Dream Dancer nodded hopefully then waved in warning. "Yes, but not just her! It is going to take a combination of Raven, you, and the marshal to set things right again."

Golden Eagle frowned thoughtfully before finally inclining his head in agreement. "Okay, I will do my part. I am not sure if I will love Raven yet, but I am willing to try it now. So tell me about this ranch we saw in the vision."

Dream Dancer smiled reassured then they talked long into the night about Ravens plans for the ranch as well as what adding his property to hers would do for the future of both of them.

CHAPTER FOURTEEN

Jed rolled out of his blankets at dawn. He stretched and yawned. He looked over at the fire pit; Rose was making breakfast already. He slipped behind some trees so that he could do his business in isolation then went to the creek with a pan and filled it with water to shave with. He gave his face a quick wash once he was finished shaving then went over and hunkered down beside the fire. He grinned at Rose as he took the coffee she handed him. "Good morning, how are you feeling this morning? Not too sore I hope?"

Rose shrugged negligently. "I am a little sore, but not too bad right now."

Jed nodded pleased then motioned enticingly. "That is good as soon as we finish eating breakfast we will go out and practice with your rifle a little."

Rose inclined her head agreeably. "Okay, I found some flour in one of the packs, so I made crapes with bacon for breakfast."

Jed smiled in delight as he rubbed his hands together eagerly. "Sounds good to me, I love crapes."

Rose dished him up some then handed him the plate. She saw Mell and Jessica coming, so she made up two more plates. She beamed proudly as she handed one to each of them then poured them a coffee. Daniel and Pam came next then helped themselves to coffee while Rose dished them up some breakfast, as well. Pat was the last one and smiled her thanks as she sat down then ate with gusto. She fixed herself up a plate and gave the extra's she cooked to the dog. There was absolute silence as they all scraped their plates clean.

Jed finished eating first then he sat back with more coffee. "Well we will take it slow today and tomorrow we will cross the river. Rose, can you swim?"

Rose looked up then sighed dejectedly. "A little, but not very well I am afraid."

Jed nodded thoughtfully and pointed at his daughter-in-law. "That is okay a little is better than nothing. I think what I will do is double you up with Pam. I will take the packhorse across. Mell you can take the white colt since he has never had to cross water before and your horse is used to unbroken horses. Daniel you can keep leading your packhorse. Pat I want you as well as your dog to go first then scout the area before we cross."

Everyone murmured assent, so Jed got up and motioned to Rose. "If you are ready we can start your lessons now."

Rose jumped up enthusiastically then went to get her rifle.

Mell watched them walk away with a laugh of humour; she used her thumb to point at her retreating husband. "Have you guys noticed that your father has managed to get out of cooking and washing dishes since we started this trip?"

Pat chuckled knowingly as she waved in disbelief. "Of course, you did not really expect him to cook or do dishes did you!"

Everyone laughed.

Pam got up then volunteered. "I will do the dishes and Daniel can help me while you guys start breaking camp."

Daniel grumbled good-naturedly at his wife as she volunteered him for the job. The others chuckled at Daniel's exasperated expression then they all got up to get ready to leave.

*****

Raven woke and got up to make coffee before reheating her fish from last night for breakfast. She checked her snares while she waited and threw a rabbit to the wolf as well as one to Bruno then put her snares away. She fed both her horses and went over to eat. She was just sitting down on her blankets when Bruno growled a warning then looked off to her left.

Brave Heart called out a challenge to the horses being led into camp by two men.

Raven snapped her fingers in demand as she called Bruno over to her. "Lay down here boy and watch."

Bruno lay close beside her blankets obediently then watched the approaching men closely, but without anymore display of hostility.

Raven got up with her rifle and cocked it in preparation before cradling it in her arms. She smiled in relief when she recognized Chief Spitting Badger as one of the Indians. She released the hammer on her rifle then dropped her arms, but still held the rifle unsure why they were here. What luck though to find him here!

Raven clasped arms with both men in greeting silently before waving in invitation for them to sit and offered them the rest of her fish. While they were eating, she went over to her packs. She took out her pipe than tobacco and walked back over to the fire to make fresh coffee. She sat back as she filled her pipe then lit it as the men finished eating. She passed the pipe to the chief to begin the ceremony if Raven had stumbled into their camp instead the chief would have used his pipe. As the next influential person, it was passed back to her, and finally it was passed to the warrior.

Ravens status as an Indian was kind of a mystery even to her. The Cheyenne considered her just a notch below a chief, but more powerful than a shaman or medicine man. She had never figured out why. After the ceremony was finished and the pipe smoked, Raven turned to the chief pensively. "Chief Spitting Badger I was just coming to your village to talk to you."

The chief nodded knowingly his face impassive. "Yes, the shaman saw the Raven coming on a matter of great importance to be discussed in private, so he advised me to come to you instead."

Raven masked her surprise quickly; it was not good to express your feelings openly to an Indian. They considered it a sign of weakness.

Spitting Badger frowned solemnly. "I know why you have come to see me Raven of the Wolf tribe, 'Protector' of her people."

Raven sighed in relief then waited patiently for the chief to go on.

Spitting Badger grimaced angrily for a moment. Suddenly his face became expressionless once more. "At the time of the last new moon one of my warriors went out to hunt, he was not seen again. Squatting Dog has not returned in all this time. The shaman had a vision two nights ago about how he died, he also said that you would be coming. So the answer to your question is no; I did not have anything to do with the massacre of the white people the shaman saw in his vision."

Raven nodded in relief, with only a slight lift of her lips to show her pleasure, but that was all the emotion she showed. She motioned in praise as well as reassurance. "That is good; I know you have been approaching my grandfather to join our winter camp. I will tell him that you did not have anything to do with it so he should let you come next winter."

The chief inclined his head relieved before accepting more coffee.

Raven excused herself and went over to her pack then took out the rabbit skin she had scrapped the other night. She also took out a set of the grizzly claws and one of the eyeteeth as well as two molars of the grizzly she had killed. She walked back then nodded at the chief in appreciation. "Thank you for coming all this way to see me. I have gifts for you both, although you will have to ask your wife to finish tanning one gift."

Raven gave the chief the claws and teeth from the grizzly. She then gave the warrior the rabbit hide.

The chief waved in pleasure pleased with the gifts before frowning disgruntled. "The Raven is extremely generous, but I did not bring a gift for the 'Protector'."

Raven nodded solemnly at him, not in the least upset over that and motioned the apology away. She knew though that she would have to help him keep his dignity by telling him that he had given her a gift of immense importance to her. "Your coming here to meet me was worth more than the gifts I gave to you. May your journey be short and without hardships!"

The two men rose then Raven clasped arms with both men, the chief first of course. They turned towards their horses, but only went a few steps when the chief stopped suddenly and said something to the warrior. The brave trotted to their horses immediately then took out something from the chief's saddle and turned back. He hurried over then handed something to Spitting Badger.

The chief walked back to Raven gravely. "I do have something for you."

The chief held it out to Raven impassively; it was a rifle with a fringed carrier.

Raven pulled the rifle out to inspect it dutifully and nodded solemnly in approval as well as acceptance. "It is beautiful!"

The chief's lip curled in a semblance of a smile that is all the pleasure he would show at Ravens approval. "It is the new Winchester rifle I traded for it yesterday with a vi'hoI."

Raven inclined her head in appreciation. "I will treasure your gift always, thank you."

The chief nodded satisfied that he had given a gift worthy of her position so was no longer shamed then left.

Raven frowned thoughtfully as she watched them go. A white man! What white man? She had not asked him, knowing that the chief would not know what the man's real name was. It was not good when the whites started selling the Indians rifles; it only meant trouble to come. She shrugged there was no use worrying about it now.

Raven turned away and swiftly broke camp. Before mounting, she wrapped her new rifle up since she had no bullets for it then stowed it on her packhorse and mounted. She headed towards the Eagle's summer camp next in relief, now way ahead of schedule.

*****

Dream Dancer left his grandmother's tepee with two bowls of porridge then walked towards Ravens and slipped inside. Golden Eagle was already awake making coffee. He smiled good morning then handed Golden Eagle a bowl of porridge. "How is your arm today?"

Golden Eagle wiggled his fingers experimentally. "Better today, but it swelled up slightly during the night so is still a little sore. I do not think

I should use it too much yet. Can you re-wrap it for me please I would not want anyone to see it yet."

Dream Dancer frowned thoughtfully wanting to see if he could do it again as he helped the Englishman with the bandages. "I will put more ointment on it tonight and see what happens."

Golden Eagle inclined his head eagerly as his young friend finished before stepping back. "Okay, but we are running late, so we better hurry to the clearing for our lessons. I think we should take the cub with us; he can play in the field while we work."

Dream Dancer chuckled impressed. "That is a good idea I never thought of that."

Golden Eagle smiled at his young friends praise, but did not comment as he asked in concern. "How is your headache any better this morning?"

Dream Dancer sighed forlornly. "Yes it is better, but unfortunately, it's still there."

Golden Eagle scowled in anxiety then motioned in dismay. "Should you have a headache after all this time?"

Dream Dancer frowned thoughtfully slightly worried himself. "I don't know. I think I just strained myself a little bringing both of you with me at the same time; I have never done that before. When I healed you last night it made me slightly light headed as well, so that could be why it is still there!"

Golden Eagle nodded uneasily before grinning at an idea. "Well if it is not gone by tomorrow you should go see the medicine man. Or better yet maybe you should try rubbing some of that ointment on your temples tonight after you do my arm; the heat from healing me might help you as well."

Dream Dancer inclined his head in approval. "Good idea, okay I will try that tonight."

They continued eating in silence.

Golden Eagle watched the cub eat his breakfast and looked over at his young friend curiously. "I forgot to ask you last night about the cub. He was acting weird after you had the vision. When I came out of the dream, you were staring at me fixedly, still as a statue. The cub jumped up suddenly then started crying loudly, that is how I knew you were in trouble. I got up and tried shaking you, when that did not work; I tried slapping you. You jerked in my arms then fell back with your eyes closed. I called your name constantly trying to help you come back from wherever you were. The cub stopped crying unexpectedly and just stood staring intently at you. After a few minutes, he curled back up against you then went back to sleep. Why did he do that? Was it my imagination or did he help you some how?"

Dream Dancer shrugged pensively; he could only speculate of course. "The bear was our spirit animal at one time. We were called the Bear tribe before my Cheyenne grandfather on my father's side died, but when they joined us, we became the Wolf tribe. The Great Spirit finds us through our spirit animals that is why I told you to make sure you had your medicine bag on. It helped the Great Spirit to find you and me when it was time. The Great Spirit often uses real animals to give messages or warnings. Sometimes your spirit animal will show up at your greatest hour of need, take the cub for instance. If the Great Spirit knew I would need extra help in the future, he could have gotten the she grizzly to sacrifice her life in order for Raven to bring the baby cub here. So that when I was in trouble the Great Spirit could help me through him."

Golden Eagle sighed dejectedly. "Your Great Spirit is just as confusing as our white God is."

Dream Dancer grinned consolingly then picked up the cub. "That is why they are Spirits or Gods. We are not supposed to understand them, just follow their teaching as best we can."

Golden Eagle shrugged dismissively and got up, as well. "I suppose you are right, let's go."

*****

Jed slowed his horse to a trot to cool him down then looked around. He could hear the river clearly now and knew they were close. They rode around a curve then slowed their horses to a walk as the river came into view. He started looking for a good campsite it was still early, but he did not want to take a chance of being caught in the middle of the river at night.

Mell rode up and pointed to the right. In the distance was a good place for a temporary camp. Jed inclined his head in agreement. They all turned towards the spot Mell pointed out. Everyone dismounted then camp was hastily made. Afterwards, they walked to the edge of the river and looked at the far shore in trepidation.

Rose stared in dismay at the fast moving water then shuddered apprehensively as she pointed grimly. "We have to cross that, I do not think it is possible!"

Jed walked over to her; he put his hand on her shoulder before smiling in reassurance. "Yes we are going to cross that, but do not worry I have crossed it before it is not as bad as it looks. All you have to do is hold on to the horse and you will be fine."

Rose nodded relieved at Jed's assurance that it can be done, but she still looked doubtful. They all went back to camp sombrely unsure what tomorrow would bring. They tried to push thoughts of what was to come away to enjoy the first early day they had since they started their journey, but their laughter was obviously strained with no pranks or jokes this night to relieve the tension.

*****

Raven slowed her horse to a trot then to a walk; they had ridden hard today, and she had not even stopped for lunch. Both horses, as well as their rider were exhausted. It was still too early to stop, but Raven figured she had better for her horse's sake. She started looking for a camp then finally found one up on a ledge. Behind the ledge rose a steep hill, which would be difficult to climb, it gave her some protection. She rode up to it and jumped down off her horse. She unsaddled both horses then rubbed them down before she set up camp. She decided to look for some fresh meat so grabbed her rifle and walked cautiously through the underbrush around the base of the hill. She spotted a doe in the distance, but it was too large for her needs. So she kept going until she spotted three pheasants. They were the perfect size, so she shot all three then walked over and picked them up before heading back to her camp. When she got back, she threw one pheasant to each of her animals then sat down and cleaned her own bird. She built up her fire then put the final bird on a spit to roast.

While Raven waited in anticipation for supper, she saddled the packhorse again so she would be ready to go in the morning and made her bed up. When the bird was cooked, she sat back down to eat then sat back to enjoy her coffee once finished.

Raven let thoughts of Golden Eagle surface; she shivered as she remembered their night of lovemaking. She could not figure out what had come over her that night maybe it was the alcohol. She could have easily used her training to get away from him, but she had not. Except for a brief half hearted effort at first, she had actually melted against him. She could not blame it all on him either. He had given her plenty of chances to pull away or to tell him no, but she had not she had actually encouraged him in the end. She trembled in pleasure remembering the feel of his hard muscled body pressed against her. She had enjoyed every minute of their lovemaking and had not wanted to leave him in the morning.

Raven frowned thoughtfully as she considered Dream Dancer's vision then sighed contemplatively. She recalled seeing Golden Eagle as a Lord in England and he had looked good in his fancy clothes, but he also seemed unhappy at the same time. She remembered seeing herself suckling an infant, she had known before she had seen Golden Eagle that he was the father. She could not help thinking about how good that had made her feel.

Raven shook herself then threw away her cold coffee. She banked the fire and crawled into the blankets, to try sleeping. Try as she might though to banish thoughts of Golden Eagle her last thought before she slept was about him.

*****

Golden Eagle and Dream Dancer walked towards the corrals then saw Black Hawk already there waiting for them. The mare was running around the corral nickering at the stallion.

Black Hawk motioned curiously at Golden Eagle. "Well how did your visit with Devil go last night?"

Golden Eagle grinned unperturbed that his horse was being stubborn. "He let me walk up to him, but as I reached out to touch him, he moved away. When I sat down, he came over to me and ate out of my hand again."

Black Hawk nodded pleased then waved towards the paddocks enticingly. "Why don't you go over and try touching him again."

Golden Eagle turned quickly then walked over to the studs corral and climbed in.

Devil turned to face him as soon as he entered then stood still watching him.

Golden Eagle crooned softly to the stallion in persuasion and walked towards him slowly.

Devil watched him as his nostrils flared for a scent, but this time he did not walk away.

Golden Eagle stood beside him then reached out to touch the stallion in awe.

Devil quivered in response a little at the feel of a humans hand on him but did not turn away.

Golden Eagle scratched the stud's neck and proceeded to rub his hand all over him. He touched the stallion's legs but did not try to lift his feet yet or go behind him not sure, if he would kick. He stepped back not wanting to push him too quickly then turned and left the corral ecstatically.

Golden Eagle could not stop smiling as he walked up to Black Hawk then gestured in excitement. "Did you see that I finally got to touch him?"

Black Hawk chuckled at Golden Eagle's eager question. "Yes, I did see congratulations. Now tonight and tomorrow I want you to go in with the stud every chance you get and touch him, but next time try to pick up his feet then handle them as well."

Golden Eagle inclined his head in excitement. "Okay."

They turned back to the mare and Black Hawk motioned in explanation. "Today I am going to saddle my mare again. I will put the sacks on her for a bit, when she stands still for that I will try lying on her back. If it doesn't take her long to get used to that, I might try getting up on her to get her used to having someone on her back."

Golden Eagle nodded then watched Black Hawk walk into the corral with the mare.

*****

Golden Eagle chuckled as he watched the mare follow Black Hawk like a little puppy as he walked back to them finished for the day. "She learns fast."

Black Hawk nodded pleased. "I am not going to do anything more with her today, always end your lessons on a positive note, so you two can go have an early supper if you want."

Golden Eagle smiled thankfully. "Okay I will go in with my stud then we will take the cub out for a bit before supper."

Black Hawk inclined his head and turned away without comment to brush down his mare.

Golden Eagle followed by Dream Dancer walked to Devils pen.

Seeing the water bucket empty in the corral Ravens brother took it out. "I will go get him some water while you go in with him."

Golden Eagle nodded distractedly before climbing over the fence. He walked towards the stallion crooning softly. Devil let him touch him again, but this time he picked up his feet. He touched the stud all over then turned and left still not wanting to force his horse too quickly.

Dream Dancer was just coming around the corner when Golden Eagle climbed over the fence. While his young friend put water into the stallion's corral, Golden Eagle went to the shed then took out some hay for his horse. Once they were done, they turned and went to Ravens together.

The cub was awake when they entered, so Dream Dancer picked him up then they went back out into the trees. The cub went to the bathroom before ambling over to a tree that was dead. It was lying on its side, and the cub scratched at the tree insistently but was too small yet to move it.

Golden Eagle smiled then pushed it over for him. Underneath were grubs, worms and insects. The cub ate while the two friends sat talking about England.

Dream Dancer frowned thoughtfully. "When my father's will was read there was a long list of estates, but I was only eleven at the time so did not pay much attention."

Golden Eagle nodded as he tried to remember back then he ticked them off on his fingers as he talked. "Well let's see if I can remember. You have a townhouse in London, Oxford, and Windsor. You have two castles one is in West Summerset about thirty to thirty-five miles from Clevedon; you can see the coast of Wales from there. The castle was built on the cliffs, which overlooks the mouth of Severn it goes to the Bristol Channel then out to sea. You own all the land in Summerset and all the serfs, as well. You also own a castle in Wales at Conwy not far from the border of Snowdonia. Your grandfather hardly ever went to his castle in Wales they say that Snowdonia is haunted people who go there never come back. You will probably spend the first few years at your townhouse in Oxford since that is where the best schools are. I would like to make some suggestions though on what you should do after you arrive in England, it could mean the difference between staying the Earl of Summerset or losing your title."

Dream Dancer grinned eagerly. "Please do I am not sure what to do so anything that might help me will be very much appreciated."

Golden Eagle frowned contemplatively. "Well before you leave you will need to gather every document you have to take with you, the late Earl's marriage as well as death certificates are very important. Your father's birth, marriage, as well as his death certificate is also important. Yours plus your sister's birth certificates, as well as a copy of your grandfathers will, do not forget your fathers also. Then the first thing you need to do when you land is go to your townhouse in Windsor and go put a request in to see the Queen right away. When she grants you an audience, make sure you take all the papers I have listed with you then give them to her. I wish I had my trunks here so I could show you how to dress properly and give you some lessons on how to behave in the presence of the Queen."

Dream Dancer smirked devilishly. "I know where your trunks are grandfather hid them. He said if you are going to be staying here for the time being you should be cut off from your old way of life until you became used to the new one."

Golden Eagle chuckled at his young friend's best imitation of his grandfather's voice. "Okay before you go, I will give you some decent clothes then when you arrive have your butler get some new clothes made up for you as soon as possible. The Queen will leave you sitting for a few days so you should attend some of the parties while you are waiting. Now stand up you will be wearing a sword on your right side since you are left handed as your grandfather was. As you walk into the room where the Queen will receive you do not look around, stare straight ahead and keep your right hand loosely on the hilt of your sword. When the person who is guiding you, probably the secretary stops drop to one knee then bend down with your hand on your sword hilt like this."

Dream Dancer watched closely and imitated him.

Golden Eagle nodded satisfied. "Good but you will need to practice so that your movements are more fluid, not jerky. Now when you go to some of the parties or balls you bow slightly to the host then take the host's wife's hand in yours and bend over it before saying, 'charmed my Lady' then straighten and walk in. Remember that you are an Earl so the only people more powerful than you are, is the Queen, any children she has, her husband of course, and a Duke. Now the Queen right now is Victoria, her husband is Prince Consort Albert; we do not have a king at present. The Prince is powerful but only as far as the Queen lets him. The aristocracy is made up of King or Queen, Prince or Princess, Duke as well as a Duchess, Earl with a Countess, Viscount with a Viscountess, Marquees with a Marchioness, and Baron with a Baroness. All the offspring's of the nobles are called Lords or Ladies. Most likely, the Queen will be in Windsor Castle since that is where they spend most of their time, but if she is not you will have to go wherever she is to see her. Your grandfather was out here because he was in exile; he angered the old King who at that time was King George the fourth. So be extremely careful what you say to any of the royal house. Like her father Queen Victoria has a quicksilver temper it can flare up when you least expect it. Remember she can let you have your estates back since they were never actually taken away or she can banish you just for being a Summerset.

She can also send you to prison or cut off your head with a flick of her hand. In England, she is all powerful."

Dream Dancer grimaced dejectedly. "I am not sure I will remember all this it is very confusing."

Golden Eagle grinned decisively in promise. "You will remember I guarantee it, from now on every night before we go to bed I will tell you more than give you some history lessons as well as etiquette lessons. I will have you so well versed in court manners nobody would even suspect that you are part savage. Your fair colouring will help as well but make sure you are very upfront with the Queen nobody else needs to know, but she does."

Dream Dancer smiled appreciatively. "Okay thank you, but we better get back supper should be ready."

Golden Eagle nodded and they took the cub to the tepee before going to Giant Bear's for supper.

CHAPTER FIFTEEN

Golden Eagle woke early then looked past the fire pit to where Dream Dancer was still sleeping. He smiled delighted this was the first time he had woken before him.

Golden Eagle wiggled his fingers experimentally and grinned wider. His arm was almost fully healed thanks to his young friend's magical touch. He thought of last night with Dream Dancer; they had gotten back from supper then Golden Eagle had gone to visit his stallion again. Afterwards, they took the cub to the lake and they all had a bath before going back to Ravens for some more history lessons on England's Royalty.

Dream Dancer had rubbed more cream into his arm as they talked with the same results as before. The heat sensation had gone from the tips of his fingers all the way up into his shoulder. Raven's brother had rubbed some into his temples afterwards; it seemed to help him too. He had still felt slightly light headed after healing him again, so they had pondered the possibility that the healing was coming from deep within Dream Dancer so was taking some of his strength from him. If that were the case, he would have to be extremely careful; a more serious injury might kill him!

Dream Dancer had cautioned him not to use the arm yet if he tried to use it too soon he could damage it further, but maybe in another day or two he would have full use of it again.

Golden Eagle rolled out of his blankets then built up the fire it was chilly this morning, and he could hear rain falling outside. The cub woke, so Golden Eagle passed him a cooked squirrel, which he wolfed down. He got dressed in his heavier set of buckskins that were waterproofed then headed out the door. He went to the corral first and fed his horse then touched him again. He finally turned away heading for Giant Bear's next to get their breakfast. He scratched at the tepee flap and heard a muffled. "Come in."

Golden Eagle ducked inside then grinned over at Golden Dove.

Golden Dove smiled back and started dishing up some porridge as she asked in Cheyenne. "How are you this morning? Where is Dream Dancer?"

Golden Eagle frowned in concentration as he answered back hesitantly in Cheyenne. "I am fine this morning a little wet since it is raining. Dream Dancer is...um...still sleeping."

Golden Dove chuckled as she looked at Englishman's soaked hair then handed him two bowls of porridge and a folded piece of paper. "It looks as if it's pouring not just raining you are soaked you know! Here, can you please give this to Dream Dancer for me."

Golden Eagle inclined his head in agreement, as he laughed with Golden Dove. "You are right it is pouring out. I will give that to your grandson, thank you for breakfast."

Golden Dove beamed in delight. "You are welcome."

Golden Eagle turned then left the tepee and walked to Raven's wondering what was in the note. He ducked inside before grinning at Dream Dancer cheerfully, pleased with himself for getting breakfast for his young friend for a change. "Good morning."

Dream Dancer chuckled at his friends soaked appearance. "Good morning to you too you are up awful early today."

Golden Eagle laughed in satisfaction as he handed Dream Dancer his bowl of cold porridge. "First time I woke up before you."

Dream Dancer smiled dismissively at his friends smug look then pointed at the paper curiously in Golden Eagles hand. "What is that you have there?"

Golden Eagle passed his young friend the note and sat down. "I do not know, your grandmother asked me to give it to you."

Dream Dancer nodded his thanks then opened it and read while he ate his breakfast. When he finished he handed it back to Golden Eagle. "It is just a list of supplies needed from the ranch, which means I will be leaving in a couple of days, but I will be back again."

Golden Eagle frowned thoughtfully then read the list contemplatively. "That is a lot of supplies; does your sister have enough? If Raven gives this every year how does she keep up and what about money for extras, I am sure she does not charge your grandfather for anything?"

Dream Dancer shrugged not worried in the least. "Usually Grandfather does not need so much. He only gets supplies in the winter most of the time, but now that he will be staying for the rest of the year, they need a little extra. You are right though she does not charge them for anything, but he makes sure the women make dream catchers, buckskins, Indian saddle blankets as well as other Indian products that the whites crave then gives them to her for payment. She sells them and uses the money to get things like coffee that we cannot grow or other necessary staples that usually my people cannot get. We have talked about the future though eventually grandfather will have to stay here year round. It is getting too dangerous for them to move around now that the government is trying to drive the Indians on reservations. So far, he has managed to stay away from them, but as more whites come, they steal more land. It is not looking promising for the Indian Nations in the future."

Golden Eagle handed the list back as he sighed grimly what could they do it was a difficult situation. The Queen had no voice here it was too far away anyway for her to do anything about it. So going to her would do no good. Besides there were too many people in England that wanted out, there was no way they could stop them. He shook off his thoughts not wanting to think about it anymore then got up. "Well let's go for our lessons, dress warm because it is pouring out."

Dream Dancer groaned unenthusiastically and dressed as he asked his friend optimistically. "Do you think my uncle will cancel the lessons today since it is raining out?"

Golden Eagle chuckled sympathetically then shook his head negatively. "I hardly doubt it, but we will wait and see what he says."

Dream Dancer scowled shrewdly without much confidence knowing his uncle the way he did. He picked up the cub then they headed out the door.

*****

Raven woke and hurriedly dressed then broke camp she did not even take the time to eat. She looked around for Bruno and his she wolf, but neither was around. She frowned they would have to catch up to her, or they were gone. She nudged her horse into a canter then looked up irritably it was clouding up fast, and she could see lightning in the distance. She knew she was in for a good soaking; she shrugged in exasperation nothing she could do about it then rode on.

*****

Mell woke up first so started breakfast.

Jed joined her a few minutes later and smiled his thanks when she handed him a coffee. He looked up then frowned in concern. "It looks as if it is going to rain; I hope it holds off until after we cross the river."

Mell scowled anxiously before waving decisively. "I hope so too, but we have to cross today we have already lost too much time."

Jed heaved a sigh uneasily and shook of his unpleasant feeling not wanting to upset anyone as he smiled at his daughter then at Jessica. "Good morning how are you two feeling this morning?"

Jessica grinned good-naturedly. "Just great!"

Pat looked up at the sky wearily and smiled hesitantly at her mother as she handed her some porridge then turned to her father. "I feel fine, but I do not like the looks of those clouds coming. I am going to eat my breakfast and cross the river right away with Silver Tip so we can scout around. I think we better get across before that storm hits."

Jed nodded thoughtfully as he motioned in anxiety. "I was thinking the same thing! I think I will go with you as well it will be faster with two of use scouting. Rose will just have to forgo her lessons for today. After we look around, I will come back across then lead everyone else over."

Jed turned to Mell and waved around the camp expectantly. "Have everything as well as everyone all ready to go as soon as possible!"

Mell inclined her head then handed him a bowl of porridge without saying anything, she was getting those forewarning feelings again. She shivered in response; she tried to ignore it as best she could, but was unsuccessful. They had no choice but to navigate it today time was running out for Giant Bear they had to get to him now before it was too late!

Jed and Pat were just finishing their breakfasts when Daniel with Pam following sat down. Rose came next then smiled her thanks when Mell handed her a bowl of porridge and a cup of coffee.

Jed with Pat a step behind left then quickly saddled their horses; they mounted and rode to the edge of the river. Pat whistled for her dog then waited for her.

Mell walked up beside them in concern still trying to ignore her foreboding feelings. "The river is getting rougher so please both of you be very careful."

The two nodded and urged their horses into the water without a word.

Mell stood there watching then looked around as she felt someone take her hand in support. She smiled at Pam, and her son then turned back to watch apprehensively.

Jed led the way; he turned to look back at his daughter in warning. "It gets deep ahead as well as a little rough so get ready for a swim."

Pat nodded but did not say anything as she fought to keep her horse under control. She saw her fathers horse plunge into the water and saw him drop out of the saddle then swim beside his horse holding onto the saddle horn. She kicked her horse impatiently before slapping him sharply with the reins in rebuke.

He nickered in fear and backed up a step then obediently plunged in.

Pat copied her father and slipped out of the saddle.

Silver Tip swam up beside his mistress but soon foraged ahead.

Pat saw swirling water just ahead so tightened her grip on the saddle horn. She realized that the undertow was stronger now just by the way that the water was reacting. She was buffeted against her horse but had been prepared for that. A piece of driftwood floated towards her, so she kicked it away from them before it could touch her horse.

Pat saw here father climb back on his horse, she sighed thankfully then waited a few minutes before climbing back on her horse just as they stepped up into shallower water. Finally, they were across safely.

Jed looked across at his wife and waved in reassurance to her knowing she would not leave until she was sure they were okay then turned right to explore that part of the river.

Pat and Silver Tip turned left to explore their side.

*****

Mell watched the whole ordeal from the opposite riverbank then sighed in relief when her husband and daughter reached the other side safely. She did not relax entirely though until she saw her husbands indication that they were unharmed.

Mell squeezed her daughter-in-law's hand in thanks for holding on to her then they all turned and started breaking camp to get ready for their turn to cross.

*****

Golden Eagle followed by Dream Dancer went into Raven's then both fell on their beds in exhaustion, wet clothes and all. Golden Eagle groaned in agony. "I do not think I am ever going to learn how to fight with a knife. You seem to be learning way faster than I am."

Dream Dancer chuckled in sympathy. "Well I have a confession to make. When I use to watch Black Hawk and Raven do their moves, I would go somewhere private then try to copy them. So I already have a few years of doing this behind me."

Golden Eagle sighed relieved. "Well I feel a little better now."

Golden Eagle stood up and grimaced down at himself irritably. "I am soaked right through, oh well I have to go back out to feed my horse then go for my lessons so I might as well stay in these soggy clothes."

Dream Dancer chuckled teasingly and added more fuel to the fire. "I will just stay here to dry out while you are gone."

Golden Eagle grimaced dejectedly at his young friend then slipped out of the tepee as Dream Dancer laughed mischievously after him. He went to the shed for feed, and after putting the hay in Devil's pen went in then approached him.

Devil snorted at him forlornly as he stood with his rear end to the wind.

Golden Eagle crooned softly to the stud in sympathy as he ran his hands up the stallion's neck and scratched behind his ears. He moved his hands back down the stallion's neck then touched his sides, before running his hand down the horse's leg and lifted each front foot. He brought his hand back up the horse's leg then down one side of the horses back. He stood to the side a little just in case the horse kicked at him and scratched the stud's hindquarters just above the tail; he smiled in delight when Devil pushed against him for more scratching. He ran his hand down the horse's side then down his back leg before picking up one foot and went around to the other side then picking up the other one. He playfully pulled his horses tail to see what he would do, but Devil just pushed against him wanting another scratch. He obliged him and walked up to Devil's head then scratched his ears and patted his forehead before leaning forward then kissed the horse on the nose.

Devil woofed indignantly through his nostrils and bobbed his head.

Golden Eagle chuckled then held out his hand and let Devil sniff then nibble on his fingers looking for grain. He turned and clucked to the horse, Devil obediently followed him around the pen. After giving Devil some oats, he climbed over the fence then walked to Giant Bear's for his lessons.

*****

Raven pulled up and jumped off her horse then went to her packhorse to grab her rain slicker. She quickly drew it over her head as the rain started coming down harder. She sighed in disgust as she got back up on her horse. She would ride a little further and set up an early camp. If she remembered correctly, there was an old miner's shake up ahead. It would give them some protection from the pounding rain as well as the lightning.

Raven hunkered under her rain slicker in misery then nudged her horse into a canter as she continued doggedly on.

*****

Mell and her group stood on the bank then watched Jed swim back towards them beside his horse. It was just starting to rain, but darker black and purple clouds were coming fast; they could also see lightning in the distance. The river was getting higher as well as choppier as the wind started picking up. Jed reached them, so Mell released the breath she had not known she was holding.

Jed waved to Daniel as well as Jess insistently. "You two can cross now, but watch for floating debris or water snakes. They do not usually live in fast water, but watch for them anyway sometimes they get caught as the river rises then get swept down river."

The two nodded at the information as they nudged their horses forward. Daniel was leading a packhorse and Jess was leading Rose's horse.

Jed went over to join his wife as he watched his son followed by his sister-in-law go out into the rushing river. He lowered his voice so only she could hear him as he turned to his wife then motioned in concern. "I don't know about this; that river is getting worse, and the storm is moving in faster than I thought was possible."

Mell took his hand and squeezed it in reassurance. "We will make it love do not worry so much."

They stood on the riverbank together then watched in trepidation, neither relaxed until the two made it safely to the opposite bank.

Jed turned to his horse and tied the packhorse to the back of his saddle then rummaged inside his saddlebag and pulled out a small rawhide rope. He walked over to Pam's horse; he tied the rope to the back of the saddle then made a loop. He turned to Pam and Rose in warning. "Okay Pam when you get to the deeper water than have to swim hold onto the saddle horn. Rose you grab this strap and hold onto it as you slide off the horse; all you have to do is kick your legs the horse will do the rest. I will ride in front with Mell riding behind you; push any debris out of your way. Whatever you do, do not panic. Just hold on the horse will get you to the other side safely."

Pam mounted then Jed lifted Rose up onto the back of Pam's horse.

Jed mounted his own horse before turning and looked back at his wife in encouragement; he faced forward once more then nudged his horse into the water. He entered and frowned apprehensively as lightning flashed closer; the rain was now almost a solid sheet as it fell harder. Suddenly the wind picked up howling fiercely; he looked upstream into the distance then saw the water moving faster as more debris started floating towards them. Horse and rider got to the edge of the drop off then plunged in; they were committed now no turning back. He slipped out of the saddle and looked behind to make sure his packhorse was okay. Once reassured he watched Pam with Rose clinging tightly to her, jump in then successfully drop out of their saddle one on each side of the horse. He anxiously stared past them at Mell fighting with the white colt. He sighed in relief when both horses plunged into the deep water. He turned back just in time to push a piece of driftwood out of his way.

*****

Rose and Pam slipped off the horse one on each side.

Pam yelled loudly in question trying to be heard above the rushing water as well as the fierce wind. "How are you doing Rose?"

Rose called back nervously. "I am doing fine Pam."

Rose kicked her legs hard as she pushed pieces of wood out of her way. She had a hold of the strap in a death grip than she shivered in panic as a lightning bolt flashed just ahead on the distant shore, not too far away from them. A loud clap of thunder boomed out only split seconds after the lightning hit.

The horse squealed in fright and tried to turn.

All of a sudden, the strap Rose was holding came loose then she went under as the current pulled her down relentlessly. Rose squealed in shock as she floundered trying to rise to the surface desperately.

*****

Pam held onto the saddle horn for dear life as the lightning flashed, and the thunder boomed just a ways on the opposite shore. She grabbed desperately at the horses reins as he turned trying to bring him back around. She heard a frightened cry then pulled herself up enough to see over her horse, she saw Rose go under suddenly. Hastily Pam let go of the saddle horn and swam around then plunged in. She grabbed Rose by the shirt pulling her upwards; once they surfaced, she grabbed Rose around the chest holding her backwards trying to keep them both afloat. She sighed in relief when Rose sputtered and took a deep breath.

Pam looked around, but could not see her horse anymore. She groaned apprehensively then tried to push against the current, but was unsuccessful. She could not get them both across by herself!

Rose turned her head and looked up at Pam in terror then shouted in apology. "I am sorry the rope let go."

Pam smiled in reassurance trying to keep the fear out of her voice as she pleaded desperately. "It is okay, but we need to get to the far shore, and I cannot do it alone. I need you to turn over then hold my hand; I will keep you afloat I promise. We both need to kick as hard as we can and try to steer towards the shore! Can you do that?"

Rose nodded grimly; she grasped Pam's hand trustingly as she turned then kicked as hard as she possibly could, trying not to be a hindrance. They were making some progress when a piece of wood floated by just in front of them.

Pam screamed in painful surprise unexpectedly unable to move.

Rose held onto her desperately as she pulled herself closer to see what the problem was. "What is it Pam what happened?"

Pam shuddered in agony. "That piece of driftwood is actually a tree under the water; a branch I did not see pierced my side. I cannot go any further I am stuck you will have to go on alone."

Rose saw the blood pooling around Pam and shook her head in horror. "No, I will not leave you!"

Rose looked around in despair then saw a piece of a tree coming swiftly towards them. It was bobbing up and down but staying above the water. She released Pam's hand then lunged for it hoping to get it before it was swept past them. Luck was with her as she grasped it, and kicking her legs as hard as she could manage as she steered it towards Pam.

Pam was still tangled up in the tree, but between the two of them, they managed to get her loose. She grabbed onto the other side of the log Rose was clinging to thankfully, they pushed away from the tree then both kicked their legs hard.

Suddenly, Rose felt the branch tip and looked over fearfully to see Pam sinking under the surface. She lunged towards her then caught her by the hair before she could drop out of sight. She heaved up with all her strength and grabbed Pam around the waist as she broke the surface then pulled her up onto the log that Rose had somehow managed to keep a hold of.

Pam coughed weakly as she spit out water trying to clear her lungs and pulled herself up. "I don't know how much longer I will be able to hold on!"

Rose held onto the branch with one hand then swung around so that Pam was between her and the log. This way she could stabilize Pam against the branch with her body plus still maintain a grip on the log. She grabbed the branch on the other side of Pam to help keep her in place.

Pam sighed in painfully relief, finally feeling secure she trustingly lost consciousness knowing Rose would get them safely across.

Rose clung to the driftwood in desperation; but in this position she could not steer it or lessen her grip to push obstacles away, or she might lose Pam for good this time. Jed would never forgive her if she did not get Pam safely to shore. She looked up imploringly as she mumbled a prayer to the Great Spirit under her breath. Suddenly finding strength she did not know she had she kicked desperately trying to get to shallower water. She watched in horror as a large branch came rushing towards them at a rapid pace. She positioned herself so that she could protect Pam, this way it would hit her instead. She grunted in surprise then gasped for breath when it connected just under a rib. She heard a loud snap and she screamed in painful surprise. She tightened her grip desperately as she felt herself almost lose her grip on the log as well as Pam. She was just losing consciousness when thankfully she felt hands pulling her out of the water.

*****

Raven looked around but could not see anyone. There were no fresh horse droppings or footprints, so she dismounted then walked up to the old miner's cabin and pulled open the door. It was totally abandoned as she had thought, so she took both her horses inside with her. She would wait out the storm here then get an early start in the morning she hoped.

Raven just finished unsaddling her horses when she heard a persistent bark at the door. She opened it and smiled down at Bruno thankfully. "Decided to join me did you, well come in make yourself at home."

Bruno trotted in then went directly towards the fireplace.

Raven watched him circling around and around in amusement as he tried to find a good place to lie in, he dropped down suddenly then promptly went to sleep. Shaking her head, she chuckled at him in amusement and went back to work getting a fire going then ate supper before curling up in her blankets to sleep.

*****

Golden Eagle with Dream Dancer following went back to Ravens and plopped down in front of the fire in relief. Golden Eagle sighed irritably still soaked to the skin. "It has been a long wet day, but finally it is over; my arm hurts a lot tonight though! How is your headache?"

Dream Dancer added more wood to the fire then smiled over at his friend and started undressing. "Strip down to your loincloth I will put some cream on your arm."

Golden Eagle nodded then did as he was told.

Dream Dancer sighed thankfully, as he answered Golden Eagle's question. "My headache is gone thanks to your good advice about rubbing your ointment into my temples. I think your arm hurts so much because it is so damp outside."

Golden Eagle inclined his head appreciating the praise as he sat back down so that Dream Dancer could unravel the binding from his arm. He stared down at his arm in amazement; it was extremely difficult to believe that only last week it had been swollen to twice its normal size.

Dream Dancer grinned in satisfaction. "Your arm looks good the swelling is completely gone now."

Golden Eagle watched Dream Dancer rub the ointment into his arm as had happened before his young friend started chanting and Golden Eagle felt the same hot tingly feeling travel up his arm then into his shoulder. He closed his eyes blissfully as the heat warmed the rest of him up, as well.

Dream Dancer sat back pleased; he was only slightly light headed this time. He could feel that the Englishman's arm only needed one more healing touch. He looked at Golden Eagles ecstatic expression and laughed knowingly. "You can leave the bandage off tonight, but you should still bind it during the day at least for a couple more days then I think you can go without the bandage after that."

Golden Eagle opened his eyes reluctantly and nodded in agreement. He smiled gratefully at the young Earl then changed the subject. "Okay let's get back to your lessons on England. The Queen's full name is Alexandrina Victoria; she goes by Victoria though. She is the only child of Edward Duke of Kent and Victoria Maria Louisa of Saxe-Coburg. They were only going to call her Victoria, but George the fourth, her uncle who was next in line for the throne insisted that she be named Alexandrina. That way she would have her godfather's name as well; Tsar Alexander the second, of Russia is his full name. She was born on the twenty-fourth of May, eighteen-nineteen. Her father, the King, died when she was eight months old. An ambitious Irish officer befriended Victoria's mother; his name is Sir John Conroy. He would be the power behind the throne once Victoria became Queen, until she turned eighteen anyway. Lucky for England, her uncle King George the fourth did not die until twenty-seven days after Victoria's eighteenth birthday. She became Queen in eighteen-thirty-seven; as soon as she became Queen, she banished Conroy from the Royal Court. Lord Melbourne was prime minister, so he took over Conroy's office then became the power behind the throne until eighteen-forty when she married her cousin Prince Albert of Saxe-Coburg. Several attempts have been made on the Queen's life so far including at least two in eighteen-forty-two that I know of."

Dream Dancer listened raptly as Golden Eagle continued, unsure if he wanted to go to England now though. It did not seem as if it would be a very pleasant place to be. He shrugged what would be, would be! The Great Spirit must have a good reason for him to go there, until told otherwise he would go.

*****

Mell made it to the opposite shore and rushed up to her husband in fear. "What happened? The girls were in front of me one moment then gone the next!"

Jed shook his head unknowingly. "It looked to me like Rose panicked and went under! Pam must have gone after her."

Daniel grabbed his father's arm desperately pleading in despair. "Well let's go find them right now!"

Jed put his arm around his son consolingly. "I am sorry they could be anywhere at this point, we will camp here tonight. It is pitch black out right now, so we will look for them first thing in the morning."

Daniel wrenched away furiously. "I will find them by myself then, without your help!"

Daniel stalked away, but stopped short when his sister grabbed his arm to stop him.

Pat feeling her twin's pain as her own, but knowing it would be difficult to find them in this storm, urged her brother to reconsider. "Dad is right Daniel besides in the morning Silver Tip can track them, but not in this rain. It will be much faster that way, running around blindly in this storm right now would be a useless exercise. It is already so dark we might ride right past them and never know the difference. We could be miles away before we even realized it then we would have to backtrack, which could kill them both. They are both in very good physical condition if they huddle up together as soon as they get to shore, they should be fine until morning. Pam is Cheyenne, Daniel, even though you forget that sometimes. She can survive in this, or even worse!"

Daniel sighed in frustration as his mother walked over and took his hand in comfort then nodded her agreement with the others. "We will find them tomorrow I promise!"

Daniel scowled reluctantly, but knew his sister was right to scold him. He did forget a lot of the times that his wife was Indian and could look after herself. He sighed forlornly as he inclined his head grudgingly. Everyone turned back then went to the camp Pat, and Daniel had set up earlier. Nobody felt like eating so they all crawled into their bedrolls then tried to sleep.

Daniel clutched his bible desperately as he prayed feverishly begging God as well as Jesus to look after his wife. If she died, he did not know what he would do. He looked up imploringly. "Please God, not her; I do not think I could handle that!"

Uneasily he drifted into a troubled sleep. His dreams were filled with the mocking laughter of something or someone he could not see fully. "Is your faith strong enough Preacher?"

Loud menacing taunting made him toss, and turn all night. In the morning, he would be unable to remember his dream, only a vague sense of uneasiness that would follow him around for days afterwards.

CHAPTER SIXTEEN

Raven woke early then smiled up at her horse as he nudged her awake impatiently. She looked out the only window and sighed, thankfully the storm was moving off as she saw the sun peeking over the windowsill. She pushed her horse's nose away with a chuckle. "Okay I am up already."

Brave Heart snorted as if to say it's about time.

Raven laughed at him as she got up reluctantly then went over and opened the door for Bruno. She saddled Brave Heart then tied the packhorse on a long rope to her stallion's saddle blanket so he could eat and took them over to the door then held it open for them. "Okay, out you go."

Brave Heart nickered as if in thanks and went out to eat while he waited for his mistress patiently.

Raven hastily cleaned up the mess; she might need it on the way back then ate a hurried breakfast before she mounted and galloped away.

*****

When Daniel got up it was barely daylight, he rummaged around noisily so that everyone would get up to. There were dark circles under the Baptist preacher's eyes from lack of sleep then he shivered in anxiety wondering why he felt so agitated as well as edgy.

Pat was the first one to the fire and sat down; she regarded her brother then frowned apprehensively at him. "It is still raining I do not know if Silver Tip can track very well in this. We will try it anyway and hope for the best."

Daniel scowled grimly as he made porridge, but did not comment; he was going dog or no dog he did not care. He looked up as he wiped the rain out of his eyes he could see clearing off to the west, but it was still some distance away yet. He turned back to his cooking resolutely not saying a word.

Jessica then Mell came next followed a few minutes later by Jed.

Pat looked at her mother and grimaced in concern as she made coffee.

Mell smiled in reassurance then reached over before squeezing her hand calmly. "It will be fine dear, do not worry so much."

Inside though Mell was anything but calm, her outward appearance was only for show, and they all knew it. She blamed herself slightly; she had known it was not a good idea to cross, but she had pushed her nervousness aside then urged the crossing anyway. If anything happened to her daughter-in-law, she would always blame herself.

Breakfast was made and eaten in total brooding silence.

*****

Rose was rudely awakened by a kick in the backside; she groaned in denial then turned over and looked up into the unsmiling eyes of a hideously painted Blackfoot Warrior. She screamed in terror then tried to roll away desperately.

The Indian grabbed Rose by the hair unmercifully and hauled her back. He pulled her face up closer to his then grinned in delight at her fear.

Rose cried out in pain as her broken rib protested at the sudden jerk; she looked up at the Indian in confusion as he spoke harshly to her. She shook her head uncomprehendingly. "I do not understand you!"

The Indian grunted in irritation and motioned to the fire before bringing his hand up then making a gesture for eating, he pointed at the fire once more in demand.

Rose nodded in understanding and carefully got up holding her side as she limped over to the fire obediently. As she got closer, she could see a pile of furs on the other side. The bundle thrashed around then moaned pitifully. She rushed over quickly in fear and fell beside the furs then lifted the edge away from Pam's face as she examined her critically. She whispered distraughtly as tears of terror streamed down her face. "I am so sorry Pam, I tried!"

Rough hands grabbed her from behind and hauled Rose off.

Rose looked up in despair at the Indian standing above her as he waved furiously for her to move away from Pam.

The Indian brave pushed a reluctant Rose over to the fire in demand.

Rose knelt down obediently in front of it.

The brave handed Rose what looked like remains of a rabbit they must have had last night for supper.

Rose ate hungrily not even pausing for a breath since she was starving, she saw three more warriors came out of the trees leading horses, and she sighed in relief as she saw one of their horses with a travois trailing behind him.

Two of the Indians walked over and hoisted Pam onto the travois.

The Indian standing above Rose beckoned impatiently for her to come then he pointed at his horse in demand.

Rose nodded and got up painfully then limped over to the horses. She gasped in agony as the Indian lifted her up roughly before leaping up behind her. She looked around at the grotesquely painted warriors and figured that these must be the Blackfoot Mell had talked about. She looked back at the river in sorrow than wished she were still in it. As the Indians nudged their horses into a painful trot, she prayed desperately that Mell would find them. She had little hope though as they were spirited further away.

*****

Raven looked around and finally found a campsite for lunch. She had lost a half a day because of the rain but the chief showing up unexpectedly had saved her one or two days at least, so she was still ahead of schedule. She could see the mountains ahead now thankfully; she hoped to reach the Eagle Tribes village sometime tomorrow night. She made a hasty meal then fed her horses before changing her bandage on her leg, another couple of days and she could remove the stitches as well as the binding. She mounted again then rode on.

*****

Golden Eagle and Dream Dancer entered Raven's tepee then both sighed in relief at being done that lesson for today. Dream Dancer started making coffee while Golden Eagle fed the cub and changed into dry clothes since it had stopped raining. They just sat down to have a quick cup of coffee before Golden Eagle had to go for his lessons with Golden Dove when a scratching was heard on the flap. Golden Eagle sighed plaintively then put his coffee down. He went over to the door and opened it for Black Hawk than Giant Bear. The chief and his son came in then squatted around the fire.

Dream Dancer handed each a cup of coffee and sat back to sip his own.

Giant Bear spoke first as he waved towards the opposite side of the village. "Golden Eagle the medicine man wants to look at your arm again."

Golden Eagle inclined his head in agreement; he looked towards Dream Dancer briefly then smiled in reassurance at his frightened expression.

Black Hawk waited for his father to finish and spoke next. "After you are done with your lessons from my mother we are going to start training your stallion."

Golden Eagle sat forward eagerly then motioned in anticipation. "Are you sure he is ready?"

Black Hawk inclined his head decisively in encouragement. "Yes you have made good progress with him, and soon Raven will return so we must get him ready to ride before then."

Golden Eagle beamed enthusiastically and finished his coffee.

Black Hawk rose then left.

Giant Bear beckoned for Golden Eagle to come.

Golden Eagle spared another quick glimpse of comfort to Dream Dancer and followed Giant Bear to the medicine mans obediently. They entered, as before they sat around the fire.

The old man unwrapped Golden Eagle arm then probed at it in awe, he looked at the Englishman in puzzlement. He turned and spoke rapidly to Giant Bear in excitement.

The chief looked at the medicine man in doubt before translating for him with a frown of uncertainty as he turned to Golden Eagle inquisitively. "Your arm has healed fast; way faster than we thought was possible, it should still have been swollen what has caused it to heal so fast?"

Golden Eagle shrugged dismissively as he stared at the medicine man with an expressionless face as he lied impassively. "I put that ointment you gave me on three times a day, and every time I put it on it got better. I also heal very fast."

The medicine man shared a dubious look with Giant Bear; the old man finally nodded reluctantly, not sure, if he should believe him or not then re-wrapped the arm thoughtfully as he frowned troubled. "You do not need the sling but leave the bandage on two more days, and you can remove it as well."

Golden Eagle grinned in delight at the idea of having more freedom without the sling always getting in his way as Giant Bear translated.

Giant Bear scowled at Golden Eagle suspiciously. He did not believe the Englishman's explanation that he healed fast or that the ointment was the reason he had healed even faster, but what other conclusion is there!

Golden Eagle left the two confused men to try figuring out what was going on. The Englishman went for his lessons whistling in delight at having outsmarting the chief. It felt good, to damn good! He frowned thoughtfully; Dream Dancer would not approve he was sure, but he shrugged with a grin of pleasure it did not make him feel that guilty.

*****

Daniel sat tensely in his saddle as they all gathered around Pat and her dog hoping for the best. He was not just hoping he was murmuring a prayer to God under his breath asking for his assistance.

Pat took a shirt from Pam's saddlebags then held it out for Silver Tip to smell.

Silver Tip sniffed the shirt and looked up at Pat for instructions.

Pat squatted down then grabbed her dog by her ruff and brought her nose close to her face trying to convey her urgency. "Track Silver Tip, go find Pam girl!"

The large dog yelped then turned up the river and raced off.

Pat mounted as they trotted after the dog staying close.

Mell rode up beside Pat in question; it was still drizzling slightly, but the clear skies were getting closer. "Are you sure she can track in the rain?"

Pat shrugged unknowingly not sure, but it was worth a try. "I do not know, but the girls had to have exited the river somewhere if I know Pam it won't be too far away. Once we find where they left the river Silver Tip will have no trouble finding them."

Mell nodded satisfied then fell back a little, as they trotted upstream but stayed close to the riverbank looking for any sign of the girls. They spread out a little to explore a wider area. It took several hours before Silver Tip found the blood soaked log where the girls had exited the river.

Jed and Mell jumped off their horses then walked around the area carefully reading the signs.

Mell came back a few minutes later with a look of fear on her face that she tried hard to hide, but was unsuccessful. "It looks as if the girls were holding onto that log over there; one of them was hurt bad enough to bleed. We found many Indian tracks around here; it looks to me as if they had been here for several days, probably fishing. I would imagine that they thought it was their lucky day, when the girls washed up to shore. Once they dragged the girls out of the river, they went southwest. Silver Tip has the scent now so we will follow her then see where she leads us."

Pat and the others nodded soberly then prayed hard as they followed Silver Tip deeper into the woods. Two hours later, they rode into a clearing where the Indians had camped for the night.

Mell and Jed again dismounted then walked around searching.

Jed came back a few minutes later and waved so that everyone would dismount. "It looks as if there were four warriors. One of the girls slept by the fire the other one slept over there. The one by the fire was hurt bad enough that they had to use a travois to carry her. I want everyone to grab a quick bite to eat it might be the last time we will have a chance for a hot meal until we find the girls."

Everyone nodded as Jed got a fire going than Mell started lunch. They hunkered around the fire waiting for hot coffee still chilled from the rain earlier, but thankfully, it had finally stopped. All except Daniel he rummaged in his saddlebags until he found his holster and guns, he had brought them just in case.

Daniel stared at them for a moment undecided; that sense of foreboding returned stronger than ever. Shaking of his trepidation, he strapped his gun belt in place before taking each gun out and checked them over as he twirled them experimentally then dropped them into the holster. Quickly he grabbed both and drew them to get a feel; it had been a long time. Twirling them again, he dropped them back in one more time. He took out his rifle then checked it over as well; suddenly he turned as he heard an ominous knowing laugh. He cocked his rifle reflectively looking around uneasily, but there was no one there, he let the hammer down confused.

Mell and Jed exchanged a worried look, but Pat was the one who walked over to talk to her brother. She put a hand over her twin brother's hand to stop him then frowned deeply concerned. "You do not have to do that Daniel we will find the girls and get them back safely. You do not need your guns!"

Daniel jumped slightly in surprise then flushed guiltily and sighed heavily as he looked at his sister deadly serious. "I know, but if I have to use them to get my wife back I will. The good Lord knows I try to live my life by his word but sometimes it is just not enough so I must choose between what I know is right by human standards or his teachings. If I must kill to save my wife then I will, but I am praying to God profoundly that I will not have to make that choice."

Pat sighed sorrowfully and knew there was nothing she could say now that would change his mind. She squeezed his hand in reassurance then went over to sit beside her mother dejectedly praying as well that her brother did not have to do something he would regret later.

Mell looked at her in question

Pat shrugged and shook her head warningly. "Leave him be it is his decision to make!"

Mell nodded unhappily then ate quickly.

Everyone remounted and followed as Silver Tip led the way.

*****

Golden Eagle walked back to Ravens after his lessons then ducked inside. He smiled at Dream Dancer as he walked over to the fire and sat down then accepted a cup of coffee.

Dream Dancer frowned in agitation as he motioned in demand wanting to know what Golden Eagle had said. "Well what did the Medicine Man have to say?"

Golden Eagle grinned reassuringly and could not help but chuckle as he remembered the two old men's doubtful faces as he left. "He was very surprised at how fast I heal, he said I could take off the bandage in two more days, I told him that it was the cream he gave me that healed me so fast. I do not think he believed me though."

Just then, Black Hawk stuck his head inside the flap. "Come on you two it is time."

Golden Eagle drained his cup eagerly in anticipation and got up with Dream Dancer then followed Black Hawk.

Black Hawk stopped at Devil's pen and turned to Golden Eagle. "I put my mare as well as another stud in the other pen for a distraction; see how your stallion is prancing around then calling out challenges. You must get his attention focused on you just as we did with my mare."

Black Hawk handed Golden Eagle the whip.

Golden Eagle nodded in anticipation and took the whip as he opened the fence to start the first day of training. He whistled in demand as soon as he entered the paddock.

Devil turned for a moment then turned away as he called out another challenge to the other stallion.

Golden Eagle cracked the whip suddenly, and Devil jumped in surprise then took off around the pen with a squeal of anger. The determined Englishman ignored his stallions rage as he took a step in front of Devil to turn him around. He pointed the whip in the opposite direction so that the stud would see it, but he had to crack the whip twice before his horse would turn. Twice more he turned him before lowering the whip then let the stud stop.

The mare nickered across at Devil, and he turned away abruptly to answer her.

Golden Eagle cracked the whip in demand then started running him again relentlessly.

Dream Dancer and Black Hawk smiled at each other in admiration as Golden Eagle refused to relent. It only took about an hour for the stallion to stand for Golden Eagle. Both men were impressed at what a quick learner he was.

*****

Jed called a halt as soon as Silver Tip started growling.

Pat called her dog over then shushed her hurriedly.

Everyone dismounted and gathered around.

Jed frowned troubled then waved to the south. "There is a Blackfoot summer camp just ahead it looks as if that is where the girls are. Mell and I will go scout out the encampment. I want all of you to set up camp here, but absolutely no fire, after we look around we will be back then plan a course of action."

Everyone nodded except Daniel; he stared at his father insistently with a stubborn look. "I am coming to!"

Jed looked at Mell and saw her nod in agreement. He turned back to his son then pointed at him in warning deadly serious. "Okay but no heroics we are just looking right now. I want your promise that you will not do anything without our permission or I will leave you here!"

Daniel frowned angrily but inclined his head furiously not wanting to be left here. "Fine you have it!"

Pat took their horses reins with a grimace of trepidation she could feel her brothers resentment, and it worried her.

Mell took off her white buffalo robe; it was too easily seen then handed it to Pat with a reassuring look. "He will be fine I will not let him do anything foolish I promise."

The three slipped into the woods soundlessly and cautiously walked forward looking for sentries. Jed stopped periodically to listen then continued on when he did not hear anything. He held up his hand suddenly and motioned them all down without saying a word. They squatted immediately then crawled forward slowly to a small hill that would give them a good view of the whole encampment. The three lay flat and looked around vigilantly.

Jed leaned over then whispered in Mell's ear first. Next, he turned to his son and pointed then leaned closer in explanation. "There's the travois that must be where the Medicine Man or Shaman is located. So we know where one girl is at, I do not see the other one."

Mell leaned close to Jed and pointed to the left before gesturing towards the right in warning. "They have two sentries out, one to your left as well as one to your right further down."

Jed nodded then whispered cautiously. "They do not really need them see the dogs walking around the camp they are trained to give warning of intruders. Come I have seen enough lets go back now."

They warily inched back and quietly with their guard up walked back to camp, none of them said a word. As soon as they got back, the other two crowded around to hear what was being said.

Jed frowned thoughtfully. "Well we know where one is, but we are not sure how badly she is hurt or which one it is. We do have a couple of things to our advantage. First, the Blackfoot are highly superstitious plus their sacred animal is a white horse, which we happen to have two of. Second is that I have had dealings with the Blackfoot before. I saved a chief son once, but not with this tribe. I hope that they have heard about that incident. We will camp here tonight then first thing in the morning Mell, Daniel and I will go into their village."

Jed turned to Mell inquisitively then waved towards the horses. "Which horse do you want to trade for the girls?"

Mell sighed irritably at possibly losing two horses both sons of Lightning on this trip. "I will give them the colt if I must, I cannot very well ride him the rest of the way he is too young yet for such a strenuous ride even though I was working on him, and he is green broke. I can give Raven my horse when we get to Giant Bear's if I have to."

Jed inclined his head in agreement then motioned in caution. "Okay but you will have to ride one of the other horses into camp, or you might lose both horses."

Mell nodded grudgingly.

Jed frowned as he gestured at their packs. "We can't have a fire so everyone get some jerky and whatever else that you can find to eat in the saddlebags. Try to get whatever sleep you can manage it is going to be a tough day tomorrow."

Everyone ate quietly then went to bed except Mell and Jed.

Jed turned to his wife speculatively once they were alone. He knew these people extremely well from his earlier years in Montana. He also knew that his wife would be the key to their success or failure tomorrow. "I want you to wear your white buffalo hide tomorrow; I need you to be as dramatic as possible. With their spirit animal, as well as the Cheyenne's spirit animal around you plus your white hair, I am hoping we will not even need to trade your colt. It's too bad you could not ride the colt in then rear him up at the appropriate time, but he is too unpredictable for that. I think we better put both our badges away as well I am not sure, but I think this is the same band of Indians the army was searching for not too long ago. They might take exception to the badges."

Mell eyed her husband keenly; she knew he was using her to scare the Blackfoot into releasing the girls. She chuckled eagerly; she was always looking for a challenge and leaned forward for a passionate kiss; it might be their last, so she made it count. She pulled away breathlessly then took his hand and led him to bed.

*****

Raven looked around then found a good defensible campsite, she dismounted and made camp then she unsaddled both horses and rubbed them down before feeding her animals. She rummaged in her pack for her supper since she did not feel like hunting. After she ate, she saddled her packhorse then crawled into her blankets. She thought of Golden Eagle and wondered how he had taken her slipping away without saying good-bye. She had thought about him a lot lately; she just could not seem to get him or their one night of lovemaking out of her head. She finally fell asleep but even in her sleep there was no respite from him as her dreams replayed their night of lovemaking once again.

*****

Golden Eagle sighed as he entered Raven's tepee for the night. He stirred up the coals before adding more wood as he waited for Dream Dancer to come in with the cub. He thought of Raven as he waited then couldn't help wondering where she was at and if she was okay. He had dreamed about her last night, actually he had dreamt about her every night. She was so beautiful their one night of lovemaking had been so intense even magical to him. Thankfully, Dream Dancer came back in interrupting his thoughts as he put the cub down.

The cub waddled over to Golden Eagle immediately; he curled up beside him then promptly fell asleep.

Dream Dancer laughed in delight. "I think he likes you."

Golden Eagle nodded and patted the cubs ebony soft curly fur lovingly. "I like him to."

Dream Dancer sat down then sighed thankfully before grinning inquisitively at his friend. "So how does it feel to start training your own horse?"

Golden Eagle smiled in pleasure as he motioned in excitement. "It feels great; he is a fast learner to. It only took an hour to get him to pay attention to me and to follow me around without a rope. But then he was following me yesterday looking for grain, so I guess it does not really count."

Dream Dancer chuckled and got up to put Golden Eagle's ointment on his arm. "Everything counts with a horse, looking for grain is different then following you around because he wants to. Here let me put some stuff on your arm and let's go to sleep early. It is going to be a big day tomorrow."

Golden Eagle inclined his head in agreement then undressed, as had happened before the tingling heat started from his fingertips before going all the way up to his shoulder.

Dream Dancer sat back with a smile of satisfaction he hardly felt any wooziness this time. He frowned thoughtfully, each time he healed his friend the light-headedness had gotten less as if he were not putting out as much power maybe that meant Golden Eagle was fully healed. "I can feel that you do not require anymore healing your arm is completely healed now."

Golden Eagle wiggled his fingers and twisted his wrist before stretching out his arm experimentally. He opened then closed his hand into a fist a few times and shook his arm, nothing no pain at all. "I think you are right I don't have any more pain at all."

Golden Eagle impulsively reached over then hugged Dream Dancer ecstatically. "Thank you for helping me."

Dream Dancer hugged him back and pushed him away pleased that he had been able to help. After all, his people had done it to him in the first place. "You are very welcome I am glad I could help. Now go to bed!"

Golden Eagle smiled at Dream Dancer slight flush of pleasure then nodded without comment. He crawled under his fur obediently and with no more bandages, he fell asleep almost immediately. As he slept, he dreamt of Raven again.

CHAPTER SEVENTEEN

Rose was rudely awakened by a kick in the back; she screamed in pain then curled up protectively.

The woman standing above Rose snickered in extreme pleasure. She reached down and grabbed Rose by the hair cruelly before hauling her to her feet unceremoniously.

Rose staggered after her holding onto her tortured ribs, she was bent slightly trying to keep her hair from being ripped out of her head. She bit her lip to keep from crying out again, not wanting to give the woman the satisfaction of knowing she was still hurting her. She was dragged out of the tepee then hauled towards a group of women.

The women parted, and Rose was thrown to the ground in-between them. The woman that hauled her over pointed to a scraper in explanation than to the hides in demand. Rose nodded dejectedly in understanding as she picked up the scraper and went to work.

*****

Raven woke early then promptly broke camp. She should hit the outskirts of the Eagle tribe by dark if all went good today. She saddled her horse and checked to make sure all traces of her being there were gone; satisfied she mounted then rode out.

*****

Golden Eagle woke and looked across the fire; Dream Dancer was just getting up. He smiled over at his young friend. "Good morning."

Dream Dancer grinned back. "Good morning, my friend."

They both got dressed then Golden Eagle stocked up the fire and put wood in to made coffee.

Dream Dancer turned towards the door. "I will get breakfast."

Golden Eagle nodded as he got a fish for the cub that was just waking up then gave it to him. He sat and looked down at his arm in pleasure. It seemed strange not to have it wrapped or tied to his side. He flexed his fingers experimentally then twisted his wrist around and around in delight. He grinned relieved when he felt no pain at all.

Dream Dancer came in twenty minutes later then handed him his porridge, they sat together in companionable silence to eat.

*****

Mell woke first and hurriedly pulled out jerky, hardtack, as well as a couple cans of beans for their breakfast. They would have to eat everything cold with no coffee to wash it down.

Jed walked over wearing his buckskins.

Daniel then Pat arrived next, with Jessica following a few minutes later.

They all grumbled about the lack of coffee.

Mell just grinned placatingly as she handed out the cold food. There was more complaining, but everyone ate it.

Jed grinned in admiration at Mell, as he looked her over with a chuckle. She had changed to the buckskins that Pam had made for her a couple of years ago. The front of the shirt was intricately designed with a buffalo done in white beads. A large grizzly standing on its hind legs done in black on the back of the shirt gave it a dramatic look. Pam had told them that she had made them to represent the relationship between Mell and Giant Bear.

Mell had left her white medicine bag hanging in clear sight; her white buffalo hide was folded neatly beside her, waiting to be put on. She had braided her hair in two braids Indian style they fell to just below her waist. The fact that her hair was white now added to the startling affect she created.

Jed smirked knowingly; he could not wait to see the effect she would have on the superstitious Blackfoot.

Mell saw the approving smile on his face then she laughed at him in pleasure as she got up and twirled around flamboyantly. "Do you like my new look?"

Jed chuckled in satisfaction. "Yes I think you will give the Blackfoot nightmares. Can you still speak their language?"

Mell frowned thoughtfully as she sat back down; it had been a long time since she had used it. "Yes, not as well as I used to though, but good enough to be understood I think."

Jed nodded reassured as they ate quietly finishing their cold meal in haste.

Once finished eating Mell put on her white buffalo robe before mounting Pam's horse.

Pat handed her mother the lead rope to the white colt then scowled up in caution worried for them. "Be careful!"

Mell smiled grimly down at her in warning. "We will! I want you two to clean up this camp and stay hidden until we return, be ready to go as soon as you see us coming."

Pat inclined her head in understanding as she watched the three most important people in her life ride out. Make that four as she saw Silver Tip trotting beside her mother's horse. She opened her mouth to call her dog back then closed it without saying anything as the dog disappeared with the trio. She turned to Jessica as soon as the others were out of sight. Without saying anything, they cleaned up all traces of them being there then hid themselves as well as all the horses.

*****

Golden Eagle and Dream Dancer went into Raven's tepee.

Golden Eagle stocked the fire then fed the cub while his young friend made coffee. They sat across from each other as soon as the coffee finished brewing.

Dream Dancer handed Golden Eagle a cup before pointing down at his arm curiously. "Well how is your arm holding up?"

Golden Eagle grinned in relief as he flexed his fingers. "It is a little sore from the exercises I was doing, but not unbearably sore. Do you find that the last two days the exercises we have been doing are not as painful as they use to be?"

Dream Dancer nodded with a chuckle. "You are right, and I think that we are getting better at them also."

Golden Eagle inclined his head in agreement then finished his coffee and got up. "I have to go for my lessons; I will see you in a couple of hours."

Dream Dancer watched him leave before draining his own coffee. He picked up the cub. "Come on Cuddles let's go for your daily swim."

*****

Mell looked down then saw Silver Tip trotting beside her horse. She opened her mouth to send the dog back to Pat, but closed it when Silver Tip looked up at her with a penetrating stare. It was as if the dog were saying I am coming and nothing you say can stop me. She chuckled down at her then nodded her consent with a smile. "Okay you can come too, but absolutely no fighting with the other dogs unless they attack you first."

Silver Tip gave a little yelp of understanding and Mell laughed in delight.

Jed snickered in amusement. "I think she understood everything you said."

Mell nodded decisively with a smirk. "I think so too."

Daniel who was riding behind them never said a word or even cracked a smile. He just brooded quietly fighting with himself as well as his beliefs; occasionally he swore he could hear laughter.

They crested the hill they had hid behind last night then started down.

Jed heard a shout and saw the Blackfoot gathering as they watched them curiously.

The dominant female hound slunk forward with her hair all bristled in challenge at the strange scent of another female.

Silver Tip growled at her in warning.

The female hound took one look at the large black bear of a dog then tucked her tail between her legs with a whimper of fear and raced off.

Silver Tip just ignored her after that.

Mell gazed down for a moment then nodded in approval at Pat's dog before looking back up.

Jed nudged his horse forward a little and took the lead. He stopped at the edge of the crowed then waited quietly. When all the Blackfoot in the village were gathered, and silence fell, he called out in command his face expressionless. "I wish to speak to your chief!"

A man stepped forward immediately; he crossed his arms as he drew himself up imposingly his face impassive. "I am Chief Broken Horse! Why have you come to my village?"

The chief was relatively short, but he had a daunting stance; it made him look larger than he actually was. His hair was mostly grey and done in two braids, which reached down to the middle of his back. His face was weathered with deep imbedded lines crisscrossing in many directions showing that he had an extremely difficult life. He had a scar running from the corner of his right eye down his cheekbone then it curved until it reached his nose. It was shaped like the hoof of a horse; whatever had caused the injury had also crushed the chief's nose, which gave him a funny way of speaking.

Jed dismounted and handed Daniel his horse's reins before he walked over to the chief. "I am called Grey Wolf."

Jed stopped speaking as he waited for the crowed to hush. He smiled inwardly to himself showing emotions here could be fatal; good they had heard of him! He waved behind him, to introduce his family. "This is my wife White Buffalo as well as our son Daniel."

Mell clucked to the white stud colt in demand hoping he would remember.

The white stallion reared up then pawed the air dramatically.

Mell watched the awed looks of the Blackfoot and secretly she grinned, just the effect she wanted. She clicked her tongue again in demand, which was his cue to settle quietly. She got down off her horse then also handed the reins to Daniel before walking calmly up to Jed leading the colt.

There were exciting murmurs from the Indians as they finally got a good look at Mell and the horse she was leading. Several of them stepped back in fear murmuring uneasily about a she-devil.

Silver Tip followed closely beside Mell then sat when Mell stopped and gazed around vigilantly. The fur on her neck was bristled slightly in warning, but other than that, she showed no other signs of hostility.

The whispers of unease started again as the Indians stared in amazement at the huge black dog that looked like a miniature grizzly as she stayed close protecting the white woman without any urging.

Daniel had nodded at the introductions but did not get off as he held both his parents horses just in case they had to make a quick get away.

The chief grunted impressed as he looked at Mell, and the white colt expressionlessly trying not to show it. "I have heard of you Grey Wolf but not for many, many moons. The Blackfoot in the south still talks about the time you killed ten warrior's in their own village without them even knowing you were there then saved the chief's son a few minutes later after killing so many of his warriors."

Jed nodded solemnly remembering also. "They had stolen my son! I was close to the chief's tepee when I heard a child crying in fear. A wolf had snuck into the camp and was trying to drag the child away. So I killed the wolf to save the child, I do not kill children or blame them for their fathers mistakes. I did not know at the time that he was the only son of the chief."

Chief Broken Horse inclined his head eloquently, but that is all the emotion he dared show as he waved in demand uneasily. "You were then named after the grey wolves just as silent and deadly when stalking your prey. We have not stolen anything from you Grey Wolf! So why have you come?"

Grey Wolf shook his head guardedly. "No you have not stolen from me, that's why I came openly in peace! But your warriors did find an Indian woman as well as a half-breed that was separated from us in the storm; they were swept away by the raging river. One is my son's wife, the other one I was escorting to her tribe."

The chief nodded thoughtfully. "I know of the two you speak of. One I do not think will live; the other one is my son's new slave."

Jed frowned disturbed at the notion that one of them was hurt that badly. He kept his face unreadable as he pointed enticingly at the white colt. "We will trade our sacred white horse for the two women."

Mell urged the colt forward then clucked so that he would rear again in a spectacular show. She made sure that the colt was positioned in such a way that it looked as if he were trying to strike out at her.

The chief looked the colt over and hid his admiration as well as a slight tinge of fear as he reached up then stroked the scar on his face. The colt reminded him of the white stallion that had almost killed him as a child. It was not up to him though, but up to his son. He finally shrugged impassively. "You can take the one in the shaman's tepee, but you have to talk to my son about the other one."

The chief signalled out two warriors. "Go put the woman back on the travois and bring her here."

The two men trotted off immediately.

The chief turned back to them then waved negligently trying to prove his generosity to the feared Grey Wolf. "I will give you this woman since she will probably die anyway."

Jed inclined his head in thanks. "And which one is your son?"

A man pushed forward arrogantly then drew himself up before folding his arms across his chest in refusal. "I am, and I do not wish to give up my slave."

Jed studied him closely; he was slightly taller than his father was but not as tall as Mell. He was quite husky; he also had impressive arm muscles for an Indian. He looked to be about thirty, he was good-looking, but not handsome. His hair was just past his shoulders and was worn loose in pride.

Jed waved towards the colt enticingly. "Not even for the white colt?"

The Indian looked the colt over then eyed Mell up and down insolently. "I will trade my slave for the horse as well as the white woman!"

Jed frowned in anger, he had known that the man would try this trick; he was too arrogant for his own good. He bent over a little as Mell touched his arm then listened as she whispered in his ear.

He looked down at her incredulously. "Are you sure?"

Mell nodded decisively in reply; she knew the looks of the brave all to well, he would not trade. He was too full of pride and arrogance to be honest when dealing with others figuring he should get his way every time.

Jed looked back at the arrogant Indian then smiled in temptation. "I have a better idea, a knife fight between my wife and you; if she wins we take your slave as well as the colt then leave, if you win you can keep your slave and the white colt."

The villagers all started talking at once in excitement; it was unheard of for a woman to fight a brave.

The chief held up his hands in demand for quiet. "Are you sure Grey Wolf my son has not been beaten for many moons, plus he is thirty years younger. I would not want to see your pretty wife hurt or killed then have the Grey Wolf stalk my warriors for revenge."

Jed nodded expressionlessly as he swore solemnly. "I am sure! I will make a vow to you now that no matter what happens I will not take revenge. Besides my wife has never been beaten and I think your son needs a lesson."

Jed had lowered his voice a little so only the chief could hear that last part.

Chief Broken Horse looked at his proud son; he had tried talking to him several times over the years. He was extremely arrogant as well as full of pride they were not good traits in a future chief, but he would not listen. Maybe if, the white woman beat him he would become a better man than a good chief in the future. He nodded his mind made up and motioned in agreement. "As you wish!"

Jed turned to Mell then inclined his head in permission.

Mell smiled grimly before taking the colt over to her son and handed him the reins.

Daniel looked down at her in dismay. "Are you sure mom? I probably should be the one to challenge him to a fight since it is my wife who is his slave."

Mell put her hand over her son's leg in comfort then squeezed in reassurance. "Yes I am sure! Your job is to help people, and my job is to hurt people!"

Daniel sighed resignedly, but in relief too. He looked up as the warriors came up to them bearing the travois between them. When he saw his wife lying there looking as white as death he cried out then jumped off his horse before rushing over to her.

Mell grimaced thankfully at least she would not have to worry about him doing anything stupid anymore. She tied her colt to Daniel's saddle horn before walking back over to Jed and stood beside him calmly.

Jed bent over as he whispered softly in question. "Are you sure about this? He is a lot younger than you are, and he has pretty big arm muscles for an Indian."

Mell nodded decisively. "It is the only way now!"

Jed scowled helplessly; she was right of course, they could not back out now without severe penalty. "Okay, but remember that I love you."

Mell smiled up at him then cupped his left cheek tenderly with her hand. "I love you too."

Mell gave her husband a quick kiss of reassurance and turned away before walking towards the man she was to fight. As she got closer, she assessed his strengths as well as his weaknesses quickly. He was strong in the arms but weak on brains. He had a slightly longer reach than she did, but she was taller and had longer legs. He should be easy to beat as long as she stayed out of his reach. She did not want to kill him then get the chief's back up, but she would do so if left with no other choice. She stopped not too far away from him and heard Jed come up behind her so she took off her buffalo robe then handed it to him. She tucked her medicine bag away under her shirt.

The Indians fearfully caught sight of the white buffalo on the front and then the black grizzly on the back of the buckskin shirt. Excited whispers of a she-devil quickly started up again.

Mell blocked them out of her consciousness needing all her attention on her prey.

Jed hid his grin of delight having heard them whispering fearfully of a she-devil. He took a piece of sinew then tied Mell's hair together in one long rope before tucking her hair under the whip that she was wearing as a belt, to keep it in place. She had tied the whip loosely so that one tug and the whips snake like coils would loosen then be ready for use at a moments notice.

Mell took out her knife and stood patiently waiting for the chief's son to stop bragging to the other men about how fast he was going to put her on the ground.

Jed feeling Mell's readiness backed away quietly, praying silently.

All the other Indians formed a circle around the two combatants then waited expectantly. The Indian women clustered together whispering in anticipation. This was the first time any of them had seen a woman and a man actually fight. Secretly, deep down they all hoped White Buffalo would win, but none of them dared voice it aloud. Every woman there had felt the cruel backhand of the chief's son at one time or another.

The chief came over then stood beside Jed regrettably. "Grey Wolf as much as I would like to see my son lose some of his arrogance, I can still call this off and give you back your women."

Jed shrugged at the chief's concern. "Thank you but it is too late for that. Besides, you have never seen my wife fight. Just watch then you will know why the Cheyenne named her White Buffalo."

The chief nodded thoughtfully as he recalled his enemy's awe of the sacred white buffalo. For a white woman to be named as such, she must have extremely powerful medicine. Now he was beginning to be afraid for his son. He turned to watch in dread.

Mell stood relaxed and waited patiently for her opponent to come to her.

The brave strutted towards the woman arrogantly; he had no doubts whatsoever that he would lose.

Mell turned her knife around so that the handle was tucked against her palm with the blade resting against her arm. As he advanced closer, she bent her knees slightly then lifted up on the front of her feet so that her heels were just slightly off the ground. That way if she needed to pivot she could do so instantly.

The warrior stopped close and smiled insolently at Mell before lunging forward knife first.

Mell had been waiting for this, so she sidestepped neatly than as the knife and his hand went past her she brought her free hand down in a fist against his wrist.

The warrior drew back in amazement with a hiss of pain.

Mell waited patiently still relaxed as she watched the warriors eyes narrow. She rocked back on her heels a little, as the warrior came back, but this time a little more cautiously. She paid close attention to his eyes as they circled each other. It was not long before he gave himself away as his eyes flickered down to her left shoulder suddenly. She calmly waited as he lunged for her, at the last moment she pivoted around his arm so that her back was pressed against it. Still turning, she hit him hard in the back with her elbow. She continued pivoted the rest of the way around so that she was now facing his back as he staggered forward incredulously.

The warrior growled in rage then swung around to find her.

Mell figured it was time to end it; the warrior was so enraged now that he charged her like a bull. She knew if he got those muscular arms around her, he would crush her to death. She patiently waited until he was close enough, and suddenly she jumped up then kicked out with her long legs catching him directly in the face.

The kick toppled him backwards; he landed in a dazed shock as he shook his head trying to clear it.

Mell seeing her opportunity to finish it jumped on him so that her legs straddled his chest. She made sure that his arms were pinned down as well before she held the knife to his throat dramatically. She sat like that for a moment breathing heavily. Suddenly she grasped the knife in both hands and lifted it over his face then brought the knife down with all her might. At the last possible second, she moved slightly. The blade went whistling past his head as she buried it to the hilt in the dirt.

The knife was so close to his head that it nicked his ear slightly and made it bleed.

Mell stayed like that for a dramatic moment letting the silence of surprised disbelief intensify then suddenly she sat up with both arms raised above her head and gave a blood curdling scream of victory before she called out in his language fervently. "Now you are dead!"

Mell lifted herself of him then stepped back before smiling down at the warrior in approval. She held her hand out to help him up hoping he would take it and there would be no hard feelings.

The warrior looked at the hand offered to him in disdain then rolled away without accepting her help.

Mell shrugged regretfully and bent down to pull her knife loose from the dirt.

"MELLL!"

Mell looked up in surprise as she heard her name screamed in warning by Jed. As she looked up the chief's son, his knife stabbed down towards her face. She turned her head away instantly, but not fast enough, as she felt the sting of the knife as it cut a deep furrow across her cheek.

The knife dropped to the ground suddenly in shock as Silver Tip jumped for the Indian then toppled him backwards. She grabbed him by the throat squeezing slowly, not in any hurry to kill him wanting him to suffer. Enraged at what he had done to the leader of her pack.

Mell ran over fearfully then grabbed the dog around the neck pleadingly trying to lift her off the unfortunate warrior. "No Silver Tip, please do not kill him!"

Silver Tip let go instantly at the pleading note in her leader's voice and backed away obediently from the choking Indian.

Jed rushed over apprehensively then looked at Mell's face in concern as he dabbed at the blood with a soft cloth that someone handed him.

The shaman pushed through the crowd immediately and looked at Mell's cheek. "It will need to be treated come with me White Buffalo, I will help you!"

Mell inclined her head in agreement then giving Jed a reassuring look she trotted off after the shaman with Silver Tip following closely beside her.

Jed turned to the man on the ground angrily, but did not say anything as the crowd parted to let his father through.

The chief stood over his first-born son silently for a long moment. He finally shook his head in disappointment. "You have shamed this tribe and me for the last time. I had hoped that time would curb your boastful arrogance then help you gain some wisdom before it was time for you to become the next chief. Now I no longer have that hope you are no longer my son. You will live on the edge of our village as an outcast no longer will you be welcomed in my tepee."

The chief turned towards Jed shamefaced as he motioned in apology. "I am sorry Grey Wolf your wife fought with honour. My wife will bring you the slave; you and your family will always be welcomed here. I hope this incident will not stop your friendship with the Blackfoot."

Jed nodded solemnly then clasp arms with the chief. "I accept your apology and would be honoured to visit you again on my return."

Jed looked up as he heard his name then smiled as Rose limped painfully towards him holding her side. When she was close enough, she flung her arms around him ecstatically. He stroked her hair in reassurance and whispered encouragingly. "Daniel is seeing to his wife go join him please."

Rose nodded in agreement then slipped away silently.

Jed watched in relief as he saw Mell coming; except for a paste on her cheek, she looked unhurt.

Mell walked up beside her husband and grinned teasingly. "I am fine another scar to add to my many others that is all."

Jed sighed comforted then put his arm around her.

Mell turned her gaze to the chief in concern. "The dog did not hurt your son too much I hope?"

Chief Broken Horse shook his head negatively as he frowned decisively in anger. "He is no longer my son he has dishonoured this tribe. You fought bravely as well as with honour if it had been me, I would not have spared his life. You have your women back as promised so are free to go in peace."

Mell inclined her head in farewell before clasping the chief's arm in goodbye. "Thank you Chief Broken Horse."

Jed followed closely by Mell walked over to Daniel and Rose.

Mell bent down to Daniel then whispered encouragement. "We can go now the shaman gave me some medicine for Pam. I will tell you what to do later."

Mell turned to Jed calmly wanting to get out of there as soon as possible before something else drastic happened. "Bring your horse over and we will tie the travois on."

Jed turned away then got his horse quickly. After the travois was securely tied, he lifted Rose onto Mell's horse so that she was behind her.

Rose cried out in agony as Jed lifted her.

Mell looked back at her in concern. "What is the matter?"

Rose took a little hesitant breath; large ones were just beyond her ability now as she held onto her side. "I think my ribs are broken!"

Mell frowned in worry. "I will look at it later."

Rose nodded mutely not wanting to stay here either.

Once everyone was mounted, Mell and Jed waved to the chief one final time then urged their horse's on without looking back.

*****

Dream Dancer smiled over at his uncle in delight. "Devil is learning fast."

Black Hawk inclined his head in approval as he watched Golden Eagle turn the stud once more. He called out instructions to Golden Eagle. "Let him go around once more and stop him. When he stops go up to him then touch him all over and cluck to him to see if he will follow you again."

Golden Eagle did as he was told.

Black Hawk watched intently before nodding to himself impressed; the stallion was a fast learner and would be ready to ride soon. He watched Golden Eagle touch the stud then Devil followed him obediently. He beckoned so that Golden Eagle would come over. "That is enough for today tomorrow we will do the same thing, and we will bring our noisemakers too. If he responds fast, you can try putting the blanket then bridle on him."

Golden Eagle smiled in anticipation and went back into the center of the pen to gather his things.

Dream Dancer opened the gate for him in excitement. "Wow your stallion sure learns fast. At this rate, you will be on him in three or four days at the most."

Golden Eagle grinned eagerly at Dream Dancer's enthusiasm. "I sure hope so."

Black Hawk walked over then took his gear back. "You two are invited to my tepee for supper."

Dream Dancer frowned in worry. "Are you sure Gentle Doe is up to the company?"

Black Hawk waved in unconcern. "Mom is helping her prepare supper so that she does not have to do anything."

Dream Dancer inclined his head in agreement. "Well in that case we accept! I will just help Golden Eagle with the cub and we will be there shortly."

Black Hawk inclined his head then left.

Dream Dancer followed by Golden Eagle rushed to Ravens to get ready for supper.

*****

Jed's party reached the area they had left the other two girls.

Mell whistled to let them know it was safe to come out.

Pat and Jess hurried forward with the extra horses.

Mell got down off Pam's horse then helped Rose down also. She turned to her daughter. "Help Rose on her own horse please, but be careful she is injured. I want to travel a little further before we make camp we are going to need a fire tonight."

Pat nodded without speaking questions could wait until later. She helped Rose up before mounting her own horse and they rode on in silence.

*****

Golden Eagle with Dream Dancer close behind got back to the tepee two hours later. Dream Dancer took the cub out while Golden Eagle made coffee. They both sat down across from each other than Dream Dancer smiled sadly. "I have to leave tomorrow."

Golden Eagle nodded dejectedly. "I know."

Dream Dancer looked at Golden Eagle intently worried about him. "Will you be okay? Do you want me to try healing your arm one last time? I noticed that you were favouring it earlier."

Golden Eagle smiled in reassurance and shook his head negatively. "I am fine; the arm is only a little sore from using it so much today. The muscles have to work a little harder to catch up with my other arm; I will put a little of that cream on. Besides, if I do not show at least a little weakness to your grandfather, he would start asking me questions that I will not answer."

Dream Dancer grinned relieved that his friend was not in any real pain than smirked teasingly. "Okay I might see you in the morning, if not take care until I get back and no fighting with my grandfather!"

Golden Eagle chuckled at his young friends teasing then stocked the fire before putting on some cream and going to his own blankets to sleep.

*****

Jed found a good campsite then called a halt.

Pat and Jess hurriedly made camp while Daniel helped Jed remove the travois then put Pam down beside where the fire was going to be.

Mell helped Rose down and took her behind her horse for some privacy. "Lift up your shirt so I can see your side before it gets too dark."

Mell winced in sympathy at the dark purple colouring then gently probed the wound. "Take as deep of a breath as you can and exhale as far as you can."

Mell kept her hand on the wound as Rose did as instructed. She frowned then motioned for Rose to lower her shirt. "One is broken I think or very badly cracked, but I do not feel anything sticking out. Your lungs are not pierced luckily, and I do not hear any rattling when you fill them with air. So I will bind them tomorrow before we start riding again just to give them some support from the constant motion. We do not want the jarring to move any jagged piece that might be there into your lung."

Rose nodded glumly.

Mell motioned towards the fire. "Go sit, I do not want you to move around too much right now. I need to tend to Pam."

Rose sighed in aggravation again she was useless then holding her side she limped painfully to the fire obediently.

Mell went over to Pam's horse and removed the package the medicine man had given to her then went over to Pam. She knelt on the ground beside her daughter-in-law before opening it. She smiled hopefully up at Jed. "Can you help the girl's while Daniel and I see to Pam? Rose might have a broken rib, so I do not want her doing anything until I have a chance to wrap it."

Jed frowned apprehensively one being hurt was serious enough, but two would make travelling difficult; he turned away obediently.

Mell smiled in reassurance at her son. "Can you remove Pam's fur as well as her shirt please?"

Daniel nodded then did as instructed. While he was doing that, Mell selected three packages of dried leaves and got up to go see Rose. Heating water for them to make tea would not be too strenuous for her. She walked around the fire then handed two packets to her first and finally the other one as she explained what she wanted her to do. "Rose can you steep a pinch of these two packets in some water for tea, make enough for both you as well as Pam. I also need you to make a paste with this one; I will need some warm water as well."

Rose inclined her head thankfully; glad to be of some use at least than went to get some water from the stream.

Mell went back to Pam and knelt down so that she could remove the bandage wrapped around her ribs while Daniel lifted her carefully. She explained to Daniel as she unwrapped the binding what the shaman had told her about his wife. "The shaman said Pam has a broken rib, which is a bit of a cause for worry because it is protruding inward, so it is to close to her lung. He said she must be kept as still as possible, so that the rib does not puncture another hole in her soft tissue. Now Rose told me that, in the river, Pam was snagged on a tree, which was hidden under the water. A branch punctured a hole in-between the ribs, which caused one rib to break. The shaman thinks the branch either scraped her lung or maybe put a little hole in it but not all the way through the lung. That is why she is wheezing a little, if it had gone all the way through she would be cough up blood depending on how large the hole is. Since she has not coughed up blood yet, he does not believe it went all the way through. If that rib moves though, it could pierce the same hole then make it bigger. Rose is brewing some tea, when it is cooled off enough you must put a little tea in your mouth and dribble it into Pam's mouth a little at a time she should swallow reflexively. If not you will have to stroke her throat to make her swallow. She must have the tea three times a day as well as some water. At least once a day she should have broth given in the same manner. Rose is making a poultice as well for Pam's wound it needs to be washed three times a day then the poultice put on before we re-wrap her ribs."

Daniel had listened quietly to Mell talking while he gently held his wife up so that his mother could remove the binding. When she finished talking, he sighed grimly in concern. "But will she make it?"

Mell looked at his son in sympathy before shaking her head sadly. "We do not know, all we can do is pray for the best, but you must be prepared for the worst. If she gets pneumonia, she probably will not survive it."

Daniel nodded bleakly without saying anything else.

Rose came over with warm water as well as a cloth, so Mell cleaned Pams wound while Daniel gave her medicine and a little cool water to drink.

Once finished they squatted around the fire to eat themselves.

Everyone enjoyed the hot stew Jess prepared immensely, but they were all too tired to talk. They fell into their blankets in exhaustion as soon as they possibly could.

*****

Raven sighed in relief as she looked for a hidden defensible camp. The Eagle tribe was just over that ridge then down into the trees for a bit before reaching a clearing. She wanted to scout it out first, but it was much to dark to see, so she would have to wait until morning. She found what she was looking for and made a quick camp.

There was a stream just behind Raven's camp, so she decided to go for a bath after her animals were looked after. When she returned, she rummaged in her pack for supper. She did not want to have a fire this close to the Eagle camp. She ate jerky with some hardtack then crawled into her blankets and promptly fell thankfully into a dreamless asleep.

CHAPTER EIGHTEEN

Golden Eagle woke then looked around for Dream Dancer, but he was already gone. He got up and stretched then quickly dressed before building up the fire to make coffee. The coffee was almost done when Dream Dancer ducked into the tepee with breakfast.

Golden Eagle smiled enthusiastically; he was glad his friend was still around. "I thought you left already."

Dream Dancer grinned back reassuringly and handed Golden Eagle his breakfast. "I could not leave without saying goodbye first."

Golden Eagle beamed in satisfaction. "I am really glad you did not go yet."

Golden Eagle dribbled a little honey in his porridge then ate in silence. He was not all that hungry, so he only ate half and put the bowl down. He looked over at Dream Dancer inquisitively. "Are you coming for your lessons this morning before you leave?"

Dream Dancer nodded decisively. "Of course…"

Dream Dancer did not quit finish what he was going to say as he laughed in amusement instead then pointed down at Golden Eagle's side for him to look.

Golden Eagle looked down inquisitively and saw the cub eating the rest of his porridge. He looked back at Dream Dancer incredulously with a chuckle. "I did not think he would like porridge."

Dream Dancer smirked in humour then pointed at the jar. "It is probably the honey, bears love honey."

Golden Eagle grinned in delight. "Good I will give him porridge in the morning instead of a fish one less thing I have to do at night before bed."

Dream Dancer inclined his head in approval. "That is a good idea. Now that the cub is finished we better go for our lessons."

Golden Eagle nodded as he lifted the cub before standing up as they left the tepee.

*****

Mell and Daniel woke to the smell of bacon frying.

Mell reached over to check Pam; thankfully, she was sleeping peacefully. She smiled at her son in reassurance. "She is still sleeping so go eat then we will check her wound and give her some medicine."

Daniel sighed in relief as he yawned tiredly then got up.

Neither of them had gotten much sleep last night since they both slept beside his wife, his mother on one side and him on the other. Pam had woken them both up several times groaning then thrashing in her sleep; they had taken turns throughout the night administering to Pam's needs.

Daniel walked to the fire and smiled teasingly at his father. "You cooked breakfast!"

Jed grinned up at his son ignoring his wittiness. "Well since we need to go a little slower I decided I better cook it since I was the first one up."

Daniel hunkered down before accepting the plate of bacon and flapjacks his father handed him in gratitude.

Jess followed by Pat came next.

Pat smirked at her father incredulously, but did not comment. "Everything is ready to go."

Jed nodded then gave each of the girl's a plate.

Mell and Rose came next.

Mell looked at her husband disbelievingly then exclaimed in shock as she held onto her chest dramatically as if having a heart attack. "You cooked breakfast!"

The others all laughed at Mell's amazed stare.

Jed gave his wife a dirty look. "I do cook sometimes!"

Mell just smiled in delight at his injured tone and helped herself to coffee than the food without further comment.

Jed waited until everyone finished eating as he sighed thoughtfully. "Well, we are definitely going to have to slow down now! I want to leave a little earlier from now on, and we will ride a little later if we can. If we have no more problems we can still make the next town in four days. We are still in Blackfoot country so be prepared though most of the tribes are not as friendly as the last one was. We will have to try keeping Pam as quiet as possible."

Daniel grimaced in dismay then motioned for everyone to go ahead. "Maybe you should leave us behind; we can always catch up later."

Mell shook her head emphatically surprised her son would even suggest such a thing. "No way would I ever leave you or my daughter-in-law out here by yourselves."

Jed nodded decisively, reluctant to leave anyone behind. "I agree with Mell, besides we were going to have to slow down anyway. Our horses need to stay in reasonably good shape just in case we have to outrun the Blackfoot. We can tie the travois between my horse and Mell's. This way Pam is not being bounced on the hard ground. If we have to make a run for it as well, we do not have to worry that she will get hurt anymore than she is now or fall off without us notice. Tomorrow after we get out of the tree's it is relatively barren from there so it should not be a problem for the horses to carry Pam that way. It will also be very hot for the next few days with not much water so be prepared for that too! I want everyone to fill up every container we have with water before we go."

Daniel inclined his head in relief; he had not actually wanted them to leave him, but he felt that he had to make the offer anyway. "Okay, I will give Pam her medicine right away."

Mell got up to help her son.

The others finished breaking camp, and Pam was tied behind Jed's horse again.

Daniel put his gun belt on again before mounting; he frowned disconcerted as he heard that strange laughing again, but this time it was different it had more of a satisfaction sound to it now. He stared grimly at the others as they gazed at him in disapproval, but he refused to say anything not ready to talk about it yet.

Mell looked at Jed in bafflement, but neither said anything respecting their son's decision as they turned their horses then they were on their way once more.

*****

Raven woke just before dawn so swiftly broke camp; she picketed the packhorse so he could eat but could not wander off. She turned to Bruno in demand. "You stay here boy and guard the packhorse while I go scout the Eagle tribe."

Bruno whined plaintively at being left behind, but obediently layed down then watched the horse.

Raven mounted Brave Heart, and they trotted away from her camp.

*****

Golden Eagle with Dream Dancer walking beside him went back to Ravens quietly both amerced in their own thoughts. As they got closer to the tepee, Dream Dancer sighed dejectedly as he waved ahead of them. "It looks like grandfather is here already."

Golden Eagle looked up sadly then saw the wagon and horses already waiting outside Raven's for Dream Dancer. He frowned in aggravation. "I will miss you while you are gone. Try to hurry back will you?"

Dream Dancer grinned at the plaintive note in his friend's voice. "I will try."

Dream Dancer ducked into the tepee before putting the cub down then started to gather his things.

Golden Eagle went over to talk to Giant Bear.

Giant Bear smiled in greeting as he motioned at his arm in doubt still not believing the Englishman's reason for the fast recovery. "How is your arm doing today?"

Golden Eagle sighed in irritation as he put on a good show of being in pain; he held onto his wrist and slowly flexed his fingers. "It is fairly sore today from all the exercising I have been doing. I will put some more of that cream the medicine man gave me on it tonight."

Giant Bear nodded with a frown of displeasure, but still he could not figure out how he had done it. "That should help it. How is it going with your stallion any progress yet?"

Golden Eagle grinned at the thought of his horse then dropped his arms. "Yes, he is a fast learner. Black Hawk figures we can probably put the saddle blanket and the bridle on him today or tomorrow."

Giant Bear nodded in satisfaction. "That is good."

Dream Dancer finished his packing then came out. He walked to his grandfather to clasp his arm in goodbye. "I will see you in a few days."

Giant Bear inclined his head. "Okay, you be careful."

Dream Dancer turned to Golden Eagle next, they embraced in farewell. "I will see you in a few days also."

Golden Eagle chuckled in warning. "Yes, and do not get into any mischief while you are gone."

Dream Dancer laughed as he remembered the jokes he had played on his friend. "Now that is not something I can promise!"

Golden Eagle smirked knowingly then helped his young friend put his things in the wagon before waving goodbye forlornly. He turned away walking sadly towards Giant Bears tepee. He would miss Raven's brother as well as their talks about Indian's and England. He reached Giant Bear's then ducked in for his lessons with Golden Dove.

*****

Raven reached the edge of the trees and dismounted; she tied Brave Hearts reins together then put them over his head. So if she had to call out to him, her horse would not trip nor become caught in a tree. She whispered softly in command. "Stand, Brave Heart!"

Raven turned away and melted into the tree's without a sound. She walked forward cautiously, so quiet that not even the animals realized she was there. Every once in a while she would stop to listen then go in another direction as she slipped past the sentries like a ghost unseen and unheard.

Raven reached the edge of the trees without incident then cautiously peered out. She looked left and right thoughtfully then spotted what she was looking for off to her right. It was a small hill overlooking the village; she could hide behind it while she watched them. She backed away from the opening and angled to her right. Suddenly she stopped then squatted down behind some bushes as she heard rustling off to her left.

Raven held her breath and waited as she watched two warriors walk out of the trees where she had been standing only a moment before. She held perfectly still as they disappeared from view then she quietly went further. She judged that she was near the hill so went back to the edge of the trees to look out.

The hill was just ahead of Raven, and she sighed in relief. So far so good, now she had to cross an open space then she would be safely hidden behind the hill.

Raven looked around and did not see anyone, so she crouched in readiness. She was just about to run out when she heard a raven squawk loudly in rebuke. Instantly, she dropped down then waited. She stayed there for five minutes before she heard warriors trot past her hiding place. After they had gone by, she got back up and reached for her medicine bag thanking her spirit animal for the warning.

Raven cautiously peeked out again, but not seeing or hearing anything more she crouched down again then left her hiding place. She raced across the open area in a half crouch. Once she reached the hill, she ran behind it before climbing up. She saw some rocks ahead, so she hurried behind them and stopped to catch her breath.

Raven looked around cautiously, but all she saw was another pile of rocks off to her left. They were higher up though, just past that was the top of the hill. It would be the perfect place to hide so that she could watch the village. She explored the rocks a little more carefully then noticed a niche that was hidden. If she had to hide, she could crawl in there and nobody would see her. Satisfied that she knew the area well enough she warily made her way to the top of the hill. When she judged she was close enough she dropped onto her stomach as she peered over the edge.

The view from up here was even better than Raven had at first thought, she could see the whole village and the people clearly. She identified the shaman's tepee as well as the chief's tepee right away. Next, she looked for Howling Coyotes but did not see it anywhere. She counted tepees before shaking her head in puzzlement when she only counted thirty, there should have been at least another fifty tepee's down there.

Raven looked at the chief's again then stiffened as she saw a white woman come out; she was blonde and did not look very tall from this distance. Raven could not see her face; she wondered if that were Janet. She did not want to get her hopes up though; the Eagle tribe had a couple of white women in their camp from before. That was one reason they were refused when they asked to stay on Raven's ranch. Two of the white women had not wanted to stay or be adopted they wanted to go home instead. The Indian brave's who owned them did not want to give them up, so they had left.

Raven backed off then went to her hiding place; she took out some jerky and ate while she was thinking. She decided to go get her horse as well as her packhorse then she would come around on the other side of this hill so that nobody would see her. That way she could watch the village for the rest of the day and hopefully, get the chief alone to talk to him. She sat back then relaxed as she ate making plans.

*****

Jed started looking around contemplatively; he found what he was looking for a few minutes later, a good defensible campsite for lunch. Everyone dismounted, and a hasty meal was prepared.

Mell with Daniel's help unhooked the travois then moved Pam over to the fire while the others made a meal.

Mell took off Pam's shirt before washing the wound. She looked at Daniel in concern. "She has a slight fever hopefully it will not last, go over and ask Rose if the medicine is ready."

Daniel got up then left, he came back a few minutes later and handed his mother the paste for Pam's injury.

Mell put the paste on before wrapping a clean bandage around Pam; she redressed her then covered her with a fur. She took her white buffalo hide and put it around Pam as well for added warmth hoping to sweat the fever out.

Mell sat back then looked at her son and motioned towards the cup he was holding. "Give her the medicine then come and have lunch."

Daniel nodded distractedly after his mother; finally, alone he bowed his head in prayer desperately pleading to God as well as his son Jesus to help his wife. When he was finished, he put some tea in his mouth then dribbled a little at a time in. Once the tea was all gone, he sat back and looked up imploringly once again. He felt a slight shiver flow down his spine as he prayed then smiled as he felt another presence beside him comforting him in his time of need. He stayed that way for several minutes before reluctantly opening his eyes once the feeling was gone. He felt lighter in spirit though as his faith, that he had thought lost, was renewed once more.

Daniel remembered a passage in his bible that he had forgotten; being a pastor, he should not have forgotten it. It was in Romans five, verse three, four and five; 'We can rejoice, too, when we run into problems and trials, for we know that they help us develop endurance. And endurance develops strength of character, and character strengthens our confident hope of salvation. And this hope will not lead to disappointment, for we know how dearly God loves us because he has given us the Holy Spirit to fill our hearts with his love.'

*****

Mell went over to the fire then accepted a bowl of stew and ate hungrily.

Jed eyed his wife then frowned in concern. "How is she doing?"

Mell sighed apprehensively. "I am not sure yet, she is getting a fever which worries me. If it turns into pneumonia, we could be in trouble!"

Everyone finished eating sadly and repacked to go.

Mell took a bowl of stew to her son; she eyed his serene expression curiously but did not ask before smiling in approval knowing he had found his inner peace once more.

Daniel ate all of it except the broth then patiently fed his wife using his mouth. Thankfully, he got her to take all the nourishing broth in the bowl. When he was done, they reattached the travois to Jed's horse.

Daniel walked over to his horse, and as he walked, he was undoing his gun belt. He put them away for good this time; his faith was now stronger than it had ever been and even if his wife were to die today, it would not ever be shaken again. He looked around then smiled serenely as he heard a groan of disappointment from somewhere but again there was nobody around. Never again would he hear that mocking laughter. A few minutes later, he forgot about it as if it had never happened.

Jed and Mell exchanged relieved smiles they had both been worried when their son had strapped the gun belt back on the next morning after retrieving Pam.

Daniel's twin sister Pat rode up to him after he mounted then winked at him in joy having felt his faith as it became stronger. "It's about time; you had me worried there for awhile!"

Daniel sighed dejectedly as they followed the others. "I was worried to; my faith has never really been tested before now though. I have watched my parishioners in my church as one tragedy, or another tested them. Some walked away stronger in their faith, but others lost their faith completely. I have never understood fully how they could walk away from God. It frustrated me being unable to help them to see that Jesus will forever stand by them. Now at last I fully understand what I preach about in my church, of course I have always believed, but until now, I have felt unsatisfied. My first reaction, especially since I am a preacher, should have been to trust in God as well as Jesus but I did not. I strapped my guns on instead, so I thought I was lost for sure, but today I realized that Jesus understood and was still standing by me regardless of my mistake. Just because, I am a Pastor, does not mean I am not allowed to make errors in judgement as well."

Pat nodded in understanding as they continued on in silence.

*****

Golden Eagle ducked out of Giant Bear's tepee then walked back to Raven's. Golden Dove had mentioned that he had better start walking the cub around the village so he could get used to other people and the camp dogs. She had also advised him to take Cuddles over to where the children played. That way they could play with the cub, to keep him occupied while he was at his lessons or working with his horse. He had expressed his concern about the dogs hurting the cub or one of the children possibly getting hurt. But Golden Dove had reassured him when she told him that the dogs, as well as the children, were used to bear cubs in the village this was not the first time they had one.

Golden Eagle ducked inside then walked over to the sleeping cub; he grabbed a fish and woke the cub to feed him. When Cuddles was done eating, the Englishman picked him up then took him out back to his favourite tree. After the cub finished Golden Eagle called him to come.

The five camp dogs eyed the cub curiously, but only one came over to sniff at him curiously. They walked past the shaman's tepee and out into the open where Golden Eagle could hear children laughing.

When the children caught sight of the vi'hoI coming with the cub they all quieted then gathered in a group.

Golden Eagle bent down and picked up the cub then walked over to the children. When he was close, he stopped and spoke hesitantly in Cheyenne. "My name is Golden Eagle."

The boy who brought water to his horse stepped forward then pointed at himself. "My name is Little Beaver."

Golden Eagle inclined his head at the introduction. "Dream Dancer has gone home, so I was hoping you would play with the cub in the morning and afternoon so that he will not get bored by himself."

Little Beaver eyed Golden Eagle as well as the cub then huddled with the other children for a moment. He turned back to the Englishman and nodded his head in agreement. "I will come for the cub just after the sun rises; I will bring him back to you before the sun goes down."

Golden Eagle smiled in relief. "That is good; his name is Cuddles, thank you!"

Golden Eagle put the cub down to see what the children would do. He watched in satisfaction as each child went to the grizzly cub to be introduced.

Little Beaver picked up the cub after introductions were finished then they disappeared.

Golden Eagle turned before going to look for Black Hawk.

*****

Raven looked around cautiously than not seeing or hearing anything, she ran back across the clearing and into the trees. When she was hidden away again, she grinned pleased with herself. She moved ahead slowly, sometimes she would stop then listen closely before veering around a sentry. About halfway back to her horse, Raven stopped dead in her tracks and waited tensely. She could feel the hair at the back of her neck rising in warning, she stood there perfectly still not move a muscle for a good ten minutes. Only her eyes moved as she looked for whatever was causing her reaction; she caught movement not far ahead, if she had kept going on her current course she would have walked right into a sentry. She backed away quietly then turned to her right and went around. She exited the trees suddenly with a sigh of relief then found where she had left her horse; swiftly she mounted and rode off.

*****

Jed stopped then beckoned Mell forward. "The tree's stop just ahead after that it's all open country for awhile. Even though it's early I think we should camp here for tonight, it will give Pam a little break and hopefully the fever will abate a little by morning."

Mell sighed relieved then motioned decisively. "Yes, I think we all need a good nights sleep before riding through open Blackfoot territory."

Jed nodded, and the camp was set up for the night.

*****

Giant Bear walked over to Black Hawk then stood there watching Golden Eagle work his horse. He turned to his son in concern. "How is Gentle Doe doing?"

Black Hawk smiled in relief. "She is doing fine so far."

Giant Bear waved towards the paddocks inquisitively. "Good, how is Golden Eagle doing he seems much calmer the last few days."

Black Hawk grinned in agreement. "Yes he is. Dream Dancer was good for him, and training with me, as well as teaching his own horse helped also."

Giant Bear nodded pleased. "He will start training with Running Wolf in two days too."

Black Hawk inclined his head in satisfaction. "That is good now that Dream Dancer is gone it will keep him busy."

Black Hawk looked at his father curiously, he had not dared go over much since the night the chief had told his wife what he had done. "How is mother doing?"

Giant Bear scowled in irritation then shrugged dejectedly. "I do not know she still will not talk to me unless she has to. Which reminds me you and your wife are supposed to come over for supper with Golden Eagle?"

Black Hawk nodded distractedly then walked to the fence before calling out instructions. "Golden Eagle you can stop him soon and take him to the middle of the pen then try to put the saddle blanket on him."

Golden Eagle waved in acknowledgement.

Black Hawk moved closer to his father and frowned inquisitively. "Have you changed your mind yet on forcing the two to marry?"

Giant Bear shook his head decisively in disagreement. "No, I have not changed my mind."

Black Hawk sighed in exasperation then motioned in warning. "Well, I wish you would do so! Forcing those two to marry is going to backfire in your face. It will cause a catastrophe even you would not want to contemplate."

Giant Bear grimaced in apprehension and frowned in alarm. "What do you know that I do not?"

Black Hawk shrugged in forewarning. "I am not sure what will happen exactly I just have a bad feeling about all this."

Giant Bear stood quietly beside Black Hawk worried more than ever now. For some reason, the shaman was apprehensive as well. The Great Spirit had been silent lately, way to quiet with no visions forthcoming. Now Black Hawk was getting feelings it was time to talk to the shaman again. He turned to Black Hawk. "I will see you later."

Black Hawk nodded and watched his father leave before shaking his head in disapproval. He had known that his father would not listen, but it was worth one more try. He shrugged then turned back to Golden Eagle and watched him walk towards the stallion with the blanket.

*****

Black Hawk walked up to the fence and called out in encouragement. "Golden Eagle get him to follow you around the pen for a few minutes then take off the blanket and rub him down. That will be enough for today we are suppose to go for supper soon."

Golden Eagle inclined his head in agreement towards Black Hawk then smiled in satisfaction as the stallion followed him around and barely paid any attention to what was on his back. After two rounds around the pen, he took off the saddle blanket then rubbed his horse down before gathering everything and leaving.

Black Hawk let him out then took his things. "Go get cleaned up a little and meet me at my fathers for supper."

Golden Eagle nodded then went to get ready.

*****

Raven arrived back at camp and unhobbled her packhorse before tying him to Brave Heart then she remounted. She looked down at her dog. "Come on Bruno and be quiet."

Raven rode around the village giving it a wide birth, she could not help but wonder what was going on. The Eagle tribe had out twice as many sentries then they need this close to their own village. The only time a village had that many sentries out was when they feared attack or was in enemy territory. So who would attack them out here? The last she had heard the army was busy running after the Blackfoot for destroying a wagon train a month ago. Which meant that the Blackfoot were too busy running away from the army so did not have time to strike here.

Unless, the chief feared Raven would bring warriors and attack them. This would mean that they knew about the attack on Golden Eagle's party.

Raven reached the hill she had watched the village from then dismounted and walked ahead of her horse clucking in encouragement. "Come on Brave Heart you have to climb a little."

Brave Heart obediently followed his mistress up the steep terrain.

Raven got to her pile of rocks than moved the horses in front of them so that they would not be seen. It was fairly level here so the horse's would have no problem staying close to her. She went to the packhorse first and took out hay, as well as oats that were carried for this purpose just in case feed was unavailable. After feeding the horse's she took out some jerky than cakes to give to her dog.

Raven crawled back up to the top of the rise and peeked over, it was still extremely quiet down there; the War Chief still was nowhere to be seen. She went back to her horses then made a bed for herself; she would wait until morning and hopefully, get the chief by himself so that she could find out what he knows. Her mind made up she rolled herself in her blankets then slept.

*****

Golden Eagle escaped Giant Bear's tepee and went back to Ravens. The cub was already sound asleep with a half-eaten fish lying beside him when Golden Eagle entered. He smiled down at the cub then banked the fire for the night and curled up beside Cuddles to sleep.

CHAPTER NINETEEN

Mell woke first then checked on her patient; she shook her head in concern Pam's fever was getting worse. She reached over Pam and shook her son.

Daniel woke immediately then looked up at his mother in fear.

Mell smiled reassuringly and crooked her finger for him to follow her. They went over to the smouldering fire; he built it up again while Mell got water then started coffee. She made breakfast as Daniel put a large pot of water on the fire to heat for Pam's sponge bath; he took a smaller bowl and added water for her tea. Mell finished making the porridge then set it on the fire to cook. She looked over at her son inquisitively. "Can you stir the porridge while I go wake the others?"

Daniel nodded and watched his mother get up then leave, he smiled in delight after his mother she was still in her buckskins, and they made her look remarkably striking. He stirred the porridge then added the medicines to the boiling water for tea. He let it steep for a few minutes and removed the pot from the fire just before it started boiling again. He reached over then checked the bath water it was not quite ready yet, so he left it on a little longer while he stirred the porridge.

Mell came back a few minutes later to take over breakfast duty once more.

Jed and Jessica arrived with Pat then Rose not far behind.

Jed smiled at his wife hopefully. "How is Pam this morning?"

Mell sighed in sorrow as she motioned grimly. "Not very good since her fever is worse, but at least her wound is healing."

Jed frowned apprehensively and gestured inquisitively. "Will she be up to a long ride?"

Mell shrugged then grimaced uneasily. "I do not know, but we need to get her to a doctor soon. We will have to tie her securely so that if we need to trot or run she will not get bounced as bad."

Jed nodded calmly even though he did not feel calm. He had a feeling time was running out. "We will keep it to a walk as much as possible today."

Mell inclined her head in relief.

Daniel took the bath water and tea over to his wife while everyone ate.

Mell made the paste before heating up some broth they had saved from last nights stew while she ate then took them over to her son.

Daniel smiled sadly at his mother as she knelt down beside Pam.

Mell sighed at her son's downcast face and reached out then squeezed his hand comfortingly. "Go eat breakfast while I sponge Pam down, the tea and broth should be cool enough when you get back."

Daniel finished undressing his wife before leaving.

Mell tenderly washed Pam down then after checking her injury she put more paste on and re-wrapped her ribs. She tightened the dressing a little more this morning to give Pam's ribs more support if they had to run then dressed her once more. She just finished when Daniel came back carrying a cup of coffee for her. She grinned in pleasure as she sat back and accepted the coffee gratefully. "Thank you everything should be cool enough now."

Daniel nodded then knelt down beside his wife; he put a little tea in his mouth and dribbled a little at a time into hers.

Mell watched as her son put his lips gently on his wife's then released some of the liquid into her mouth slowly. She sighed relieved as Pam reflexively swallowed the tea; he did the same with the broth.

Daniel sat back in concern and waved anxiously. "Why has she not responded yet?"

Mell frowned uneasily as she shook her head perplexed. "I do not know the shaman could not find anymore wounds or any bumps to her head. He figures when her body heals itself enough it will let her know then she will wake up."

Daniel absently stroked his wife's hair away from her forehead; he scowled in fear as he looked over at his mother in dread. "Her fever is getting worse is there anything we can do for that at least?"

Mell sighed negatively and motioned in explanation. "We are already giving her the medicine for fever. I think we will strengthen the dose a little when we stop tonight though."

Daniel nodded at his mother then smiled sorrowfully up at his father as he came towards them carrying some rope.

Jed handed the rope to Mell. "Better tie her down now it is time to go."

Mell inclined her head, and they secured Pam tightly to the travois.

Jed with Daniels help lifted it between them then carried Pam to the horses.

Mell brought her horse over beside Jed's and held him still while the women secured a rope on each saddled horn than a cord to the back of the saddles so that the travois rested between her and Jed's horse.

The two men eased the travois down carefully holding their breaths apprehensively.

Jed's horse threw his head back then snorted in uncertainty at the unfamiliar weight as his saddle leaned slightly to the right.

Jed stepped in front of him as he stroked his horse in comfort. "Easy now, Two Socks!"

The horse bent down for a scratch before settling down.

Mell turned towards Jed worriedly. "I think we better walk in front of them for a bit to let them get used to moving together especially with the travois moving between them."

Jed nodded in agreement at the good idea as they lead the horses out into the open cautiously. Keeping the horse's evenly spaced proved to be no problem since both horses were used to travelling together.

The travois bumped Mell's horse a little that caused him to jump in surprise.

Mell murmured reassurances to him, so he obediently settled down. After walking for half an hour with no more problems Jed nodded to

Mell, so they mounted. They tried to keep most of their weight on the opposite side of their leaning saddles, so that they did not lean, quit as perilously.

Daniel watched anxiously unsure if this was such a good idea as the horses moved together with Pam strung in the middle precariously.

Jed kept the horses to a walk for an hour. He turned to look back at Daniel in warning. "We are going to trot for a while so that the horses can get used to the travois."

Daniel nodded fretfully.

Jed looked over at his wife. "Okay ready."

When Mell nodded, Jed gave the command. "Now!"

Mell and Jed kicked their horses into a trot at the same time. The travois bumped around way too much, so Mell moved her horse over a little to tighten the ropes more. The travois steadied as the horses got into a rhythm that kept them at an even distance. She sighed in relief as both horses adjusted to the travois with no real fuss.

Jed turned to Mell again. "Okay let's canter for ten minutes then go back to a walk."

Mell nodded as she waited.

Jed gave the order, so they both kicked their horses into a canter.

Jed's horse tried to rush forward past Mell's, and Jed had to hold him back.

The travois bumped into Mell's horse again, so she moved him over a little more.

Daniel watched in dismay as his father fought with his horse then finally got him under control. He watched the travois hit his mother's horse in fear. He held his breath anxiously praying as he watched her try to keep control of her horse before heaving a sigh of relief as both horses adjusted and the travois steadied between them.

Jed sighed in satisfaction as he called out to Mell. "Okay a trot first then walk."

Mell waited and together they pulled up as they trotted then went into a walk.

Jed smiled in approval over at Mell. "We will walk until just before we stop for lunch, and we will try this again at that time."

Mell frowned in relief glad she did not have to do this again for a bit as they continued on.

*****

Raven woke then sat up, she looked up at the sky, but it was still to dark to see. She got up to feed both her horses before rummaging in her pack for her and Bruno's breakfast. When she judged that it was light enough, she climbed back up the hill then looked down. The village was just coming awake, and she watched the women coming out first to start their chores.

Raven stiffened when she saw the same white woman come out of the chiefs with two buckets for water then disappear between the tepees towards the creek. She stood up to slip down and intercept her then dropped back down as two other women followed her to the creek. She sighed in disappointment and settled back to watch the chief's tepee once more. She saw the chief's wife with their daughter come out then leave.

Raven got up again and looked down the hill speculatively. If she slipped down to her left, she could sneak up to the chief's from behind. She dropped back down in irritation as she watched the chief come out of his tepee then head over to the shamans. She frowned in frustration and settled back down to wait for another opportunity.

*****

Golden Eagle woke to a cold nose stuck in his face nudging him awake impatiently. He laughed as he pushed the cub away. "Okay I am up Cuddles what's your problem this morning. Are you hungry already?"

Golden Eagle rolled out of his blankets then got dressed, he walked over to the corner where the bucket of fish was and took out a small one then hit it with the butt of his knife before giving it to the cub to keep him busy while he went over and got them some porridge. He left the tepee then walked towards Giant Bears.

Golden Eagle was halfway there when he heard horses galloping into the village. He looked up and jumped out of the way, as two white men almost knocked him down. He hurried after them curiously. He slowed down as he got to Giant Bear's tepee then watched the white men storm in.

Black Hawk came running up to Golden Eagle. "Come on it looks like trouble."

Golden Eagle nodded in relief at being included and rushed after Black Hawk. They went inside, but immediately the Englishman stepped into the shadows so that he would not be noticed then listened quietly.

*****

Giant Bear jumped up as the two white men stormed into his tepee. He scowled in angry reproach as he waved in demand. "What is the meaning of this Jake you are supposed to be at the ranch?"

Jake shook his head urgently. "I am sorry Giant Bear, but the sheriff and half a dozen men are on their way here right now. We raced ahead of them to warn you as soon as we found out!"

Giant Bear frowned uneasily. "It is too soon Raven is not back yet!"

Giant Bear looked up as Black Hawk came in. In his agitation, he did not see Golden Eagle slip in too. "The sheriff is on his way here with six men. It will be at least another two weeks before Raven gets back, any suggestions?"

Black Hawk thought for a moment then nodded grimly. "First off we will have to hide Golden Eagle, if they see him they are going to want to know what happened to his guides. Since the sheriff only came with six men he is probably just coming to look around and to ask questions, we will let him know that Raven is looking into the matter. I will try to stall him for two weeks until she gets back."

Giant Bear inclined his head gloomily. "Okay, I will let you handle it then."

Giant Bear turned to Jake. "Are you going to stay and help convince the sheriff?"

Jake grimaced in agreement then gestured sharply in reassurance. "You will need us here as back up, I will help anyway I can. I already posted men all around to make sure nobody comes in or out of these hills without me knowing. I left Shorty in charge until I return."

Jake turned to the other guy and waved towards the entrance. "Dan, go take your position but stay hidden unless I tell you otherwise."

Dan nodded then left.

Golden Eagle stepped forward wanting to help too. "I can tell them it was not your village that attacked me. I could also tell them you saved my life!"

Black Hawk looked at Golden Eagle in surprise; he had forgotten he was there. He shook his head negatively. "No, the whites would not care if they saw you it would give them an excuse to drive the Indian's out and Raven too for harbouring us."

Golden Eagle nodded with a frown of apprehension. "Okay, I will hide over where we train in the morning."

Giant Bear looked at Golden Eagle in shock. "You will hide yourself without a fight or someone having to watch you?"

Golden Eagle scowled at the chief's incredulous look obviously he did not know him very well. "I promised Raven I would wait for her, I always keep my word! Besides I do not want to jeopardize my sisters only hope of rescue!"

Jake turned to Golden Eagle then looked him up and down speculatively. "So you are the man who is causing all the fuss."

Golden Eagle nodded with a smile, as he looked Jake over. Dream Dancer had told him Jake looked after the ranch when Raven was gone. He stuck out his hand for a shake. "Names, Devon Rochester or Golden Eagle here."

Jake inclined his head in greeting then clasped Golden Eagles hand in a firm handshake. "I'm, Jake Shannon."

Golden Eagle frowned thoughtfully wondering how much time he had. "How long before the sheriff gets here?"

Jake sighed disgruntled. "About half an hour."

Golden Eagle nodded relieved and turned to Golden Dove. "Is there any breakfast?"

Golden Dove smiled in encouragement as she waved down at the waiting food. "Porridge is ready whenever you are."

Golden Dove had seen the Englishman walk in but had not said anything watching him knowingly. She had guessed some time ago that he knew everything by the way he had been acting lately. The fact that he never showed any surprise or asked any questions when he had seen Jake had confirmed it for her. What he was going to do with that information worried her a little, he was so hard to understand sometimes. She knew he was just bidding his time until his sister was returned to him, what would happen after that was anyone's guess.

Golden Eagle walked over to the fire then dished up two bowls of porridge.

Golden Dove lifted her eyebrows in surprise.

Golden Eagle grinned and shrugged with a chuckle of delight as he explained. "I found out yesterday that the cub likes porridge with honey."

Golden Dove nodded but did not say anything.

Golden Eagle took the bowls of porridge then left.

*****

Raven sighed annoyingly this was not working at all; she had sat in this spot all morning and watched the village. Not even one occasion had presented itself to get the chief or the white woman alone. She went back to her horses then rummaged in her packs for something to eat. She sat with her back to the rocks thinking furiously as she ate her lunch and fed her dog. She could sit watching the village for the rest of the day or she could take a chance then ride in so she could confront the chief directly, sitting around was defiantly not doing her any good and time was running out. If the sentries were out watching for her though, Raven could be dead before she reached the village. Then another idea came to her, and she got up then tied the packhorse back onto Brave Hearts saddle. "Come, Brave Heart."

Raven led her horses back down the hill; when they reached the bottom, she turned to Brave Heart in command. "Stand, Brave Heart."

Raven snapped her fingers in demand to Bruno. "Come Bruno, but stay close to me."

Raven and Bruno inched their way around the hill then she crouched and cautiously looked around. Not seeing anyone she raced out of her hiding spot then into the tree's for cover. She crouched there for a bit and not hearing any outcry, she cautiously made her way back to the spot she had seen one of the sentries hidden. When they were close enough she drew her knife then crouched in readiness, she put her finger to her lips to show the wolf that he needed to be quiet.

Raven held her knife tucked against her arm so that if she needed it, it would be ready. They inched their way forward, but when she got to the location she was looking for the lookout was gone. She frowned irritably and looked around; he had to be here somewhere. She spotted movement to her left, so she went in that direction.

The sentry Raven was looking for was standing beside a tree relieving himself.

Raven motioned the wolf to stay then crept soundlessly up behind the man. She stood up behind him suddenly and put her arm around the sentry's throat then held the knife up threateningly so that he could see it. "Why are there so many sentries around the village?"

The warrior looked to the side and saw the wolf crouched ready to jump at him if he threatened the woman holding him in anyway. He held up his hands showing he was no threat as he answered her calmly already knowing who she was. "The chief has banished our War Chief Howling Coyote; he has threatened revenge against us."

Raven eased her grip on the sentry in relief then stood back. The warrior flipped his loincloth back around himself and turned to face Raven expectantly. He nodded impassively as his suspicion was confirmed then he pointed at her. "The chief has also been waiting for the Raven, 'Protector' of her people!"

Raven stiffened instantly in surprise. "Why?"

The Indian shrugged uncaring. "I do not know the chief told us that when you come we are to bring you to him immediately."

Raven narrowed her eyes dangerously. "Not if I come, but when I come?"

The warrior scowled knowingly. "The chief seemed certain that you would come here since he has something you want."

Raven nodded as she waved so that the brave would go first. She snapped her fingers in command and Bruno obediently walked close to her side watching the Indian closely. When they reached the open area then exited the trees she gave a whistle for her horse to come.

Brave Heart galloped around the hill and ran to his mistress leading the packhorse. He stopped beside her then followed closely.

The Indian brave looked the horse up and down in admiration. "I am going to come to see you when we move to our winter camp to trade for one of your horses."

Raven, not actually caring about horses or trading right at this moment still answered distractedly anyway, not wanting to discourage him. "I have many that are for trade."

The warrior inclined his head then continued to lead the way.

*****

Jed and Mell slowed their horses to a walk. He waved towards Mell's right. "There is a hill over there with large rocks at the bottom for protection we can camp there for a quick lunch."

Mell looked at where he was pointing then looked over her shoulder at the others. "You guys go ahead of us to start setting up camp we will follow."

They galloped away while Mell and Jed followed more slowly.

*****

Golden Eagle watched quietly from his hiding place, as the sheriff with six men rode up to the village. All the Indian's gathered behind Giant Bear, Black Hawk, as well as Jake curiously.

Golden Eagle had kept the cub with him today instead of letting him go with the children this morning. The cub wiggled in his arms trying to get down.

Golden Eagle held him tighter then whispered consolingly. "Quiet now Cuddles you can play later."

The cub settled down, so Golden Eagle turned his attention back to the meeting.

*****

Giant Bear, Black Hawk, and Jake stood in front of the villagers then watched as the seven vi'hoI rode towards them. When they were close enough, Black Hawk and Jake stepped forward.

The sheriff moved his horse in front of the others then called a halt.

Black Hawk nodded to the sheriff cordially. "What can we do for you sheriff?"

The sheriff looked around at all the faces in the crowed searchingly when he did not see the Englishmen or guides he was looking for he turned to Black Hawk. "We are looking for three white men as well as two white women they have disappeared. I was hoping you would have seen them?"

Black Hawk shook his head negatively as he kept his face impassive. "Why would they come here?"

The sheriff frowned in suspicion. "They were not coming here, but were on their way to Raven and Edward Summerset's place then just disappeared without a trace."

Black Hawk shrugged unknowingly. "I am sorry they did not stop here on their travels."

The sheriff sighed in irritation and inclined his head expecting that answer as he looked around again curiously. "I was led to believe that there were more of you here than Raven was telling us?"

Black Hawk smiled calmly as he motioned behind him. "All of the Wolf tribe are here there are no more of us."

The sheriff nodded and frowned thoughtfully. "Why are you still here shouldn't you be gone for the summer?"

Black Hawk waved dismissively. "Raven asked us to stay until she comes back; she said if you come here we are to answer all your questions truthfully. We are also suppose to tell you that she will be back in two weeks with news on what had happened to the people you are looking for. She said for you to come back here at that time."

The sheriff looked around again at all the faces; he stiffened suddenly in question then turned back quickly to Black Hawk. "You have a white woman here? I was led to believe that you do not steal women anymore!"

Black Hawk shook his head negatively in reassurance. "She was not stolen that is my mother; a white Preacher married the chief and Golden Dove legally. You can contact him at Smyth's Crossing in North Dakota if you want to check."

A man off to the sheriff's left urged his horse forward impatiently. "Sheriff he is lying!"

Black Hawk whispered softly to Jake. "Who is that?"

Jake sighed softly in annoyance. "His name is Charles, he is our neighbour unfortunately. After Raven's parents died he tried to get her to sell out to him, but she refused of course. When Raven was old enough, he tried to get her to marry him, but she laughed in his face in public. Since that day they have been enemies, but he still keeps harassing her to sell to him."

Black Hawk nodded as he turned back to the conversation. He assessed the man as he sat there arguing with the sheriff. His horse was taller than the sheriff's was, yet the man still only reached the sheriff's nose in height. He was in his late forties and almost totally bald. He had a sharp beak of a nose that he held at a lofty position so that he could look down at people. He reminded Black Hawk of a little weasel his voice was high pitched with a whining aggravating tone.

The sheriff frowned angrily at the annoying Charles. "I told you that I will handle this if Raven says that she will be back in two weeks with news it is good enough for me! Since both the guides were her friends, I am sure she will do everything in her power to find them for us."

Charles scowled back furiously then pulled his gun. "If you can't do your job I will!"

Black Hawk stiffened as the vi'hoI levelled his gun at him.

*****

Raven and her prisoner reached the village then walked to the chief's tepee.

The brave scratched at the door and stood back for her to enter.

Raven waved at her horse anxiously. "Can you make sure nobody gets too close to him? He goes absolutely crazy when anyone comes near him so I would not want anyone to get hurt."

The warrior nodded as the chief's wife opened the flap.

Raven ducked inside then looked around quickly. The chief was sitting in front of the fire, and the white woman she had seen earlier was sitting quietly behind him.

The chief waved in invitation for Raven to sit across from him.

Raven dutifully sat then waited as the chief lit his pipe.

The chief blew smoke in the air to the Great Spirit and down at the ground to Mother Earth before blowing smoke to the right then left. He passed the pipe to Raven, so she repeated the ritual. The pipe was put down, and the chief looked at Raven solemnly. "Raven of the Wolf tribe, 'Protector' of her people is welcomed here. I have been expecting you!"

Raven nodded impassively. "Chief Red Eagle is also welcomed at the Wolf tribe."

The chief inclined his head in relief then pointed behind him. "You have come for the vi'hoahI?"

Raven nodded decisively. "Yes, and for the War Chief!"

Chief Red Eagle frowned in anger as he gestured sharply in finality. "I banished Howling Coyote as well as all his followers when I was told what they had done. In these troubled times with the whites killing so many of our people, it is not good to call attention to ourselves. Already the whites outnumber us, if we do not learn to live in peace with them the Cheyenne will be no more. We must stand together at this time, not bicker amongst ourselves. Had I known what Howling Coyote had planned I would have put a stop to it. Unfortunately, I did not find out until after it was done. When I banished the War Chief, I would not let him take the vi'hoahI with him knowing you would come for her. Now he has turned on us, I fear he has a bad spirit inside him, he is full of hate for anyone who goes against him even his own people."

Raven smiled slightly in respect. "Chief Red Eagle is wise, he sees the future true. I have been to a white school; they taught us that for every white person here now, they have many more where they come from. If we are to survive, we must learn to live in peace. The Badger tribe has also seen the future true so wishes to join me, if you wish you could also join with us. As long as you live on my land, nobody can drive you out. I have approached other chief's, but only your tribe as well as the Badger tribe see the future. The rest wish to kill more whites to drive them away, this will not happen they will all die including the women plus all their children."

The chief inclined his head sadly. "You speak passionately as well as truthfully. I have been approached by other chief's on banding together to drive the whites out. I have tried to talk them out of such a foolish plan, but they refuse to listen."

Raven nodded grimly. "We have also been approached, only one tribe has broken away from us so far. They left to join the war against the whites which saddened me greatly as I watch them all die slowly."

The chief sighed in understanding then pointed as he gave directions. "When Howling Coyote left I sent one of my warriors to follow him. He said that they are only one and a half days towards where the sun sets than a half-day towards where the sunrises. They took fifty tepees with them in total."

Raven scowled thinking quickly; she had almost walked right into their camp. Well, at least they are back the way she had come, and it would be closer to her village than here. She smiled up at the chief's wife as she handed her a bowl of stew. "Thank You."

The chief's wife smiled back shyly at Raven and handed her husband then the white woman a bowl, lunch was eaten in complete silence. Not once did Raven talk to, except for a cursory glimpse when she first entered, or pay any attention to Golden Eagle's sister not wanting to offend the chief. Until Janet was given to Raven, she was still his slave.

*****

Jed turned back and checked to make sure no evidence of their presence was left. When he was satisfied, he nodded then they moved off. Jed motioned for Pat, as well as Jess, to take the lead. Mell and Jed were in the middle with the travois between them plus both packhorses were tied to their saddles now. Rose with Daniel brought up the rear; he was leading Pam's horse while Rose was leading the white colt. They rode now in complete silence carefully watching as well as listening vigilantly for any hint of danger.

*****

Golden Eagle listening intently to the conversation going on with the sheriff from his hiding place, sounds echoed loudly in these mountains. He smiled in approval at Black Hawk's answers he had not told one lie. It was true that they had not visited the village; he had been found somewhere else. It was true that Raven would be back in two weeks with answers. He even told the truth about the Wolf people all being here; the sheriff did not ask if there were other tribes staying here. He put the squirming cub down then whispered softly. "Okay, but stay close and be very quiet."

Golden Eagle turned away then frowned in concern as a small white man started arguing with the sheriff, he could not catch everything they were saying from this distance. He jumped up immediately outraged and even took a step forward as the white man pulled his gun then levelled it at Black Hawk threateningly.

Golden Eagle squatted back down in surprise as he watched the grizzly cub that he had just put down go streaking towards the horse's bawling loudly. He held his breath as he watched the sheriff's horse rear in fright.

*****

Black Hawk stared in shock as the cub raced towards the horse's crying loudly.

The horses reared and screamed in fright throwing some of their riders then bolting with others.

Charles landed hard on the ground before rolling a few times. When he stopped, he levelled his gun at the cub.

Black Hawk and Giant Bear ran forward to grab Cuddles, but it was too late as a gunshot rang out then the cub fell to the ground dead.

The only one still on his horse was the sheriff, after getting his horse under control; he jumped down and raced to the scene but was too late to save the cub. He was the first one to reach Charles though, so he kicked the gun out of his hand then reached down to haul him to his feet furiously.

When the sheriff kicked the gun out of Charles's hand, Black Hawk and Giant Bear stopped then waited to see what would happen next.

Charles growled at the sheriff indignantly as he sputtered angrily. "How dare you touch me?"

Charles's words were cut off, as the sheriff's right fist connected with his jaw, and he landed back on the ground groaning in pain. The sheriff stood over Charles seething in anger. "I have a mind to throw you in jail!"

The sheriff turned to two of his men then pointed down at Charles in disgust. "Get this riffraff back on his horse and out of my sight!"

The two men hurriedly did as they were instructed. The sheriff watched them gallop off in satisfaction, he had wanted to do that for a long time now then he grinned in pleasure. He sobered and turned to Black Hawk in apology. "I am sorry this happened."

Black Hawk walked over to the cub then knelt down beside him sadly, he turned the cub over, but he was dead. He looked up at his father and shook his head grimly. "He died saving my life as I saved his."

Giant Bear nodded in sympathy but did not say anything. He looked at the sheriff intently. "You tell that white man if he ever comes here again he is a dead man!"

The sheriff nodded not blaming the chief in the least. "I will warn him, again I am sorry. Tell Raven if she gets here earlier than two weeks to come and see me right away. If she does not I will be coming back to see her."

Black Hawk inclined his head in agreement then watched the sheriff, and the rest of his men leave.

*****

Golden Eagle sat down hard on the ground in horror as he watched the cub race towards the horse's then die as the bullet meant for Black Hawk killed him instead. He wanted to applaud the sheriff as he punched the little chubby white man in the mouth. As soon as the sheriff left, Golden Eagle raced over to the cub and knelt down. "I am sorry I tried to keep a hold on him, but he kept squirming to get down. I was afraid if I did not he would cry out then they would find me."

Black Hawk put his hand on Golden Eagle's shoulder consolingly. "It is okay he gave his life to save me. I will skin him and stuff him so that Raven can keep him always. The Great Spirit has plans for all his creatures, be they human or animal. Now we know why the cub was put in my path; he was meant to save me as I saved him."

Golden Eagle nodded thoughtfully it was the same thing Dream Dancer believed. "You might be right, but I am going to have two very angry people on my hands when they return."

Black Hawk shook his head negatively. "I do not think so they will understand. Go have some lunch then we will work on your stallion afterwards."

Golden Eagle nodded and followed Golden Dove to her tepee.

*****

Raven finished her second lunch of the day then sat back. Janet was already finished hers so Raven looked over at her and waved for her to come over then sit beside her.

Janet meekly walked over and sat with her head lowered in fear.

Raven put her finger under her chin then raised her face so that she could see all of her. She hissed in anger when she saw Janet's face and turned furiously to the chief. "Who did this to her?"

The chief sighed sadly. "She was like that when she came here only worse; some of the swelling has gone down; I would guess Howling Coyote did it. The shaman said that her cheekbone is broken other than that there does not seem to be anymore wounds."

Raven scowled in relief as she turned back to Janet. Her left eye was black and blue just under that was a cut on her cheekbone she would have a scar for life. Her lower lip was badly swollen, as well as cracked; she looked just like her brother only more feminine. She sighed in sympathy then motioned knowingly as she switched to English. "Your name is Janet Rochester is it not?"

Janet frowned in surprise and nodded eagerly. "It was once, but I have been married, so it is Lady Janet Clevedon now, how did you know?"

Raven smiled oh yes she had forgotten about that. "I have come looking for you. You have a very worried impatient brother waiting in my village for your return."

Janet's face lit up in disbelief. "My sister is she there to?"

Raven shook her head sadly. "I am sorry your sister's heart could not take the shock it stopped beating."

Janet put her head in her hands then quietly mourned for her sister.

Raven sighed and stroked her hair in sympathy. Janet was older then her brother in age, but Raven knew just by looking at her that she was far from experienced about the world. Her inexperience was clearly going to be a problem on their way back to her village.

The chief scowled in puzzlement. "Why is she crying?"

Raven smiled reassuringly. "This is the way white people mourn for their dead. I just told her that her younger sister died!"

The chief nodded in understanding. "I will have a horse saddled, and supplies gathered for your trip back tomorrow. Tonight you are welcomed to share our tepee."

Raven shook her head negatively in apology. "Thank you, but I must get back as soon as possible."

Chief Red Eagle frowned in disappointment then turned to his wife. "Get Raven provisions and a horse for the vi'hoahI."

Raven turned to Janet inquisitively. "Wipe your tears now you will have to grieve later. Do you know how to ride?"

Janet looked up then inclined her head affirmative.

Raven sighed in relief. "Good if you have anything here you want to take go get it."

Janet shrugged mournfully. "I have nothing but this dress."

Raven grimaced at the rag and turned to the chief hopefully. "Do you have a boy who is about the white woman's size? She will need buckskin pants as well as a shirt."

The chief nodded then got up.

Raven rose as well and pulled off her necklace then handed it to the chief. "Give this to him in trade tell him it is from a grizzly that I killed."

The chief smiled, extremely pleased and left.

Raven sat down to wait impatiently.

*****

Jed spotted a suitable campsite so called out to Pat. "Pat there is an outcrop off to your left go check it out as a possible camp for the night since there is no moon out we will have to stop or possibly injure one of the horses."

Pat inclined her head in agreement as she rode off with Silver Tip following.

The rest of Jed's group followed, but more slowly.

Pat came back a few minutes later. "It is a good place there is even a little stream behind us for water."

Jed nodded thankfully. "Okay, let's stop for the night then."

*****

Raven looked over at Janet and sighed in annoyance. Janet had said that she could ride, but she failed to mention that she could only ride sidesaddle. Luckily, the chief had made sure the saddle blanket had a girth as well as stirrups. Indians did not use them, but Raven always made them special for the ladies then provided each horse she traded with one. She moved closer to Janet to try to give her lessons as they rode along. "You have to relax there is no difference riding astride, move with your horse. The only thing different is that you direct your horse with your legs now not just the reins."

Janet frowned plaintively. "It feels so strange riding like this in England ladies do not ride astride and horses have bits in their mouths so that we can control them. We never use our legs to control a horse it is unheard of."

Raven nodded irritably then waved grimly, of course she only fibbed a little since women in the towns still rode sidesaddle. She did not have the time though or the inclination to get a spoiled white girl a sidesaddle. "That is true in England, but not out here. Now take a deep breath, and let it out then relax slowly. Good! Now squeeze with your legs gently as she walks, so she picks up a little more speed. Good now close your eyes and feel her moving under you. Slowly move with her, not against her."

Raven watched in approval as Janet slowly relaxed then started to move a little more in time with her horse. "Okay, open your eyes and squeeze a little harder with your leg's to get her to trot."

Janet did as she was told.

Raven smiled pleased. "Good now inhale then exhale slowly and relax again. Feel the movement of your horse then rock your hips to the movement."

Janet relaxed and grinned in delight at Raven. "That feels much better not so jerky."

Raven started looking around for a good campsite; they had been riding for about four hours now it was getting dark with no hint of a moon. She spotted a good place then turned to Janet. "Okay to slow your horse lean back slightly relax in the saddle and ease back on the reins gently a little, do not jerk them."

Raven watched as Janet did as she was told then the mare slowed to a walk. She nodded and turned her horse to the camp she had picked out. She dismounted then went over to help Janet she looked up at her. "Okay on all horses I train, and this happens to be one, you can mount or dismount on either side of your horse. Or you can push yourself back over her hindquarters then slide down her backside, and she will not kick or move."

Janet laughed at the mental image of herself sliding backwards then landing on her rump on the hard ground. "I think I will stick to dismounting on the left side for now thanks anyway."

Raven nodded not surprised. "Okay, so stand up in your stirrups and lift your right leg over the horses back then slowly lower it until you reach the ground."

Janet did as instructed and smiled in satisfaction at doing something right.

Raven grinned in approval. "Do you know how to unsaddle a horse then rub them down as well as how to check their feet?"

Janet shook her head negatively. "No, we had stable boy's who did that for us."

Raven shook her head in disbelief at how useless women in England were. "Okay, you can watch me tonight but after that you will have to tend your own horse. The first thing you need to learn out here is that your horse is your life. Without a reliable horse, you are helpless. Some Indian's can even outrun a horse at long distances so for you to try to outrun an Indian on foot is futile. So, before you eat, sleep, or even get yourself a drink of water your horse must be seen to first."

Raven looked over at Janet, to make sure that she was paying close attention. She turned back to the mare satisfied at Janet's intent concentration. "Now watch as I take the bridle off the horse and the saddle. The bridle, as well as the saddle blanket should be put somewhere clean. That way you do not get any dirt on it, usually I find a low hanging branch or a log to drape them on."

Janet nodded then watched closely as Raven took off the bridle and the saddle blanket.

Raven draped them on a branch close by; she smiled at Janet. "Now the second most important thing to do for your horse is to check their hooves, Indian horses do not have shoes. To do that you stand at the side of your horse facing backwards then you run your hand down her leg and pull up on the hair just below her fetlock. She will lift her foot for you when you pull. This horse is well trained though so all you have to do is touch her leg then say 'up'. See how she automatically lifts her foot without any fuss. Now see the grooves in her hooves you need to clean out all the mud inside so that she does not get a stone in her foot. A stone in her hoof would make her lame if left to long it could damage her hoof and cause her to be crippled for life."

Janet nodded watching intently as Raven cleaned all four hooves without any fuss from the horse. She then followed Raven and helped her unload the packhorse.

Raven took out oats then showed Janet how much to give them and how to hobble a horse so that they would not stray. She dug into one of the packs then pulled out a brush she had made and handed it to Janet. "I use this to curry my horses."

Janet grinned in relief. "I know how to use that."

Raven nodded pleased. "Good I will let you brush down your horse as well as the packhorse. Oh, before I forget stay away from my stallion he was wild when I found him. Only a few others besides me can get close to him. While you are combing the horses, I will get a fire started then make supper. Tomorrow I will show you how to set up camp and what to look for in a good one."

Janet nodded then did as she was told.

*****

Golden Eagle walked back to Ravens and ducked inside. He looked around expectantly forgetting for a moment then sighed in dismay as he remembered that the cub was dead. He dropped down onto his fur and sighed sadly, as he gazed around at the empty tepee. It seemed so bare now; first Raven had left then Dream Dancer and now the cub. He laid back to sleep thinking about Raven.

*****

Mell smiled at her son in relief as she finished bathing Pam. "The fever is down."

Daniel sighed thankfully. "Well that is good news anyway."

Mell nodded at her son before smiling up at her husband as he handed her a bowl of stew. "Thank you."

Jed handed his son a dish too. "I heard you say the fever is down?"

Mell beamed in relief. "A little, enough to give me hope anyway."

Jed grinned thankfully. "Good, we made better time today than I thought we would, so tomorrow we will keep to the same routine walking most of the time. Periodically we will trot and canter to keep the horse's used to the travois."

Mell inclined her head in agreement distractedly. Jed left, so she finished dressing Pam then sat back to eat her supper.

Daniel ate all the meat and vegetables then fed the broth to his wife followed by some water and her medication. Finished they covered Pam with furs then went to the fire for a coffee.

Mell gave the good news to the rest of them and sat back then listened to everyone talking as well as laughing for the first time since they had lost Pam and Rose. She banked the fire then took the first watch as everyone else went to bed.

*****

Raven looked over at the sleeping Janet and sighed they had not talked much after supper. Janet was still healing from her ordeal, so Raven had fed her then sent her to bed. She lay down in her blankets as she looked up at the stars reflectively. She would have to teach Janet as they travelled, and hopefully still make good time. At least it was keeping her mind off Golden Eagle as well as what she should do about him. She turned over then sighed as she slipped into sleep, no one could help her now though as she relived her one night of lovemaking again.

CHAPTER TWENTY

Golden Eagle woke and rolled out of his blankets, he quickly dressed then looked at the dying embers in the fire pit. He shrugged and left the tepee since the cub was not there anymore he did not have to come back until later tonight. He had been informed last night that after he had his breakfast he was to train with Black Hawk then Running Wolf would come for him and teach him how to track, wrestle, hunt, shoot a bow, as well as how to live off the land. His lessons with Golden Dove would now take place at night after supper. He reached Giant Bear's then scratched on the flap and entered when permission was given.

*****

Mell was jerked awake by a moan of pain; she quickly rolled out of her blankets then knelt down beside Pam. She felt Pam's forehead and grimaced uneasily she was burning up.

Daniel dropped down across from his mother. "What is wrong?"

Mell looked at her son earnestly in fear then waved towards the creek. "Go get me some cool water. Pam is burning up, and I need to bathe her to cool her down. Wake the others while you are doing that."

Daniel nodded grimly then jumped up and hurried away.

Mell bent over then murmured soothingly to Pam while she took off the furs and undressed her. She looked at Pam's healing wound there was no red marks around the wound, so there was no blood poisoning. Nor was there any pus to indicate that it was infected in any way. She was totally baffled, why did she still have a fever?

Rose came over then squatted down in concern.

Mell smiled at her reassuringly. "I need you to make some more medicine, but add an extra pinch to strengthen it a little more."

Rose nodded and left.

Daniel brought the lukewarm water then knelt down beside his wife.

Mell looked at her son in dismay extremely confused. "It is not the wound that is causing the fever thank God! We need to sponge her down to cool her off and after she gets her medicine we need to pile blankets on her to sweat out the fever. It would be a good idea if you stripped then crawled in with her as well, the extra body heat might make the fever break sooner."

Daniel nodded praying desperately as they worked on Pam.

*****

Raven got up out of her blankets and added more wood to the dying embers. She looked over at Janet, but she was still sleeping. She made coffee then started breakfast.

Janet rolled out of her blankets with a groan of pain and looked over at Raven as she shook her head dejectedly. "I am never going to get used to sleeping on the ground."

Raven smiled consolingly then waved her over. "Yes you will now come over here and have a coffee."

Janet obediently moved to the fire then poured herself a cup.

Raven stirred the porridge and got up then went to one of her packs and rummaged inside until she found the two packets she was looking for. She went back to the fire then opened both packets; she grabbed a handful of each before throwing them in the pot with the porridge.

Janet watched curiously. "What are you putting in there?"

Raven smiled teasingly. "Nuts and raisins of course!"

Janet lifted her eyebrows in surprise. "Where do you get raisins or nuts out here?"

Raven shrugged dismissively. "We harvest the nuts ourselves then I trade for the raisins."

Janet nodded that made sense and sipped her coffee with a grimace tea would have been preferred.

Raven stirred the porridge then looked at Janet intently hesitating to ask but needing to know. Of course, she had been married before so a maiden head was not the issue. "Your face is banged up pretty bad. He did not hurt you in any other way did he?"

Janet looked at Raven in confusion before blushing as she finally caught her meaning. She shook her head emphatically. "No, he was going to but the chief took me away from him before he could!"

Raven sighed in relief and dished out some porridge then handed it to Janet before dishing up some for herself. They ate in silence both immersed in their own thoughts.

*****

Mell looked down and sighed at her son relieved then beckoned him to come out. "The fever has broken you can crawl out of there now. Bring me some warm water after you dress so that I can sponge the sweat off and we can go."

Daniel nodded then rolled out of the furs thankfully as the sweat poured down his face in rivulets. The preacher put his pants on, but not his shirt as he went for water; He desperately needed to cool down as well.

Jed walked over with two bowls of porridge then handed one to Mell. "How is she?"

Mell grinned pleased. "The fever broke; I just want to sponge the sweat off before we go."

Jed sighed gratefully and stood back as his son came then put the warm water down beside his mother. Jed handed Daniel a bowl of porridge and looked back down at Mell. "I will tell the others to break camp."

Mell inclined her head distractedly then finished her porridge before taking the furs off Pam again to wash her down.

*****

Golden Eagle sat down and sighed in exhaustion.

Black Hawk walked over then squatted down beside him inquisitively. "How is your arm doing?"

Golden Eagle grimaced as he moved his fingers experimentally. "Not to bad, only a little sore."

Black Hawk nodded in approval. "You are doing very well, and you learn fairly quickly. In another week or two, you will not need any more instructions. You should be able to continue on your own soon then you can put your dance together whenever you feel that you are ready. From that moment on you will start using your knife, tomahawk, coup stick, and bare hands."

Golden Eagle smiled in thanks at Black Hawk's praise. "I used to box in England plus I like to fence I think that helped in my training with you, but do you really think I will be ready soon?"

Black Hawk grinned decisively. "Yes!"

Golden Eagle beamed in pleasure then got up as Running Wolf walked into the clearing.

Black Hawk stood as well and grinned at his son. "Do not be too hard on him today Running Wolf, he has been training hard this morning."

Running Wolf grunted noncommittally, but did not say anything as his father left. He handed Golden Eagle a bow, a quiver full of arrows as well as a rifle. "The bow with the arrows is yours to keep. I made them for you; the rifle is my grandfathers so you can return it after our lessons."

Golden Eagle inclined his head in surprised pleasure. "Thank you for the gift."

Running Wolf turned impassively without saying a word then beckoned Golden Eagle to follow him.

Golden Eagle frowned in disapproval after the unpleasant rude Indian brave; he shrugged dismissively as he did as he was told.

*****

Jed and Daniel carried the travois over to the horses. After it was securely tied, Jed turned back to make sure all trace of them were gone.

Everyone else mounted then waited.

Satisfied Jed nodded in approval before mounting his own horse. He turned to Mell. "Ready."

Mell nodded, and they nudged their horses into a walk.

*****

Raven looked over at Janet then smiled in delight. "You are riding well today, how do you feel?"

Janet grinned at the praise and chuckled in satisfaction. "I feel very good thank you. I am even starting to like pants as well as riding astride."

Raven inclined her head, not surprised. She spotted the ledge that she had stayed at a few nights ago. She turned to Janet before pointing for her to look. "You see that ledge over there?"

Raven waited until Janet saw it then continued. "Look at it closely and tell me why it would make a good spot to camp."

Janet studied the area carefully then smiled hesitantly. "The hill I think behind the ledge it is straight down so nobody would be able to sneak up from behind."

Raven nodded encouragingly. "Very good, now what else do you notice about it?"

Janet frowned in concentration and brightened. "There are lots of trees below on both sides so it would be hard for someone to sneak in without giving themselves away. Which would mean that there is only one good way in or out? That would make it easy to defend."

Raven grinned impressed. "You are absolutely right; there are two other reasons, one is that even though you cannot see it from here there is a little stream for water. The tree's are the other reason if there are tree's around there are animals for food so if you are being chased you could defend that ledge for a long time. Always look for camps that are only assessable one way preferably with water close by with access to food."

Janet smiled shyly at the approval then changed the subject curiously. "When will we get to your village?"

Raven frowned in concern. "I have to find the Indian's that attacked you first and scout them out. We should find them tomorrow night, if we have no difficulties it should take us one day for scouting or possibly two. So we should be at my tribe in seven or eight days hopefully."

Janet shuddered in revulsion. "Do we have to go there? Can't you just take me to my brother first?"

Raven shook her head negatively. "No, I am running out of time as it is. I did not come just for you. My whole tribe is in danger if I do not find the killer's the army will come into my village and kill everyone in it."

Janet sighed distressed. "I would not want that to happen."

They rode in silence after that.

*****

Jed held up his hand to stop everyone then sat there listening quietly. He turned suddenly and motioned silently to Daniel so that he would come forward then they both dismounted. He handed his reins to Daniel before leaning forward to whisper cautiously. "Get up on my horse if we are not back in twenty-five minutes ride on quickly and we will catch up!"

Daniel nodded uneasily then mounted his father's horse.

Jed untied Pam's horse from Daniel's saddle, and Mell dismounted grimly then handed her horses reins to Rose before mounting Pam's horse. He beckoned Pat to come forward next. "Stay here with your brother, if we are not back in twenty-five minutes get everyone moving southwest as quickly and quietly as you can."

Pat nodded mystified then took out her rifle.

Jess followed her lead and sat tensely.

They were not sure what was up, but something had spooked their parents.

Jed mounted Daniel's horse then turned north.

Mell waved silently in reassurance to the others, and they galloped away. She had listened to Jed's instructions, but knew better then to talk.

Jed led her towards a hill about ten minutes away from the others and to the north of where they waited. They crested the hill then stopped incredulously.

Mell gazed down in horror at the carnage-taking place below.

Jed moved his horse closer as he whispered in concern. "Are you okay?"

Mell nodded mutely as her horrified stare swept the valley. The army had come across a Blackfoot summer camp, so they were killing everyone including women and children.

Jed looked around in disgust then stiffened in surprise before leaning close to Mell again furiously. "There are no warriors down there only old men, women, and children."

Mell gazed around grimly then nodded in agreement, as she pointed to the north. "The braves are coming now, they are over there. I can't count them from this distance, but there must be at least a hundred braves."

Jed looked in that direction and turned to her as he whispered urgently. "Let's get out of here; it is too late to stop this now!"

Mell nodded sadly as they raced back; they jumped off the horse's then Daniel remounted his own after tying Pam's horse back onto his saddle.

Jed mounted and pointed so that Pat would precede further south away form the carnage that was occurring. He let her head south for half an hour then waved her back to them.

Everyone gathered close, so that they would all be able to hear.

Jed sighed dejectedly. "The army is north in a valley murdering women and children again, as we watched about a hundred braves were galloping to save their families. I want to get as far away from here as we can so we will not stop for lunch today but keep on riding."

Jed turned to Pat, but included everyone. "We are far enough now so you can start going straight west again, but keep your rifles out as well as ready just in case!"

They all nodded tensely in agreement then they were off again.

*****

Raven pulled up and pointed to her left. "We will make a quick camp there for lunch. I want to show you how to use a rifle while we are stopped."

Janet frowned grimly, but finally nodded in agreement.

Raven dismounted then hobbled the packhorse so that he could graze. She turned and motioned so that Janet would follow her.

Janet dropped the reins of her horse since she was trained to stay then helped Raven gather wood before watching avidly as her rescuer built a fire.

Raven pointed to the packhorse. "Grab the bacon and beans out of the left saddlebag please, while I gather what I need for lunch."

Janet inclined her head then jumped up to do as she was told.

Raven got up as well and went to the right saddlebag then took out a coffee pot, two skillets, as well as coffee. She put the coffee as well as the beans on to cook once she returned to the fire. Afterwards, she grabbed her rifle, and a box of bullets then waved so that Janet would follow her again before walking into the trees. She found a good-sized tree and took out her knife then made a sizeable X in the center and walked back to Janet. She showed Janet how to load as well as unload the rifle. "Always make sure your safety is on when loading or you might accidentally shoot someone! Here, you try it."

Janet grimaced in distaste not really liking guns then tentatively took the rifle from Raven and slowly loaded then unloaded it.

Raven smiled pleased. "Good! Do it a few more times but try to be a little faster while I go stir the beans and put the bacon on."

Raven took her time then walked back to Janet who was just reloading again. She smiled at Janet teasingly. "How many times have you loaded since I left?"

Janet smiled proudly. "That was my second time."

Raven chuckled impressed she was a quick study. "Not bad I want you to put the gun to your shoulder. Make sure the gun is held very tightly or you will get bruised very badly from the recoil."

Janet frowned attentively and tucked the gun against her shoulder then waited for further instructions.

Raven put her hand out and touched the sight on the rifle. "This is what you want to line up to make your shot. Center this in the middle of the X on the tree then gently squeeze the trigger when you are ready."

Janet did as she was told and jumped in stunned shock at the pain in her shoulder; she almost dropped the rifle in amazement as the deafening noise reverberated through her skull.

Raven laughed at the astonished look on Janet's face. "You have to hold the rifle tighter against your shoulder. Try a few more times then come join me at the fire for lunch."

Janet sighed unwillingly, but did not refuse as she repeated her efforts several more times until she felt that her teacher would be satisfied.

*****

Golden Eagle limped towards the corrals and sighed plaintively. He was exhausted, but he still had to work with his horse yet then eat and have his lessons with Golden Dove before he could even contemplate going to bed. He walked around the corner then forgot all about his pain and fatigue as his stallion neighed at him in greeting. He grinned in pleasure as he walked over to join Black Hawk by the fence.

Black Hawk smiled teasingly at the late Englishman. "Your horse has been standing exactly in that position for the last half an hour watching for you intently without moving a muscle."

Golden Eagle laughed in delight then shrugged in apology. "I am sorry I am late but your son is definitely hard to please and would not let me leave until I got it right."

Black Hawk nodded curiously. "What were you having trouble with?"

Golden Eagle sighed dejectedly. "Walking soundlessly through the underbrush as well as the bow it is giving me lots of trouble. It did not seem to matter what I did, I could not hit the target."

Black Hawk chuckled consolingly. "Well I cannot help you with being stealthy that will come with practice as well as time, but I might be able to help with your bow. When you first pick it up you have to relax then take a few deep breaths and blow them out all the way. As you are blowing each breath out think of another part of your body relaxing. After you are completely relaxed, lift your bow then sight on your target. Think of the arrow as an extension of your arm with the tip as your finger and decide where you want your finger to touch then visualize the arrow already touching that spot. Make sure to exhale slowly as you let the arrow go gently, do not jerk the string! It might seem strange and slow to do this at first, but once you hit your target a few times, it does get easier. After a while you will automatically relax when shooting, without even being aware that you are breathing properly."

Golden Eagle grinned in thanks. "I will try it tomorrow."

Black Hawk nodded pleased as he waved him away. "Good now get in with that stud then get to work, he has been waiting for you patiently. If everything works out good today, tomorrow you should be able to get up on him."

Golden Eagle smiled in anticipation as he picked up the equipment waiting for him before going into the pen with his stallion.

*****

Pat rode back to the others since she had been scouting ahead. She went straight to her mother and father then waved to their left. "About an hour from here there is a decent campsite with water. Behind that is a steep hill with trees on one side for cover, but the rest is very open which I do not like. I climbed it to look around, but did not see anything better. I suggest we make camp there even though it is a little early since we did not stop for lunch."

Jed looked at Mell for her opinion and turned back to his daughter at Mell's nod. "Lead on."

Pat rode ahead as everyone followed her.

*****

Raven looked over at Janet. "We will stop early so you can practice with the rifle again. I also want to teach you how to move around a little quieter. Tomorrow we will reach the outskirts of Howling Coyote's hiding place so I will not be able to give you anymore lessons until after we leave there."

Janet nodded relieved then sighed with a painful grimace. "An early camp sounds good to me."

Raven chuckled in sympathy, and they rode on.

*****

Black Hawk turned as he heard footsteps behind him then smiled at Jake. "Well hello there Jake, where were you hiding all day?"

Jake stopped beside Black Hawk and watched the white man curiously, as he worked with his horse. He did not say anything for a long time then turned and answered Black Hawk. "I was out seeing to my men. One of them saw Charles break off from the others then head north."

Black Hawk frowned thoughtfully. "That is the direction Raven went."

Jake inclined his head apprehensively. "I know."

Black Hawk stepped forward and called to Golden Eagle. "Put the saddle blanket on him if he does not fuss try putting the sacks on."

Golden Eagle waved in acknowledgement

Black Hawk moved back to Jake then sighed inquisitively. "Do you have any idea why he would go that way?"

Jake shrugged unknowingly. "He could have gone the long way back to his ranch so that he would not meet up with the sheriff again."

Black Hawk chuckled as he nodded. "You could be right the sheriff gave him quit a wallop."

Jake watched the white man for a few minutes and turned to Black Hawk curiously. "What is going on around here anyway? Your father has hardly said two words to me! Who is the white man?"

Black Hawk grimaced then told Jake everything he knew.

When Black Hawk finished Jake shook his head uneasily. "Your father is making a big mistake if he tries forcing Raven to marry!"

Black Hawk snorted in agreement. "Don't I know it, but he will not listen to anyone."

Jake scowled in contemplation. "I worked for the Summerset's since before the old Earl died. I helped raise that girl she is like my own daughter. I taught her everything she knows about cattle as well as running a ranch. She is as stubborn and pigheaded as her English grandfather was, if she refuses to marry this Englishman I will stand behind her all the way!"

Black Hawk smiled in appreciation at Raven's foreman he was as reliable as they come. "You are a good man Jake, I know you love Raven like a daughter. I have to tell you though that Raven is falling in love with the Englishman, but because of my interfering father she will never admit it."

Jake grinned pleased. "Are you sure?"

Black Hawk nodded decisively. "They have already spent one night together, but like you said Raven is as obstinate as they come."

Jake's smile widened in delight. "Well it is about time that Raven fell in love, I will definitely have a long talk with this Englishman to see if I approve."

The two men turned chuckling to watch the unsuspecting Golden Eagle.

*****

Jed looked around then nodded in approval at his daughter's choice.

Everyone dismounted, and the camp was hastily made.

Jed with Daniel's help unhooked the travois then set it beside the fire before helping set up camp.

Mell built up the fire and put water on to heat for Pam's sponge bath while Daniel bent over his wife then started to undress her.

Pam moaned and opened her eyes.

Daniel smiled in relief down at her then smoothed her hair back tenderly. "How are you feeling love?"

Pam moistened her dry cracked lips as she whispered painfully. "Thirsty, and sore!"

Daniel nodded elated then looked over at his mother. "Pam is awake will you bring some water please!"

Mell grinned in delight and filled a cup with cold water then brought it to her son. She handed the cup to Daniel as she knelt down and watched as he tenderly lifted his wife's head then held the cup to her lips.

Pam drank all the water before shifting with a groaned of pain.

Daniel eased her down and sat back.

Mell smiled at Pam teasingly. "You gave us quite a scare young lady! How do you feel?"

Pam grimaced uncomfortably. "My side hurts quite a bit other than that I feel okay, what happened?"

Mell turned to her son and gestured towards the fire. "Will you bring the tea as well as the warm water here while I check Pam's wound?"

Daniel nodded then went to the fire.

Mell finished undressing Pam while she explained everything that happened.

Pam sighed grimly when Mell finished. "I do not remember much except going after Rose and getting tangled in that tree."

Mell chuckled not surprised in the least. "You were unconscious for most of it."

Mell smiled at her son as he handed her the bowl of paste for the wound. "Thank you."

Mell washed the wound then looked at it closely and nodded thankfully. "It is healing nicely although it is turning some intriguing colours"

Pam lifted her head to look as best she could then grimaced at the pain movement caused. "It sure does not feel as if it is healing."

Mell grinned and put more medicine on it then re-wrapped Pam's ribs. "It might not feel that way right now, but believe me it was a lot worse a couple of days ago."

Mell redressed Pam and smiled up at her husband then the others as they gathered around. "It looks as if Pam is going to make it after all."

Smiles of relief could be seen on all their faces.

Pam looked up at Rose and whispered earnestly. "Thank you for saving my life!"

Rose smiled down at Pam teasingly. "You saved my life first!"

Pam giggled slightly, unable to laugh. "I guess that means we are even."

Rose inclined her head in agreement.

Daniel stroked his wife's cheek enticingly. "Instead of a sponge bath would you like me to take you to the creek for a real bath?"

Pam nodded eagerly. "Yes please."

Daniel picked up his wife carefully then turned to his mother. "Will you bring us some soap and give me a hand?"

Mell got up to follow her son.

The rest went back to their chores.

*****

Raven found what she was looking for then they dismounted.

Janet helped with the horses and Raven taught her how to set up a camp.

Raven pointed out all the edible plants in their area although most of them were not ready yet.

Janet paid close attention eagerly soaking up everything like a thirsty sponge.

Raven handed Janet her rifle. "Go do some target practice while I cook supper."

Janet nodded then left.

*****

Golden Eagle grabbed the rifle out of his tepee and walked to Giant Bear's for supper then his lessons. He scratched on the door and waited politely for permission to enter.

Golden Dove smiled at him as she pushed open the flap. "How are you doing today?"

Golden Eagle grinned back. "Tired, how about you?"

Golden Dove chuckled sympathetically. "I am feeling good. Come sit then eat."

Golden Eagle propped the gun against the tepee wall and walked over then sat by the fire.

Giant Bear and Jake walked in next then sat across from him.

Golden Eagle waved so that Giant Bear would look in the corner. "I brought your rifle back."

Giant Bear looked at the rifle and harrumphed in unconcern as he turned to Golden Eagle then shrugged dismissively. "Keep it I have more."

Golden Eagle frowned angrily at the rebuff, but his good manners prevailed, and he mumbled irritably. "Thank you!"

Golden Dove handed our bowls of stew than quiet descended as supper was eaten in complete silence.

*****

Raven kept cooking pretending she did not hear Janet approaching behind her. At the last moment Raven turned. "Better, but not good enough!"

Janet sighed dejectedly and shrugged. "When did you first hear me approaching?"

Raven grinned in approval. "About ten minutes ago."

Janet smiled forlornly then propped the rifle against a tree and sat down across the fire from Raven. "Better than last time though."

Raven inclined her head in agreement. "Much better! How did you make out with the rifle?"

Janet grimaced, very unsatisfied. "I hit the tree three times, but not even close to the X."

Raven beamed in encouragement at the disgruntled Janet; she tried to hard. Raven could not figure out why either, but shrugged inwardly to herself it was not her business. "That is definitely an improvement if you want I can teach you how to shoot a bow?"

Janet's expression brightened. "Could you? I would really like that."

Raven nodded and handed Janet her supper. "Yes I can, but not until after we leave the war chief's hiding place."

Janet nodded soberly then ate quietly.

*****

Mell smiled down at Pam and bent over then kissed her forehead. "Get some sleep dear we will talk more tomorrow."

Pam nodded and grinned up at her. "Okay, goodnight mom!"

Pam turned to her husband as she took his hand pleadingly. "Stay with me please."

Daniel inclined his head before lying down then carefully put his arm under his wife so that her head was on his shoulder. He kissed the top of her head and sighed in contentment. "Goodnight, I love you!"

Pam snuggled closer then whispered sleepily. "I love you too."

Mell left the two of them alone and walked over to the fire then sat down across from her husband. "Where are Jessica and Rose?"

Jed smiled then waved towards the creek. "Doing dishes."

Mell snickered teasingly.

Jed put on an injured expression. "What! I offered to help, but they refused."

Mell poured herself a coffee. "I will take first watch if you will take second."

Jed nodded thoughtfully. "Okay Pat can take third watch, and Jess can take last watch."

Mell inclined her head in agreement then smiled as Jess, Pat and Rose walked to the fire. She gave both girls their schedules.

Jess nodded then poured Rose and Pat a coffee as well as one for herself.

Rose cleared her throat hopefully. "What about me can I take a watch?"

Mell shook her head negatively. "No, you are still learning you are not ready yet for a watch. Besides which your rib is not fully healed yet, if it makes you feel better you can cook breakfast in the morning."

Rose sighed dejectedly. "Okay."

Mell refilled her coffee before getting up. "Goodnight, everyone."

Mell sauntered towards a large rock at the edge of the trees then sat there sipping her coffee.

Jed watched her walk away and threw the rest of his coffee out before banking the fire for the night. They all got up then headed for their beds.

*****

Golden Eagle got up to leave.

Jake stood up as well. "Mind if I sleep in Raven's tepee with you?"

Golden Eagle looked at Jake in surprise and shrugged in agreement. "No, I do not mind."

Jake smiled in thanks. "I will just collect my bedroll from my horse then join you shortly."

Golden Eagle nodded and left.

Giant Bear got up apprehensively. "Jake I do not want you to talk about the ranch to Golden Eagle because he does not know about it yet."

Jake inclined his head thoughtfully. "As you wish, but I think that man knows more than you think."

Giant Bear scowled grimly. "What do you mean?"

Jake waved dismissively. "Just a hunch I have nothing that I have heard definitely."

Giant Bear sighed in agitation. "Just watch what you say to him."

Jake turned and noticed the rifle still propped against the tepee. "Golden Eagle forgot his gun I will take it with me."

Giant Bear nodded then sat back down.

Jake picked up the rifle and went to get his gear then walked over to Raven's, he scratched on the flap.

Golden Eagle opened it and held it while Jake manoeuvred his belongings in. He took his rifle from Jake. "Thank you I forgot it."

Jake nodded then put his stuff down opposite to Golden Eagles and made his pallet.

Golden Eagle put some wood on the fire then made coffee.

Jake walked over and sat across the fire from him.

Golden Eagle handed him a cup of coffee then poured some for himself.

The two men sat there eyeing each other speculatively.

Golden Eagle was the first to break the silence as he motioned inquisitively. "So you are Raven's foreman?"

Jake chuckled and nodded in delight. "I guessed that you knew more than you were letting on."

Golden Eagle smiled and shrugged in agreement. "Well I could understand Cheyenne sooner than I let on. I had a hard time speaking it though. When I saw Dream Dancer, it did not take me long to figure out who he was. He looks just like the old Earl!"

Jake frowned thoughtfully and eyed the Englishman curiously. "That he does, I take it you do not want Giant Bear to find out that you know."

Golden Eagle smirked grimly. "No, I do not want him to know yet. I want to see what he has planned first."

Jake looked at Golden Eagle intently. "How come you have not tried to get away?"

Golden Eagle shrugged dismissively. "I made a promise to Raven. Plus I am curious to see what the old man is up to."

Jake harrumphed in disbelief then could not help tease him a bit. "Are you sure that is the only reason. It might not have anything to do with a raven haired she devil would it?"

An instant picture of Raven came to mind, and Golden Eagle instantly hardened in desire. He shifted to hide the evidence of his arousal from the other man. He grimaced reluctantly. "I have not spent enough time with her to decide yet."

Jake smiled knowingly then drained his coffee letting the uncomfortable Englishman off the hook before going to bed.

Golden Eagle banked the fire as he too went to bed.

*****

Raven turned on her back for the fifth time and sighed as she looked up at the stars. She just could not sleep tonight every time she closed her eyes an image of Golden Eagle would appear. She sighed in frustration then closed her eyes and let the vision come.

As sleep overtook her, the dream started like the one of old with her standing in a field as Golden Eagle rode towards her. At the last minute, he reached down then pulled her up in front of him. He bent his head as he captured her lips in a searing kiss before stopping his horse and swung down with her still in his arms. He tenderly placed her on the ground as he started to make love to her. She sighed in pleasure then gazed up at him as he stood up. She cried out suddenly in denial as he started shimmering before fading. She jumped up and rushed towards him, but he was gone. She looked around in desperation then saw that she was no longer in a field, but was now standing on a dock watching a ship leaving port entirely dejected.

Raven jerked herself awake with a small cry of despair. It took her a moment to realize where she was; she looked around and saw Janet still sleeping in relief. Raven curled up in a ball then wiped the tears away as she sighed apprehensively finally she fell into a dreamless sleep.

*****

Mell looked around and frowned something was bothering her, but she was not sure what. She undid the whip from around her waist before coiling it in her hand loosely then walked into the tree's. She decided to make a circle through the tree's and around the camp. She had learned a long time ago to trust that little voice inside her head as well as the shivers of warning coursing down her spine that at this moment said something was seriously wrong.

*****

Jed woke abruptly; he lay there rigidly until he was sure the threat was not immediate. He reached over then grabbed his gun belt that was always hanging on a limb close to his head in easy reach as he got up cautiously and strapped it on. He bent next to pick up his rifle that was never far from his side before going to Rose first. He put his hand over Roses mouth so she would not cry out then bent down to whisper urgently. "Grab your rifle and slip behind the tree to your right, please stay hidden there!"

Rose nodded mutely in fear as she did as she was told without questions.

Jed looked towards Jess, but saw Pat already talking to her. He started towards his son then stopped suddenly as four men walked into the camp with rifles trained on him.

The biggest man stepped forward. "Do not even think about that, put down dat rifle."

Jed slowly bent over and put the rifle on the ground then stood up with his hands in the air. "What do you want?"

The leader scowled at him incredulously. "What do ya think I want? You hoses are what we want and food."

Jed discreetly looked around, but did not see Mell or Pat's dog. He jerked his attention back to the four men not wanting to give anything away. He eyed their dirty ripped uniforms knowing immediately that they were survivors of the infantry attack they had seen earlier. They all had wild desperate looks on their faces; Jed knew the four men were going to kill all of them; they could not afford to leave witnesses.

Jed saw movement behind the four men then tensed in readiness.

A whip whistled eerily in the silence..."SNAP!"

The burly man screamed a warning to the rest just as he heard the loud crack of the whip, but he was too late as the snake like coils curled around him locking his arms against his sides.

Silver Tip attacked the fourth man in the line.

Jed's gun cleared leather, and two shots were fired.

The third man too stunned to react fast enough turned slightly then dropped his gun with a shriek as he grabbed his right shoulder in pain.

Jed turned slightly, and saw Pat walking towards him with a smoking pistol.

Rose came running then stopped beside Jed.

Jed smiled at her in reassurance. "Grab some rope out of my saddlebag so I can tie these men up."

Rose nodded and ran off with Jess following to help.

Pat walked over then grabbed all the guns before she called her dog off.

Jed grinned in relief at Mell standing behind the stocky man keeping tension on the whip. "Well it is about time, what were you waiting for one of them to shoot me?"

Mell smiled back teasingly. "I thought of it!"

Mell's expression sobered. "Is everyone okay?"

Jed nodded placatingly. "Everyone is fine."

Mell frowned as she jerked the whip a little tighter in anger. "What do you want to do with these men? We do not have time to take them with us."

Jed scowled thoughtfully. "Well we are only about a day or a day and a half away from the next town, which is where the army is based if I remember correctly. So we will doctor the two up who are bleeding then tie them securely so that the army can come and get them after we report this incident."

The burly man grunted in fear as he tried to fight the whip.

Silver Tip dropped to her haunches then growled menacingly in warning.

The big man immediately stopped fighting and took a hasty step back.

Pat looked at the man as she grinned in warning. "I would not move if I were you."

The man suddenly froze then watched the dog warily.

Daniel walked up to his father.

Jed motioned in concern. "How's Pam doing?"

Daniel grinned in humour. "She slept through the whole thing."

Jed sighed relieved. "Good she needs her sleep."

Rose and Jess ran up to Jed then handed him all the rope they could find.

Jed inclined his head in approval before walking up to the leader and uncoiled the whip from around him. He marched the man over to a tree then tied him securely.

Jed came back a few minutes later and turned to Rose. "Reheat the stew then feed these men, give them each some water also. When you are finished go back to bed."

Rose nodded, and Jess followed her to help.

Jed turned to the other outlaw who was unhurt then tied him up, as well.

Daniel walked over and checked the man with a hole in his hand. The bullet had gone straight through. Daniel grinned at his mother. "I suppose this was father's handiwork?"

Mell chuckled as she coiled her whip up. "Of course it was!"

Daniel sighed in admiration. His father was not as fast as his wife or son, but his accuracy was excellent. "Will you grab some bandages so I can wrap this?"

Mell inclined her head in agreement then trotted off.

Daniel went over to the last man and ripped open his army shirt then examined the wound.

Jed walked up behind his son. "That bullet will need to come out."

Daniel frowned in agreement before pointing at the fire. "Can you put your knife in the fire to heat it please?"

Jed went over obediently and shoved the knife in the coals.

Mell came back then expertly bandaged the man with a hole in his hand. When she finished Jed pushed him towards a tree and tied him securely.

Daniel took the last man over to the fire before pushing him down, so that he was sitting. He took the knife out of the fire to cool then cut off a piece of wood so that the man could bite on it.

Rose, Jess, and Pat took a bowl of stew then went over to feed the other three.

Daniel beckoned to his father to come forward and hold the man down for him.

Jed pushed the man on his back then held him tight while Daniel put the piece of wood in the outlaw's mouth before probing at the wound with the knife.

Daniel grunted in exertion as the man lifted up in pain trying to get away from him. He did managed to grasp the bullet despite the other mans unwillingness to cooperate. As Daniel pull it out the man mercifully lost consciousness, not once, had he cried out. He applied some of the paste that was left from Pam's poultice earlier then wrapped the shoulder.

The man came to, so Daniel fed him then gave him some tea before Jed took him and tied him up with the others.

Mell banked the fire before smiling at everyone. "Good job everyone, now go to bed! Jed will take over the watch then Pat and finally Jess for the last watch."

They all nodded before wandering off to their beds.

Mell smiled then stood up with Jed as she kissed him tenderly. "Goodnight love."

Jed hugged his wife and turned her then smacked her bottom. "Go to bed."

Mell smiled saucily over her shoulder at her husband, and made sure to give a little wiggle as she turned away with a teasing giggle.

CHAPTER TWENTY ONE

Raven woke then sighed disgruntled she had not slept that good last night. Nightmares of Golden Eagle going back to England had woken her in the middle of the night. She could not afford to be having nightmares right now this close to the war chief's camp. If someone had heard her last night the two of them could have been in tremendous trouble. Raven shook of her thoughts before getting up and added more wood to the last of the embers. She put the coffee on then made some porridge. She left it to thicken while she went to check on the traps she had set last night. She had caught three rabbits, so she threw one to the wolf and one to Bruno then she took the third one back to camp.

Janet was already pouring coffee, so she poured a second one and handed it to Raven. "Good morning."

Raven mumbled irritably. "Morning!"

Raven sat down with a weary sigh then took a sip of her coffee. Feeling slightly better, she took out her hunting knife and skinned the rabbit.

Janet watched carefully intrigued then reached over and stirred the porridge.

Raven fashioned a spit before putting the rabbit on it to cook.

Janet dished them up their breakfast.

Raven scrapped the skin and rolled it up then handed it to Janet; she wanted to give Janet something to keep her busy after they stopped. "Put this in your saddlebag, I will teach you how to cure it tonight."

Janet nodded in pleasure as she stroked the soft silky rabbit fur. "Thank you."

Raven waved in warning. "We should find Howling Coyote tonight so you will be unable to practice with the rifle until we are on the trail again."

Janet sighed dejectedly she truly did not want to go anywhere near that man and risk being caught by him again. She ate quietly watching Raven fugitively; she was so strong, unlike any other woman Janet had ever met. After the attack, Janet would have given anything to go home to England. Now though she was not that sure. In England, her older husband had pampered her; of course, she had loved it in a way. At the same time though, she had hated it. When her husband died her father stole everything from her, she had been powerless to stop him. Unfortunately, that meant that she was at the mercy of her fathers whims; it had been degrading. She never wanted to feel that helpless or dependent on anyone ever again. Looking at the independent Raven so sure of herself, without a man telling her what to do or what to wear she wanted to be just like her. Strong, unconventional, she was also absolutely fearless!

*****

Golden Eagle woke first; he stirred up the embers before adding more wood. He put on coffee then left the tepee and heading to Giant Bears to get breakfast. He scratched on the flap then entered when it was lifted for him.

Golden Dove beamed cheerfully in delight. "Good morning."

Golden Eagle smiled back. "Morning, is breakfast ready yet?"

Golden Dove grinned before motioning curiously. "Yes it is. Is Jake still sleeping?"

Golden Eagle nodded. "Yes he is I will take him a bowl as well."

Golden Dove chuckled as she waved him over in invitation. "Okay, help yourself."

Golden Eagle filled two bowls and turned to leave. "See you tonight Golden Dove."

Golden Dove walked over then opened the flap for him. "Okay, see you for supper."

Golden Eagle ducked out and hurried to Ravens. He pushed his way inside then smiled over at Jake. "Morning Jake, did you sleep well?"

Jake inclined his head as he accepted the porridge gratefully. "Yes I did thank you."

Golden Eagle sat across from Jake and put some honey on his porridge then extended the jar to Jake. "Would you like some?"

Jake shook his head negatively. "No, thank you."

They ate breakfast in silence.

Jake drained his coffee before getting up to go. "I have to go check on my men. I will see you tonight."

Golden Eagle nodded goodbye and put his empty bowl down then poured himself a coffee. As soon as he drained his cup, he put the fire out and left for his lessons with Black Hawk.

*****

Rose finished making breakfast then smiled across the fire at Daniel who after making the paste and tea for his wife was waiting patiently for the porridge so he could feed her before his mother came to help with administering the medication. "Can you wake everyone please breakfast is ready."

Daniel inclined his head then left to wake the others. He came back to the fire when he was done and dished up some porridge for Pam as well as for himself then left.

Mell and Jed walked over then helped themselves to some porridge and coffee before eating hastily.

Pat followed closely by Jessica came last.

Rose finished her breakfast then took a bowl plus a cup of coffee to one of the men. Pat and Jess finished then followed Roses example before walking over to help feed the deserters.

Mell smiled at Jed hopefully knowing they all needed a break. "You said last night we should reach the next town soon?"

Jed nodded thoughtfully. "We should be there really late tonight or tomorrow morning sometime. It was just an army outpost at first, but a town grew around it. We can find a doctor there to look at Pam and Rose then wire the Montana Marshal and let him know about that sheriff in the border town. I think we should spend one night in town as well for a much-needed break, even if we have to stay a whole day."

Mell frowned in agreement she did not quite like the thought of losing an entire day though then shrugged resignedly. "I really do not like that idea, so hopefully we can reach it tonight instead. The horse's are exhausted though, and so are we. I guess it will have to do; I better give Pam her medicine than we can go."

Jed watched his wife pick up the paste and tea that Daniel had left by the fire. He drained his coffee then got up and started breaking camp.

*****

Golden Eagle fell down on the hard ground then stayed there as he laid back breathing deeply in exhaustion.

Black Hawk chuckled in sympathy as he sat down beside him. "My son is coming. Did you bring your rifle, bow, and arrows?"

Golden Eagle groaned dejectedly then sat up reluctantly. "Already! Yes, they are leaning against a tree over to your left. Your son sure does not say much."

Black Hawk smiled in agreement, as he gestured in reassurance. "He takes the responsibility of being the next chief very seriously too much so sometimes. Do not take it personally he is like that with everyone."

Golden Eagle grinned then motioned teasingly. "Well by the look of your father it is going to be a long time before that happens."

Black Hawk shook his head negatively disagreeing. "Not really father is talking about handing over leadership to Running Wolf next year."

Golden Eagle looked at Black Hawk in surprise. "Why is he sick or something?"

Black Hawk shrugged negligently at the surprised look on the Englishman's face. "No, he is not sick just tired he says. My mother wants him to give it up as well."

Golden Eagle stood up without commenting as Running Wolf walked into the clearing and beckoned impatiently for Golden Eagle to follow him. He waved goodbye to Black Hawk before collecting his things then walked behind Running Wolf obediently.

Running Wolf led him to the same target area they had used yesterday and pointed to the rifle wordlessly.

Golden Eagle nodded then put down the bow and quiver of arrows. He lifted the rifle then aimed before firing. He shot ten times before hitting the center on the eleventh shot. He was better with a pistol or a sword never having shot a rifle.

In England, the preferred method of duels was with a sword or a duelling pistol. You and your opponent were placed back to back then walked until told to turn by a third party and you would spin around as fast as you can then shoot your opponent. Marksmanship was essential to survival, and he had been one of the best with a pistol.

It was different out here he had been told, they used a gun holster. In order to use the gun you had to be able to get the revolver out of the pocket. Golden Eagle had tried it a couple of times, but he had a hard time with getting it out first. He shook off his thoughts as he turned to his teacher inquisitively.

Running Wolf grunted in approval before pointing at the bow next.

Golden Eagle smiled proudly undeterred by Running Wolf's silence now that he knew it was not personal. It had taken five shots less than yesterday to hit the center. He took out ten arrows and stuck them in the ground in front of him. Making sure that they were within easy reach then took one and notched it.

Golden Eagle remembered what Black Hawk had told him yesterday, so he stood there for a few minutes relaxing his body as he breathed in then out deeply before lifting the bow and sighted down the arrow. He imagined the arrow already in the center of the target then gently let go of it and watched in amazement when the arrow hit the target. It did not go exactly where he had aimed, but at least he had hit the target this time.

Running Wolf frowned in annoyance as he crossed his arms in front of his chest in disapproval. "You have been talking to my father."

Golden Eagle grinned in delight unrepentant as he nodded in satisfaction. "Yes, he gave me some advice last night."

Running Wolf snorted in irritation then uncrossed his arms and pointed to the rest of the arrows without saying another word, but the look on his face told Golden Eagle he would be giving his father an earful.

Golden Eagle chuckled knowingly then resumed his lessons.

*****

Raven slowed her horse and turned right then moved into the trees.

Janet followed obediently without a word she dismounted when Raven did.

Raven turned to Janet in warning. "We will have a quick lunch here before continuing on. From the time we leave here, until I tell you there will be no talking unless it is an emergency. Keep the rifle with you at all times, you can lay it across your saddle but make sure the safety is on. Do not shoot at anything unless it is impossible to avoid it. Try to be as quiet as you possible can."

Janet nodded soberly before helping Raven with lunch.

*****

Mell and Jed stopped their horses as one then looked at each other uneasily.

Jed sighed in agitation as he asked his wife's opinion. "How many?"

Mell shrugged thoughtfully. "I would guess about fifty horses."

Jed inclined his head in agreement. "I figured that as well."

Mell and Jed dismounted to change horses.

Jed walked over to Pat then pointed south. "There are a few trees off to your left it is the only cover for miles out here. Take everyone over there and have some lunch. We will wait for those horses. Keep your guns handy but do not shoot unless you have to."

Pat nodded calmly as she waited for Daniel to mount his father's horse before picking up the reins to her mothers. She looked down at her dog. "Stay with mom Silver Tip."

Silver Tip whined plaintively then obediently went to Mell and sat beside her horse.

Mell leaned down from Pam's horse as she smiled in reassurance at Silver Tip. "We will not be long girl."

Silver Tip yipped at her in response then obediently followed as Jed and Mell moved their horse's a little further away from the others hiding place then stopped to wait.

Mell squinted and looked ahead then turned to Jed. "Army I think."

Jed frowned thoughtfully before motioning knowingly. "Either looking for those four deserters or riding out to find out what happened to his men. Do you have your badge pinned on?"

Mell nodded that she did as they lapsed into silence while she removed her fur so that her badge and guns were plainly visible. She tucked the fur behind her then waited patiently.

About a quarter of a mile off the man in the lead called a halt, he left everyone behind before riding towards them with only one other person curiously. He had seen the others veer off so wanted to check it out, although he figured they were just taking precautions. It never hurt to be careful out here though.

The major eyed the man and woman waiting for him. He noticed the marshal's badge on the woman then the deputy marshal's badge on the man. He smiled in delight as he waved towards them before looking at his aid in humour. "Well a woman marshal does not that beat all Simmons."

The man beside him snorted in derision but made no comment.

Mell overheard and narrowed her eyes in anger.

The major lifted his hands in apology seeing the furious look not wanting to offend anyone. "I meant no disrespect ma'am. It is just a bit of a novelty to see that is all."

Mell relaxed, at the major's conciliatory tone before assessing him.

The major eyed her just as boldly then smiled in appreciation at the picture she made with those beautiful buckskins on. He noticed the white fur behind her and grinned eagerly as he motioned hopefully. "Mind if I see the robe behind you."

Mell inclined her head in agreement then lifted the buffalo skin so he could see it.

The major whistled in awe never having seen a white buffalo before. "You must have done something pretty spectacular for the Indian's to award you a white buffalo hide, especially being a white woman and all."

Mell shrugged dismissively, but ignored the invitation in his voice to talk about it as she tucked it securely behind her. She pointed at herself then towards her husband in introduction "I'm Marshal Brown and this is my husband Deputy Marshal Brown."

The major inclined his head respectfully then returned the introductions in kind. "I am Major Sinclair, and this is my aid Simmons. What are you folks doing out here if you do not mind my asking?"

Mell smiled pleasantly then answered vaguely. "We came from North Dakota, and were going to the Bitterroot Mountains to visit friends."

The major sighed in relief before waving towards the east. "Well maybe you two can help me then I am looking for an army squad of about thirty. They were supposed to be back two days ago, and they have not been seen since."

Mell shared a knowing look with Jed, but Jed was the one who answered. "As a matter of fact major we saw them from a hill about two days back."

Mell snorted in disgust then took over the telling. "Your squad had come across a Blackfoot summer camp and they were killing everyone in it. Unfortunately there were only women, children, as well as a few old men in it, so they found easy prey."

The major's face turned purple in anger. "Damn that Tucker I should have known better than to send him on a scouting expedition. I will kill him when I find him."

Jed shook his head regretfully. "Well I do not know if very many of your men lived since we saw about a hundred braves riding to help their families. I do however know that at least four survived since we left them tied to a tree after they came into our camp last night and tried to kill us for our horses!"

The major grimaced angrily in hope. "One would not happen to be a large burly black haired man with slightly curly hair would it?"

Mell nodded decisively. "Yep, that was the leader of the four."

Major Sinclair grinned then turned to his aid in satisfaction before turning back. "Good Tucker lives now I can hang him for insubordination as well as for killing innocent women and children. We will go get those men then find out if anybody else survived. Thank you for your information, I need statements from you both if that is possible?"

Mell nodded in agreement before gesturing towards where the rest of her family was gathered. "We were just stopping for lunch would you care to join us?"

The major shook his head negatively. "No thank you, but if you are going to be in town tomorrow you can drop off your statements at the sheriff's office instead of at the army barracks if you prefer."

Mell pointed in the direction they had come. "They are that way major about six hours away, good luck."

The major tipped his hat cordially in farewell. "To the both of you as well marshal, and deputy marshal."

Mell watched the major ride back to his men then leave with a final salute. She looked down at Silver Tip. "You were not needed this time girl go find Pat."

The dog barked happily and raced off towards his mistress.

Jed chuckled in grim approval. "The major was not looking to happy with his man that is for sure. I definitely would not want to be in Tucker's place right about now. I probably would have ended up liking that major if I stayed around here for any length of time. He had not said squaws, but women."

Mell smiled in agreement, as they rode towards the others then motioned inquisitively at her husband. "Will we ever be without prejudices against the colour of people's skin?"

Jed shrugged unknowingly before gesturing grimly. "Hopefully one day, Mell."

They rode back to their group in silence after that.

*****

Golden Eagle sighed tiredly as he came around the corner, but perked up as his stallion neighed at him in greeting. He walked up to Black Hawk and leaned up against the fence for a little break.

Black Hawk smiled enticingly. "Are you ready to get up on that horse today?"

Golden Eagle nodded eagerly as he straightened forgetting about his weariness in his excitement. "I sure am."

Black Hawk chuckled as the Englishman's face lit up. "Okay, I want you to put him through his paces then saddle and bridle him. Lead him by the reins again to make sure he understands you when you say 'whoa'. When you are satisfied, put the sacks on him then put him through his paces once more. If he does not balk too much, I want you to stand up in the stirrup and get down again. If you feel confident, you can sit on him then dismount and take the blanket off then lay on him bareback. Afterwards, you can call it a day if you want."

Golden Eagle gathered everything he would need before going to work without complaining once about being too tired.

*****

Raven rode ahead of Janet quietly keeping a vigilant watch.

Janet followed with the packhorse, so that Raven's horse was unencumbered and could react promptly when his rider told him to.

Raven frowned pensively as she looked around for a place to hide Janet, so that she would be safe while she did some scouting. Howling Coyotes camp should be about half an hour to forty-five minutes from here; she judged from the chief's description of the area. She did not want to get any closer than that.

If Janet was not so ignorant, she would have camped closer to the war chief's camp, but this will have to do. She turned right into the forest and followed a small game trail until satisfied then she stopped and dismounted.

Janet waited for the prearranged signal then dismounted also.

Raven walked over close to her and talked softly. "We can talk quietly now, but no yelling sounds travel far out here. I want you to unsaddle the packhorse, rub him down then feed him. After he is finished eating saddle him again just in case we need to make a hasty retreat. Do the same with your horse and make sure to tie both horses securely, so that they do not wander off. You can have half the rabbit I cooked this morning with some cakes that are in the saddle packs on the packhorse, but absolutely no fire. Set out three or four traps as I showed you, I am going scouting. If you get bored you can take the skin I gave you out then take four sticks and stretch the hide out before scraping it like I showed you this morning then leave it like that till I get back."

Janet nodded silently terrified as she watched Raven disappear with her wolves trailing her. She shook off her fear, angry with herself for allowing her emotions to gain control and did as she was told.

*****

Golden Eagle stood beside the stallion murmuring reassurances as he put his foot in the stirrup. He lifted himself up a little and waited. When the stud looked back curiously, but did not move the Englishman stood up all the way.

The stallion shifted uneasily not liking that then snorted in warning.

Golden Eagle stroked his neck and murmured assurances. The stud finally stood still, so the Englishman got down then stood up again. Devil did not object this time, so he got down and went back to the other side again then stood up in the stirrup once more. When his horse stood obediently, Golden Eagle lifted his leg and straddled him cautiously.

The stallion shifted uncertainly, but the Englishman rubbed his neck then talked to him soothingly. Devil stood still, and Golden Eagle dismounted. He repeated his actions one more time then stripped the saddle of the horse before taking the bridle off and walked over to Black Hawk elated.

Black Hawk grinned as he watched the stallion following Golden Eagle. He turned in admiration towards the Englishman; he actually did not need to ask him the question it was written all over his face, but he did anyway. "Well how do you feel?"

Golden Eagle smiled in delight as he waved eagerly in pride. "Great did you see that? He hardly even fussed when I sat on him."

Black Hawk nodded with a chuckle. "Yes I was very impressed. Rub your horse down now then meet me for supper at my tepee instead of mothers then we will celebrate."

Golden Eagle nodded and went back to work.

*****

Jed looked around in concern before turning to Mell. "We will have to camp here it's a little more open than I usually like, but I never noticed anything better. At least we will have a steep hill behind us with water available. We were delayed a little too long this afternoon by the major, with hardly any moon it is not a good idea to continue on."

Mell inclined her head in agreement then sighed in disappointment; she had hoped to get to the town tonight.

Everyone dismounted and helped set up camp.

Rose started supper; it was not long before everyone gathered around the fire except for Daniel and Pam.

Mell poured two coffee's then went over to them.

Pam scowled at her husband in angrily demand. When she saw Mell coming, she motioned entreatingly in hope. "Mother tell this lummox that I want to get up and sit with the others."

Mell chuckled at the two of them. "Well if you are feeling good enough to argue with your husband I guess it will be all right."

Mell turned to her son then compromised a little. "Pick her up and set her on the log in front of the fire that way she will not be walking yet."

Daniel nodded in relief before lifting Pam effortlessly then walked over and gently put his wife on the log.

Jed smiled in delight at his daughter-in-law. "Well it is nice to see that you are feeling good enough to join us Pam. We have really missed you since you have been hurt."

Pam ginned thankfully at her father-in-law. "Well I am definitely glad I feel better as well."

Pam looked up then inclined her head in thanks at Rose as she handed Pam a bowl of stew. She ate slowly enjoying the laughing and joking going on around her then sighed blissfully as her husband put his arm around her.

*****

Raven moved ahead soundlessly and she grimaced in apprehension, they had camped closer to Howling Coyotes camp then she had thought.

She had only walked for about fifteen minutes when she almost stumbled into a sentry.

Luckily, Bruno had sensed him and growled softly in warning.

Raven dropped to her stomach then slithered forward. At the edge of the tree's she stopped, and looked out of her hiding place. She looked around then saw the war chief's tepee in the center and the others positioned around it.

Raven nodded to herself in satisfaction, this would be a good spot to watch. She slithered backwards then got up and headed back to her camp. It was getting too dark to see much of anything right now, but at least Raven now knew where they were. Tomorrow she would come back for the day to watch them. She walked around the sentries then broke into a trot.

Raven needed to move them further away, especially if she were going to have another nightmare. The sentries would have heard Raven if they had been this close last night.

*****

Janet jumped up in fear as she pointed her rifle in the direction of the rustling noise. She sighed in relief as Bruno walked in first to give her warning before Raven showed herself.

Raven making sure the inexperienced Janet would not kill her by mistake finally walked out of the tree's.

Janet dropped down to the ground shakily grateful that Raven was back.

Raven squatted down beside her and accepted the water canteen plus the plate of cold food for supper that Janet had made her. She sighed plaintively as she looked at Janet in warning. "The sentries are only about fifteen minutes away, so please try to be quiet. I want to move us further away so let's eat then you can follow me. Afterwards, I will show you how to tan your hide before we go to bed."

Janet nodded wordlessly in fear and waited then got up and stayed close to Raven as they moved deeper into the trees.

*****

Golden Eagle had gone to Black Hawk for supper, but Gentle Doe was not feeling well so he had left with Black Hawk to eat at his mothers instead.

Golden Eagle slipped into Ravens then smiled at Jake when he handed him a cup of coffee. "When did you get back?"

Jake shrugged in unconcern. "About twenty minutes ago."

Golden Eagle nodded and sat across the fire from Jake then asked curiously. "How are your men doing?"

Jake smiled in reassurance. "So far they are all okay; nobody tried to slip past them to get in here yet, but they will try sooner or later I am sure."

Golden Eagle frowned thoughtfully in worry; he did not have any food available here. "Did you eat?"

Jake inclined his head placatingly. "Yes, with my men. How did your training go today?"

Golden Eagle grinned eagerly. "Better I even sat on my horse today, and he did not buck once."

Jake nodded impressed then banked the fire for the night. "That is good! I will see you in the morning."

Golden Eagle nodded as he drained his coffee before following Jake's example and went to bed.

CHAPTER TWENTY TWO

Golden Eagle left Raven's tepee then walked to Giant Bears. He scratched on the flap and entered when it was lifted for him. He looked at Black Hawk's worried expression then frowned uneasily. "What is the matter?"

Black Hawk sighed in despair before running his fingers through his hair in distress as he paced. "Gentle Doe was complaining of back pains last night. So the medicine man and shaman are with her now they think she is in labour already."

Black Hawk stopped talking fearfully then turned to the door as his mother walked in. "How is she mom."

Golden Dove sighed grimly as she shook her head in worry. "Not good our suspicions were correct she is in labour already."

Black Hawk scowled in despair before motioning in fear. "Damn it, it is too early! She will not be in her eighth month for another few days."

Golden Dove nodded sadly. "It could still be a false labour we will not be sure for a few hours yet."

Black Hawk grimaced in hope, but he knew deep down that it was fruitless. He started his pacing once again in agitation. He stopped suddenly and turned to Golden Eagle as if just remembering why he was there. "You will have to practice on your own today."

Golden Eagle inclined his head having already guessed that before grabbing two bowls of porridge then left.

*****

Mell walked over to Pam and helped her stand up in alarm. "Are you sure you can walk?"

Pam chuckled teasingly as she nodded decisively. "Yes my right side hurts like the dickens, but my legs are fine they are not broken you know."

Mell nodded still concerned then kept a firm grip on Pam as they walked to the fire for breakfast.

Pam sat down before sighing in annoyance at the pampering. "Honestly, I really am feeling better."

Jed and Daniel walked over to the fire then helped themselves to bowls of porridge.

Mell handed Pam a bowl before sitting down with the others.

Pat, Jess and Rose all came together talking as well as giggling. Everyone was in high spirits knowing a night in a bed was only a few hours away.

Jed included everyone in his smile as they all sat down to eat. "It is about five hours to the next town at this pace. We will stay one night there then it will be a two to three day ride to the town just before Raven's ranch I think. We will stop at the ranch first and see if anybody is home. Then two days to Giant Bear's winter camp so we should be there in five or six days at the latest. If nobody is there either, we will have to find Giant Bear's summer camp. That might be a little difficult without someone to help us find it. However, we will cross that bridge when we come to it no use worrying now about it. Even with all the delay's we have had we are still making pretty good time."

Pam sat straighter confidently as she motioned pleadingly. "I would like to ride now."

Mell and Daniel both shook their heads in denial, but Mell was the one who spoke. "No, when we get to town we will take you to see a doctor, Rose too. If he says it is okay you can ride after we leave town, but only if he agrees."

Pam wilted unhappily then nodded grudgingly. "Okay."

Mell smiled encouragingly at her before turning to the others. "Okay everyone let's get going the faster we get there, the sooner we can have a hot bath!"

Everyone chuckled at Mell's ecstatic expression at the thought of a bath. They all nodded eagerly in agreement, but they could not help teasing their mother unmercifully about her inability to stay awake in a tub as camp was quickly dismantled.

*****

Raven rolled out of her blankets and looked towards Janet, but she was still sleeping. She went over to the packhorse before taking out some cakes then grabbed her extra canteen. She slung the container around her shoulder and nibbling on one of the cakes as she quietly left with Bruno following closely.

Raven broke into a trot as soon as she finished eating then slowed, as she got close.

Silent as a whisper Raven skirted the sentries and slipped back to the hiding place she had found last night. She parted the bush in front of her, but everything was still quiet. If she did not see anything by tomorrow, the two of them would have to leave regardless. She settled herself more comfortably than watched hopefully.

*****

Golden Eagle sighed tiredly as he laid down on the ground for a moment hoping. He waited for Running Wolf for a bit, but finally decided that he was not coming. He got up before grabbing his rifle, bow, and arrows then headed to the practice area by himself.

Golden Eagle put everything down except for the rifle and started shooting. After the sixth shot, he hit the center. Elated he shot another ten bullets, but only hit the center twice more before lowering the rifle then picking up the bow.

Golden Eagle put ten arrows in front of him tip down in the dirt before breathing deeply relaxing himself. He lined up his shot as he carefully let the arrow go gently. He hit closer to the center with his first attempt than he had with all ten arrows yesterday. He jumped up and down in excitement then stopped abruptly in embarrassment as he looked around. Of course, no one was there to see him. Shrugging he quieted and continued on calmer now.

*****

Jed raised his hand in warning before stopping his horse. Everyone else halted as well then Jed pointed ahead in relief. "There it is! It is called Little Rock because of the mountains behind it, which are called Little Rocky Mountains. It is about an hour away as soon as we get into town we will drop off Pam, Rose, and Daniel at the doctors. The rest of us will go on to the sheriff's office. I hope that we will find it calmer than the last two towns we have been in! Is everyone in agreement?"

They all nodded with smiles of anticipation.

Jed chuckled at the optimistic looks on all their faces. "Good lets go."

Mell and Jed kicked their horses into a trot.

Mell looked down at Pam encouraging. "Not much further dear."

Pam sighed in irritation as she swayed between the horses. The movement was almost making her sick to her stomach. "Good, I am getting tired of staring up at the sky all day."

Mell laughed in sympathy, but did not say anything more.

*****

Golden Eagle walked to Ravens then dropped off the rifle, bow, and arrows. He had hit the target ten times with the arrows today, but only one got close to where he was aiming. It was still a better improvement from two days ago when he could not even hit the target.

Golden Eagle smiled at his stud as the horse trotted over to the gate then nickered at him in greeting. Since Black Hawk would not be here today, he decided to play with his stallion for a bit since he did not have any equipment to work with anyway. He walked into the corral and raced across the paddock playfully.

Devil chased him for a moment then turned away uninterested.

Golden Eagle waited until he moved a bit further before sneaking up behind him and grabbed his tail then gave it a yang as he ran across to the opposite side of the pen.

Devil spun and chased him to the other side of the paddock before nudging him playfully with his head.

Golden Eagle laughed in delight then fell down on the ground playing dead.

Devil pushed at him a few times uncertainly before dropping onto his knees and lying down beside his master.

Golden Eagle chuckled in humour then turned himself and propped his head up on the stallions neck then promptly fell asleep.

*****

Raven sighed irritably as she shifted so that she could get to her cakes and canteen. She took a large drink then cupped her hand and poured water in it for her dog. She broke the cake in half then fed some to Bruno before eating the other half. She lay back again and pushed the bush in half to re-assume her watch.

The only excitement today had been the changing of the sentries other than that nothing had happened. She would wait until dusk before making her way back to camp. She shifted to get comfortable as she laid there quietly without moving an inch.

*****

Jed and Mell eased their horses to a walk as they entered the town. They got a few curious looks from the townspeople, but nothing threatening. He pointed to a man sitting on a step whittling so they headed towards him. He smiled down at him then tipped his had cordially. "Excuse me can you point me towards the doctor in town?"

The man nodded and spat in the dirt then pointed with his knife ahead of them, but did not look up even once. "Sure can three doors down on the left hand side."

Jed tipped his hat politely once more. "Much obliged."

The man grunted before going back to whittling uninterested.

Mell and Jed turned up the street then pulled up to the hitching rail and everyone dismounted. Jed with Daniel's help unhooked the travois as Mell opened the door for them; she waited until Rose walked in then followed her inside.

Everyone else stayed outside.

The man behind the desk looked up inquisitively before jumping out of his chair as he hurried to a door to his left. "In here please!"

Jed and Daniel followed him then laid the travois on the bed.

Pam frowned in aggravation. "I could have walked you know!"

The doctor smiled down at her placatingly. "You let me be the judge of that young lady! I am Doctor Michael Andrews."

He shook Pam's hand before turning to the others.

Mell stepped forward next and shook the doctor's hand. As she made introductions, the doctor shook hands with Jed, Daniel then Rose.

Mell smiled at the handsome young doctor as he turned back to her before pointing to her son. "We will let Daniel explain while we go to the sheriff's office, we will return afterwards to see how the girl's are."

The doctor nodded as he pointed in the general direction. "The sheriff's office is up two buildings."

Mell and Jed thanked him then left.

They walked up the street with Mell and Jed leading while the other two girls followed quietly. Mell unhooked her whip then coiled it in her hand as she took the lead.

A man of about fifty looked up and smiled good-naturedly in welcome. "How are you folks today, what can I do for you?"

Mell eyed the sheriff for a bit, quickly assessing him then relaxed and put her hand with the whip down at the genuine integrity she saw in his eyes. She introduced everyone then tensed for a scathing remark.

The man nodded knowingly and smiled in pleasure as he pointed at her then Jed. "I know who you both are, although you are a little older now. I only saw you from a distance, but I still remember seeing you use those guns once."

Mell lifted her eyebrows in surprise as she shook her head baffled. "I do not remember you."

The sheriff chuckled not surprised; he had not wanted anyone to see him at that wild time in his life. "I was just passing through one of your towns when you and at that time your fiancé gunned down two hired guns that were looking to take over your towns. Miller's Creek I think the town was called. You both inspired me so much that I quit the gang I had just started riding with then came home here and became the next sheriff. It was the best decision I ever made."

Mell shared a pleased look with Jed then both turned back and grinned in delight at the sheriff.

The sheriff sighed plaintively at his lack of manners as he stood up then shook everyone's hands in greeting before chuckling. "Well I guess I should give you my name as well, I am Sheriff Peterson. Please have a seat and tell me how I can help you? I am very curious to hear what brings you to my hometown?"

They all found seats then Mell explained about the dirty sheriff in the border town and about the massacre at the Indian village.

*****

Golden Eagle woke suddenly then jumped up incredulously as he looked up at the position of the sun. He must have slept for a good hour and not once did Devil move.

Devil lifted his head to look up at his master then laid his head back down as if to say he did not want to get up yet.

Golden Eagle chuckled and knelt down before lying across Devil's neck then scratched him all over.

Devil snorted through his nostrils gently in pleasure and did not move a muscle enjoying the scratching immensely.

Golden Eagle getting an idea laid full length on Devil then clucked for him to get up. "Come on old boy up you go!"

Devil reluctantly lifted up onto his knees.

Golden Eagle straddled him and leaned forward then put his arms around the stallion's neck so that he would not fall off. "Come on boy up you go all the way."

Devil slowly got up with him his master clinging to his neck.

Golden Eagle smiled elated before whistling so that the stud would walk around. After one round around the pen, the Englishman sat up all the way and let Devil wander wherever he wanted to go. Leaning forward again, he put his arms around his horses neck then whistled for a trot.

Immediately Devil responded as he trotted around the pen.

After a few minutes, Golden Eagle again sat up in anticipation. He let his horse go his own way not trying to lead him yet. He did the same thing again, but this time asked for a canter. He halted him finally and jumped down then put his arms around the stallion's neck in gratitude as he gave him a giant hug in gratitude before heading for his tepee.

*****

Raven sighed in disappointment and slithered backwards, it had been a fruitless day today. It was starting to get dark out so Raven headed back to camp. She stopped suddenly then crouched at a rustling ahead as a sentry walked by close to her hiding place.

The sentry stopped suspiciously instantly on guard as he felt another's presence.

The Indian looking around cautiously and Raven held her breath then grasped her knife before taking it out of her pouch in readiness. Raven and the lookout both heard a growl of anger off to their left.

The brave saw a grey-wolf ahead, slink by with a rabbit in her mouth. He chuckled at his jumpiness then continued on.

Raven breathed a sigh of relief as she slipped around him soundlessly.

The brave was totally unaware that Bruno's mate had just saved him from certain death.

*****

Janet jumped up in fright as she pointed her rifle in the direction of the rustling. Again, she saw Bruno first before Raven stepped out and Janet sighed in relief before lowering her rifle.

Raven's eyebrows rose in surprise.

Janet shrugged in embarrassment. "I was starting to get worried, which made me a little jumpy."

Raven nodded knowingly then looked down at her wolf. "I will leave Bruno with you tomorrow to keep you company."

Janet inclined her head thankfully; several times today, she had almost shot her rifle in reflex. She did not tell Raven that though knowing her rescuer would be angry at her foolishness. "That will make me feel better, thank you."

Raven smiled hopefully, she was starving as she motioned eagerly. "Did you catch any rabbits today?"

Janet beamed in pride before wrinkling her nose with a shudder of distaste. "Two of them, I gutted and skinned them both, even though it was absolutely disgusting then scraped the hides and staked them out as you showed me."

Raven could not help but laugh at the unlady like face Janet made then went over and looked down at the two hides. She noticed a few slices where Janet had punctured the skin, but for her first time she had done well. She smiled in approval then turned back to her inquisitively. "Very good did you reset the snares?"

Janet drew herself up at the compliment before inclining her head regally trying not to show how pleased she was. "Yes, I figured you would want more for your animals."

Raven chuckled not fooled by Janet's regal attitude. "Good girl, go check the snares and I will show you how to build an underground oven so that there is no smoke."

Janet grinned in delight at the thought of hot food then did as she was instructed quickly in anticipation.

*****

Doctor Andrews finished with Rose before walking back into the room where Pam was waiting patiently. He looked down at Pam solemnly. "So let's get these clothes off and have a look at you."

Pam nodded as she sat up so that the doctor could help her remove her shirt then he unwrapped her ribs and draped the cloth across Pam's breasts when she laid back down to spare her some discomfort.

He ran his hands expertly across her ribs then down under the rib cage before going across the top of her stomach to the other side. He looked a little closer at her belly suddenly as he smiled in delight. "Expecting are you I would say about six months."

The doctor stopped talking suddenly as she glanced away quickly and looked over at her husband before biting her lip uneasily.

The doctor moved back out of the way knowingly as Daniel marched up to the bed then glared down at his wife in anger. "You are pregnant and you did not tell me! How could you endanger yourself like that with a baby on the way?"

Pam sighed unhappily in apology as she lifted a beseeching hand before placing it on her husbands arm. "I wanted to tell you! I went to the doctor the day I stopped to see your mom that is when we compared dreams, but with all the rushing around to get ready to go I just never got the chance. Besides I knew that if I told you, you would not have let me come."

Daniel scowled furiously then waved in frustration. "You are darn right I would not have let you come!"

Daniel turned to look at the doctor grimly before motioning in fear. "She has not hurt the baby has she?"

Doctor Andrews smiled reassuringly. "I do not think so, but let me finish my examination and I will let you know."

Daniel nodded briskly then backed off.

The doctor took out his stethoscope and bent towards Pam then mouthed silently. "I am sorry."

Pam smiled sadly, as she shrugged at his apology the damage was done now.

Doctor Andrews listened to her lungs first before putting the scope on Pam's stomach and listened intently. He stood up with a touch on her shoulder in reassurance. "Well young lady I think you are very lucky. Your lungs are clear no rattle or wheezing now, so they were not punctured all the way through. Your baby has a very healthy heart rhythm. Your third rib was broken, but it is healing nicely. Your wound is almost completely healed, so I do not think you need a travois anymore. Just be careful mounting or dismounting, no heavy lifting while you are pregnant if you can help it. Keep bandaging your ribs for another week just for the support while you're riding then you should not need it anymore."

Daniel walked up to the doctor in question as he gestured uneasily. "Should she be riding in her condition?"

The doctor chuckled in amusement at the anxious father to be. "Of course she can, I am a firm believer in lots of exercise until around the seven and a half to eighth month. After that no riding, but walks as well as light exercise are still needed."

The doctor helped re-bandage the ribs then helped her with her shirt. He was just helping her to sit up when Jed and Mell entered.

Mell smiled at Pam hopefully then turned to the doctor. "Well how are both girl's doing?"

Doctor Andrews started with Rose first. "Rose's rib was not quite broke all the way. I would say that a sliver of the bone was still attached so was holding the rib in place. Wrapping it also helped to keep it from further damage that is why she was not as bad off as Pam. So she does not need the binding anymore as long as she is careful not to re-injure it again."

The doctor pointed at Pam next with a smile of satisfaction. "This young lady can ride again as long as she keeps her ribs tightly bound for another week. Since you are her mother-in-law congratulations are also in order on the upcoming birth of your grandchild in three to three and a half months I would say."

Mell grinned knowingly then nodded in delight at hearing that the child she had suspected Pam was harbouring was okay. That was what had kept the fever from abating for so long; it was not the injury causing it, but the baby. "I know I could not help but notice."

Daniel sucked in a shocked breath in anger as he waved incredulously. "Mother! Why didn't you tell me?"

Mell shrugged grimly. "It was not up to me to tell, and since I was not sure for awhile there that she would even survive I did not want to make it worse."

The doctor inclined his head in approval. "You are very wise. If you do not mind could you tell me where you are headed?"

Mell smiled inquisitively. "We are headed to Earl Summerset's ranch just outside the next town. Malta I believe it is called, on the border of the Milk River. Why?"

Doctor Andrews sighed relieved; he had hoped that was where they were headed. He motioned hopefully. "No kidding, I am headed that way tomorrow too. Mind if I ride along with you it's not safe going alone."

Mell looked at Jed for permission then saw him nod. She turned back to the doctor and motioned in caution. "You can come if you like doctor, but we are in a bit of a hurry so we will be riding hard. We are hoping to make the next town in two days at the most. Earlier if we can, we will be riding at seven in the morning if you still want to come meet us at the hotel."

The doctor nodded decisively. "I will be there."

Mell inclined her head in goodbye then they left.

*****

Golden Eagle walked over to Giant Bears and ducked inside when the flap was opened for him. He looked around then spotted Black Hawk. "How is she?"

Black Hawk turned an anguished look on Golden Eagle. "I was just in there. I had to make the choice of either saving my wife or my son, although it was not really much of a choice since my wife made me swear to save the baby. She was in so much pain that I could only stand to stay in there for a few minutes. I left right after I told them to save the baby."

Golden Eagle walked over and put his hand on his friends shoulder in comfort. "If you need to talk at any time come see me."

Black Hawk nodded in thanks then turned away.

Golden Eagle walked over to the fire and saw a pot of stew so dished himself up some then decided to take extra just in case Jake was back and had not eaten yet. He grabbed another bowl then left quietly.

*****

Raven walked over and with Janet's help they uncovered the underground oven then lifted the two rabbit's out and the tiny wild potatoes they had dug up earlier. They were not very big yet since it was only the beginning of their growing season, but large enough for them. They rapidly filled in the hole so that no smoke could escape.

Janet inhaled deeply at the heavenly smell then sighed ecstatically in hunger. "I am starving!"

Raven chuckled in agreement, as she cut one rabbit in half and put it on Janet's plate then put the rest on her own. She split up the few potatoes they had found before they dug in enthusiastically.

Janet groaned in pleasure as she bit into the rabbit and juice squirted down her chin. "I will have to remember how to cook this way it is absolutely delicious."

Raven grinned in delight as she nodded. "A lot of times we cook deer, pig, or cattle this way whole then have a big feast."

Janet sighed blissfully. "I hope I am around the next time you cook this way, it is fantastic!"

Raven laughed knowingly, hoping she would stay as well as they finished their meal in silence.

*****

Jed ushered everyone into the hotel before walking up to the desk. "We need three rooms please. We also have a dog with us."

The hotel clerk looked at the huge dog and his eyes widened in fear. "I think you mean a bear is with you! Is it house broke?"

Jed smiled reassuringly. "Yes, she is house trained."

The clerk looked at the badge on Jed's shirt in reluctant agreement then handed him three room keys. "Sure deputy marshal you can keep the dog with you, but she is not allowed in the dining room."

Jed inclined his head in thanks before signing the register. "That sounds fair enough. I would also like to know if we could have supper in our rooms and a bath would be nice as well."

The clerk pointed towards the back of the hotel.

Jed could see a door leading out as he turned to look in that direction.

The clerk continued in explanation when Jed turned back to him. "There is a male bathing room out back. We have tubs in the rooms already for the women; I will send the boys up to fill them. I will also send up supper right away."

Jed turned back then nodded in thanks as he flipped the clerk a silver dollar. "Much obliged sir."

The clerk's smile widened as he expertly caught the coin. He shook a little bell hidden under the counter, which was only used for such a rare occasions as a tip.

A boy of about fifteen rushed into the room in disbelief, it was not very often he was called by that bell. "Yes sir."

The clerk pointed to Jed. "Get these folks their luggage and show them to their rooms."

Jed smiled at the boy. "You can show us our room's first then go down to the stables and ask the stableman for our saddlebag's, but do not touch the packhorse's please."

The boy beckoned them to come, so they followed him to their rooms gratefully.

*****

Golden Eagle walked back to Raven's then shouldered his way inside. He saw Jake sitting by the fire, so handed him a bowl of stew and sat across from him; he smiled over sadly.

Jake frowned knowingly. "Gentle Doe is worse?"

Golden Eagle nodded grimly. "Yes, Golden Dove thinks she will die sometime in the early morning if she lasts that long. I was just leaving the tepee when she stopped to tell me not to come back tonight for lessons. She was just on her way to go get Black Hawk so that he could sit with his wife for the duration of her life."

Jake frowned gloomily then handed Golden Eagle a coffee as they ate in silence.

Golden Eagle scrapped his bowl clean and drained his coffee before getting up to tired as well as depressed to talk. "I am going to bed. Goodnight."

Jake nodded before banking the fire then followed Golden Eagle's lead.

*****

Raven used dirt to clean her plate and rinsed it with a little water there was no stream around here, so they had to make do. She sat on her pallet after she put the plate back in the saddlebag then sighed in irritation as she looked at Janet in annoyance. "There was nothing today nobody came in, and nobody left. I will watch tomorrow again, but if I do not see anything useful we will still have to leave anyway."

Janet nodded forlornly not looking forward to another day spent sitting around waiting then lay down disgruntled. "Okay, goodnight."

Raven grimaced uneasily hoping not to have a repeat of the nightmare from the other night. She yawned and layed down then fell into a dreamless sleep almost immediately.

*****

Jed walked into his hotel room after his bath and chuckled knowingly as he stared down at his wife in the tub fast asleep. He stripped then walked over and picked her up tenderly before putting her in bed then climbing in beside her and snuggling up. A few minutes later, he also slept.

CHAPTER TWENTY THREE

Mell woke then purred in pleasure as her husband ran his hand down her chest and belly then teased the curls at the junction of her thighs. She pushed back against him in encouragement.

Jed arched his hips and pushed his engorged manhood against her buttocks enticingly. He scooted over a little further then lifted Mell's leg backwards over his and pushed up then entered her moist womanhood from behind.

Mell groaned in delight as she rotated her hips.

Jed pushed up inside her harder before nibbling on her neck. He put his arm under her head so that he could play with her breast at the same time. He continued stroking her bud of pleasure gently as he ground his hips against her faster. He moaned ecstatically as he felt Mell's first tremors of ecstasy peeking. Once he felt her let go of her control, he let his go also.

Mell cried out as she felt the tremors inside her intensify and gasped in satisfaction when she felt her husband lose his control too.

Jed dropped his head on his pillow panting for a few minutes in exertion then disentangled himself from his wife and lay on his back.

Mell turned as she curled up against him then purred deep in her throat like a contented cat in satisfaction. "Hmm that is definitely a nice way to say good morning."

Jed chuckled in agreement, as he nudged her playfully in humour. "Sit up and I will comb your hair out before we go downstairs."

Mell groaned, but not in pleasure this time, it was now a gasp of agony at the thought of her hair. "I fell asleep again didn't I?"

Jed nodded sympathetically before laughing at her pained expression. "Pass me the brush, luv, I will get all the tangles out for you."

Mell sighed plaintively then did as she was told and reached towards the nightstand then passed the brush to Jed. She sat up before turning her back to her husband and put on a stoic expression as he methodically attacked the stubborn knots in her long white hair.

Every time she had a bath, she would fall asleep in the tub then Jed would have to carry her to bed. Her kids thought it was hilarious and were constantly teasing her about it. She did not think it was funny though the next morning when Jed had to try getting all the tangled mess straightened out

*****

Raven woke then sat up reluctantly. She was not actually looking forward to another day of lying perfectly still and watching hoping to hear or see something that might give her a clue as to why they had attacked Golden Eagle's party. She sighed perturbed before going to the packhorse then grabbed her canteen, more cakes, and half the rabbit from last night.

Raven looked down as Bruno trotted over to her. "You stay with Janet."

Bruno whined plaintively, but immediately went over to the sleeping Janet before lying down close to her then watched Raven disappear without him forlornly.

*****

Golden Eagle woke quickly as he jumped out of his blankets in fear thinking they were under attack as more and more shrieks shattered the silence.

Jake looked up at Golden Eagle sadly then handed him a cup of coffee. "Gentle Doe died a few minutes ago."

Golden Eagle dropped down across the fire in distress. "Are we under attack as well?"

Jake shook his head negatively. "No, they are grieving! I guess I should tell you before you go out that Indian's do not grieve as we do, we cry usually for a long time. They grieve for two days only, today they will shriek out their grief and cut themselves. Depending on how close a relative or friend you are, is how much you cut yourself! For some, it will only be two or three shallow cuts. Running Wolf will probably cut himself up to seven times since she was his mother. Black Hawk will cut himself up to ten times or more. I have seen Indian's die because their grief was so strong that they cut themselves one too many times then they bled to death. Tomorrow they will keep shrieking, but not as powerful or severe. There will be no more cutting themselves though. The ones closest to Gentle Doe will cut off their braids during the burning of the pier. In the evening, they will have a funeral with everything she needs to go to the spirit world placed around her so that it can be burned at sunset with her. After the fire dies, they will not mention her name aloud again, and it is disrespectful for others to mention her name also. In the morning, it will be as if the death never occurred unless someone else dies of their wounds."

Golden Eagle sighed uneasily. "I am glad you warned me Golden Dove did talk about their funerals a little, but she never told me about cutting themselves. Should I go out there then follow their example, or will it cause trouble?"

Jake shook his head negatively. "No, you would not be welcome right now and you did not know her that well. Just go do what you did yesterday, but slip around the back. Tomorrow you will be expected to attend the funeral, but that is all they will expect from you. Golden Dove brought some stew for us to eat later, so come back here after you are finished for the day."

Golden Eagle nodded grimly in relief as he finished his coffee then grabbed his stuff before leaving.

*****

Mell and Jed left their room then headed down to the dining room. They entered and looked around expectantly, spotted the kids sitting in the corner they went over.

Mell smiled warmly down at the doctor in greeting. "Decided to join us did you Doctor Andrews?"

The doctor beamed up at her enticingly. "Please call me Michael all my friends do."

Mell sat before inclining her head in agreement. "Only if you call me, Mell! Have you met everyone?"

Michael nodded then motioned curiously. "Yes I did. Do you mind if I ask why you folks are headed to Earl Summerset's?"

Mell shook her head that she did not mind at all before pointing at her daughter-in-law. "Pam happens to be Raven and Edward's aunt, since she married our son we are now related by marriage."

Michael grinned over at Pam.

Everyone sat quietly as they waited for the waitress to finish taking their order then to pour them coffee.

After she left Jed cleared his throat inquisitively. "Why are you headed to Malta Michael, if you do not mind me asking?"

Michael shook his head it was no secret. "They have no doctor in town, so I go out there every two weeks and administer to the sick. I always try to find others going because it is too dangerous travelling by myself."

Jed nodded at this simple explanation then quiet descended as their breakfast was served.

*****

Raven slipped into her hiding place and parted the bush as she did a quick survey, but nothing had changed since last night. Everything still seemed quiet, so she settled herself more comfortably then continued her vigil. She sighed dejectedly she had a feeling it was going to be a long day.

*****

Golden Eagle sighted on his target; the Englishman let go of the shaft and watched in dismay as it flew past the target then hit a tree some distance away. He sighed miserably and gave up; he just could not concentrate with all the wailing in the distance.

Golden Eagle sat down as he thought of his own mother. She had died giving birth to his younger sister, so he knew what it would be like for Black Hawk's new son. He still missed her it had left a massive hole in his life when she died.

His father had changed for the worst after that becoming harsh as well as demanding. Sometimes he wondered if he were wrong in his reasoning though maybe his father had always been that way, but his mother had kept him from seeing it by sheltering him.

Golden Eagle pushed thoughts of his mother away then turned his thoughts to Raven instead. Her coal black hair and dusky skin made the light misty green of her eyes even more vivid; her beauty was unmistakable. He wished she would hurry back so that he could see her again. He treasured their one night of lovemaking, even dreamed about it often. He hoped that he would still feel that tingling sensation when she returned. He really did hope so! Golden Eagle frowned thoughtfully still thinking of her as he got up then collected all his gear and headed for Raven's tepee.

*****

Jessica rode up to the doctor as she smirked knowingly. "You are not a very good rider, are you? I see you do not wear guns, but have a rifle. Do you even know how to use it?"

Michael looked at Jessica calmly then smiled in aggravation as he answered her disdainfully. "I am not the greatest horseman so I usually go by buggy, but I can still keep up if that is what you are worried about. As for not wearing a gun, I am in the business of saving lives not taking them. The rifle is only for wild animals and yes I know how to use it."

Jessica scowled angrily at his sarcastic tone then kicked her horse into a gallop and surged ahead.

Michael sighed plaintively as he watched her expertly manoeuvre her horse. He shook his head regretfully then wondered why she did not like him, nobody else seemed hostile towards him only her.

Michael smiled widely as he thought of the challenge she would make. He could not help reflecting seriously about trying to get past her hostility. She was an extraordinarily beautiful woman, so he itched to see what she was hiding beneath that hat and baggy men's clothing she was wearing. He loved challenges.

*****

Jessica slowed her horse down before walking him to cool him off a little. Her brow puckered in puzzlement as she sighed perplexed, why did the doctor annoy her so much? Especially when he looked at her with a frown of disapproval at her attire, never before had it bothered her. She turned slightly then sighed grimly as the object of her displeasure rode up beside her.

Michael smiled smugly as he pointed behind them. "Your sister said to tell you we are stopping for lunch just up ahead, so you are to wait for everyone else."

Jessica nodded irritably as she stopped her horse and waited for the others.

Michael looked at Jessica teasingly then smirked devilishly. "You ride well, and I see that you have a rifle as well as guns. Do you know how to use that rifle? If you do not, I can teach you."

Jessica frowned angrily then tossed her head haughtily. "Yes, I know how to use my rifle. I wear guns, but I do not usually use them because I do not need them. I have other ways to protect myself."

Michael snorted in disdain. "I bet you do!"

Michael fell silent as the others caught up.

Mell grimaced at Jessica in confusion before shaking her head in disapproval. "You should not have ridden off like that Jessica you are supposed to be protecting the packhorse and Pam!"

Jessica nodded at the rebuke in regret. "I am sorry, Mell, it won't happen again."

Mell inclined her head in forgiveness at the apology.

Jessica glared angrily at Michael for having witnessed the reproach from her beloved sister then jerked her horse around before falling back into place without another word to the doctor.

Pam smiled sympathetically at Jessica, but did not say anything.

Mell and Jed stopped at the spot they had picked out for a camp then a quick lunch was made.

*****

Raven sighed in irritation, she was just about to move back and eat when a disturbance occurred at the war chief's tepee.

Howling Coyote came out then stood with his arms folded staring off to his left. The two sentries who had caused the uproar stood behind the war chief and waited.

Raven watched in puzzlement then tensed as she heard three horses approaching. She watched as one man and two packhorses loaded with goods rode up to Howling Coyote.

The white man dismounted before a heated debate occurred, but strain as she might she could not hear anything. Raven eyed the vi'hoI horses thoughtfully they looked familiar. She stared at the white man again then sucked in a shocked breath as he turned giving her a better look at him. She knew that man, it was Charles her neighbour. What was Charles doing here anyway; he hated Indian's with a passion!

Charles raised his voice angrily, enough for Raven to hear him this time. "I am telling you the white man was not there you were not supposed to kill him. That Englishman would not know the difference between one Indian and the next!"

Howling Coyote spoke again, but too low for Raven to hear

Charles scowled grimly as he answered loudly frustrated. "I could not get them to do anything. It seems the sheriff talked the townspeople into waiting until Raven returned. Damn it since it did not work I want you to go attack the ranch as well as Raven's grandfather. I brought more rifles; I want them off that property now, I need that gold!"

Raven sucked in a shocked breath as she watched the war chief shake his head no. Not needing to learn more since Raven knew that Howling Coyote did not have enough men to attack her ranch or the Wolf tribe she slipped out of her hiding place then past the sentries before rushing back to her camp.

Raven made a lot of noise in warning so that Janet would not shoot her before rushing up to her. She whispered urgently as she beckoned Janet to hurry. "Get your horse saddled quickly we have to leave now!"

Janet nodded fearfully before doing as she was told without asking any questions. Afraid her nightmares were coming true, and the war chief was coming after them.

*****

Golden Eagle whistled to his stallion then smiled in delight when the horse obediently came to him. He led him towards a log in the center of the corral and laid on Devil's back more confident now after yesterdays playing around. When he did not fuss the Englishman turned slightly so that he was facing front then grabbed his horse's mane and sat up.

Golden Eagle whistled his command to walk, but did not direct the horse wanting the stud to become familiar with him on his back without any pressure at first.

Devil pranced for a moment unsure about the man sitting on his back then calmed as Golden Eagle stroked his neck and whispered reassurances.

Golden Eagle smiled in pleasure as they walked twice around the pen then he whistled for a trot and finally a canter then a walk once more. He dismounted and played with his horse for a bit before lying down to see if his horse would lay with him again. When he did, the Englishman laid his head on Devil's neck then fell asleep again, but for only a few minutes this time. He straddling him after a good scratch and urged his horse to get up with him clinging to his neck once again. He walked, trotted then cantered around the corral before jumping off and headed towards his tepee. He was starving, so hopefully some supper would still be waiting since he had not eaten since this morning.

*****

Mell looked over at her husband in aggravation then frowned in disapproval. "Jessica is acting weird today. I have never seen her so distracted before."

Jed smiled knowingly before winking suggestively. "I think it has something to do with a good looking doctor."

Mell sighed plaintively. "You could be right I think we should stop soon?"

Jed inclined his head in agreement before pointing to the left. "Over there looks like a good spot, and it's not far."

Mell gazed in that direction then nodded in agreement and called to Pat. "Go scout out those tree's off to your left, if it is okay we will camp there tonight."

Pat nodded then whistled to her dog, and they raced off. The others followed more slowly waiting for Pat's signal that it was all clear. Jed sighed in relief as Pat beckoned them to come. They all dismounted before setting up camp.

*****

Raven pushed their horses hard, but slowed as dusk descended then walked the horses for half an hour to cool them down. There was only half a moon tonight so not bright enough to see to keep riding. She turned to the right and left the main trail before dismounting in a grove of trees.

Janet still not saying anything helped Raven set up camp. When supper was cooking, she sat across the fire from Raven then eyed her curiously. "Well what happened?"

Raven sighed grimly. "It seems that a white man, my neighbour actually, was the one who arranged the attack on you and your brother."

Janet frowned angrily as she thought back. "Yes, I remember now. I was still dazed so thought I was seeing things when a white man came into our camp two days after the attack. What did you hear?"

Raven grimaced in anger then told her everything she had heard.

Janet shook her head furiously in anxiety. "Are you sure they will not attack the ranch or your people?"

Raven nodded decisively the war chief would not be that stupid! Would he? She finally shook her head confidently. "I am very sure that they will not because they do not have enough warriors for an assault. Plus, my ranch is too close to the town for Howling Coyote to take the chance that the army would show up. Even though the war chief used the white man to get back at me, he knows I am too powerful for him to fight openly. I have too many chiefs on my side so he will not risk challenging me openly. As for the white man, he has been after me to either marry him or sell out to him since my parents died. I have walked those hills around my grandfathers all my life, and I have never seen any hint of gold anywhere."

Janet frowned in thought. "Could it be on my brother's place than so that is why they took me as a hostage?"

Raven started to shake her head negatively, but stopped suddenly and scowled grimly. "Not on his land, but up against it. There is a place though that borders our land that could have gold. I suppose he would need both properties in that case, but since your brother was selling the land anyway; my neighbour did not feel threatened by him. I would guess that they took you as insurance that he would sell the place cheap in exchange for your life."

Janet nodded distastefully. "He probably figures if the place with the gold is on the border of both places it is likely that some gold could be on our place as well, or if it is a cave it could run all the way into my brother's hills too."

Raven inclined her head in agreement then dished up some supper. She handed it to Janet before getting some for herself. "Eat it is still four or five days back to my people, we will be riding hard only stopping when we have no choice. We must hurry just in case I am wrong and Howling Coyote decides to attack. Starting tomorrow we will start your lessons again."

Janet nodded as she ate quietly lost in thought.

*****

Golden Eagle sat across the fire from Jake then smiled his thanks as he handed him a bowl of stew.

They ate quietly before sitting back to enjoy their coffee.

Golden Eagle sighed grimly in worry. "Did you find out whether the baby lived or not?"

Jake nodded relieved. "He lives, but he is a little small. He should make it though."

Golden Eagle sighed thankfully, as he waved vaguely around. "Well that is good news anyway. Did you go out to see your men today?"

Jake inclined his head that he had before motioning curiously. "So far everything is quiet and no sign of Raven yet. How is the training going with your horse?"

Golden Eagle smiled in delight at the thought of Devil. "Very well I was up on him yesterday, today as well. I walked, trotted then cantered him around the paddock with me on him, but I did not try to guide him yet."

Jake grinned in approval. "Good with that kind of progress you should be riding him fully in a day or two."

Golden Eagle nodded eagerly. "I will work with him a little more tomorrow before the funeral."

Jake banked the fire without comment before waving. "Goodnight."

Golden Eagle went to bed too. His last thought was for Raven to hurry home, he was getting anxious to see her again.

*****

Jessica sighed and walked slowly towards the small lake trying to figure out what it was about the doctor that made her so uncomfortable as well as very unsure of herself. She reached the edge of the lake then looked down at the inviting water. She looked around and not seeing anyone decided to take a swim.

Jess removed her hat letting her slightly wavy fiery red hair cascade down her back to just above her hips. She took off the oversized men's vest then removed her boots, and pants before standing straight. She looked down at herself contemplatively.

Jess was not skinny by any means, but she was not fat either. Her backside was a little bigger than she liked, but her hips and waist were just right. Her breasts were a little small, but she was sure they would fit nicely in any man's hand. They were pert then thrust up invitingly, with just a touch of rose in the center. He legs were really long, and shapely. She also had nice firm muscles in the calves, but they were not overly muscled. Her feet were a little bigger then she would have wished for, but the fourth toe curled to the side a little which made them look attractive.

Jessica sighed and walked into the water. When she was deep enough, she ducked under the surface then swam under the water for a few minutes before surfacing. She went around the tree's jutting up from the edge of the lake and stopped in surprise treading water as the man of her thoughts earlier stood on the beach gloriously naked.

The doctor's hair was dark brown with a slight curly at the ends. It was pretty long brushing the top of his shoulders. His neck was muscled, but not too thick. His shoulders were broad which tapered down to a muscled chest as well as surprisingly large arm muscles for a doctor. There was a light dusting of hair in the middle of his chest, but that was it. His waist was narrow which emphasised his nicely rounded firm buttocks. His legs were long nicely muscled as well. It was the sight of the appendix at the juncture of his thighs, which had Jessica squirming in embarrassment, as it jutted up from the foundation of brown curls.

Jessica sucked in a shocked breath then her eyes widened as his shaft started to grow. She jerked her eyes up and saw a knowing smile cross Michael's face as he watched her blush grow until her face was almost the same shade as her hair. She hurriedly spun around then swam back to where she had left her clothes.

Michael dove gracefully into the water and with powerful strokes easily caught up to Jessica just as she was leaving the water. He ran up behind her before spinning her around then he was kissing her with unleashed passion.

Jessica grabbed his broad shoulders to hold herself up as her legs buckled from the sheer pleasure of the kiss.

Michael eased Jessica down onto the soft sand and followed her. He lay fully on top of her before pushing his knees between her legs so that she would open them wider to accommodate him.

Jessica groaned in passion then denial as Michael left her lips and captured one of her breasts in his mouth suckling gently, but urgently.

Michael propped himself up a little so that he could bring his hand down between their bodies so he could touch her most intimate secrets.

Jessica cried out in delight as he stroked her bud then arched her hips up for more.

Michael moved to her other breast and gently lapped at it as his fingers pressed her bud a little harder. His mouth left her breast then moved down her belly nibbling all the way, as he moved towards his goal. He pushed her legs up and dipped his head to taste her sweet nectar.

Jessica arched up before crying out in shocked pleasure then felt a pressure building up inside her. It was almost painful, but at the same time, it felt pleasurable. Unable to keep it at bay any longer Jess let go and she saw stars as she cried out her intense gratification.

Michael scooted back up before kissing her tenderly then probed until his engorged manhood found her moist opening. He lifted his head and looked down at Jessica with intense desire. "I want you, but only if you want me too!"

Jessica shook her head in denial pushing weakly against his shoulders half-heartedly trying to get away.

Michael watched her closely then waited until she looked back up before pleading desperately. "I need you!"

Jessica met his gaze and gloried in the blaze of passion she saw in Michael's light golden brown eyes. Unable to resist the passion any longer Jessica nodded in agreement.

Michael sighed in relief as he pushed his manhood a little deeper inside her. He held himself still so that her body would adjust slowly to his intrusion. Once he felt her relax, Michael entered her a little more until he felt the barrier that he had known would be there. The doctor's intense gaze kept Jessica prisoner for a long moment until Michael dropped his head then kissed her long and tenderly.

Jessica's body lost its tension at the tender kiss then she arched her hips just as Michael entered her fully. She whimpered in pain and pushed against him trying to get away from it.

Michael held perfectly still then brought his mouth down to her ear and whispered soothingly. "There will be no more pain I promise, trust me!"

Jessica nodded hesitantly then felt Michael move his hips ever so slightly. When there was no pain, just pleasure Jessica groaned arching against him.

Michael felt her response and thrust himself inside her a little more fully. When she moaned in surprise peeking once more, he lost control then captured her lips again in a more demanding kiss as his hips thrust against her repeatedly.

Jessica wrapped her legs around Michael gasping in pleasure as he drove into her fully. She felt the pressure building inside her again, but this time did not fight it as she soared among the stars once more.

Michael felt her release so let his own control evaporate as he spilled his seed deep inside her. He dropped on top of her and tried to get his breath back to normal. He had slept with a few women, but he had never felt this level of satisfaction before or this sense of well being. He lifted up in anxiety then looked down at Jessica. Her eyes were closed, and her head was turned away from him.

Michael sighed hoping she did not regret this before rolling off her then gathered her close, and stroked her hair in contentment. He frowned grimly. "I am sorry I never meant for this to go so far."

Jessica tensed in his arms then sat up.

Michael sat up as well and moved so that he would be facing her.

Jessica looked away from him saying nothing.

Michael put his finger beneath her chin then turned her head, so that she was looking at him. He saw her lips tremble, and he grimaced uneasily. "Are you okay? I did not hurt you too badly did I?"

Jessica shook her head emphatically in denial.

Michael's scowl eased a little in confusion. "What is the matter then?"

Jessica sighed forlornly and shrugged dismissively. "You must think me pretty inept if you regret taking it this far."

Michael looked at Jessica in disbelief then roared with laughter. When she frowned at him he laughed harder; he just could not help it. He got himself under control finally and sighed as he wiped the tears away. "I did not mean it like that. I meant that I had not wanted it to go this far yet. I wanted to woe you a little first then for us to get to know each other a little better. Believe me you were not inept I have never felt such intense joy and pleasure in my life."

Jessica frowned in relief. "You are not sorry or disappointed?"

Michael shook his head negatively. "No I am not sorry, but I thought you might be. It happened so fast, plus you were a virgin so I figured that you might be upset with me."

Jessica shrugged in confusion. "I am not sure yet how I feel. Like you said it happened so fast."

Michael nodded knowingly. "Fair enough, how about a swim. We can talk more a little later."

Jessica nodded then followed him into the water. When the water reached the inside of her thighs, it stung a little, but the discomfort faded after a few minutes. They played in the water for a bit before

Michael took her hand leading her into shallower water. He proceeded to make love to her one more time, but this time more slowly.

*****

Mell paced back and forth mumbling under her breath in rage the whole time.

Jed reached over then took his wife's hand in comfort before standing up trying to appease his wife. "It was bound to happen sooner or later."

Jed stopped the rest of his sentence and stepped back as his wife rounded on him.

Mell drew a fierce breath. "Later would have been preferable when they were married or better yet with someone closer to home!"

Jed sighed knowingly then nodded grimly. "Oh, so that is the real problem is it? Love does not always choose someone close to home. You knew that eventually she was bound to find someone to love and not necessarily close. You must let her find her own way she is a full grown woman after all."

Mell bit her lip in sorrow then turned away dejectedly. "I waited my whole life to have a sister now she will probably move far away, and I will not see her again."

Jed shook his head sadly. "You know that Jess is more your daughter than your sister! It is your daughter you are upset about losing not your sister. If it was Patricia moving that far away you will still feel the same way."

Mell frowned unhappily, as she turned back to Jed. "I suppose you are right."

Michael and a giggling Jessica chose that moment to come into the firelight. They both stopped short at the angry glare they received from Mell.

Mell folded her arms across her chest grimly then stared daggers at the two of them. "Where have you two been?"

Jessica eyed her sister uneasily and knew that she was already aware of what had happened. She straightened before stepping forward furious now herself. Mell was always trying to be her mother, instead of her sister. "We were down at the lake swimming if it's any of your business, you are not my mother!"

Jessica regretted that little outburst of defiance as soon as she read the pained look that flashing across Mell's face.

Mell turned away before marching off in despair.

Jess sighed in regret then turned to Michael. "I better go talk to her, stay here!"

Michael nodded and watched her hurry away.

Jed drew himself up to his full height then waited.

Michael tensed as his possible future brother-in-law towered over him.

Jed smiled reassuringly as he waved at the fire. "Relax; I am not as upset about this as Mell so how about a strong cup of coffee no better yet a shot of whisky will calm our nerves better."

Michael sighed in relief and relaxed a little as they headed to the fire; it was going to be a long night.

*****

Jessica hurried after Mell, she found her sister sitting on a stump at the edge of their camp. She hesitantly advanced then sat on the other end of the stump. Jess sighed in remorse and motioned in apology. "I am sorry; I should never have said what I did. You have always been more like a mother to me than a sister. I was just caught off guard that you already knew before I had a chance to talk to you first."

Mell shook her head grimly. "You do not need to apologize, you are right I am not your mother."

Jessica frowned curiously. "How did you find out?"

Mell grimaced in anger. "Jed and I went to the lake for a swim."

Jessica sighed dejectedly then turned to her sister imploringly. "Oh! Mell it happened so fast and I'm very confused do you think you could be my sister instead of my mother just this once."

Jessica stopped as she fought a sob back then felt Mell engulf her in her arms, so she finally let her confusion take control as she sobbed quietly.

Once Mell's sister stopped crying, she let Jess go before picking up her hand and gave it a tug in invitation. "Come on let's go for a walk so that we can talk."

Jessica nodded then got up.

They walked and talked for over an hour.

Mell had to struggle with herself at first since the motherly instinct in her was strong, but she did manage to let go of it finally then they chatted like sister's for the first time. Both exhausted mentally, they went to bed sharing a new relationship that both had needed and found at last.

CHAPTER TWENTY FOUR

Golden Eagle woke then sat up as he listened intently. He heard only occasional outbursts of grief, but it was more subdued less frantic now. He sighed in relief and got up then built the ember up into a good fire before putting coffee on.

Jake woke and rolled out of his bedroll before going over to the fire then sitting across from the Englishman.

Golden Eagle poured Jake a coffee and handed it to him. He just finished pouring one for himself when he heard a scratching on the tepee flap. He put his cup down then jumped up quickly to open the flap hoping to see Golden Dove or Black Hawk.

An old Indian woman thrust two bowls of porridge at him before turning and walked away, without even speaking. He sighed in disappointment then carried the porridge over to the fire and handed one to Jake.

They ate quietly then sipped their coffee reflectively.

Jake sighed thoughtfully. "There will be a big feast tonight after the funeral to honour the dead; it is really a celebration of life to the ones left alive."

Golden Eagle inclined his head and drained his coffee before getting up. "I will see you at the funeral tonight then."

Jake motioned in warning. "Oh, make sure you dress in your ceremonial clothing if you have any."

Golden Eagle nodded as he turned to leave. "Yes I have some, see you later."

*****

Raven got up and made a hasty breakfast then woke Janet before sitting down and dishing up their porridge. They ate quickly as well as quietly then broke camp and saddled their horses. It was not until they had been on the trail for about half an hour that Janet urged her horse to catch up to Raven.

Raven looked at her inquiringly, but never said anything.

Janet sighed curiously then motioned inquisitively in question. "Do you have any idea what you are going to do about your neighbour when we get back?"

Raven shook her head negatively. "No, I am not sure yet. Most of it depends on how things have progressed since I left."

Janet nodded and fell back into place as they continued on.

*****

Mell woke then stretched and reached over for Jed, but remembered he was on sentry duty. She sighed than thought of last night and her new budding relationship with Jessica as she smiled in relief. They had chatted then giggled like sisters instead of like mother and daughter; Mell would be eternally grateful for this new relationship. Jess in all likelihood would marry the doctor now then move away, but they could still visit once the railroad made it this far.

Mell got up and went to the lake to wash her face then went back to camp and hurried over to the fire.

Rose smiled at Mell. "Good morning, I am making crapes with bacon again."

Mell smiled eagerly then rubbed her hands together in anticipation. "Hmm, sounds delicious! Is coffee ready yet?"

Rose handed her a cup before pointing behind her. "Jed just left to wash up and shave said he would be back soon."

Mell nodded before pouring coffee into her cup then sat back with a sigh of pleasure.

Michael came striding into view, but hesitated when he saw Mell. He finally walked forward, nobody liked a coward he could not help thinking.

Mell hid her smile in her coffee cup and ignored the doctor.

Jed with Jessica following came next then Pat walked over with her dog.

Daniel and Pam came last.

Michael jumped up then hurried to Pam needing to get away from Mell's disapproving stare. "How are you feeling this morning? Did your fever return or any more pain?"

Pam smiled reassuringly as she shook her head negatively. "No, I'm fine. Just a little stiff from riding that is all."

Michael nodded in relief and went back to his coffee.

They all sat around waiting for breakfast, when everything was finished they all helped themselves. After eating, they quickly broke camp then continued on their way.

*****

Golden Eagle eyed the target and smiled proudly. Three arrows were on the edge of the bull's eye, he was certainly getting better. He took three more arrows out then put them in front of him; he wanted to try firing more rapidly. He took out a fourth arrow and shot it then grabbed another and shot it too. He grabbed the third arrow waiting for him quickly. Just as he pulled the arrow back into position, he heard a rustling off to his left so turned slightly until he spotted the buck watching him curiously.

Golden Eagle never even hesitated as he lined up then let the arrow go. He watched in fascination as the arrow hit the buck just behind his front leg and in-between the ribs imbedding deeply.

The buck made one giant leap then fell dead.

Golden Eagle whooped in delight before running over and took out his hunting knife to slit its throat. He chanted the Cheyenne thank you to the Great Spirit then to the buck's spirit. He had only learned this song recently and he was not sure he even got it right, but he continued doggedly. He carefully cut open the buck's stomach then pulled out the insides being careful not to break open the stomach or the intestines not wanting to taint the meat.

Golden Eagle got everything out without breaking open anything and he grinned in relief before cutting the liver out. He sliced it in half, then one-half he cut again and still chanting he buried two pieces of the liver. Grimacing in distaste, wondering if he could even do it the Englishman took a bite of the last piece then almost gagged at the salty warm metallic taste as the blood ran down his chin, but he did manage to eat it all.

Golden Eagle put everything that Running Wolf had told him they used back into the cavity of the deer. He sat back and sighed in pleasure at making his first kill then he frowned thoughtfully wondering how to get the deer back to his tepee. He thought for a few minutes before untying the rawhide rope around his waist. He would tie it around the antlers and drag it back.

Golden Eagle sat back again then sighed dejectedly. That would not work if he dragged it the hide would not be any good. He grimaced in distaste, but knew he would have to carry the thing on his shoulder. He tied the rawhide rope around the buck's stomach to keep everything inside until he could get back to camp. He knelt down and hoisted the deer up onto his shoulder then cringed as the blood dripped down his neck before slithering under his shirt.

Golden Eagle shrugged in resignation and stood up slowly. The deer was heavier than it looked, and his legs almost buckled from underneath him. Hoisting it in a better position in determination, he trudged back to camp knowing it was not far. He was almost ready to fall over from exhaustion when he stepped out of the trees then walked into the center of the village.

Four Indian women and two braves rushed towards him.

The two braves took the deer from him, they grunted in exertion as they lifted the heavy carcass clear of his shoulder. The braves looked at Golden Eagle with new respect at having carried such a large deer all the way here on his own.

One of the women stepped forward. "We will use the deer for the feast tonight if you have no objections."

Golden Eagle bowed slightly in pleasure. "I would be honoured."

The woman inclined her head solemnly then asked curiously. "The hide, do you want it when it is finished?"

Golden Eagle thought for a moment before pointing towards the chief's tepee. "Please give it to Golden Dove as a thank you gift for teaching me your language and customs."

The woman nodded in approval then turned and disappeared.

Golden Eagle hurried back to his tepee before ducking inside.

Jake was just pouring coffee for himself. He looked up in surprise as he arched his eyebrows in shock at the blood all over Golden Eagle. "What happened to you?"

Golden Eagle fell more than sat down and sighed in exhaustion. He quickly explained what had happened then accepted the coffee Jake handed him.

Jake smiled in admiration when the Englishman finished and chuckled as he held out his hand for a shake. "Well congratulations on your first kill."

Golden Eagle shook the offered hand in gratitude. "Thank you! I just came to change before I went out to work with my horse."

Jake shook his head negatively. "Do not change; just go out as you are. Your horse needs to learn to work with the smell of fresh blood so this would be a good opportunity for him to learn."

Golden Eagle grimaced unhappily not looking forward to staying dressed in these clothes any longer then drained his coffee cup and got up to go. "Good idea, see you later."

Jake waved then smiled after the retreating Englishman. Yes, he showed considerable courage and determination at carrying that heavy buck around. He will be a good partner for Raven.

Jake also happened to like him; he also knew that if the old Earl were still alive he would highly approve of Golden Eagle. Raven's foreman banked the fire then left to check on his men.

If Raven could read Jake's thoughts, she would be groaning in dismay.

*****

Mell slowed her horse a little and let the doctor catch up.

Michael tensed, as he got closer to Mell. He had known this moment would happen eventually, but he had hoped it would be later.

Mell looked at Michael out of the corner of her eye. "You are going to marry her of course!"

Michael stiffened uneasily then gestured in appeasement. "If that is what she wants?"

Mell looked at him fully for the first time since this morning with a demanding glare. "And is it not what you want?"

Michael cringed at Mell's menacing voice, but answered evenly not backing down. "We need some time to get to know one another before we make that decision."

Mell leaned forward intently with a dangerous scowl. "Are you telling me you are willing to bed my sister, but not marry her?"

Michael shook his head swiftly then held up his hand apologetically. "No, that is not what I am saying. I said if she wants to get married I will gladly marry her, but I will not force her into marriage if she does not want it."

Mell frowned grimly before waving angrily. "What if she is pregnant?"

Michael sighed in relief now on more firm ground being a doctor and all. "It is not likely that she got pregnant from a first encounter, but if she is I will think of something."

Mell nodded decisively as she gestured at him in warning. "So there will not be a repeat of last night then?"

Michael shrugged grimly in apology still not back down. "I cannot promise that, it is up to Jessica."

Mell grimaced furiously.

Michael held up his hand to forestall Mell from interrupting him. "All I can promise is that we will not make love again until after we have discussed the possibility of a child first. That is all I can promise you at this time."

Mell stared intently at Michael before pointing at him threateningly. "If she becomes pregnant I promise that you will marry her whether either of you like it or not. My father will be down here with a rifle if you do not and believe me, you would not like the results. If you think my husband is big wait until you meet my father!"

With that threat hovering on the air, Mell kicked her horse ahead then caught up with Jed. Jed looked over at his wife and saw the infuriated frown on her face then sighed forlornly obviously Michael had not appeased her anger only made it worse. He looked up at the sky and grimaced then looked around for a campsite for lunch. He finally beckoned Pat forward when nothing looked promising. "Please go ahead of us and find a camp it is going to rain soon, I would like to eat before then."

Pat nodded and whistled for her dog then galloped off.

Mell looked up at the sky before grimacing uneasily. "Last time it rained we almost lost two of our party."

Jed smiled reassuringly. "At least we do not have to cross any water this time."

Mell inclined her head without speaking as they urged their horses on when they spotted Pat waving them over to her. Everyone dismounted as a temporary camp was set up.

*****

Golden Eagle whistled in demand a second time at his stud; Devil had not liked the smell of the fresh blood right from the first and still showed his displeasure.

Golden Eagle had went over to Giant Bears then got some equipment so that he could saddle his horse this time. It was a good thing he did or he would not have gotten anything done with him tonight.

Devil frisked before finally obeying the whistle and with a snort of unease, he walked up to his master.

Golden Eagle put Devil through his paces spending over two hours with him, until satisfied he stopped his horse then jumped down and gave him a good rub down. Once done he headed back to Ravens to drop off the stuff then grabbed his ceremonial buckskins. He finally left the tepee before heading over to the creek for a bath.

*****

Raven and Janet put on their parkas before they remounted their horses, it was not raining yet but it would be soon. She waved Janet up beside her. "While we are riding I will give you some language lessons then tell you some of our history to pass the time."

Janet inclined her head eagerly bored back there by herself. "I would like that."

Raven nodded pleased before continuing Janet's training.

*****

Mell and the others pulled their parka's on then mounted as they left camp. They had only ridden for about half an hour when the skies opened up, and within minutes, they were all soaked to the skin. She sighed grimly. "I suppose we will have to stop early."

Jed nodded thoughtfully. "Probably before dusk I would imagine. Tomorrow we will ride hard, no stopping for lunch so we should reach Malta around supper time if all goes well."

Mell inclined her head in agreement. "Sounds okay to me, but I would like to go as far as we can today."

Jed smiled knowingly then they urged their horses into a faster pace.

*****

Golden Eagle walked back to his tepee and sighed forlornly as it started to rain. He ducked inside quickly then smiled dejectedly at Jake. "It is raining out not a very good night for a funeral."

Jake nodded as he eyed Golden Eagle's buckskins in surprise. "Where did you get those?"

Golden Eagle looked down in delight. "Raven gave them to me. She said if I have to marry her at least I could do so in decent clothing instead of the rags I was wearing at the time."

Jake smiled in appreciation. "Well they certainly fit you well, almost as if she had made them for you. The eagle on the front also suits your name."

Golden Eagle chuckled remembering her reaction to his name. "I know and wasn't she furious when I wore them to my adoption then was named Golden Eagle."

Jake grinned at the mental image of Raven angry. "I can well imagine; I have seen her like that plenty of times believe me. Well let's go."

Golden Eagle nodded before following Jake out.

*****

Raven sighed plaintively, she was soaked and the horses as well. She chuckled softly to herself as she looked over at Janet fugitively; she looked like a drowned rat. They had quit talking about an hour ago too wet as well as miserable to talk any longer.

Raven motioned enticingly to the unhappy looking Janet. "We will stop early then camp; tomorrow we will have to skip lunch to make up some time."

Janet nodded wearily without debate as she followed Raven into the trees thankfully.

Raven showed Janet how to build a shelter of tree limbs as well as underbrush. After eating, they curled up under the cover to sleep.

*****

Jed nodded to the right. "We will camp over there."

Everyone sighed in relief totally wet through.

Jed, Daniel, and Michael made a hasty shelter large enough for everyone to crawl under for some protection then after eating jerky and cakes they fell into their blankets then slept.

*****

Golden Eagle stood quietly watching as the fire burned down on Gentle Does pier. It had actually been a magnificent display of skill by the shaman as well as the medicine man as they danced asking the Great Spirit to receive Gentle Does spirit.

Golden Eagle had looked curiously at some of the things on the pier to be burned with Gentle Doe; this was done to help her on her journey he knew. Some of the things surprised him like food, flint for fire, as well as a knife. He would have to ask Golden Dove later what the meaning of those items was.

Black Hawk, Running Wolf, Giant Bear, and Golden Dove all stood in front of the crowd.

Golden Eagle heard them chanting as each cut off their braids, Giant Bear as well as Mary cut theirs to just below their shoulders. Black Hawk then his son cut theirs just above their shoulders that gesture would be the last show of mourning for Gentle Doe.

Black Hawk and Giant Bear took the lead then everyone followed as they headed over to the tepee that was used for meetings. It was the largest building in the village and could seat up to a thousand people. Raven had it built in the style of a tepee with hides covering it. It was a permanent structure so never moved being too large.

Golden Eagle made his way over to Black Hawk then sat beside him silently as he shook his head to remove some of the water before slicking his soaked hair back.

Black Hawk was staring off into space in sorrow. He was not paying attention to anybody or the fact that he was soaked with little rivulets of red dripping down his body.

Golden Eagle looked over as he grimaced in sympathy; Black Hawk was only wearing a loincloth since his whole body was riddled with cuts and some were still bleeding.

A woman walked over with a bundle in her arms then tried to give it to Black Hawk, but he turned away.

Golden Eagle lifted his arms to take the baby. "I will take him."

The woman looked at Golden Eagle intently for a moment unsure if she should let him have the baby or not, but finally nodded and handed the boy to him. "I will return soon to feed him."

Golden Eagle inclined his head in agreement then held the baby tentatively at first before easing the blanket away so that he could see the boy's face. He peeked up at Black Hawk and saw him staring at his son with an anguished look.

Golden Eagle quickly uncovered the rest of the baby before Black Hawk could look away. He looked up then smiled at Black Hawk in pleasure. "He has blonde hair like your mothers, although it will probably darken a little later. What are you going to call him?"

Black Hawk reached out and touched the baby's golden fuzz then his expression softened a little. "Little Buck."

Golden Eagle nodded in approval as he handed the baby over to Black Hawk before he could argue.

Black Hawk took his son and gently cradled him in his arms then watched as the baby opened his eyes and regarded his father for the first time. He smiled down tenderly then watched puzzled wondering if his son were going to cry as the baby's face scrunched up and he promptly farted.

Golden Eagle laughed in delight at the expression on Black Hawks face.

The baby his job done then closed his eyes and went back to sleep.

The woman came then took Black Hawk's son as supper was brought into the tepee and passed around. She gave Golden Eagle a grateful look having seen him give the baby to his father. She took him from Black Hawk then left.

Black Hawk looked at Golden Eagle inquisitively. "I heard you shot a buck today and carried it all the way here on your shoulder. That is why I named my son Little Buck."

Golden Eagle nodded pleased by that then explained what had happened.

Black Hawk ate quietly as he listened to the Englishman's story. When Golden Eagle finished his tale, Black Hawk inclined his head in approval. "Congratulations you are now a full Cheyenne and have earned your name."

Golden Eagle smiled proudly at his friends praise then finished eating.

After the food was removed, the shaman stood up and walked to the fire then turned and beckoned to the Englishman to come to him.

Golden Eagle looked at Black Hawk inquiringly unsure.

Black Hawk just smiled in reassurance then nodded for him to go.

Golden Eagle walked to the shaman and frowned in puzzlement as the shaman shaking his ceremonial staff circled him chanting.

The shaman finished his dance then turned to Golden Eagle as he pointed at the crowd; he looked at the Englishman intently. "You will now tell everyone of your first kill as a Cheyenne."

Golden Eagle understood now, to the Cheyenne he was now a man and had earned his name. He remembered Raven as she told her story, so Golden Eagle not only told the story but for the first time he acted it out. When he finished they all cheered their approval. The shaman walked over to Golden Eagle then waited for silence before chanting again and held open his hand. "This is a piece of the antler off your first kill; you will put it in your medicine bag then keep it with you always."

Golden Eagle pulled out his medicine bag and opened it. He took the antler then with a serious expression, befitting the occasion. He solemnly put the antler in his medicine bag. The ceremony over, Golden Eagle walked back to Black Hawk proudly. He sat back down beside him with a smile of delight.

Black Hawk grinned back in respect. "You learn quickly your dance was very good for your first time. Have you kept up your training and working with your horse?"

Golden Eagle inclined his head eagerly. "Yes I did, I have ridden my horse three times now just inside the paddock though."

Black Hawk motioned in warning. "I will be with you tomorrow."

Golden Eagle smirked in satisfaction. "Good I have missed you."

Black Hawk got up. "See you tomorrow then."

Golden Eagle watched him go before getting up and leaving too. He entered his tepee, but Jake was already asleep. He stripped out of his ceremonial clothes, with only his loincloth on he dropped onto his bed then slept.

*****

Raven jerked awake at the soft low intense growl her dog was making, she grabbed her gun before reaching over and touched Bruno reassuringly. Bruno looked at her then whined as Raven bent forward and whispered. "What is it boy?"

Suddenly Raven heard a loud growl coming from the trees where the she wolf was probably sleeping. Raven tensed instantly in fear as she heard a vicious scream off to her left. She saw a streak of grey as the female wolf ran towards the sound.

Raven tried to hold onto Bruno, but he broke her hold then raced after his mate. Raven lunged for her dog, but knew it was useless. "Damn!"

Janet woke abruptly in confusion as she heard the screams and growls getting louder then Ravens salvage curse. "What's happening?"

Raven jumped to her feet and looked down at Janet. "Stay here, keep your rifle ready."

Raven barely waited for Janet's nod of understanding before she took off after her wolf. She followed the sounds through the trees then slowed as she came to a space and peered out cautiously. It was a good thing the rain had stopped, with a three quarter moon she was able to see quite clearly into the clearing.

Raven grunted in amazement as she watched the two wolves fighting a cougar. What was a cougar doing here at this time of year? Usually they were higher up in the mountains having their young. If it were a male, he would still remain close to the den to protect the female. They only came out of the hills in the winter when hunting was scarce.

Raven watched as Bruno went behind the large cat then attacked from the rear as the female wolf tried to get at the cats throat. She was really puzzled by the wolf's actions. Usually wolves did not challenge a full-grown cat. She finally got her opportunity to shoot it, but knew it would be too late to save the female wolf as the cat sprang on top of her before the bullet hit and the cougar fell dead.

Raven trotted out of the trees then called to Bruno immediately concerned. "Come over here, boy."

Bruno obediently went over to Raven.

Raven cautiously walked towards the cougar when she was close enough she nudged the cougar with her rifle, but it was dead. She pushed him over and saw the female wolf lying there with her eyes staring off in death. She sighed sadly then patted Bruno in sympathy as he nudged his mate and sat back on his haunches then howled his grief.

Raven left him alone as she took out her hunting knife and walked over to the cougar. Before skinning him, Raven checked his mouth then scowled in fear. She sheathed her hunting knife quickly and hurriedly went back to Bruno. She ran her hands through Bruno's thick fur looking for any type of scratch or open sores. Finally, her inspection completed she sat back then sighed in relief. She checked Bruno's mouth next to make sure he had not bit through the cat's thick hide. Seeing no sign of the cat's blood on her dog, she got up and checked the cat's hind end where her wolf had been attacking the cat but saw no puncture wounds.

Raven sat back then sent a silent prayer of thanks to the Great Spirit for saving her dog. If Raven had found any evidence that the cat had scratched or bitten him, she would have had to put him down in case he had caught rabies from the cat. As it was, she would still have to keep an eye on him for a couple of weeks just to make sure.

Raven sat quietly for a moment staring in disappointment at the beautiful cat grimly before sighing dejectedly, she would have to bury both the cat and the wolf. Rabies was highly contagious even to humans so the hide would be useless. Raven got up then snapped her fingers in command. "Come on Bruno."

Bruno whined and nudged his mate once more then obediently followed Raven.

Raven called out to Janet as she got close to camp before walking out of the trees.

Janet sighed in relief as she lowered her rifle. "What happened? And what was making the screaming sound? I have never heard anything make such a hair-raising sound before. What was it?"

Raven sighed then went to the packhorse to find something to dig a hole with. "It was a cougar that came out of the mountains because he was sick. He killed Bruno's mate before I could shoot him."

Janet sighed sadly at losing the beautiful wolf that had shadowed them all this time, but refused to come closer. "Can I see the cougar? I have never seen one before?"

Raven inclined her head in agreement, as she grabbed her axe and a small shovel that she always carried then two rawhide ropes. "You can help me bury them too."

Janet frowned puzzled. "Why are you burying them won't the scavengers eat them?"

Raven grimaced in disgust and disappointment. "The cat had rabies."

Janet frowned as she got up to follow Raven. "What is rabies?"

Raven stopped then looked down at Bruno. "You stay here boy!"

Bruno whined dejectedly, but obediently went back to the fire and layed down.

Raven started walking again as she tried to explain. "Rabies is highly contagious. Usually it is a dog, wolves, bats, raccoons or skunks that carry the disease. They pass the disease on by biting another animal or by passing any type of fluid from their bodies. Humans can also catch rabies; it usually results in a very unpleasant death."

Raven stopped at the edge of the trees then turned to Janet cautiously. "Do you have any open sores or cuts on your hands or arms?"

Janet put her hands out so that Raven could examine them.

Raven checked them carefully, but did not see anything and nodded. "Good they look okay. We will dig a hole here under this tree big enough for the cougar as well as the wolf. I will show you what to look for in a rabid animal after the hole is dug."

Janet nodded as they got to work. Two hours later Janet sighed in relief then sat down hard on the ground. Raven walked over and sat beside her. "That should be deep enough. We will tie the front legs then back legs of the cat together before dragging him over here. Do not touch him if you can help it and do not whatever you do scratch yourself on his claws or touch any place that has blood or fluid around it."

Janet frowned uneasily then took the rope Raven handed her and they both walked over to the cat. The Englishwoman walked closer to Raven when she beckoned her over.

Raven squatted down beside the cats head then pointed to his muzzle. "See the foam and saliva around his muzzle this is what you would look for. When you see an animal foaming at the mouth like this, do not hesitate just shoot it. Another indication of rabies is an animal's willingness to attack anything it gets close to. Take the cat for example; if he had come into our camp, he would have attacked us immediately. Usually though a cougar will not come close to humans unless he feels threatened or has cubs close. Rabies causes animals to go utterly crazy so never trust an animal with this disease. Just shoot it; okay let's get these animals into their grave.

Janet nodded grimly as they carefully tied the rope around the cats legs then dragged him over to the grave and dropped him in. Then they went back for the wolf.

Raven grabbed the wolf's tail; Janet grabbed a hind leg, and they hauled her over to the grave then dumped her in. Raven frowned thoughtfully as she stared down at the shallow grave, not liking the fact that another animal could uncover them easily. She turned to Janet uneasily. "Go get a burning branch out of the fire I think we should set them on fire for a bit first in precaution."

Janet nodded and raced back to camp while Raven grabbed wood as well as underbrush then threw it on top of the animals. A few minutes later Janet was back, and she dropped the burning branch inside then they watched in satisfaction as both animals burned. Raven waited a good half hour letting them burn to a crisp; It took them another half an hour to fill in the grave. Once done, both women stumbled back to camp exhausted as well as filthy from the mud and soot.

Raven grabbed a canteen to wash her hands then her face, with no water around it would have to do, before handing it to Janet. "We have about an hour until dawn. Get some sleep tomorrow we will camp early and have a bath."

Janet sighed in relief then fell into her blankets, instantly she was asleep. Raven was only a few minutes behind her as she also fell into an exhausted dreamless sleep.

CHAPTER TWENTY FIVE

Raven stirred the porridge before getting up and walked into the trees. She searched then found a nice straight long branch about a half-inch thick. She used her hand axe she cut it close to the base of the tree. She headed back to camp while she stripped all the little branches off. She walked into the opening then sat by the fire and took out her hunting knife to peel the bark off the branch.

Janet dished up some porridge for both of them then handed a bowl to Raven.

Raven put the branch down and accepted the bowl. After she had eaten, she grabbed the branch again to smooth it so no notches were noticeable. She stood up then turned to Janet as she motioned up. "Stand up so I can measure this branch."

Janet nodded curiously and put her bowl down then stood up. "What are you making?"

Raven put the branch against Janet and made a mark where she wanted it. "I have an extra bow string with me, so I am going to make you a temporary bow."

Janet smiled widely in ecstatic pleasure. "Thank you."

Janet frowned in puzzlement then sat down again. "I never knew Indian women were allowed to handle weapons."

Raven frowned thoughtfully. "You are right and wrong all at the same time. Earlier in our history, women were not allowed, but we have become more resourceful as our people dwindle. But most women do not want to change so adhere to old ways; many of the younger women go with their husbands when they are on the warpath they even participate if the battle goes badly for them. I am an exception I have been training as a warrior since I was a small child. Pour us a coffee then I will explain how I became a warrior while I finish this bow. It is only temporary just to practice with later a proper bow will be made for you, if you wish to continue using one."

Janet nodded vigorously in anticipation as she listened eagerly to Raven's life story.

After Raven was done, she watched Janet practice loading and unloading her rifle for a few minutes then got up with a satisfied nod at Janet's progress and started breaking camp.

*****

Golden Eagle stirred up the fire then made fresh coffee.

Jake got up with a sniff. "Hmm smells good, it is always a good omen when you wake to the smell of coffee brewing."

Golden Eagle laughed in delight. "It is only good when you do not have to be the one who is up first to make it."

Jake smiled contentedly. "Well you could be right."

Jake was half way to the fire when he stopped and changed directions at a scratching on the tepee flap. Jake opened it before stepping aside in pleasure. "Good morning, Golden Dove. You brought breakfast, here let me help you with those bowls."

Golden Dove chuckled knowingly. "Trust you Jake to be the first one at the door when it comes to food."

Golden Dove ducked inside after being relieved of the two bowls then smiled at Golden Eagle as she came towards the fire. "Good morning."

Golden Eagle poured her a coffee and handed her the cup after she sat down. "Good morning to you too!"

Golden Eagle accepted his bowl of porridge from Jake with a nod of gratitude. "Thank you."

Golden Dove grinned into her coffee cup as she watched the two men eating with quiet gusto. Both totally absorbed in their breakfast they never even heard the scratching on the door.

Golden Dove put down her coffee then got up. "I will get it."

Golden Eagle looked up in surprise and smiled his thanks.

Golden Dove lifted the flap out of the way. "Good morning Black Hawk, come on in."

Black Hawk ducked inside then kissed his mother on the cheek. "Good morning!"

Golden Eagle hastily put the last spoonful in his mouth before grabbing another cup and poured Black Hawk a coffee. He handed it to him. "Good morning, how is the baby today?"

Black Hawk grimaced with a chuckle. "Good morning, and in answer to your question he is already letting me know who rules the tepee."

They all laughed at Black Hawks pained expression.

Golden Dove stood back up then grinned down teasingly. "Well I must go I have to finish tanning my new deer hide and baby-sit my new grandson while you boys get to play."

Golden Eagle smiled up at her inquisitively. "Do you like it?"

Golden Dove beamed down at him in pleasure as she gestured in delight. "Of course I like it! I already know what I am going to make out of it. First, I am going to make the baby an outfit then a small pair of moccasins before making a pair for you, Jake, and myself if he would like a pair. I should still have enough left over to make a pair for Black Hawk then possibly for my husband as well."

Golden Eagle nodded in satisfaction. "Thank you I could use another pair."

Black Hawk inclined his head in agreement. "I would be glad to accept another pair if you have enough."

Jake smiled widely in agreement. "Well I have always meant to ask you or Raven to make me some, but there was just never an opportunity before. So thank you I would be proud to wear them."

Golden Dove grinned happily and waved before she left.

Black Hawk turned to Golden Eagle after his mother was gone then motioned in praise. "Thank you for giving that hide to my mother. You should have seen her face when she was given the hide and told it was from your first kill."

Golden Eagle beamed delighted then gestured earnestly. "It was the least I could do after she has taught me so much about your language and customs."

Jake finished his coffee before getting up. "Well I have to make my rounds see you two later."

Black Hawk got up too. "We have to get going also, but if you come to the corrals later Jake we can all go for a ride before supper."

Jake nodded in satisfaction at being included. "Sounds good to me see you later."

Golden Eagle waved at Jake then banked the fire and quickly grabbed his stuff then followed Black Hawk out.

*****

Jed walked over to Roses blankets and gently touched her shoulder not wanting to scare her. "Wake up Rose."

Rose turned over with a yawn. "I am awake."

Jed chuckled with a smile as her yawn almost drowned out her vow. "Will you make breakfast while I wake everyone else?"

Rose rolled out of her blankets in agreement then got up.

Jed went over to Jessica next and noticed an extra body lying beside her. He shook his head in disapproval; he was glad that he had found them instead of Mell. He pushed Jessica's shoulder a little more forcefully than he normally would have.

Jessica jerked awake and looked up into Jed's grim face then blushed as she realized Michael had turned in his sleep and had cuddled against her. She turned away from Jed then mumbled irritably. "I will wake him!"

Jed grunted in anger before marching off.

Jessica sighed in exasperation as she sat up and nudged Michael impatiently.

Michael woke then smiled up at Jessica. "Good morning."

Jessica scowled angrily before waving grimly. "You rolled over in your sleep, and Jed found us sleeping together if it had been Mell she would have been furious."

Michael frowned apologetically. "I am sorry."

Jessica got up then put a little space between them as she shrugged dismissively. "Forget it come on I can smell breakfast."

Michael got up and rolled his blankets up solemnly as he eyed her curiously. "Have you thought about my proposal?"

Jessica nodded uneasily, not sure, if she wanted to accept or not. "I have, but I have not made up my mind yet."

Michael grimaced impatiently then motioned in bewilderment. "Well what is the problem, either you love me and want to get married or you do not!"

Jessica interrupted with a shake of her head in confusion. "It is not as simple as that. You refuse to move to Dakota with me, but you expect me to leave everything as well as everyone I love behind then move here with you!"

Michael sat down and put on his boots as he sighed in frustration. "I told you I have responsibilities here I just can't leave both towns without a doctor!"

Jessica harrumphed in anger then bent over and rolled her own bedding up. "You make it sound as if you are the only one with responsibilities, but I have them too this is a big decision I need more time!"

Michael got up angrily in disappointment. "Fine we will be in town soon then we will be going our own separate ways again. If you come to a decision you know where to find me."

Michael grabbed his bedding and stalked off to his horse muttering furiously to himself.

Jessica watched him go then quickly wiped her eyes so that know one would notice the tears. She left her bedroll where it lay before turning as she headed to the fire dejectedly.

Rose handed Jessica a bowl of porridge before pouring her a coffee.

Everyone sat quietly pretending they had not heard most of the argument between Jessica and the doctor.

Jed looked up at the doctor curiously when he arrived. "How much further to Malta?"

Michael frowned in thought then looked around. "We travelled further and faster than I usually do. I will say around three or four o'clock if we hurry."

Jed grimaced in thought as he nodded his head decisively. "That is what I figured; I have decided to change our plans. Mell, Doctor Andrews, and I will go into town. Pat I want you to give the town a wide berth then take everyone else with you and make camp a few miles away from town. We will take Silver Tip with us so that way we can find your camp afterwards."

Mell scowled in puzzlement then motioned curiously. "Why the change?"

Jed shrugged nervously. "Just a precaution!"

Jed got up quickly now that they had decided on a plan of action. "Okay let's break camp."

Everyone nodded, soon not a sign was left that anyone had been there at all.

*****

Golden Eagle looked around quickly, not seeing Running Wolf anywhere he cautiously took a step forward. He saw a brief flicker of movement off to his left, so he dropped into a crouch then waited. Not seeing or hearing anything more the Englishman shifted his coup stick a little and moved to his left knowing Running Wolf had gone in that direction. He took another careful step then froze. Quickly dropping to the ground, he rolled and brought his stick up, but was not quite fast enough as Running Wolf hit him first with his stick.

Running Wolf nodded impassively down at him. "That was better!"

Running Wolf held out his hand to help the Englishman up.

Golden Eagle smiled elated at the praise then accepted the assistance offered to him. He stood up and absently rubbed his shoulder where the coup stick had struck him.

Running Wolf smirked as he watched Golden Eagle rub his shoulder. "You may go no more lessons today."

Golden Eagle noticed the smug look in annoyance then quickly dropped his hand. "It is still early yet?"

Running Wolf shrugged expressionlessly. "It is, but my father wants you to go see your horse early today."

Golden Eagle nodded eagerly remembering Black Hawks statement about going riding. "I will just go grab my things."

Running Wolf shook his head negatively. "Go! I will put everything in your tepee."

Golden Eagle inclined his head in thanks before sprinting back to the village.

Black Hawk was waiting impatiently for him at Devils paddock. He let Golden Eagle catch his breath before waving for the Englishman to look at the equipment. "This is a gift from my mother and me. We started making this gift for you when you first started training your horse."

Golden Eagle stared in disbelief. The saddle blanket had eagles embroidered on both sides with his family crest just below it. The saddlebags had a wolf with ravens embroidered to represent his relationship with the Wolf tribe as well as Raven. The rifle cover also had eagles on it, but they were done in beads. Even the bridle was beautiful in its simplicity. The headstall was made out of soft supple leather than died black. The reins were also died black before being braided intricately to give it an unusual look. Golden Eagle ran his hands over the reins and knew that the braid would keep his hands from slipping even if his hands were wet. He turned to Black Hawk in awe as he grinned in appreciation. "These are beautiful, thank you! I will cherish them always."

Black Hawk smiled knowingly at the elated Englishman. "I am glad you like your gift. Now get in with your stallion then put him through his paces. I want you to get on him and ride him at a walk, trot then a canter. If you have no difficulties, we will go out for a ride when Jake gets back."

Golden Eagle nodded ecstatically and grabbed his new equipment then let himself into the pen.

*****

Jed stopped his horse and turned to the others. "Okay this is as far as you go. Pat will lead everyone around the town."

Jessica moved her horse forward pleadingly. "I need a moment with Michael before we go."

Jed inclined his head in assent knowingly.

Jessica turned her horse then beckoned the doctor to follow. When she was sure, they were far enough not to be heard by the others she dismounted before putting her horse between her and prying eyes.

Michael followed her lead then dismounted and waited expectantly.

Jessica smiled hesitantly now unsure of herself. "Can you wait for my decision until I get back?"

Michael sighed in disappointment; he had hoped for more. The doctor looked down at Jessica's pleading look before finally nodding grimly. "I do not have much choice! You be careful, I am not sure what is going on, but I have had the feeling since I started this journey with you that this visit is not just a social call between friends or family. Try to stay out of trouble if you can."

Jessica smiled reassuringly; she stood on tiptoe then kissed the doctor goodbye.

Michael drew her closer and deepened the kiss, reluctant to let her go.

Jessica broke away suddenly then mounted she looked down at him in earnest. "I promise to have an answer for you when I return."

Michael nodded grimly as he mounted. He looked at her one more time solemnly before letting his love for her blaze to the surface so she could see it. "Just remember that I love you."

Jessica sighed forlornly as she turned away before galloping back to the others.

When Michael rode up, everyone was gone except for Mell, Jed, and the dog.

Mell looked at him expectantly.

Michael shrugged dejectedly. "She still has not given me an answer maybe you can talk to her."

Mell shrugged undecided, she did not think she should interfere yet then they all turned before heading for town.

*****

Black Hawk watched as Golden Eagle, and Devil cantered past again then turned expectantly as he heard footsteps behind him.

Jake walked up and smiled eagerly at Black Hawk. "Well it looks as if we will be going for that ride after all."

Black Hawk nodded thoughtfully then turned back to watch Golden Eagle. "Your horse is a gelding right?"

Jake inclined his head reassuringly.

Black Hawk grinned in approval. "Good I will use a gelding, as well. We do not want the stud acting up today."

Jake chuckled in agreement. "My horse is ready when ever you are. I left him saddled and tied to the other corral."

Black Hawk stepped up to the fence then beckoned to the Englishman. "Okay Golden Eagle you can stop over here."

Black Hawk waited and grinned up at him when he obediently stopped. "Give your horse a rest for a bit while I go saddle my horse."

Golden Eagle beamed excitedly then jumped down off his horse. "I will just walk him while I wait."

Black Hawk turned and left.

Jake went over to his horse then untied him before walking back towards Devil's pen.

Golden Eagle walked his horse until he saw Black Hawk coming. He opened the gate and led Devil out.

Black Hawk trotted up to Jake then waited as Devil decided to neigh a challenge to the other horses.

Golden Eagle pulled down sharply on the reins and slapped Devil on the nose lightly. "None of that now!"

Devil snorted in rebuke then shook his head, but he did settle down.

Golden Eagle smiled in approval and patted the stud then mounted.

Black Hawk chuckled in satisfaction as he turned his horse and took the lead.

Devil did not like following, so he tried to surge ahead.

Golden Eagle pulled tightly on the right rein until Devil's head was almost touching his foot. This caused Devil to spin in circles until the Englishman felt Devil relax then he released the reins as they walked behind Black Hawk again.

Black Hawk and Jake waited patiently then walked their horses forward when Devil got close.

Devil decided to try once more to take the lead, so Golden Eagle had to pull the right rein in again. He snorted in indignation when he was finally allowed to go forward again.

Jake rode up beside the Englishman then smiled knowingly. "Does not like to follow does he?"

Golden Eagle laughed in delight. "No, why don't you drop back a little and follow behind us to see what he does?"

Jake nodded before slowing until Devil was far enough ahead so that if he kicked at Jake's horse he would not get hurt then fell in behind the stallion.

Devil tensed angrily and tried to stop; when that did not work, he tried to back up.

Golden Eagle kicked Devil in the ribs hard. "None of that nonsense now let's go!"

Devil shook his head indignantly, but eventually moved forward.

They rode like this for about ten minutes then Jake trotted back up beside Devil.

Black Hawk kept this pace for a few minutes before kicking his horse into a trot.

Devil tried again to leap forward, but his master reined him into a circle immediately.

Black Hawk then Jake stopped to wait again patiently before starting out at a trot again when Devil settled down.

Black Hawk maintained the trot for about fifteen minutes before kicking his horse into a canter.

Devil behaved this time thankfully he did not try to take the lead.

Golden Eagle reached down then patted him on his neck in praise.

Black Hawk slowed his horse after about ten minutes before halting. He turned to the others. "We will go back now, this time I want everybody together nobody out in front."

Jake and Golden Eagle turned their horses around quickly. They walked for a few minutes then Black Hawk nodded for the trot.

Devil promptly tried to take the lead, so the Englishman had to rein him into a circle. Once Devil settled down, they went back to a walk before picking up the trot again. He behaved, so Black Hawk maintained the trot for a moment before he nodded, and they picked up their pace. They were getting close to the paddocks, so Black Hawk called out. "Go back to a walk now."

Black Hawk smiled at Golden Eagle as they slowed. "That is good for today put your stallion away; we will meet you for supper in a bit."

Golden Eagle smiled pleased with his horse then turned away.

*****

Jed slowed to a walk as they entered the outskirts of town.

Mell undid her whip before coiling it loosely in her hand.

The first row of houses on the right was dark, but they were not too concerned until they passed the store on the left that was also black without a single person in sight.

Mell and Jed exchanged uneasy glances when they heard the faint murmur of people talking excitedly ahead. They rounded a corner then stopped in surprise at the large group of people talking and shouting at something a man standing on a wagon had shouted.

Jed looked around uneasily then spotted the sheriff standing on the porch of the sheriff's office with a rifle cradled in his arms. He pointed him out to Mell, and they turned left towards the hitching rail then dismounted.

Mell stepped up onto the porch before looking down at Silver Tip in demand. "You stay and guard the horse's girl."

Silver Tip obediently layed down, watching them closely.

Mell stopped abruptly in shock before she could even take an extra step as the sheriff tuned to look at them. She turned to Jed with an incredulous scowl. "I know that man wait here!"

Jed frowned then watched his wife go back to her horse and dig around her saddlebag for a moment then took a packet out that she had brought with her for Giant Bear and Mary. She tuned back then took the lead as she whispered to her curious husband. "I will explain later."

Mell approached the sheriff cautiously. She was not entirely sure if this were what the white buffalo was suppose to tell this man, but she was pretty sure. "Good afternoon sheriff, mind if we talk in your office for a moment?"

The sheriff appraised Mell and Jed, but the only sign of surprise at finding a woman marshal was one eyebrow lifting curiously. He looked at Andrews then smiled cordially. "Hello Doc did not expect to see you out this week."

Michael shrugged dismissively then returned the sheriff's smile. "It was pretty quiet at home, and since these folks were on their way here I decided to tag along."

The sheriff looked one last time at the throng of townspeople then sighed uneasily before turning to his guests with a pleasant nod. "Come on in folks I have coffee on."

Mell followed and took a chair where he indicated. They all waited quietly as the sheriff handed coffee out then poured himself one and sat behind his desk with a sigh of relief. The sheriff sipped his coffee then eyed his visitors curiously before sitting forward inquisitively. "Name is Jeffrey Lane; I'm the sheriff of Malta. What can I do for you folks?"

Mell smiled as she made introductions. "I am Marshal Brown; this is my husband Deputy Marshal Brown. We are from North Dakota. We are on our way to the Summerset Ranch for a visit."

The sheriff scowled in concern. "I was afraid of that right now you are riding into the middle of what could be another war between the Indians and whites."

Mell frowned in puzzlement then motioned hopefully. "Can you tell us what is going on sheriff?"

The sheriff nodded and sighed grimly. "Just a little over four weeks ago, an Englishman with two ladies got off the stage coach then asked around for a guide to lead them to Earl Summerset's Ranch. Two brothers from town who are friends of Raven's agreed to take them. They never came back and all traces of the five of them disappeared. The townspeople automatically blamed Raven's grandfather as well as his people for killing them. I took a few men out to the village, but Raven was away looking into the matter. We did not see any white people there except for the chief's wife plus a few half-breeds. I have managed to stop the townspeople from calling in the army so far, but as you can see from the crowd out there. I can't keep them from going out there themselves much longer."

Mell shook her head disbelievingly as she handed the sheriff the packet to look at; she had been right. "Well sheriff, I can guarantee you that Giant Bear would not have done it. I know also that he would not allow his people to do it either."

The sheriff shrugged sceptically as he opened the package curiously. "You were not here so how would you know?"

Mell smiled as she waved to the papers. "There are two reasons why I know he would not have done it. The first is that as you can see about twenty-seven years ago I personally deputized Giant Bear as a deputy sheriff. He was never released from that oath; it was a mistake that I had made when I deputized him. He swore for as long as he lived, instead of as long as he wore the badge. I never told him I made a mistake so as far as he is concerned he is still under oath. The second reason is that the Englishman who came here was Lord Devin Rochester from England; it was because of Giant Bear that he was here. We got in touch with Lord Rochester for Giant Bear then asked the Englishman to come here. Giant Bear was hoping Raven, and Devin would like each other then get married. He would not do anything to jeopardize that."

The sheriff frowned in thought. "For many years now I have heard rumours that Giant Bear was deputized at one time. I think it was from a friend of Raven's who told me, but I had no proof."

Mell reached into her pocket and pulled out a letter then handed it to the sheriff. "I brought this along just in case. It is a letter from our present mayor's office in North Dakota, where Giant Bear was deputized. It not only confirms that he is still a deputy in the books in North Dakota, but that he was also legally wed to his wife Mary. I had the mayor include that just in case it was needed."

The sheriff nodded as he bundled up the papers and handed them back then took the one from the mayor. "That was a good idea since I had asked who the white woman was since the agreement was no white captives were allowed to be taken. Do you need this one? If you do not I would like to keep it I need to show it to the townspeople to try calming them down."

Mell smiled in agreement. "Yes you can have it."

The sheriff took a key out of his pocket then unlocked the bottom drawer before putting the letter inside and re-locking it. He sat back up then eyed Mell before gesturing in warning. "If you are going to help your friends I would hurry if I were you. I can only hold the townspeople here one maybe two more days if we are lucky."

Mell inclined her head in agreement, and they stood up then shook hands. "Thank you for the information sheriff we will see you in a few days."

The sheriff nodded and shook hands with Jed.

Mell turned to the doctor. "We will probably see you as well in a few days. Take care of yourself."

Michael frowned grimly; he had known there was more to this story than what they had let on, now he was worried for Jess. "You take care of Jessica for me as well."

Mell smiled reassuringly as she went back out to her horse while Jed said goodbye.

Finally, they were on their way out of town with Silver Tip leading. She led them straight to Pat without wavering in her path.

Mell and Jed dismounted as Daniel took the two horses then fed and watered them while they went to get supper from Rose. Mell repeated the conversation she had with the sheriff in-between bites of food.

Jed finished eating first. "Well let's pack up; if we hurry we can reach the ranch by midnight tonight. The sheriff told me where to find a secret game trail that is only passable by a horse, very few know about it according to him. We will stay at the ranch for the rest of the night and head out to Giant Bear's first thing in the morning."

Everyone nodded agreement then within minutes not a hint of them could be found.

*****

Raven slowed her horse before turning to Janet. "The horses are exhausted, so I want to stop a little early, and I am disgustingly dirty."

Janet nodded forlornly. "Good you are not the only ones tired I am almost asleep in the saddle."

Raven chuckled then turned into a grove of trees to her left. She had stayed here before and knew that there was a creek further back in the trees. She walked her horse forward until they were hidden then dismounted.

Janet more comfortable now with Raven's routine helped set up camp.

After eating the fish that Raven showed Janet how to catch with her hands, they both went to the creek for a quick bath. Once back in camp to tired to talk, they rolled themselves into their sleeping furs and fell asleep almost instantly.

*****

Golden Eagle handed Jake a coffee then sat back with his own and yawned. "Boy am I ever tired, tonight."

Jake chuckled at the Englishman's gargantuan yawn that almost drowned out his words. "You look tired too. Why don't you go to bed, I am going for a bath then I am going to bed as well."

Golden Eagle nodded and drained his coffee cup. "Bank the fire before you go to bed for me, please."

Jake nodded then finished his coffee before leaving.

Golden Eagle undressed and crawled into his fur, he never heard Jake return.

*****

Jed slowed his horse wanting to cool him down a little; all the horses were foam flecked. It had not taken them long to get through the hidden trail then into more open territory so that they could pick up speed. Now since the horses were all breathing hard from the demanding ride, he figured it was best to slow down. He turned to Mell in warning. "The ranch is just ahead there should be sentries around here somewhere."

Mell nodded knowingly keeping a sharp look out, but it was not long before they saw a horse and rider approaching cautiously. She waved so that everyone would stay back, while only the two of them rode ahead to meet the man.

The man stopped in front of Mell then smiled pleasantly in greeting. "You must be Melissa and Jed Brown. Edward told me to keep a lookout for you; he said to tell you that he could not wait any longer. When you arrived I was to take you to the ranch then provide you with anything you needed."

Mell smiled in delight Dream Dancer was up to his tricks again. "Well all we need tonight is a bed and directions to Giant Bear's village in the morning."

The guard nodded then turned back up the trail. "My name is Eric Johnson. Please follow me."

Jed waved to the ones waiting, and they all followed. He turned to Eric curiously not even asking how the Earl knew they were coming familiar with his predictions. "When did Edward leave?"

Eric smiled apologetically. "Yesterday morning, the Earl with two other wagons left carrying supplies up to the village."

Jed inclined his head in disappointment if the rain had not stalled them they might have made it in time. They arrived at the barn then dismounted.

Mell handed the white colt to the head stableman. "This is Raven's new stallion we brought him along since she will probably need him this year."

Steven nodded relieved; he would put the stud in with the mares that he had just brought back just in case some of them were not bred. "The name's Steve and you are correct we do need him. Thank you I will take care of him as well as the rest of your horses. I will also have them saddled ready to go first thing in the morning for you. Johnson will take you to the house then show you to your rooms. There is food in your rooms waiting for you and breakfast will be served there in the morning."

Mell smiled gratefully. "Thank you."

Johnson beckoned to them, so they followed him to the house.

CHAPTER TWENTY SIX

Jake woke first so built up the fire; it was a little chilly in here this morning as he warmed himself then put the coffee on. He left and headed for Giant Bear's tepee. He looked up at the sky as he waited then he sighed in annoyance. He scratched on the flap again waiting for permission to enter. When the tepee door was lifted, he ducked inside.

Golden Dove beamed at Jake cheerfully. "Good morning."

Jake smiled forlornly in warning. "Morning, I am not sure if it is good though it looks as if it might rain again and it's down right chilly!"

Golden Dove grimaced dejectedly without comment then dished up some breakfast for the two men.

Jake accepted the two bowls gratefully. "Thank you."

Golden Dove nodded before walking over to the tepee entrance and held it open for him. "Say good morning to Golden Eagle for me."

Jake inclined his head in agreement then left. He immediately broke into a trot as the wind picked up and threatened to cool off his breakfast. He reached his destination then ducked inside the tepee.

Golden Eagle was pouring himself a coffee; he looked up and smiled at Jake before pouring him a coffee too.

Jake handed Golden Eagle his bowl then accepted the coffee cup in return. "Thank you Golden Dove said to say good morning."

Golden Eagle nodded pleased before smiling his thanks for the message. "You are up early?"

Jake grimaced miserably. "The wind woke me, and it is getting worse. I think we are in for a big storm."

Golden Eagle scowled grimly. "That figures."

Golden Eagle lifted his cup to take a sip of his coffee then jumped in surprise and sloshed the coffee all over himself as a loud clap of thunder sounded almost right above him.

Jake laughed in sympathy as he noticed coffee dripping off Golden Eagle's shirt.

The flap opened swiftly as Black Hawk stumbled in. "Well I think this will be a good day for staying inside today. I already told Running Wolf not to expect you."

Golden Eagle wiped at the front of his shirt then smiled in delight. "Good I could use a day of rest. I have not had one since my arm healed."

Black Hawk nodded in agreement before sitting down beside the fire and smiled his thanks at Jake as he was handed a cup of coffee.

Jake sighed in disappointment. "Well some people have all the luck. I still have to go out in this to do my rounds."

Black Hawk watched Golden Eagle smile smugly at Jake then cleared his throat at an idea. "On second thought I think we might ride along with you. Not only will it give Golden Eagle a change of scenery, but it would be a good test for his stallion."

Jake watched the smug look disappear on Golden Eagle's face, so he grinned at him in satisfaction.

Golden Eagle sighed in vexation before grinning good-naturally and poured them all another cup of coffee.

*****

Raven jumped out of her blankets in fear before rushing over to Janet then shook her awake none to gently in panic. "Hurry and get up we have to get out of here now."

Janet sat up then stared at Raven in shocked surprise at having been awakened so rudely. "What's wrong?"

Raven hurriedly grabbed everything that was loose and started stuffing it in the saddlebags even dirty dishes. "There is a lightning storm coming we have to get across the creek now. If we are lucky, we can get to the cabin I used on my way here before the storm hits now no more questions! HURRY!"

Janet sensing the urgency in Raven's voice did not argue anymore and swiftly rolled her blankets up then saddled her mare.

Raven threw the packsaddle into place before whistling for her stud.

Bruno raced to Raven and whined in urgency then raced off before returning to his mistress and whining again impatiently.

Raven nodded grimly as she threw her saddle blanket on her horse. "I know Bruno I am hurrying as fast as I can!"

Raven's stallion neighed loudly as his nostrils flared in fear before pawing the ground nervously.

Janet then finally Raven were mounted in record time.

Raven turned one last time to Janet. "Stay as close to me as you can and whatever you do, do not get separated from me! We are now in a race for our lives! Remember also to trust your horse if you get into difficulty she can find her own way!"

Janet nodded in alarm then rode up beside the packhorse that Raven had tied to her saddle; hopefully she could keep close to him, which in turn would keep her near Raven.

Raven rushed them as fast as she dared through the trees.

*****

Mell and the rest of her party all met in the hallway.

Johnson stumbled into the house as everyone was dressing. "We are in for a mighty big storm. You might want to stay one more night then leave in the morning."

Mell and Jed looked at each other then both shook their heads, but it was Mell who spoke. "No, we need to get to Giant Bear's as soon as possible."

Johnson nodded not arguing with them. "Okay your horses and supplies are all waiting for you. I will accompany you to the trail that Dream Dancer took it's not the fastest way to go, but you might be able to catch up to him. Once on the trail, keep following it because it will lead you right to Giant Bear's winter camp. You will see cairns of rocks periodically there are supplies in the ground under them if you get into any trouble."

Jed inclined his head in thanks as they headed out.

*****

Jake led them up a steep incline then gave three sharp whistles.

A man stepped out of the shelter of trees and beckoned them to follow him. They soon found themselves in a little hidden camp, so they dismounted in relief at being out of most of the wind. They all hunkered down beside the campfire then accepted cups of hot strong bitter coffee.

Black Hawk smiled across the fire at Golden Eagle as Jake talked softly to the sentry. "Well your stud is behaving better today; he has not tried to take the lead even once. This storm does not seem to be bothering him much either."

Golden Eagle nodded pleased before chuckling in disagreement. "Yes he is doing very well, but the storm is bothering him a little. A couple of times I thought for sure he was going to buck. Especially when the lightning flashed, and the thunder boomed just ahead of us a couple miles back. His whole body was twitching I could feel his muscles bunching under me, so I thought for sure I was in for it. I kept stroking his neck though keeping him distracted it seemed that as long as I talked to him soothingly he behaved."

Black Hawk inclined his head pleased then drained his coffee as Jack beckoned them to follow. They remounted, and Jake turned east heading up higher into the hills.

Jake sighed in relief then motioned thankfully. "No problems here, we will circle around until we come to the trail heading to Raven's ranch and go up that trail until we get back to the village."

Black Hawk sucked in a shocked breath at Jake's reference to Ravens ranch before quickly looking at Golden Eagle to see his reaction. Except for a raised eyebrow at his stunned intake of breath, no surprise was evident on the Englishman's face. He gestured grimly. "You already know about the ranch?"

Golden Eagle grinned perceptively. "I have known almost as soon as I met Raven's brother, we have many portraits of the late Earl when he was younger. Dream Dancer is the splitting image of his late grandfather. I also saw the ranch in a vision that Dream Dancer helped me have."

Black Hawk sighed in disgust. "I told my father you knew a lot more than you were letting on."

Golden Eagle shrugged dismissively. "I also know it was your father who brought me here to begin with."

Black Hawk eyed Golden Eagle intently as he waved uneasily. "And this does not upset you?"

Golden Eagle frowned as he shook his head resignedly. "At first I was very angry, but then Dream Dancer helped me have a vision. In the vision, I was shown the ranch, Raven, a little boy, and a newborn baby before I saw myself smiling proudly at my wife. I am still not sure if that is what I want, but I am willing to give it a try now."

Black Hawk nodded relieved then sighed sadly, as Jake called out to the next sentry. "Well at least you are willing to try, and that is all anyone can ask of you."

*****

Raven looked back then saw Janet's horse slowing so held her own horse back until Janet was even with her. "Why are you falling behind?"

Janet sighed wearily, not sure, why there was such a need for such haste as she motioned in exhaustion. "She is too tired; I do not know how long she can keep up this pace."

Raven looked behind them and grimaced in panic. She turned back to Janet anxiously as she pointed over her shoulder the way they had come. "I am sorry, but she has got to keep going there is a forest fire raging behind us! If we can get across the creek it will keep the fire from following us further."

Raven looked up as she felt the first rain drops falling then scowled grimly. "This rain will be a little help with the fire, but not much. The fire has been burning to long, and this forest has many dead trees as well as a lot of old growth to keep it fuelled. It is not much further, so please try to keep up."

Janet glanced back in surprise not having realized what was behind them then saw the smoke for the first time before hastily turning back to Raven and nodded with a stark look of shock on her face. They kicked their horses into a faster pace then pressed on.

*****

Jed stopped beside Johnson before grimacing in irritation. "Is the weather like this all the time out here?"

Johnson shook his head negatively. "Not really, once maybe twice a year a storm like this will blow in from the Rockies, but they never last long. I will be leaving you here, about six hours up the trail there is a camp set up for just this type of emergency. I would suggest you stay there tonight it is about half way between the ranch and the village. This lightning as well as the wind will only get worse before it gets better so be careful you do not want to lose one of your horses. Or one of your companions if lightning hits one of the trees in your path."

Jed looked at Mell then saw her nodded in agreement.

Jed turned back to Johnson as he held out his hand. "Thank you and we will take your good advice."

Johnson warmly clasped Jed's hand then tipped his hat to the women before turning and galloping away.

Jed turned back to the trail before following it grimly keeping a close lookout for lightning.

*****

Jake slowed for their last stop then whistled before waiting, but nothing happened.

Suddenly they heard two shots ring out and a scream of pain.

Jake spurred his horse forward in anxiety with Black Hawk right beside him in an instant as they galloped towards the gunshots.

Golden Eagle stayed behind them letting the experienced warriors stay in the lead. When he saw both men take out their rifles, he did also.

Black Hawk veered right then went after someone fleeing on a black horse.

Jack veered left after another man.

Golden Eagle was about to follow Black Hawk when he noticed a horse standing alone; he was riderless with a man lying beside him face down. He went immediately to the downed man in concern, when he got close; he jumped of his horse and knelt beside him then gently turned him over.

Golden Eagle sucked in a shocked breath it was not a man at all, but a sandy haired youth about seventeen or so. He immediately ran his hands over the boy looking for wounds, he found two one in his left shoulder and one in his right leg. He checked the shoulder injury first then noticed that the bullet had gone straight through and out the back. He got up quickly before rummaging in one of his new saddlebag then found two pieces of clean doeskin clothes that Black Hawk had given him, it was carried for just such an emergency he had been told. He knelt down again and wrapped the shoulder in a hasty bandage to stop some of the bleeding.

Golden Eagle turned to the leg wound after. He had to use his knife to cut away the pants then expertly probed the wound. The bullet was lodged in the fleshy part of his leg and would have to be dug out, but not here. He wrapped the leg then looked up as Jake and Black Hawk returned with both men tied to their saddles.

Jake grimaced in guilt as well as in fear. "Is he okay?"

Golden Eagle nodded as he finished tying the bandage. "Two bullet wounds neither fatal, but one bullet will have to be dug out."

Black Hawk frowned thoughtfully as he eyed the boy. "That's your son is it not Jake?"

Jake nodded forlornly. "His mother is going to kill me for leaving the boy alone on guard duty. I really did not think anybody would try anything here though, it is the worst place to try reaching the village from."

Black Hawk frowned thoughtfully. "You are right this is a bad spot for anyone trying to sneak into the village, it's way too open. The camp where Raven got that grizzly bear is not far from here, the herbs that I need are not far from there. Golden Eagle please lift the boy up to his father then take the lead rope of the other horse so that Jake can hold his son until we reach the camp."

Golden Eagle helped Jake mount with the boy in front of him. He walked over to the horse of one of the men who had shot the kid and glared up at him. The man was staring at the Englishman with a horrified stunned look on his face. "You are supposed to be dead!"

Golden Eagle scowled grimly. "I do not know you how do you know if I'm supposed to be dead or not?"

The man visibly gulped as he realized he had spoken aloud.

Black Hawk grimaced pensively then shook his head warningly. "Later Golden Eagle we must see to the boy first. Questions will just have to wait."

Golden Eagle grabbed the lead rope and walked back to his stud.

Devil snorted then pranced in place as his master got closer with the mare.

Golden Eagle frowned at his horse threateningly. "I am not in the mood for your antics Devil, behave yourself!"

Horse and rider stared at each other intently for a bit then Devil snorted softly as if in apology before standing quietly as Golden Eagle mounted.

Black Hawk watched all this and shared an amused look with Jake as Devil settled down without a fuss. He jumped down then grabbed the reins of the kid's horse and tied him behind his saddle before picking up the lead of the other man's horse that he held captive then vaulted back onto his own and took the lead.

*****

Raven pointed up ahead in relief.

Janet nodded as she saw the fast moving water ahead. It certainly did not look like a stream. She slowed to a trot and looked behind her before frowning uneasily.

The rain was coming down harder now, but the forest fire still raged behind them even closer than it had been. All morning as they ran for their lives they saw wild animals running in every direction as well, mostly in panic.

Raven turned back to the creek that should have only been a trickle, but was three times its size and getting higher. She slowed to a walk.

"The stream is already running pretty fast, but should not reach up to the horses bellies yet I hope. Give your mare her head then hold onto your saddle and her mane. She will follow the stud with no direction from you."

Janet nodded nervously and did as she was told. The mare had a remarkably long mane, so Janet wrapped a handful around her hand twice just to be on the safe side. As Raven's stud stepped into the water, the mare obediently followed him without even a hesitation. The Englishwoman clung to the saddle, and the mare's mane with a death grip then held her breath uneasily as the mare daintily picked her way into the middle of the stream. The mares, left front foot slipped out from under her suddenly, and she stumbled.

Janet almost went sailing over the mare's head, but she had the presence of mind to release the saddle then push up on the horse's neck with her free hand.

The mare righted herself and scrambled over the edge onto dry land then stood there quivering for a long moment.

Janet had to wait until she settled down before she could get her to move forward.

Ravens head jerked up in shock as she listened intently for a moment at a roaring sounded in the distance. She cupped her hands around her mouth then shouted at Janet desperate to be heard. "Get out of this gully now! HURRY!"

Suiting words to action Raven dug her heals into her stallions sides and bent low over his neck.

Janet's mare sensing the danger as well galloped full out beside Raven.

Raven sucked in a shocked breath as she turned her head slightly then saw the wall of water rushing towards them. She looked forward again hastily and saw the edge of the gully coming up fast. If they could make it up that hill, they would survive. It was almost as if everything happened in slow motion all of a sudden. The closer they got to their goal the closer the water got to them.

Raven was just thinking they were not going to make it when her stud started straining upwards. The feeling of slow motion stopped suddenly as everything begun speeding ahead again then the stallion gave a tremendous leap over the lip of the gully.

Brave Heart came to a dead stop suddenly before sliding backwards slowly as the packhorse tied to the saddle slipped at the edge and started pulling them back to the lip of the gully.

Raven grabbed her knife out of its sheath then reached over to cut the line to save herself and her horse, but the packhorse righted herself then lunged upward to safety.

Janet and her mare reached the rim of the gully at the same time as the packhorse. Her horse slipped then started sliding backwards. She screamed in terror as the mares two front legs buckled under her and she was almost thrown from the saddle for the second time. She thanked God than for the fact that her hand was still wrapped in the mare's mane. She remembered what Raven had said about trusting her mare, so she dropped the reins on the mare's neck and let her find her own footing as Janet clung to her desperately.

The mare struggled back up to her feet then tried to jump over the lip again. After the second failed attempt, she squealed in rage and surged upward. Once on flat land again the mare raced full out in terror with a clinging Janet unable to stop her.

Brave Heart called out to her so she slowed then finally turned around and trotted back to him before standing against him quivering in fear.

Raven was sitting on her horse staring in awe down below.

Janet looked as well then gasped in surprise. The tidal wave that had tried to catch them had swept everything in its path ahead of it, trees, rocks, and animals nothing was immune to its power. She shook in delayed shock then turned to Raven incredulously. "How could this happen?"

Raven sighed in relief that they had made it in time and turned her horse before trotting off. She looked over at Janet and shrugged dismissively as the Englishwoman kept pace with her wanting answers. "Sometimes a rock slide will dam up a creek, which is why it gets smaller as time goes on. Then nature takes a hand, and rain will fall so heavily in the mountains that the rocks cannot contain it. Soon the water starts seeping through the rocks until they break loose then all that water comes rushing down to fill in the stream once more. Normally that stream behind us is so deep you have to swim across, but about five years ago it started diminishing so now we know why."

Janet shook her head in wonder. "This is a strange land you live in I am not sure if I want to stay here very long."

Raven grinned in comfort before nodding in agreement. "This land is salvage and brutal at times, but it has amazing beauty too. You just have to know where to look for it, if you two decide to stay I will show you many wonders plus teach you how to survive out here if you would like."

Janet smiled shyly at Raven. "If I stay I just might take you up on your offer."

Raven pointed ahead enticingly. "The cabin is just over that rise. We will stay there tonight then leave first thing in the morning. Hopefully the rain will stop by morning."

Janet beamed in excitement to herself. She might have lost one sister, but she felt like she now had another sister. This one though was not sickly! Janet felt a moment of guilt and sorrow as she sent a silent apology to her dead sister, but still could not help feeling elated at the same time. Raven might be younger in years, but her experiences far exceeded her own which made Janet feel younger. Instead of making her angry, it actually felt good; she might just stay here after all. The Englishwoman followed Raven towards the cabin, happier then she had ever been in her entire life.

*****

Jed pointed to his left, and Mell looked at the campsite that Johnson had recommended then nodded in approval. The wind was so strong now that the trees were bending alarmingly, and the rain was coming down so hard that they could not see more than two feet in front of them. The campsite had a sanctuary not only for themselves, but also for the horses. Quickly and quietly, they tended to their horses first then went into their own shelter and saw to their own needs.

*****

Black Hawk held up his hand to halt everyone then cocked his head and tried to listen. He backed his horse up until he was even with Jake then handed him the lead rope to his prisoner's horse. "There is someone up ahead, stay here. If either men calls out shoot them."

Jake nodded and took his revolver out of his holster then pointed it at the man beside him.

Black Hawk looked over at the Englishman before lifting an enquiring eyebrow.

Golden Eagle grimaced at Black Hawk, but quickly followed Jake's example and took out his rifle then pointed it at the other man.

Black Hawk satisfied jumped off his horse, within moments he disappeared.

After what seemed like an eternity to Golden Eagle, Black Hawk returned he grinned up at Jake. "Looks as if our supplies are here, but one of Dream Dancer's horses pulled up lame so they are camped here as well."

Jake sighed in relief then tossed the lead rope back to Black Hawk before he re-holstered his gun.

Golden Eagle put his rifle away as well thankfully.

They both followed Black Hawk eagerly.

Dream Dancer jumped up in amazement as they entered the clearing. He had not seen his uncle sneak into his camp. The two hands Dream Dancer had with him lowered their guns when they saw Jake and grinned at him.

Golden Eagle was off his horse first, within seconds he had Dream Dancer in a hug.

Black Hawk was right behind him then gave his nephew a hug also. "It is good to see you boy."

Jake cleared his throat noisily. "Would one of you mind giving me a hand please?"

Black Hawk grimaced in apology. "Sorry Jake, Golden Eagle can you take the boy while we secure the prisoners."

Dream Dancer looked surprised for a moment as he looked at the prisoners behind Black Hawk speculatively before turning away. Seeing Golden Eagle gently lifting Jake's boy down, Dream Dancer quickly motioned for his friend to accompany him. He led him over to a shelter and motioned for the Englishman to go ahead of him. "Put him in here please! How bad is he hurt?"

Golden Eagle ducked down under the cover then carefully placed the boy on the furs. "He was shot twice; a bullet went through his shoulder and out the other side. The second bullet is in his left leg, it is still in there. The bullet went into the fleshy part so it should not be a problem getting it out. Neither wound is life threatening unless infection sets in."

Dream Dancer waved calmly towards his wagon. "Under the seat to your right is a saddlebag, bring it to me, please. Oh, put your knife in the fire to heat as well."

Golden Eagle nodded then did as he was told.

Jake walked over and ducked under the shelter.

Dream Dancer moved over so that Jake could kneel by his sons head.

Jake watched his young boss closely as the bandage was removed.

Dream Dancer looked up in surprise as a light materialized beside him then saw Black Hawk grinning at him. He smiled back thankfully in relief. "I forgot I had an oil lamp in my wagon."

Dream Dancer turned back to his patient and gently probed at the shoulder injury.

Jake slid forward and lifted his son, so that Dream Dancer had his hands free.

Dream Dancer nodded his thanks distractedly, but did not say anything. He probed at the wound in the boys back before grunting in satisfaction. The hole in his back was larger than the hole in the front, which was a good indication that the bullet had went all the way through. The wound looked clean, but he was not taking any chances it would have to be disinfected.

When the Englishman brought Dream Dancer his saddlebag, he took out a bottle of whisky and sat it beside him then took out a packet of leaves. He opened the package and looked; satisfied he had the right one he put that down beside the whisky. He rummaged around then pulled out bandages. He grabbed a packet with a red ribbon tied around it then looked up at his uncle in warning. "Put a pinch of this in some water to steep. Only a pinch mind you it is very strong, and we do not want to kill him."

Black Hawk took the package with an understanding nod then left.

Dream Dancer turned back to Jake. "I'm going to pour some whisky on both sides of his wound so make sure you hold him tight."

Jake frowned queasily as he got in a better position after helping Dream Dancer remove his son's shirt before nodding that he was ready.

Golden Eagle sat on the boy's legs careful not to get too close to the leg wound.

Dream Dancer uncorked the whisky and poured a generous amount on the front of the wound. Jake's son groaned then twitched, but otherwise did not move.

Jake lifted the boy up and held tightly so that Dream Dancer could pour some more whisky on the back of the wound. His son's body arched this time as he screamed in pain, which caused him to briefly, gain consciousness then mercifully; he passed out.

Dream Dancer grimaced in sympathy. He immediately packed both sides of the wound with the leaves he had waiting and put a pad on each side of his shoulder to keep them in place before bandaging the wound. He then tied the boys arm to his chest to keep him from moving it at least for tonight.

Jake gently lowered his son back onto the blankets.

Dream Dancer sighed, grateful to have one injury done with before moving down and with the help of the other two men gently pulled the boys pants off. He unwound the bandage then sighed in relief as he probed the wound and found no muscle or bone injury. He sat back as he smiled at the Englishman in respect. "You were right the wound is not serious, he should heal without even a limp. How did you get to be so knowledgeable?"

Golden Eagle grinned as he remembered when he was younger. "I used to fight a lot of duels back in England. My aim was not very good at first so at least once a week I would end up at the doctor's office getting a bullet dug out, or having stitches from being stuck with a sword. Fortunately none of my duels was to the death only to first blood."

Jake stroked his son's hair trying to calm him then sighed happily at the good news that his boy would not have a limp. He absently listened as Golden Eagle replied to Dream Dancer's question before grinning and looked up at the Englishman enticingly. "The old Earl taught me how to fence so if you ever want to practice with someone I will be happy to poke a few more holes in you."

Dream Dancer laughed in jesting. "You better watch him Golden Eagle he is very good, he taught me as well."

Golden Eagle rubbed his hands together in glee then smiled in challenge. "Well I have two foils in my trunks at the village, so if you two want to try me I will oblige both of you."

Dream Dancer and Jake looked at each other incredulously then at Golden Eagle, and both spoke at the same time. "You are on!"

Black Hawk brought the tea just then, so Dream Dancer got down to business.

Jake lifted his son a little so that the young Earl could get some tea into his boy.

Dream Dancer sat back when he was satisfied that the boy had drank enough. He motioned to the Englishman so that he would bring him the knife. He doused the knife in alcohol and watched the steam rise for a bit then satisfied he turned to Jake. "Hold him still, please. Golden Eagle I want you to lay across his lower legs, make sure to hold them tight, even with the pain killer I gave him this is going to hurt."

Jake and Golden Eagle did as they were told.

Dream Dancer doused the wound in whisky again then took the still steaming knife and gently inserted it inside the injury then searched as fast as he possible could.

The boy jumped violently screaming as the knife entered his wound.

It took Dream Dancer a few precarious minutes to find the bullet and get it out of there without losing it. He withdrew the knife then done with it he dropped it on the ground. He grabbed the whisky bottle and poured a generous amount onto the wound before putting his leaves on top then a pad to keep them in place before wrapping a bandage around the wound.

Once done Jake lifted his son again so that the young Earl could give him the rest of the tea.

Dream Dancer put some furs around the boy before grabbing the whisky bottle and handed it to Jake. "Here take this I want you to go get drunk with Black Hawk."

Jake smiled sickly at Dream Dancer. "Do I look that bad?"

Dream Dancer nodded with a chuckle. "Go! I will stay with him."

Jake stood up, but stumbled a little as he left with Black Hawk.

Dream Dancer grinned at Golden Eagle. "Actually, he did better than I expected him to do. But I did not want Jake or my uncle to see what I was going to do next. Can you stand inside the opening and block their view a little."

Golden Eagle nodded in understanding then did as he was asked.

Dream Dancer started chanting quietly before putting one hand on the boys injured shoulder and one hand on his leg wound. Still chanting he started rocking slowly. He could feel the heat radiating from his hands then he stopped suddenly, he did not want the boy to recover too quickly and raise questions. He gave the boy just enough of himself to prevent any infection from developing as well as to start the healing process.

Dream Dancer stood up then had to lean on his friend for a moment.

Golden Eagle steadied him before smiling in sympathy. "Come on let's go get some of that whisky before the others drink it all."

Dream Dancer smirked teasingly. "Well I would not worry about that too much; I have another bottle stashed away."

Golden Eagle laughed in delight as they went to the wagon and got the other bottle.

They all sat in the pouring rain then got roaring drunk before they all passed out.

CHAPTER TWENTY SEVEN

Raven woke slowly and listened intently for a bit, not hearing anything she got up then opened the door before peering outside hopefully. It was still drizzling a little, but she could see the clouds breaking up in the distance. She sighed in relief and let the three horses go outside. She called Bruno then shooed him out too. She closed the door then added more wood to the last of the glowing coals to make a good cooking fire. She put on coffee and porridge to cook, when it was ready they ate she woke Janet. After eating, the two women quickly saddled up and let.

*****

Golden Eagle groaned in agony before sitting up slowly. He closed his eyes briefly then dropped his head in his hands trying to stop the world from spinning. He massaged his temples slowly trying to alleviate some of the pain.

Dream Dancer smiled in sympathy as he poured him a cup of tea. He had made the tea knowing that everyone would have a hangover. He got up and walked around the fire then squatted in front of the Englishman holding the cup out enticingly. "Here have some tea it will help, I promise!"

Golden Eagle opened one bleary eye and eyed Dream Dancers smiling face distrustfully before reaching out then took the cup offered to him. He took a hefty swallow and almost choked in surprise. "Ague this stuff is awful!"

Dream Dancer laughed in delight as he got up. "The cure is always worse than the disease. It will help though; now drink it all while I make breakfast."

Jake moaned in pain as he stumbled towards the fire. "Did somebody say something about food? I could not eat even if I wanted to."

Dream Dancer grinned teasingly and poured Jake some tea. "Here have some it will help."

Jake grimaced knowingly. "Your famous remedy it tastes worse than the hangover makes me feel."

Dream Dancer chuckled in agreement. "It might taste bad, but it works."

Jake nodded grimly holding the cup tentatively trying to get the courage to drink it. "I know I have had it a few times. How is my son doing this morning?"

Dream Dancer smiled in approval. "Good he has already had breakfast. I gave him some more painkillers, and he is sleeping. There seems to be no infection so far which we should be thankful for."

Jake sighed in relief then could not put off drinking the tea any longer. He looked down and took a deep breath in preparation before lifting the cup as he downed his tea in one swallow. He shuddered in response at the bitter sour taste.

Golden Eagle finished his tea reluctantly then smiled up at Black Hawk as he came stumbling towards the fire. "Good morning."

Black Hawk dropped down beside the fire and poured himself some tea then downed it. He shuddered before turning to the Englishman grimly. "Morning, now I know why you white men called that excuse for alcohol rotgut."

Golden Eagle laughed in agreement.

Dream Dancer dished up bacon and eggs for everyone then they all sat back enjoying their breakfast now able to eat. The young Earl especially took pleasure in the laughing teasing jokes they were all handing out.

*****

Mell was up first, so decided to celebrate their last day on the trail with the bacon and eggs that the ranch hand had given them. With the last of the flour, she also made flapjacks.

Jed walked over and poured himself coffee. "The others are all up, so they are seeing to the horses."

Mell inclined her head relieved as she finished making the batter before pouring some in the steaming pan. "It will seem strange when we get there to be able to stay in one spot for more than a day."

Jessica and Patricia strolled up to the fire then sat together.

Pat poured them a coffee and sat back. "I agree with mother it will seem strange, but I am defiantly not going home for at least two weeks. I need a rest."

Jessica chuckled knowingly then sipped her coffee quietly.

Pam and Daniel strolled up to the fire before sitting on a log.

Rose sauntered in last.

Daniel reached over then poured all three of them a coffee.

Jed smiled at them before turning back to Pat in reassurance. "Well I think we can go the long way back this time. We can catch the train part of the way home since we are not in a hurry to get there, if it is running yet that is."

Patricia frowned incredulously. "We could have taken a train here! How far out of our way would it have been?"

Jed grimaced in sorrow. "A week to ten days, if I had known that Pam was pregnant we would have taken the extra days. When Mell and I talked about it, we decided to go the shortest way because she felt we did not have an extra week to spare. After talking to the sheriff, it turns out that she was right."

Pam shrugged dismissively as everyone looked at her. "It turned out better this way even though I got hurt. We made excellent time."

Jed sighed plaintively. "You are right we got here faster than I figured we would even with all our problems, but I still wish you would have told us."

Mell finished breakfast before handing out plates then shook her head in disapproval at her husband. "What is done is done no use dragging it in the mud over and over again? Eat so we can get to Giant Bear's village sometime today."

Jed nodded at the rebuke then took his plate of food from Mell.

Everyone ate quietly after that.

*****

Golden Eagle put out the fire and walked over to the lead wagon then joined Dream Dancer and Black Hawk.

Black Hawk frowned at his nephew in caution. "The big bay mare balked a little when I put her in the traces to pull the wagon, so I will ride beside her for a bit to make sure she does not act up. I split the prisoners up one in each of the other wagons. Your wagon horse is not badly hurt, but he picked up a rock somewhere so his front left foot is a little bruised. Jake with Golden Eagle's help can scout ahead. When we get back to the village, I think we had better send out two braves to guard this entrance. We better be prepared just in case there is still vi'hoI lurking about."

Dream Dancer inclined his head at his uncle in agreement then asked curiously. "Did they tell you anything?"

Black Hawk frowned as he shook his head negatively. "No, but one of the prisoners recognized Golden Eagle. He says that he has never seen the man before last night."

Dream Dancer looked at Golden Eagle inquisitively; his friend shrugged in confusion.

The young Earl sighed perplexed. "Did you check their saddlebags?"

Black Hawk shook his head grimly. "No, I figured I would wait until we got back to the village for that."

Dream Dancer sighed thoughtfully before turning to climb into the driver's seat and called over his shoulder. "Let's go then!"

Golden Eagle and Black Hawk smiled at each other at the sound of impatient command in the young Earls voice then mounted.

*****

Jed held up his hand to stop everyone as he sat listening and sniffing the air.

Silver Tip growled a warning, but hushed when Pat told her to.

Jed turned in the saddle in caution. "Mell come with me everyone else take out your rifles, but stay here."

Jed turned back to Mell as she took out her whip in precaution then they moved forward vigilantly. Silver Tip invited herself along and walked beside Mell's horse. They walked around a bend in the trail then came to an empty campsite.

Silver Tip walked around sniffing the ground curiously.

Mell and Jed dismounted; she walked over to the fire pit then put her hand on the rocks, but quickly snatched her hand off again when the rock almost burnt her fingers.

Jed walked around looking at the signs before turning to Mell. "It must have been Edward looks as if he stayed in this spot last night. Over to your left six horse's came into camp in the night, one was carrying a heavy load. There is a bullet on the ground with blood on it, so someone was hurt. They have not been gone very long."

Mell inclined her head in agreement and pointed at the fire pit. "The rocks in the fire are still very hot since this spot is sheltered from the wind, I would say about two hours maybe three at the most."

Jed nodded thoughtfully. "I will get the others. We can decide then if we want to stay here for lunch or try to catch the wagons."

Mell continued to look around until the rest of her party gathered in the clearing.

Jed beckoned to Mell. "They want to press on."

Mell mounted immediately and Jed led them out of the clearing.

*****

Raven beckoned to Janet. "Do you want to stop or press on? If we do not stop for lunch, we will stop early for the night."

Janet nodded preferring the early night to food right at this moment. "Let's keep going I am not very hungry anyway."

Raven kicked her horse back into a fast trot in agreement.

*****

Black Hawk galloped past the two back wagons then slowed beside Dream Dancer's wagon and jumped off his horse onto the wagon seat without stopping. His horse stayed beside the wagon patiently waited for his master. Black Hawk pointed behind them. "We are being followed a large party maybe an hour behind us, they are riding pretty fast. It could be the sheriff again."

Dream Dancer looked back then squinted in concentration before turning back to Black Hawk with a smile of relief. "No, not the sheriff it's White Buffalo and Grey Wolf!"

Black Hawk's eyebrows rose in amazed surprise. "Your talent is getting stronger if you can tell that from this distance! Tell me then what are Aunt Mell and Uncle Jed doing here?"

Dream Dancer shrugged dismissively in concern not wanting his uncle or anyone to know how much his powers had grown. "I had a dream that they were coming awhile back. After the dream, I could sense them getting closer, but not how close. I do not think that my powers are getting any stronger it is only because I dreamt about them; that is why I know who was behind us."

Black Hawk nodded in understanding not suspecting his nephew was telling him an untruth. "Well since you are sure it's them, I think we should stop here then make lunch and wait for them. Do you happen to know why they are here?"

Dream Dancer smiled in relief as his uncle accepted his explanation without suspicion. "To save us!"

Black Hawk frowned then eyed Dream Dancer in surprise. Knowing he was not going to get a straight answer by the stubborn look on his nephew's face he vaulted back onto his horse. "I will get Jake and Golden Eagle while you set up camp."

Dream Dancer grinned in delight at his uncles annoyed look then he stopped the wagon.

Black Hawk galloped ahead spotting Jake he whistled sharply.

Jake looked behind him curiously and saw Black Hawk coming towards him so called out to the Englishman to get his attention. "Black Hawk wants us to stop."

Golden Eagle trotted back towards Jake immediately then they waited.

Black Hawk slowed his horse as he pointed over his shoulder the way they had come. "We are stopping for lunch, we have company coming."

Jake frowned in surprise. "Do you happen to know who it is?"

Black Hawk nodded in irritation. "Dream Dancer says it's White Buffalo and Grey Wolf."

Jake's eyebrows rose in disbelief. "I did not know they were coming."

Black Hawk shrugged as they walked their horse's towards camp. "Nobody except Dream Dancer knew I guess."

Golden Eagle looked away guiltily. Black Hawk caught the look on the Englishman's face then scowled in exasperation. "Well maybe not only my nephew."

Jake looked at the Englishman in disbelief. "You knew they were coming?"

Golden Eagle sighed uncomfortably as he nodded in apology. "Yeah I knew."

Black Hawk threw his hands up in the air in vexation. "Secrets everyone seems to have them lately."

The rest of the trip was done in silence.

*****

Silver Tip growled in warning, but was too late as three shadows stepped out of the trees.

Jed and Mell cleared leather in an instant.

A grinning Black Hawk threw up his hands in mock surrender. "I give up do not shoot!"

Mell smirked at Jed before they re-holstered their guns.

Pat called Silver Tip over so she would not attack the men.

Mell jumped off her horse then raced to embrace Black Hawk ecstatically. He swept her into his arms and twirled her around in pleasure laughing. Mell squealed in delight like a child then pushed away to look him over closely. "My darling Tommy, I have missed you all these years! How have you been? How is your pretty wife? How are your father and mother?"

Mell stopped her questions immediately at the look of sadness that appeared on Black Hawk's face then she noticed his shorter braids.

Black Hawk smiled sadly in reassurance. "We camped just ahead when Dream Dancer told me White Buffalo was coming. Why don't you wait till we get back there before I answer all your questions?"

Mell more subdued now already guessing that Tommy's wife had died; nodded and walked back to her horse then mounted.

Black Hawk and the others walked into the trees to get their horses.

Golden Eagle's stud called a challenge to Mell's stallion and tried to rush forward. He cursed at Devil angrily as he just about ran him over then pulled down hard on the reins until the stud's nose was even with his master's chin. "Stop that this instant!"

Devil snorted furiously and tried to throw his head back up.

Golden Eagle stepped to the side then pulled Devil's head with him.

Devil refused to budge, so the Englishman swung the end of the reins in a circle and slapped Devil on the hindquarters until he turned fully around. Golden Eagle took another step to the side, this time Devil followed without any prompting. He kept turning until he was back to where he had started. The Englishman held the reins loosely waiting for his horse to act up again. When Devil behaved himself then stood quietly, he sighed in relief before mounting.

Mell chuckled knowingly. "Training a new horse are you?"

Golden Eagle grimaced in aggravation. "Yes, this is only his third day out of the corrals."

Mell smiled shrewdly. "You must be Devon Rochester."

Golden Eagle inclined his head in agreement. "It is Golden Eagle here, and you are Melissa Brown or White Buffalo as Dream Dancer calls you."

Mell nodded then they rode the rest of the way in silence. She dismounted once they entered the makeshift camp and shook hands with everyone as introductions were handed out. Then they all sat around the fire talking excitedly as they waited for lunch. She waited until everyone calmed down and they were sipping coffee before turning to Black Hawk inquisitively. "So tell me what happened to your wife?"

Black Hawk sighed sadly then told her everything.

Mell grimaced in condolence before reaching over and gave Black Hawk a hug. "I am so sorry for your loss. Has the baby taken some of the pain away at least?"

Black Hawk nodded solemnly as Mell released him. "More than I thought was possible; at first I did not even want to look at him it just hurt too much. Golden Eagle would not let me get away with that though. Once he took the baby himself, and I saw him I just could not help myself then took him."

Mell smiled at Golden Eagle in thanks before turning to Dream Dancer and patted a spot beside her invitingly. "Come sit over beside me."

Dream Dancer smiled shyly then got up from across the fire before walking over to White Buffalo. "I have heard a lot about you from my grandfather and Black Hawk."

White Buffalo smiled in delight then hugged Dream Dancer. "Well I have heard a lot about you too and your extraordinary gifts. Now tell me how did you know we were coming?"

Dream Dancer pushed away from Mell then eyed her pensively before looking over at Golden Eagle for permission.

The Englishman understanding the questioning look nodded in complete agreement.

Dream Dancer turned back to Mell. "I dreamt that you were coming to save us, after I had the dream I could feel that you were getting closer. Not exactly how close though until you were right behind us, but closer from one day to the next."

White Buffalo frowned thoughtfully. "Well your grandfather never told me about that gift."

Dream Dancer shrugged unknowingly. "I do not think I could do it again I think this was a special case sort of a once only event."

White Buffalo listened grimly to Dream Dancer's account of his dream before sighing pensively. "Well it sort of goes with the dream Pam and I had."

Seeing Dream Dancer confusion White Buffalo smiled in apology. "Well I guess I should call her Morning Star here."

Dream Dancer smiled at his aunt then turned back to White Buffalo. "Can you describe your dream for me?"

White Buffalo sighed grimly as she thought back. "I was very confused at first; it was not until Morning Star told me that she had the same dream that I paid more attention to it. I kept seeing a white buffalo turning away from a village one minute and deaths would happen. The next minute I would see the white buffalo going towards Giant Bear then saying, 'they must not be forced to marry'. The white buffalo would repeat the saying over and over almost in a chant. But I do not understand, who is not supposed to be forced to marry?"

Dream Dancer smiled widely in pride at being proven right. He shared a look with the Englishman then turned back to White Buffalo. "My grandfather is trying to force Raven and Golden Eagle into marriage. If I had more knowledge into what my grandfather was thinking it might help to give me a better picture of what's happening, but all I can do right now is speculate."

Black Hawk cleared his throat as he interrupted. "I can help you with that; father confided in me the day Golden Eagle started his training."

Dream Dancer nodded pleased. "Good. You start then I will finish with what I know."

Grey Wolf got up and poured everyone more coffee as they all listened attentively to Black Hawk story.

Dream Dancer listened closely; occasionally he would nod as if he knew what was going to be said next. When Black Hawk finished, the young Earl sighed grimly in relief. "Well now I know my theory was sound. I had the same dream as the shaman, but after talking to Golden Eagle we decided that the dream meant something different."

White Buffalo frowned in confusion. "How can you both have the same dream, but get different answers?"

Dream Dancer shrugged then tried to explain. "Well it is a little complicated, but like I told Golden Eagle a shaman is not infallible. The Great Spirit gives us visions to help us. Sometimes a vision is meant to be acted on and sometimes it is only a reassurance that something will happen. There have even been a few shamans who would only interpret a dream that he liked they would ignore anything else. It is up to the shaman to decide whether to act or sit back then wait. Only time and experience can say whether the shaman interpreted the dream correctly."

White Buffalo grimaced thoughtfully. "I think that I understand now, what you are saying is that we should not have interfered in this situation if we had not contacted Golden Eagle he would have come on his own."

Dream Dancer grinned pleased that she figured it out on her own. "Correct that is exactly right. Let me tell my story now then you be the judge."

White Buffalo listened closely. She was nodding at the end of Dream Dancer explanation as she finished her beans before putting the plate down. "Yes I agree with you and Golden Eagle. One thing I think we should think on is that the deaths we all see are not physical they will not actually die, but it could be a death of your beliefs or maybe the death of the Cheyenne as a whole."

Dream Dancer frowned in thought. "That would make a lot of sense since all the other Indian Nations, even the Cheyenne that are not living with us, are being driven onto reservations. The few that are still free, only want to continue fighting the whites, so they too will die. So if the Cheyenne living here lost Ravens protection they would end up dying on reservations also. Or as you say, it could be our beliefs since we are different from the other Cheyenne tribes. We believe in living in peace instead of trying to drive the whites away. We have adopted some of the white mans ways too thinking that the only way to survive is through adapting to the changing world. Many Cheyenne do not even consider us Cheyenne anymore. They call us, 'Friendlies', thinking it's a degrading thing to us, but it is not."

Grey Wolf interrupted. "So what can we do to stop Giant Bear from making such a fatal mistake then loosing Raven's protection?"

Dream Dancer shrugged grimly. "I am not sure; I could not go to my grandfather and the shaman myself before because to them I am still too young as well as untrained. The shaman would say that I was wrong then all that would have done was to separate Golden Eagle and me. I think at the time Golden Eagle needed me as much as I needed him in order to understand the situation. Between us, I think we learned more plus accepted more of what was happening then if we would not have been able to get to know one another. That is why I think I was given the dream about White Buffalo saying to hold on she was coming, or I might have been tempted to try interfering which would have caused more problems."

Golden Eagle smiled fondly at Dream Dancer. "He is right at first all I wanted was revenge. My hatred was growing daily at being forced to stay here and marry someone not of my choosing. I now feel no more hatred; I am also now willing to try working things out. I think we all need to go back to the village then talk to Giant Bear and the shaman. Now that you are here they will be more willing to listen."

White Buffalo sighed contemplatively. "I agree if that does not work we will have to come up with a better plan."

Dream Dancer stood up quickly. "Okay let's try it."

Everyone helped break camp then they were on their way.

*****

Golden Dove watched her husband pace for a moment and picked up a moccasin she was working on before trying to ignore him. Finally, she could stand it no longer, as she growled in frustration. "Will you sit down or do something."

Giant Bear frowned down at his wife in aggravation. "I cannot help it they have been gone for over a day anything could have happened to them."

Golden Dove shook her head reassuringly. "They are fine, probably holed up somewhere to wait out last night's storm."

Giant Bear stomped to the door before turning to his wife in disbelief. "That might be true, but they should have been back this morning. I am going to go look for them."

Golden Dove sighed plaintively as her husband left. She was a little nervous herself, but hid it better than her husband did. She grimaced in fear and turned back to her sewing to distract herself from her apprehension.

Giant Bear was organizing a search party when one of the sentry's came galloping in. "There is a large party approaching."

Giant Bear nodded in relief then frowned hopefully. "Is it Black Hawk?"

The lookout inclined his head solemnly. "He has three wagons with him and some vi'hol. Two are prisoners."

Giant Bear scowled in surprise. "Put the horses away then one of you go get the shaman."

Giant Bear walked to the beginning of the trail as he waited uneasily. He saw them coming and grimaced thoughtfully as he counted. Well the three wagons must be the supplies, but who were the others.

The shaman arrived a minute later then stood beside his chief grimly.

Giant Bear heard a familiar war whoop so turned to the shaman in excitement. "Send Little Coyote to get Golden Dove. White Buffalo and Grey Wolf are here."

The shaman nodded apprehensively then left.

Giant Bear turned back to the galloping rider and grinned in delight as Grey Wolf jumped out of his saddle in front of him. "Blood brother it is good to see you again."

Giant Bear embraced his friend then stood back to look at him perceptively. "Well I see you are finally starting to get a few grey hairs."

Grey Wolf laughed in delight as he pulled one of Giant Bear's short braids. "Not as grey as you, old man!"

White Buffalo pushed her husband aside in demand. "Let the rest of us say hello too."

Grey Wolf staggered in exaggeration.

Giant Bear smiled knowingly as he enfolded White Buffalo in a big hug. "Still pushing your husband around, I see."

White Buffalo chuckled as she squeezed her blood brother affectionately. "Of course, and he would not have it any other way."

White Buffalo pushed away then stepped back in pleasure. "Look who else I brought."

Giant Bear smiled widely in pleasure as he gave his daughter a long lingering glance before gathering her in his arms. "My Morning Star how beautiful you look, just like your mother."

Morning Star laughed and cried at the same time. "I have missed you something fierce I'ho."

Morning Star pushed away then beckoned to her husband. "You remember my husband Daniel."

Giant Bear nodded and clasped his son-in-law's arm in greeting. "I only met him once since he grew up, but yes I remember him."

Daniel beamed solemnly. "Nice to see you again, sir."

Giant Bear shook his head in distress. "Not sir, please call me Giant Bear, or I'ho which means your father."

Daniel nodded in pleasure then moved away.

Patricia squealed in delight and flung herself at Giant Bear. "Uncle Bear, I have missed you I have not seen you in many years."

Giant Bear laughed in humour as he lifted Pat of her feet. "Little Owl you are the only one who dares to call me Uncle Bear. But you have grown so big I will have to think of another name for you."

Patricia stepped back with a shake of her head in denial. "Oh no you don't, I love the name you gave me."

Giant Bear grinned in pleased. "Good from now on your Cheyenne name is Little Owl."

He turned to Jessica next as she stepped up a little more reserved than the others and gave him a hug. "How are you Giant Bear it has been a while since I have seen you?"

Giant Bear smiled at the image of her mother then grinned as he stepped back. "Red Sparrow, you are still the splitting image of your mother. You can call me Uncle Bear to if you like."

Red Sparrow nodded in excitement. "Okay, I would like that."

Giant Bear looked over her head as he smiled at the lovely vision behind Red Sparrow. "And who is this lovely lady?"

Red Sparrow turned then introduced her friend. "This is Black Rose. We helped her leave from a white town and brought her with us since she is Cheyenne. We figured you could help her find her family."

Giant Bear grinned then took Rose's hand in greeting. "I will see what I can do."

Rose smiled shyly. "Thank you."

Giant Bear turned to Grey Wolf. "What are you doing here?"

Grey Wolf sighed warningly. "Remember you told me that the white buffalo was supposed to save you in the future."

Giant Bear inclined his head slowly having forgotten about that as he remembered the conversation they had before he had left their ranch to come home.

The others all wondered off to greet the villagers and give them some privacy.

Giant Bear sighed grimly. "Yes, I remember."

Grey Wolf smiled placatingly. "Well now is the time."

Giant Bear frowned incredulously. "You have come to save us from the whites?"

Grey Wolf shook his head negatively. "No, we have come to save you from yourself!"

Giant Bear scowled in confusion, before he could ask what his friend meant by that his wife trotted around the corner then shouts of greeting and squeals of joy drowned him out.

Grey Wolf smiled in reassurance then leaned forward and whispered. "We will talk later."

Giant Bear nodded thoughtfully as he watched Grey Wolf trot over to Golden Dove for a welcoming hug. He heard an angry shout suddenly then turned to see the Englishman holding something as he shook one of the prisoners.

Black Hawk and Dream Dancer each grabbed an arm then held the raging Englishman back.

Giant Bear trotted over, he arrived at the same time as Grey Wolf and White Buffalo. "What is going on here?"

Golden Eagle shook free of the restraining hands. "This piece of scum has a shirt, brush, plus several other articles of my sisters. There is even a bloodstained shirt sleeve that was ripped off me during the battle."

Grey Wolf frowned thoughtfully for a bit as he eyed first one then the other prisoner. "Evidence, they were planning on hiding evidence in or around your village."

White Buffalo nodded agreeing with her husband. "You are probably right since the sheriff and villagers will be here tomorrow. If they found all that evidence in your village, they could call in the army without anymore questions asked."

Golden Eagle scowled angrily. "They did not find me when they came last time so whoever is trying to frame Raven's people must be getting desperate. Where did you get this stuff?"

The prisoner that had first recognized the Englishman looked away mutely.

Golden Eagle grabbed the prisoner again then shook him violently.

Black Hawk stepped forward to stop him, but stepped back again when White Buffalo held up her hand and motioned him away.

Golden Eagle shook the man again in rage. "You will answer me, or I will skin you an inch at a time until you do! Believe me living with the Cheyenne has taught me how to do it plus keep you alive for a long time while you suffer."

Black Hawk choked then coughed to hide his amusement and Dream Dancer had to turn away to hide his smile.

The prisoner paled visibly as he trembled in terror. "I do not know anything. I was just told to plant these things in the village."

The other prisoner broke in hurriedly. "Shut up you idiot."

White Buffalo stepped in front of the other prisoner then pushed her buckskin jacket away from her marshal's badge. "I would be quiet if I were you. There are now many witnesses including me to your crime and talking just might save your life from a hangman's noose."

The man scowled in disbelief. "You can't hang us for carrying stuff we found."

White Buffalo smiled nastily. "Oh, but I see you still do not understand! Since you shot Jake's son, who happens to be white; we can probably use the evidence you have to convict you of the murder of Golden Eagle's sisters as well as the guides."

The man frowned angrily then turned away mutely.

White Buffalo turned back to the Englishman. "Continue your questions."

Golden Eagle nodded and turned back to the other prisoner. "Who told you to put these here?"

Dream Dancer had turned to look at the man White Buffalo was talking to then stared thoughtfully. His forehead smoothed as he remembered where he had seen him before, and he interrupted Golden Eagle's questioning. "I know you!"

Golden Eagle whirled around at Dream Dancer's statement.

The man grimaced in denial at Dream Dancer then shook his head in fear. "I do not know you?"

Dream Dancer nodded decisively. "You just do not remember me, I was a lot younger. You came to the ranch with Charles when he was trying to get Raven to marry him. I remember you because you kicked my dog and broke his rib."

The man scowled uneasily then hurriedly looked away. "You must have confused me with someone else."

Dream Dancer shook his head negatively. "No, I am right I distinctly remember that scare under your left eye."

Black Hawk frowned thoughtfully. "Charles is the same man who shot the bear cub instead of me."

Dream Dancer inclined his head sadly. "Yes, Golden Eagle told me about that. Charles is our neighbour and a real pest, when Raven laughed in his face after he proposed to her he started coming over trying to get her to sell out to him."

White Buffalo eyed the prisoner speculatively. "Is there a reason for this?"

The man shrugged irritably. "I am just a ranch hand I do not know anything, I just do as I am told."

White Buffalo nodded then turned to Giant Bear. "I do not think they know anything important. Do you have somewhere to keep them until the sheriff shows up tomorrow?"

Giant Bear scowled grimly. "Yes, and I will put a guard on them as well."

Golden Dove walked over to them. "Come the women want to put the supplies away. A tepee is being erected for our guests also. We can talk later at supper."

Giant Bear sighed in aggravation knowing he would not get any answers now.

White Buffalo motioned inquisitively. "Do you have a place to bathe around here?"

Golden Dove nodded then beckoned to her friend. "Come with me I will show you."

Giant Bear waved to some braves standing off to the side then gave them instructions for the prisoners and their guest's horses.

White Buffalo went to her horse then grabbed her saddlebags before following Golden Dove talking excitedly. The others followed Mell's lead and the braves led the horse's away.

Giant Bear watched his guests following Golden Dove then turned as the shaman walked up to him. "Well what do you think?"

The shaman shrugged uneasily. "I did not see this only your daughter and her husband were supposed to come, so I have no answers for you."

Giant Bear nodded in confusion then turned to help his braves. "I guess we will have to wait to hear what they have to say."

The shaman nodded and followed his chief extremely disturbed.

*****

Raven pulled up then turned to her left. "We will camp here tonight. If we get up early, we can be at the village sometime around two or three if we do not stop for lunch."

Janet nodded in relief and followed Raven. They quickly set up camp together. When finished eating, they both crawled into their blankets then slept.

*****

They settled in the ceremonial tepee talking excitedly as they ate supper, drinks were handed out afterwards.

Giant Bear frowned at the Englishman dismissively. "We will be speaking privately you can go back to your tepee now."

Golden Eagle shook his head negatively with a stubborn mulish look on his face, but White Buffalo was the one who spoke. "No, he will stay this concerns him as well."

Giant Bear scowled angrily before addressing White Buffalo. "He does not know anything and must not know for now!"

White Buffalo smiled in sympathy at her blood brother. "He already knows everything, he knew before I came."

Giant Bear grimaced furiously before looking at his son in anger.

Black Hawk shrugged defensively. "Don't look at me, I only just found out yesterday that he already knew."

Giant Bear then turned his heated gaze on Dream Dancer.

Dream Dancer smiled in apology at his grandfather. "Yes, he knows although I did not tell him everything."

Giant Bear turned to the Englishman and looked at him enquiringly confused.

Golden Eagle smirked slyly, but refused to answer.

Dream Dancer elbowed his friend in the ribs in rebuke.

Golden Eagle grunted slightly as his young friends elbow connected hard then sighed in apology. "Well he made me suffer enough."

Dream Dancer lifted an eyebrow in reproach waiting.

Golden Eagle shrugged in annoyance. "Oh very well, I have portraits of the late Earl at home and Dream Dancer is the splitting image of his grandfather. So I started piecing things together on my own."

Giant Bear sighed aggrieved. "I knew it was a mistake letting Dream Dancer come here."

Dream Dancer shook his head negatively. "No, it was because of me that Golden Eagle learned to accept the bad situation you put him in."

Giant Bear nodded thoughtfully. "Yes, you had a very calming effect on him."

Giant Bear turned to White Buffalo without further comment. "Why have you come?"

White Buffalo smiled grimly. "I came to save you of course."

Giant Bear frowned uneasily. "Come to save me how?"

White Buffalo sighed thoughtfully then eyed the chief pensively trying to decide how to frame her answer. Finally, she decided to be direct. "I have come with a message from your Great Spirit; I am to tell you 'they must not be forced to marry'!"

The shaman jumped up in wild disbelief as he waved furiously in denial. "That is a lie my dream stressed if they do not marry the whites will kill everyone even Raven and the vi'hoI! What does a vi'hoahI know the Great Spirit would not tell her anything?"

Dream Dancer shook his head in disagreement then stood up as well before pointing at the shaman. "You are wrong; I had the same dream as you did what you saw was Raven turning away from her people because you forced her to do something that you should not have. The deaths of our people are only a forewarning of what will happen if Raven withdrew her protection. The death of the raven and eagle above them meant that their Indian spirits would die within them, not that they would die physically."

Giant Bear scowled then turned to the shaman in confusion. "Could he be right?"

The shaman harrumphed in contempt before stopping thoughtfully as he recalled his dream. He sat back down staggered never had he been wrong before as he nodded reluctantly. "Yes, it could be interpreted that way."

The shaman eyed Dream Dancer curiously with new respect. "We have never had the same vision before how did you reach your conclusions?"

Dream Dancer sighed grimly as he sat down also. "Well I know my sister very well, and she is as stubborn as they come. If you tried to force her to do something, she would find a way to get back at you. When she got hurt by that grizzly, she told me that if she were forced to marry she did not know if she would be able to continue helping the Cheyenne."

Giant Bear grimaced furiously at the shaman. "I told you something was wrong."

Dream Dancer nodded decisively. "Yes, for one thing you should not have interfered when the Great Spirit gave you that vision about Golden Eagle."

Giant Bear frowned apprehensively things were going from bad, too worse. "How do you know about that? Why do you think we should not have contacted Golden Eagle?"

Dream Dancer waved dourly. "Well I only guessed at first until Black Hawk confirmed it this afternoon. We figured that the Great Spirit gave you that first vision as a reassurance that somebody had already been chosen for Raven, not for you to interfere. Golden Eagle told me he was already thinking of coming here. Since his sister had a very weak heart we figured if things had progressed on there own that she probably would have passed on in England. This would have been the last straw for Golden Eagle then he would have moved here on his own. But because you drew him here before his time, circumstances changed. He got drawn unwillingly into a fight that was not his own."

Giant Bear frowned troubled before turning to the shaman. "Well what do you think?"

The shaman's face creased in thought as he ran through all his visions; he remembered seeing the golden eagle at Ravens naming ceremony and he shrugged, sceptical. "He could be right although I am not completely convinced yet I will have to think about it some more."

Giant Bear nodded and turned to his grandson inquisitively. "What do you suggest?"

Dream Dancer smiled in satisfaction at being asked his opinion. "I think you should withdraw your request for Raven and Golden Eagle to marry then let them work it out on their own."

Giant Bear sighed in relief; he had wanted a way out of this almost since the beginning anyway. He turned to White Buffalo next, but already knew the answer. "And your opinion is?"

White Buffalo inclined her head in concurrence. "I agree with Dream Dancer."

Giant Bear turned to Grey Wolf then saw him nodding his agreement with the others. Giant Bear turned to the shaman last. "Do you agree?"

The shaman sighed reluctantly. "Yes, I believe they are right at least for now."

Giant Bear turned to the Englishman. "You are released if you do not wish to marry my granddaughter you are free to go."

Golden Eagle grinned in delight pleased to have a say as he released the breath he had been holding in relief. "Do you mind if I stay and finish my training first?"

Giant Bear's eyebrows lifted in surprise. "I figured you would leave if the opportunity presented itself."

Golden Eagle shrugged dismissively. "In the beginning I probably would have jumped at the chance, but I have made many new friends here so would like to stay if it is okay with you?"

Giant Bear inclined his head in consent. "You can stay as long as you wish it is the least we can do for you, keep all your gifts as well."

Golden Eagle smiled his thanks then shared a satisfied glance with Dream Dancer.

Grey Wolf sighed glad to get that over with. "Now that this situation is cleared up I think we better talk about the sheriff. He should be here tomorrow with some if not all of the townspeople."

White Buffalo nodded grimly. "He is right even though we do not think all the dreams are connected with the death of your people at this time, he still posses a threat to you."

Golden Eagle frowned in worry. "I do not like the fact that Raven's neighbour is the same one who tried to shoot Black Hawk plus sent his men to plant evidence against you. I also do not understand how he got the evidence in the first place."

Dream Dancer scowled incredulously at a disturbing thought. "Do you think he had something to do with the ambush? I know he has been getting pretty nasty with Raven lately because she refuses to sell to him, but killing innocent people is not his style either?"

Giant Bear grimaced angrily. "You could be right that it is not his style, but he did not actually have to do the killing maybe he paid the Indian's to do it. I wonder what is so important about Raven's land that would drive him to such desperate measures."

White Buffalo pondered grimly before turning to her husband. "Remember about ten years ago we had a similar situation. It was a drought year and water was getting more precious than gold. One neighbour had a natural spring that came out of the hills through his land and onto the next neighbours land. They ended up in a war over it; one neighbour kept trying to buy out the other, but he would not sell. Suddenly his cattle started dying then his ranch hands started mysteriously disappearing. We had to step in and put a stop to it."

Grey Wolf nodded remembering. "Yes, the neighbour got so desperate he ended up killing a few people then he was hung for his crimes."

They all turned and looked at Dream Dancer expectantly. He shrugged unknowingly. "As far as I know there is no problem with water for anyone. We do have good grazing land for cattle, but nothing to kill for."

White Buffalo sighed dejectedly. "It could be almost anything."

Golden Dove stood up satisfied at how events had turned out, maybe now she could let her husband back into her bed. "Well it is late I think tomorrow we should send out a hunting party for fresh meat so we can cook a big feast for all the townspeople coming out."

Giant Bear nodded in agreement, as everyone got up. "That is a good idea we can also roast a whole pig in the underground oven too."

White Buffalo grinned eagerly not having roast pig in a long time then turned to Dream Dancer in demand. "If you think of anything that might cause him to go after the land let me know."

Dream Dancer nodded decisively. "I will goodnight."

Hugs and kisses were exchanged then everyone went to bed.

CHAPTER TWENTY EIGHT

Golden Dove smiled in sympathy as her daughter told her all about their trials to come here. Every once in awhile White Buffalo or one of the others would include a few more details. It was so lovely to have her best friend as well as her daughter around. The men had all went hunting except two braves who were sent out to show the sheriff and townspeople here safely.

All the Indian women of the village were preparing an enormous feast. Golden Dove felt a little guilty sitting around talking instead of helping them. The women had shooed Golden Dove away though, allowing the chief's wife to go visit with her friends.

Golden Dove hugged her daughter after she finished in joy at having another grandchild. "Well congratulations how far along are you?"

Morning Star smiled in delight at her mother's ecstatic expression then hugged her back. "The end of my six months I think, Daniel thinks we should stay here or at the ranch until after the baby is born."

Golden Dove nodded in excitement at being present for at least one of her grandchildren's birth. "We would love for you to stay, and if you decide to stay at the ranch I will go stay with you when it is getting close to your time."

Morning Star grinned pleased. "I would like that."

Golden Dove turned to White Buffalo. "How long will you be staying?"

White Buffalo sighed hopefully. "I am not sure yet at least two weeks we are hoping. I have to wire the marshal's office then see if they need me yet!"

Golden Dove grinned teasingly. "How much longer are you two planning on staying marshal and deputy marshal?"

White Buffalo chuckled in amusement. "Still as perceptive as ever I see. We have not made an official announcement yet, but we are thinking of retiring in a couple of years."

Little Owl shared a stunned look with Red Sparrow at this startling revelation.

White Buffalo smiled at the twos surprised looks. "What did you think we would never give it up?"

Little Owl laughed in delight. "Well we were starting to wonder. Who will be your successor?"

White Buffalo shrugged mischievously. "I will be making two recommendations, you of course; Dusty will be the other one."

Little Owl scowled furiously. "That stuck up piece of work; he will wreck everything you have done."

White Buffalo's eyebrows rose startled at the angry answer. "You use to like Dusty what happened?"

Little Owl frowned grimly then waved in annoyance. "He got too big for his britches, is what happened. He figures since he is so good looking women should fall at his feet in awe."

White Buffalo and Golden Dove shared a meaningful glance then White Buffalo nodded knowingly to her friend. Her daughter was falling in love.

Little Owl saw the look the two shared and glared at both of them in exasperation.

White Buffalo wisely changed the subject.

*****

Raven frowned impatiently at Janet then mounted in anger. "Hurry up we are so close now I want to get there before supper."

Janet sighed in frustration Raven had been irritable all morning. Twice now, she had snapped at her. She mounted trying not to feel hurt at Raven's tone as she reminded herself that Raven was just anxious to check on her people. So she mutely followed Raven without comment.

Raven was aware of Janet's hurt feelings, but was getting worried. What would she find when they arrived, she sighed to herself apprehensively then tried to shake of her mood. Once they were on their way Raven's mood lightened so she started giving Janet more language lessons trying to appease the pain her new friend was feeling.

*****

Dream Dancer smiled fondly at the Englishman as he laughed boisterously at a joke Black Hawk was telling him. He looked more comfortable now with all the angry lines that had been his constant companion since Dream Dancer had met him gone. If anything, it had made him look more elegant or maybe nobler would be a better word. His hair had lightened considerably since he was spending more time in the sun as a lock kept falling down into his eyes, which gave him a rakish air.

Jake and Running Wolf both pulled travois's loaded with a buck each, they had broken off from the main hunting party then had gone west instead of north and to their good fortune had stumbled onto the two bucks eating in a gully.

Dream Dancer sighted dust ahead then slowed until Golden Eagle and Black Hawk caught up as he pointed. "Others are coming!"

Black Hawk shaded his eyes as he squinted so he could see better. "It looks like the other hunting party is on their way back also. We should meet up with them soon."

Dream Dancer nodded as they kicked their horse's into a trot.

*****

Golden Dove looked up then called out at a discreet scratching on the tepee flap. "Come in!"

Little Badger poked his head in. "The hunters are back they had a good hunt."

Golden Dove nodded pleased as they all got up to follow the boy out.

The braves who were not loaded down galloped into the village whooping in triumph.

Giant Bear smiled in satisfaction down at his wife when he rode up then he dismounted. "We got two young buffalo and Black Hawk's party got two bucks."

Golden Dove grinned pleased then hugged him before turning and beckoned the hunters to bring the animals over to the butchering area.

White Buffalo hugged her husband eagerly. "You did well I have not had buffalo in a long time."

Golden Dove overheard as she was passing by so stopped. "Well then we will just have to cook up some for you."

They all turned before looking up as they heard a horse galloping quickly into camp.

Giant Bear and Grey Wolf walked over to meet the rider immediately.

The sentry jumped off his horse in excitement. "The vi'hoI are coming, they should be here just past the suns highest point."

Giant Bear nodded in approval. "About three hours do you know how many are coming?"

The lookout shook his head negatively. "No, but most of them are men with only a few women, but no children. It is taking them longer because of the wagons for the women."

Giant Bear frowned solemnly then turned to Grey Wolf. "It is probably the women who are related to the guides who were killed."

Grey Wolf sighed in agreement and smiled at the guard before they turned away then headed back to the others.

White Buffalo looked at her husband grimly as he rejoined them. "What is the news?"

Grey Wolf repeated the sentry's message.

White Buffalo nodded sadly and turned to Golden Dove. "Do the women need help?"

Golden Dove grinned in delight at the offer. "I was just on my way anyone who wants to can come along also to help out."

All the women nodded as they followed Golden Dove.

Giant Bear looking more relaxed then he had been in a long time smiled at all the gleeful hunters. "The hunt was such a success we have a surprise for you all, please follow me."

Golden Eagle looked inquiringly at Dream Dancer, but he just shrugged perplexed as he followed his grandfather.

Dream Dancer had watched his grandfather closely today before they had broken off to go their own way to hunt. He had noticed that the worry lines on his grandfather's old craggy face had smoothed out. Dream Dancer knew he was feeling relief at having released Golden Eagle and Raven from their forced union.

Giant Bear turned then faced the men when he reached the sweat lodge. "We will have a purifying ritual to thank the Great Spirit for providing us with food. For those of you who have never done this before you will strip to your loincloth; the shaman will perform the ceremony on each of us before we enter."

Golden Eagle smiled at Dream Dancer enthusiastically. "Well this will be a new experience for me. I've never been this way before; I did not even know these tepees were over here."

Dream Dancer pointed vaguely behind him as he undressed eagerly. "There are two more tepee's set up on the other side of this hill for the women. Sometimes we have a communal sweat bath with both men and women together, but usually it's separate."

Golden Eagle nodded then finished undressing as he watched the shaman chant and shaking a ceremonial staff around Jake. The shaman was dressed only in a loincloth with a wolf pelt draped around his shoulders. His face was painted in intricate detail almost but not quit the same style as Dream Dancer had on his face the night they had visited the spirit world together. He stepped up next then listened as the shaman chanted, but he could hear no recognizable words. Finally, he ducked inside and gasped in shock as a wave of heat hit him full force. It took him a moment to catch his breath then another minute to be able to see vague shapes ahead of him through the wall of steam.

Dream Dancer entered behind him and led him to a seat.

The shaman entered last then immediately he sealed the opening closed so that nobody else could enter. He walked over to the steaming rocks and poured more water on them to increase the moisture as well as the heat as he continued chanting.

Dream Dancer leaned over so he could whisper softly. "After we finish here we will run down to the creek then jump in, it is a cold shock when the water hits your steaming flesh. Clean clothes will be ready for us when we get out of the creek."

Golden Eagle nodded without answering before looking down at himself in fascination as the sweat and dirt ran down his body in rivulets. He still found it a little hard to breathe though.

*****

Raven jumped off her horse then bent down to look at the tracks before looking back up at Janet in concern. "Somebody leading a horse came by this way late last night, and they were in an awful hurry. See how far apart the tracks are that means they were at a full gallop, if you look closely you could see an indent of a shoe, which means the horse, has a white owner. Indians do not shoe their horses.

Janet got off her horse curiously then examined the tracks closely before looking up at Raven and nodded that she understood.

Raven walked further then studied the ground again in interest; she beckoned and pointed out more intriguing tracks for Janet. "Look at these tracks here, see how close together they are all of a sudden it looks like the horse stumbled here then picked up the gallop again. Whoever it is; is in an awful hurry and does not care if the horse dies."

Raven mounted thoughtfully as she frowned disgruntled.

Janet followed her lead after looking curiously at the tracks.

Raven kicked her horse into a canter then looked over at Janet when she caught up. "It is probably my neighbour, Charles! It would not surprise me one bit that he would run his horse into the ground and not care."

They rode silently for about an hour then Raven slowed again as she pointed into the sky so that Janet would look up at the birds circling above something. Raven took out her rifle, and Janet followed her lead then draped the rifle across her saddle. She looked for Bruno in anxiety and saw him off to her left. "Bruno come boy, stay beside me."

Bruno trotted over to his mistress then followed her obediently.

Raven nudged her horse into a trot and kept her rifle ready just in case. She heard a shriek of fear, which meant whatever the birds were after, was still alive, so she kicked her horse into a gallop.

Janet caught her breath in horror as they crested a ridge then saw a horse lying on its side kicking feebly trying to get back up. The vultures to impatient to wait for the horse to die tried to get close enough to eat.

Raven lifted her rifle as she shot it into the air, which gave Bruno permission to drive the vultures away.

The ugly vultures lifted into the air with heated squawks at being deprived of their dinner by the barking dog and his companions.

Raven dismounted then knelt down beside the horse and felt along his legs for any breaks. Not finding any, she put her hand on his heaving side then one on his chest.

Janet knelt down beside the horse's head before stroking him soothingly to keep him quiet as Raven examined him.

Raven looked at Janet before pointing at the packhorse. "On the right hand side of the saddlebag there is an extra halter rope, please bring it here. We need to get him up on his feet, and walking slowly."

Janet nodded in concern then quickly jumped up hurrying to do as she was told. She rushed back and handed Raven the halter then a lead rope. "Will he be okay?"

Raven shrugged not sure yet and slipped the halter on then with the two women urging and pushing him the horse got to his feet reluctantly then stood there trembling in exhaustion. Raven sighed as she looked up at the sky and frowned. Another couple of hours they would have been back at the village, but with the exhausted horse needing them it would take a little longer.

Raven sighed grimly then looked over at Janet. "I am going to walk him slowly, while I do that I want you to make a fire and cook us something to eat. I also want you to put a handful of oats in a bowl with some water then cook it until it is a mush, after it cools I will feed it to the horse. I am hoping if we walk for a bit he will make it back to the village where he can be tended to properly. He has been winded badly, but he is salvageable. He is a nice looking stud, but that is all he will ever be now though. This is Charles's prized stallion, he has won many races with him, but he will never be able to race again. A few months in a pasture with slow exercise he will be ride able, but only at a slow trot and not for very long."

Janet nodded then watched Raven patiently persuade the reluctant horse to take a trembling step and another. She turned away before doing as instructed as she started setting up a temporary camp.

*****

Golden Eagle shivered as he dressed in the ceremonial clothing that had been left there for him. He looked at a shivering Dream Dancer then laughed as he hopped on one foot trying to get his pants on as fast as possible. "Well that was something I would not want to do every day. I thought my heart was going to stop when I jumped into that icy cold water."

Dream Dancer grabbed his shirt and immediately put it on before answering. "We do not do it very often in the summer it is more of a winter thing once the ice freezes our bathing area."

Golden Eagle nodded as he followed Dream Dancer up the path.

Everyone else had already left they were the last ones.

Dream Dancer topped the hill first then waited for the Englishman as he spied dust in the distance. He pointed it out to Golden Eagle when he reached him. "Looks like the townspeople are almost here, let's hurry!"

Golden Eagle nodded, and they broke into a fast trot.

Dream Dancer saw his grandfather with the others as they gathered at the edge of the village waiting, so he headed that way.

Giant Bear looked at his grandson then at Golden Eagle in disapproval for their tardiness as they stopped beside him on his left, but made no comment. He turned back to watch the townspeople getting closer. Jake, Running Wolf, as well as Black Hawk stood on the right hand side of Giant Bear. White Buffalo and Grey Wolf moved close to Golden Eagle so that they would all show a united front to the sheriff, both had their badges pinned on in plain sight.

The shaman, Golden Dove, with the rest of White Buffalo's party was right behind the chief. The villagers surrounded them, but stayed at a discrete distance.

Black Hawk pointed off to their left, so they all turned to look towards the dust as a horse galloping full out raced towards the townspeople. Whoever was riding the horse finally reached the sheriff then stopped as a heated discussion took place.

Dream Dancer harrumphed angrily as he waved towards the exhausted horse. "It is my neighbour Charles. I wonder where he is coming from, and look at his poor horse."

Black Hawk frowned in concern at seeing such a beautiful animal in such distress. The tall leggy chestnut mare was so lathered in sweaty foam that you almost could not distinguish her colour. Her sides heaved in agony as she tried to draw in a breath. Her head hung in exhaustion; she looked as if she were about ready to fall over dead on the spot.

*****

The sheriff watched Charles gallop towards him, but did not stop until the man pulled up right in front of him then would not let him pass. He scowled angrily as he eyed Charles horse before shaking his head in sadness at the poor creature's condition. "Where have you been and why did you ride your horse into the ground to get here?"

Charles frowned angrily at being rebuked in front of the townspeople, but let it go. "Two of my men snuck into the village then found evidence of the massacre in their possession."

The sheriff scowled in doubt as he eyed Charles's horse speculatively the man defiantly had not come from his ranch or his horse would not be in such a condition so how would he know. Charles looked around the sheriff searching for his men, but could not find them. He grimaced in annoyance the two men were supposed to be around to back up his story.

The sheriff moved his horse around Charles. "Do not worry if there is any evidence I will find it."

Charles fidgeted at the sheriff's dubious voice and walked his mare beside him.

*****

Giant Bear leaned over then addressed White Buffalo. "That is Raven's neighbour Charles."

White Buffalo frowned in disapproval and eyed the man coming towards them speculatively; she shook her head in pity for the horse disliked the man instantly as she took his measure. She had an uncanny way with measuring people and rarely was she ever wrong in her assessment. It had given her an edge as a sheriff then as a marshal. What she saw in Charles was an avid greedy do not care about anybody but yourself, individual. He also had a cruel streak hidden, but noticeable if you looked at his horse's sides closely enough and noticed the wicked spur marks.

*****

The sheriff walked his horse gradually to allow Charles's horse a chance to cool down, but then he could walk no further as he pulled up in front of Chief Giant Bear before dismounting respectfully.

White Buffalo and Grey Wolf walked up to the sheriff then shook his hand in greeting.

Charles frowned in puzzlement as the two white people greeted the sheriff as if friends and he scowled in concern when he noticed the badges pinned to their buckskin shirts. He jumped off his horse then waited impatiently for introductions.

Not all the townspeople had come, but the ones that did dismounted before milling around waiting. The mayor as well as the town council was all here of course, plus the wives of the two missing guides. There was several friends of the women present plus a few supporters of Raven. They all totally refused to believe Charles men when told that Raven's family had murdered the Englishman, his family, and the guides.

Giant Bear regally stepped forward then waited for quiet before speaking loud enough to be heard by all. "Sheriff if there are no objections my braves will take all the horse's and wagon horse's to be fed then watered and they will put them in the two corrals off to your left to wait for you since you are all welcomed to a feast in your honour that we have prepared. We have a ceremonial tepee where we will all be able to eat together and talk about your concerns if it is agreeable."

The sheriff looked at Mell then saw her nod in agreement. He turned back to face the chief. "I will be honoured to share in your feast."

Giant Bear nodded and beckoned to Little Badger then spoke in Cheyenne. "I want you to take the big mare the little man is riding and give her special attention."

Little Badger nodded solemnly before walking over to Charles then reached for the horse's reins.

Charles hid the reins behind his back. "No dirty Indian whelp will touch my horse!"

There were shocked intakes of breath, even from the villagers at such an ignorant comment.

Golden Eagle took an angry step forward, but stopped short as Dream Dancer grabbed his arm to stop him.

The sheriff calmly passed his reins to a brave who walked up to him before turning with an angry frown to Charles. "That is fine Charles you can stay here and guard the horse's while the rest of us go eat then talk!"

Charles scowled furiously at being outmanoeuvred before thrusting the reins of his horse at the boy without further protest. The boy led the mare away not having understood the words the vi'hol had said so had just stood there waiting patiently.

Giant Bear grimaced in anger and turned to the sheriff. "That man is not welcome here!"

The sheriff inclined his head in apology then motioned in conciliation before explaining. "He is under my protection this once only; after we leave here he will not return ever!"

Giant Bear looked at Black Hawk who nodded in agreement since it was his right to demand Charles leave since he had almost shot him once already. He turned back to the sheriff irritably. "Black Hawk has agreed, but only if he is relieved of all weapons will I allow him to go any further."

Charles frowned at being ignored, but was smart enough to allow the sheriff to handle this. He was sure that the sheriff would not leave him defenceless, but he was shocked when he saw the sheriff nod in concurrence.

The sheriff turned to Charles and held out his hand in demand. "You will give me your guns."

Charles shook his head furiously. "No way!"

The sheriff stepped in front of Charles menacingly. "You will give me your guns or you will get on your horse then leave this instant!"

Charles nodded reluctantly before taking out both his guns and handed them to the sheriff.

Giant Bear nodded in satisfaction as the sheriff handed the guns to his deputy for safekeeping then he beckoned to the sheriff to follow him. "Come we will eat before we discuss unpleasantness."

The sheriff nodded as he beckoned the villagers to come as he followed the chief. He looked around curiously; he liked what he saw. The tepees were all in good repair, with no garbage lying about. He could also see that several buildings were permanent. The children were all clothed with only a few running around naked, most of them were toddlers.

The sheriff had been in a few Indian villages, but had never seen one so well taken care of or the people so well fed; they all looked in good health too. He turned to the chief curiously. "Your people look happy and healthy?"

Giant Bear nodded proudly. "That is all thanks to Raven, since we moved here nobody has gone hungry or died of diseases. She built us a cold room for our meat to keep it away from disease carrying flies. It used to be that the meat would spoil that caused more deaths in the old days than we care to think of. She also provides us with some medicines we cannot get otherwise and immunizes us against some of the diseases we are susceptible to since the white man came."

The sheriff frowned thoughtfully as he waved around curiously. "You are lucky to have her, but what do the other tribes think of you?"

Giant Bear sighed sadly. "Unfortunately most do not consider us Indians anymore they say we have become to white, so they call us 'Friendlies' now."

The sheriff grimaced in sympathy. "Yet you still leave every spring then go to your summer camp."

Giant Bear nodded grimly. "Yes we have been, but I do not think we will be going any longer. Since all the Indian tribes are now being herded onto reservations it will not be safe to leave soon, actually this was supposed to be our last year at our summer camp."

The sheriff inclined his head in approval. "I think you have made a wise decision to stay here permanently word has just come that the army will be arriving in force by fall to drive all the Indians they can find onto reservations before winter hits."

Giant Bear scowled uneasily. "It was bound to happen sooner or later."

The sheriff frowned in agreement, and they walked part of the way in silence. He eyed the building the chief was leading him towards in surprise then smiled it was shaped like a tepee, but was obviously made out of wood with hides covering the entire building. It must have taken them over a hundred hides to be able to cover the whole thing. The sheriff turned to the chief in appreciation. "Interesting building you have there."

Giant Bear smiled in satisfaction. "Yes it is Raven built it for us just after we moved onto her land. It took us a long time to gather enough hides to cover it all, but unlike a regular tepee which uses one hide to symbolize who owns it we used a hide of every animal to symbolize the people as a whole. The women stitched it together then we all gathered to put it up together both men and women. Usually it is the women who takes down then puts up our camps, but this building is different we all helped build it, so we all helped finish it. Every person had an opportunity to put their own symbol on a hide, and as you can see, there is still a lot of room for more symbols. Every child who reaches manhood then wished to stay puts his symbol on one of the hides."

Giant Bear opened the flap, and they entered the tepee together then Black Hawk followed before holding it open for everyone else to enter. Someone had lit all the oil lamps hanging on the walls as well as the central fire pit.

Giant Bear smiled at the look of awe on the sheriff's face as he looked around. "The inside is decorated by the shaman, medicine man, Raven, Dream Dancer, and me because we are all leaders or spiritual leaders. It symbolizes our spirit world, the walls also tell the story of our ancestors as well as how we came to live here plus why."

The sheriff grinned in admiration as they walked to the center of the tepee then sat beside the fire. "It is very beautiful maybe later you can explain what some of the drawings mean."

Giant Bear nodded pleased that the sheriff was interested. "I will be happy to explain it to anyone who wishes to hear."

Giant Bear waited until all were seated before clapping his hands sharply in demand. Several Indian maids entered and handed out cups to all then two more entered with water bags and filled everyone's cup. The sheriff took a sip of his beverage then nodded in approval. "This is good!"

Giant Bear chuckled in amusement at the praise. "We make our own alcoholic beverage which is not as strong or as deadly as whisky."

The sheriff smiled pleased that Giant Bear's group stayed away from whisky. He watched as the older Indian women came in, and then handed out bowls of stew. More came in a few minutes later and passed around plates heaping with different meats. There were also several varieties of vegetables available, but you could tell that they were from winter storage or bottled. The sheriff tried the stew first then smiled as he turned to Giant Bear. "This is beef is it not?"

Giant Bear nodded in agreement. "Yes it is, and there are three types of meat on the plate. They were all roasted in an underground oven. One is buffalo; the other one is deer, the last one is a whole pig."

The sheriff tried all three then smiled in appreciation. "It is very good."

Everyone finished eating, and the women collected all the dishes then left quietly. More mead was poured for those who wanted more before the sheriff turned to Giant Bear. "Has Raven returned yet?"

Giant Bear shook his head sadly. "No, we have had no word from her yet, and I am getting a little worried she should have been back here by now."

The sheriff nodded then looked over at Golden Eagle and his eyes narrowed speculatively. "I take it you are Sir Devon Rochester from England?"

Golden Eagle nodded decisively. "Yes I am."

The sheriff scowled slightly in angry suspicion. "Have you been here all along?"

Golden Eagle nodded again. "Yes."

The sheriff looked around expectantly. "The rest of your party, are they here also?"

Golden Eagle sighed sadly, as he shook his head negatively. "My oldest sister was taken captive the rest sadly did not make it, including my youngest sister!"

There were cries of anguish from the back of the crowd, but Golden Dove, Little Owl as well as Morning Star all rushed over to comfort the women. They had all been waiting in the back for that unhappy announcement.

The sheriff looked back, but seeing the women being taken care of he turned back to Golden Eagle then motioned around in demand. "Are these the Indians that attacked you?"

Golden Eagle shook his head negatively. "No when I first woke up and found myself here I thought they were, but after I talked to Raven then saw two of the Indians who had done it I realized they were not the same ones."

Charles jumped up angrily in anger wondering how the Englishman had escaped being found last time they were here. "That is a lie there is evidence here that says they did do it!"

Giant Bear clapped his hands sharply again, and two braves stepped into the tent with two white men obviously prisoners. Then two more stepped into the tent helping a teenage white boy to hobble inside.

The sheriff eyed the boy and turned to Jake curiously. "That is your son, is it not?"

Jake nodded in agreement. "He was on sentry duty when those two men showed up then put a couple of bullets in him as they tried to sneak into the village. It was a good thing for my son that we were on our way there and heard the shots. It was also fortunate for us that Dream Dancer was close by to dig out the bullet."

The sheriff eyed the two prisoners then looked up at Charles who was still standing. "Those are your men are they not, Charles?"

Charles sat down heavily and sputtered in desperation. "I fired them a few days ago."

Both prisoners gaped at their employer in disbelief then shouted out loudly. "He lies!"

Giant Bear waved to one of the braves to bring the saddlebags over. He took them with a gesture of thanks before handing the bags to the sheriff. "You might want to look in their saddlebags yourself. Marshal Brown was here when we opened them, so is a witness to the fact that we did not tamper with them."

The sheriff opened both bags and pulled out the evidence the two were suppose to hide inside the village then the sheriff turned to Charles in demand. "Can you explain why your men have all this stuff on them?"

Charles looked around wildly before jumping up again and tried to think of something to say or to find a way out, but he was trapped.

The sheriff stood up then faced him in accusation. The sheriff's two deputies stood up as well and surrounded Charles as the room hushed instantly in shock.

CHAPTER TWENTY NINE

Raven frowned grimly as she looked around expectantly; no guard had greeted them so the closer they got to the village, the more agitated she became. They entered the deserted village then Raven stood up in her saddle before looking around wildly, not a soul was in sight. She looked towards the paddocks and grimaced uneasily in amazement at all the horse's milling around. She sat back in fear then kicked her horse into a trot before jumping off her horse and eyeing the strange horses inside. She spotted the sheriff's horse immediately then spun around in fear, was she too late!

Janet dismounted and stared at Raven in consternation at the panic on her face. "Are you okay?"

Raven held up her hand for quiet as she heard the sound of a horse walking towards them, she spun around then stared at Little Badger hopefully with one of Charles's horse's. Little Badger's face broke into a wide smile of greeting as he pulled the reluctant mare into a faster pace. "Raven you are back!"

Raven knelt down and smiled at Little Badger as she tried hard to hide her fear from the boy. "Where is everyone?"

Little Badger pointed over his shoulder. "They are all in the ceremonial tepee."

Raven sighed in relief. "Can you take the horse's then put them in the big pasture, but be careful of my stud okay just lead the mares away and he will follow you? I will unsaddle them later."

Little Badger nodded solemnly. "I remember."

Raven grinned then ruffled his hair affectionately before standing up and beckoned to Janet to come with her then the two hurried on. She rushed into the tepee expecting to find the townspeople in an uproar. Instead, she saw the sheriff tying Charles's hands behind his back and everyone else calmly sitting talking in excitement at this turn of events.

Janet pushed past Raven at a shout then smiled in relief as her brother rushed towards her.

Golden Eagle grabbed his sister and swung her around in joy. "Are you all right?"

Janet cupped her brother's face as she gazed up at him adoringly. "I am now!"

Golden Eagle sighed in relief as he held her for a moment longer before setting her down. He kept his arm draped around her though to keep her close. He turned and eyed Raven in respect. "Thank you for finding my sister I will be forever in your debt."

Giant Bear walked over then hugged the confused Raven. "It took you long enough! You should have been back days ago what happened?"

Raven hugged her grandfather before pushing away and shrugged impatiently. "I had a few minor delays nothing to worry about. What is going on? I expected to see something different when I walked in here was the vision wrong?"

Giant Bear shook his head then sighed sadly in apology. "No, it was not wrong only misinterpreted I will explain later."

Raven frowned at that piece of news and looked around even more confused now then spotted White Buffalo and Grey Wolf talking to Dream Dancer. She turned back to her grandfather baffled then both eyebrows lifted in surprise. "When did Mell and Jed get here?"

Giant Bear smiled at his confused granddaughter. "They just arrived yesterday."

Giant Bear leaned closer then whispered so that nobody else could hear them. "By the way I have released you and Golden Eagle from having to marry!"

Raven's mouth dropped open in stunned surprise then snapped it shut angrily, but before she could ask any questions, the sheriff walked over and offered her his hand. "Well met Raven you are looking good as usual."

Raven turned to the sheriff reluctantly wanting to know what was happening, but not wanting to seem rude. She took his hand then smiled curiously. "Thank you! I see you have arrested Charles how did you all figure out that he did it?"

The sheriff let go of Raven's hand before hooking his thumbs in his gun belt. "Your uncle and Lord Rochester caught two of Charles's hands trying to sneak into the village to plant evidence. They shot Jake's son in the process, but luckily, he was not hurt badly. We still do not know why yet?"

Raven beckoned to him so that they could speak privately as she told him her story.

The sheriff listened thoughtfully then nodded in disgust. "Well I should have guessed it had something to do with gold Charles has always been a greedy son of a bitch. Pardon the language, what are you going to do now?"

Raven shrugged unknowingly. "I do not know yet? I will talk to Devon later and see what he wants to do since it is on both our land. Can you keep it quiet for now until we decide?"

The sheriff nodded in agreement then waved decisively. "You bet I will that is all we need is a bunch of gold hungry vultures landing in our town with gold fever."

Raven inclined her head resolutely in complete agreement. "We defiantly agree on that, I need to give my condolences to the widows I will talk to you later."

Raven walked over to Morning Star and the other women. Both widows turned as Raven approached. She reached out then took their hands in comfort. "I am so sorry for your loss."

Colleen always being the stronger of the two women spoke for both of them as they squeezed Raven's hand in gratitude at the sympathy. Both of them had already known they were gone deep in their hearts; they had come out more to find out why. They also wanted to see where they were buried or if Raven knew where the bodies were. "You buried them here I am told, we would like to see where if you do not mind?"

Raven sighed sadly having expected that then nodded decisively. "Of course, my grandmother will take you. I want both you ladies to know that I promised your husbands I would look after you. Whatever you need just let me know, and if you want to go back to Scotland, I will help you. Or if you both want you can move out to the ranch and stay with me I could always use some extra help?"

The women looked at each other in amazement not having expected that then both turned back to Raven. Colleen reached out and hugged Raven in thanks. "That is very kind of you we will discuss it first before letting you know."

Raven was relieved that the two women were taking this better than she had thought. She stepped away from Colleen and reached out then hugged Priscilla. "Let me know soon okay?"

They nodded before Golden Dove took their hands and led them away.

Raven grimaced upset then turned to her aunt and hugged her aunt in greeting. "What brings all of you here so unexpectedly Aunt Morning Star?"

Morning Star smiled mysteriously then took Raven over to her mother-in-law as she motioned teasingly. "We came to save my father from himself of course!"

Raven frowned in bafflement, but did not have a chance to ask any questions as White Buffalo enfolded Raven in her arms in greeting. "Well don't you look as beautiful as ever, what took you so long to get here?"

Raven grinned in pleasure as she hugged White Buffalo back. "I had a few delays I am afraid, but it is sure good to see you!"

White Buffalo stepped back as her husband elbowed her aside. "Do I get a hug too?"

Raven laughed then hugged Grey Wolf next.

Little Owl squealed in excitement and pushed her father aside in her eagerness to get to her friend. "I am so glad to see you, do I ever have a lot to tell you!"

Raven chuckled at her cousin by marriage as she hugged her. "I am sure you do."

Red Sparrow was next, but she was a little more reserved as she hugged Raven then she whispered in her ear. "I need to talk to you later about something very important."

Raven frowned perplexed, but nodded. She stood back before including both girls in her invitation. "You both can stay with me tonight if you want."

Red Sparrow smiled pleased as she stepped back to give Daniel his turn. "Okay I would like that."

Daniel lifted Raven right off her feet as he hugged her enthusiastically. "We all miss you guys you know!"

Raven grunted slightly at the ardent hug. "I have missed you too."

Welcoming hugs finished at last she was finally able to sit down by the fire. White Buffalo and her family sat on her right then Golden Eagle with his sister and Jake sat on her left. Dream Dancer, Running Wolf, Black Hawk, her grandfather, as well as the sheriff sat on the other side of the fire facing them.

Raven looked up with a smile of thanks when two of the women brought the newcomers food plus some mead. While she ate hungrily, she told them about the Badger Tribe being innocent as well as Red Eagle's banishment of Howling Coyote. Raven looked at the sheriff earnestly. "I can take you to where the war chief is hiding out!"

The sheriff shook his head negatively then motioned in reassurance. "Now that will not be necessary you have Devon's sister back safe and sound. We have Charles in custody; he will be tried as well as his men then probably hung. If you want, later when you get home you can come to my office and give me a written description of where they are. I will send it to the army; they can round them up if they wish."

Raven frowned uneasily as she gestured around at her people in fear. "What about my family, will the army come here as well?"

The sheriff smiled placatingly then shrugged calmly. "Not that I am aware of, but excuse me for now I must talk to the mayor for a moment I will be right back."

Raven nodded in confusion as he left before looking at her grandfather curiously. She frowned grimly as she gestured sharply in demand wanting answers now. "Okay, what is going on around here?"

Giant Bear leaned forward earnestly in apology as he raised a hand in supplication. "I am sorry Raven I was wrong to try forcing you and Golden Eagle to marry; I hope you can forgive me!"

Raven scowled forbiddingly in anger, as she thought over the last month, was it all for nothing then. She leaned forward intently before waving in aggravation. "Are you telling me the vision was wrong?"

Dream Dancer shook his head grimly as he took over the telling. They had all decided it would be best for him to tell her and he had agreed knowing how upsetting this announcement would be to her. "Not wrong Raven, but misinterpreted!"

Dream Dancer explained everything to the flabbergasted Raven.

*****

Michael stood at the back of the crowed watching Jessica longingly. He had not gone anywhere near her after he arrived. He knew she was aware that he was here, but he kept his distance not wanting to push her. He sat down dejectedly then tried hard to ignore the need to go to her.

*****

Rose frowned uneasily and turned her head away from the intense stare of the young buck sitting beside Black Hawk. He had stared at her fixedly the whole evening it was making her very uncomfortable; suddenly he was sitting beside her. She jumped slightly; she had not heard a sound.

Running Wolf moved over a little more until their legs were touching slightly.

Rose peeked at him through her lashes pretending to ignore him. The warm tingly sensation where their legs touched made her smile slightly in invitation.

Running Wolf's face softened as he looked at the beautiful Rose. "What is your name?"

Rose shook her head in confusion not understanding the language quite yet. "I do not know how to speak Cheyenne."

Running Wolf scowled perplexed she was Cheyenne also, how could she not understand him? He switched to English instantly. "I will teach you then."

Rose smiled hopefully and nodded eagerly. "I would like that."

Running Wolf leaned towards her then whispered in her ear suggestively.

Rose giggled in agreement, as they both got up before leaving together.

*****

Black Hawk had watched his son curiously off and on throughout the afternoon. He grinned knowingly as Running Wolf stared intently at the girl his aunt had brought with them. His son got up the courage to go talk to the tiny Rose finally then left. He nodded in approval; it was about time that his son found a mate. He would have to talk to White Buffalo later to find out where she came from so a formal offer for her could be made. He turned back to the conversation between Raven and the others.

Raven scowled incredulously at the grandfather then waved furiously. "I can't believe that you would think I would need your help finding a mate. I have been turning down offers for years grandfather I was not ready yet!"

Giant Bear visibly wilted as his favourite granddaughter berated him in front of the others.

Golden Eagle had been listening quietly not wanting to interfere. This was the first time since he had met the formidable chief that he showed his age. He had thought he would be delighted to see the old chief brought down a peg, but surprisingly he felt no satisfaction only pity for Giant Bear.

"RAVEN!"

Raven looked up in surprise as her grandmother towered above her in warning.

Golden Dove frowned down grimly as she motioned sharply in rebuke. "We will speak about that later in private!"

Raven turned and gazed at her grandfathers subdued appearance in surprise then sighed and nodded as she looked up in remorse. "Sorry grandmother you are right of course."

The sheriff came back a few minutes later then sat down oblivious to the strained silence around him as he grinned over at Raven ecstatically. "I talked to the mayor, the town council, and the townspeople that are here. When we get back to town, the mayor is going to start procedures with the government to make your land a reservation for your people. I hope that eases your mind about the army."

Raven stared at the sheriff speechless for a moment in amazement. "I did not think that was possible!"

The sheriff grinned in delight as he nodded in reassurance. "Of course it is! Now I am not saying the government will agree to this, but if the whole town is willing to support you, I can't see why not. Of course, Devon will have to agree as well since he is your neighbour, once he gives his approval we can get started right away. Since Charles will be hanged then his land confiscated the town will deed it to you as compensation for his crimes against you and your people. "

Raven stood up slowly almost in a dazed shock. The others around her got up as well; they all turned to face the grinning townspeople. She smiled in bemusement then motioned hopefully. "Are you sure that is what you want?"

The mayor stood up so that he could speak for all the others. "Raven, your people have been here for years now and never once have they caused any trouble. A few of us were unfortunately ready to drive them out when we found out about the guides, but we were wrong so wish to apologize by giving you this gift."

Raven with tears in her eyes went forward; the others all followed her as hugs then handshakes of thanks were passed around.

Giant Bear clapped his hands for quiet in demand as he turned to his braves. "Bring out the drums we will have a great celebration."

A cheer arose from the braves as they quickly raced out.

Giant Bear beckoned to several women that he knew could speak English and waved towards the townspeople as he gave them specific instructions.

The shaman built the fire up until it was almost touching the ceiling then one by one, the braves danced for the spellbound townspeople. The women the chief had talked to sat among the villagers and interpreted the meaning of each dance, so that they would not miss anything.

*****

Red Sparrow aware of Michael's longing gaze could take it no more, as she cornered Raven then motioned to her pleadingly. "Raven I must talk to you it is very important!"

Raven looked at the intense red head curiously before crooking her finger so that she would follow her towards the back of the tepee away from the noise and merrymaking. She frowned at the confused worried expression on Jessica's face. "What is the problem Red Sparrow you seem upset by something?"

Red Sparrow nodded forlornly as she explained about Michael as well as the difficulty she was experiencing. "I just do not know what to do?"

Raven reached over then took the bewildered red heads hand and asked the vital question. "Do you love him?"

Red Sparrow nodded grimly as she motioned decisively. "Yes, of course I do!"

Raven grinned in delight. "Well then there should be no problem if you love somebody that is all that is important."

Red Sparrow frowned unhappily, as she shook her head miserably. "But my family!"

Raven sighed in understanding having had that fear herself not to long ago, thinking she would have to go to England. She could not afford to lose the doctor either so she decided to tell Jess more about Michael, something only she knew. Hopefully, that would help her decide to stay here with him also. "That is a problem all right, but the doctor is right he can't leave his responsibilities here. Let me tell you a little secret about Michael and my people. All the townspeople here suspect, but do not really know how many Cheyenne actually stay here. Your doctor on the other hand has known since he started doctoring here five years ago, do you know how he knows that?"

Red Sparrow shook her head in confusion puzzled by where this was going. "No!"

Raven smiled trying to explain how dedicate to the people he was. "Well he knows because he comes every winter then immunizes and doctors my people against the white mens diseases. Do you know how much money it takes to get enough vaccine for all these people? Or how much he charges us to do this service?"

Red Sparrow frowned still baffled unsure what this has to do with her decision. "No!"

Raven chuckled at the bewildered Jessica as she held her thumb then index finger in a zero before putting it up to show Red Sparrow. "Zero! He will not accept a single penny for the vaccine or his time, which is how dedicated he is to all the people in both towns. I supply him with all the food he needs in return. In the five years that he has been with us not once have I seen him with a woman either and believe me there are many women in both towns that would gladly be his life partner. I have thought of it myself especially since he looks after my people, but respect we have unfortunately no love is there."

Raven laughed at the jealous look that crossed Red Sparrows face before continuing. "If he left what would my people do then? I know that your family is important to you, but someday the train will get to Michael's town. In another year or two we think, afterwards you can visit your family anytime you want. Besides it is not as if you do not know anyone here, grandmother and I can visit you or you can come visit us anytime you feel lonely."

Jess thought about everything Raven had said then reached out before hugging her in thanks. "I will be eternally grateful for your good advice, and you are right I would not want to deprive your people of Michael's generous heart."

Raven pushed Jessica away with a laugh of pleasure then waved for her to go. "You better hurry before I change my mind and go after that good looking doctor myself."

Red Sparrow chuckled not worried in the least then nodded and raced across the room searching for Michael. When she found him, she threw herself in his arms then looked at him adoringly as she framed his face lovingly. "Yes, I will marry you!"

Michael whooped ecstatically before grabbing her hand, and they escaped out of the tepee to be alone.

*****

Raven chuckled as she walked away then sat beside White Buffalo before nudging her and pointing at the door as the two lovebirds disappeared. "I think you have lost your sister to one very good looking doctor!"

White Buffalo looked then sighed knowingly in relief. She turned and smiled at Raven sadly. "Good I was hoping she would give in, but I will miss her dreadfully."

Raven nodded then motioned in reassurance. "Well I heard that the railroad was starting up again, someone somewhere bailed them out of bankruptcy again. This means that they should be here in a year or two depending on Indian raids and workers, of course."

Raven looked up in surprise as the braves started chanting for Golden Eagle insistently. She swung her gaze towards him in amazement as Black Hawk motioned for him to go up.

Golden Eagle rose, ignoring Raven's curious look then walked to the fire before dancing of his killing the buck and becoming a Cheyenne brave. He walked away when finished then smiled down at his sister in delight explaining to her what that was all about as he took a seat.

The chanting started again, and Black Hawk rose next then went to the fire to dance about the capture of the two white men who had shot Jake's son.

Janet had watched the chief's son fugitively all night in fascination. As he danced her eyes became dreamy, and she looked up at her brother seriously then pointed towards the brave insistently. "I am going to marry that man!"

Golden Eagle looked at his sister incredulously. "Black Hawk?"

Janet smiled pensively trying out his name in her head; she liked it. She inclined her head decisively at her brother. "Is that his name?"

Golden Eagle stared at his sister in disbelief before motioning in caution knowing Black Hawk would never leave here. "You are willing to stay in this village for the rest of your life?"

Janet nodded calmly as she waved negligently not upset by that at all. "Yes I am!"

Golden Eagle had a hard time imagining his pampered sister sleeping on the hard ground and living in a tepee. He gazed into her determined face then frowned his sister had changed; he could see it in her eyes. He gestured in warning. "His wife just died a few days ago in childbirth, but the baby lived!"

Janet sighed sadly at his lose before smiling in delight at the thought of a child she was unable to have any and had lamented that fact for years. "I will give him a month or so to mourn before I tell him!"

Golden Eagle laughed in delight as the unsuspecting Black Hawk made his way towards them then sat down.

Absolute silence prevailed as the drums quite unexpectedly for a few heart pounding seconds. Suddenly the banging of rocks and spears then the chanting for Raven began insistently.

Raven sighed as she got up obediently to the cheers of the waiting braves. Once in the center she began to dance and as had happened before Golden Eagle could not take his eyes of her.

Dream Dancer scooted over to interpret the dance for the spellbound Englishman. "Raven is describing the screams of a cougar then the fight between it and her wolves. She shows that she killed the cougar, but Bruno's mate is dead. She is now describing her inability to take the hide since the cougar was rabid. Desperately she frantically searches for a wound or blood on her wolf dog there is none, so Raven thanks the Great Spirit for saving her companion. She finishes by telling how the two of them burned then buried both animals. Now she is describing the escape of her and the vi'hoahI, Janet from the forest fire as well as the flood. She is showing their fight now to get to safety then their triumph as they prevailed so that the white woman can be reunited with her brother."

Golden Eagle looked at his sister after Raven finished and squeezed her in gratitude glad that she had survived all that. He turned to Dream Dancer with a nod. "Thank you!"

The braves all done the shaman let the fire die down as a few Indian women came in with furs then passed them out to the townspeople.

Giant Bear stood and addressed them solemnly. "It is getting late you are all welcomed to stay in here tonight. Tomorrow my people will make you breakfast, afterwards my braves will escort you safely part of the way back to your homes. Anyone wishing to come with me to examine the walls of this tepee before bed is more than welcomed too. I will explain what the symbols mean to anyone wishing to hear. Goodnight to all of you and may your dreams be filled with nothing but pleasantness."

The sheriff with most of the townspeople following Giant Bear eagerly listened.

Raven stood up then looked down at Golden Eagle. "You will have to take your sleeping pallet and take it to my grandmother's tepee to sleep there with the men. We women will be sleeping in mine tonight."

Golden Eagle frowned angrily having wanted to be alone with Raven, but obviously, he was not going to get his wish. He nodded grimly then got up and left sullenly.

Golden Dove stood up then faced Raven reassuringly. "We already have a tepee set up for White Buffalo as well as her family."

Raven shrugged dismissively. "Okay, but Little Owl as well as Red Sparrow want to stay with me tonight. Janet can come as well if she wishes."

Golden Dove nodded knowingly; it was obvious to her that Raven wanted to avoid Golden Eagle. "As you wish!"

Red Sparrow and Michael came back in just as they were leaving for bed. Jess spotted Daniel so went over to him before grabbing his arm pleadingly. "Will you marry us tomorrow?"

Daniel smiled down thoughtfully. "Is Michael going to stay here with us for a bit or is he leaving tomorrow with the others?"

Michael inclined his head decisively. "I will be staying Jess wants to remain until her sister leaves, so I will be staying with her as well."

Daniel grinned in relief. "Well I am not sure we will do it tomorrow then I will need to talk to my mother and Giant Bear to see when the best time is, but I promise I will marry you in the next couple of days, okay?"

Jess looked at Michael then turned back as they nodded reluctantly. "We will wait if we must."

Daniel chuckled at the downcast looks before pulling his younger aunt into a hug. "I promise only a day or two and congratulations to both of you."

Mell walked over then beckoned to Michael. "You can stay with us in the meantime."

Michael sighed dejectedly as he followed Mell out obediently.

Jessica, Patricia and Janet all followed Raven.

Spotted Owl walked up to Raven then waved towards the large corral reassuringly. "I unsaddled your horses for you everything is in your tepee."

Raven nodded her thanks before turning away.

The girls followed Raven but just before they entered; Golden Eagle waylaid them. "Raven I need to speak to you in private please!"

Raven turned to the girls and pointed at the entrance to her tepee in reassurance. "Go, I will be there in a minute."

They left obediently then Raven turned to the Englishman curiously.

Golden Eagle shifted nervously unsure what to say now; he cleared his throat before gesturing hopefully. "What do you want to do now that we do not need to get married to save your people?"

Raven sighed in irritation not actually having thought of it up until now. She shrugged grimly not wanting to talk about it, but she could tell by his face that he wanted an answer tonight. "Go our separate ways I guess. I am sure you and your sister want to return to England soon."

Golden Eagle frowned angrily as he waved in disbelief. "What about our one night together, can you pretend it never happened!"

Raven scowled decisively. "Of course, it was only the alcohol anyway!"

Raven turned away in finality then was brought up short in disbelief as Golden Eagle grabbed her and ground his lips against hers in demand. She struggled for a bit then melted against him as her passion flared once again.

Golden Eagle did not relent until he felt her body respond to his. He wrenched himself away and stood there for a moment breathing heavily. Without another word, he spun around before marching off his point made.

Raven stood there stunned as he left unexpectedly then shivered in desire as her body tingled all over wanting more. She ignored her body in disgust at its treacherous betrayal of her feelings. She did not want to love that man and that was final. She marched into her tepee her mind made up.

The girls talked then giggled for an hour until finally they fell into their furs around midnight for some much-needed sleep.

*****

Raven sat up with an anguished cry as her nightmare returned. She looked around, but thankfully, she had not disturbed anyone. She wiped the tears away furiously; Golden Eagle had left her again. She rocked herself forlornly, what would she do if he actually did go! Did she really, deep down want him to leave? Just thinking of the anguish she felt in her dreams as well as the empty hopeless feeling that she would have to live with made her shiver. Maybe she should give her and the Englishman a second chance; she could not live with herself if she did not for at least for a few months. This resolution in her mind, she layed down then dropped quickly into a dreamless asleep.

CHAPTER THIRTY

Raven woke with a feeling of peace and tranquillity as she thought of her decision last night. It was as if a massive burden had lifted of her shoulders as she got up eagerly looking forward to the future. She started a fire for coffee then just as she hoped the smell of the coffee roused the others.

The four girls sat around the fire laughing as they enjoyed the company talking excitedly about how bright the future looked for Raven and her Cheyenne tribe.

Raven called out in exasperation at a scratching on her door as it interrupted them. She did not want to go yet enjoying the company of other women for a change, instead of men. "Come in."

Golden Dove poked her head in then beckoned them to follow her impatiently. "Come on girls the townspeople are waiting for you so they can have breakfast."

They all jumped up before rushing out in anticipation as they followed Golden Dove. She led them into the tepee and immediately the sheriff then the mayor got up to shake everyone's hands, afterwards they all found seats around the fire pit. Coffee was handed out to the late comers.

Raven smiled around as she included everyone in her look. "I hope you all slept good last night."

The sheriff spoke for the villagers. "Yes we did, thank you."

Food was brought in by the women and passed around. There were smiles of delight at the eggs, bacon, slices of pork from the pig last night, as well as the bannock that was being handed out. Absolute quiet descended as everyone ate with silent gusto.

Raven looked around then frowned in surprise Golden Eagle, Jake, Black Hawk, and her brother were missing. She shrugged inwardly to herself they were probably out somewhere training or knowing her brother as she did, causing mischief somewhere.

Golden Dove smiled at her granddaughter in approval; she looked different this morning more relaxed without that angry scowl she had carried around since this mess had started. She looked over at her husband next then her expression softened, she had let him back in her bed last night. His face also showed his relief at having everything put back to rights.

Golden Dove looked down at her plate as she frowned in concern. She wondered if her granddaughter knew about Golden Eagle, maybe that is why she looked so happy this morning.

After everyone had finished eating, one more coffee was poured so that they could all relax before the long journey back. The sheriff finally stood as he shook hands with Raven, Giant Bear, the marshal, and everyone else as goodbyes were said.

Giant Bear led them out towards the paddocks then gestured at the sheriff in explanation. "I had my brave's saddle your horse's and hook up the wagons for you."

The sheriff inclined his head in approval. "Much obliged."

Colleen walked over to Raven then touched her arm to get her attention. "We decided to accept your offer and go stay with you at the ranch. Neither of us has family or anything in Scotland anymore if the offer is still available that is?"

Raven reached over then hugged Colleen in reassurance. "Of course it is! I will have cabins built for both of you right away. As soon as they are ready I will let you know."

Colleen nodded in relief as she went over to Priscilla. They got into their wagons now with no more worries about the future. The three prisoners were put in the wagons with the women also. There was an armed guard riding right behind the wagon watching them closely

The sheriff mounted and looked down at Raven to confirm the conversation they had yesterday. "Come in to my office as soon as you can since the Englishman has given his consent for the reservation. Devon also said that you have full authority on his land as well now that he has gone back to England. Whatever you decide to do is fine with him, he said for you to send him a letter in Sussex then he will sign any legal forms you need signed."

He tipped his hat cordially before turning away without further discussion leading the villager's home, unaware of the bombshell he had just dropped on the unsuspecting Raven.

Raven frowned in confusion as she turned to her grandmother inquisitively. She motioned in bewilderment. "What did he mean by that?"

Golden Dove sighed resignedly; well that look on her granddaughters face answered the question she had asked herself earlier. Raven obviously did not know he was gone. She reached over to take her granddaughters hand in sympathy, but there was no easy way to tell her this. "Golden Eagle left last night dear, he said he was going back to England. Dream Dancer, Jake, and Black Hawk went with him to Malta. He went to catch the stage there then he is going to the first town that has a railroad so that he can take a train to Boston. He left instructions with the sheriff so that the land was given to you in trust; you could do anything you want with it except sell it of course."

Raven scowled incredulously she had not even considered the fact that he would leave during the night without Janet. She waved over at Janet in bewilderment. "But he can't be gone, Janet is still here!"

Janet stepped forward with an angry grimace as she gestured sharply furious at her brother for his desertion. "Well I did tell him last night I was staying here, but I did not think he would be leaving in the middle of the night without saying goodbye to me at least!"

Raven looked at White Buffalo in panic wondering what to do now as that sense of hopeless despair settled over her almost immediately.

White Buffalo sensing Raven's desperate wretchedness and understanding stepped forward quickly. She pointed towards Malta in demand. "Well do not just stand here! Go get him!"

Raven shook her head undecided; she could not force him to stay if he wanted to go! Could she?

Jessica grabbed Raven's arm in pleading. When Raven turned to her, Red Sparrow squeezed her arm in encouragement. "What did you tell me just last night if you love him that is all that matters? I agree with my sister go get him before it's too late!"

Giant Bear stood there helplessly watching his granddaughter's anguished expression not sure, if he should say anything or not. Afraid to interfere again, but as the minutes ticked by he could not take it anymore. He stepped forward when Jessica released her then grabbed her arms as he shook her trying to get her to see sense. "Raven you must follow your heart! I was not going to say anything because I had already messed things up for you once, but now I think I must! When you were a child, the shaman saw you as the 'Protector' of our people, but he also saw a golden eagle by your side. We did not know what it meant at the time, I now know though that you and Devon were meant for each other right from birth. Please do not throw away that love because this old fool made a mistake. Your mother had that love with your father; I also have that kind of love with your grandmother. Now go before you regret this for the rest of your life!"

Raven stared at her grandfather grimly then suddenly she threw her arms around him ecstatically and gave him a fierce hug before racing towards her tepee. As she ran, she whistled urgently for her stallion.

Brave Hearts head lifted at the urgent request then raced towards the fence at a full gallop. Clearing it in one mighty leap, he raced towards his mistress's tepee.

Raven came out a few minutes later and quickly saddled her stallion, luckily her saddlebags were still full not having gotten around to emptying them. She vaulted onto his back before galloping out of the village without once looking back. A life without Golden Eagle would leave her miserable for the rest of her life. She frantically prayed to the Great Spirit that she would not be too late.

*****

Golden Dove reached over then took her husbands hand as she smiled at him in praise. "You did well love that was a very nice speech you made."

Giant Bear hugged his wife in appreciation, as he looked around at all the admiring grinning faces around him. He stood straighter; his dignity restored to him once more as he beckoned everyone to follow him.

They all turned away, each one of them prayed that Raven would make it in time as they went back to the ceremonial tepee. Already they were discussing when the best time for a triple wedding would be. Since Daniel would not only marry Jess and the doctor, but Running wolf wanted to marry Black Rose also. Now hopefully, Raven would be marrying Golden Eagle too.

*****

Dream Dancer frowned uneasily as he looked over at his friend as they approached the stagecoach building. "Are you sure this is what you want Golden Eagle?"

Golden Eagle nodded decisively as he gestured in finality. "I am sure!"

Dream Dancer looked at his uncle then over at Jake grimly, afraid of what would happen next.

Black Hawk shrugged sadly at his nephew's despairing expression. "It is his choice we cannot force him to stay here. That was tried already with almost disastrous consequences!"

Dream Dancer wilted in agreement, as he sighed forlornly, his uncle was right of course. They all dismounted before following Golden Eagle inside and waited while he paid for his ticket. They took seats to stay with him until it was time to leave all of them were reluctant to leave him just in case he changed his mind suddenly.

Black Hawk turned to Golden Eagle inquisitively as he gestured curiously. "Are you taking your stallion with you?"

Devon frowned thoughtfully unsure if it were a good idea to expose his horse to the rigours of ship life. "I do not know if I should, do you think he will be okay on a ship?"

Dream Dancer leaned forward then nodded in reassurance as he looked around his uncle so that he could talk to the Englishman. "Sure he will I will be taking my horse's with me. Just tie him to the back of the stage coach."

Golden Eagle inclined his head in relief. "Good I would hate to leave him here."

They all got up as the stagecoach driver beckoned them to come; it was time to go. Once outside Jake stepped forward first as he clasped the Englishman's hand firmly in parting. He shook his head sadly in sorrow. "You take care of yourself; I am sorry it did not work out between you and Raven."

Golden Eagle scowled grimly in warning then motioned in anxiety. "You take care of her for me and if she needs anything you have my address just send me a letter or telegram."

Jake sighed unhappily in agreement, as he stepped back to let Black Hawk say goodbye next.

Golden Eagle embraced Raven's uncle then released him. Black Hawk smiled sadly, as he moved back. "You keep up your training now you hear."

Golden Eagle gestured decisively. "You bet I will!"

Dream Dancer waited for his uncle to finish, and then grabbed his friend in a fierce embrace of farewell. "I will miss you blood brother take care of yourself."

Golden Eagle stepped back reluctantly as he grinned fondly. "I will, do not worry so much I will be seeing you next fall in England remember."

Dream Dancer nodded sorrowfully and stepped back as they watched their friend tie his stallion to the back of the stage before disappearing inside.

The burly driver cracked his whip loudly in demand before snapping the reins as he bellowed insistently. "Get up there!"

Jake turned to the other two with a disgruntled smile then waved up the street in invitation. "Come on you two I will buy you guys a drink so that we can drown our sorrow in alcohol. They say it is the best medicine for broken hearts, we can have lunch while we are at it."

Dream Dancer and Black Hawk agreed gloomily before untying their horse's as they walked across the street then down past the sheriff's office and into the saloon.

*****

Raven cut across the country it was shorter than the way the sheriff went, but it was impassable by wagon. Even with this shorter route, she still would not get to Malta until midnight if she were lucky. She knew that she would not find Golden Eagle there, he was probably already on board the stage.

Raven did hope to catch him in the next town though; if he got on a train before she could get to him, it would be too late. She bent closer to her stallion's neck asking for more speed desperately at the idea that she might never see him again.

*****

Jake looked at Black Hawk blearily. "I tink we're drunk!"

Black Hawk laughed uproariously in amusement as he slapped Jake consolingly. "I tink we are beyond dat me friend. What's the time anyways?"

The large red headed Irish saloonkeeper chuckled as he refilled their glasses. "It is eleven or there abouts."

Dream Dancer groaned as he stared at the whisky in his glass as if it were going to jump up and bite him. He was not even sure if he could drink it without falling over. "I tink we's should goes or I might ends on floor!"

Black Hawk snickered then putting on a stoic expression; he grabbed his glass one more time and raised it to his companions in a toast to their friend. "Ere's to Devon may is trip ome be with no ardships."

The other two nodded decisively in agreement then reluctantly downed the whisky before turning for the door as they waved goodbye to the saloonkeeper. They were only half way across the saloon weaving badly when the doors flew open violently as a desperate Raven rushed in having seen their horses tied outside.

The three men stopped guiltily as Raven rushed up to them in a panic. "Where is he?"

Dream Dancer wobbled slightly as he tried to focus on his sister. "Goners took stage at noonish."

Raven eyed the three men in disapproval; obviously, they had been here all this time since they could hardly stand up straight. She beckoned them back to the counter impatiently and frowned at Sam. "We will need four coffees, something to eat to please."

Sam nodded with a grin of understanding. "Sure Raven, coming right up. Oh, by the way what happened out at your place I have not seen hide nor hair of the sheriff or mayor?"

Raven waved calmly in reassurance. "They should be here tomorrow sometime; probably late depending on how often they stop."

Sam inclined his head in relief, but did not ask any more questions knowing that he would find out more from the sheriff as soon as he got to town. He turned away then went into the kitchen in order to see if there was stew left from earlier.

Raven motioned to the three men, and they went to sit at a table in the back were they would not be disturbed. She sat forward intently then pointed at the three of them in anger. "One of you could have woken me to tell me he was leaving. Or better yet you could have stopped him at least until morning!"

Black Hawk shrugged in aggravation. "What ya want us to do hog ties im for's ya!"

Dream Dancer chuckled at that thought he had wanted to earlier, but he sobered as his wild sister swung her gaze towards him in anger. He raised his hands placatingly. "He tolls us you does no want im to stay."

A pretty slightly plump brown haired barmaid brought the stew. She peeked over at Dream Dancer longingly.

Jake seeing the look elbowed Black Hawk knowingly and tipped his head for him to look discreetly so that Raven would not notice.

Black Hawk smirked in delight then nodded slightly at Jake in drunken humour.

Raven waited until the barmaid left before motioning in annoyance, not having noticed the byplay between her uncle and foreman. "Well none of you are sober enough to come with me so stay here until I get back. Hopefully, I can catch the stage before or in the next town."

Dream Dancer hiccupped then smiled eagerly in foolish delight. "Yous chang yours mind abouts Evon?"

Raven nodded decisively. "Yes I did!"

Black Hawk and Jake grinned at each other. Jake snickered knowingly; he poked Ravens uncle hard, in an I told you so manner. He leaned over slightly then whispered conspiringly, or thought he did anyway. "Women day chang dar minds at da last moments!"

Black Hawk laughed in agreement.

Raven scowled ferociously at the two drunken men having heard that loud whisper and leaned forward in demand as she pointed at them in challenge. "Is that supposed to be funny?"

Both men turned to Raven, with identical innocent bleary looks.

Raven harrumphed in disgust as she put the last spoonful in her mouth before rising angrily. "I must go, wait here until noon tomorrow if I am not back by then you can head home."

The three nodded as Raven rushed out.

Black Hawk chuckled in delight. "Didst no pay da bill do she?"

Jake laughed knowingly in agreement before nudging Black Hawk suggestively as he pointed over at the barmaid standing at the bar still sending longing glances at Dream Dancer.

Black Hawk nodded in permission so Jake got up and walked over to her then discreetly passed her some money.

Lily slipped the money in her bodice with an incline of her head of assurance and pleasure then walked over to help Dream Dancer up. "Come on honey, I will show ya to your room."

The young Earl looked down at his uncle and foreman in confusion. "What's about yous?"

Black Hawk chuckled then waved for him to go. "We knows where our room are, you's goes with Lily."

They both laughed drunkenly in delight as Dream Dancer stumbled on the stairs.

Jake yelled out to the barkeep as he banged on the table insistently. "Mores whisky Sam we's now celebratin!"

Sam snickered knowingly in approval as his barmaid disappeared upstairs with the young Earl and obediently brought the other two another whisky.

*****

The sun was coming up when Raven reluctantly slowed her horse; they all needed a rest as much as she could wish differently. She looked down at Bruno. "We will walk for half an hour then stop for a rest I promise."

Bruno yelped tiredly in agreement. Raven laughed as she looked down; Bruno's tongue was hanging out on the left side of his muzzle, and it looked hilarious.

Raven reached down then patted Brave Heart's sweat encrusted neck in apology. "How are you holding up old boy?"

Brave Heart blew hard in a loud woof through his nostrils almost in rebuke as he breathed heavily in exhaustion.

Raven grimaced in agreement almost asleep in her saddle. She crested a hill and saw a valley down below with a creek. It was not a large creek so easily fordable, she decided to cross first then make a quick camp for something to eat and hopefully a couple hours of sleep. It was a little to open down below for her liking, but with Bruno around to give warning of any danger or of strangers coming, it would have to do. So she shrugged resignedly then trotted down the hill and across the creek.

Raven unsaddled her horse then rubbed him down; afterwards she checked his legs and hooves before satisfied she fed him. She rummaged in her pack for jerky as well as hardtack. She sat on her bedroll then fed half her lunch to Bruno.

Suddenly Bruno growled and got up before looking up at the top of the hill intently that they would be climbing after a brief rest.

Raven jumped up with her rifle ready then looked up.

On top of the hill, stood a horse with a rider, they were staring down intently at them. The sun, an abnormally large orange ball of fire just rising over the opposite hill shone directly on him. The position of the sun and rider made the horse he was sitting on appear white, as did his hair.

Raven inhaled in shock then dropped the rifle before racing towards the hill and to the man of her dreams

*****

Devon looked down speculatively, but the sun was almost blinding him so he could not see anything.

The coach he had taken yesterday had finally reached the next town early this morning. He had gone into the hotel to eat, after being informed that it would be an hour or two's wait as they changed the exhausted horses. He had tried sleeping in the coach, but every time he closed his eyes, an image of Raven would appear.

Devon had walked into the hotel grumpy very out of sorts, but felt better after he ate. He was drinking one more cup of tea when a woman walked in; he caught his breath in hope until the black haired lady turned then met his grey eyes with her blue ones.

Devon's heart plummeted instantly in disappointment so he got up and paid for his breakfast before leaving. He walked to the stage then stopped in excitement as a woman with black hair done in two long Indian braids stood arguing with the driver. She turned away angrily and stared at Devon disgruntled for a moment before stalking away furiously. He wilted as the brown eyed woman marched passed him.

Devon walked up to his horse then stroked him soothingly. Devil shifted uneasily before nudging his master impatiently as he craned his neck staring longingly back the way they had come.

Devon sighed forlornly at his horse and looked back also. Suddenly, without thought or hesitation he untied Devil then turned him around before jumping up and galloped out of town heading back the way they had come. Now here he sat looking down hopefully one more time at another black haired woman.

The sun blinded Devon for a moment, so he had to shade his eyes to see anything. He saw the woman running suddenly then he kicked his horse in excitement down the hill screaming her name. "RAVEN!!"

Raven stopped, as the horse got closer and lifted her arms up as he bent than swooped her up in front of him kissing her ecstatically as she clung to him.

Devon stopped his horse and jumped down before holding his arms up for Raven. He knew that if she accepted him now it would be forever. No longer would he be called Devon, but from this day forward, he would be known as Golden Eagle a Cheyenne brave of the Wolf tribe.

Without any more hesitation, Raven slid into his arms gladly. Golden Eagle gently laid her down in the grass whispering love words in between kisses.

Raven clung to him crying in relief, refusing to let him go afraid he would disappear again as he had in her dreams.

They made love ferociously unable to get enough of each other; afterwards they both fell asleep unable to stay awake for another moment. As sleep claimed them, a grinning ecstatic Dream Dancer chanting a love song entered both their dreams. In his hand was a dream catcher with their likenesses painted inside. They both knew this was no dream as the most powerful shaman in history lifted the dream catcher up towards the Great Spirit. Shooting stars danced all around him as if in celebration as if God, Heammawihio, their Great Spirit were pleased!

EPILOGUE

Dream Dancer hugged his sister fiercely in farewell. "I love you! I will miss you terribly while I am gone. You take care of that new husband of yours; try to keep him out of trouble. Remember if you need me I will know then come back!"

Raven stepped back and wiped tears from her eyes as she motioned plaintively. "I love you too! Are you sure you do not want us to come to Boston with you, I do not like the fact that you are going alone."

Dream Dancer smiled reassuringly at his sister as he reached out then squeezed her hand in assurance. "I will be fine Raven I must do this alone it is my destiny. Besides, you still need to help grandfather. I will write you when I get to Boston before I leave for England I promise!"

Golden Eagle standing behind Raven put his arm around his wife as he pulled her back against his side in rebuke. He looked at her chidingly as she looked up at him. "Let your brother be Raven he will make out all right. He must do what he thinks best, besides he will be riding with White Buffalo and Grey Wolf to North Dakota before catching a train to Boston. They will not let him get into any trouble I am sure!"

Golden Eagle let go of his wife as he turned to his young brother-in-law. He bowed deeply in farewell. "You take care of yourself Earl Edward William Charles Summerset, always remember my training. I know that you will do fine in England."

Edward smiled in gratitude as Lord Devon Rochester stood up then he stepped forward and clasped Golden Eagle's arm in the traditional Cheyenne way as he grinned at his new friend. "Goodbye blood brother

I will remember your teachings. You take care of my sister for me; please try to make sure she does not get into anymore mischief."

Both men chuckled knowingly at an indignant huff behind them then Edward turned away without another word and walked to his horses. There were three of them in total; the gelding he had trained then rode since he was eleven years old. A mare that was being used as a packhorse, but eventually he would breed. Plus his gift from Raven a coal black two-year-old stallion he would use in England as a stud. He had named him Cheyenne to remind him of his home roots and the other half of himself.

*****

Edward was jerked awake by the loud call of the conductor as he yelled out loudly so that everyone could hear him above the noise of the train. "One hour to Boston folks!"

Edward smiled in anticipation then sighed thankfully as he sat up with a giant yawn finally he was here. He continued thinking of his journey here; he had ridden across Montana into North Dakota with Melissa and her husband Jed. He had stayed with them for two days, but Mell was too busy getting her towns back in shape after being gone for almost two months. He had laughed when he had heard her mumbling under her breath about how incompetent her deputy marshal's were. It would have been rude of him not to stay at least two days though since they had asked him to while travelling

Edward roused himself pushing his thoughts of home away as he looked out the window in anticipation not wanting to miss anything. His first sight caused him to sigh in disappointment; it looked exactly like the towns close to the ranch except it was much bigger. It was also disgustingly dirty, compared to their villages.

The Great Spirit had promised him he would get help here; how, he was supposed to find anyone in this vast city was beyond him. Why he needed help from someone not of his own people baffled him, but he knew it would be revealed to him when the time came.

The train slowed, so Edward shook off his reflective mood then grabbed his gear that he had put on the seat beside him so nobody else could sit with him and headed towards the rear compartments where his horse's were kept. He arrived just in time as he heard his stallion scream in anger then saw him rear. He ran towards the idiot trying to lead his stud out of his stall. "Stop, get away from that horse before you get yourself killed!"

The tall burly man backed off immediately as the young fellow grabbed the lead rope away from him.

Edward's voice lowered soothingly as he talked calmly in Cheyenne to quiet the agitated stallion. The stocky black stood there quivering and blowing hard, but his ears perked forward listening attentively to his master's quiet reassurances then he calmed down once more.

The young Earl heard the other man mumble irritably under his breath as he shook his head in disgust. "Damn Indians and their horses!"

Edward frowned angrily at the man's prejudice comment, but did not criticize him it would not help anyway. As the train came to a full halt, the large door dropped to the ground. He led his stallion out then tied him securely to the hitching rail; even though he knew the stud would not stray unless spooked, there was way too much noise and people to take that chance. He raced back up the platform then went to get his mare. He tightened the mare's packs before leading her out to stand beside the stallion.

The man who had tried to lead his stallion out came with his more passive gelding, and Edward nodded his thanks then tied him up as well before heading into the train station. Once he had directions, he went back out and tied his stallions lead rope to his gelding after untying him then tied his mare on the opposite side of his saddle. He finally mounted and headed north.

His sister with the help of their lawyer had made all the arrangements for him. He would stay in Boston for three days before catching a ship to England where he would be met by another lawyer then taken to one of his townhouses. There, he would be outfitted in the proper clothing so that he could be taken to the Queen to be properly introduced.

All the arrangements were already made for his schooling; he was to start at Oxford in the fall. His English grandfather on his father's side had attended the same school. Hopefully, in a few years he would be a full doctor. At first, he had wanted to be a lawyer, but his blood brother advised him to become a doctor instead. That way he could help people with his powers, and they would not be any the wiser.

Edward looked around curiously as the buildings got smaller then cruder with a lot more garbage lying around. He noticed a group of men standing together, so he slowed curiously. He had never seen people like them before. Jed had warned him that he probably would see them here; he had called them Orientals. They had coal black hair done in a long braid down their backs some almost to their hips. They were dark skinned like his people, but their skin had a bit of a yellowish tinge. Their eyes were anywhere between a deep brown to black with a slight tilt some upward and some downward depending on where they lived, most of them wore funny looking clothes.

Jed had also told him that they were treated worse than the Indian tribes and that most laboured in mines or on the railroad. He said they were treated like slaves, so most of them died from starvation or diseases.

Edward rode on then shook his head sadly most of the time he was terribly ashamed of his white blood. He turned onto his street and continued on. As he rode along, the houses got better kept as well as more expensive. He saw the hotel so turned into the stables. He dismounted then led his horses in.

A large bulky dark haired bear of a man in an apron bustled up to him and knuckled his forehead in respect. "What can I do for ya young sir?"

Edward nodded cordially back. "I am booked into the hotel for three days can you look after my horse's for me? Be careful of the stallion though!"

The man inclined his head in agreement then turned and bellowed loudly to someone in the back. "Hey Chink comes out den take dose hoses en feed em!"

A little Chinaman came out of the back room then shuffled towards them. He put his two hands together as if in prayer and bowed slightly, but not once did he look at the big stableman. "As you wish!"

The little man walked over to the black first then unhooked his lead rope.

The stallion rolled his eyes angrily and backed away with a warning snort ready to rear up.

The Chinaman reached out then touched the stallion's nose calmly before talking soothingly to him in a strange language.

The stud's ears perked up and he calmed almost immediately as he followed the little man docilely.

Edward shook his head in disbelief that was the first time his stallion had allowed anyone near him without hardly any fuss. Satisfied his horse's were in good hands, he pulled off his main saddlebag that had some of his clothes in before turning to the stableman then tossed him a half dollar. "Please have the rest of my packs brought to my room."

Edward waited until he saw the nod of agreement from him before turning to the little Chinaman as he came to take the mare. He handed him a coin and smiled his thanks.

The little man bowed again with his hands pressed together, but a little deeper this time. "Thank you my Lord."

When the Chinaman stood back up he looked up at the young man then stared into his eyes intently for a long moment assessingly. A slight curve of his lips showed his approval before he took the mares rope and unhooked her then led her away without comment.

Edward frowned in puzzlement, when the little man had looked into his eyes; he had felt a slight tingle of something. Almost of recognition and anticipation, but he had never seen him before that he knew of. He shrugged uneasily slightly disconcerted then left. He went to the front door and entered the lobby then looked around curiously. The counter was on his left and to his right was a stairway leading up to the rooms, just past that was a door that Edward assumed led into the dinning room. He walked up to the counter then saw a little bell on top, so he rang for service.

A huge barrel of a man came out of the back rooms and nodded in acknowledgement. "Yes sir may I help you?"

Edward smiled in surprise; the man was enormous at least thee hundred pounds if not more, but he was shorter than the young Earl was. He resembled the stableman slightly, so Edward guessed that they were probably brothers.

The hotel clerk was assessing Edward just as intently, he eyed the light brown almost blonde auburn streaked hair and dark green-eyed stranger curiously. He wondered if this was the young Earl, he had been instructed to watch for. If it were, he was tall for sixteen at six foot already. The clerk liked the honest straightforward expression of the young man.

Edward reached across the counter so that he could shake the hotel clerks hand in greeting. The clerk approved of the firm, but not crushing handshake the young man gave him as he grinned knowingly. "Names, Edwin Burke."

Edward inclined his head as he released Edwin's hand. "I am Earl Summerset, but my friends call me Edward."

Edwin nodded in delight his suspicion confirmed. "I have been expecting you."

Edwin reached under the counter then pulled out his special key that only a few were ever privileged to use before walking around the counter. He beckoned the young Earl to follow him.

Edward obediently trailed the clerk; he was led towards the door of the dinning room. He turned right then walked under the main stairway that lead up to the rooms. The young Earl had not noticed the hallway on his first inspection. There was one door down the hallway, and the massive clerk almost did not fit. He unlocked the door before opening it with a flourish then waved for the young man to precede him. He handed the key to the Earl as he walked past.

Edward walked in, and his eyes widened in surprise. The room was done up in royal blue colours, it was enormous. It even had its own bathtub off to the right partially hidden by a screen. The bed was round it would hold three people comfortably without crowding each other; he was sure. He turned to the fireplace then smiled in satisfaction; they had clearly expected him today since a fire was already crackling cheerily inside. He turned with a grin of pleasure and appreciation to the innkeeper. He dug out a silver dollar for a tip in thanks. "It is beautiful!"

Edwin waved off the tip with a smile of pleasure at the young Earl's obviously delight in his room. "No need for that it has already been taken care of, so under no circumstances are you to tip anyone here.

Your lawyer already made sure that everyone was looked after. Now Susan will be here soon, she will take care of all your needs while you are here. The rest of your saddlebags will be delivered directly, so enjoy your stay with us Earl Summerset.

Edward nodded pleased, he was confident that he would. He watched the stout innkeeper close the door then dropped down on the bed with a satisfied sigh as he fell asleep almost instantly.

*****

It was getting late when Edward left the hotel to go to the saloon Edwin had recommended. He had turned seventeen yesterday, but had been unable to celebrate that fact on the train. He decided to do so tonight; he was about halfway there when he felt a prickle of warning on the back of his neck. His hand dropped to his gun immediately as he spun around looking for whoever was watching him so intently, but nobody was there.

Edward frowned perplexed as he looked everywhere, but to no avail. That feeling of being watched did not go away, however. He shrugged dismissively then turned back around and continued on. The young earl released his gun then chuckled at his foolishness. The gun was a new addition to his wardrobe and a gift from Mell. She had insisted on teaching him how to use it, but he knew deep down that he would not be able to kill anyone unless given no choice. It just was not in him, he was a healer not a killer.

Edward was close to the saloon when he heard a woman scream in terror off to his left. The dreadful sound came from an alley in-between two buildings. Instantly the young earl raced in that direction so that he could help whoever was in trouble. He was halfway down the alleyway when he heard a grunt of effort then a fainter call for help. His pace quickened as he saw two men struggling with a young woman, she was on the ground sobbing hysterically as one man held her down while the other one was in the process of raping her.

The young Earl did not even hesitate for a second as he grabbed the man lying on the woman and he heaved him bodily across the alleyway off her.

The man holding the woman down jumped up in surprise then went for his gun.

Edward was faster as his left foot rose rapidly connecting under the man's jaw.

Instantly the man dropped stunned to the ground.

The man Edward had thrown across the alley raced back towards the young man.

The young Earl crouched readying himself as both arms came up in a fighting stance that he had learned from his uncle and Mell.

The rapist wanted nothing to do with the towering stranger though. He got to his friend then helped him up before both men turned tail and fled.

Edward waited for a few moments to make sure that they were not coming back. Once sure they were gone, he relaxed his stance then dropped down beside the sobbing girl. He looked around making sure nobody was around before eyeing the girl in contemplation obviously he had been too late, and she had been raped at least once. He frowned angrily maybe he should go after those men after all to make them pay for what they had done as he looked at the girl a little more closely. She could not be more than fifteen, and judging by the coal black hair dusky yellow skin she was Chinese like the man in the stables. The Earl moved closer to the girl then rubbed his hands together chanting softly in Cheyenne.

The girl stopped sobbing suddenly as she listened to the big man above her chanting she could not understand what he was saying, but it calmed her to listen to him. She watched curiously, as he continued to rub his hands together before reaching out to her and she automatically flinched away thinking he wanted to hurt her too.

Edward never once wavered or stopped his chanting as he brought Dream Dancer to the surface then reached out with his hot hands towards the girl, not letting her fear stop him. He laid one hand on her forehead and one hand on her stomach still chanting in Cheyenne. This was only the third time he had done this, the first time was by accident with his brother-in-law then the next time had been with Jake's son after he had been shot. He was not sure he could even do it here away from his people and homeland, but he did not let that stop him as he tried to help the girl's body heal itself.

When Dream Dancer's hands touched her he was surprised to feel a burning jolt race up his arms, it took all his concentration to continue as he felt his healing powers reluctantly come to life once more. The shock was something new; he had not felt that with the other two. He felt the power in his hands wane then he released the girl abruptly as he sat back on his haunches rubbing his hands together painfully. He dropped his head in his hands for a moment hoping the slightly woozy feeling in his head would not last long. He sighed in relief as the feeling subsided after only a few minutes, she had not been hurt that badly.

The girl smiled gratefully at the strange young man sitting in front of her. She was not sure what he had done, but she felt warm and tingly. Suddenly her eyes widened in stunned disbelief at something behind him. Instantly she got to her knees then knelt with head bowed as her two small hands came together in a prayer like position and she started babbling in her own language fearfully.

Edward spun around quickly then crouched unsure what had her so upset. He looked up in surprise at the little man from the stables that had looked after his horse's.

The man stared down at the girl in disapproval as she continued to babble incoherently. Finally, his hand came down in a sharp silencing motion as he spoke harshly to her in his own language. Instantly the girl quieted, and she bowed down deeper. Now her forehead was almost pressed against the little man's feet as she listened to him respectfully.

She jumped up suddenly without warning then bowed to the Oriental man first and to her rescuer without looking at either of them then scurried away as fast as she could go.

The man stared after his granddaughter reflectively; she had disobeyed him again this time with disastrous consequences, but he would deal with her later. He turned slightly and regarded the young Earl intently staring down into the dark green eyes relentlessly. Waiting for him to turn away, as every white man had done since he had arrived here searching for his destiny. To his surprise though, the young man's gaze never once wavered. He watched in fascination as Edward's eyes darkened from a dark green to such a deep green that his eyes were now almost black. He had watched the young man kick his opponent then crouch in a fighting stance, and he had been pleased to see that. Even though the young Earl had a gun, he had never made one move towards it as he had done earlier while he had watched him so intently. It was good the boy had such good instincts; he was obviously a fighter not a killer as he had demonstrated while saving his granddaughter. Now that Edward's eyes were very black, he could feel the chaotic power radiating from him. He had felt it slightly earlier in the stables, which was why he had looked at him so intently.

Dream Dancer forced to the surface stared up just as fixedly refusing to relent then he felt his power surge in his body as his eyes changed. The power tingled in his body wanting to be released it scared him badly. This had never happened to him before the man was doing something to him.

Dream Dancer refused to look away though knowing deep down if he did; it would be disastrous for him. He knew he had to bury his power somehow; it was almost beyond his control now. So chanting softly he slowed his heartbeat down a little at a time, he could feel the blood in his veins slowing as well as he relaxed every part of his body one muscle at a time. His uncle had taught him to do this when using the bow and arrows. As his body then his heart relaxed so to did the power and Edward could feel his eyes changing back to their usual dark green. Still he refused to look away form the little man.

Unexpectedly the Oriental released the young Earl's gaze, as he stepped back he clapped twice in admiration before bowing deeply with both hands pressed together in respect. His bow this time was deeper than it had been this afternoon. "You have saved my granddaughter, I owe you a debt. To repay this debt I will accompany you on your travels and teach you how to control your powers, your mind, as well as your body. This is my destiny I have been waiting a long time for you!"

Edward frowned slightly confused then stood up to his full height and looked down at the little man who still stood bent over. "You cannot come with me I am going to England in a couple of days!"

The man stood back up then inclined his head at the Earl knowingly. "I have knowledge of this already, even if I have to pursue you from a distance I will still follow. Your powers are strong, but without my help, you will not be able to use them to their full potential. Without my help, they will also become unmanageable for you one day!"

Edward grimaced in anxiety; he had been afraid of that for so long now. He smiled suddenly before nodding pleased, the Great Spirit had not steered him wrong he had found the help he knew deep down he had needed. His sister had been worried because it had been so long since they had a shaman with Dream Dancer's ability. There had been no one to teach him how to manage the power that had just begun to grow stronger. He felt relief as the two walked out of the alleyway together.

Edward looked sideways at the little man. "What should I call you?"

The Little man looked up in amusement. "Dao Ba Zevak Hajime. The meaning of my name is complex; Dao means sword in Chinese. Ba is Vietnamese, and it means third. Zevak is Hebrew it means, sacrifice. Hajime is Japanese; it means beginning. To make it easier for you just call me Dao, or you can call me teacher if you prefer."

Edward smiled curiously, as he tried to figure out why the Oriental would have a name that means so many different things. If his people were anything like theirs a meaning or warning would be hidden in his name, but sword, third, sacrifice, and beginning just did not make much sense to him. "I take it you are not full Chinese than? Is there a specific reason for your name?"

Dao shrugged as he looked up at the Earl. "You are correct I am not full Chinese, but a mixture of cultures. Why this is so has not been revealed to me as of yet. Our names always have great meaning, but why is not always revealed to use until the end of our lives."

Edward nodded thoughtfully. "I will call you Dao in public and teacher when we are alone. You can call me Edward or Dream Dancer that is my Cheyenne name."

Dao grinned teasingly then chuckled in amusement. "I will call you Earl Summerset in public and Dream Dancer in private it suits you best."

When Edward took his teacher back to the hotel, he arranged to purchase Dao's bondage papers then freed him. In the morning, he would seek out all the papers for Dao's family as well and release them too.

The Earl had a cot put in his room for the mixed Oriental. As predicted Dao refused to leave his new students side; always he stayed one-step behind respectfully in public. In private, he became Dream Dancer's shadow teacher.

*****

Here ends the book of Raven and the Golden Eagle.

Coming soon, my third book in the White Buffalo (New Beginnings) Series:

Dream Dancer and the Celtic Witch.

Earl Edward Summerset the three quarter Cheyenne youth, known to his people as Dream Dancer, finally becomes a full doctor. He learns as he grows older the intricacies, power, and the betrayal that the English nobility is capable of! As his power grows within him, he must learn to become just like the people that would use him cold and secretive.

Dream Dancer becomes drawn unexpectedly into a battle to save a reluctant Welsh heiress from the evil clutches of her cousin. Will he succeed in helping her or will he find himself in more danger then he ever thought possible as a power lying dormant since the beginning of time comes to life as it senses a way to be released! It tries to gain control of him through the Welsh Witch; thwarted by another power it must find another way.